# HEARTS ENTANGLED IN WINTER'S FURY

## HAUNTED DARKNESS OF OUR RUIN

### BOOK ONE

## DONNA KESSLER

*For anybody who has ever felt powerless, hopeless or helpless. For anybody who has felt weighed down by grief, anger, trauma, betrayal, madness, loneliness, or their past. This is for anybody who had to deal with neglectful or abusive/addict parents, feeling invisible and pained in your own life.*

# CONTENTS

# BLURB

Amelia and Caiden don't fall in love. They crash. They bleed. They survive. They ruin each other slowly and still come back to each other.

Conditioned to hate. Cursed to crave. When survival turns brutal, and the past refuses to stay buried, they discover the most dangerous part of their war isn't the violence around them. It's the hunger between them. A tidal wave of yearning and obsession.

This isn't a romance built on softness. It's a haunting built on need; it's two hearts being forged in the dark.

# FOR READERS. IMPORTANT. PLEASE READ FOR CLARIFICATION/CONTEXT AND TRIGGERS

**TRIGGERS AND WARNING:** Please be aware that there are reasons for the way I wrote this specific timeline to give context when it comes to part 3 in the present.

Amelia and Caiden both make mistakes and take self-destructive actions in THE PAST. It is **necessary** for their character backstory, plot, dynamic, and to convey the psychological behavior of people who experience trauma, anger, hate, loss, grief, abuse, etc.

Since this is not a regular enemies-to-lovers, and since their hatred and conflict run so deep, it was important to include a huge part of it, which is senior year in part 1.

Otherwise, there would be no context or reader to character connection in the present.

And for clarification, both **Amelia and Caiden are 18 years old in the past (Amelia POV past chapters).** This is dark romance, but it is dark because of the dark things that happen to the characters. My characters are complex, complicated, emotionally damaged, and messy. It is very emotional and in-depth. Goes past the surface level of hatred, grief, rage, emotions, addiction/abuse. It is raw and extremely heavy.

It is a slow burn because Amelia and Caiden do NOT become lovers by the end of book 1 and will stay enemies through over half of book. Not slow burn when it comes to spice, because there are a

<u>few spicy scenes in there, not to convey love but to convey the passion of rage and hate.</u>

There are some hate-filled, spicy scenes due to their own inner conflict, emotional scars, and twisted issues. The first chapter scene on page 1 is written to show firsthand the dynamic.

Caiden: fueled by power, rage, hate, hunger, and control.

Amelia: fueled by grief, loneliness, fear, and helplessness in her own life. Rage and hate can parallel love and passion in a physical way (which is a recurring theme: how there is a fine line between hunger and hate)

This series portrays the ugly pain of being human. How we make mistakes, break down, make the wrong choice, give in to things like self-destruction, anger, revenge, darkness, desire, shame, guilt, loss, needing to feel good to numb the pain, self-sabotage, ache, conditioned mindsets, grief, emptiness.

It follows major themes of death, grief, loss, childhood wounds and abuse, neglect, survival, kidnapping, angst, tension, yearning, hatred, passion, revenge, inner conflict, obsession, avoidant and anxious attachment style, trauma and the consequences or affect of it, desire mixed with resentment, shame/self-loathing, trauma responses, childhood wounds of becoming you who were told to be vs. becoming who you choose, cost of growing up too early, identity crisis, addiction.

It is enemies-to-friends-to-lovers. But, it is emotionally raw, dark, painful, angsty, tense, psychological, and will tug and tear at your heart. You will ache in a huge way, cry, and feel broken yet whole all at once. You will really *feel* the pain and inner conflict of characters, and it will leave you wanting more.

Read with caution. It portrays how we can become conditioned to feel a certain way, how it is rooted in our bones from childhood, and how it is a long, painful struggle to pull ourselves out of that conditioned state, to come back to our core self.

For Amelia and Caiden, it is certainly a slowburn process. They must learn to heal from deep-rooted wounds and conditioned mindsets learned from their parents in order for them to overcome their long-standing hatred for each other.

They will either let their hatred and anger crumble into ashes, or it will tear them apart. Their slowburn progress will span over three books.

Major push/pull theme. No instant forgiveness or healing. It is a very messy journey for them to truly overcome their past and realize that they are what each other needs without any doubts.

Their hatred is real, it's raw, it's powerful, and all-consuming.

Their eventual passion for each other is on the same level. Old hatred and new passion will clash; they must decide which one will win.

This book is the first in the series. The past (Amelia POV) is during high school in senior year, highlighting the breaking point of their hatred, anger, psychological inner conflict, grief, and need for revenge. In the present is seven years later. Continuing in Amelia and Caiden's first person POV. It also has Caiden's first person POV in the past, conveying his side of it and the abusive conditioning that led to him being hateful, violent, and filled with rage.

It's a story about being conditioned, breaking, and clawing your way back to yourself.

## TRIGGER WARNINGS

Hearts Entangled in Winter's Fury is a dark, emotionally heavy romance. The darkness comes from what happens to the characters and how they cope with trauma, grief, rage, and self-destructive choices. Please read with care. It is very complex.

•Parental abuse scenes (physical abuse, verbal abuse, emotional abuse)
•Sexual assault (Part Three; involves a minor character)
•Strong language / cuss words
•Kidnapping / abduction
•Sexual content ("spice")
•Suicide and discovery of a body
•Death and grief
•Major mental health struggles (including depression/anxiety themes)
•Trauma / PTSD
•Dark themes
•Addiction / substance abuse in the family (and related fallout)
•Manipulation and toxic dynamics
•Violence, threats, and intimidation
•Blood / injury

•Weapons (knives)
•Panic attacks / trauma responses
•Bullying / humiliation
•Obsessive behavior / possessiveness
•Sexual content rooted in anger/hatred/revenge (hate-fueled intimacy; not "soft" romance tone)

*BOOK 2*
*HEARTS ENTANGLED IN YEARNING'S TIDE*
DUAL POV
(TO BE RELEASED June 26th 2026)

BOOK 3: TO BE ANNOUNCED

I always knew I wanted this story to be dark, heavy, and emotional. It's who I am and how I write. I truly hope that my readers can connect with these characters and their traumatic tragedies.

All of you book girlies with dark hearts/souls, this is for you. The ones who want to be seen, heard, and comforted. The ones who have had darkness in their lives and want to lose themselves in a book where the characters also deal with darkness, and slowly make their way through it, finding healing and comfort in each other.

That is the beauty of Amelia and Caiden. They are parallel in their pain, hurt, emotions, and trauma. They are soulmates, but it takes a long time for them to realize it.

Eventually, they soon realize that all they needed was each other. Amelia learns that she is not her mother's grief, and she is not her mother's issues. Caiden learns that he is not the shadow of his father; he is not a monster born to be cruel.

We are born into this world and thrown into our families and childhood. We are conditioned to be a certain way, act a certain way, and feel a certain way. And one day, we must either crawl out of that conditioned identity and find ourselves, or walk in our parents' shadow all our lives.

This is not your regular dark romance enemies-to-lovers. It is a dark, aching, emotional, and psychological story between two characters who grow up conditioned to hate each other in childhood, then reunite 7 years later and must survive in the wilderness together. Faced with their anger, their hate, their old wounds and resentments. Stripped to the core, forced to dissect their own minds and finally face the subconscious hunger they have always felt for each other.

It is NOT black and white enemies to lovers. Yes, there is real and consuming hatred, but there is a lot of gray area to consider when it comes to Amelia and Caiden. Their histories, their behavior, their personalities, their hatred and hunger, their grief and anger, their pain and mentalities.

Where there is darkness, there is also light. Where there is hate, there is also passion.

# PLAYLIST

# PLAYLIST

- BROKEN BY LIFE HOUSE
- WHERE IS MY MIND? BY PIXIES
- ALWAYS BY SALIVA
- CLOSER BY NINE INCH NAILS
- BITTERSWEET BY WITHIN TEMPTATION
- BLEED LIKE ME BY TRAPT
- WHERE DOES THE GOOD GO? BY TEGAN AND SARA
- BAD BLOOD BY TAYLOR SWIFT
- COLD AS YOU BY TAYLOR SWIFT
- STILL BY DAUGHTER
- YOUNGEST DAUGHTER BY SUPERHEAVEN
- SMOTHER BY DAUGHTER
- EVERYTHING I DO IS FOR YOU BY AMIRA ELFEKY
- OVER AND OVER BY THREE DAYS GRACE
- BRING ME TO LIFE BY EVANESCENCE

# PART ONE
# HER BREAKING POINT, HIS CONDITIONING, AND THEIR CONNECTION

# 1

## THE PAST

### AMELIA'S BREAKING POINT

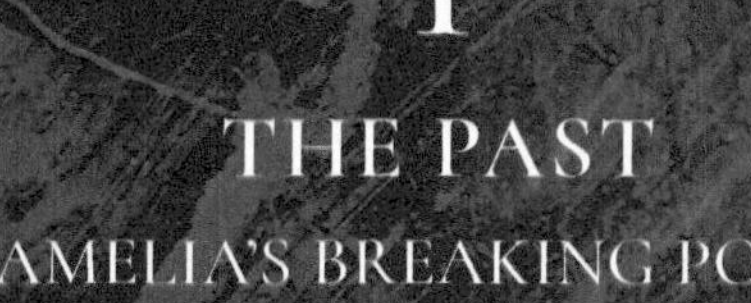

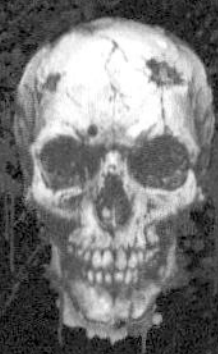

*18 YEARS OLD*

I grew sickly accustomed to the stench of liquor, its sour bite clinging to the air whenever my mother stumbled home.

In those nights, she became a stranger. Harsh, unpredictable, and so cold that I ached to flee her presence.

My stomach would clench before I even saw her, heart twitching like a trapped bird. She drifted from room to room in a glassy haze, muttering at empty chairs, and I felt my chest hollow out.

I wanted to vanish.

Sometimes that same stench trailed behind Caiden at school.

It hit me like a slap when he barged into class with his sour breath, rumpled shirt, and bruise blossoms on his cheeks. My pulse skittered as if he were a coiled spring, waiting to snap at me.

I hated him so fiercely, but a tiny voice in my skull whispered that maybe there's more beneath that anger. It crawled through my ribs, a silver hope that he wasn't all cruelty.

Then my fists clenched, and the spark died.

He'd proven time and again he was nothing but a coward masking fear with fists.

He chose me, always me, for his playground brutality. He prowled the halls like a beast, and I was the trembling prey.

Every taunt carved me smaller. When I saw him near, my knees went rubbery. I'd drop my head and weave through corners, willing the ground to swallow me whole.

This wasn't the kind of hate you grow out of. This was the kind you carry around like it's a part of your bones.

That afternoon, I spotted him first. Back turned, jaw clamped tight as he leaned toward Dante, his best friend.

My heart thundered: he'd notice me any second. Dante's gaze flicked up, met mine, and he slid me a pitying smile that felt like a lifeline.

I edged past, trying not to inhale Caiden's booze breath as it drifted after me in waves. My skin prickled.

Luck clung to me until the final bell. Then it abandoned me.

I'd almost made it out of the back lot when I sensed him behind me. His shadow stretching over my spine.

My pulse hammered, ears roared. I tried to push past, but his bulky body pinned me against the brick wall. Cool stone dug into my shoulder blades.

"Hey, Langston," he snarled. "Where do you think you're going?" His breath was a toxic blend of whiskey and malice.

I squeezed my eyes shut, mouth dry. How could no one else be here?

"Leave me alone," I whispered. My voice cracked, but I willed it steady. I fought his weight, but strength flooded from my body.

"Why? That's no fun, Amelia." He leaned closer, and I tasted the booze on my tongue. His voice was low and dangerous. "Are you scared?"

"No."

My voice trembled.

"Liar," he said, his voice full of menace and hunger as he stared at me. "Liars get punished."

He closed the last inch between us. My heart hammered against my ribs.

When he kissed me, it was a bruising collision, ragged and relentless. I tried to twist away, lungs burning, but my limbs wouldn't obey.

He was reminding me that he was in control and had the power, while I was powerless.

I didn't scream or fight the way I should have. Instead, I froze.

The way a rabbit does, out in the open, as the hawk's shadow hardens over its neck.

He was all muscle and hate, shoving me deeper into the brick as if he wanted my bones to fuse with the wall. With my arms trapped, even my knees could barely buckle; all that was left to surrender was my breath. My last weapon, gone.

"Fuck off," I finally snapped, nails raking his arms,

"Fuck," he whispered, and the heat in his voice made my stomach lurch. "You're feral today." He pressed the length of his body against mine, hips pinning me so hard I thought he'd shatter my pelvis.

He smashed his lips against mine again, filled with anger.

"You taste like fear," he slurred, and I saw, for a split second, the wreckage inside him: a hunger to ruin and be ruined in turn.

His grip tightened until spots fuzzed the edge of my vision.

My tongue was a shard of glass, my mouth glued shut with something worse than terror.

Shame. And hunger.

I managed to twist my head, catch a glimpse of the lot. Empty except for a dying robin flapping in the gutter, wing broken.

I saw myself in that bird: ugly, helpless, only good for suffering.

For a minute, all I could be was a body: heat wrapped in terror, ribs cinched so tight my heart might splinter. The world narrowed to the stink of booze and his darkened anger.

I understood exactly what my mother meant when she said some men were born hollow and lived only to swallow the light out of girls like me.

Somewhere distant, a voice cut through: "Dude, c'mon. Leave her alone. You're drunk. You shouldn't even be here."

I looked to see Dante, his hand trying to yank Caiden away.

Caiden growled, shoved off, and staggered away with Dante behind him as he shoved him forward.

Dante looked back at me only once with pity and concern.

Light flooded back into my vision, and I sagged against the wall, trembling so hard I thought I might shatter.

Tears slicked my cheeks, hot and shame-laced. I scrubbed at them, but they tracked stubbornly over my jaw. The taste of defeat was sour in my mouth.

I wondered if soap or water could ever wash away the memory of his hands on my skin. Raw disgust coiled in my belly. At him, at myself for feeling so powerless.

I bolted to my car and floored the pedal, vision blurring with each passing streetlight. By the time I pulled into my driveway, my chest felt hollow, every breath a ragged gasp.

Inside, the house reeked of cigarettes and vodka. Mom's usual aftermath.

Empty bottles were clustered on the counter. My fingers brushed the scarred walls, the faded nails, and holes where pictures once hung. Those scars whispered stories of chaos, but nothing comforted me.

Lillian emerged from the hallway, dead eyes behind smudged mascara. She offered a flat, "Hey, Amelia."

I met Lillian's eyes, searching for a sign that we could be allies, at least for tonight. All I saw was the same mask I wore in every mirror.

Her silences cut sharper than words. I wanted to scream: Mom's out again. Maybe gone for nights this time. But I only managed, "Where's Mom?"

Lillian shrugged. "With some guy. Said don't wait up." She slipped away, and I realized how much I wanted to shake her, demand we be sisters again.

But I was too tired.

I fled to the bathroom and slammed the door, ripping off my clothes.

Under the dribble of tepid water, I scrubbed until my arms stung, fingernails raw.

Steam coiled around me as I collapsed against the tile floor and wept until my lungs trembled. My reflection in the mirror stared back. Eyes red-rimmed, skin blotched. I imagined bugs crawling beneath my flesh, proof that I wasn't safe in my own body.

I didn't deserve any of this, and yet here I was, alone. No gentle hand to brush my hair, no voice to whisper words of comfort. My mother's love was as vanished as my father's. Abandoned. It pressed on my chest, a weight I could neither lift nor escape.

———

Later that day, I faced my evening shift at the bookstore, the weight of the day still clinging to me like a second skin.

As I drove through the familiar streets, an unsettling sensation prickled beneath my skin, as though I might peel away the layers of myself at any moment.

Now, rolling up to the shop's faded brick façade, the scent of paper and ink seeped through the cracks in the door, anchoring me.

The bell chimed as I entered, and for a moment, the day's chaos melted away.

Michelle looked up from the stacks. Concern rippled across her face. "Hey, you okay? You look pale." Her gaze traced the dark crescents under my eyes.

"I'm fine," I forced a smile, throat tight.

*Fine.* The word tasted metallic as I imagined Caiden's mocking grin, the memory of roaches scuttling under my skin after our last encounter. The lie slipped out too easily.

I turned to the boxes at my feet. New arrivals. My fingers brushed over glossy spines.

Thrillers and memoirs, self-help guides promising salvation.

My pulse rattled in my ears. I longed to dive into one of those pages, to escape into a world where endings were happy, and hope was guaranteed.

But here, reality clung to me like a shadow. No one could feel the ache I carried, the suffocating loneliness that trailed me down every aisle, every street corner. If I surrendered to that darkness, it would swallow me whole.

I sliced open a box and pulled out a memoir about a girl who survived an abusive and narcisstic father.

My lips curled.

Father. A ghost. I used to cling to the idea that he'd come back someday.

Next came a self-help guide, its bright letters promising healing.

My heart clenched at the memory of giving this very book to my mother on her birthday; she had exploded and stormed out in a rage. Lillian and I should have known better than to corner her with care.

I learned my lesson. Never corner a druggie. Let them figure it out on their own time.

"Hey, Amelia."

I looked up from the battered cardboard box at my feet, my fingertips brushing over the cracked leather spines and faded gold lettering of old volumes, and saw Dante standing in the fluorescent glow of the bookstore aisle.

He had that way of appearing out of nowhere, like a shadow slipping between stacks of paper, and my pulse stuttered.

"Dante, hey." I forced the corners of my mouth into a smile, though my chest felt tight. The scent of aged paper and dust motes drifting in the lamplight did nothing to calm my nerves. "What are you doing here?"

He shrugged, hands shoved into the pockets of his worn denim jacket. His dark hair fell into his eyes as he glanced around the quiet shelves. "Just need to pick up a book for English class."

A low thrum of curiosity made me tilt my head. He didn't strike me as the reading type, more a pranks-and-skateboards guy, but maybe I was wrong. "Oh? What book?"

He licked his lips, gaze flicking back to me. "And Then There Were None. Is it in stock?"

I nodded and pushed off from the box, weaving between rows of tightly packed fiction. My fingertips danced over author surnames—Austen, Bradbury, Christie—until I drew her from the shelf: a crisp hardcover clad in Christie's name.

I slid it out and offered it to him.

"Thanks." He accepted it with a small smile. The paper felt cool against my palm. "Is it a good book?" Genuine curiosity flickered in his eyes.

I swallowed, trying to mask the tight coil of emotion in my throat. He was Caiden's best friend, an alliance bound by loyalty I could never break. "It's... interesting," I said, trying for casual.

He laughed softly, the sound warm in the hush of the stacks. "Cool. If I'm going to read this, I have to like it."

A polite smile curved my lips, though my heart thumped so loudly I was sure he could hear it. Dante had rescued me not long ago, but friendship with him felt forbidden, like tasting sugar when my enemy held the recipe.

"Well, I hope you enjoy it," I whispered, turning to leave.

He stepped beside me, concern knitting his brow. "Hold up, are you okay? I've been thinking about you. I felt terrible about what happened."

A metallic tang rose in my mouth.

Panic, shame, and anger all at once.

I clenched my jaw until my teeth ached. "I'm fine." The lie slipped out on a bitter note. "You helped me. I'm grateful. But Dante... you're his best friend, and I'm the girl Caiden hates."

His shoulders sagged, but he shook his head. "Just because I'm his friend doesn't mean I hate you. I've known you a long time. As for Caiden, he's just dealing with a lot right now."

I crossed my arms, a cold laugh catching in my throat. "Like what? Plotting new ways to hurt me?"

He flinched, just a flicker of hurt in his dark eyes, and part of me felt triumphant. But then he spoke softly: "It's not just you. At home, his father's not kind."

I frowned. "Then maybe he should take it out on someone who can stand up to him."

"Amelia, I'm really sorry." His apology trembled between us.

I wanted to tear down my walls, let him see the tremor in my heart, but I couldn't. "It's fine. What do you want from me, Dante?"

He inhaled deeply and met my gaze with an intensity that made the world hush around us. Every beat of my heart echoed in my ears. "I want you. I've wanted you for a long time, Amelia. You know that."

Silence draped over me like a heavy curtain. To be wanted by him felt like both rescue and ruin. If Caiden ever knew –

I shivered, imagining dark eyes gleaming.

"Dante, I can't," I whispered, voice barely more than a breath.

His shoulders slumped, sadness softening his features. "I know. I just needed to say it."

He stepped close, the warmth of his body brushing mine, and pressed a quick, gentle kiss to my cheek, longer than a friend's touch, before squeezing my hand.

My heart fluttered, torn between terror and longing.

Without another word, he turned and vanished around the corner, leaving me alone among the silent shelves.

I couldn't have him. I was doomed to fall into a pit of loneliness, cut off from love and belonging. Maybe if things were different, we could have been something more.

———

The rest of the day passed in a dreamlike haze: the ghost of his lips on my skin, the ache of hope and heartbreak entwined in every heartbeat.

Inside our house, the usual fog of cigarette smoke and stale gin hit me. I stood in the entryway, listening; no sounds except the rhythmic tick of the kitchen clock, the hum of the fridge, and from somewhere in the gloom, a muted snore.

Mom.

She'd passed out on the couch, mascara streaked like a bruise beneath each eye. A tremor ran up my spine. I couldn't decide if it was hatred or pity that moved me.

My head kept replaying Dante's confession, the earnest tremble in his voice, and how it felt to be wanted, even for a moment.

I tried to imagine a world where I wasn't just a victim, but I failed.

In the absence of noise, the memory of Caiden's hands on my body looped through my mind like a bad film, every detail amplified and distorted.

Maybe the ocean, if I could swing it. I could see myself on a windblown campus, wearing sweaters that didn't smell like mom's cigarette haze, talking to people who didn't know the taste of violence.

Maybe I'd invent a new self, one who was never prey.

———

Later that night, I crept into the dimly lit living room. My mother sat slumped on the couch, a half-empty bottle of wine resting on the table beside her. The television cast shadows on her face, emphasizing the lines of fatigue etched into her skin.

"Hey, Mom," I said softly, crossing the room. Her eyes remained glued to the screen, the same rerun of a show she'd probably seen a dozen times already. I waited for her to look at me, to ask about my day, but the silence hung thick between us.

"Hi, Amelia," she murmured, her voice distant. I swallowed hard, feeling the edges of loneliness creeping back.

"I'm going to my room," I said, retreating before the ache in my chest could become unbearable.

I passed Lillian's door, my sister's sanctuary. I hesitated, wondering if she was home. The sound of muffled music wafted through the crack beneath her door. I knocked lightly, but there was no answer.

Disappointed, I slipped into my own room, the walls painted a shade of blue that was meant to soothe me, but tonight it felt like a prison. I pulled out my sketchbook, flipping through the pages to find solace in art.

But as I drew, my thoughts wandered back to Caiden. The way his eyes had narrowed, that sneer plastered on his face.

After a while, I heard my mother's voice drifting, slurred and shaky, calling for Lillian. I strained to listen, filled with concern for my sister, who had been struggling to find her own way in the world.

"Lillian? Can you come here?" Mom's voice was softer now, almost pleading.

I could hear Lillian's footsteps, slow and hesitant. "What is it, Mom?" she asked, the weariness in her tone was clear.

"I just... I need someone to talk to." There was a long pause, and then I heard the creak of the couch as Lillian sat down beside her.

"Okay, I'm here," Lillian said, her voice steady, but I could sense the tension in her words. "What's going on?"

"Nothing... just feeling a bit down, you know?" Mom replied, her voice laced with the familiar sadness that always accompanied her substance usage.

I could feel the bile rising in my throat. It wasn't just "a bit down." It was an endless cycle of despair that had trapped our family in a suffocating embrace.

I wanted to intervene, to tell Lillian to walk away, but I knew she wouldn't. She was always the one trying to save Mom, to pull her back from the edge.

Yet, she was also the one to carry the weight of my mother's anger and drug-infused outbursts.

Some days, my mother was kind to Lillian. The air crackled with tension on other days, as her screams of accusation and blame filled the house. Spitting words of resentment, laced with venom and spite.

While I, the younger child, was a mere shadow in the house. Neglected and forgotten by my mother, who chose the path of drugs after my father left, curling into her sorrows and trauma, allowing it to consume her.

The conversation continued in hushed tones, and I felt helpless as I retreated into my sketchbook. I drew the familiar strokes of trees and landscapes, my emotions bleeding onto the page.

But as I sketched, my mind kept drifting back to Caiden.

I finished my sketch, the ink smudging slightly as I pressed my palm against the paper, lost in the swirl of emotions.

I had to find a way to navigate the tangled web of my life between my mother, my sister, and Caiden.

But as I closed my eyes, exhaustion washed over me, and I let the darkness take me. The weight of the day settled into my bones, and I knew tomorrow would bring its own battles.

But for now, in the quiet of my room, I could pretend that everything was okay.

# 2

# THE PRESENT

## AMELIA

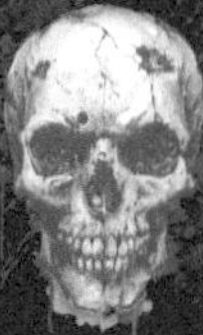

*25 YEARS OLD*

The thunder tore across the sky like a wounded beast, its deafening roars rippling through the frigid air, each crack a blow to my chest, sending jagged icicles of fear racing through my veins.

My body, cold as carved marble, trembled with each echoing boom. Around me, the world felt warped. Every shadow stretched into unfamiliar shapes, every footstep on unseen ground felt aimless, as though I were stumbling in a vast, directionless void.

I hurled my voice into the blackness, a raw, ragged plea for rescue, but the darkness swallowed it whole. No answer came. I was utterly alone in a suffocating sea of night.

A stinging wind snapped at my exposed skin, its icy fingers tearing through the thin fabric of my clothes, leaving me raw and quivering. Above me, the trees stood like skeletal sentinels. Gnarled branches twisting skyward, black as old bone, each twig scraping the air like the talons of a ravenous horror.

Rain began to pelt me, cold needles dancing on my scalp, then driving into my flesh with increasing fury, as though the storm itself sought to shred me apart.

I squinted into the void, praying for the slightest glow—a distant star, a fraction of moonlight—but the sky offered nothing but impenetrable black. It pressed down on me like a living blanket, its weight crushing, its silence absolute.

Every path I ventured twisted back into more lifeless gloom, the leafless forest a labyrinth of despair. It felt alive with malice: the bark of every tree seemed to pulse with a hidden heartbeat, and I could almost sense eyes tracking me from the shadows.

A cold dread pooled in my gut, each footfall louder than the last, echoing across the emptiness where no creature stirred, where not even an owl dared break the hush.

Then the earth beneath my feet began to change. The damp soil darkened, blooming into a thick, congealed crimson that sloshed underfoot like grotesque syrup.

A metallic tang bloomed on my tongue, and a rancid stench flooded my nostrils, yanking me back to the memory of finding my sister's lifeless body in her bed. My heart slammed against my ribs as I stumbled backward.

A shape materialized a few paces away, and my hand flew to my mouth as a strangled scream ripped from my throat. Terror rooted me to the spot, my limbs refusing to obey.

The figure stepped into the weak, flickering gloom: my sister, blood-soaked and battered, her pale skin mottled with bruises and wounds that oozed dark rivulets. Her once-lustrous hair hung in greasy tangles across her shoulders.

I could hardly bear to look, yet I was powerless to look away.

Slowly, she rose to her feet, each movement stiff and unnatural. Her eyes, once warm and familiar, now glowed with a feral red light. As if embers of rage burned behind her dead gaze.

In a motion so swift it left me breathless, she seized a handful of my hair and yanked my head back. Her lips curled into a savage snarl, revealing stained teeth. The fetid odor of decay surged from her like a physical blow.

Her hand, white and cold as marble, pressed against my throat. Ice spread across my windpipe as she squeezed, her face inches from mine.

I tasted the stench of earth and blood and an otherworldly rot that clung to her. She resembled a spirit returned for vengeance, every line of her face twisted in hate. "My death is all your fault. If you weren't so cowardly, I would still be alive!"

Her words reverberated around me, sharper than knives. All your fault. All your fault. The accusation hammered at my mind, and tears burned behind my eyes. I was helpless, my sobs breaking free in ragged gasps.

In an instant, the world shifted. The forest dissolved, replaced by a sheer, rocky precipice. The sky above roiled with dark, bruised clouds. My pulse thundered in my ears as I realized what was coming.

Without warning, Lillian, a figment of my own grief, shoved me over the edge. I plummeted into the abyss.

For a moment, I felt nothing but the wind rushing past, a curious peace settling over me before terror returned in a final, breathless gasp as I hurtled toward the unforgiving rocks.

Then everything blackened.

A strangled scream tore from my throat, and I snapped awake, heart hammering, chest heaving. Morning light flooded my room, soft and ordinary, dissolving the nightmare-like mist.

I lay on the floor beside my bed, trembling as my eyes adjusted to the gentle dance of dust motes in the sunbeams.

*It was just a dream*, I told myself, the same mantra I repeated every dawn when my past surfaced in horrors too vivid to be mere slumber. I forced myself up on shaky legs, determined to shake it off and greet the day as though the nightmare held no power over me.

Temptation nudged at me to reach for the cabinet in my kitchen, to pour myself a bottle of wine to dull the distress, but I shook my head at the thought. I was not my mother.

My friend Cathy often insisted that I was an alcoholic because of how frequently I indulged in wine at night.

"To be an alcoholic, it must completely ruin your life and leave you in shambles. Believe me, I know," I would respond matter-of-factly. Just because I drank in larger quantities now and then did not make me an alcoholic. I had my life together, despite all the hardships I had endured.

People claimed one could live a seemingly perfect life yet still feel profoundly unhappy. They said it was possible to achieve every ambition and still grapple with a persistent sense of despair.

My life was close to perfect. I earned a good income as a writer. I had a lovely, suitable home. Each day unfolded with the same simple routine. I savored the aroma of freedom, relishing the opportunity to do my own thing, far removed from the misery of my past.

I had believed that running away and starting anew would heal me, that I could forget the trauma and heartache and become someone else entirely. But this was not a fairy tale. I had not encountered my prince charming or lived happily ever after.

The shadows of darkness still haunted my vision, trailing behind me and whispering in my ear during moments of silence and solitude.

From time to time, happiness enveloped me like a delicate veil. I wore it like a safety blanket, hesitant to peel it away, fearful of what lay buried beneath the mask. If I didn't delve too deeply into the horrors of my past, I was fine. I could wake up and live the illusion of a perfect life.

Almost.

I cleared my mind of the heinous dream that had haunted me, focusing instead on preparing for the day ahead. My current best friend had asked to meet this morning, claiming she had exciting news to share in person.

Sabrina had been my savior when I first moved to this town. As my real estate agent, she had helped me find a home, and our bond had blossomed during that process.

Without her, navigating a new place would have been infinitely harder. Although she was a few years younger than me, it never felt like a barrier.

Two hours later, I arrived at the town's beloved café. The rich aroma of freshly brewed coffee and sweet pastries washed over my senses the moment I stepped inside. It was a quaint little establishment, filled with friendly workers and warm customers. I spotted Sabrina sitting at a table by the window, sunlight illuminating her auburn hair like a halo.

The café's amber morning light pooled around us as Sabrina swept in, her laughter rippling through the air like warm honey. "Amelia! How are you?" she called, rising from her table to enfold me in a quick, buoyant hug. I inhaled the faint bouquet of her rose-scented shampoo and the rich aroma of espresso, then eased into the rattan chair across from her.

"I'm alright," I said, brushing a strand of hair behind my ear. "Had a weird dream last night, but let's skip that. What's up with you?"

Sabrina's grin bloomed. She held her hand aloft, palm tilted so the overhead light danced across a single, enormous diamond. The gem sparkled like a shard of starlight.

"You're engaged?" I whispered, leaning forward, eyes wide as I took in the ring's fire.

"Yes!" she gushed, cheeks flushed pink. "Shane proposed, finally! I'm over the moon to be his wife."

A genuine smile curved my lips as happiness radiated from her face. Then she paused, her voice dipping into excitement so bright it made the coffee steam swirl. "But that's not the best part. I want you to be my maid of honor."

Silence settled between us for a heartbeat. My heart pounded in my ears. Sabrina pressed on, voice softening with warmth. "You know I don't have siblings, and my circle's small. You've been my rock since you moved here. I couldn't imagine anyone else besides me."

I blinked against a surge of emotion. No one had ever asked me that before. "Sabrina, oh, I'm honored. Yes, I'd love to."

She whooped softly, clapping her hands. "Yay! You're the best!" Her eyes shone like emeralds as she sipped her cappuccino.

"I'm really happy for you," I managed, though a dull ache tugged at my chest. Lillian's absence, her lost wedding day, flickered through my mind in a wave of grief. Sabrina must have seen it.

"Hey, everything okay? You seem... distant." She tilted her head, concern furrowing her brow.

I swallowed. "I've been wrestling with bad dreams and old scars."

Her gaze softened. "I'm sorry. Have you thought about therapy?"

I rolled my eyes, recalling sterile offices and surface-level questions that never reached my wounds. "Therapy doesn't cut it. I need something more real." I glanced away, ashamed.

Sabrina chewed her lip, then sat forward, eyes alight with determination. "Okay. I have an idea, something to pull you out of this funk."

I raised an eyebrow, skeptical. "Oh? And what's that brilliant idea of yours?"

"Well..." She stretched the word, considering her next choice of words. "Shane wants to take a bonding trip with his half-brother and suggested I come along since we're engaged. He thinks it could be a cool experience for us."

I sat, processing the information and struggling to connect the dots of how this would help me. "Wow. I didn't know Shane had a half-brother. How did that happen? And where do I fit into this?"

She chuckled, sipping her drink. "I was getting to that. Basically, his mom was unhappy in her marriage and got pregnant by somebody else, from what Shane said, because her husband was an abusive cheater. She ended up leaving town with Shane's dad since she was already pregnant. He only found out recently after discovering an old picture at his mom's house. The guy is about four and a half years older than Shane, around your age!"

The midday sun filtered through the café's tall windows, casting honeyed patterns over our table. I traced the rim of my iced latte with a slender finger, watching condensation drip onto the polished wood. "Damn," I muttered, pressing my mug to my lips. "That must've been weird for him, finding out his mom had another kid. But, seriously, what does this have to do with me?"

Sabrina let out an exaggerated tut, her manicured nail tapping the cup between us. "Oh, Amelia, my sweet, clueless friend," she chided, eyes dancing. "I was hinting that you should come along with us! I'll need someone to chat with while they're off talking boy stuff. And who knows? This half-brother might be cute."

My heart fluttered in spite of my caution, curiosity sparking beneath my skin. The idea of tagging along with two near-strangers both alarmed and intrigued me. I swallowed, my voice a measured calm. "That could actually be interesting. So you haven't even met this guy in person? Where are you headed?"

Sabrina leaned forward, a grin playing on her lips. "It'll be a blast, like a never-ending double date." She waggled her eyebrows, and her laughter tumbled out bright as bells. "Shane's video-chatted with him a few times and told me all about him, but no real-life meet-and-greet yet. Shane tracked him down on his own, so proud of him for that."

I studied Sabrina's radiant excitement: the way her eyes sparkled, how a rosy flush colored her cheeks.

A pang of longing tugged at me. Would I ever know that kind of effortless happiness? Engagement rings and breathless declarations of love felt like fairy tales I'd never belong to.

But I tucked the sadness away, reminding myself: Sabrina thrived on sunshine; I was the black cat perched in her shadow, and somehow, it balanced us.

"That's wonderful," I said, forcing a bright note into my voice. "Truly. So where's this trip happening? Tell me more."

Sabrina clapped, the sound echoing like high-fives in an empty hallway. "A wilderness retreat! Imagine winding trails through towering pines, the scent of fir and damp earth. While the boys rough it, building campfires and having survival lessons, we'll bask in the spa, do sunrise yoga, soak in the hot springs. We're thinking of piling into Shane's SUV. It's massive, room for four, and all our bags. He said it's about two weeks, but I'll confirm."

I let the image settle. A silent forest, steam rising from a natural pool, morning light through the trees. I had always craved an escape into nature. "Sounds amazing. I'm a sucker for greenery. Do you know how much it costs?"

She waved her latte in a casual arc. "Expenses are on Shane. You know he's rolling in it."

I lifted an eyebrow, my tone teasing. "Marrying him for his money, are you? Very generous of him."

Sabrina laughed, warm and light. "He is loaded, yes, but there's a reason. He's the perfect lover." She sighed, gazing off as though picturing him now, hand in mine.

I smiled, letting amusement and genuine happiness mingle in my chest. "I'm really happy for both of you. I think I could go. It might be fun."

She squealed, scooting across the bench to give me a side hug. The fabric of her sundress brushed my arm. "Yay! You won't regret this, Amelia. I'll text you all the details once Shane confirms times and routes."

"Great," I said, sipping my latte as the rich coffee buzz tickled my senses. "I could definitely use some joy, and I'm curious about this mystery brother."

Sabrina's grin stretched from ear to ear. "Me too! Shane even said he's thinking of moving here; his life's not great where he is now. Wouldn't it be fun to have him around?"

I nodded, picturing an extra branch on our small circle of friends. "Yeah. I bet Shane would love a bit of family close by."

She gathered her things and stood. "I have so much to plan, but I'm thrilled you're coming. Watch for my text!"

We parted behind the café's counter, each slipping into our own cars. I settled into the driver's seat, the engine purring beneath me, and watched the urban bustle fade. Doubt flickered at the edge of my mind: Was I wise to plunge into the unknown?

But then I inhaled deeply, released a shaky laugh, and whispered, "Fuck it."

I deserved a break. I deserved to disconnect. With that, I pulled out onto the road, sunlight dancing across the dash as I steered toward new memories.

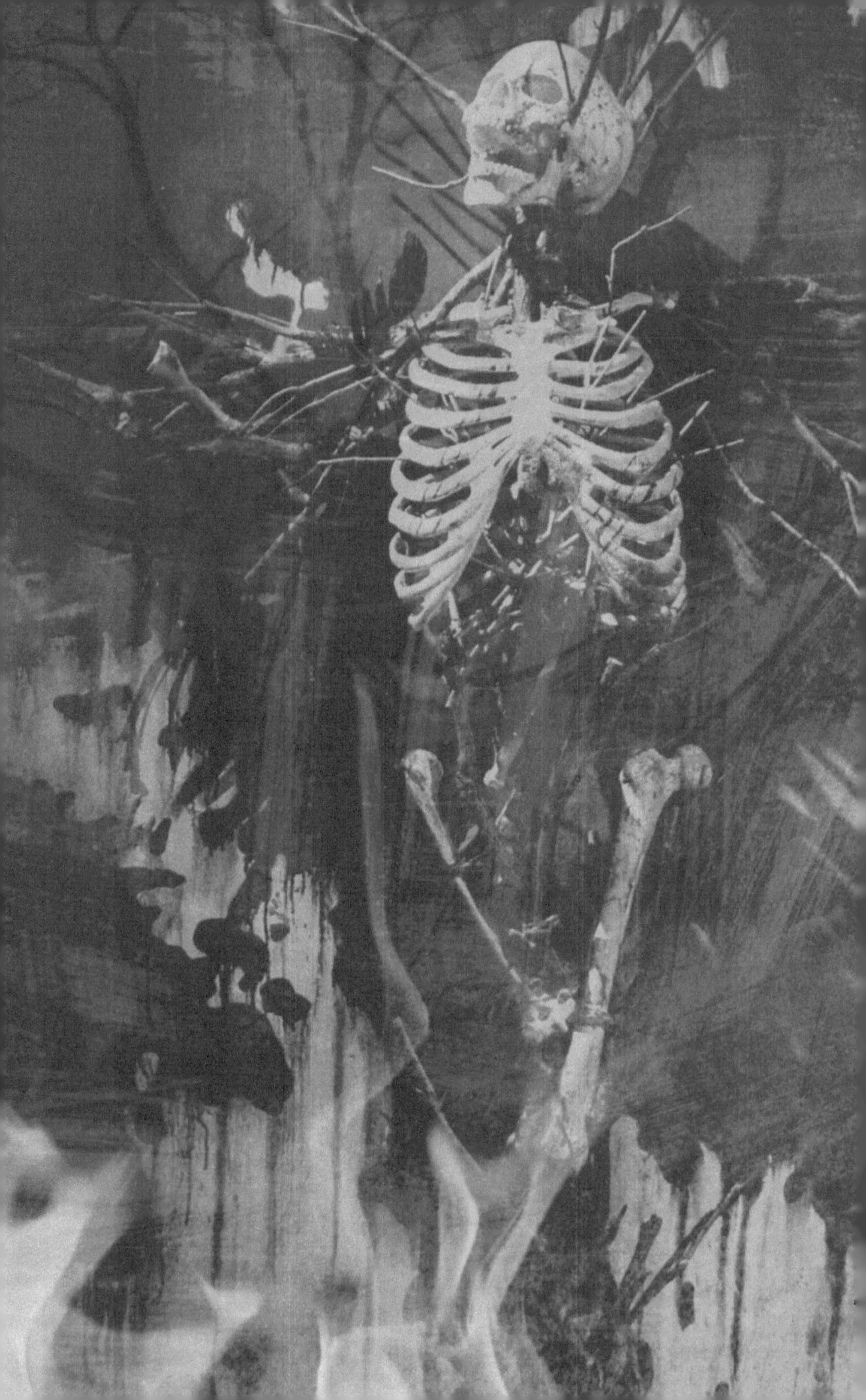

# 3
## THE PRESENT

### AMELIA

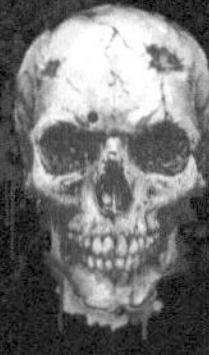

 morning of our wilderness retreat finally dawned.

Our expedition would span two full days, hugging the winding blacktops from our sleepy North Carolina town through rolling foothills, across sunlit plains, and into the soaring Rockies of Colorado.

Already, I braced myself for the cramped hours ahead: me, my perpetually chatty best friend Sabrina, her upbeat fiancé Shane, and some mysterious stranger I'd never met. Oh, the joy.

I tried to summon a spark of optimism. Maybe he'd be tall with soft eyes, maybe our conversation would flow, maybe I'd finally discover someone who saw past my walls.

But that hopeful flicker sputtered almost as soon as it appeared.

I pulled a handkerchief from my pocket and dabbed at my palms, reminding myself how foolish I was to crave acceptance, to dare imagine I might be worthy of affection. Better to resign myself to solitude. A lonely soul destined to fade away.

A hollow ache settled in my chest as I rolled my suitcase's frayed leather handle between my fingers, its familiar scuffs reminding me of every trip I'd taken alone. Each hesitation knotted my stomach tighter. I inhaled, lungs trembling, and whispered into the quiet room: "Get it together, Amelia. You're a grown woman. Act like it."

Sabrina had promised to swing by in thirty minutes. I typed out a quick text—'I'm ready; you can come get me now.' Almost immediately, her response pinged back. Too quick. I had no time left to steel my nerves.

Minutes later, the door swung open with its creaky welcome, and in burst Sabrina, pure kinetic energy in a sundress, her auburn hair catching the morning light like embers. "Amelia! Are you excited? This is going to be incredible!"

She enveloped me in a hug so enthusiastic I stumbled back against the wall. I patted her shoulder awkwardly, plastered on a grin. "Yep. All packed. Let's roll."

With a delighted squeal, she flung my suitcase toward her car parked out front, where wildflowers bowed in the breeze. I'd traveled light—one large duffel and a small backpack—and Sabrina clucked. "Are you sure that's all? I feel so excessive with my two stuffed trunks." She shook her head in mock dismay. "You're so efficient, Amelia."

If only she knew how empty I felt beneath my poise. I fluttered my eyelids and offered half a smile. "I've got everything I need." The lie felt heavy on my tongue.

She laughed, slid behind the wheel, and cranked up the stereo. Melodic country tunes poured through the speakers as I eased into the passenger seat, keys jangling in Sabrina's hand.

The engine roared to life, and we tore off, the car lurching forward like a roller-coaster plunging into adventure I wasn't sure I wanted.

When we finally pulled into Sabrina and Shane's sunlit suburban cul-de-sac, my heart pounded. I sat frozen, gripping the door handle. Sabrina glanced over. "You coming?" Her tone was all cheer.

I managed a shaky nod. "Just... nerves." My fingers drummed a staccato on the vinyl seat.

"Relax, Amelia. Deep breaths. And hey, Shane's brother's there, too. He's kind of... cute." She winked, genuine excitement sparkling in her eyes.

I forced a nonchalant shrug. "Great. Can't wait."

She bounded from the car, her dress swirling, and I followed with my baggage. Inside, their front hall glowed with gentle lamplight. Hardwood floors gleamed beneath an ornate console table, and fresh lilac blooms perfumed the air.

My own home sprang to mind. Bare walls, forgotten postcards, shadows pooling in the corners. My heart sank at the contrast.

"In here, Amelia!" Sabrina called from the living room, voice buoyant. I squinted against the midday glare filtering through tall windows. Dust motes danced in the shafts of light, painting the room in gold.

Sabrina leaned against Shane's broad shoulder, their laughter blending like cherished music.

Opposite them sat a solitary man in a leather armchair, his posture stiff, eyes wide as he stared at me.

In that instant, my world constricted. My pulse thundered in my ears, breath turned to ice in my lungs, and the back of my neck prickled with remembered dread.

There, framed by soft sunlight, was Caiden Baxter. Tall and familiar, every memory of him rushing back like a tidal wave.

My heart stumbled and faltered.

My voice died in my throat. I stood paralyzed, the past colliding violently with the present, unable to tear my gaze away from the one face I never wanted to see again.

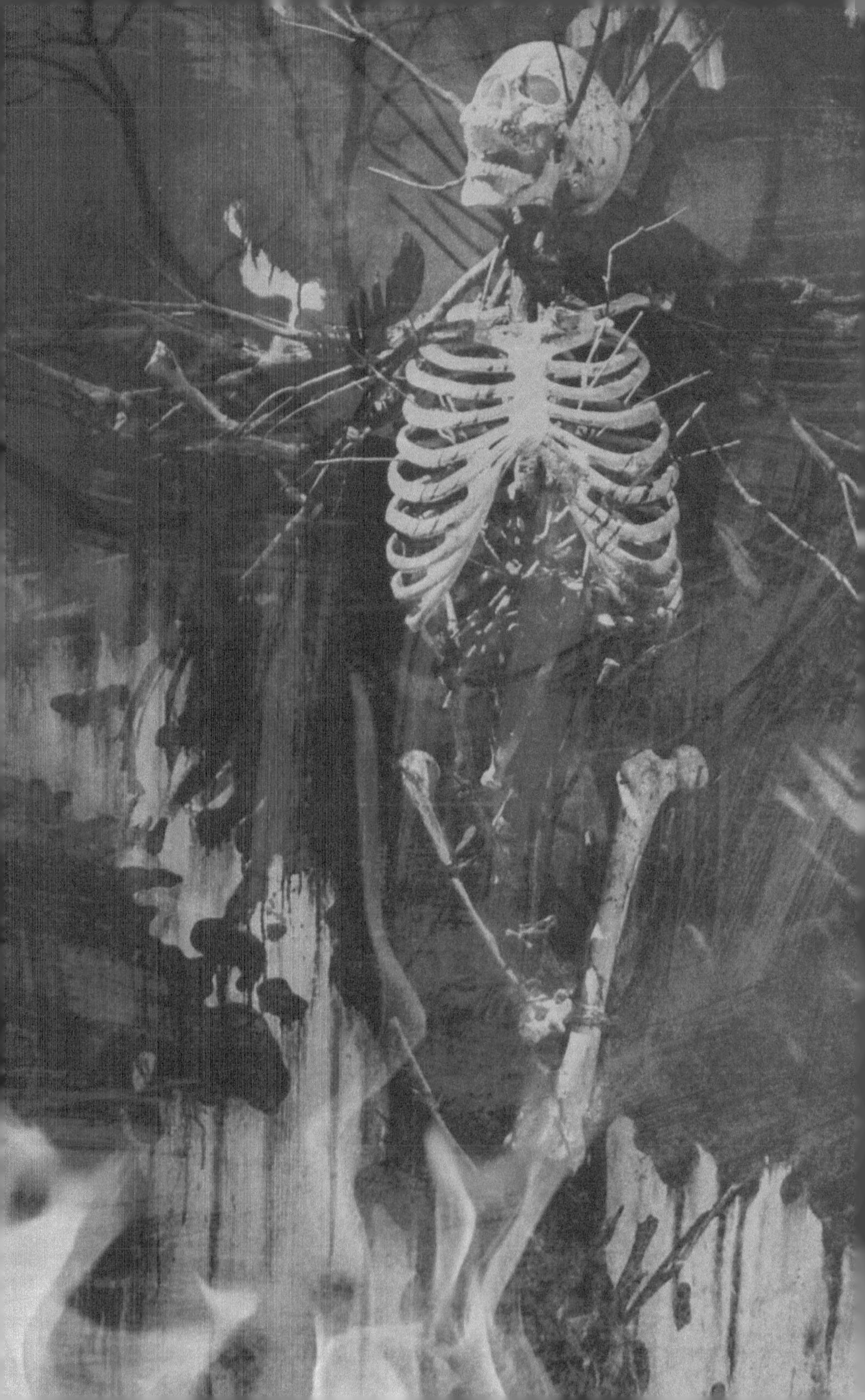

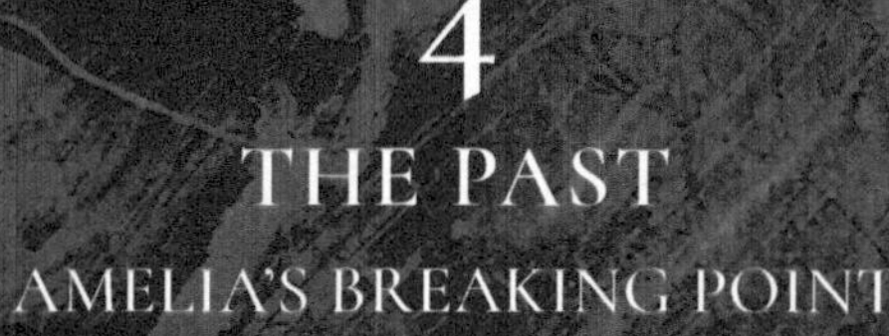

# 4
## THE PAST
### AMELIA'S BREAKING POINT

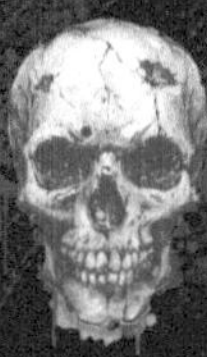

Everyone at school knew about Mom. Whispers trailed after me like vultures, curiosity and pity colliding in their eyes. Most steered clear, either intimidated or repelled by the messy fragments of my life.

I rounded the corner to the classroom door.

*Thwack.*

My toe caught something solid. One second, I was upright, the next, I was tumbling onto a pair of scuffed Converse.

"Whoops. My bad," Caiden drawled, voice dripping with disdain.

I scrambled upright, fists clenching at my sides. He looked down at me with those coal-black eyes. Cold and empty caverns where light dared not tread. "Sorry? Are you even capable of remorse?" I spat, studying the cruel smirk curving his lips.

"Not really," he shrugged. "Doesn't look like you mind."

My jaw clenched so tight it ached, but I forced myself to breathe slowly. A handful of students had paused to watch; I refused to give them the triumph of my reaction.

Caiden had mastered the art of feigned innocence. He'd done it before, in fifth grade. He'd shoved me off the playground steps, leaving me with a bruised arm and no apology.

The teachers believed his smooth lies, where he deemed me clumsy, and I hated him for it.

"Why do you have to be such a bastard?" I yelled as he pivoted to leave. Tears stung my eyes, and my voice cracked on the word "bastard," raw and broken.

A flare of anger painted my vision in dark crimson. He paused, his back rigid, then spun around and stalked toward me.

I felt his breath, warm and tainted, brush my face. "You'll never understand my pain, Amelia," he hissed, eyes blazing with something like fury. "So don't pretend to."

My heart thundered. "You're not the only one who hurts," I shot back, voice steady with the weight of all the mornings I'd spent praying for strength. He didn't answer.

He simply turned and melted into the tide of students pouring into the halls.

"I loathe you," I whispered after him, but the words dissolved into the swirl of pre-class chatter.

When pain and hatred churn between two people, there are only two roads: you face the inferno together and try to rise above, or you run until it consumes you.

Between Caiden and me, the embers of resentment sputtered into flame.

Let the war rage, Caiden. Let it burn until one or both of us fall.

———

Home was meant to be my refuge, a safe harbor, yet the thin walls and simmering tempers transformed it into a pressure cooker ready to explode at any moment.

My mother drifted through rooms like a ghost, cloaked in a haze of exhaustion. Her eyes were distant, sunken behind dark, weary circles that told tales of sleepless nights.

Lillian was either hiding in her bedroom or slouched on the couch, headphones clamped tightly over her ears to drown out reality.

Above our roof, black storm clouds seemed permanently anchored, heavy and ominous, threatening to unleash chaos at any moment.

They were at it again, and I was not surprised; it had become a familiar refrain in my life. "I'm over eighteen, so stop trying to tell me what to do," Lillian's voice crackled with irritation.

Peering around the corner, I saw them locked in a battle of glares in the living room, expressions like daggers.

"I don't give a fuck if you're eighteen. You still live in my house, so you will obey me," my mother's voice was a whip crack, cutting through the tension.

"That is such bullshit logic, Mom! Get over yourself. You're barely even here most of the time to claim this as your house," Lillian countered, her words dripping with contempt.

"If you do not like it, then you can just get the hell out. It was your decision to drop out of college and move back in," my mother shot back, her voice a mix of frustration and resignation.

Silence settled like a heavy fog, and I was about to turn away when a sound, unmistakable in its violence, echoed through the room.

I spun around, heart pounding, to see my mother holding her own face, her expression a mix of shock and disbelief.

Lillian's hand hovered in the air, trembling.

My mother's eyes went flat and cold, as if all the anger had been drained out in one cruel siphon. She didn't move, didn't even lower her palm from her stinging cheek, just stared at Lillian in shock.

Lillian shrank in on herself, mouth working, then she backed up until the backs of her knees hit the sofa. "I didn't mean—" she started, but her voice was a strangled croak. She pressed a fist to her mouth, eyes fixed on the red bloom spreading across my mother's cheek.

I watched, paralyzed. My body wanted to fly at Lillian, to shield our mother from more, but the rest of me just stood there, wooden, like I was watching actors on a sound stage.

My mother recovered first, turning her back on us both, her steps stiff and unsteady. The kitchen light caught the wet tracks on her face, and for a moment, I saw her not as a monster, but as a woman undone by her own life, her daughters grown wild and bitter.

Lillian's breathing quickened. "She started it," she muttered, almost childlike, but the words dissolved into a dry sob. She sank to the carpet, fingers clutching at her temples.

From the kitchen came the crash of glass, my mother shattering a cup, maybe on purpose, maybe not.

I realized I was holding my own breath.

The house shuddered with silence. I crept past Lillian toward my room, trying not to disturb the air.

I could still feel the echo of Caiden's hands on my skin, the heat and shame of it lingering like radio static.

At my desk, I opened my sketchbook and tried to let it out the only way I knew how.

But all I could manage was a pathetic tangle, a wild, unfocused bramble instead of the careful portraits I used to make.

My wrist ached from the pressure, but it didn't dull the noise inside my chest. I tore the page out, crumpled it in my fist, and shoved the sketchbook away.

The walls stifled me. I needed air, the kind that froze your skin and made your lungs remember how to work.

I grabbed my cardigan and slipped outside, letting the front door whisper shut behind me.

I didn't have a destination. My sneakers found the sidewalk, then the sloping curve of the street, then the dirt path that wound past the soccer field and into the old park.

A single swing creaked in the empty playground, chain links singing a metallic lullaby to no one in particular.

I wandered aimlessly, brushing my fingertips along the ridged bark of an elm. The world was locked in a gray half-light, neither day nor night. I felt invisible, a ghost in my own life.

That's when I saw him. Dante, alone, hunched on a half-rotted bench with his elbows on his knees, watching the puddles at his feet.

A cigarette dangled from his lips. The glow of it caught the last scraps of sunlight and set his shadow flickering on the ground.

He looked up, his expression startled for a heartbeat, then softened into something almost apologetic. "Hey," he said, voice rough. "You okay?"

I nearly laughed. The answer was written all over me, and he could see that. My lips parted, but nothing came out.

Dante flicked the cigarette away, grinding it into the gravel. "You can sit, if you want."

I hesitated, then folded myself onto the bench, keeping a careful slat of distance between us. The silence buzzed.

He leaned forward, elbows on knees, and spoke without looking at me. "Is it your mom again?"

"Always." The word came out small, like a cough. "Or my sister. Or both. Or some other fucking cosmic joke."

He nodded, slow and grave. "You want to talk about it?" His voice was low, respectful of the dark.

I wanted to. I wanted to spill every broken thing in my chest onto the mud and let it rot there, feeding the worms.

But I just shook my head. "I don't know how."

He let that hang for a minute. A breeze whipped a strand of hair across my face, and I tucked it behind my ear, suddenly aware of how hunched and childish I must look.

The breeze enveloped me, and I wished I could float into it, fly away into some other reality.

The wind picked up, raking through the empty swings and making them squeal.

I shivered.

Dante shrugged off his jacket and draped it over my shoulders. His warmth lingered in the cotton threads.

I tugged the sleeves over my fists, felt the heat seeping into my bones.

"It's not going to get better, is it?" The question was a pebble dropped into a vast, black well.

He didn't flinch. "Maybe not soon. Maybe not ever. But sometimes it helps to have somebody who gets it." His words were careful.

The gesture gutted me. I shook under the weight of his kindness, anger, and shame tangling in my throat. I wanted to tell him to take it back, to stop pretending I was worth the warmth.

Instead, I crushed my fists in the jacket's sleeves and stared at my sneakers.

"You don't have to babysit me, you know," I said, voice small and watery. "I'm not going to break."

He scuffed his boot against the gravel. "That's not why I'm here."

"Then why are you here?" I pressed. "Is this some guilt thing? You feel sorry for the girl with the fucked-up family?" My words came out sharper than I intended, but I was tired of being a charity case, tired of people acting like I was a kicked dog in an ASPCA commercial.

Dante's jaw flexed. "I don't pity you, Amelia." He said my name like it hurt him.

He looked so tired. I wondered what it cost him to be good when his best friend was Caiden. What it cost him to be the one in their duo who still had a soul.

The silence grew, crawling between the slats of the bench, pressing in on my chest until I had to speak or suffocate. "He hates me, you know. Caiden. I don't even know what I did."

Dante shook his head. "It's not about you." He ran a hand through his hair. "His dad, he's worse than you can imagine. Caiden learned early how to hurt before he got hurt. He thinks if he makes you the target, he'll be safe." His voice darkened. "He's not. Nobody is. Somebody's always bleeding in his house."

"I can't handle being someone's punching bag forever."

Dante's lips curled in a sad smile. "I know. But you take it. Every day. That takes guts. More than you think."

The wind cut through my sweater. I huddled deeper into his jacket, a borrowed shell. "Some days, I want to disappear."

He didn't say anything for a while. I wondered if he, too, ever wanted to vanish, if the world's rough edges ever dug into him the way they did me.

"I feel like that too, sometimes. My dad works too much, drinks often, and my mom is always stressed. It's nothing like your situation, or Caiden's, but it weighs me down some days." Dante leaned back on the bench, his head turned sideways to look at me.

"I'm sorry. I didn't know."

He shrugged, as if it wasn't a big deal. "I get through it, I tell myself that it could be worse."

I wanted to believe him.

But my anger wouldn't grant me peace; it hungered, gnawed, begged for someone to blame.

"Maybe I should just stoop down to Caiden's level next time," I said. The words surprised us both.

"I wouldn't blame you," he said. "But you're not like him."

Wasn't I? I could feel it deep in my marrow, that sickness, that generational rot.

Maybe I was just another version of my mother, bottling up poison until it overflew and scorched everything in its path.

I stared at the raw crescents my nails had left on my palm, thinking I should cut them short before they hurt someone else.

Dante's hand hovered, hesitant, then landed on mine.

I let it stay, neither flinching nor grasping, and we sat like that for a long time, listening to the wind try to tear the world apart.

The sky overhead bled from iron gray to navy, and the streetlights flickered awake, casting cones of sickly gold onto the crumbling sidewalk.

The world shrank down to the bench, two bodies pressed close but separated by an ocean of silence.

I thought of all the times I'd watched other girls orbit each other, arms slung over shoulders, mirroring steps, swapping secrets like friendship bracelets. Their laughter was a language I'd never learned. I wore this isolation like a badge.

Dante's jacket weighed on me, a tangible reminder of kindness I could neither accept nor repay.

My fists balled up in the warped sleeves, skin itching, and I let myself picture what it would be like to lean into him, to rest my head on his shoulder, to cry until the ache hollowing out my chest spilled onto his shirt and left a stain.

But I couldn't. I wouldn't. I didn't even know how to start.

My teeth ached with the effort of holding myself together. I didn't realize I was rocking, just a little, until Dante's hand landed gently and steadily on my knee.

"Hey," he murmured. Warmth, simple and unassuming, radiated from his palm. "I'm not going anywhere, okay?"

I managed a nod, small and jerky. I was afraid that if I tried to speak, I'd scream.

"I know you think nobody sees you," he said, eyes fixed on the scuffed toes of his boots. "But I do."

My throat tightened.

His words should have comforted me, but instead they scraped at some raw place inside.

People always leave. They get tired of the mess, or bored, or just forget. You could count on that as surely as sunset.

The swings squealed mournfully. The sky overhead pressed down, bruised and swollen with the promise of rain.

I wanted to believe him, but all I could see was the way I flinched from loud voices, how easily I cried, how I let people trample my boundaries until nothing was left but a muddy doormat.

"I should go," I said finally, hating the way my voice trembled.

I peeled off the jacket, holding it out to him like an apology, but Dante shook his head. "Keep it. I've got others."

He said it like he believed I'd be cold again, like I'd need it.

I bundled the jacket close, wrapping myself in its borrowed armor, and walked home through the blue dusk. Every footstep sounded too loud.

I wanted to evaporate, just drift up through the clouds and never come back.

Inside, our house was dark except for the jaundiced glow of the kitchen. I stood in the doorway, invisible, while my mother scrubbed at a wine stain on her shirt.

Lillian crouched on the floor, gathering shards of glass into her palm, not bothering with a dustpan.

Nobody looked up when I closed the door. It was like I wasn't even there.

I drifted to my room.

I laid on my back and tried to name the shapes on my ceiling, to convince myself the shadows were just dust and not monsters with outstretched arms.

The world outside darkened by degrees, one streetlamp at a time. I let my mind drift, searching for a safe place, but everything ended up looping back to the moment at the wall, to Caiden's hands and the taste of his hate on my tongue.

# 5

## THE PAST
### AMELIA'S BREAKING POINT

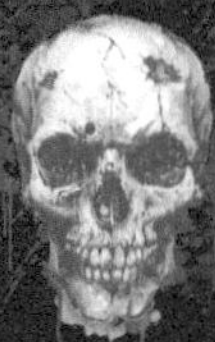

Today, we were taking a field trip for history class. The same class that Caiden and I shared.

I woke with dread in my heart.

The sky outside was corpse-pale, unconvincing in its cheeriness. I dressed in silence, layering myself in dark cotton and denim, bracing for the long day ahead.

I shrugged into my faded hoodie, the cotton threadbare and soft against my skin, then wrestled into jeans that were too small.

My footsteps echoed through the narrow hallway as I passed Mom's door. I paused, heart thudding, and peered inside.

She sat on the edge of her bed, a small amber lamp flickering beside her, hunched over the nightstand. Lines of fine white powder glistened on the oak surface.

She pinched a rolled-up dollar between trembling fingers, bent her head, and inhaled. A quiet sniffle escaped her as she turned, revealing hollows beneath her eyes and cheeks pulled taut over sunken bones.

The woman I once knew was gone, replaced by a pale ghost who drew poison into her lungs.

My breath hitched. I pressed a hand to my heart and vowed, with every last echo of dread, never to follow the same path. I would not lose myself in haze and emptiness.

As I stood there, a figure peeled out of the shadows behind Mom. Tall, angular, features swallowed in half-light.

My pulse hammered, and I stumbled back as he latched the door shut, severing me from refuge.

The man's smile glistened. He watched me with a hungry clarity that made my skin try to crawl away from itself.

"Hey there. You Judy's little one? Don't think we've met." The man's eyes glittered. "You want a bump? First one's free," he said, and patted the pillow beside him, like I was a dog he wanted to coax closer.

He grinned at me with catlike, unblinking eyes, then made a show of licking his lips. His hair was a greasy halo, and the way he leaned against Mom's dresser made my skin crawl.

"Don't be a bitch, Amelia," Mom muttered, voice thick with contempt. "Take a bump and get to school, okay? Jesus." Her hand was already reaching for the next line, knuckles white, veins spidering blue beneath the thin skin.

I wanted to vomit.

I offered a bitter smile and ducked into the bathroom, locking the door with shaking hands.

I stood there for a long time, forehead pressed to the cold metal of the lock, listening to their laughter seep through the drywall.

My palms sweated, my teeth buzzed. I didn't dare move. I could see the needle's shadow in my mind, hovering at the edge of the mirror.

Once I felt it was safe, I tiptoed through the rest of the house, hoping to find Lillian waiting with sleepy warmth.

Instead, her door lay shut; soft snores leaked through the crack. Disappointment was a bitter chord in my chest.

I stepped outside into the cool morning, the ache in my gut swirling like storm clouds.

The wind nipped at my ankles, pulling at the loose threads of my jeans, and I thought about how the cold made every memory sharper, how every passing day carved me thinner.

At the curb, a battered yellow bus squatted beneath maples, students crowding at its door in a loose, shuffling pack.

I almost wished Dante could be here, but he wasn't in this class with me, leaving me alone with Caiden, his best friend.

Mrs. Grant, our history teacher, perched at the top of the bus steps, clipboard in hand, yelling names over the tangled chatter.

I kept my eyes on my sneakers and handed her my permission slip, not trusting my hands not to shake.

She barely registered me.

I squeezed past a cluster of soccer girls, their laughter bright and mean, and picked an empty seat near the back. I pressed myself to the window.

Ten minutes passed. More students filtered in, filling the seats with the chaos of young bodies and too-loud voices.

My thoughts drifted, webbing out across the parking lot, and I almost didn't notice when a person sat next to me.

I looked to see Caiden, his rigid frame so sudden and large.

The air tightened between us as he sprawled, elbows wide, thigh pressed hard against the outer edge of my jeans.

I looked around helplessly to see that all other seats were filled.

Caiden didn't say a word at first. He just let his gaze burn a hole in the back of the vinyl seat in front of us, jaw flexing, fists opening and closing on his knees.

I used all my willpower not to flinch when his hand twitched within inches of mine, fingers curling as if about to break the seat in half.

I mustered my voice, brittle with effort. "You planning to murder me in a bathroom, or just maul me before we get to the next stoplight?"

He snorted, eyes not moving. "You'd like that, wouldn't you?"

I could have laughed, then. I almost did. But the sound stuck dry in my throat, a piece of brittle straw that wouldn't dislodge.

I narrowed my eyes at the window, refusing to let his stupid, smug words find their mark.

"Your obsession with me is getting embarrassing," I said. "Maybe try therapy instead of homicide."

That got a reaction. His hand twitched again, and then he forced a little noise. A chuckle. "You're so full of yourself. You really think I spend my nights plotting ways to ruin you?"

"You already ruined me," I said. The words slipped out before I could choke them back. I could feel his gaze then, pinning me to the grimy glass, as if he'd pressed my skull to the window and peeled back my scalp to see the softest bits inside.

"Listen, Amelia," he spat. "You keep pushing, and you're gonna find out exactly how much worse it can get."

I turned, finally meeting his eyes. They were black holes, the kind that devour everything and spit it back as ice.

"I'm not scared of you," I lied, my lips wearing a smile I'd never felt.

"You should be." The words hung between us, and he must have caught my body shrinking away from him, a reflex of terror.

"Relax," he muttered after a minute, voice lower than I'd ever heard it. "I'm not going to touch you."

I squeezed my fists. "You already did," I said, too quiet for anyone but him to hear.

He rolled his head against the seat, eyes boring into me, black and bottomless. "Don't flatter yourself. I was drunk and angry at the world."

A bitter laugh twisted through me. "Right. Because you only bother with the ones you think matter."

His jaw worked, and for the first time, I saw the tiniest crack in his mask. "Whatever."

We rode in silence. The bus rattled over frost-heaved roads, windows fogged with ghosts of breath and the lowing of other people's easy laughter.

I pressed my forehead to the glass and watched the trees blur, bare as bones, their shadows a tangle of accusations over the dead fields.

At the front, Mrs. Grant's voice wheeled above us, something about colonial history, about how the field trip would "bring the past alive." Her words snagged in the thick air, but never made it past the bubble of us in the back row. We were going to some old, historic battlefield with a museum.

Beneath the roar of voices and the hollow laughter, I caught his breathing, just a little too loud, like he had to prove he was still alive.

"You know," he said, after a mile of silence, "it's funny how all those times you talk back, stand your ground. You think you're righteous."

I didn't answer.

He leaned closer, his mouth almost at my ear, his words were molten. "But no matter what you do, your mom's still a junkie, and your sister's still a fuck-up, and you're still the trash everyone steps over on their way to something better."

The words should have gutted me, but I'd heard them all before. In my own voice, in the cracked mirror above the bathroom sink.

I stared ahead, eyelid twitching, refusing to blink.

I let my head thud, lightly, against the cold pane. I let him see that I wouldn't even give him the blink, or the tremble, or the tears. I could feel him watching for a reaction, the whole ride, like a hungry fish circling the wound.

I let the poison eat its way through me. The worst thing you could do with someone like Caiden was show them the wound.

The bus jerked to a stop on the shoulder of some godforsaken back road, its tires crunching loose gravel.

Caiden's thigh pressed harder against mine as the bus's movement shoved us both sideways.

Mrs. Grant barked a warning, her lips puckered in the rearview. "Settle down, please! We'll be at the fort in twenty minutes." Her voice bounced around the metal shell, paper-thin, always on the brink of tearing.

Outside, the sun clawed through the haze, slicing the world into slabs of icy blue and dust. I watched crows fight over something mangled in the ditch.

I wondered if the other students could see, if they cared, if they'd ever know what it felt like to be the smallest thing picked by the world.

Caiden didn't speak. He just flexed his hand, tapping the tips of his fingers against his thigh, one-two-three, restless, drumming some primitive code he probably didn't even know he was broadcasting.

I tried to picture where his mind went when he wasn't plotting ruin. Did he ever dream? Did he ever wish for anything but the next hit, the next fight, the next day to dawn?

He caught me watching him, and his eyes flared before he clamped his face back into the steel I always expected.

His jaw ticked.

"You got a staring problem?" he said, voice low.

I shrugged, not looking away. I knew if I blinked, he'd win. I wasn't about to lose, not today. "Do you get off on making people miserable?"

He arched a brow, like this was a stupid question. "The world's miserable, Amelia. Some of us are just honest about it."

I rolled my tongue along my teeth, hating how raw his words left me. "Maybe some people don't want to drown in your truth."

He grinned, all wolf, no heat. "Maybe they need to learn how to swim, then."

He thumped his head back on the seat, a grim laugh rattling loose. "You know, you act like I'm some kind of monster. But I've seen real monsters. You wouldn't last a minute in my house."

I wanted to fire back, tell him what he already knew: that my own house was a graveyard, and I'd slept in enough empty beds to know every inch of the dark.

But I didn't. I just closed my eyes and let his words chill me.

The bus rolled on. Every pothole rattled my bones.

My hands were cold and damp, the skin along my wrist burning from where I'd picked it raw the night before.

I curled my fingers, digging my nails into my palm, and counted the seconds until we arrived.

The fort hunched on the hill like a decaying tooth, all weathered wood and bristling fences. The bus hissed and shuddered like a dying animal as Mrs. Grant's shoes clacked down the aisle.

"Pair up with your buddy, please, and stay together for the tour!" she trilled, her breath a fog on the air. "This place is like a maze if you're not careful."

I rose, hoping to melt into the tide of bodies clogging the aisle, but Caiden blocked me, one broad hand gripping my shoulder with a pressure just shy of pain.

"What are you doing?" I spat, part of me bracing for him to shove me into the seat again, to snap something in me that hadn't already splintered.

"Not like you have any friends here," he sneered. "If I don't stick with you, you'll vanish in five seconds flat. Think of it as a mercy."

I twisted under his grip, but he didn't let go, just marched me down the steps and into the raw wind.

The chill cut through my layers, needling my bones. I hunched up, arms crossed, wishing I could shed my skin and leave it behind.

The rest of the class milled around the entrance, snapping photos or huddling in cliques. Caiden steered us toward the far edge of the group, his grip loosening only after he was sure I wouldn't bolt.

A faint dusting of snow crusted the ground, shushing our footsteps as we crossed the courtyard. The fort loomed overhead, log walls blackened by age, windows like gouged-out eyes.

I could almost hear the echo of old violence, musket fire, and shouted orders, men shivering in the picket line before being ordered forward to their deaths.

Inside, the fort reeked of varnished pine and something older, a sour musk that seemed to leach from the floorboards themselves.

Our class funneled into the first chamber, where a guide in period garb waited.

The words were meant to impress, but nobody cared. Half the class drifted to their phones, the glow of screens brighter than candle lanterns mounted to the wall.

Caiden trailed behind me, sometimes so close I could feel the heat of him. Other times, he vanished into the blind spots only to materialize at my shoulder, breath ghosting against my ear.

I hated how my skin tightened every time. I hated that he could still make me feel anything at all.

He followed me through narrow hallways, into the belly of the barracks. The ceiling pressed low, trapping the air between us, forcing us into proximity.

I traced the grain of the wood with my fingertips, counting old knife marks, wondering which were scars from battle and which were just bored boys carving up history.

"Bet you feel right at home," Caiden sneered, voice low enough for only me to hear. "Place reeks of loss. Suicide vibes, you know?"

"Yeah, actually," I shot back, "I was just thinking about how much this place reminds me of you. All the ghosts, the endless hunger for more pain."

He snorted, a harsh puff of air, but he didn't flee. For a blink, his gaze flickered, hurt, maybe, or just the surprise of finding himself a punchline for once.

He grabbed for the next insult and found nothing, and that empty beat between us swelled until I could hardly breathe.

I drifted to the back of the group, where Mrs. Grant's voice dissolved into static, and the tour guide prattled on about "harsh discipline" and "a culture of obedience." The words bled into the walls, into my bones.

I trailed my fingers along the splinter-gouged banister of a spiral stair, wondering if the stains in the wood were blood or just the slow seep of rain through the centuries.

When I looked back, Caiden was two paces behind, hands in pockets, eyes fixed on the floor.

He looked like a statue, carved from anger and cold. I thought about all the times I'd fantasized about shoving him down a flight of stairs, watching him crumble, and felt the old giddy pulse of vengeance.

But the longer I looked, the more I saw the animal gravity in his slouch.

He was so alone that he didn't even realize how alone he truly was.

"You gonna keep following me?" I asked, not turning.

"Not much else to do," he said, voice drained of venom. "You're all I've got for this damn field trip."

We shuffled after the group, through narrow passages where the low ceilings threatened to break our skulls.

The tour guide, a reedy grad student in a secondhand blazer, corralled us into a cramped meeting hall and fired up a projector.

The first slide was a sepia photograph of men in ragged uniforms, faces ghostly and hard. "This," he intoned, "is where the Regiment made their last stand in 1777. You can almost feel the memory of suffering in the air."

He wasn't wrong. Every inch of that place felt haunted.

Caiden folded his arms and leaned against the splintered wall, eyes hooded as he scanned the room.

When the guide gestured for everyone to break into pairs and explore, Caiden slid in front of me so fast I nearly tripped into his back.

"You don't have to stalk me," I said. "I can find my own way."

"Yeah, sure." He didn't even look at me. "Just don't want to explain to the cops when they find you curled up in a supply closet. Again."

I bristled, memory stinging my scalp. "That was one time. And you're the one who locked me in, jackass."

He shrugged, not even pretending to care. "You were pissing me off."

We trailed the group through narrow, echoing corridors. Half the class dissolved into the museum gift shop, but Caiden herded me toward the back stairs, away from the slouching chaperones.

"If you're gonna murder me, at least do it somewhere scenic," I muttered. My sneakers scuffed over warped floorboards, each groan of wood a complaint.

Caiden said nothing, just kept a pace a step behind, herding me up the narrow stairwell. The air at each landing grew colder, closing in hard.

At the top, a low door opened to a catwalk strung with icicles, the sky above gray as a spent shell casing. Wind whipped over the parapet, slicing my cheekbones.

He followed me out, lighting a cigarette with hands that shook slightly.

"For real?" I gestured to the 'No Smoking' sign staked in frosted mud. "Don't you ever get tired of rules you're going to break?"

He squinted into the wind, exhaled smoke that spun away in ribbons. "Only if they're boring."

The lighter clicked shut, metal on metal.

We stared out over the old battlefield: a patchwork of dying grass and rust-stitched mud, the memory of slaughter covered thinly in frost.

I half-expected to see spectral uniforms crawl from the trenches, bayonets, and bones. Instead, I saw a murder of crows rocket up from the trees.

He sat on the edge of the catwalk, feet dangling, cigarette balanced between two fingers. I stayed standing, arms wrapped tight, wishing the cold could reach in and hush every muscle.

"You know," he said finally, "I expected you to try harder to get away from me."

I laughed, the sound torn raw by the wind. "I don't give you the satisfaction if I don't have to."

He peeled his eyes off the horizon, settled them on me. "Why are you so obsessed with not letting anyone see you scared?"

I flinched. "Because you'd sniff it out and eat me alive."

He grinned, a slow, leeching thing. "You're not wrong."

"Look, you can go back down. Smoke your cigarette in peace. I'll wait five minutes before I go in, so we don't have to pretend to be on speaking terms."

I shifted my weight to the balls of my feet, ready to spring away the moment he loosened his attention.

But he just watched me, eyes narrowed like a predator testing the fence.

He looked over the bay, cigarette ash falling onto frozen dirt below. "My old man says people like you, people who break easily, are why the world's a joke. Maybe I just wanted to see if you'd prove him wrong."

I clenched my fists. "I'm not broken."

"Sure."

He stubbed the cigarette out, flicked the butt over the rail.

I trailed after him, down another set of shuddering stairs into the bowels of the fort.

Past the ropes and plexiglass that guarded the "authentic" rooms, down a corridor that shivered with the cold breath of history.

The air was darker here, denser. The only light came from a distant exit sign, bleeding red against the stone.

A trickle of other students moved through, their voices echoing from the next chamber, but Caiden led me the opposite way, into a hall bricked off from both ends.

He stopped, one hand drifting along the rotten timbers as if searching for a secret panel. He found a door—unmarked, uncurtained, slightly ajar—and nudged it open with his boot.

The room beyond was pitch black, the kind of dark that eats sound and reason.

I hesitated, every primal instinct screaming to turn back, but Caiden's silhouette filled the threshold.

He stepped inside, then waited, daring me.

I followed, because I couldn't let him have the last word.

He let the door fall shut.

The blackness was absolute, the kind that presses in on your bones and makes you doubt the shape of your own limbs.

I reached out, groped for the wall, and found only a chill that ran straight to the marrow.

I could hear him breathing, slow and deliberate. Then he laughed, low and cruel, the sound bouncing crazy off the stone.

"Freaked out yet?" he whispered.

"Hardly," I lied. My voice skittered along the walls, thin as moth wings. I pressed myself into the thick black, willing my body to freeze, to become an animal at rest so he couldn't taste my dread.

"Sure you're not broken?" he crooned. The darkness amplified every scrape and whisper, made his words crawl under my skin like centipedes. "You're shivering."

"Maybe there's a draft."

His footsteps echoed, three—no, four—paces away, then circled behind me.

With no sight, every sense sharpened; I could feel the displacement of air as he drew near, the faint electricity of him, the way the room seemed to pulse with his orbit.

I remembered being six, hiding in a closet when my mother raged through the house, the pitch-black womb both sanctuary and executioner.

Here, the dark was not empty: it was inhabited, predatory.

He moved closer, presence like a shifting draft in the void. "You ever wonder what hell feels like?" he murmured, the words cutting from somewhere behind my left shoulder. "Not the Sunday school version. The real one."

His breath was damp and sour, clouds of it blooming against my neck.

I tried to steady my voice, but it trembled into the void. "Sure. Hell is being trapped with someone you hate."

His laugh slithered over my skin. "But you didn't run. You followed me in. Makes you wonder which of us is more fucked up. Your self-worth must be pretty damn low."

I swallowed the bile, refusing to give him the sound of fear. I didn't have an answer for him. I didn't even know why I followed him.

Maybe I do have low self-worth.

Of course I did. Years of being neglected by my mother and tortured by Caiden–it did some terrible things to me.

Footsteps, quick and predatory, then his hand braced the wall right beside my head. I could feel the heat of him even through the cold, the pressure of his chest hovering just out of collision range.

I imagined Caiden's hands around my throat, like a noose, his thumbs digging into the soft shelf beneath my jaw, pinning my voice inside my throat.

The image sickened me, not because I thought he would, but because I half-wished he'd try.

At least then I'd have a reason to see myself as a survivor instead of just a scavenger.

He slammed his fist against the wall, the bang echoing like a gunshot.

I flinched, barely, but still didn't give him what he wanted.

"You're such a little masochist," he snarled. "You'd rather take a beating than admit you're scared."

The word rattled around my skull.

Was that what I was? Was that why I stayed in rooms with people who hated me, why I followed him down the stairwell and into this coffin of a room?

Maybe. Maybe I was just sick enough to like the attention, even if it meant being chewed up and spit out.

"You're projecting," I said, voice barely a whisper. "You want me scared because you're terrified of being alone with yourself."

I heard him move, the air shifting as he paced the small box of darkness. Suddenly, his hand found my shoulder, heavy, not painful, but enough to root me in place.

I flinched, but he didn't let go.

"Don't flatter yourself," he said, but the words rang hollow.

We stood, two satellites locked in orbit, neither willing to break the pull.

"God, you're a freak," he said, the words trembling with something rawer than anger. "Anyone else would be pissing themselves right now."

I remembered, in that instant, crouching in a closet while my mother's boyfriend slammed her through drywall, the sound of violence both muffled and amplified by the dark. How I'd pressed my palms over my mouth so hard my teeth left blood in the skin, just so I wouldn't make a sound. How I'd become a ghost, and how that had saved me.

"I've met worse monsters than you," I said, voice flat.

"I'm the worst kind of fucking monster you'll ever meet. Believe me."

He inched closer. I felt his breath first, then the heat of his body, then the fine tremor of his hands as they landed on either side of my head, pinning me without touch.

It was so black I could feel my pupils flaring, the useless straining for light.

Time had no measure in that dark room, maybe a minute, maybe an hour. I only knew that every inch of my skin felt peeled and raw, exposed to the wet rot of history oozing through the stones.

"Get away from me," I hissed.

He let out a snort, but didn't budge. "You'd like that, wouldn't you?" The chill between us vibrated, a dark, pulsing thing, his silhouette looming blacker than everything else. "Make a scene, Amelia. Scream. See if anyone comes."

I refused him, even as my lungs fluttered and a new, deeper panic wormed through my veins. Not fear of him, but the sudden, suffocating certainty that I'd always end up like this, trapped in a box with someone who wanted to see how much damage I could take before I broke.

I'd been screaming for years, and nothing ever came except more darkness.

"Knew it. No fight left in you."

The hands left the wall, but I could hear him circling, a wolf in a pen, waiting to lunge if I dared run. "You want to know what my dad does to me when I can't fight back?"

No. I didn't want to know.

But I pictured it anyway, in full high-def misery: the bruises, the raw-throated mornings, the way his voice sometimes hit the exact same pitch as my mother's boyfriends when the violence was just getting started.

Misery recognizes itself, even in people you hate.

He didn't say it, but I could taste it in the air: the memory of pain, the slow drip of it, how it seeps out and stains every inch of your life. I hated him for making me feel it. I hated myself for understanding.

My body was lit up with static, every nerve jangling. "Open the door," I said.

He stood unmoving, his shape a hulking smear in the void. "Bet you can't even find it," he whispered. "You'd die in here, you know. They used to bury the weak ones in the walls."

I almost believed him.

I pressed my back to the wall and tried to slow my breathing, but every gulp of air was thick with mildew and dread.

Caiden's steps whispered over the floorboards, circling so close I could have spit and hit him.

My hands fumbled at the wall behind me, searching blindly for seams or latches, anything that might break the spell of his darkness.

He let me grope around, savoring it, his own breathing settling into a predator's hush. "You remind me of a mouse, you know that?" he murmured, voice syrup-thick and hateful. "Scurry, scurry. But there's nowhere for you to go. Not this time."

The air in the blackness started to thicken, a velvet sack pulled over my head, suffocating and absolute.

I could hear my own heart, roaring in my ears, and it told me I was prey.

This was what he wanted: to see what shape my terror would take when no one was watching. The horror wasn't that he might hurt me, but that I might beg him not to.

I let myself slide to the floor, knees curling tight to my chest. I wouldn't give him tears, but the tremor in my arms said enough.

He prowled the small perimeter, boots dragging over the planks, every so often pausing to let the silence press harder.

He crouched, I could feel the heat of him, the animal patience of a true sadist. "You know, I could keep you here all day." His breath soured the air. "No one would care. Not even your own goddamn family."

"My family's garbage," I said, hating him for making me say it. "But at least I'm not a copy of my father, like you are."

He went still. I heard him exhale, long and hollow.

"Shut up," he said, voice stripped of affect. "You don't have any right to talk about him. About me."

"Then let me out," I said, louder, more desperate than intended.

My hand scraped the wall for anything. Nail, knob, even a splinter to dig under my skin so I had pain I owned, not pain he gave.

He didn't move. "Make me."

Hatred and terror warred inside my chest, a chemical cocktail. I rose, fists balled, pushing blindly along the edges with my knuckles.

I moved along the frozen plaster, splinters raking my fingertips, and the panic at my throat threatened to choke me.

I remembered the way my mother used to pace outside my childhood closet, her voice a low, hungry croak, waiting for me to come out so she could finish the fight. I'd lasted hours that way, feeding off the darkness until it tasted like home.

This dark was worse. There was no promise of morning, just Caiden, circling, hungry to see me crumble.

I could hear him crouch, knees popping, the hiss of his exhale close enough that I imagined his lips at my ear. "You're not even worth hating, you know that? You think you matter, but you're a nothing. You're a ghost."

I flinched at the word. "You're wrong," I said, but the syllables wavered, thin as thread.

He crawled closer, boots scuffing, then crouched, so close that his heat pressed against my side. "Ghosts don't feel pain," he whispered. "But I know you do." And his fingers brushed my wrist, deliberate, not gentle.

"Let me go," I rasped, voice cracking. "Let me go, Caiden. I fucking mean it."

He didn't answer. He just stared, his face inches from mine, a mask of hate and hunger and something so lonely it hurt to witness.

I tried to wrench free, but his grip was iron. Rage and shame and terror carved me open.

I pictured the bus, the empty house, the way my mother flinched from noise.

Nobody came for me, not really.

But I screamed anyway, a wild, animal sound that tore my throat raw and bounced crazed through the black.

The scream was a mix of a shriek and words. A chant of "let me go, let me go, let me go, leave me alone."

He flinched. Not much, but enough. "Jesus, Amelia," he breathed, and his grip loosened just a millimeter.

"Is this what you want?" I gasped, eyes leaking hot tears I refused to let fall. "You want to see me break? You want to feel like a man? Go ahead, hit me. Do it."

His hands trembled. He released me, like I'd turned to fire.

"I don't want to hurt you," he said, but his voice was so small I almost missed it.

I had no words. My throat was burning, along with the blood pumping through my bones. I couldn't trust myself to talk without weeping.

He released me, and for a fraction of a second, the world hung upside down. Me, gasping, with my hands clawed open, him, an outline of feverish anger, sucking in air like a swimmer who just breached the surface after too long underwater.

The dark rushed back in, thick as tar.

We stayed like that, orbiting the same patch of empty space, the only noise the ragged echo of our breathing, until I could finally hear my own heart slowing.

My knees ached from the stone floor. My wrists burned in the ghost of his grip.

"Fine," he muttered, voice shredded. "You win."

He fumbled at the wall and, after a scrabble that sounded like he was tearing at his own skin, found the latch.

Light stretched in, bulb-bright and savage, slicing the black into trembling strips. I blinked, eyes watering, face streaked with tears I couldn't remember making.

He watched me, unreadable, breathing hard. "You want out? Get out."

His lip curled, but the old pleasure in it was gone. He pointed to the door with a flick of his chin.

I stumbled to my feet, legs numb and shaky, and swept past him without looking up. I leaned into the wall, fighting not to be sick.

He followed, but kept a careful distance, like he was the one afraid to get too close.

I wiped my face with the back of my sleeve, the salt of tears biting the raw skin under my eyes. My hands wouldn't stop shaking.

I hated that he'd seen me like that, hated more that I'd made a sound, given him exactly what he'd wanted.

I pressed my shoulder to the cinderblock, clawed breath after breath, but the ghost of his hands still clung to my wrist.

The sensation was so vivid I dug my nails in, leaving red half-moons as proof I could still feel something of my own.

He leaned against the wall across from me, slouched, arms crossed, eyes fixed on the floor. He didn't gloat. He looked smaller, drained, maybe even ashamed, but I didn't trust the angle of his mouth.

I watched him through the blurred halo left by light-starved pupils, refusing to blink, waiting for the next punch.

"You done?" he asked.

I wanted to say something venomous, something that would bruise him. Instead, my voice came out flat. "Go to hell."

His lips twitched, a hint of the old wolfish sneer. "Already there, sweetheart. Thought you'd noticed." He rolled a shoulder, shrugged, and started down the corridor, boots echoing off the stone like a slow drumbeat. "You coming, or you gonna sit in the dark all day?"

I straightened, wiped my cheeks again, and followed two paces behind, the distance a shield I could cling to.

We emerged into the fort's central courtyard. The sky above was flat and iron, the sun a bare rumor behind clouds.

Kids in our class milled near the cannon, a little cluster of noise, but their laughter sounded distant, underwater.

Mrs. Grant was at the periphery, her mouth a hard slash, watching the pair of us like she sensed what we carried with us from the dark.

A gust of wind bit through my sweatshirt, cold and vengeful. The taste of the dark still clung to my mouth, copper and rot.

I wondered if the others could see it on me. The stink of freshly-peeled nerves, the way my hands kept closing themselves into little fists, over and over, as if I could squeeze out what he'd put there.

I hunched my shoulders, expecting Caiden to close in, to pick up our war where we'd left it.

Instead, he just paced along the edge of the ground, hands deep in the pockets of his jacket, head bent.

I wanted to believe the dark had scared him too, that there was something left in him that could feel shame, but the memory of his hands—hard, sure, wanting—kept replaying behind my eyes.

I drifted to the far side of the fort's yard.

Beyond the fence, an expanse of churned earth and dying grass sloped toward a tangled line of woods. The ground was pitted with hollows and mounds. Trenches, probably, or the remains of the old burial pits the guide had mentioned in passing, voice grave and theatrical for the benefit of bored high schoolers.

I imagined corpses stacked tight as cigarettes, the dirt too cold to let them rot, all their stories reduced to bone and bloodstain. I wondered if they haunted the place, if they ever wished for vengeance or simply wanted to be left alone.

I pressed my hands to the frozen rail at the fence's edge, the sting of it snapping me back into my skin.

I thought: if I stood here long enough, maybe the cold would work its way in and soothe every wound, every memory, until I was blue and hard and too numb to care.

A crow perched on a splintered picket, watching me with the derision of someone who'd seen it all before: girls unraveling, boys turning to dogs, the world never bothering to notice either way.

It cawed, a single dry syllable, and flapped to a post farther down, keeping its distance but never taking its eyes from my hands.

I realized I was still trembling. I pressed the heel of my palm into my thigh, grounding myself in the spike of cold.

A memory surfaced. The day after my father left, I'd sat alone at the kitchen table.

The whole house had the sickly-sweet tang of rotting fruit, and in that morning light, every object seemed edged in shadow, as if the sun itself was sick to its stomach.

My mother had been in her room for hours, door locked, the sound of her crying a constant, low-pitched whine through the drywall.

I'd sat motionless, listening for the world to crack open and end, but nothing had happened. The clock had kept ticking. The fridge had kept humming and I'd realized, with a clarity that hurt, that I was the only one who noticed.

That same loneliness had followed me here, to the fort, trailing me like a disease. Even with the courtyard swarming with kids, the sound of their laughter a rotten froth over the hard earth, I felt isolated, a cold spot in the middle of a fever.

Alone, drowning in my darkness, forever.

Back in the bus, I scrabbled for the window seat and crammed myself against the shuddering glass.

The sky was a morbidity, blue turned to lead, clouds low and morbidly thick, swallowing the sun before it could die a proper death.

I pressed my forehead to the cold, letting the vibration of the engine rattle my thoughts into something empty.

After a while, I realized Caiden wasn't next to me. The seat was vacant, and I was alone for the first time all day.

I wanted to feel relief, but all I felt was a slow, numbing dread creeping up my bones.

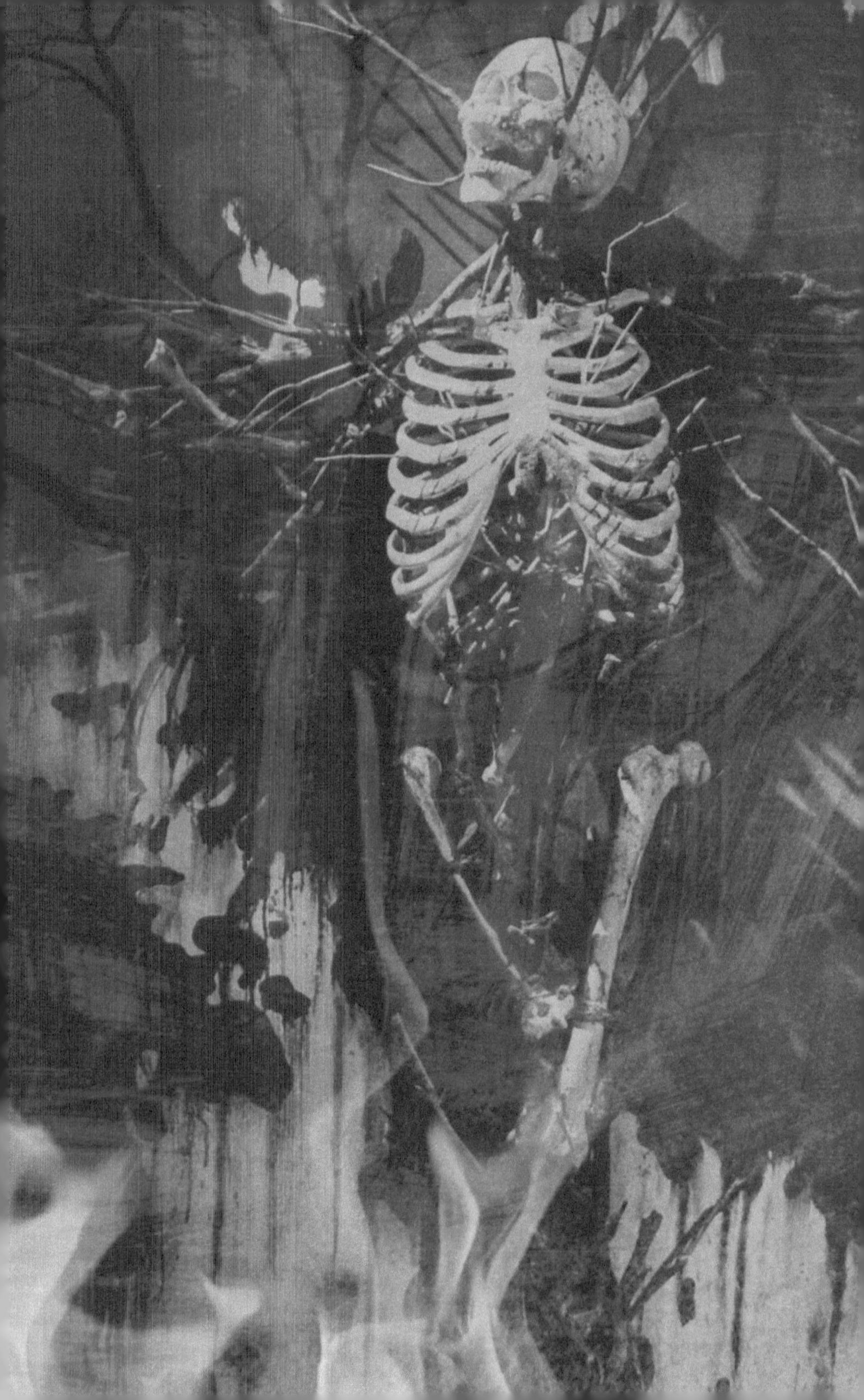

# 6

## THE PRESENT

### AMELIA

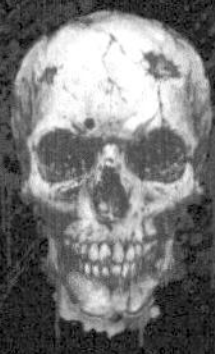

The walls tilted, and the floor seemed to ripple beneath my feet; a wave of nausea rose in my throat. Every breath felt as if I were underwater, and yet I couldn't tear my gaze from him.

He sat there in the half-light, like a dark statue come to life.

His jaw more defined, cheekbones sharper, and shoulders broader than I remembered. His brown eyes, cold and haunted, bore into me with the same taunting intensity that had stalked my dreams for years.

I was rooted to the spot, drawn to him by some terrible fascination, as though I peered into a car crash through shattered glass, unable to look away.

Panicked, I forced out a whisper, "I can't do this." My legs trembled, and I bolted for the door, my footsteps echoing on the hardwood.

I scanned the driveway. No car, no escape.

My heart hammered; my ribs felt tight as cords.

I sank against Sabrina's sleek black sedan, palms flat against its cool, metallic finish. My chest heaved as I fought for calm. "Honey, are you okay?" Sabrina's voice floated through the open window, soft with concern. I closed my eyes, picturing myself dissolving into the pavement.

*Please go away*, I thought, but guilt wove through me like barbed wire. She'd invited me on this trip, insisted it would be fun, paid for

59

everything. While I was on the brink of collapse because of a man I never wanted to see again.

"I... I felt sick," I managed, my voice a croak. Images of Caiden Baxter, my high school tormentor, swirled in my mind. How could I explain that seeing him was like reopening an old wound? Words failed me.

Sabrina's brow furrowed. "C'mon inside. I'll get you water, maybe something for your stomach." She reached for my arm, gentle but insistent.

"I don't think I can go on this trip," I blurted. "I'm sorry." My voice cracked.

Her lips parted, disbelief shimmering in the lamplight. I closed my eyes and took a shuddering breath. I'd promised her, and I was supposed to be a grown-up. This rivalry between he and I happened years ago, after all.

"Wait—no. I'll go. I just need a minute." I opened my eyes and forced a smile.

Sabrina's relief was a warm breeze; she pulled me into a hug. "Thank you, Amelia. Really. Take your time."

She stepped back and left the door ajar. I watched her disappear inside the yellow glow.

In the threshold stood Caiden, framed by lamplight, his face inscrutable. My pulse thundered. I forced myself to look away, focusing on the cool night air brushing my cheeks, on drawing slow, steady breaths.

Summoning every ounce of courage, I stepped forward. The threshold felt like the edge of a cliff, but I crossed it.

"Amelia? Are you feeling better?" Sabrina's voice rang through the foyer, crisp with worry.

I nodded, swallowing hard, and gave her a shaky smile. "Yes. I just needed air."

From the corner, Shane emerged, warmth in his grin. "Hey, Amelia. So glad you're here, for Sabrina, especially."

He laughed lightly at his own joke, and I offered a courteous nod, heart pounding as I braced myself for the days ahead.

"I was honored to be invited. I'm so happy for you both," I said, my voice smooth as glass, hiding the quake beneath. My smile felt brittle, stretched too thin. Every nerve in my body buzzed with the knowledge that Caiden would be here.

Shane's expression lit up. "Now that you're feeling better, I can finally introduce you to my half-brother." He waved theatrically. "Caiden, this is Amelia."

Caiden stood like a marble statue in the doorway, silence clinging to him. I offered my hand, determined to seem composed. "Hi! Nice to meet you."

He blinked down at my outstretched hand as if trying to remember its purpose. My pulse spiked.

Inside, that gawky teenager I once was clawed at my nerves, begging me to bolt. I shoved her back, forcing calm as I maintained my smile.

Sabrina, ever the instigator, nudged him. "Go on, Caiden! Amelia won't bite, unless you ask nicely."

At last, he took my hand. His grip was unexpectedly warm and firm, a spark crackling through me. I swallowed, heart pounding.

"Nice to meet you, Amelia," he murmured in a low, velvety tone. "This will be an interesting trip."

Polite enough on the surface, but I caught the flicker of something colder in his voice. Hardness edged with disdain. We held each other's gaze, locked in a silent, unspoken challenge.

I forced my jaw to unclench.

Sabrina clapped her hands. "Okay! Introductions done, let's hit the road!" She darted around us, gathering duffels and suitcases with the fervor of a child on the brink of vacation.

"Caiden, help me with these bags before Sabrina pulls a muscle," Shane laughed. Caiden nodded and hoisted a heavy pack. I stood to the side, heart still racing from our brief contact.

I grabbed my suitcase, its cool handle grounding me, and slung my backpack over my shoulder.

Outside, the air carried the crisp scent of pine. The Toyota Sequoia gleamed in the late afternoon sun, its black exterior polished to a mirror shine. Inside, charcoal leather seats and warm wood accents beckoned, scenting the air with new-car freshness.

"So, seating arrangement?" I asked, handing off my bags to Sabrina.

"I was thinking you and I take the back row, boys up front," she said, stowing my things neatly. "We might switch so Shane isn't stuck driving."

I nodded, gripping my hands together to still their tremor. The thought of sitting beside Caiden ignited my nerves.

"Alright, let's hit the road!" Shane called from the driver's seat. Caiden slid into the passenger side, and Sabrina whisked to the rear, claiming the seat behind Shane. That left me nestled closest to Caiden.

The engine roared, and the Sequoia rolled forward.

Through the windshield, the world unfurled in streaks of green and gold. My breath caught. My heart drummed a warning. There was no running now. The past was here, inches away, and I would have to face it.

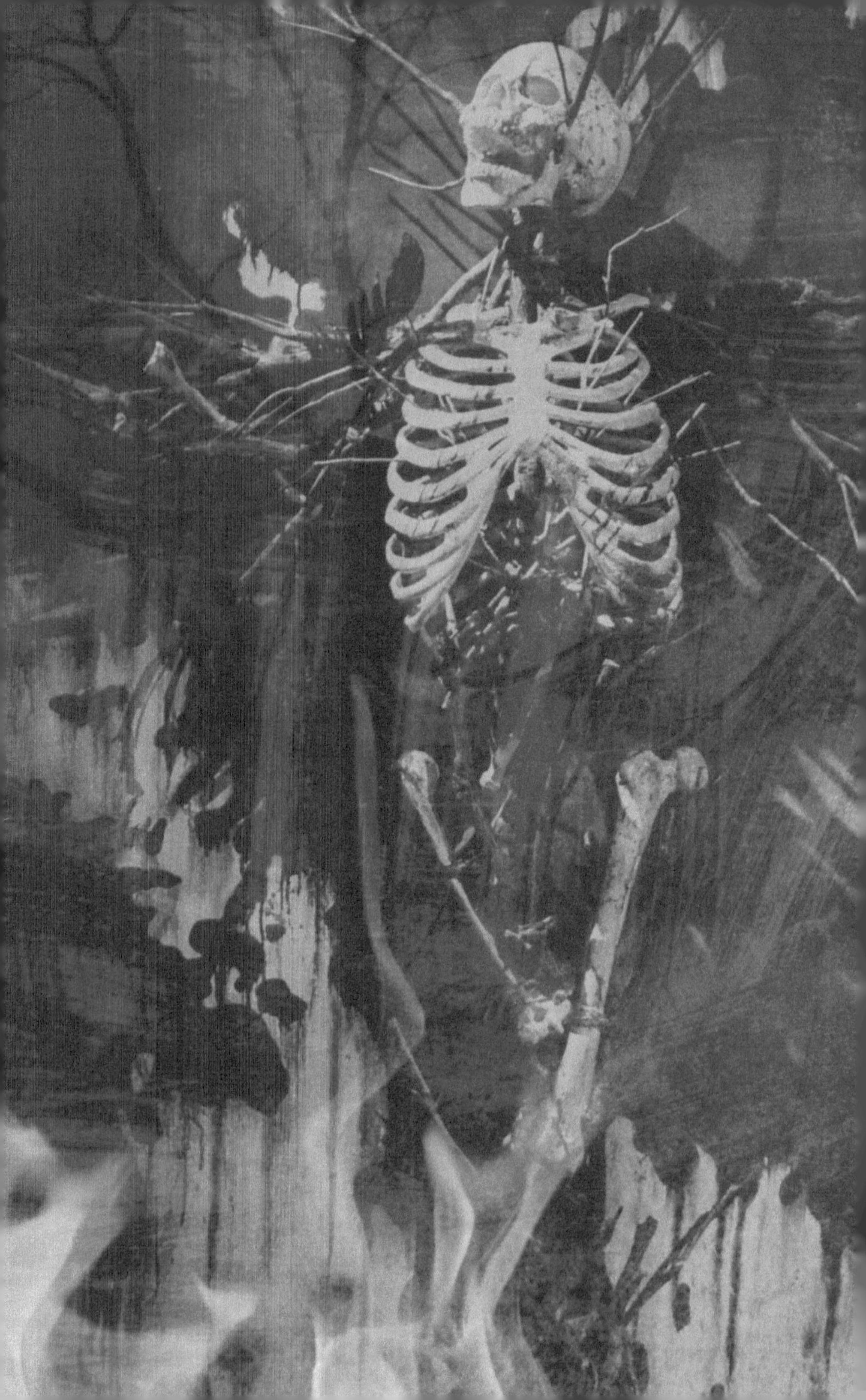

# 7

# THE PAST

## AMELIA'S BREAKING POINT

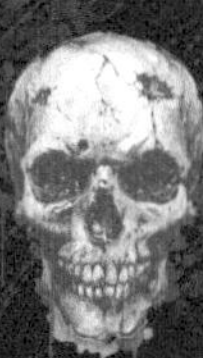

THE ROAR OF VOICES DRIFTED LIKE A BOMB THROUGHOUT the house. I winced as I listened to my mother and Lillian snapping at each other like wild beasts.

I had sensed something terrible would happen today as soon as I saw my mom using drugs early in the morning.

Nothing good ever emerged from a drug binge.

"What is your fucking problem, Mom?"

"You are my problem! You kids ruined my fucking life!"

Something metal crashed against the wall, sending a jarring sound echoing through the house. Silence followed, then cries and more terror-filled yelling. Another object was thrown. I couldn't endure it.

Every night felt like a descent into hell, and the days were no better. I shut my eyes and let out a long breath.

One day, I would escape and never return.

The walls here were too thin, the air too thick with all the things we never said. Some days, I dreamed the drywall would collapse beneath the pressure of our secrets, bring the whole house down in a pile of splintered remains.

Then, maybe, we could start over and get it right.

But the world doesn't give second chances to families like mine.

The tears came slow and silent. Not the racking, gasping kind, but the ones that slid out without permission, soaking the threadbare carpet under my cheek.

When the shouting dulled to a low, guttural moan, I snuck out of my room and padded down the hallway on bare feet. The carpet was sticky from some spill; I had long ago stopped asking what it was.

The living room looked like a crime scene.

Mom sat slumped on the arm of the couch, mascara smeared. Lillian lay on her stomach, clutching a throw pillow with white knuckles, lips pressed tight to keep in the animal noise.

Mom caught me in her periphery and jerked upright. "What're you looking at?" she spat, dragging a sleeve across her wet face.

I shook my head and shrank into the wall, wishing I could melt through it.

She staggered to her feet, swaying, then advanced on Lillian, voice cracking like a whip. "I gave up everything for you ungrateful shits."

It didn't sound like her at all. Barely human. She was somewhere else behind her eyes, watching the scene on a busted projector while her body moved on autopilot.

Lillian rolled over, not even trying to wipe her face. There was blood at the corner of her mouth. "You never gave up anything. You just took and took."

Mom's hand lashed out, catching a fistful of Lillian's hair and yanking her upright. Lillian didn't scream, just stared back, daring Mom to hit her again.

For a second, I saw the whole past play out in their locked stares. The way Mom used to stroke Lillian's hair and sing to her, back when warmth was still possible.

"Don't touch me," Lillian sobbed, flinching away. Mom's shadow blotted out what little light leaked in from the kitchen. She bared her teeth, the shape of a woman stretched so thin that bone glimmered beneath the surface.

"I should have left you both at that hospital," she howled. "You and your goddamn sister are leeches, every last one, just like your father." Her fingers flexed, trembling with some animal urge.

For a moment, I thought she might strike Lillian's bowed head, but instead she spun and hurled the nearest mug against the far wall. Porcelain exploded, shards tinkling over the floor. "Look at me!" she shrieked, words slurring into one another, language unraveling with her self-control. "I could've been something. I could've had a life. But you—both of you—just take and take and take—"

Lillian lifted her face, eyes red but cold. "That's enough, Mom. You're high."

"Don't you dare talk to me like that, you little—"

"Enough!" Lillian's voice had the sharp edge, and for a split second, Mom reeled back in surprise.

Somewhere in the kitchen, a faucet dripped. The smell of wine, sweat, and bitter narcotics filled my nose.

I felt myself floating above it all, watching from the cracked paint of the ceiling, like a ghost haunting the wreckage of the only home I'd ever known.

Mom let go of the fight and stumbled into the kitchen, just barely missing the doorframe.

I wanted to follow her, to see if the monster had eaten her whole or if there was a scrap of my mother left in there, but Lillian curled a hand around my wrist and pulled me down next to her on the floor.

I let her, my body loose and numb.

We listened to the sounds of pill bottles being shaken, cabinet doors slamming.

The refrigerator opened, then shut. A glass fell and shattered. The kitchen light flicked off and on, off and on, in a sick little rhythm.

A scream built behind my teeth, but I buried it and let my eyes burn instead. Someday, I would scream until the world heard me, until someone came to dig me out from beneath all this ash.

I waited until the house fell into a dead hush.

My mother was passed out and left a mess. We were the ones who had to clean up after her drug-infused rage.

The only noise was Lillian breathing, slow and uneven, like she was learning how for the first time. I reached over and squeezed her hand, and after a moment, she squeezed back.

We didn't say anything. We didn't have to. I wanted to comfort her, to say that I would always be there.

But I couldn't speak, because words meant nothing in this house. Words were walls and doors, things to be locked and battered down.

I slipped out the back door, my phone cold in my hand. My legs took me down the block, where the pavement burned with memories and the streetlights flickered on like nervous glances.

I texted Dante on my flip-phone with trembling fingers.


Amelia: Can I come over?

Dante: Dad's not here. Mom's home but she won't bother us. Want me to meet you halfway?

Amelia: No I need to walk. See you soon.


I let the phone drop into my pocket and moved through the dusk as if the air would swallow me.

The town was quiet, all the houses dark and hunched against the coming cold. The only sound was the soft thwack of my shoes and, far off, a siren screaming for nobody in particular.

His house was exactly two blocks away. The paint had peeled back to gray in most places, and the front walk was littered with busted yard toys and last year's Christmas lights.

But it was warm inside, and I could pretend, for an hour or two, that I belonged somewhere.

Dante answered the door before I could knock. He wore a frayed T-shirt and sweatpants, hair wet from a recent shower.

"You okay?" he whispered, but I shook my head and stepped past him into the warmth.

We didn't go to his room, because his mom's bedroom was right across the hall and he said the walls were thin.

Instead, we headed down to the basement where Dante's dad kept a pool table, a couch and a battered old TV. It was cold and smelled like laundry soap, but I didn't mind.

Down here, the world above felt impossibly far away.

Dante led me to the far corner, away from the naked bulb and the mildewed laundry basket and gestured for me to sit on the threadbare couch.

He grabbed a fleece blanket from the arm and draped it around my shoulders, tucking it in with a gentleness that made my eyes prickle.

Then he sat down, a careful foot or two away, and waited.

I don't know what I looked like, but he must have seen something in my face that scared him.

He didn't say anything right away, just drummed his fingers on his knee and watched the carpet, quiet.

There was a deep sense of panic clawing its way through my skin, as if to say, 'you're not safe anywhere.'

After a while, when my hands stopped shaking so badly and my heartbeat lessened a bit, Dante offered me a can of Sprite from the mini fridge under the stairs.

I opened it and drank, the cold sweet fizz scraping the raw places in my throat.

"It was bad, huh?" Dante said, his voice a low hush.

I nodded, not trusting myself to speak.

He reached over, slow and uncertain, and put his hand over mine. His palm was warm, and I didn't pull away this time.

"You can stay here tonight if you want," he said. "I'll make up the guest bed, or we can both crash here."

I wanted to say yes. But I also wanted to curl up and disappear, to claw my way out of my own skin and escape whatever I was carrying.

Instead, I just stared at the pool table's green felt, torn in one corner and patched with duct tape. A perfect circle of cigarette burn in the center. I wondered if the scar would ever fade.

"My mom was scary tonight. I just need a break from it." I admitted, ashamed of appearing so vulnerable and shaken.

He looked at me with a tenderness I didn't deserve, which made me want to punch something, maybe even him. "You can stay as long as you need," he said, voice full of that rare patience that I always wanted but couldn't accept.

I tried to say thank you, but my throat squeezed shut around the words.

All my life, I had a warped sense of love.

Love wasn't soft, kind, or pure. Love was filled with screams and terror. It was bloody and dark.

I said, "If I stay here, she'll get pissed. She'll take it out on Lillian."

He didn't argue. "You could tell someone, you know. I could help."

"I don't want help. Not from anyone." My own voice sounded mean, not like me. "I just want it to stop."

There was a pause while I stared at the cracked ceiling, counting the web of pipes and the water stains spreading like bruises. I wondered if it would be easier if I just disappeared. Would my mother notice? Would Lillian feel relief?

He squeezed my hand, thumb circling the bone. "You ever want to talk about it, you can."

"I don't want to talk," I said, and then, "Maybe I just want to forget."

Dante nodded, a small, sad smile on his lips. "I could distract you. We could watch something? Or I can blast music until you can't hear yourself think."

He was trying. His hands were gentle, and his voice was soft, and for a moment, I hated him for being kind when the world was so ugly.

But I found myself leaning into his shoulder, just enough to feel the warmth of him through the fleece. He didn't say anything, just let me rest there.

"It's okay. All I want is to feel safe for once in my life."

My head drooped against Dante's shoulder, the wool of his fleece scratchy but solid. The panic receded at the edge, like a dog that might bite again at any moment, biding its time.

There was a comfort in Dante's silence, in how he didn't press for explanations or try to fix me. He just waited, breathing slow and steady, tethering me to the here and now.

The Sprite can went warm and sticky in my hand, but I cradled it anyway, needing the small chill, the sugar burn.

I tracked the ticking of a basement clock, the way the second hand jerked its way around. The only other sound was the rattle of pipes as the furnace kicked on, and the hum of the fridge, always hungry for more.

We didn't move for a long time. I think we both knew if we did, the moment would shatter and everything I was holding back would flood the room.

So, we sat, hunched together on the battered couch, while the clock's juddering heartbeat measured out the infinite, empty seconds.

Eventually, Dante reached for the remote, turning on the old TV.

The static flickered across our faces, throwing us into silhouette. He didn't bother with the volume. It was only there to fill the air, to say: here is something harmless, something not meant to wound.

His hand was still on mine, and that felt stranger than anything. I didn't know what to do with it.

I wanted to squeeze back, to prove I was still capable of caring about another person, that my insides weren't all burnt resin and rot.

But my fingers wouldn't move. I just sat rigid, letting a strange numbness creep up my arm, into my chest, until I couldn't tell if I was breathing or not.

I must have drifted. The basement light was off, the TV's blue glow replaced by a dark silence.

My eyes snapped open and for a disorienting moment, I didn't know where I was. The air was cold, but the weight behind me was warm and solid, a body curved along the length of mine.

Dante's arm bracketed my ribs, his hand splayed gently, not possessive but anchoring, the way you might keep a page from blowing away in the wind.

For the first time in my life, I woke up not to the drone of my mother's rage or the sulfur stink of pills, but to the slow, steady rhythm of someone else's breathing.

It was so startlingly gentle I almost panicked; my chest seized, all the old alarms blaring to life, and for a second I considered biting him, or running, or just screaming until the house shook.

But the warmth of Dante's palm soaked into me, and I pressed my lips together, trying not to make a sound.

It felt good, too good, in a way that terrified me.

Like if I let it in, even for a second, I would need it forever. I'd be ruined.

His chin nuzzled my shoulder. The heat of him, the way his knees hooked the back of mine, the gentle flex of his fingers at my hip, every bit of contact was a reminder that some people could want you without trying to break you.

I wanted to let it happen. To be touched and not torn. But even in dreams, the coil of panic lived at the base of my skull, waiting for a reason to strike.

I lay as still as I could, counting the seconds between his breaths, then the seconds between mine. I lost track, let the numbers unravel, and drifted back to a muted sleep.

This time I dreamed of nothing at all.

When I woke again, it was morning, and the daylight was leaking around the edges of the little window well, painting the cement floor with a weak, gray light.

I shifted, and Dante stirred behind me, groaning and stretching. I tried to squirm free, but his grip only tightened, dragging me closer.

I glanced at the clock and realized it was nine in the morning.

Thankfully, it was Saturday, so no school.

Yet, I had the urgency to leave.

I squirmed away from the warmth of Dante's body, my movements quick, almost frantic. I could feel the static of his skin linger on mine, a phantom touch that made my teeth clench.

Affection wasn't something that I was used to. It was foreign and cold. An immense sense of panic overcame me. I thought about the neglect of my mother. The abandonment of my father. How nothing is safe, and everybody leaves.

*Leave them so they can't disappoint you.*

Disentangling myself from the couch, I stood, arms folded, shivering in the clammy basement air.

My heart thudded in my chest, a warning drum: *Don't get used to this. Don't you dare.*

Dante blinked awake, confusion fogging his features. "Hey," he rasped, voice thick with sleep, "where are you going?"

"I can't stay here," I said, the words rushed and jumbled. "I just —" I searched for something true, something that wouldn't make me sound weak. "I need to breathe."

He sat up, rubbing his eyes. For a long moment, he was silent, watching me with a gaze that tried to pin me down. "You can tell me what's wrong, you know."

His tone was gentle, but there was an edge of desperation that made me want to run.

I shook my head, hugging myself tighter. "I can't... I just can't." My voice crumpled at the end, and I hated myself for it. "I'm gonna go home."

Dante stood, hands outstretched but not quite touching me. "You don't have to. You can stay as long as you want, Amelia. Nobody's gonna make you—"

"Please," I whispered, voice raw. "Don't."

He stopped, shoulders dropping.

For the first time, I saw hurt flicker across his face, but it slipped away as soon as it came.

Dante's arms hung at his sides, all soft threat and apology. He looked so much like a kicked dog I almost laughed, but my lungs were full of splinters. I left before he could say goodbye.

Dante didn't follow. I knew he wouldn't. He was good like that. He knew when to back off, when to let my spiral run its course.

Still, I hated leaving him in that half-lit basement, empty arms dangling at his sides, not knowing if he'd ever get to hold me again.

I hated that I already missed the warmth of him, the way his breath had tucked itself into the curve of my neck like an apology.

But I couldn't have that. It would never last, and it would only end in tragedy.

The neighborhood was empty. No cars humming past, no neighbors scraping frost from windshields, no distant shouts of kids too young to know what bruises lasted longest.

It was just me and the crows, picking at the bones of the morning.

I imagined every family inside, each one a snow globe of warmth and noise and normalcy, and I wanted to shatter every single one.

My hands shook, so I stuffed them in my pockets. I tried to walk slowly, but my body kept speeding up, as if I could outrun the memory of Dante's hand on my hip.

The ache in my chest had sharpened into something new: shame. For needing, for wanting, for letting myself believe, even for a second, that I could have something soft.

The wind whipped hair into my mouth and eyes, but I barely noticed. The taste of old Sprite lingered on my tongue.

I tried to focus on that.

As I approached the house, a stinging sensation pinched deep in my gut.

My mother's car was missing, but Lillian's broken-down vehicle was in the driveway. I approached the front door with caution.

I stepped inside, an eerie silence immediately wafting through the air. Nothing seemed out of place, yet a gnawing dread clawed at me.

I made my way toward my room, passing Lillian's door. It was cracked open, and I peeked inside, freezing at the sight before me.

Shock coursed through my veins, and nausea churned in my stomach. A torrent of emotions surged through me like lightning.

My sister lay sprawled on her bed, and beside her lay my worst enemy.

Caiden.

The chilling realization hit me hard: they were both naked, their clothes were strewn haphazardly across the floor.

Would I run, or would I explode in fury?

The answer became clear.

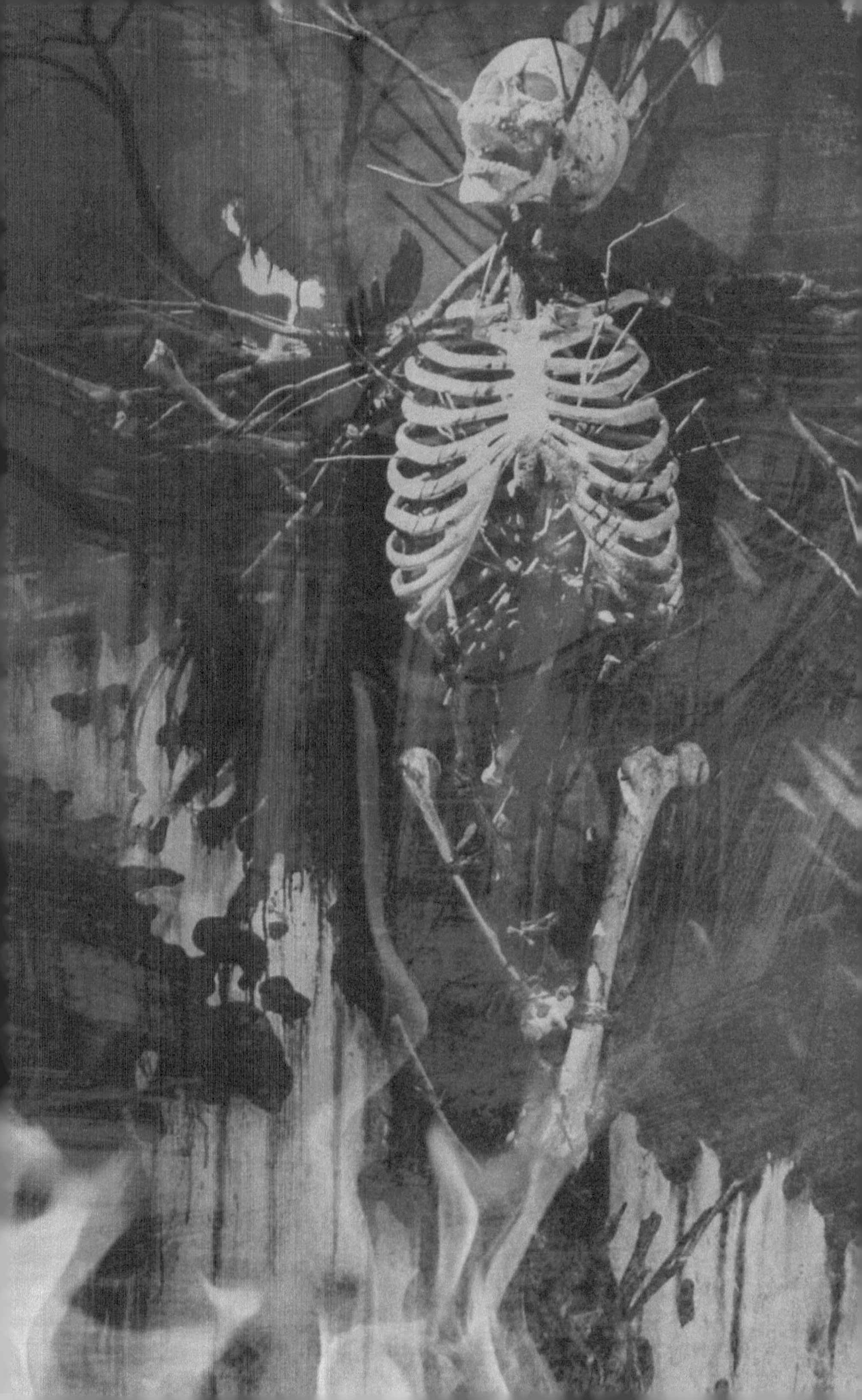

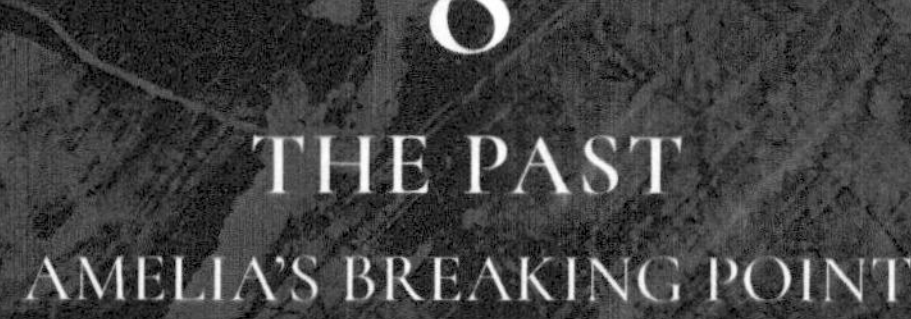

# 8

## THE PAST

### AMELIA'S BREAKING POINT

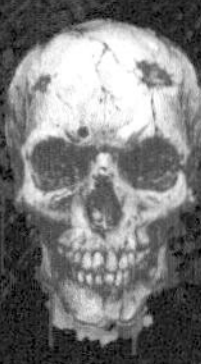

A WAVE OF CRIMSON RAGE, BLISTERING AND ALL-consuming, swept over me, turning every nerve into a flame.

My sight blurred, edges melting into a red haze, and the taste of bile rose in my throat as my lungs constricted against a belly-twisting convulsion of nausea.

The room felt too small, the wallpaper crawled toward me, tilting the air so each inhale sounded like the snap of a tightening noose.

Betrayal, I realized, was a fragile blade, its initial incision barely noticeable before it gouged out a cavern of ruin, a disaster teetering on the brink.

To be deceived by a stranger was to let a momentary wound bleed and then scab over, forgotten in time's dull ache.

But when that knife twists in the blood of family, the cut never heals. It festered raw, throbbing with every heartbeat, and once that barrier shatters, everything splinters into shards, impossible to realign.

"What the fuck is going on?" I shouted, my voice loud enough to wake them from their slumber.

Lillian stirred, groggily looking up from where she lay, her arms splayed across Caiden's bare chest, a sight that felt like a punch to the gut.

"Lower your voice; my head hurts like hell," Lillian grumbled, covering her head with a pillow, trying to retreat back into her cocoon of denial.

I took a moment to analyze the area around her bed, and my heart sank as I noticed the scattered bottles of vodka on the floor.

A surge of anger coursed through me, my mind racing with the horrifying thought that Caiden had gotten her drunk, then taken advantage of her.

I was gone for one damn night, and everything had gone to shit.

How did this happen? How had Caiden managed to manipulate my sister into sleeping with him?

A darker conclusion began to take root in my mind, one that sent my heart plummeting further. What if Lillian had slept with him willingly, despite knowing how much I hated him?

That would be the ultimate act of betrayal. I desperately hoped it wasn't true. The thought alone felt like a knife twisting in my gut, as if I had lost everyone I cared about.

"Get up, dammit, and explain yourself!" I stormed over, yanking the blankets off her, exposing her to the harsh reality of the morning.

"Amelia, calm down! It's not a big deal," Lillian said, her voice thick with sleep as she squinted in my direction, the remnants of last night still heavy on her.

"Yeah, Amelia, get over yourself," Caiden chimed in, completely awake now, his voice dripping with sarcasm.

I snapped my head in his direction, and fury ignited within me, hot and raw. "Get the fuck out, Caiden, before I do something I regret."

"Why should I?" he challenged, a dangerous glint in his eyes, testing me as if he knew I would break if pushed far enough.

"Because I'll snap your fucking neck if you don't leave."

My voice was cold, and I realized I had crossed a line, but the monster inside me had taken over, and I didn't care anymore about what came out of my mouth.

He had gone too far, and just looking at him made me want to put my fist through a wall.

To my surprise, he listened, stepping back and leaving me alone with my hungover sister.

Once he was gone, I let my defenses crumble, breaking down as I turned to Lillian.

"How could you?" I asked, my voice small and ruined, barely above a whisper.

"It doesn't matter," she replied quietly, her gaze fixed on the floor, as if it held the answers to questions we both feared to ask.

"You know damn well that it matters."

She finally looked at me, her expression hardening. "No, Amelia, it doesn't. I'm a grown-up, and I made a choice. I went out to a bar and came across someone who could make me feel better. Stop acting like Mom and let me live my life."

Her words cut through me like a knife, and I suddenly felt as if I didn't know her at all. She used to be my safe space, someone I could count on and run to for comfort.

But now, all I could think about was how far away she felt, even though she was sitting right in front of me.

"How did it happen?" I asked after a few moments of deafening silence, the weight pressing down like a rock on my collapsing chest.

"We were both drunk. Things happened. It doesn't matter."

Disappointment surged through me, and I shook my head. "It does matter because you're my sister, and you're supposed to be there for me. You listen to me talk about how vile Caiden is, yet none of that made any difference, and you still slept with him."

The words slipped out slowly, sadness scattered in the syllables. I didn't bother to hear her try to defend herself.

I wiped the tears that threatened to spill and turned to my bedroom, seeking solace in the familiarity of my surroundings.

There were so many unsaid words between Lillian and me. The feeling I had after the initial shock that coursed through me was almost like standing on the edge of a cliff, staring down into an abyss, an overwhelming sense of dread.

It only takes one step to either pull back and walk away from the impending disaster, or you fall and shatter.

I knew I had to take that step back, or else all hell would break loose.

Betrayal was a terrible thing. To give your trust and love to someone only for them to squash it and tear it up right in your face, then act as if it were no big deal, was heartbreakingly cruel.

Trust was like a delicate flower that must be handled with care, or else it would wither and die.

The question I had to ask myself was how I could ever forgive her for this? That was the thing about betrayal: you either forgave or you didn't. It all came down to how deep the pain ran and how horrific the act truly was.

*But everybody makes mistakes,* the small voice in my head reminded me.

Maybe one day, I would wake up and find the answer to the question that hung in the air between us.

It shouldn't be such a hard decision. But it was.

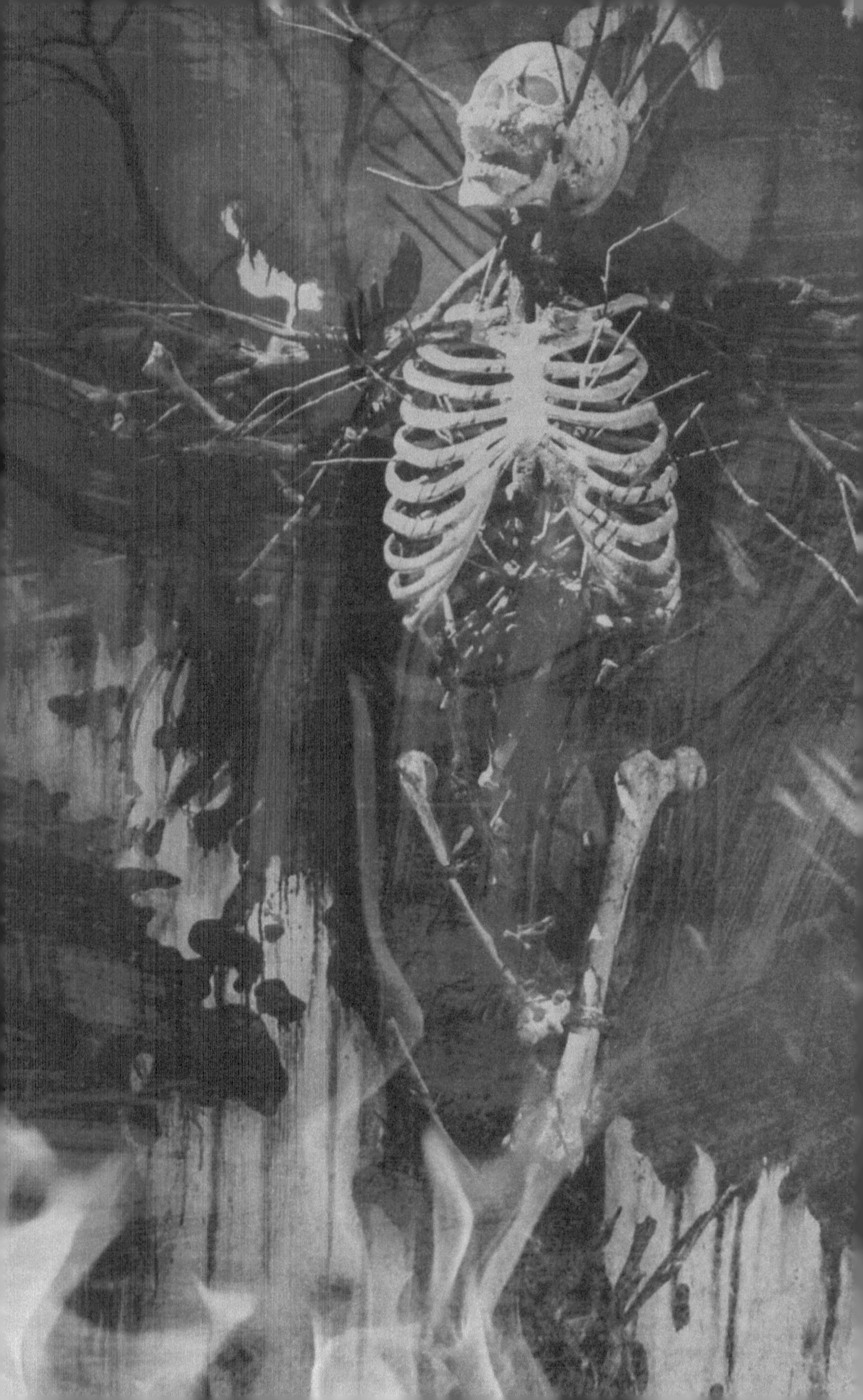

# 9
## THE PRESENT
### AMELIA

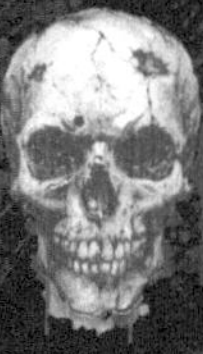

W E  W E R E  N E A R L Y  A  D A Y  I N T O  T H E  D R I V E ,  T H E  M I L E S
stretching out behind us like an endless path. Caiden and I had
managed to avoid conversing, each of us wrapped in our own
thoughts.

Sabrina, ever the social butterfly, had offered a convenient excuse
to the others: I was shy and needed time to warm up to strangers. It
was a simpler explanation than the reality, which lingered
between us.

"I was thinking we could spend the first few days just chilling in
the spa. Then, maybe we could all go on some adventures in the
wilderness!" Sabrina's voice danced through the car, a constant
stream of chatter that filled the awkward void.

Now, she had drifted back to planning activities.

"That sounds good to me," I replied absently, my gaze fixed on
the back of Caiden's head. The sight of his dark locks, so familiar yet
so distant, stirred a sense of dread within me, a creeping sensation
that snaked its way under my skin.

He was engaged in conversation with Shane, their words washing
over me like distant waves.

"Have you started looking for places to live yet?" Shane asked, his
voice steady and curious.

Caiden shrugged, the movement almost rigid. "Sort of. I haven't
found much yet. Been busier with packing."

Shane's response was immediate, filled with a brotherly warmth. "You can feel free to crash at our place until you get on your feet."

Caiden shook his head; a stubbornness etched into his features. "No, I couldn't do that."

"Don't be so stubborn, man. We're family; that's what family does. We help each other."

I sensed a bitterness creeping into Caiden's tone as he replied, "Yeah, well, you got the better life with my mom. I was stuck with the asshole who made my existence a burden."

In that moment, the anger I had felt toward him faded, replaced by a delicate sorrow. I had forgotten how deeply damaged Caiden was, how cruel his father had been.

He had not had it easy. Neither had I. Yet a small voice whispered within me, reminding me that he didn't have to take his anger out on me.

"Sorry, man. I didn't mean to hit a nerve. But you won't be a burden to us. You're my half-brother, and I want to help you out," Shane offered, his tone genuine and concerned.

Caiden sighed, running a hand through his hair in a gesture of resignation. "Yeah, okay. I'll think about it. Thanks."

He had always been a man of few words, and I hadn't expected to witness a heart-to-heart between him and Shane.

I remained in a daze, barely absorbing Sabrina's excited stream of words. The simmering flames of frustration within me continued to bubble, coursing through my veins like an infection.

"Anybody need to use the bathroom?" Shane's voice cut through the thick atmosphere of the car.

I peered out the window into the unfamiliar territory, noting that the sun had dipped below the horizon, leaving a canopy of shimmering stars scattered across the black sky. Their silent twinkling brought an odd sense of comfort amidst the chaos.

"Sure," I replied, seizing the opportunity to escape the suffocating tension.

Caiden and I still hadn't exchanged a word, and I hoped it would last.

The cold air of the small gas station sliced through the heat of my body as I stepped inside. I searched for a sign leading to the restroom but found nothing.

Wearily, I approached the front counter, where a bearded man stood, his gaze lifting to meet mine with an unsettling grin.

"How can I help ya, young lady?" he asked, his voice dripping with a drawl that made me wish for a jacket.

"I need to use the restroom," I replied, my voice small and squeaky. His grin widened, a predatory glint in his eyes.

"Sure thing, anything for a lady like you. Bathrooms out back; here's the key." He handed me a wooden stick with a key attached, his gaze lingering longer than comfortable.

"Great, thank you!" I said hurriedly, eager to escape his lustful scrutiny.

I glanced outside, spotting Sabrina and Shane engaged in conversation beside the car, their silhouettes barely discernible in the darkness. A solitary light hung by the front door of the gas station, casting feeble illumination over the scene.

I walked around to the back of the building and spotted a small shed marked with a bathroom sign. The structure appeared dingy and uninviting, a sketchy cube that made my stomach churn.

The door creaked as I entered, revealing a grimy interior with dirt clinging to the sink and walls.

Once I finished, I hastily washed my hands, eager to return to the clean safety of the car. As I opened the door, I found the man from the front counter waiting for me by the entrance, a smirk playing on his lips.

"Fuck," I whispered under my breath. Darkness enveloped me, a thick cover that concealed my presence. The building loomed above like an ominous cloak. I opened my mouth to shout, but my voice vanished into the void.

*Thump. Thump.*

My heart raced, pounding against my ribcage, while my mind froze in terror.

The man's hands glided over my skin, his toothy grin dangerously close, and an unsettling sensation of invisible bugs crawling across my flesh sent shivers down my spine.

"You're such a pretty thing," he grumbled, pressing me against the wall, its rough surface jabbing uncomfortably into my back.

"Please," I whispered, desperation lining my voice.

"You want more, little girl?" he taunted, his breath hot and foul.

I shook my head vigorously. "No. Please leave me alone."

I pushed against his chest, but he remained immovable, a grotesque statue.

"Feisty little thing," he murmured, his hands continuing their sickly exploration. I repeated my plea, but he ignored me.

"I think she wants you to leave her alone." The voice cut through the darkness, and my eyes snapped open.

Even in the dim light from the bathroom door, I recognized Caiden's tall figure. His voice was calm, but I longed to read his expression, to know what he thought of this nightmare.

A wave of déjà vu washed over me, recalling years ago when I had found myself in a similar position with Caiden. His hands had once touched me too, leaving a coldness that cascaded through my body.

"Mind your own business, boy!" The man's weight shifted as he turned toward Caiden, the threat momentarily lifted.

"It's late. The lady and I need to get moving, so how about you crawl back into the hole you came from?" Before the sleazy gas station clerk could respond, Caiden seized my arm and dragged me around the corner of the building.

"I didn't ask for your help," I protested, pulling back and glaring at him. He had no right to swoop in and play the hero.

I should have felt grateful, but I didn't.

"Well, you got it anyway," he replied, determined to keep pulling me along. I resisted, digging in my heels.

"What's the matter with you? Huh? You pop back into my life, say nothing, and now you're saving me from the molester?"

I hoped he would fuel my fire. I craved a fight, needed to scream, needed something to release the tension coiling within me.

"Stop being so childish. Maybe you should thank me, or perhaps I should've let him feel you up." His eyes, dark and intense, met mine.

"Yeah, you would've liked that, wouldn't you? Watching me helpless and hurting, just like old times." I knew it was pretty and immature of me to say, but I couldn't help it. I felt as if I were that edgy, teenage girl again.

Caiden shook his head, the moonlight illuminating his face and revealing a clenched jaw, irritation etched into his features. Good.

"I don't have time for this shit," he grumbled before striding toward the car, leaving me standing in the shadows.

The creepy guy lingered nearby, and a shiver of unease coursed through me. I groaned and hurried after Caiden, who walked with a purpose.

"Oh good! You found her. We can get back on the road now," Sabrina exclaimed, her energy seemingly boundless as she hopped back into the car.

We followed her, and soon the engine hummed back to life, pulling us onto the road once more.

Tension hung heavily in the air between Caiden and me, thick enough that I could almost sense his anger radiating from the back of his head. Neither Shane nor Sabrina seemed to notice a thing.

Hours slipped away. My eyelids drooped, fatigue creeping in as silence enveloped the car, broken only by the low volume of music. Sabrina was nearly asleep in the seat beside me. Finally.

The landscape blurred past, clouds swallowing the starlight, and my gaze became lost in the darkness beyond the window.

It resonated with the swirling emptiness inside me, a void that deepened painfully with each passing day. Caiden's presence only intensified it.

"There's an exit coming up with a motel. I'm going to call it a night," Shane announced, his voice breaking through my thoughts. Sabrina mumbled an incoherent response, barely roused from her slumber.

The car slowed, veering down a narrow road. Up ahead, I spotted a sign for the motel, a solitary beacon in the night. The area was sparsely populated, save for the motel and a few other scattered buildings.

The car came to a halt, and I glanced at the structure before me. It was a long, one-story building, with rooms lined up side by side. A separate building stood nearby, presumably the check-in area. Trees surrounded the property, standing like silent sentinels.

I grabbed my backpack, containing some clothes, essentials, and a few books, and followed the others to the office.

I hoped there were enough rooms to accommodate us. A handful of cars dotted the parking lot, and with each vehicle I counted, my hope dwindled.

"Hey, I was wondering if there's any room for us tonight?" Shane inquired, stepping to the desk.

The man behind the counter squinted, raising an eyebrow. "Depends. How many rooms do you need?"

"I'd like my own," I interjected before Shane could speak for me. He nodded in my direction, a silent show of support.

The clerk laughed, a sound laced with mockery. "Well, I have two rooms available. Both single beds."

"Seriously? Jeez, why are so many people needing a room tonight?" My own grumpiness seeped through, irritation coloring my tone, prompting another chuckle from the clerk.

"Well, young lady, we're a small town. Lots of folks need a getaway place quite often. Most of the rooms booked belong to locals."

"I need to share a bed with my man. Sorry, Amelia. But maybe you and Caiden can use this night to bond," Sabrina chimed in, her voice teasing.

To her, Caiden was just an attractive guy I could fall for, settle down with. She had no idea of our history. I couldn't blame her.

"Actually—" I started, but was cut off by another voice.

"That's going to have to work. Sorry, I'm too tired to go back and forth on this." Shane's gaze flicked to me, an awareness of my discomfort lingering in his eyes.

I stood there, helpless, as Shane paid and collected the keys. I remained frozen even as they turned to leave the office.

"Amelia! Are you coming?" Sabrina called back to me, concern tinged with impatience.

I blinked. I could sleep in the car, but I craved the comfort of a bed. With a sigh, I slumped my shoulders in defeat. "Sure." I followed them into the enveloping darkness.

Shane handed Caiden the key to our room, and I watched as they disappeared inside, leaving me alone with the beast.

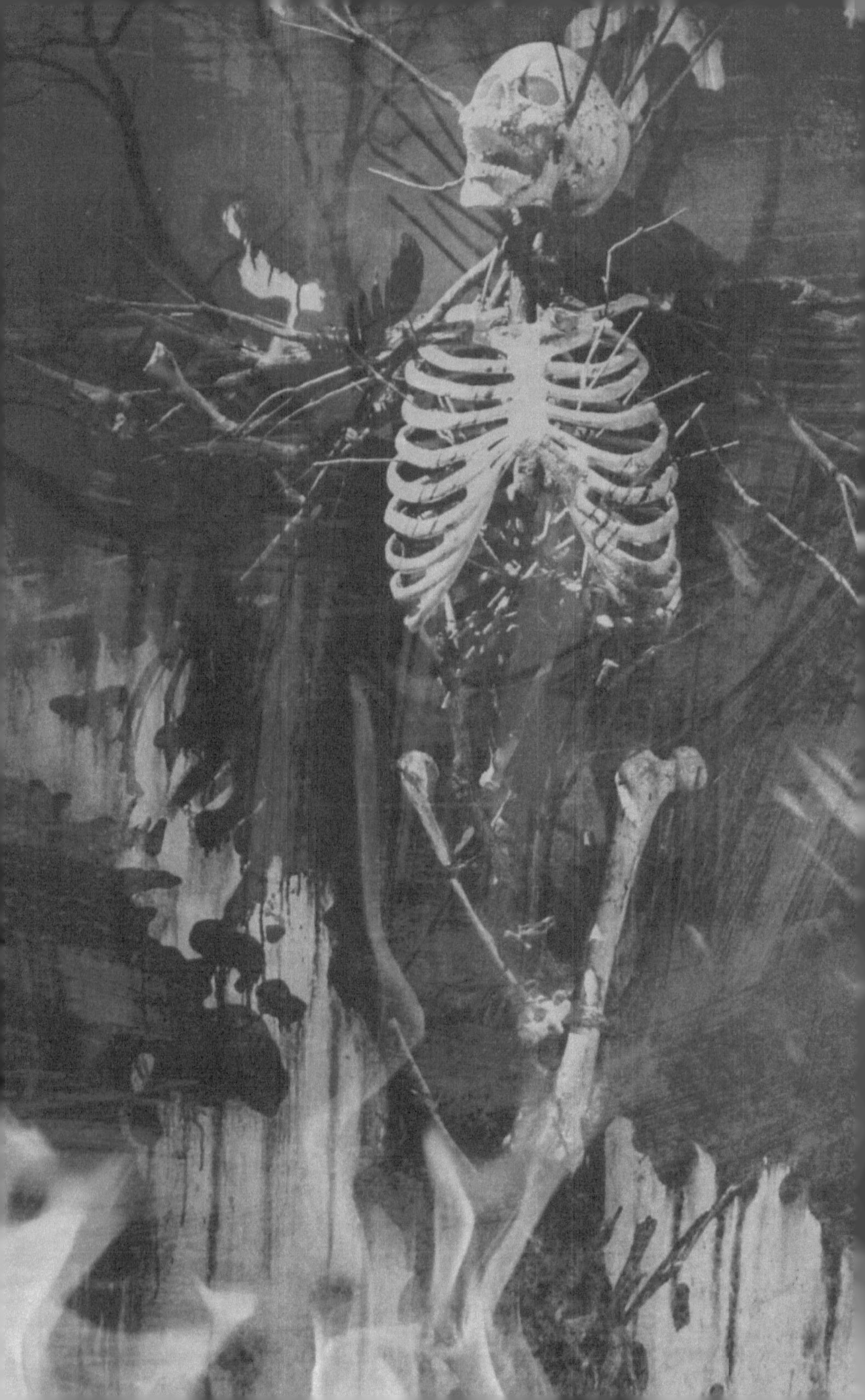

# 10

## THE PRESENT

### AMELIA

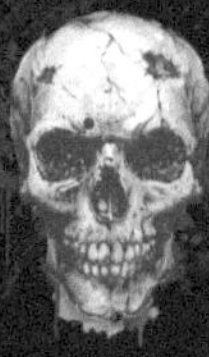

"Are you coming, or are you just going to lie out here in the dark?" Caiden's voice cut through the air. He stood in the threshold, one hand braced against the chipped doorframe, his posture rigid.

I hugged my arms across my chest, feeling the last warmth drain away. "Sleeping out here in the dark is more appealing than staying in that room with you."

He sighed, and the slam of the door echoed. Anger coiled in my gut, a thing demanding release. But I bit back the eruption, squared my shoulders, and tapped once on the scuffed wood.

When the door finally creaked open, Caiden's dark eyes met mine. They looked like cold embers in a spent fire.

I forced a polite tilt of my head. "Thank you." I stepped inside.

The room was cramped and bare: a single, rumpled bed centered against a peeling wallpaper wall; a small nightstand with a flickering lamp; a boxy television perched on a cheap dresser; and a tiny door leading to an equally small bathroom.

Just the barest bones of a place to crash.

Still, I didn't feel saved. The place felt more like a trap. Four walls closing in on me, a cell where I'd be forced to breathe the same anxious air as Caiden all night.

We avoided each other's eyes as we took turns in the bathroom, our feet padding over the thin blue carpet, water dripping from the faucet like a metronome. We might have been older now, but defensiveness made us dance around each other like frightened children.

I cleared my throat and decided to shatter the silence. "So, which one of us is going to sleep on the floor?"

He leaned against the dresser, arms crossed. "What makes you think I'd do that?" His tone was teasing, dangerous.

"There's no chance I'm sharing that bed with you. I'm the lady, remember? I deserve the mattress."

Caiden's scoff was short and harsh. "Maybe if you acted like one. Sleep on the damn floor then." He dropped onto the edge of the bed, flexing his fingers as though that small victory fueled him.

My anger flared hotter. Flames licking at my chest, screaming into my blood.

"Seriously? You're such—" I managed before he snapped back.

"Ungrateful bitch," he spat, springing to his feet. "I risked my neck to get you away from that dirtbag. Forgive me for not rolling out a red carpet after you bitched me out." His eyes glowed with accusing fire.

Exhaustion blunted my retort. I turned on my heel and yanked open the little closet cabinets. No extra blankets, just the thin bedspread and two lumpy pillows.

I grabbed one, pounded it flat, and dropped it onto the carpet. My back already throbbed at the thought of sleeping on the floor, but I forced myself to appear indifferent, even as a hurt ache settled behind my ribs.

The girl I'd once been wanted softness, wanted safety in someone's arms. I shut my eyes, willing down the sting of unshed tears.

The lamp clicked off. Darkness pooled around me. I lay on the thin pillow, listening to Caiden's breathing. Steady, untouchable.

The rough carpet pressed cold against my shoulder blade.

I turned over once, twice, searching for comfort that refused to come. Finally I sat up and peered at the bed, studying his still form. My eyelids felt heavy, my muscles screaming for rest.

Quiet as a shadow, I slid across the floor and eased myself onto the mattress, inching as far from him as possible. When the springs groaned under my weight, I froze.

Caiden shifted, a low grunt escaping him, but he didn't wake fully.

My body sighed as it sank into the soft indifference of the bed. Relief washed over me, and sleep pulled me under before I remembered where I was, or who lay beside me.

Sunlight spilled through the blinds, strips of gold striking my face. I stretched, blissfully unaware, until warmth, unexpected and startling, bloomed against my side.

My heart jolted awake, muscles tensing in panic. I snapped my eyes open and froze. His arm was draped across the mattress, fingertips brushing mine, his skin hot against my temple.

"Oh my god!" The shriek tore from me as I bolted upright. Caiden shot up too, blinking in confusion.

My cheeks burned as I scrambled to yank my T-shirt down and tug my pajama shorts into place. The room felt smaller, the air too thick. I pressed my back to the wall, staring at him in horrified silence.

He cleared his throat, voice low: "Didn't we agree to sleep separately?"

"Yeah." My voice came out tight and breathless. "But the floor was killing my back, so I fell asleep. Let's just forget it happened."

"I'm not planning on reminding you," he said, eyes still avoiding mine.

I didn't wait for more. I ducked into the bathroom, the door clicking softly behind me, and leaned against the cold tile, letting the chill chase the heat from my skin.

I splashed water onto my face, watching droplets pebble my skin in the warped mirror. My reflection looked nothing like the girl I remembered. Too pale, shadows bruising the hollows beneath my eyes, hair wild around my head like a warning. My hands shook.

I gripped the edge of the sink until my knuckles blanched, willing the tremors to recede.

It was a mistake to come here. Seven years of distance, and I still couldn't bear the sight of him. My stomach twisted as I thought of the night before, the warmth of his arm, the way my own traitorous body had sunk into the hollow he made.

I dried my face with a scratchy towel and cracked the door. Caiden was up, already dressed, his back to me as he packed his bag. His movements were stiff, every muscle wound tight beneath the faded Army T-shirt. He looked like he was preparing for a battle, not a car ride.

Neither of us spoke. We'd perfected the art of silence.

My clothes were folded in a pile at the foot of the bed. I scooped them up and retreated to the bathroom, changing quickly, wishing for armor. My hands lingered on the zipper, hesitant to return to that room, to share air with him again.

When I emerged, he was standing by the window, peering through the bent blinds at the parking lot. His posture was tense, jaw set, eyes narrowed at nothing in particular, like he could will the rest of the world into combusting if he only stared hard enough.

He didn't acknowledge me, but I caught the way his jaw flexed when I set my bag on the bed.

I wanted him to say something, to break the spell, to ignite the fight I knew was waiting for us on the tip of every word.

Instead, he spun away from the window and slung his duffel over his shoulder, exhaling like he'd just finished a set at the gym.

"Ready?" he muttered, not quite a question.

I bristled. "Yeah."

He brushed past me with the same chill he always carried. His shoulder clipped mine, a jolt of real contact that left me shivering.

Outside, the morning was cold, the sky smeared with cloud, the parking lot empty except for our car and a station wagon that looked abandoned.

I saw Sabrina jog-walking in place, arms pumping, her hair a halo of fizz in the damp. Shane stood next to her, hands in the pockets of his hoodie. He flashed us a grin, like the world wasn't caving in.

When they saw us approach, Sabrina hopped down and called, "Sleep well, lovebirds?" Her smile was wide, guileless; she meant nothing by it.

But I felt Caiden's stride falter just a fraction, and my cheeks flamed.

"Like rocks," I deadpanned, keeping my eyes on the patchy grass underfoot.

Sabrina grinned, but beneath her surface cheer, I noticed the quick dart of her eyes between Caiden and me.

"So? Anything happen?" Sabrina inquired while the men were chatting.

I shook my head and rolled my eyes. "Nope. Nothing at all."

She huffed with disappointment. "Damn. Maybe next time."

They decided that Caiden would drive this time, while Sabrina and I continued sitting in the back.

The drive was slow and long. I caught Caiden's gaze multiple times in the rearview mirror. Neither of us would hold the stare for long. My mind was a whirling hurricane, showing no signs of slowing down.

The outside world passed in a haze; I became lost in memories that I had buried deep in my mind over the years. The longer Caiden was around, the more erratic my mind became.

I was a caged lioness, pacing and pacing, waiting and waiting.

My anger needed to explode and attack, yet I felt the need to run and hide.

I glanced at Sabrina. She was completely unaware. I wondered how much longer I could keep this storm inside. How much longer could I fake politeness?

It still felt like a fever dream or a terrible nightmare. Caiden was here, coincidentally the half-brother of my best friend's fiancé. I never expected to see him again.

Vague memories of the last time our paths crossed flitted through my mind, just after graduation, before I left this place and never looked back.

It was around that time I had reached a boiling point with my mother, a day that still haunted me, echoing with the sickly expression on her face.

In the end, she had become a stranger I once knew.

———

*The walls that I had once called home were now unfamiliar, drenched in an atmosphere thick with blood and tears. Lillian's room sat empty and cold, a grave reminder of what had been lost. Day by day, my mother fell deeper into despair.*

*My graduation day had come and gone, and with each passing moment, a persistent knot in my gut urged me to leave this devastating town behind.*

*"Amelia, I need to borrow some cash," my mother's voice broke through the suffocating silence. Though I relished the quiet moments, they never lasted long.*

*"Why?" I asked, though I already knew the answer.*

*"Don't question me. When I need something, you should do it without hesitation! After all I've done for you, you should be more giving to me." She screamed and thrashed her arms like a wild beast.*

*I let out a hollow laugh, devoid of humor. "Really? Are you kidding me? What have you done for me?"*

*I recognized her fragility in that moment, but it mattered little. Her hands trembled as she scratched at her skin, her eyes darting everywhere. Unfocused, unwell.*

*"I am your mother. You do as I say. I've sacrificed so much for you and Lillian!" She persisted in her screaming, all logic out the window.*

*Something snapped inside me. "Oh yeah? Well, Lillian is still dead. And you're delusional if you think you've done anything helpful for me in the past years."*

*She shook her head, mumbling and quivering. "No. No. No." She stood on the precipice of breaking, and I pushed harder.*

*"Get over yourself, Mom. All you've done is torment Lillian and me with your drugged-up chaos. She's dead, and I'm all you've got now. But you still don't care enough to be a mother to me!"*

*"Shut up! Just shut up and give me some cash!" Her voice rose, a shrill scream, as she yanked at her hair, pacing like a caged animal.*

*"Get your own cash. I'm done with you." I stormed out of the room, grabbed my keys, and fled the house.*

*Just before I shut the door, I heard her strangled scream, followed by the sound of something crashing to the ground. More screams. She was out of drugs. Out of cash. Out of her mind. But she would find her fix. She always did.*

*My foot slammed down on the gas pedal, and I sped away, seeking solace in the only place that ever offered me a sliver of peace. The park. It was always quiet and empty, perhaps with a few children playing under the watchful eyes of their parents.*

*The air was still and warm. I kicked off my shoes, relishing the soothing sensation of my toes sinking into the soft grass.*

*In the embrace of nature's calm, I decided that I was done. I yearned for peaceful days, unburdened by the weight of my sick mother. She showed no signs of recovery, and I couldn't keep waiting for a change that might never come.*

*As I lay on the ground, I spotted a butterfly perched upon a budding flower. It looked so free and content. I surrendered to the* moment, allowing the tranquility of the blueness of the sky to envelop me. For the first time in days, a genuine smile graced my lips.

But the peace was fleeting.

The sound of footsteps shattered my moment of serenity. I jolted back into reality, anguish crashing down upon me once more. Turning toward the footsteps, I saw him. A boy, tall and lean, around my age. His head hung low, hands shoved deep into his pockets.

As he approached, recognition struck me like lightning.

I scrambled to my feet, desperate to escape before he could see me, but it was pointless.

"Amelia? What the hell are you doing out here?" Caiden's voice cut through the air, his scowl deepening.

"Hiding from reality," I replied, a frown forming on my face.

"Yeah, me too." The wind tousled his floppy dark hair. I studied his stern expression; something was different. There was no rage, just a sadness etched into his features. It reflected my own weariness.

Something shifted within me. Perhaps it was the raw vulnerability of the moment, or maybe a small part of me craved connection. I longed for someone to understand my pain, to bond over it.

"I think I'm going to leave this town," I confessed, my gaze fixed on the ground, avoiding the weight of his eyes.

"Good for you." His response was dry, lacking the usual fire.

"I'm just so tired of living with this dread. Walking past my dead sister's room. Living with a mom who's too drugged up to even function anymore. I'm exhausted, and I want out."

He took a moment to respond, staring at me with an unreadable expression, lost in thought. It was an odd circumstance to be standing here with him, no screaming or crying, just us in the wind, listening to the songs of birds.

In those fleeting moments, I glimpsed the truth of who he was. A sad and lost boy.

"Yeah, I know what you mean. Not the dead sister part, but my mom might as well be a dead phantom." He tugged at a leaf and began ripping it as he spoke, as if he could project his anger onto it.

I nodded. "I know. My father left too. I understand."

His mood shifted abruptly, a storm brewing behind his eyes. "No. You don't understand."

"I understand more than you think, Caiden."

He shook his head, anger simmering just beneath the surface. Was it aimed at himself or at me? I couldn't tell. "I don't need your pity. I don't deserve it. I'm an ass just like my dad. Get that through your head. I don't need your kindness."

Just when I thought I was breaking through, he took two steps back, and we were right back where we had always been. I threw my hands up in frustration.

"I don't even know why I bother trying to be your friend. You really need to get over yourself, Caiden. I'm not the enemy, but I don't think you'll ever realize that. I'm leaving this town, and you'll be stuck in the same place. Angry and pathetic." My words poured out harsh and rapid, the anger surging back as if it had never faded.

"Yeah. It's probably for the best that you leave. I'm never going to change. And your mom is never going to change either." Caiden spoke, not with disdain, but with a thick honesty coating his words.

I looked away, hurt swelling inside me. "Yeah. You're right." I turned to walk away, ready to leave him behind.

"Amelia."

I turned at the sound of my name, finding him standing there with a pained expression.

"What?" I snapped, weary of the back-and-forth that always ended in anger.

He clenched his jaw, glancing away as if wrestling with an internal struggle. A frustrated sigh escaped his lips.

"Nothing. Never mind. I've got to get going." Before I could respond, he turned and began to walk away. I stood there, dumbfounded by our interaction, surprised when he stopped and glanced back at me.

For just a few seconds, his intense gaze pierced through me, then he was gone, leaving only the echo of his presence behind.

# 11

## THE PAST
### AMELIA'S BREAKING POINT

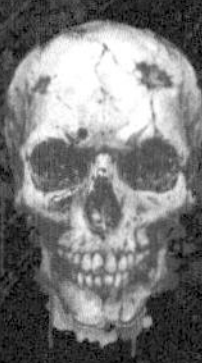

It was hard to look Lillian in the eye over the next few days. We had only exchanged a handful of words since I stumbled upon her in bed with Caiden.

She cornered me before I left for school, her expression a mix of frustration and confusion.

"You're not going to speak to me?" Lillian asked, her voice laced with annoyance.

I let out a frustrated sigh, the sound escaping me like a breath I had been holding for far too long.

What did she expect? There was a tornado of conflict swirling inside me.

One part of me wanted to reach out, to hug her and tell her it was okay, that deep down, I wasn't really mad at her.

Not truly.

But I couldn't.

My pride and anger toward Caiden wouldn't allow me to be the bigger person and let Lillian back in.

It had overtaken me at this point. My mind was a misted trench, and I couldn't find a way out of this black swamp. Someone had to bear the brunt of my fuming scorn. Someone had to take it in so it wouldn't consume me.

Unfortunately, my sister stood in the crossfire.

"I can't discuss this right now. I gotta go," I said, my voice clipped.

"Dammit, Amelia! I slept with him one time! Stop being so sensitive and move on!"

"No! If you knew what he has put me through, you wouldn't talk about this so lightly." Tremors shook my body as I spoke, the weight of my emotions threatening to spill over. She didn't understand, and I could see it on her face.

Nobody could ever comprehend this situation.

"I needed someone. He was there. It's as simple as that," she shot back, her tone defensive.

My hand stayed clenched around the doorknob, my knuckles white with tension. "No, Lillian. It's not simple at all. You don't get it."

The doorknob twisted, and I pushed it open with a harsh force, slamming it behind me.

Here I was, teetering on the edge, trying to maintain my balance. My hands quivered, a suffocating layer of hot flashes covering my skin. This was the calm before the storm.

With every second that passed, boiling anger surged within me, crashing through my body like a tumultuous wave.

One breath. Two breaths. Three breaths. Four breaths. Five breaths.

My chest heaved up and down, and I squinted to see the road through my blurry haze.

I always sensed when something, which had been building up, was about to erupt, unfurl like a poisonous creature, ready to destroy everything in its path. I could feel it in my bones, an instinctive sixth sense. It only took one or two small incidents for it to be released.

Perhaps I could swallow it down for a little longer. Perhaps it could be contained. Perhaps I could still be saved.

A small thought that felt hopeless.

Once I parked my car, I sat there for a few moments, the sun seething with heat. Everything seemed to crumble around me, as if I had been spinning too quickly in a chaotic dance.

I lingered in the parking lot, pacing around my car and wondering if I could just hop back in and drive away from all of this.

As I began walking toward the front doors, I caught sight of him. Caiden stood there with Dante, flanked by a few others near the side of the school, surrounding the courtyard where students could eat their lunches outside.

The raging beast inside me, which had kept quiet for too long, pushed me forward to where they stood.

"I bet you're proud of yourself, Caiden," I spat, my voice sharp.

Dante tried to signal to me that I shouldn't be doing this, but I didn't care at that moment.

"What are you babbling about?" Caiden replied, his tone was nonchalant, which only fueled my anger further.

The way he spoke to me, with such disdain and mockery, made me feel small, stupid, and utterly inadequate. It was a burden that pressed down, becoming increasingly difficult to bear with each passing moment.

He ought to know that a gentle soul like myself still possessed a breaking point.

When pushed past those limits, a shadowy rage erupted, a darker side unleashed.

"You slept with my sister, asshole!" I flailed my arms in the air, desperate to slap some sense into him.

"So what?" He shrugged, rolling his eyes as if my outrage were a mere annoyance.

"It's bad enough that you torment me. But involving yourself with my family and invading my house? That's too far." The tension was rising like a storm brewing.

"Stop being such a baby about it. Maybe you should be more attractive, and I could sleep with you too." His words touched something rotten inside of me.

I let out a screech that sounded more wounded than I intended. That arrogant bastard thought he was god's gift. He believed he could get away with anything, convinced he hadn't done anything wrong.

"Fuck you, Caiden! Why can't you just own up to something for once?" I stepped closer, pressing my face into his space, daring him to challenge me.

For a fleeting second, I saw a flicker of intimidation before it vanished, replaced by his usual bravado.

"I don't have to explain myself to you," he replied, dismissing me with a wave of his hand.

"Well, you need to! You owe me some explanations, dammit!"

"Leave me the fuck alone." He turned to walk away, his back a wall I couldn't penetrate.

"Amelia, it'll be okay. You just need to leave him alone before this situation gets out of hand," Dante said, but I glared at him, my heart pounding.

"You're going to defend this piece of shit? Really?"

He sighed, his expression turning sad. "No. I just don't want him to hurt you."

"It'll be the other way around," I shot back, yelling after Caiden. I snatched a pebble from the ground and threw it toward him, missing him by inches.

Caiden turned to look at me, and for a moment, I stood there, heaving and feeling like a wild animal, red-faced and vibrating with fury.

An expression I couldn't quite read flickered across his face before he turned again, disappearing into the throng of students roaming the walkway.

"You are such a coward!" I screamed, tears streaming down my face. It was impossible to explain to these people why I was exploding so badly.

"C'mon, Amelia. Let's take a walk," Dante suggested, dragging me away before I could unleash my fury again.

My energy drained suddenly, and I leaned into him, feeling completely spent. Caiden had exhausted every fiber within me.

"Why is he so cruel?" I whispered, defeated.

"Lots of reasons," Dante replied, always so vague about it.

"Whatever. I hope he rots in hell one day," I said, disdain lacing my tone.

We arrived at Dante's car, a run-down vehicle like mine. "I think we can afford to skip one day. You shouldn't be going into class like this," he said, looking at me carefully, as if afraid I might snap at him too.

"Yeah, I can't be here right now. Just take me somewhere else." I exhausted all my fight, and now I wanted to decay.

"I'll drop you back off later so you can get your car."

I nodded, settling into the cushioned seat of the car, grateful for the momentary escape.

"Nice ride," I said, trying to make some sort of normal conversation.

He chuckled, starting the engine and giving it a pat on the wheel. "Not really, but it'll work for now. I bought it for three thousand dollars. Thankfully, I'm good with cars, so I was able to fix it up."

I stared at the dashboard, at the way the speedometer needle trembled with every pothole, the way Dante's hands stayed ten-and-two, white-knuckled even when the road was empty.

We drove in silence until the town blurred behind us, the dense woods hemming the highway in on both sides like the world was closing its jaws around us.

My head was so full of static, the only thing I could do was watch the trees streak by and try not to let the pressure inside me blow out the windows.

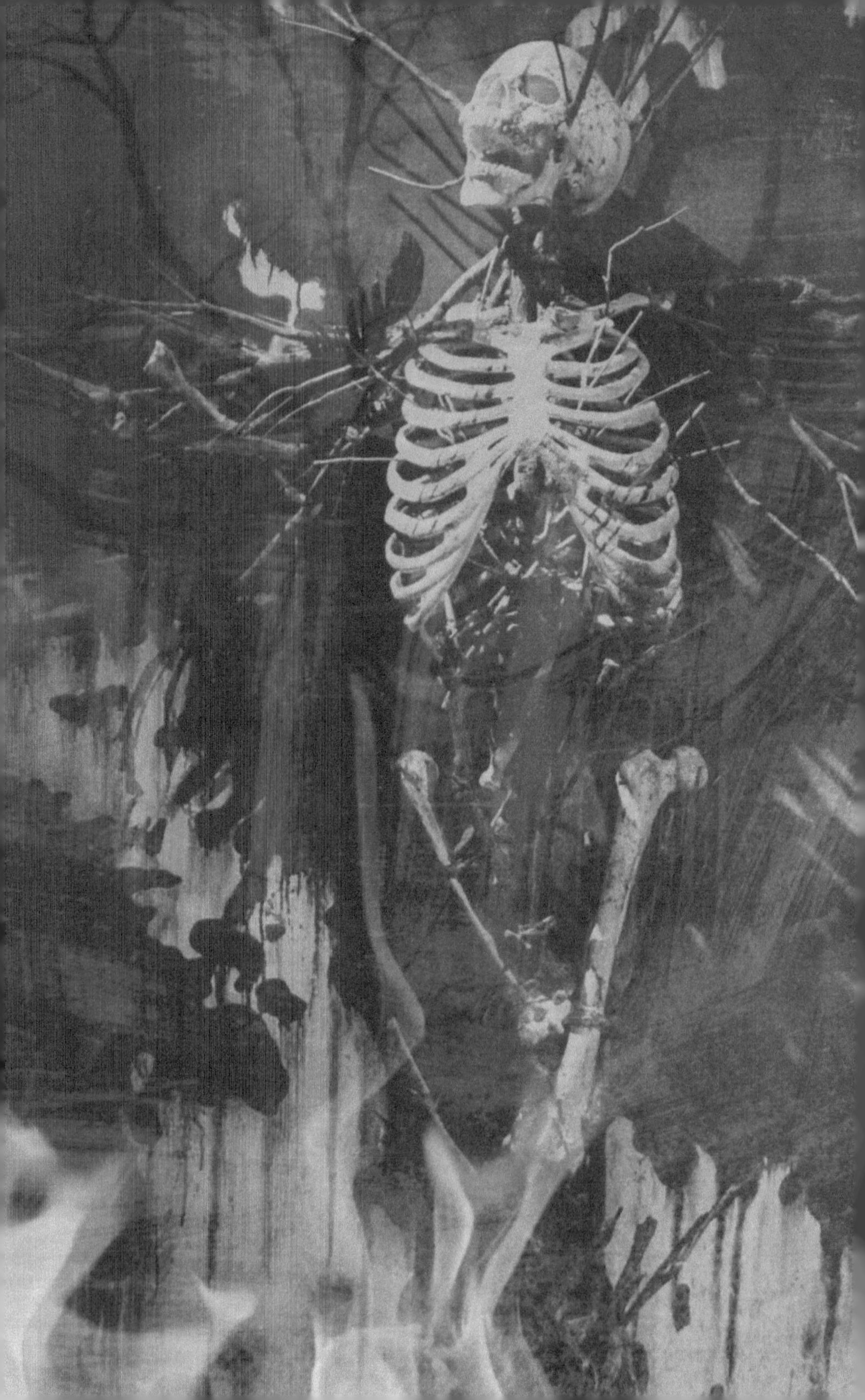

# 12

## THE PAST

### AMELIA'S BREAKING POINT

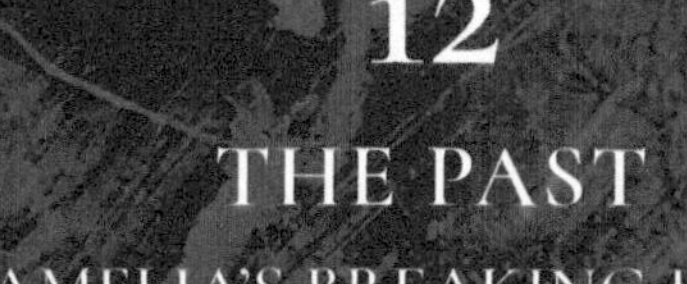

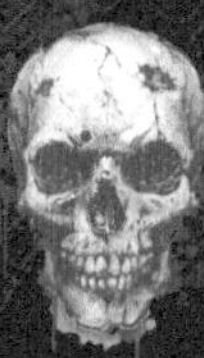

As the days passed by, my heart grew colder, and I felt as if a breaking point was heading my way.

I was in the kitchen, staring at the blue-black bruise on the apple in my palm, when Mom drifted in on silent feet and opened the fridge, the glass bottles rattling like teeth. She didn't look at me.

I watched her pour orange juice into a mug already crusted with last night's wine, and I thought: this is what it means to inherit suffering, to watch someone lose themselves so slowly you almost get used to the vanishing.

She caught me watching. Her eyes were slits drawn tight, but there was a flicker of embarrassment under the surface. An old, familiar shame. "What? Never seen a woman drink her breakfast?"

She forced a smile that was more snarl than anything.

I wanted to fight her, to scream, to tell her she was hollowing us out one sip at a time, but my rage had burned itself into embers. There was nothing left but the tired, brittle bones of disappointment.

Instead, I shrugged and took a bite of the bitter apple. "You should probably eat something."

She laughed. "Food makes me sick." She drank, wiped her mouth, and looked past me to the window, where the ice rimmed the edges and made the yard look like a frozen battlefield.

A silence grew between us, one that felt like it might swallow the whole house.

I let it bloom, then said, "Everything makes you sick because you are sick, Mom. Addiction is just sucking the life out of you, day by day."

I knew the words would cut, but I didn't flinch. I wanted to see if she'd bleed, or if, like me, she'd finally gone numb to pain.

She set her mug down with a hard clink and leaned her elbows on the counter, pinching the skin between her brows. "You always were a little bitch," she said, but her voice was thin and losing altitude. "Even as a baby. Wouldn't let me hold you, wouldn't stop crying."

I shrugged, letting the words bounce off. "Maybe I sensed what was coming."

She slumped, staring at the fridge as if expecting it to open a portal and suck her away. Her eyes were glassy, red at the rims. "It wasn't supposed to be like this, you know." Her fingers traced the spiral of a water stain on the countertop. "I used to think I'd be different. My mother was trash, her mother was trash. I thought I was better."

I wanted to say she never had a chance, not with that bloodline, that she was always bound to end up here.

But I kept it in, holding the bitterness in my molars.

Instead, I looked at her, really looked, and for a second I saw not the monster but the animal. Tired, cornered, desperate for a way out.

"Then be better," I said, voice flat. "Quit. Get help."

Her laugh was a soft, wet hiccup. "Easy for you to say."

I dropped the rest of my apple in the trash and turned to leave. "It's not easy for anyone, but it's what you have to do if you don't want the sickness to consume you until you're nothing but a rotten corpse."

She blinked, twice, and I saw the old machinery of maternal guilt trying to grind back to life. "Shut the fuck up," she muttered. "You want to see me dead? Is that it?" The desperation in her voice was a hairline fracture widening with every word.

I leaned against the counter, arms folded. "No. But you're doing a pretty good job of that yourself." The words felt good, cruel, and honest, buzzing in my mouth like bees.

I braced for a slap, or a glass thrown, but she only stared, lips pursed, chin trembling.

The silence stretched.

She broke first, as always. "You think you'll get out, that you're so fucking pure."

For a second, I wanted to say yes, maybe I did. That I could still choose a different story, a different ending.

But the truth was there in my mouth, sour as bile: I was made from her. My veins ran with the same rage, the same hunger for oblivion.

Maybe I'd never get free.

So, I shrugged, and we watched each other across the kitchen, two ghosts in a house that had never been a home.

I wanted to look away, to calcify myself against the spectacle, but I kept my gaze locked, holding her in the crosshairs of a daughter's impossible love.

Her shoulders curled forward, like a rat, and she pressed the heel of her palm so hard into her eye socket that I half-expected to see blood.

"I'm sorry," she choked, voice slurred and lurching. "I'm so fucking sorry, kiddo. You don't understand—"

I cut her off. "You're right. I don't. I never will."

———

At school, I kept my head down, headphones on. The world shrunk to a single hallway, the floor vibrating with other people's footsteps but never quite touching me.

Dante hovered in the periphery—at lunch, after school, in the parking lot—but I kept him at the exact distance required to keep either of us from falling into something irreparable.

I didn't want to be anyone's project, and I especially didn't want to be the reason anyone else broke.

Caiden haunted me, day by day. His presence was a fungus: invasive, resistant, metastasizing through all the cracks I'd tried to wall off.

He appeared just as I stepped out of homeroom, an unmoving pillar of violence at the end of the hall. But when he saw me, he straightened like a snake tasting the air.

I side-stepped, hoping to merge with a passing group of girls, but he shifted his weight to block the nearest branch of hallway. The girls peeled off, and I had no choice but to walk right at him.

"Look at you, Little Miss Tragic," he spat. His voice wasn't even trying for the usual sneer; it was ragged, frayed. "That hair is really working for you. What'd you do, cut it with your teeth?" The line was lazy and mean, but there was blood on it.

I scowled, walking past. "How about you try a new hobby, like dying?"

He grabbed my elbow and yanked, hard, spinning me around. "Don't fucking walk away from me," he hissed. "You think I'm a joke? That I'm not real?"

In that moment, I recognized the look in his eyes: raw, wild, like a rabid coyote at the bottom of a pit.

I jerked my arm free, and his grip left a white mark on my skin. "You're not a joke. You're a cautionary tale." I tried to keep my voice flat, but the tremor betrayed me.

His mouth twisted. "You have no idea what I am."

I wanted to laugh, but my jaw was stiff. "Sure, I do. I've seen enough battered dogs to know when one's about to bite the hand that won't feed it."

He lunged closer, jaw working, so close his breath burned bitterness into my eyes. "Maybe if you tried to be nice for once, people wouldn't hate you so much."

I wanted to spit at him, to scream, but I just shook my head. "People don't hate me because I'm not nice. People hate me because you tell them to."

"I swear to god, you think I control the whole universe." His voice crackled dangerously. "Earth to Amelia: nobody gives a shit about you. You could disappear, and they wouldn't even pause to blink."

"Same could be said for you," I said. "The world would keep spinning. Your dad would just punch a new face."

The words landed. He went still, lips parted, a dumbstruck moment where I thought he might actually hit me. Instead, he just breathed hard, the fight leaking out slowly. For an instant, he looked like he might cry. Or kill me.

"You don't know shit about me," he finally muttered.

"I know what fear smells like," I said. "I grew up inside it."

"Maybe. But you don't know my fear. I could show you, then you'd really know."

We stood there, locked together by hate and something else, gravity pulling our bones too close for comfort or escape. Every muscle in my body screamed to hit him, but instead I just made my breathing slow, even, until the pulse of dread shrank to a pinprick.

"I'm not scared of you," I said, and hated how much I wanted him to believe it.

He stared, the black wells of his eyes glittering with emptiness. "Liar," he said, almost gentle. "You're scared of everything."

The bell rang, breaking the moment. I slid past him, brushing his arm just long enough to feel the shudder run through his body. His heat lingered on my skin.

———

Now, it had been almost three weeks after the night Lillian and Caiden detonated my last scrap of trust, and I came home to find Mom on the living room floor, curled around a bottle of cheap gin. The TV was on, but the volume was muted. She was mouthing the words in the dark.

"Mom?" I asked as I walked over to her frail shape, afraid that she had finally lost what was left of her sanity.

Her lips moved, but no sound came out. I reached down, nudging her shoulder, and she startled awake. Her eyes were wild.

For a moment, she didn't recognize me.

Then her features slumped into a kind of relief.

"You're here," she said, and it was almost a plea.

She tried to sit up, but her legs didn't work right. The bottle rolled away, sloshing onto the carpet, and I had a flash of how a crime scene tech might catalog this mess: one adult female, collapsed, surrounded by evidence of slow self-destruction.

I knelt next to her, uncertain whether to help her upright or just let her stay collapsed, where the air was safely close to the ground.

She reached for me and caught the sleeve of my sweatshirt. "Don't go," she said, the words sticky and slow. "Everyone leaves. I can't take it anymore."

I closed my eyes and inhaled, waiting for the rest.

"Your father, that prick, he left. Lillian's gone now, too." She began to cry. "She left this morning. Just packed her shit and went."

A black balloon of silence expanded between us. I didn't trust myself to speak.

"She said she had a place with her friend. I think she's lying." Mom's head drooped. "It's my fault. I ruin everything. I did it to her. She said I'm poison."

She wailed as she spoke, and I crumbled amongst her weeps, feeling the walls close in further around my lungs.

She grabbed at my wrist and would not let go. She was less than a mother now. Just a banshee in a bone-white t-shirt, eyes so raw they looked peeled. "You don't leave me, Amelia," she said, voice shaking from some vein-deep wound, "If you ever go, I'll die. You'll see. You'll be the one to kill me in the end."

I could not breathe. Her grip was a shackle of guilt.

For a second, I saw the whole future unspool, a straight line from this room to a hundred empty apartments, a thousand bottles, my own face reflected in cracked glass, always running, never free.

The room was close, fetid. I felt the heat of her collapse. I tried to peel my arm away. She would not let loose. "I mean it," she kept saying, "I mean it, I mean it—" each repetition smaller, a heartbeat losing pressure.

I don't know how long I stood there, tethered to her grief, staring down at the top of her head, the scalp visible through thinning hair.

I wondered if she realized how small she'd become, how easily one could break her if they wanted. How easily she'd let herself be broken.

My skin crawled. I wanted to vanish between the floorboards.

Finally, I twisted my wrist hard and she let go with a yelp, fingers curling back to her own chest, sobbing into her knuckles.

I stood, watching her unravel across our borrowed beige carpet, and thought for the first time that maybe she was right: maybe she'd never be anything but poison, and maybe I was next in line to inherit the taste.

Maybe daughter's were only meant to carry their mother's grief.

When I finally made it to my room, I pressed my back to the door and slid down to the carpet, knees hugged to my chest, forehead against the cool hollow of my arms.

I tried to slow my heart, to dislodge the cold lump stuck behind my ribs, but it wouldn't move.

I wanted to scream, to shake the walls until the house collapsed and buried all the ghosts for good.

Instead, I sat there, breathing shallow and fast, until my stomach cramped and my tongue tasted of copper.

Eventually, there were no more sounds from the living room. I pictured her there, fetal, curled around the empty, shatterproof bottle, eyelids flickering with dreams of before.

The shame of it—my shame—was a gluey, sluggish thing. I let it harden around me, a second skin I'd never be able to peel off.

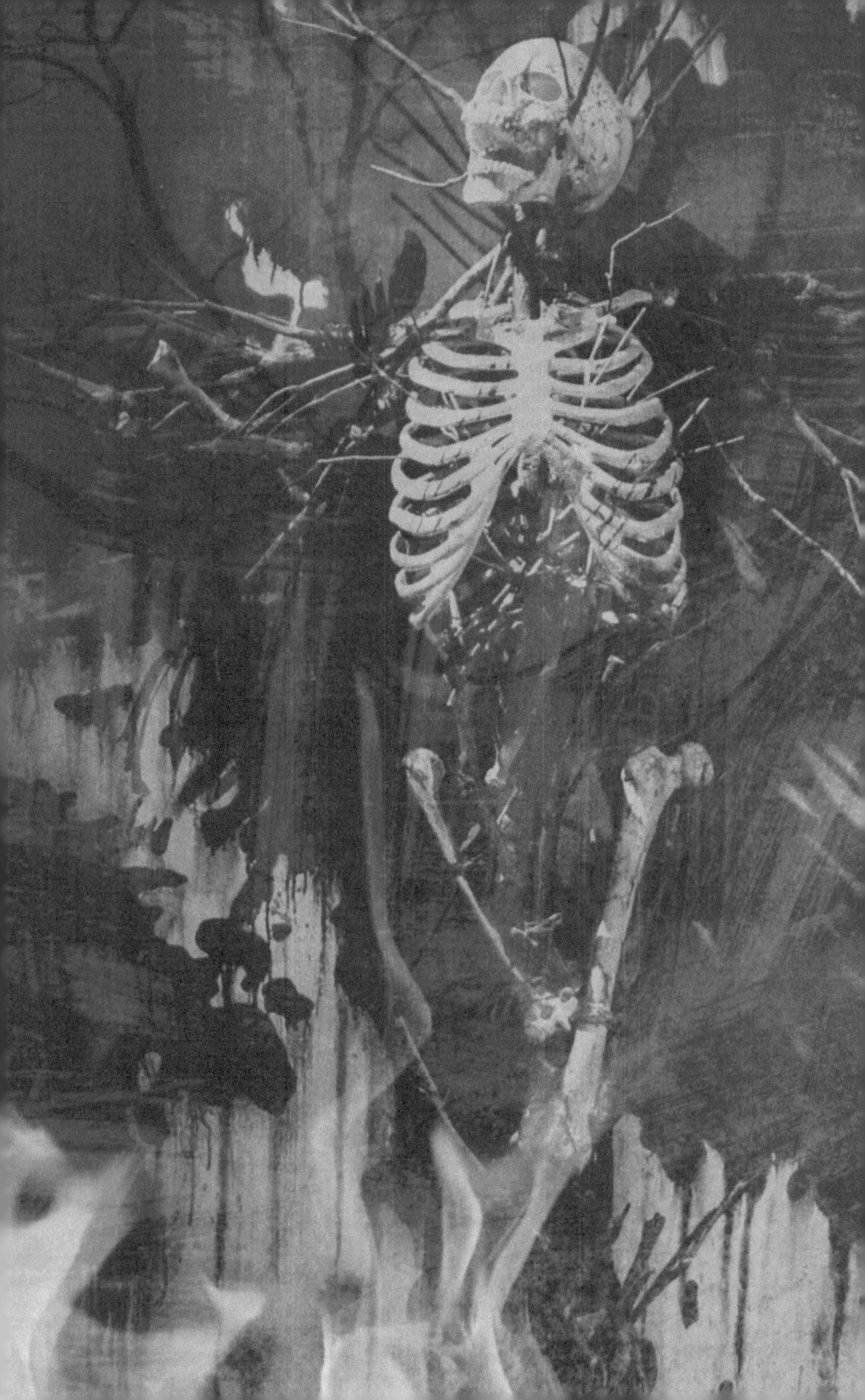

# 13

## THE PAST

### AMELIA'S BREAKING POINT

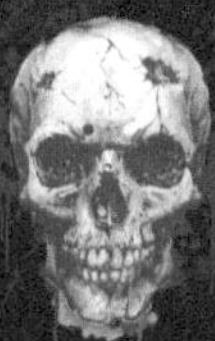

I finally decided I would visit Lillian.

Since the day of her departure, the emptiness within me had grown wider, a void I couldn't ignore.

Today, I received a phone call from Lillian. She said she had something to tell me, but didn't want to say it over the phone.

When she left, I hadn't bothered to reach out. I figured she would contact me when she really needed to.

And now, she had.

So, I would have to push down whatever resentment still lingered inside me to visit my sister and hear her out.

I wondered if my mother would want to see Lillian. I looked around the house for her, but she had already left.

A note on the kitchen table stated that she had gone to work. Thank goodness she still had her job.

Barely.

I drove a few miles to the apartment complex where Lillian was staying, trying to shake off the nagging feeling of dread that settled in my stomach. She had told me her roommate would be gone for the day, so it would be just the two of us.

As I parked in an open spot and made my way to her door, I knocked and waited, my heart pounding in my chest. The tension hung in the air as I tapped my foot anxiously against the pavement.

When the door finally creaked open, Lillian stood before me, looking worn and despondent. The deep heaviness that seemed to sit upon her shoulders was unmistakable.

"Come in," she said softly, her voice lacking its usual spark.

We settled onto the small, gray couch, the fabric worn and faded. I waited for her to speak, the silence stretching painfully between us.

"How have you been?" she asked, her gaze fixed on the floor, avoiding mine.

"Pretty much the same since you last saw me," I replied, forcing a smile that felt more like a grimace.

"Sorry to hear that," she murmured, her words showered with shame.

I sighed and stood up, the frustration bubbling within me. "I didn't come here to talk about how I am. You told me you had something to tell me."

The fear was evident on her face. Lillian bit her lip, then put her hands on her head, shaking it as if trying to dispel the thoughts tormenting her. Suddenly, her composure cracked, and tears began to flow, her cries echoing throughout the sullen atmosphere of the room.

"I feel like I'm in a hellish loop. I mean, is this karma for something?" Her voice was a mix of hysteria and despair, shaking as she spoke.

"Karma? For what?" I asked, my heart aching for her.

She wiped her eyes, her expression transitioning from fear to resignation. Nothing could prepare me for what she said next.

"I'm pregnant. Again."

A pause settled in the air, thick and suffocating.

"What?" I managed to whisper, my heart plummeting.

"I said I'm pregnant."

"I heard you. How are you pregnant?" My mind raced, reeling from the shock.

"Amelia, you're not hearing me. I'm pregnant. The last person I hooked up with was Caiden."

The world around me went blank, numbness seeping into my bones. It couldn't be true. She couldn't be pregnant with Caiden's child. The thought twisted my insides like a knife, and I felt my body shuddering as a wave of unease swept through me.

I had been teetering on the edge of sanity, and now it felt like I had fallen into darkness.

"You're lying," I said, more to convince myself than her. This had to be some sick, twisted game that Caiden had orchestrated. He manipulated her, then forced her to tell me this.

"I'm not lying! I swear I never meant to get pregnant," she pleaded, her voice thick with distress, the faint sobs punctuating her words.

"You're pregnant. With Caiden's child?" My voice trembled, and with each repetition, the weight of it pressed harder against my chest.

"Yes," she confirmed, her gaze breaking under the weight of the truth.

Saying it out loud was almost comical, like something straight out of a twisted joke.

I must be dreaming, I thought, because this was not possible. This was a scenario I couldn't wrap my mind around.

I pinched my arm, hoping to wake up from this nightmare, but the pain was all too real.

Thankfully, I realized, he was eighteen. So, it wasn't a crime, at least not in the eyes of the law.

In my eyes? It was the worst crime.

"What are you going to do?" I finally asked the question hanging among us after a few moments of foreboding silence.

"I think I'm going to keep it. I'm not strong enough to have an abortion. I just couldn't live with the guilt, Amelia."

The words hit me like a freight train. She was keeping Caiden's child, a child conceived out of desperation and poor choices. A stiffness began to form in my chest, a mixture of anger and heartbreak.

"Are you going to tell Caiden?" Despite asking, a part of me already knew the answer.

"No. He will not raise this child with me." She shook her head.

"Good to hear." A surge of satisfaction coursed through me, but I also felt a pang of guilt. I wanted Caiden to know, to see the look on his face when he found out he had impregnated my sister.

I wanted to know if he would care or be concerned, anything that would show me he had a soul buried beneath that bravado.

"Well, you need to tell Mom," I said, my voice steady despite the chaos swirling inside me.

"That's funny. You know she won't like it," Lillian replied, her tone laced with bitterness.

Our mother has not been incredibly supportive these days. But surely, she couldn't be heartless enough to turn away her knocked-up daughter?

"Let's just hope that she's having a good day." It was an unpredictable game, we couldn't win, dissecting her moods. I didn't think my own mother even knew what to expect when she woke up, especially when it came to her emotions.

We had a few more hours until our mother returned from work. In the meantime, I took Lillian to a late lunch, anything to distract us from the cloud hanging over us. It was all I could do for her at this point. Guilt gnawed at me like a persistent insect. If it wasn't for the war between Caiden and me, this most likely wouldn't have happened to my sister.

He denied it, but I knew that some part of him had slept with Lillian with the intention of getting under my skin. And it had worked.

"It will be different this time," I said, trying to infuse some hope into the conversation.

"Hm?" Lillian hummed quizzically, tracing random shapes on the table with her finger.

"This baby. It isn't going to end badly like it did when you were in college. We'll figure this out."

"I hope so." Her voice was devoid of any hope, as if her life was already over.

My heart broke for her. Lillian was still so young, just a few years older than me. She had so much potential to be the best version of herself. I wanted to make her see that this didn't have to ruin everything.

"Easier said than done," she replied, her gaze distant, as though she were already lost in the storm of uncertainty.

After we ate, I walked Lillian back to her apartment. Our mother's car was in the driveway when we arrived, and both of us held our breath as we headed inside.

We gravitated toward the bedroom, our mother making a habit of retreating there after work, letting herself rot in her own misery.

I gave a silent nod to Lillian, feeling a prick of sadness as I knew we would come out of this in ruins.

Lillian pushed open the creaking door and stepped inside the room. The smell of cigars and trash immediately assaulted our senses.

We walked along the carpet, which had once been a snowy white but was now stained brown and gray.

Mother stood by the stained window with ripped curtains, staring out into the distance as if she were in a daze. She didn't even hear us walk in, only noticing us when Lillian slowly tapped her shoulder.

"Mom?"

She turned around, her eyes glazed and unfocused. There was a moment of silence as she processed our presence, and I could feel the tension crackling in the air.

"You're back," she stated flatly, her voice devoid of warmth.

Lillian took a deep breath. "I... I have something to tell you."

"Get to it," our mother replied, impatience evident in her tone.

"I'm pregnant," Lillian finally blurted out, the words hanging in the air like a death sentence.

Mother's expression shifted to one of disbelief, and the silence stretched painfully between us.

"Get out," she said coldly, her voice sharper than a knife.

"Excuse me?" Lillian's voice trembled, and I could see the hurt flash across her face.

"I said, get the hell out. I don't want an irresponsible and disrespectful child living in my house." She screamed, pointing her finger to the door.

The horror of our mother's words washed over me like a cold wave, and I felt my own heart sink. How could she turn her back on Lillian in her time of need?

I watched with an aching heart as Lillian's composure crumbled, her body shaking as she choked back sobs. "Please, Mom, I am so sorry. Just let me stay! I can't bring this burden on my roommate."

"That's not my problem. Like you said, you're over eighteen, so you're not my problem anymore."

Lillian's tears fell freely now, but our mother turned her back, staggering out of the room.

I was horrified to see my sister treated like this, cast aside like a piece of trash. My mother was a stranger now, a cold-hearted and bitter figure who had given up long ago.

"It'll be okay," I whispered, placing a hand on Lillian's stiff shoulders.

"You're wrong," she stated, her voice breaking. I could see her hope fading, the light in her eyes dimming.

"What now?" I asked, desperation creeping into my tone.

"Take me back." She was already walking toward the front door before I could stop her, my heart racing as I followed.

Once I dropped her off at her apartment, a wave of despair crashed over me. I hoped for a miracle, but I was no fool. I'd rather be prepared for disappointment than have high hopes and feel utterly devastated.

As I drove away, everything hit me at once, dragging me down into a pit of despair. A weight as immense as a freight train crashed into my mangled body, sending me tumbling into darkness.

I hit a boiling point. I was a volcano beginning to erupt, and I could feel my hatred toward Caiden growing stronger.

The next day, I found him at school, walking alone through the halls.

"Caiden, we need to talk."

I approached him, determined.

"I don't want to," he said, his tone flat, as if I were an inconvenience.

"That's too damn bad!" I snapped, stepping into his path.

"Move." His glare was furious, but I stood my ground.

"Have you heard the news? Lillian is pregnant with your kid."

His eyes widened for a fleeting moment before the wall he had built returned, hard and impenetrable. "I don't care," he stated coldly, his mouth set in a straight line, devoid of remorse.

"Well, you should, because now my mom kicked her out just because she got knocked up. She's struggling; have some damn sympathy!" My face flushed with anger, my hands trembling at my sides.

"That's not my problem," he shot back, the callousness in his voice igniting my fury.

"Dammit, Caiden! Why do you have to be such a cold bastard?" I pushed against his chest, my words spilling out in a torrent of emotion.

He shrugged, irritation flashing across his features. "Look, I didn't mean to get her pregnant, but it's done now, and it's not my problem. So, get out of my face."

I watched him turn, his back a wall I couldn't penetrate. "You're a coward! I hope karma bites you in the ass one day," I screamed after him, tears welling in my eyes. It was impossible to explain why I was exploding like this.

"I'll let you know when it does," he sarcastically grumbled, then pushed me out of the way and continued walking with his hands stuffed in the pockets of his shorts.

I watched him leave, resentment piling up. I had gotten nowhere with him, and I felt as if I had let Lillian down.

The late-afternoon light slanted through the tall windows of the bookstore, dust motes drifting in the golden beams.

It was quiet, just the soft scrape of my sneakers on the hardwood floor and the distant hum of the register. Since it was a school night, customers were few, so I lost myself in restocking: sliding worn paperbacks and glossy new hardcovers back onto their shelves, aligning their spines until they formed a perfect row.

I ran my fingertips over each title and, not for the first time, wished I could climb inside one of these stories and live an entirely different life for a while.

"Everything all right, darling?" Nina's gentle voice broke my reverie. She leaned on the end of the shelf, her strawberry-scented perfume mingling with the musty smell of old paper.

I swallowed hard. Her concern made the ache in my chest widen as if I might start crying. "Not really," I admitted, pressing a novel flat against my heart. "My sister's pregnant, completely unplanned. We don't know what to do."

"Oh, Amelia." Nina's soft brown eyes filled with sympathy. "That's always a heavy thing to bear."

I bit my lip. "I feel so terrible for her."

Nina gave a small, knowing smile, her hands steady as she helped me line up another row of books. "Sometimes it works out for the best," she said, voice warm with memory.

"Why do you say that?"

"I was in my twenties when I found out I was expecting my daughter, totally unexpected." She paused, straightening a stack of poetry volumes. "I was terrified. But fifteen years later, she's the miracle I never knew I needed."

I let her words settle around me. I'd never understood the depth of a mother's love. "I guess I hadn't thought of it like that."

"Your sister will, too," Nina assured me, brushing a strand of hair behind her ear. "The moment she holds that baby, regrets vanish. She'll see the blessing in it."

I shrugged, trying to believe her. "I hope you're right. She wants to keep it, at least."

"She should. It'll be hard, but every challenge has its purpose."

We traded a few more polite observations until my shift ended.

My nerves were fraying, so I texted Dante to meet me.

In our little town, gossip was a wildfire, and before long everyone would know about my sister's condition.

Outside, a small coffee shop glowed under string lights a couple of blocks away. I found a wooden bench beneath a flickering lamppost and waited, the cool evening breeze tugging at my hair.

The comforting hiss of the café's espresso machine leaked onto the sidewalk, and the rich aroma of roasted beans drifted around me.

Then Dante appeared. His easy smile lighting up the dusky street. My heart pounded as I stood and wrapped him in a quick hug, craving the safety of his arms.

"What's up?" he asked, settling beside me. His jacket smelled like cedar and something familiar, something like home.

I took a steadying breath. Maybe he'd already heard. Better to rip off the bandage. "Caiden got my sister pregnant," I blurted, voice tight. "He won't admit it's his responsibility, and it's driving me crazy."

Silence fell.

I watched the lamplight dance on his profile. He stared into the distance, brow furrowed, as if wrestling with words.

My scalp tingled. I wanted to lean in, press my lips to his cheek, bury my face in his neck.

Finally, he exhaled. "I'm so sorry, Amelia. I wish I could change him."

I searched his face. "He won't even listen to you?"

Dante shook his head, letting his hand hover before he placed it gently over mine. His touch was warm, tentative. "Caiden has his own demons. He trusts me enough to joke around, but when it comes to serious advice, he shuts down. I've tried everything."

I clenched his hand, butterflies erupting in my chest. "I don't know what to do."

"I know." He squeezed my fingers. "Just... sit with me for a while."

We did. The street grew quieter as night deepened. We talked in fragments and let the comfortable silence slip in between us like a soft blanket.

After ten minutes, Dante spoke as he gazed at the flickering café sign. "I've hated watching from the sidelines."

I looked at him, puzzled. "What do you mean?"

"When Caiden bullies you," he said, turning to meet my eyes. "All those times I just stood there."

My throat tightened. "You did step in, sometimes. I'm grateful."

He offered a shy, earnest smile, his dark eyes glimmering. "A woman as kind and beautiful as you doesn't deserve that. You deserve happiness, Amelia."

My cheeks burned. Compliments like that felt foreign, especially coming from someone like him.

I whispered, "Thank you. That means more than you know."

He tucked a loose lock of hair behind my ear. "I care. I hate seeing you hurt."

"I'm glad," I breathed. Most people would have turned away. But he didn't.

"I won't," he promised. "Not anymore. You can count on me."

His words wrapped around me, steady and sure. Sitting there in the fading glow of the lamp and the scent of coffee, I felt something shift inside: a quiet hope that, in time, everything would be all right.

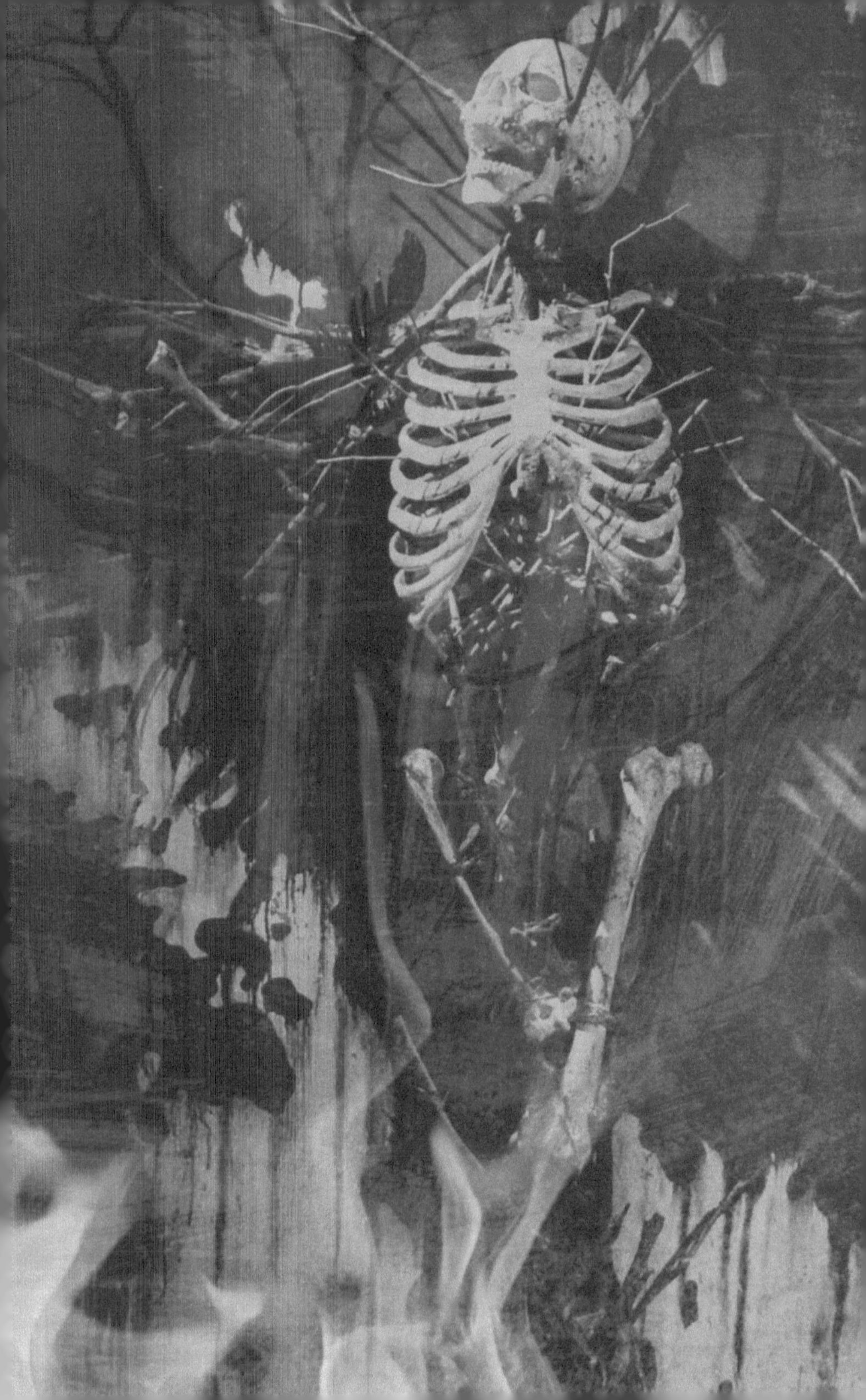

# 14
## THE PAST
### AMELIA'S BREAKING POINT

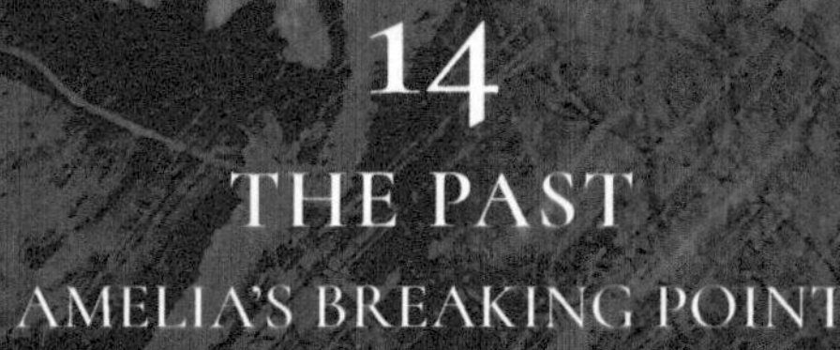

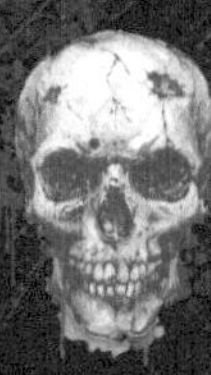

CAIDEN WAS A DARK FORCE FROM WHICH THERE WAS NO escape. Deep crimson streaks stained my skin, a constant reminder of his presence, and the mere thought of him constricted my throat, my lungs sinking into an abyss of despair.

I could not evade the deadly disease of his torment.

Because of him, my relationship with my sister had crumbled into dust.

She suffocated alone beneath the judgmental stares and cold glares of the townsfolk. The thought of her, and the unborn child she carried, twisted my heart with an unbearable tightness.

Sleep eluded me; nightfall was a cycle of restless tossing and turning, plagued by visions of terror and haunting whispers. If it wasn't for the war that raged between Caiden and me, he would never have felt compelled to breach the boundaries of intimacy with my sister.

The weight of it all pressed down on me like the force of a thousand stones. The blood of her ruined life stained my hands.

She was all I had left, and now I found myself slipping into a cloak of darkness.

What do you have when everyone slips away? That question lingered in my mind like an ominous crow, watching and waiting.

Sometimes, we were meant to be dead stars, left behind,

belonging nowhere. The sky above me was perpetually webbed with empty shadows.

A deep yearning washed over me, a longing to escape to a peaceful place where sunlight glimmered and my heart swelled with joy.

Life was growing weary. Each day, I struggled to find anything to hold onto that would propel me forward.

Just make it to graduation. Freedom was so tantalizingly close.

By the time the school day ended and I reached home, my heart hammered so fiercely I thought it might break free.

I stumbled into my dimly lit room and let myself fall onto the rumpled mattress. The air felt thick, suffocating, like my grief had taken physical form and pressed me to the sheets.

I curled inward, craving to vanish beneath the threadbare quilt, to lose myself for hours.

The lure of my mother's prescription pills glimmered temptingly, but I steeled myself; I wouldn't sink that low.

Instead, I surrendered to blank, thoughtless oblivion.

When I finally surfaced, the world had shifted from afternoon light to the bruised purples of dusk. My eyes burned, my limbs ached, and an insistent growl rumbled in my gut.

Checking my phone, I noticed a missed call and a voicemail from Lillian. I opened it eagerly, remembering our last conversation when she'd confided that her roommate had left, leaving her alone in that apartment, struggling.

Silence hung for a few agonizing seconds, broken only by her soft breathing and the sound of muffled crying.

"Amelia," her voice trembled through the receiver. "I tried calling, but you didn't answer, so I guess I'll just tell you this over voicemail. I—I don't think I can do this anymore. I have nobody, and I can't raise a child. I just can't. There's nothing for me. I'm done trying. I love you, Amelia. I'm sorry things turned out the way they did. I didn't mean any of it. I hope you find a way out of that shithole of a house, though I won't be there to witness it."

Her words, choked with sobs, sent a chilling premonition of impending doom through me, like a physical weight settling on my chest.

"I tried so hard to be there for you, but my emotions got in the way. I could only focus on myself for so long. I'm so ashamed and regretful."

A long pause followed, filled with sobs and hiccups. The impending dread coiled tighter around my heart.

"I'm sorry. I can't make you understand. There's nothing left in me to give or fight for. Goodbye."

The line went dead. Panic surged through me, gripping my throat and twisting my gut into knots. I grabbed my keys and bolted toward the front door, leaving my mother sitting silently, her haunted eyes glazed over.

I sped to Lillian's apartment, weaving through traffic and disregarding stoplights. I pleaded with the universe for her safety. My heart raced dangerously fast, pounding against my ribcage like a caged animal.

Tears blurred my vision; it couldn't be. She couldn't have given up. We needed each other.

When I finally arrived, I parked haphazardly, barely within the lines. The door swung open easily, and I rushed inside, desperate to find her before it was too late.

I burst into her bedroom, searching frantically for any sign of life. There she lay, a silhouette against the crumpled sheets, still and silent.

"No, please don't let it be," I whispered, racing to her side. My throat tightened, panic flooding my veins.

"Lillian! Wake up, come on, I'm here!" I shook her gently, watching her eyes for any flicker of awareness. Her skin felt cold to the touch, the warmth escaping her body like mist on a cold morning.

Tears streamed down my cheeks as I shook her again, urgently, but deep down, I knew.

She was gone for good.

A wave of dread crashed over me, consuming my entire being.

"Lillian, please, oh no, please open your eyes." I could think of nothing else. I could not breathe. Everything became hazy, my vision a blur. Lillian lay there, and I lost hope.

My sister was dead on an ordinary weekday, and it was all my fault.

I sank to my knees, the rough ground scraping against my skin as I felt myself shatter into a million pieces.

My body shook with silent sobs, the sheets twisted in my grip; the scent of lavender, from the fabric softener, barely masking my despair as my face remained buried in them.

Chills coursed through my helpless body as despair enveloped me.

At last, an empty numbness descended. I lay beside my dead sister, the weight of grief crushing me, the passage of time meaningless.

It dawned on me that I needed to call 911. They arrived swiftly, laying her body in a black bag before zipping it shut.

I watched, shattered, as her face disappeared from view, realizing that I would never see her again.

That realization broke me further; I would never share another moment with her, never engage in our small, meaningless chats.

She would forever be reduced to a decaying pile of flesh and bones beneath the earth, forgotten by everyone.

Memories of her flooded back, leaving me breathless. I recalled her joyous laughter, her carefree smile. The lips that were now fading would never lift into a bright, beaming grin again. I remembered the days we played outside as children, sharing our secrets under the open sky.

The police spoke to me, their voices laced with sympathy. I heard words like "pills" and "quick," but I wasn't truly listening. I sat there, a blanket draped over my shoulders. Paralyzed.

My mind raced, then fell blank. Fury consumed my thoughts, directed at myself for abandoning her. It ignited a blazing path of blame toward my mother and Caiden, erupting like a volcano.

There were too many people to hold accountable, but deep down, I knew the fault lay with me. If only I had reached for the phone in time, if only I could have talked sense into her.

Regret clawed at me, a sickening sensation that scratched at my skin and pounded at my head. I shouldn't have gone to sleep.

Instead of channeling my guilt and anger inward, I redirected it toward Caiden in that moment.

This had begun with him. I didn't want to confront the pain and guilt gnawing at me; it was suffocating. Lillian must be avenged.

This was the last straw. My sanity had crumbled into shattered pieces. Emptiness consumed me, my vision clouded with a paralyzing rage. I had overflowed into a raging tidal wave, threatening to flood everyone and everything in my path.

The solitude of my grief morphed into a ferocious fog, wrapping around me like a disoriented fog.

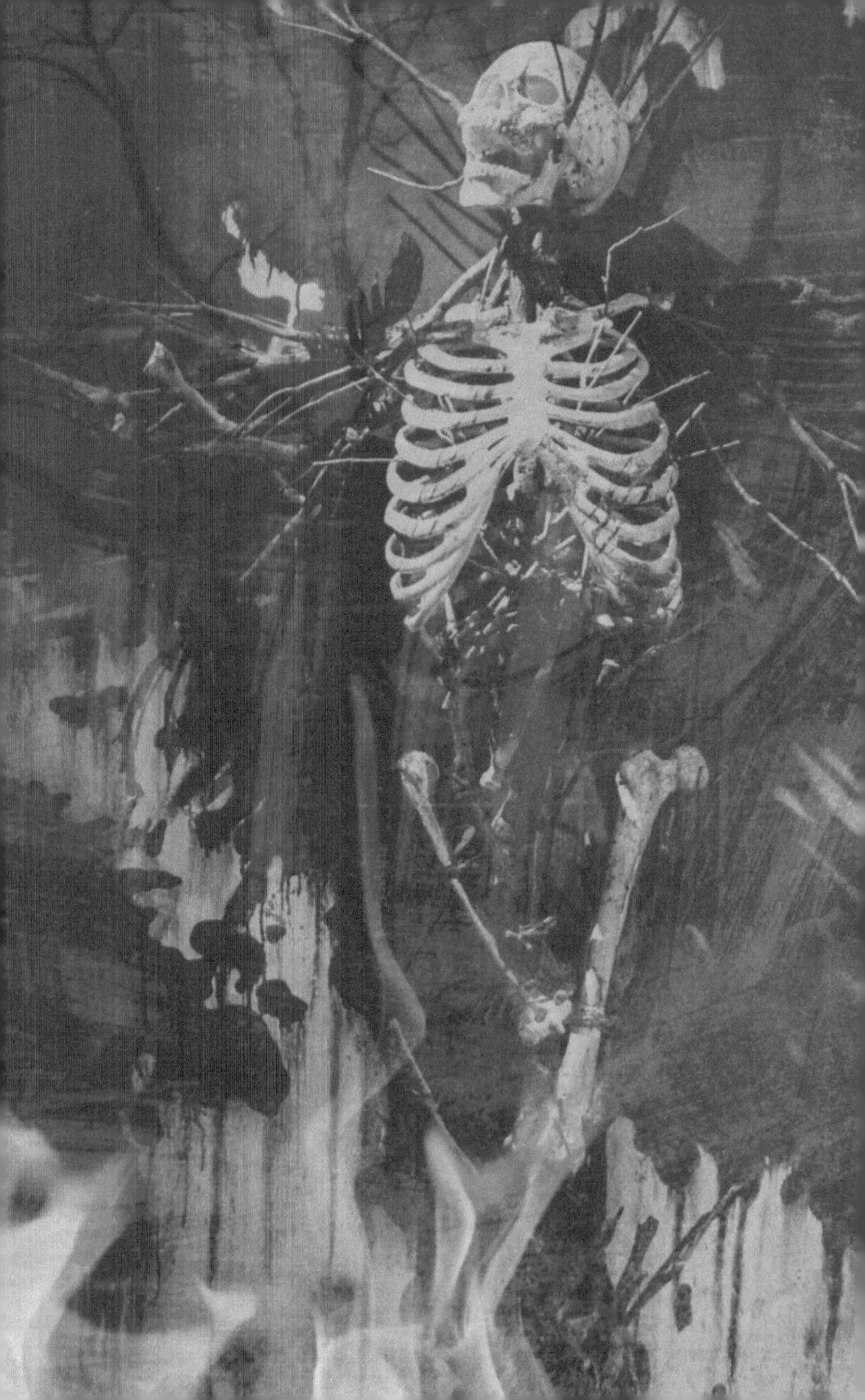

# 15

## THE PRESENT

### CAIDEN

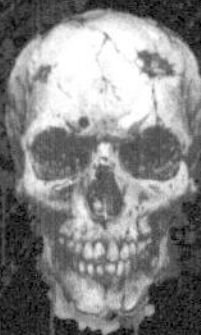

I thought Colorado would heal me, being in fucking nature, but all I felt was rage. Hot, burning rage.

I hated this. Hated the smiling and the fake warmth, hated the sound of my half-brother's voice and the way Sabrina chattered like every day was made of spun sugar. Hated most of all the fact that she was here.

Her.

Amelia fucking Langston.

She looked older. It'd been years, and I mean years, since I'd seen her up close. Her hair was darker, but her skin looked even more like it would shatter if you pressed too hard.

I shoved my hands deep in my pockets, clenching and unclenching my fists, and let Shane give the tour.

The "wilderness retreat" was just a cluster of cabins, a main lodge building, a few activity areas, and a bunch of hiking trails curling off into the trees like veins.

Sabrina did her best to make it seem fun. "Look! Mountains everywhere, I can't even believe it! Wait till you see the river."

Shane grinned. "They do group dinners at the lodge, but if you want to crash early, there's a kitchenette and a stocked fridge. Caiden, you want to check what they've got? I know you hate surprises."

That last bit was supposed to be a joke. I didn't laugh.

Instead, I shrugged, rolled my shoulders, and made a beeline for the mini-fridge. Needed something to do with my hands, anyway.

When I turned around, Amelia was standing just inside the threshold, eyes dragging over every corner of the room, already measuring the exits. Her hands twisted at the strap of her bag, knuckles almost white. She caught me staring and her mouth tightened, cheeks flushing up pink.

For the briefest second, we were alone. Sabrina and Shane outside, loading up firewood or whatever.

I didn't say a word. Maybe if I didn't move, she wouldn't provoke me. But she did, always did.

"Something on my face?" Her tone was flat, not even trying to be nice.

I laughed sharply. "Didn't realize you still knew how to look people in the eye."

A little color drained from her cheeks. Quick, the way she used to flinch when something crept too close. She lifted her chin anyway, getting brave. "Didn't realize you still needed to intimidate everyone just to feel alive."

We stood there, breathing each other's poison.

"I don't need you to be afraid of me," I ground out, voice barely above a whisper. "That's never what I fucking wanted."

She hung there, suspended, like a thread about to snap. Her voice was softer, but harder, too. "Didn't stop you, did it?"

No. It didn't. I remembered the way I used to chase her down the hallways at school, remembered every time I'd spit venom just because my father told me to. Some nights the shame ate my guts.

But that wasn't today. Today, I could feel the heat under my skin, the urge to push, to see if she'd still break. To see if I could break her.

Before I could say another word, the door banged open. Shane, arms loaded with logs, Sabrina trailing behind laughing at something he'd said.

My hands unclenched.

Fake smile, teeth bared. "We're all set in here," I said, loud enough for them to hear.

Sabrina's eyes lit up. "Oh, yay! I thought you two would want some time to get acquainted."

I nearly choked. Amelia made a noise like a cough, but she covered it with a polite smile.

"Yeah," she managed.

No one knew. They didn't suspect a thing. I could murder her in broad daylight, and my brother would just smile and tell me to pass the ketchup.

Sabrina and Shane spouted endless optimism—"Look at the view! Let's go down to the river! Who's up for s'mores?"—while Amelia and I trailed behind, cold shadows flickering between our boots.

Every word from her scraped against me. Every sideways glance made me want to throw something, just to see it break.

It didn't help that every so often, I'd catch myself looking.

Disgusted with myself, I turned away, picking up rocks and hurling them into the river. Each splash was a shot of adrenaline, cold and clean, but it did nothing to clear the thoughts in my head.

After a while, Shane drifted over and clapped me on the shoulder. "You good, man? You seem... I don't know. You okay?"

I shrugged him off. "Fine. Just not big on forced group bonding."

"Ha. I hear that." He dropped his voice. "Between you and me, Sabrina's been planning this trip for months. She thinks nature'll make us all best friends, but I think she's more nervous that you'll scare her off."

I glanced at Amelia. She was quietly talking with Sabrina, voice so soft I couldn't catch the words.

When we regrouped, Sabrina was full of plans. "Tomorrow, we do rock climbing, but tonight? Movie night, pizza, and then maybe some drinks. I want to hear all your wildest stories, Caiden."

Great. Nothing I wanted more than to sit around telling military stories while Amelia listened in the dark.

But I played along. We all went back to the cabin and took turns with the shower. When Amelia passed by me in the narrow hallway, shoulder brushing my arm, I felt it all the way down to my elbow.

Neither of us said a word.

At dinner, everyone tried to pretend we were normal. I drank two beers, maybe three, just to give my hands something to do.

Sabrina recounted a story about getting lost in the woods as a kid. Amelia actually laughed, a quick, pained sound, and for a second, she looked at me like she wanted me dead.

I smirked into my bottle. She'd have to try harder than that.

Afterward, when Shane and Sabrina left to go clean up the kitchen, I found myself alone with her in the living room, shadows trembling along the wood-planked floor.

I waited. Knew she'd speak first.

"You're the same as always," she said, voice harsh and low. "Still trying to make everyone else as miserable as you are."

I let the anger rise, boiling up from the old place. "That's rich, coming from you. Last I checked, you were the queen of freezing everyone out. You like it, don't you? Being the victim."

Her eyes flared. "Fuck you," she whispered, but it was a hiss, not a plea.

"Already did," I shot back, not even sure what I meant anymore.

She recoiled, color draining, but her chin didn't waver. "Keep it up, Baxter. Just try me."

I leaned closer, not really meaning to, but unable to resist the gravity. "Baby, you wouldn't survive ten minutes alone with me."

Her laugh was hollow as a grave. "Wouldn't want to."

But her breath came quick, nostrils flaring. Like she did want something. Like if I reached out, she'd let me touch her throat.

I stood up, looming over her, fists tight at my sides. She didn't flinch. Respect, in a sick way.

"Let's get one thing straight," I said, voice controlled but barely. "We pretend for them. But you start shit with me again, I won't hold back."

She nodded, lips pressed thin, and for half a second, the hatred between us felt like the only thing alive in the room. Feral as a starving dog.

I walked away, slamming the door behind me.

Outside, the cold bit into my ears, but it was nothing compared to the heat coiling in my spine.

I hated her. I wanted to see her bleed, and I wanted to put my mouth on her skin. I wanted to make her say my fucking name. I wanted to survive this trip without giving anything away. I was wired, on edge, every nerve tuned to her frequency.

She knew it too. I could see it in the way she didn't back down, in the way her eyes tracked me across the room.

We weren't done. Not even close. Let Shane and Sabrina play at being happy campers. Me and Amelia, our story was dirtier, messier. More fun.

And I was ready to let it burn.

———

Night came fast in the mountains. It flattened everything, made the world smaller, like the cold had come to close its fist around us. You could feel the darkness pressing in through the windows, aching against the glass, hungry to get inside. The only light was from the fire and a couple of overhead bulbs that sputtered and buzzed.

We gravitated back to the lounge after dinner, because none of us wanted to admit how tired or fucked up we'd gotten from a single day together in the wild. Shane turned on a movie and tried to be the world's best host, making popcorn, pouring drinks, keeping the conversation fizzing.

Amelia walked in last, right when I thought maybe I'd gotten my head on straight. She wore tight black leggings that stretched over her hips, over the lines of her thighs. The shirt was soft, thin, clinging to her chest. The outline of her tits was impossible to ignore. I tried, fuck me, I tried. But my eyes were heat-seeking; every inch of her body was a punch in the face.

She didn't know what she was doing to me. Or maybe she did. Maybe that was the whole point.

If so, she was winning. Even the shame was addictive.

She took a seat at the end of the sofa, legs folded under her, hair falling over her cheek. She hugged a pillow like a shield, but it didn't do shit to hide the way her body fit together.

Sabrina made a show of digging through her phone. "Okay, ground rules. If anyone falls asleep on movie night, they owe the group breakfast."

Amelia smiled, just the barest twitch, the one I remembered from high school that meant she was about to get mean. "Guess Caiden's our breakfast guy, then. Or are you planning on staying awake this time?"

Her eyes glinted, daring me.

I smirked. "I'll stay up if the company's worth it."

Shane just laughed, clapping me on the shoulder. "Look, I

can't promise much, but I did spring for the highest cabin package. At these prices, they should have housekeepers to tuck us in."

I grunted, more sound than laugh. My gaze kept snagging on Amelia, like I was trapped in some fucked-up gravity field. Every time she shifted, the shirt moved with her, nipples visible against the fabric for a heartbeat, then gone. My mouth was dry. My hands itched to do something. Grab a drink, crush a glass, maybe even close over her throat.

You don't get to want that. Not with her. Not after everything. Still, I watched.

The longer we all sat there, the worse it got. Sabrina wanted to play games, dragged out a deck of cards, making us do "icebreaker questions." Shane steered every answer into a joke, but all I could think about was the pulse in my jaw, how every muscle in my neck locked up whenever Amelia spoke.

"What's your most irrational fear?" Sabrina asked at one point. She looked at me, then Amelia.

Amelia's voice broke the silence. "Drowning. I hate water. Just being under it. Not breathing."

I remembered the time I shoved her at the lake, all those years ago. Watched her go under, gasping like a fish, eyes wild. She never forgave me for that. Not that I blamed her.

Shane's eyes landed on me. "What about you, Caiden?"

"Losing control," I said, and if I'd had a knife, I could've carved the words into my own skin.

Amelia's gaze cut to me.

*You want to see what happens when I do lose it?* I almost said it out loud.

But I kept the mask up. I had to.

At one point, I went for another beer in the kitchen. She followed, of course she did, stalking me like prey.

We were alone in the narrow galley, counters catching gold from the hallway lamp. Her back was to the fridge; she looked at me like she wanted to peel something raw off my bones.

"You keep staring," she said, voice a whisper. "You want something?"

I stepped closer, letting the door fall shut behind me. "Not from you."

"Liar." Her lips barely moved. The challenge made my pulse stutter.

I could smell her. My hands braced on either side of her, trapping her for just a second.

"I don't want you," I lied. "Not in any way that's nice."

She swallowed. "Good. I'd hate to see you try."

I let my gaze rake over her. She stiffened. I knew she felt it. My disgust, my need, the thing between us that had never really died, just gotten sicker. It's been a fucking while, too, since I've been this close to an attractive woman. Probably since my ex kicked out.

"Don't flatter yourself," I hissed, stepping away before I did something irreversible.

But even as I walked off, I could feel her eyes drilling holes in my back.

Back in the lounge, the fire burned low, shadows licking at the walls. Shane and Sabrina cuddled up on the loveseat, oblivious to the war happening six feet away.

Amelia watched the flames and pretended not to notice me watching her.

But she did.

We all pretended so fucking hard.

The movie ended. Sabrina and Shane peeled off to claim the "honeymoon suite." Their laughter faded down the hall.

Me and Amelia, left in the half-dark.

She stood up, hugging herself, eyes flicking over me with something like hate. Or want. Or both.

I blocked her path on purpose.

She glared. "Move."

I didn't.

"What, Langston? You scared?"

She glared harder. "I've survived worse."

"Oh, I know."

Her jaw trembled, just for a second, before she leaned in close enough for me to smell the heat on her skin, her anger.

"You think I'm scared of you?" she spat, barely holding it together.

I let the words slow, drip like poison.

"You should be."

But I didn't touch her. Didn't even breathe.

She shoved past me, brushing my arm, a quick scrape of nails through my shirt. It lingered.

I chased it, all the way to my room.

I slammed the door. Sat on the edge of the bed. Looked down at my hands. Still shaking.

The darkness pressed in and refused to let go. Somewhere in the house, I heard her door shut. Echoed in my teeth. We were both prisoners of this. We always had been.

# 16

## THE PAST
### CAIDEN'S CONDITIONING

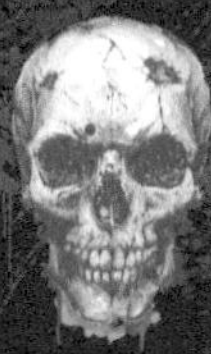

**4 1/2 YEARS OLD**

I trembled, huddled in the corner of the dimly lit room, my wide eyes reflecting a mix of fear and confusion as my father's bulky figure stumbled toward me.

"You're such a stupid boy! You're just a reminder of her."

His hand came crashing down onto my face. A sting of pain erupted as a bottle of beer shattered against the wall, glass scattering like my shattered sense of safety.

"Please, Dad, calm down," I whimpered, my voice barely a whisper beneath the roar of his fury. I felt the familiar swell of my face, a painful reminder that I had grown all too accustomed to.

Everything around me felt overwhelming. Too loud, too frightening. My father's voice spilled forth like a torrent, each word drenched in rage.

"She left because of that whore, Judy, and now I'm stuck with you and this empty, sad house."

He swayed unsteadily, mumbling to himself as he waved his arms through the air, a tempest of confusion and anger. He snatched another beer from the coffee table nearby, the cold bottle glistening ominously in the dim light.

I wished desperately for silence to drown out the chaos that had become my existence, but I felt powerless against the storm of my father's wrath.

It felt red and maddening, an unrelenting tide that threatened to consume me whole.

"You need to understand that, boy. It's Judy's fault, not mine. Your mother left because of that fuckin' wench!"

Each accusation dripped with venom, slicing through my heart, deepening the chasm of fear and helplessness.

My father paused mid-rant, collapsing onto the worn couch, his body sinking into the cushions as if the weight of the world pressed upon him.

I remained frozen in place, acutely aware of the unpredictability that defined him. Living under the same roof felt like navigating a treacherous minefield, where each word could trigger an explosion.

I longed for my mother to return, to envelop me in her warmth and assure me that everything would be okay. But now, my father had transformed into something monstrous.

"You need to avenge your mother, son."

Confusion clouded my mind, but I nodded along, my small frame quaking. He spoke as if she were gone forever, cloaked in an unshakeable darkness.

"Make your father proud and take action, Caiden."

He took another deep swig of beer, the liquid sloshing dangerously close to the rim.

"You hear that, boy? Do something right for once in your life!"

Tears slipped silently down my cheeks, each droplet a testament to my helplessness. I nodded as his drunken, slurred words washed over me, a chaotic symphony of commands that made no sense.

Yet I understood one thing. Compliance was necessary. I had to be a good son, because the alternative was too terrifying to contemplate. If I disobeyed, the repercussions would be brutal.

I wanted desperately to make him proud, clinging to the hope that perhaps, if I achieved something, anything, he might finally see me, might finally love me.

Maybe if I found someone Judy cared about and inflicted pain upon them, it would be enough to win his approval. Maybe, just maybe, I could transfer the burden of my own suffering onto another.

"Okay, Dad," I murmured, my head bowed, limbs still trembling as if I were caught in the aftermath of a storm.

I could feel the blood trickling from my lip, warm and sticky, pooling at my chin, a vivid reminder of the mark he had left upon me.

I wished for it all to end, but deep down, I feared that this torment would stretch on for many more years to come.

# 17

## THE PAST

### CAIDEN'S CONDITIONING

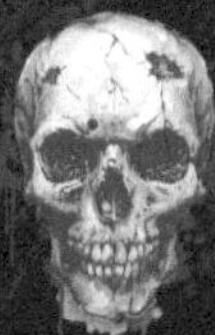

**10 YEARS OLD**

I used to make a wish every night before bed. I yearned for my mother to return, to wrap her arms around me and shield me from my father's wrath. In my dreams, her warmth enveloped me like a comforting blanket, the kind that promised safety and love.

But eventually, that fragile hope drained away, leaving only a hollow ache in its wake. There was no safety net for me, only survival and the constant need to hide in the shadows.

Each day, I faced the beast that was my father alone, a solitary warrior in a battle that felt never-ending. God forbid I ever took my anger out on the man who had become my tormentor.

I spotted her before she saw me. Her head hung low, golden brown hair framing her somber expression.

For a fleeting moment, a pang of sadness welled inside me as I considered her sadness. I had heard the whispers about her family, and in a way, I could relate. I, too, knew the ache of a parent leaving.

I shook my head, as if to dispel the thoughts swirling within. My father's voice echoed in my mind, a harsh reminder of the past. A permanent sting throbbed beneath the surface of my skin, a painful testament to his viciousness.

145

I could vividly recall the first time I saw Amelia Langston. It had been in the woods, where sunlight filtered through the leaves.

She had been crying, her tears glistening like jewels on her cheeks, yet the way the light danced upon her face made my heart flutter unexpectedly. Her hair was a cascade of shimmering gold caught in the sun. I remembered thinking how beautiful she was, unsure of what to do with that realization.

I had yearned to be friends with Amelia once upon a time. She was quiet and sweet. Seeing her was my favorite part of school. Her smile, her laughter, her innocence. It provided a brief respite from the storm that raged within me.

Yet behind her eyes lingered a profound sadness, a darkness that beckoned me to reach out, to comfort her. But I hesitated, uncertain of how to acknowledge it. At that tender age, everything felt new and overwhelming. I was just a small, helpless boy.

Then everything changed when my father's monster slowly became unleashed. Each time I saw Amelia, a wave of nausea washed over me.

It started small, after my mother left. I could recall talking to Amelia, being friendly with her, not feeling the tidal waves of rage and hatred.

Now, at age ten, that friendliness had vanished.

The phantom of my bruises pulsed beneath my skin, igniting a heat that spread across my face.

My feelings for her became a weakness, a source of shame painted in dark hues. Wanting to be her friend, to harbor affection for her, seemed wrong. It would infuriate my father, and in that moment, it felt as if it would make me a bad son.

Those thoughts dragged me down into an abyss of despair. I craved approval from my father, longed for sparks of affection to light up his eyes, rather than the familiar glint of rage and disappointment that had become all too commonplace.

In a moment of resolve, I made a promise to myself. I would bury those tender feelings so deep within that they would never see the light of day again. I slaughtered them in my mind, scattering their ashes to the wind.

Amelia Langston became my enemy. Amelia Langston also became my pathway to redemption.

"Hey, Caiden!"

I turned to see my friend, Dante, jogging toward me, a welcome distraction from the storm brewing inside.

"What's up, Dante?" I responded, a smile breaking through the heaviness. Dante was the only bright spot in my life, a friend who provided solace from the horrors lurking at home.

"Want to come to my house for dinner? We could kick around a soccer ball too." Dante grinned as if he had no care in the world.

A perfect excuse to escape the beast that awaited me. "Sure, I'll walk with you."

The small town was quiet and unassuming, a place where crime was almost nonexistent. Most houses lay within walking distance, a feature I appreciated. I enjoyed the tranquility of the breeze and the peaceful solitude that accompanied my walks home.

As we began our path toward Dante's house, a shadow flickered inside me. I loathed my father for what he had done to me. I resented Amelia for being connected to Judy. And I despised myself for my inability to stand up against my father, for allowing that darkness to shape me into a monster.

"Hey, Dante, watch this."

A sudden surge of reckless energy coursed through me as I quickened my pace and collided with Amelia. She let out a startled cry, tumbling to the ground, landing in a puddle of mud.

For a fleeting second, regret flickered within me, gnawing at my conscience.

I shoved it away just as swiftly, convincing myself I had made the right choice. Perhaps now, when I recounted the incident to my father, it would spare me from a beating that night.

"What did you do that for?" she exclaimed, her voice tinged with hurt. I wore a smug smile, reveling in the moment.

"Just felt like it." A laugh escaped me as I glanced at Dante for validation, but Dante's expression was not one of amusement. Instead, he looked at Amelia with pity.

My nostrils flared. I kicked mud toward her, watching her cringe as she whimpered. Dante was my friend, not hers. I couldn't bear the thought of him feeling even an ounce of pity for her.

"Hilarious," she muttered, annoyance lacing her words. She stood, anguish settling in her eyes, and turned to walk away.

"Yeah, go cry to your druggie mom! Oh wait, she probably won't care!" I shouted, my voice dripping with malice, relishing the sting of my words.

"That was harsh," Dante remarked as he began to stride forward.

I shrugged, feigning indifference. "I thought it was funny."

"Yeah, okay. C'mon, I'll race you!"

Laughter bubbled up within me as I chased after Dante, the heaviness of guilt momentarily forgotten, replaced by the thrill of our youthfulness.

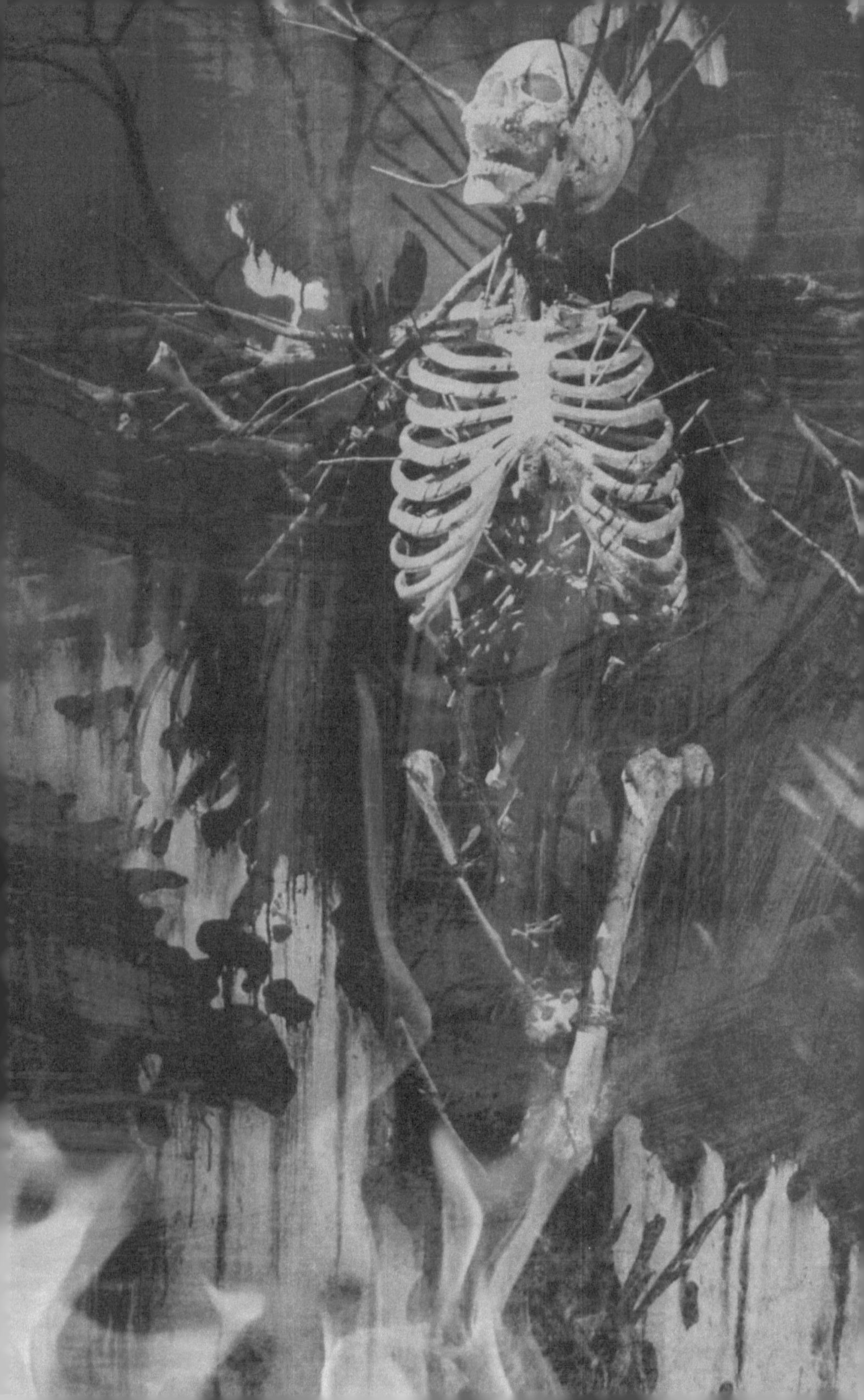

# 18

## THE PAST

### CAIDEN'S CONDITIONING

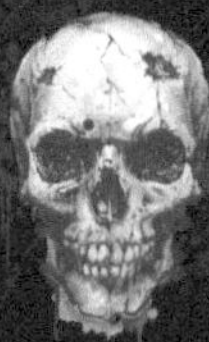

**12 YEARS OLD**

This anger consumed me like an untamable fire, leaving a scar that would never heal. It swelled and pulsated every second of the day, infecting my veins and pushing me deeper into sin.

She was a vision of sweet softness, and I hated it. I wanted to ruin her until she was just as damaged as I was.

Deep down, I knew it wasn't fair to her. I was a monster for unleashing my anger on her, for unleashing my father's anger on her. Everything about her seemed to succumb to it.

I recognized that truth, yet I still pushed her every day. My innocence had long been extinguished, leaving me incapable of feeling empathy or sympathy. "Kill or be killed," I repeated to myself throughout the day. Her fault. All her fault.

Smash.

The sound of glass fragments clinking against the ground pierced the air. I peeked into the room, only to shrink back immediately upon seeing my father in one of his rage-fueled moods.

As long as I kept my promise to remain an obedient son, I could stay clear of his violence, most of the time.

Bruises still came, but not as often.

"What are you looking at, boy?" My father's face was a deep shade of red, clearly out of his mind.

Before I could escape, he grabbed me by the shirt and threw me to the ground.

"Why don't you put yourself to some use and clean this shit up?"

I froze, gulping and shutting my eyes, bracing for the next hit. I may have been taller and older, but inside, I remained the same scared child. Paralyzed by fear and pain. My younger self lurked within me, silent and trembling.

My father kicked me with his foot. "Get on with it! Obey me!"

I sprang to my feet, grabbing a broom, and hurriedly sweeping up the glass, slicing my hand in the process.

"Damn it! You're getting blood all over the goddamn floor. Get the fuck out of here!"

He hurled a bottle at me, and my heart pounded in my chest. With weakened legs, I sprinted toward the front door and out into the open. I grabbed my bike, hopped onto it, and rode far away from the beast.

Blood gushed from my flesh, but I hardly noticed. Adrenaline and terror overwhelmed me. I rode until I could go no further, my bike collapsing alongside my body in the park onto the cool grass. I lay there, heaving breaths while staring up at the sky.

The clouds drifted slowly, and the cold wind froze my skin. I remained there until I heard footsteps approaching.

"Caiden?" A small voice broke through the silence. It reminded me of the way I would approach my father. Terrified, anticipating something terrible.

I turned my head and saw her standing a few feet away, her hair whipping around her face in the harsh wind.

Still, I didn't speak. I merely stared, still slightly numb from the recent events.

"You're bleeding," Amelia stated, her voice soft yet steady. She stood firm, not backing away. Why wasn't she running? Didn't she fear me?

Slowly, I sat up, wincing as I caught sight of the trail of blood. The wound stung, yet I felt no urgency to return home and tend to it.

"Yeah. I cut myself." I didn't bother to elaborate. I just wanted to be alone.

I glanced at her again. She was nibbling on her bottom lip, as if contemplating whether to say more. She did.

"Do you need help?" she asked softly, her voice barely a whisper in the wind.

"No. I don't need help. Especially not your help. Now fuck off." I didn't want her kindness. I didn't deserve it. I wanted her to loathe me. At least that would make it easier to be cruel to her, to feel no guilt for my words and actions.

Her expression shifted, hurt flashing across her face before frustration took over.

"Fine. I was trying to be nice. It looked like you could use a friend but never mind."

"We're not friends!" I snapped, now standing on slightly wobbly legs.

"I know!" she shot back. "But just because you're cruel to me doesn't mean you're not deserving of kindness. I guess I was wrong, though."

I clenched my teeth and glared at her. "Yeah, don't be kind to me. I don't want it. Just let me suffer in peace."

"Jerk," I heard her mutter before she turned and stormed away.

I was left alone with my bitter thoughts and the merciless wind. I wasn't sure how long I sat there, but it must have been a while.

Soon, darkness fell around me. My stomach howled for attention, and my skin felt like ice.

For a fleeting moment, I allowed myself to entertain a vulnerable thought. I wanted her to come back, to feel her warmth envelop me, to be wrapped within it. Then memories of my mother surfaced, a longing for her touch.

But none of those things were accessible. They were impossible to obtain. I put up my guard again and walked home, dragging my bike beside me.

My father would be passed out by now, but safety was never a guarantee.

I was always teetering on crackling ice, waiting for it to shatter, for me to plunge into the cold depths below. It was inevitable. Collapsing into an endless black hole, nobody around to save me.

Nothing else mattered anymore except survival, holding on until a day came when I might not feel so broken. Hoping for a day when I could start anew, when I could feel love wholly and without fear.

But hope was a delicate thing, easily crushed. That dream was fading, becoming a mere hallucination. A delusion.

Hopeless. Helpless.

Those were my thoughts as I stepped inside the house of horrors, passing by my father, who lay passed out on the floor.

I crawled into bed, not bothering to eat or clean my cut. My body ached, and my head felt hazy.

I thought about my father. The lessons burned into me. Never show weakness, never back down, never let them see what's really inside. I was supposed to be better than her. Stronger. But I wasn't. Every time I tried to wreck her, it just made the mess inside my head worse.

The rage built up, pounding in my chest, until I wanted to hit something, rip the whole goddamn school apart, just so I didn't have to feel this way.

But I did nothing.

I watched the halls empty, watched the light die, watched the world move on without me.

All I could think about was her. Amelia. The way she looked at me, even after everything. The way she tried to hold on, in spite of me.

I hated her more than anything.

But underneath that, there was something else. Something I could never name.

It scared the shit out of me.

So I fed the anger. I let it rot. Let it own me, the way my father owned the bottle.

Every night, the same. Every morning, the same. I pictured her the next time I saw her. I promised myself I'd be even worse. I promised myself I'd never let her win.

Because the anger, the hate, was the only thing I could count on. If I ever lost that, I'd have nothing left. Just the empty space inside. Nothing but a hollow echo of a boy who never stood a chance.

And maybe that was what I deserved. Maybe that was the only honest thing there was.

The anger. The ache. The hunger to hurt, so I wouldn't feel so fucking weak.

It's a cycle that starts every day. And I'd let it. Because that's who I was. And who I'd always be.

My last thought, before falling into a restless slumber, was of Amelia.

# 19
## THE PRESENT

### AMELIA

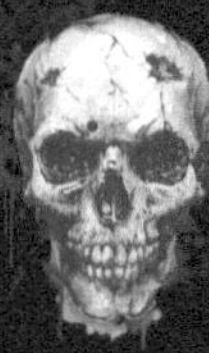

Sabrina had sworn I'd find peace here, and I hoped she was right.

The cabins loomed three stories high on a gentle slope, their rough-hewn logs glowing honey-warm in the morning light.

Inside, my room smelled faintly of cedar and old wool, comforting, if only it weren't so silent.

I pressed my back against the cool pine wall, closed my eyes, and let the resort's distant laughter and splashing pool fade into a dull hum. Solitude, at last.

Outside, the mountains reared like slumbering titans. Forests spilled from their flanks, a tangle of emerald and shadow, ribbons of silver rivers twisting through the valley below.

I settled onto our cabin's porch, its worn boards creaking beneath me, and let a breeze drift across my skin, carrying the scent of pine resin and damp earth. I inhaled deeply and smiled.

Serenity.

Then the crisp stillness shattered under the deliberate click of a front-door latch. I twisted, heart tightening, and there he stood.

Caiden.

He filled the doorway in a dark black jacket, his posture unnervingly straight, as if every muscle were wired to attention.

A stray sunbeam struck the edge of his jaw, and for a moment I wondered if the quiet confidence he wore so easily was genuine, or just another mask.

My lips curved into a scowl before I could stop it. "Why do you always manage to wreck every peaceful second I get?" My voice was low but edged with more bitterness than I'd meant to show.

He flicked his gaze my way, amber eyes narrowing. A slow smirk tugged at his mouth. "It's funny, I was just thinking you're the one killing my vibe. Like a bad scent."

I sprang to my feet, boots thudding on the porch. "Maybe you should leave," I snapped, crossing my arms so tightly my shoulder blades ached.

His jaw clenched, dark brows inching together as if to contain some inner storm. "Not happening. I'm here because of family. You're nothing but the pity guest, tagging along for sympathy."

I stepped forward, pulse pounding beneath my ribs. "She invited me to bond with her and Shane. I'm maid of honor. Get your facts straight."

Caiden's lips quirked. "Ah. So you're gonna ruin his big day too? I'm best man."

Every breath inside me felt like molten metal. I pressed my hands against the porch railing until my knuckles blanched. "You're like a virus, can't be rid of you."

His glare went to an icy anger. "And you're an annoying bug."

My tongue recoiled from the retort I'd been dying to unleash.

Then Sabrina's cheerful voice cut through the charged air, and Shane's booming laugh followed. They emerged, hand in hand, faces lit with that glowing newlywed bliss, another reminder of how trapped I was here, forced into their fairy-tale while I faced my personal villain.

"Perfect timing!" Shane called, hugging them together. "How about we all stick together today? Group hike!" His grin was so wide he looked almost feral with joy.

I managed a shrug. "Sure."

We set off along a narrow trail that sloped upward into cathedral-high pines, shafts of sunlight dancing through needles overhead. Damp moss muffled our footsteps, and the air tasted of centuries-old bark and wildflowers.

I fell behind Caiden, who strode ahead with his shoulders squared, as if clearing the path with sheer force of will. I kept my eyes on the needles underfoot, each step a deliberate refusal to meet his gaze.

The incline steepened. Rocks jutted from the earth like broken teeth; tree roots twisted across the dirt in great, gnarled hands. Somewhere above us, water tumbled over stones, its lazy gurgle rising and falling like distant thunder.

I paused at a bend and watched mist drift over the stream's surface, silver on obsidian rock, hinting at hidden cascades further upstream.

A sudden squeal snapped me back. Sabrina, frozen mid-stride, pointed into the shadows at the edge of the trail. My heart fluttered, breath catching, as I pushed past Shane and peered between the trunks.

A doe stood there, backlit by slanting sunbeams. Its ears quivered, velvet soft against a spine of dusk-brown fur. Time slowed; I could almost hear my own blood pulse in my ears as I lifted a trembling hand, afraid to break the fragile spell.

Then a twig snapped like a pistol shot. The deer bolted, hooves thundering against rock, vanishing in a rustle of leaves.

I whirled on Caiden. His eyes gleamed with satisfaction, his lips curved in a smug half-smile. I knew that sound. He'd done it on purpose.

"You scared it off," I hissed, fists clenching. "We were watching it."

"Oops. My bad," he drawled, voice silky, utterly without guilt.

Sabrina's bright voice chimed in obliviously: "Don't worry, Amelia—we'll see more wildlife soon!" Her cheer grated on me like nails on slate. I glared at Caiden, venom hot behind my eyes, longing to tear away his calm veneer and reveal the stirring cruelty beneath.

But Sabrina had already turned to lead us further up the trail, her laugh echoing through the pines, and Caiden—ever my constant tormentor—fell into step just inches behind me.

We pressed on, Shane and Sabrina bounding ahead for a moment, leaving me alone with the beast. I resorted to pretending he wasn't there, taking the opportunity to absorb everything around me.

The clouds hung in the sky, stretching across the expanse, casting a gray hue that hinted at the possibility of rain.

The weather report had assured us of a rain-free day, so I figured it was merely a temporary cluster of dark clouds.

"It's been a few minutes. I wonder what they're up to," Caiden mused, breaking the silence. He raised his eyebrows in a mischievous manner, and I rolled my eyes.

Typical men.

"I'm sure they're not doing what you're thinking." My cheeks flushed as I spoke. Just the hint of that subject with Caiden made my stomach twist uncomfortably.

Caiden opened his mouth to respond, but at that moment, Sabrina and Shane returned. I sighed with relief; moments alone with Caiden turned my blood to ice.

My heart felt entwined with darkness, the fury simmering just beneath the surface. I mustered the strength to swallow it back down.

As we neared the end of the loop, dangerous sparks simmered between Caiden and me. We were engaged in a game of who could irritate the other the most. He would say something to rub me the wrong way or shove past me on the trail, muttering a fake "oops, sorry" to make it seem harmless.

I had tried being the bigger person, but I was only human. Ahead, a low branch extended from a tree, its jagged edges threatening to snag anyone who dared to pass.

I hurried in front of Caiden, ducking beneath it just as he approached. The branch brushed against my body before snapping back, colliding with Caiden.

"Ow! Dammit," I heard him groan, disoriented. A smile crept across my face, a small victory in our ongoing game.

"You're still the same bitch you've always been," Caiden whispered bitterly, stepping back to allow Sabrina and Shane to take the lead.

"You started it," I shot back.

"I did not," he countered, his tone dripping with false innocence.

Lies.

"Yes, you did."

"Okay. Believe what you want, Amelia." My name rolled off his tongue angrily.

I turned to face him, stopping him dead in his tracks. I could feel the heat radiating from my flushed cheeks, a simmering rage boiling just beneath the surface.

"Are you kidding me? You're the one who wants to play childish games. I'm just following your lead, buddy. I never wanted to see you ever again." The tension was cold and harsh; I let it fuel me.

He offered no reaction, as usual. "I'm childish? Sure. Okay. I didn't plan to see you either. But here we are." His dark gaze pierced through me, haunting me.

"You're unbelievable. I never wanted to hate you. But you took the first step. You lit the match. I never asked for this," I screamed the last part, shoving past him and striding ahead.

The tension between us was suffocating. His very presence left me breathless and quivering, as if I had just survived a catastrophic disaster.

Caiden was my eternal darkness, bleeding out this heart of mine.

"Amelia." He grabbed my arm. His touch was cold as ice, yet it ignited a fire within my veins. Fury surged onward.

"Let go of me." I yanked my arm away, but he held fast, pulling me toward him. There was something in his expression, something intense and blazing.

"Dammit. I never meant for any of this to happen," he shouted, his brown gaze burning into me, killing me slowly.

"What—" I began but was interrupted by Shane.

"Are you both alright over here?" Shane strolled over, blissfully unaware of the storm brewing between Caiden and me.

Caiden released me with a stiff nod, stepping aside. "Yeah. We're fine. Amelia dropped something, and I was helping her find it."

I nodded, drained from our exchange.

"Okay. Well, we're close to the end of the trail now. Let's eat and clean up before the next activity." Shane told us before leading the way on the trail again.

There was more? Super.

The path ended, and we made our way back to the cabin. Before heading to my room, I glanced back at Caiden. He was already looking at me.

———

A few hours later, we gathered in the main public area near the front door. Next on our agenda was kayaking on the river.

I hesitated, voicing my concerns about the weather.

Shane waved it off dismissively. "I double-checked the weather. It'll be okay; don't worry."

Above us, the clouds continued to form, shifting from light gray to dark gray, an ominous dance of hues. I resonated with the drifting clouds, watching them float somberly, devoid of color.

We boarded the resort bus, which took us to the nearby river. Once we arrived, I followed the group to collect the kayaks, one for each of us. The river tumbled gracefully, dancing over rocks that jutted out of the surface.

"Are you sure this will be safe?" I asked, my gaze darting between the rushing water and the sky, unease coiling in my stomach. It was an echo of the same bad feeling that had shadowed me before I agreed to this trip.

"This is perfectly safe. People do it all the time," Sabrina reassured me, her comforting smile doing little to quell my anxiety.

We settled into our kayaks at the water's edge, the paddler's staff guiding each of us gently until our boats bobbed and floated free. Then, with a push off the muddy bank, we were off.

For a while the world was bright and easy. The river's surface rippled in soft undulations, carrying me forward as Sabrina's laughter tinkled like bells and Shane's voice wove between the reeds. They paddled side by side in parallel strokes, shafts of sunlight flickering across their backs.

Caiden, as always, led the way, and I trailed just behind, the warm spray of water blinking on my skin.

High above, the sun fought a losing battle with thick gray clouds. I squinted upward, spotting a flock of birds veering inland, wings slicing through the damp air.

The current rushed on. Urgent, unrelenting. Then a single droplet splashed onto my forehead, followed by another. My stomach fluttered as the droplets quickened into a steady hiss.

"Let's turn back! I must've been wrong about the weather." Shane's voice cut through the rising hiss.

I shifted my gaze and saw his kayak veering toward the bank, Sabrina weaving alongside him. Together, they began retreating from the distant, inky storm wall.

Ahead, dark rivulets of rain carved themselves down from swollen clouds.

But for now, it remained a broad sheet on the horizon. Intimidating but distant enough that there was still time.

Caiden slipped past me, his paddle carving arcs in the water. He cast a quick glance over his shoulder towards me.

"Hurry," he muttered, low-voiced urgency threading each syllable. "We've got to catch them."

I swung my torso to turn the kayak, but the current had grown fierce. The river roared around me, tugging at the hull, urging me backward.

My arms burned as I thrust the paddle into the churning water, fighting against a tide that seemed to gulp at my kayak's bow.

It all happened in an instant. My grip slipped—was it my hand or the paddle shaft?—and I caught a flash of submerged rock before the paddle clattered free and vanished into the swirling gray.

"My paddle!" I screamed, panic crawling up my throat as the rain wall advanced.

Voices rose in the distance; I thought I heard Sabrina calling my name. Through the curtain of droplets, I saw a lone figure paddling furiously back toward me.

"Hold on! I'm coming!" he yelled, his voice raw over the wind. He drew alongside, breath ragged, rain matting his hair against his forehead.

"I thought you'd leave me to drown," I said, attempting a wry edge in my tone even as adrenaline hammered in my veins.

His face remained blank. "Shane and Sabrina wouldn't let me."

I braced one hand on the gunwale and swung my legs into his cockpit, my own kayak drifting free behind me into the vortex.

Once settled, I looked around for our friends. Only the rolling gray mist and the river's hiss greeted me.

"I sent them ahead," Caiden said, settling himself to paddle again. "They'll wait at the bend."

We pushed into the current together, oars slicing through the liquid mirror. But our brief respite ended when a lump of water— like a small, angry wave—pushed against our stern, driving us back toward the heart of the storm.

Overhead, thunder cracked so close it rattled my bones, and the sky darkened until even the water seemed black.

The river became a living beast: roiling, grasping. Rain turned to sheets of needles, lashing our faces. I watched in horror as Caiden's paddle wrenched free from his grasp, tumbling into the angry depths.

In an instant his features contorted with shock and fear, an expression so raw, one which I had never seen on him before.

"Caiden, what do we do?" My voice was swallowed by gale and torrent. He stared at me, wide-eyed and wordless, as if weighing the fury of the water against our frail wooden shell.

I never imagined that this would be how I would die, trapped in a kayak during a storm with Caiden. Oh, the irony of the universe.

Ahead, I spotted a dip in the water. My lungs felt as if they had crashed into my chest.

A waterfall ahead of us. Not enormous, but enough to terrify me.

The sky roared with fury. Somewhere in the storm I screamed, but through the cacophony of the storm, it was hard to tell.

Caiden's broad shape blurred in the dark atmosphere, mere shadows in the chaos.

The dip came closer, the sky screamed louder. The kayak tumbled about, spinning uncontrollably, until suddenly it wasn't spinning anymore.

It was falling.

The sky was black, but my vision darkened further, everything plunging into silence as Caiden and I plummeted into the tumultuous waves, consumed by darkness.

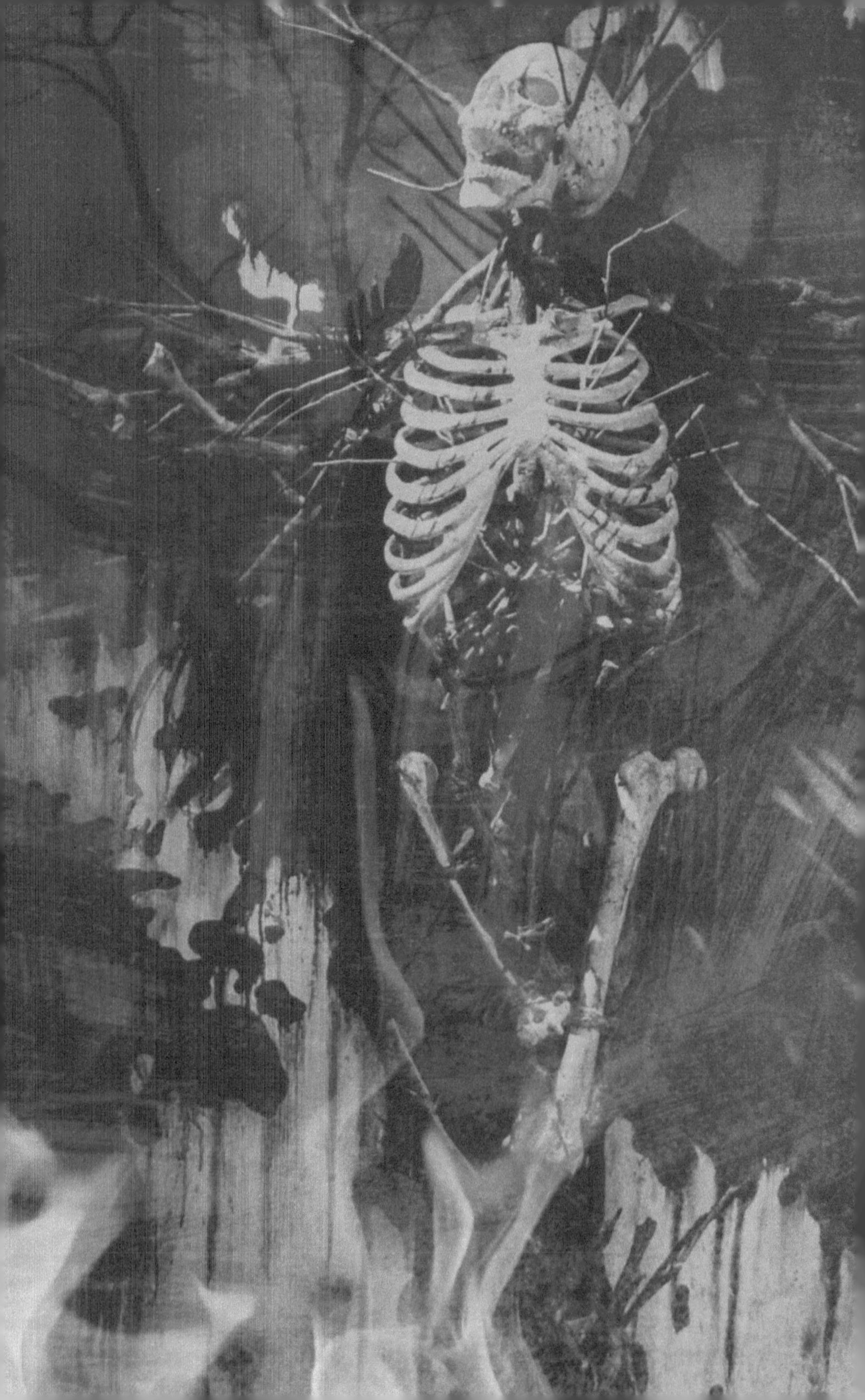

# 20

## THE PRESENT

### AMELIA

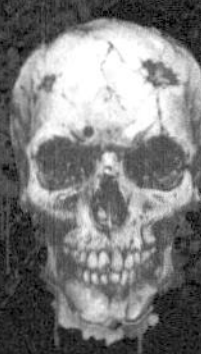

A dream so perfect drifted through my mind, wrapping around me like a warm embrace. A grassy, flowery meadow spread out in front of me, vibrant colors dancing together under a sky painted in soft pink and lavender hues.

The gentle symphony of birdsong floated through the air, carried by a softened wind that whispered secrets of serenity. In this moment, tranquility claimed my soul.

Lillian sat beside me, her face smooth and glowing, radiating warmth and familiarity. Her hair cascaded down her back in luscious waves, and she smiled, her fingers brushing against my hand with a tenderness that sent a shiver of comfort through me.

My mother occupied the space next to her, transformed from the shadowy figure I had clung to in my memories. Her once-dull hair shimmered with health, and a vibrant smile lit her lips. Her eyes sparkled like stars, and her skin no longer bore the creases of worry and wear.

Everything felt as it should be. Warm, safe, soothing.

I thought to myself, I could stay here forever. I never wanted to leave.

But then, something emerged from the distance, creeping toward us. The grass beneath my feet became drenched, and I watched helplessly as a stream of water raced around us, swallowing everything in its path.

"No!" I cried, but it was futile. The water surged, pulling them away from me, leaving me alone in the cold, wet expanse of the meadow.

"Amelia."

A whisper brushed against my ear, soft yet insistent.

"Amelia."

This time, the voice was louder. My body trembled, a chill wrapping around me like a shadow. I felt so cold. So very cold.

My eyes snapped open, and I found myself face-to-face with Caiden. A startled scream escaped my lips, echoing in the darkness. My mind was a muddled haze, struggling to grasp the reality of my surroundings.

"Amelia! Calm down. Jesus. You're alive. You're okay."

Caiden's voice attempted to soothe me, but instead, it only heightened my panic.

"Calm down? Seriously?" The memories rushed back like a tidal wave. "We're stuck in the middle of nowhere! I'm cold, I'm wet, and my head feels like it's about to explode! How am I supposed to feel okay?"

"I know," he snapped, frustration lacing his words. "I'm going to get us out of here. Just calm down. I can't think when you're freaking out like a girl."

Pure adrenaline coursed through me, igniting a fire I couldn't contain. I sprang up and shoved my palm against his chest, feeling the hard muscle beneath my fingers. "I am a girl! I have every right to have a nervous breakdown right now! You must be some kind of inhuman mutant to not feel any stress in this situation."

He shrugged, a smirk playing at the corners of his mouth. "I guess I'm just more emotionally grown than you are."

Seriously? He wanted to engage in this debate right now?

"I can't believe you." I threw my hands up in exasperation, sinking back onto the ground. I wasn't going anywhere with him. I would wait right there until someone came to rescue us.

"You should be saying 'thank you.' If it weren't for me, you wouldn't be alive," he retorted, the tension radiating from him like heat from a flame.

"What in the hell are you talking about? You're so full of yourself, as usual."

He shook his head, and in that moment, we resembled the river and sky caught in the eye of a storm. Pushing and pulling, raging and exploding. We swirled around one another like two wildfires, both desperate for control, yet knowing that ultimately, we would destroy each other.

"I came to consciousness before you. Your face was blue; your skin was cold. So cold. You were barely there. I had to perform CPR just to get you to cough up all the water from your lungs."

He had just admitted that he saved me, and yet I felt a surge of anger and humiliation.

"You should've just left me to die," I muttered, the words tasting bitter on my tongue. A part of me meant it; the dream I had was so perfect, so lifelike. Maybe I was suicidal, like my dead sister.

Had I been that close to crossing over to the other side? Was that glimpse of paradise a sign of heaven?

Caiden's eyes burned with anger, his nostrils flaring like a bull ready to charge. His fists clenched so tightly that the knuckles turned white.

"Yeah. Maybe I should have left you."

His words cut deeper than any blade. Silence enveloped us, a fog that thickened the air.

There was nothing left to say; his words had drawn a sharp line through the conversation. What could I possibly say to that?

He turned his back to me, his frustration evident as he began examining our surroundings. I sat there, helplessly drained of any determination to fight our way back to civilization.

We were far from safety, that much I knew. The drive to the river from the resort had taken a few miles, and we had been in the kayaks for nearly an hour before the rain began to fall.

Caiden and I had sailed down the river in the storm for miles before hitting the waterfall. There was no telling how long we had drifted in the water before he had pulled me out.

Yep. We were doomed.

I observed our surroundings, taking in the change in the landscape. The terrain had flattened, revealing stretches of rocky soil mixed with sparse vegetation. I desperately searched for any semblance of familiarity, but everything remained unknown.

"I think I found a good path," Caiden's voice broke through my spiraling thoughts. He stood a few feet away, tossing branches aside with a determined focus, still not meeting my gaze.

"Great," I whispered, the words barely escaping my lips. The blood felt drained from my body, leaving me still and stiff. Weariness wrapped around my spirit, and I sank onto the hard ground.

Now, he turned to face me. "Get the fuck up, Amelia."

I remained there, speechless, my eyes fixed on the river beside me, watching the water drift lazily. The sky had opened, bathing the world in a serene quiet. Yet, deep within, I yearned to return to the dreamland of a peaceful meadow, where worries ceased to exist.

"It's going to be dark soon. I'm going with or without you." Caiden stated, staring at my helpless shape.

How much time had passed? I pondered, feeling as though hours had slipped away, yet the sun was merely beginning its descent, painting the sky in hues of red and orange. The colors danced together, merging like a symphony, breathtaking yet distant.

"Go without me, then," I replied, my energy a deadened thing.

Caiden let out a strangled sound, a mix of frustration and disbelief. I didn't care if I was being stubborn or difficult; I felt no inclination to move. Perhaps I was simply too tired, too weary. If I rested, maybe I would be more cooperative.

"Fine. Have fun by yourself." His words were final and brisk.

Would he really leave me here?

As his footsteps began to fade, seconds stretched into an eternity. The sounds receded into the distance until all I could hear was the gentle rippling of the water and the frantic pounding of my own heartbeat. It was deafening.

I shut my eyes, the silence wrapping around me, terrifying in its stillness.

"Caiden! Wait!" I shot up, stumbling toward the last place I had seen him. A chill coursed through my body, the wind biting at my skin.

The once-familiar terrain now seemed ominous, filled with quiet anguish. The birds had silenced their songs, retreating into the dusk.

In a frantic rush, I followed the path he had taken, calling out his name repeatedly. I soon spotted him in the distance, standing with his back turned to me, waiting.

"Bastard! I can't believe you left me!" My breath came out in uneven huffs, panic and anger swirling within me.

"I told you that I would." He shrugged his shoulders as if it wasn't a big deal, like we were strolling through town, not in the middle of nowhere.

Confusion crashed over me in waves. He had saved me, then he had abandoned me. He had shown a small gesture of kindness, only to retract it moments later. I wondered what it would be like to peek inside his mind. He was everywhere, a chaotic whirlwind consuming me, breaking me, tormenting me.

"Jerk," was all I could muster.

"Come on," he commanded, and I found myself obeying, trudging behind him as my bones grew weaker with each passing second. His pace was strong, determined, and I couldn't help but wonder what fueled him.

As we walked, trees began to reappear, gradually surrounding us until the rushing water was no longer audible.

"Do you know where you're going?" I inquired, doubt creeping into my voice. He didn't have a map, had never been here before. How could he possibly be so confident?

"Nope."

That simple confession brought me to a halt.

"Then what are we doing? We could be traveling even further from where we should be going." My voice was hoarse, and I suddenly became acutely aware of my thirst. Each movement of my throat sent a painful reminder of my dry state.

"At least I'm trying to get us out of here. Unlike you. All you've done is complain and slow me down." He spun around, his irritation bubbling.

Two could play at that game; I was grumpy too.

"At least I'm not dragging us in circles, getting even more lost," I retorted, holding his gaze defiantly.

"You're impossible," he muttered, turning back around to continue onward. The shadows deepened as night encroached, moonlight scattering across the woods like a lantern's glow.

"I don't care what you think. I'm not going any further. I'm tired. It's dark. I want to sleep." There was no point in walking any longer.

Caiden sighed, looking around us as if he were searching for a solution, helpless.

"Fine. It is hard to navigate in the dark. We'll pick it back up at the first sign of sunlight." Caiden gave in, defeated.

I made an incoherent, irritated sound, sinking down in surrender. The bickering had grown stale, and I simply wanted to sleep.

He found a spot near me and laid down, and I followed suit, putting my arm beneath my head. It would be impossible to find comfort on this unforgiving ground.

My body ached, a chorus of complaints echoing through my muscles. As I drifted into a dreamless sleep, my last thoughts lingered on the last time Caiden and I had slept near each other.

At least in the motel, there had been the option of a bed. Now, there was no bed to fight over.

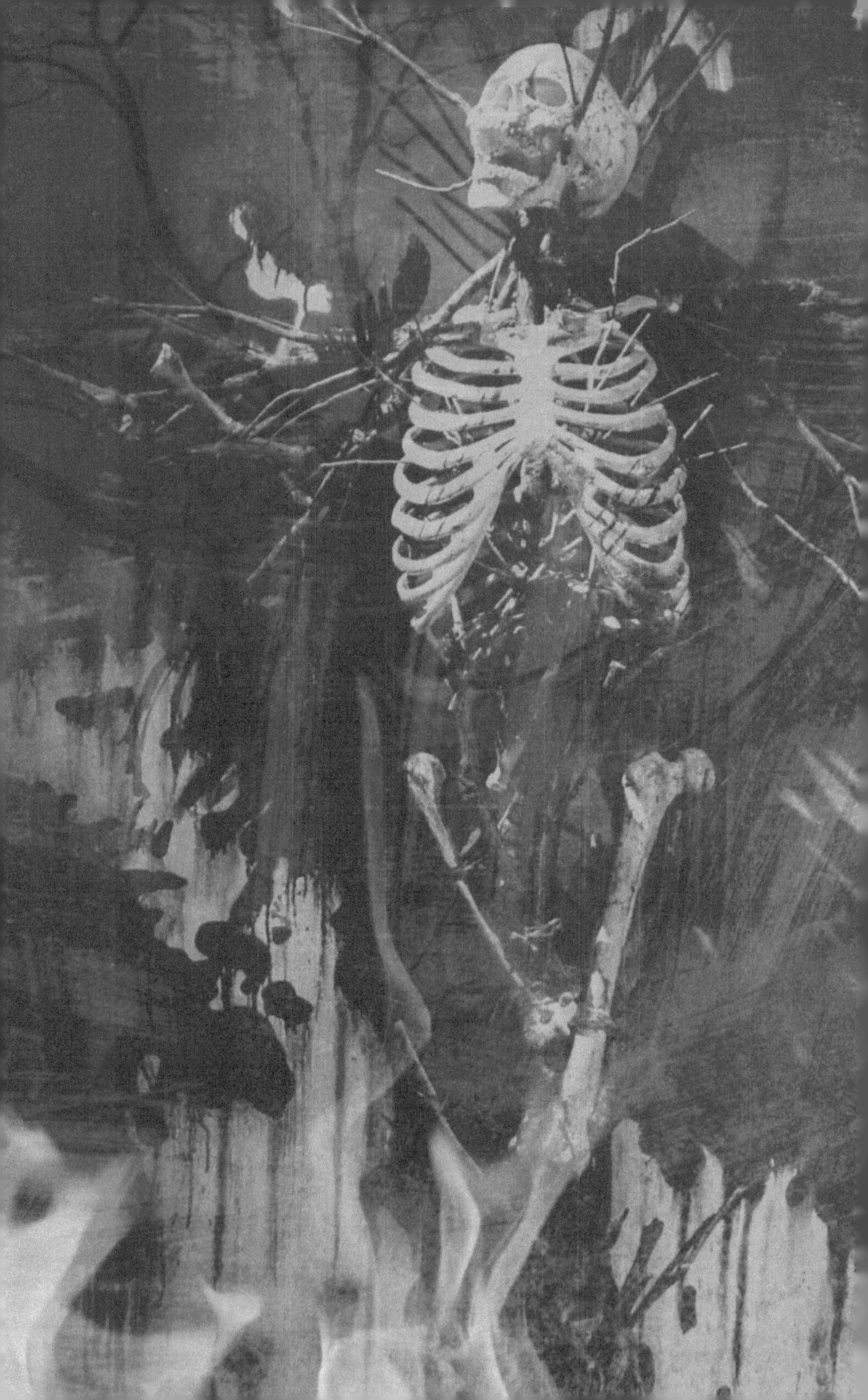

# 21

## THE PAST

### AMELIA'S BREAKING POINT

The car that carried Lillian's corpse faded into a distant speck on the horizon. It felt surreal to remember the texture of her lifeless flesh against my fingers, the acrid scent of her decomposing bones still lingering in my mind.

She was just a sorrowful memory now.

The pavement beneath me felt harsh. I had lost all sense of time as I sat in front of the apartment building, grief anchoring me to my spot, rendering reality ungraspable.

The tears had dried up, leaving my face stinging and throbbing. Puffy redness fanned across my cheeks, a testament to the melancholia swirling around me like a swarm of venomous insects, suffocating and debilitating.

Once the shock settled and fluttered away like a startled bird, I forced myself to stand. My knees wobbled, and I stumbled backward, nearly losing my balance. A woman passing by stopped, her eyes wide with curiosity and concern.

"Are you alright?" she asked.

I nodded, dismissing her with a wave of my hand, struggling to find my voice. "I just lost someone," I muttered, shaking my head as if trying to dislodge the memory of my dead sister.

"I'm so sorry," the woman said, placing her hand gently on my shoulder. I recoiled from her touch, the warmth of it sending a shiver down my spine, and I jogged to my car.

"I need to leave," I screeched hastily, desperation clawing at my throat.

The drive home resembled a frantic escape, a woman unhinged. I swerved across lanes, cutting off other drivers without a second thought. Honks blared around me, but they faded into the background; I was consumed by an urgent need to escape.

When I finally parked in the driveway, I dashed inside and slammed the door behind me. The house was cloaked in darkness, the ebony shades of shadow rattling my already frayed nerves.

I collapsed onto the dusty floor, burying my head in my hands as tremors shook my body.

The crushing silence was deafening, and I couldn't bear it any longer. I screamed, a raw, primal cry that echoed through the walls, tearing at my throat. I screamed until my vocal cords felt ragged and dry.

Footsteps approached, and suddenly, I was not alone anymore. I looked up through bleary eyes to see my mother standing above me, a frown etched on her face, hands on her hips.

"What are you screaming for? You're disturbing me!" she snapped, annoyance blazing in her eyes.

I sprang to my feet, anger flaring within me. "Oh? I'm disturbing you? So sorry, Mother!" I shrieked; my voice laced with mockery and indifference. "You should know that Lillian is dead! She's dead, and she's not coming back!"

My voice trembled, and that tightness returned to my throat. I swallowed hard, but it only pushed the anguish further up, threatening to spill over.

She froze, blinking in disbelief. "What?"

I scoffed, the bitterness rising within me. She was probably too lost in her haze to even comprehend what I was saying. A dark part of me wondered if she would be sober enough to attend the funeral.

"Lillian is dead. She killed herself because of how alone she felt. So, thanks a lot, Mom. Thanks for kicking her out when she needed you the most!"

"Oh, gracious," she murmured, holding her head as if to steady herself. She staggered back, her balance wavering.

I crossed my arms, glaring at her with venomous intensity. It was her fault. All her fault. Someone had to take the blame; someone had to face the wrath.

"Are you sure she's gone?" My mother's voice was a whisper, her pupils darting around, her focus slipping away.

"Yes, I'm sure. I found her body."

"It couldn't be," she mumbled, her words not directed at me but rather lost in the labyrinth of her own mind. Tugging at her hair, she wandered off toward her room, trapped within her muddled thoughts.

Through the walls, I could hear wailing, distant and pained, like a wounded animal. I couldn't bear to stay there any longer.

The house felt like it was spinning, Lillian's room too close for comfort, memories pressing in around me like a suffocating fog.

Before I could think clearly, my feet darted out the door. I ran until my lungs burned, until I reached the edge of the neighborhood by the woods.

A nauseating sensation twisted in my stomach, and I doubled over, retching onto the pavement. My body shuddered; my thoughts raced uncontrollably, a feral creature intent on tearing me apart.

Nobody could be trusted. Nothing felt safe anymore. The world around me felt barren and icy, dark and isolated, clawing at my ashen face.

Despite the grief that drained my energy, I continued to run. My legs carried me deeper into the woods, twigs snapping beneath my feet as bushes snagged at my clothes, nearly tripping me with each frantic step. My head throbbed from the branches scraping against my scalp, but I pressed on, each breath a desperate gasp.

Eventually, I stumbled upon the park, just beyond the tree line. I collapsed onto the grass, laying there as my chest heaved. My glazed eyes stared blankly at the colorless sky, the world around me fading into silence.

I closed my eyes, longing to slip away from the weight of it all.

A voice pulled me from my deadened trance.

"Amelia? What are you doing?"

I opened my eyes slowly. The voice was familiar. After a few seconds, it registered in my mind.

I sat up and squinted against the glaring sun. "Hi, Dante." My voice came out raspy and weak.

He knelt in front of me, lifting my chin gently with his fingers, forcing me to meet his concerned gaze. A single tear fell down my pallid cheek, and I could see the concern etched on his face.

"What happened?" His voice was soothing, wrapping around me like a comforting embrace. It was intoxicating, a blissful dreamscape amid my turmoil.

"My sister is gone. Forever." The words felt foreign on my tongue. I had never imagined I would be speaking such a painful truth so soon in my life. Was this a nightmare? If only I could wake up.

"Gone?" His voice trailed off, but I could see the understanding glimmer in his eyes. He wasn't naive.

"Dead," I stated bitterly, unwilling to elaborate further.

"Amelia. I'm so sorry. I wish I could take your pain away." His somber tone matched the air around us. Grief hung like an infection, quietly spreading, infecting everything.

He rubbed my arm comfortingly, and this time, I didn't pull away. I let his touch envelop me, not stinging or repulsive, but rather a soothing balm amidst the chaos. But it wouldn't bring my sister back.

Before I could fully absorb the moment, a voice erupted nearby, shattering the fragile calm.

"Uh oh," Dante muttered, standing abruptly, as if caught in a forbidden act.

My entire body ached as I attempted to rise, screaming at me to collapse back down, to give in to the exhaustion. A new presence loomed beside us, and I turned my gaze toward it. Hues of red ignited within my vision, my veins pulsating with anger.

Caiden had found me. And I was ready to unleash hell upon him.

Immediately, I became possessed by someone else, a different version of myself. One that was bloodthirsty, vengeful, and consumed by hatred.

It was a persona I had always feared would rise from the shadows, and now it surged forward, raw and unrelenting.

"You killed her!" My face twisted into a monstrous mask, contorted by grief and rage. I lunged toward him, ready to unleash my fury.

But then a set of arms wrapped around my waist, pulling me back with a strength that felt futile against the tempest inside me.

"Amelia! It's not worth it," Dante murmured, his voice steady yet strained as he tried to restrain me.

It was pointless, like attempting to hold back a tornado. I summoned the strength of a thousand suns, tearing away from his muscular grip, desperate to confront the source of my pain.

Caiden stood frozen, eyes wide, as if he had stumbled into a scene from a nightmare.

Before he could formulate a response, I closed the distance and slapped him hard across the face. The heat radiating from my skin felt like a toxic gas, a volatile mixture of anger and sorrow.

"What's the matter, Caiden? Are you suddenly powerless to speak?" My voice reverberated through the dimming park, an echo of anguish that pierced the stillness.

My eyes blazed with a furious intensity, shooting daggers into the man who had played a role in my sister's demise.

He merely flinched, stumbling back in shock, likely taken aback by my unexpected aggression.

I had never been the type to resort to violence, but something sinister clawed at the edges of my mind, desperate to break free.

The weight of the past months pressed down on me like an unbearable burden, snapping the fragile thread that held my sanity intact.

I was unraveling, a beast driven by an insatiable hunger for retribution.

"What the fuck was that for?" His eyes darkened, almost predatory, and he took a hesitant step forward. I could not predict his next move.

"Lillian is dead! She fucking killed herself because of you!" My body trembled like a fault line, the earthquake of my grief sending violent shakes through my veins.

All the pain I had bottled up surged forth, a molten flow of emotion, threatening to consume me.

The silence stretched between us, laced with the poison of my words. Caiden's face shifted. Was it shock? Pity? Concern? I couldn't tell. Did he feel any remorse for the loss of my sister, or was he too far gone to care?

"Sorry to hear, but that's not my problem," he muttered, his gaze shifting away from me, as if my suffering were an inconvenience he could dismiss.

"Are you serious? It's absolutely your problem! If you hadn't impregnated her, none of this would have happened! You are a monster!" My voice rose, merging with the wind that whipped around us, its chill biting at my exposed skin.

Tears streamed down my face, but the anger surged higher, pushing the sadness into the recesses of my mind, locked away for a later time.

The air grew still, the weight of my accusation settling like a dark cloud between us. He met my icy glare, and my lips trembled as I fought to keep the tears at bay.

"What do you expect from me? Do you want me to bring her back from the dead? That won't happen. She's gone; it's not my fucking problem." With those callous words, he turned, shoving his hands into his pockets, his indifference a dagger to my heart.

That was the moment I broke.

Screams erupted from deep within me, primal and raw. I collapsed to the ground, fists clutching my head as I howled in anguish.

My cries echoed through the park, a wounded and distressed animal, a grievous ode to my anger and misery. Tears cascaded down my cheeks, flowing freely like a river of despair.

"Amelia. Come on, you've got to get up and come with me. You're scaring all these people." Dante's voice was a gentle whisper amidst the chaos, but it was not enough to pull me back from the abyss.

"No! No! Leave me alone!" My voice pierced the air, a shriek of agony that tore through the fabric of my being. I felt the wetness of my nose, the salt of my tears mingling with the remnants of my shattered composure.

My chest ached, each breath becoming a laborious task as the weight of my grief bore down on me.

I was beyond the point of mere sadness; this was something darker, something hideous and grotesque.

Caiden had diminished me, made me feel small and worthless. He treated my words like the buzzing of a bothersome insect, an annoyance to be swatted away.

Just like my mother. Just like so many others in my life.

He didn't care. Nobody cared.

My thoughts spiraled faster, a tempest of confusion and sorrow.

My screams poured forth, harder and louder, my heart crashing into oblivion, lost in the depths of my grief.

I beat at the earth until my fists stung, until the skin split and mud coated my palms. I wanted to punch a hole straight through the world, let all the pain spill out and flood the park, drown all of us. Dante, Caiden, every bystander whose pitying eyes threatened to peel me open even further.

But even then, I knew the ache would not subside; it would only grow, rooting itself deeper, until it became the only thing keeping me upright.

Dante hovered nearby, a feeble north star in my constellation of loss, his hand flitting between my shoulder and the air, unsure if comfort would help or salt the wound. "Amelia," he whispered, voice trembling, "you're not alone. You're not. Please, let me help."

I tasted blood in my mouth. My voice came out warped, inhuman: "No one can help." I curled tighter, forehead pressed to the freezing ground, knuckles throbbing in the dirt. "She's dead. Lillian is dead, and she hated me, and it's my fault. Don't you get it?" The words spat out in ragged clumps. "I should have answered. I could have—"

My throat closed. The next sound was a howl, bottomless, animal.

A little girl and her mother stopped on the sidewalk, the child's face a perfect circle of terror before the mom hustled her along, shooting me a look of disgust.

I wanted to chase after them, demand they look me in the eye and see what real sorrow looked like.

Caiden just watched, expression unreadable. For a moment, one sick, electric heartbeat, I thought he looked sad.

Or maybe I only wanted him to be. More likely, he was disappointed I hadn't held up longer. That his poisons had worked faster than he hoped.

Dante knelt again, voice low, pleading: "Let me help you, please. You can't do this to yourself."

But he was wrong. I was alone because everyone I loved had been hollowed out and discarded, and all that was left were these two: the boy who had destroyed my sister, and the boy who saw saving me as a mission, the way you might try to save a bird with a snapped neck.

My wounded howls cascaded like a tragic ode to all the grief and rage that I've carried for so long.

Somewhere deep in my head, a voice, my own or maybe Lillian's, told me to get up, to stop humiliating myself, but I shut it out.

The pain was heavier here, truer. It filled my lungs, my veins, pressed hard against the inside of my skull until I thought I might split apart.

My screams were a tribute, a declaration: *Look at what you did. Look at what you left me with.*

When I finally stopped, when my throat could bear no more, I curled into myself and sobbed.

My jaw ached from clenching. Tears slicked my eyelashes and made the world shimmer, a glaze of unreality over everything.

Some small, rational part of me counted my heartbeats, wondering if I might actually die from the force of it.

I heard footsteps, Dante's again, soft and hesitant. He knelt beside me, not touching, just breathing. "I'm here," he whispered, and the words dug under my skin, almost worse than silence.

I tried to push him away, but my arms were rubber, my body a sack of wet flour. He finally caved and hugged me to his chest, crushing and awkward, but I clung to him with the violence of a drowning girl.

My nails left crescents in his skin. He didn't flinch, not even as I shuddered and sobbed, spattering his shirt with snot and spit and hot, stinging tears.

Caiden still watched from a distance, arms folded, weight shifting from foot to foot. His jaw was clenched so tight I thought his teeth might splinter.

The sun was setting behind him, a red wound low on the horizon, outlining his silhouette in blood. The sight made me want to run at him again, scratch at his eyes, take him with me into the abyss. I wanted us all to suffer equally, to drown together in the same foul river.

Instead, I let Dante hold me. My sobs slowly ebbed, leaving only the numbness, the heavy, suffocating taste of coming undone.

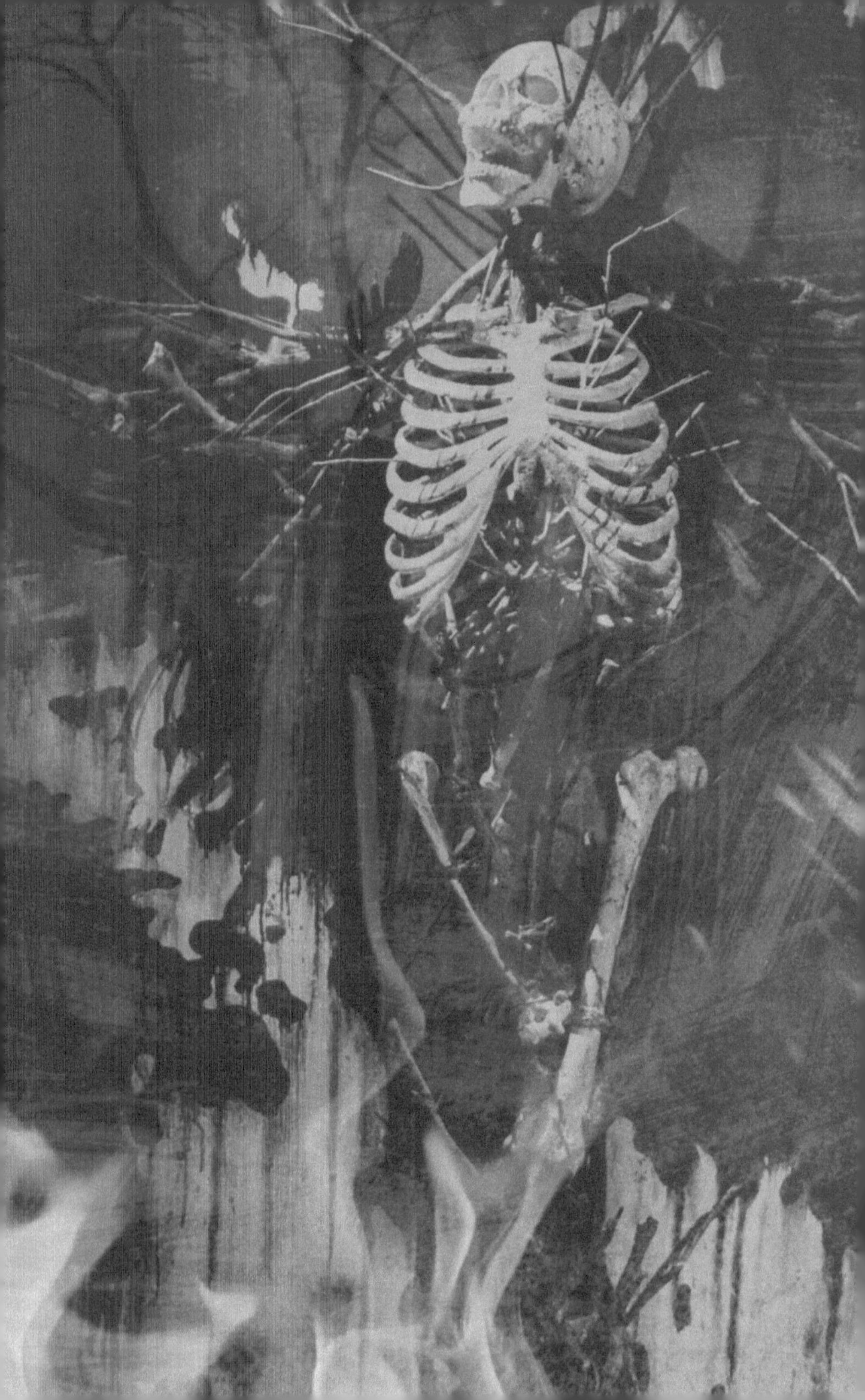

# 22

## THE PRESENT

### AMELIA

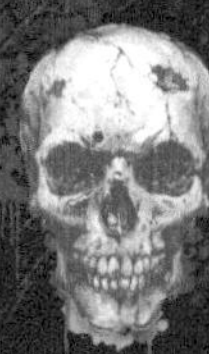

THE SUN HUNG HIGH IN THE SKY, CASTING ELONGATED shadows that danced across the forest floor like ghostly figures. Sounds of rustling leaves and distant animal calls filled the silence, but the tranquility felt like a cruel joke in the face of our grim reality.

Caiden and I had been walking for miles, our footsteps echoing in the stillness. Hours slipped by without a word being spoken between us, both too stubborn to break the silence.

It was as if we were caught in a standoff, too afraid to unravel the tension that had been simmering between us for years.

It had been almost a full day and a half since we began wandering, lost and disoriented, with no clue how to find our way back.

Caiden insisted he could navigate us out of this mess, but my faith in him was as low as the trenches of a darkened sea.

He stomped confidently through the underbrush, his pace almost too quick for me to keep up. My legs dragged wearily behind him, my hair sticking to my forehead with sweat.

A deep, rumbling noise erupted from my stomach, a reminder of just how dire our situation had become.

I couldn't sustain this much longer.

"Come on, Amelia. Pick up the pace," Caiden grumbled, never bothering to adjust his speed for my dwindling stamina.

"Maybe if you could slow down, we could avoid tiring ourselves out too quickly," I retorted, glaring daggers at his back.

"I'm not interested in slowing down. I'm interested in getting back to civilization." His tone held no room for debate, but I bit back anyway.

"How do you expect to get out of here alive? We have no supplies. Nothing to help us." If only we had thought to pack essentials before kayaking into this nightmare. If only I had listened to that persistent voice of anxiety that warned me against it.

"I'll find a way. I was in the military."

A daunting thought clawed at my mind. What if he decided to leave me behind to save himself? Or worse, what if he turned on me? I shook my head, desperately trying to rid myself of those terrible images. He wouldn't do that. Would he?

"When did you join the military?" I asked, trying to fill the silence with conversation. It was better than spiraling into my dark thoughts.

His body was tense, rigid as if horrid memories were playing in his mind. "Around nine months after graduation. I stayed for a little while after you left, but I had to get the hell out of that town. Most importantly, away from my asshole father."

"What did your father do to you exactly? I've heard rumors, but it was always different things I would hear." I saw an opportunity to dig into him, so I took it.

He stopped and spun around, anger swirling in the depths of his eyes. "I'm not talking about my father. Don't make me go there."

I shrank back at his intensity. "Sorry. You brought it up. I figured I could understand you a little better since we're stuck out here."

"Well, stop trying. I'm not discussing the horrors of his actions with you." He took a deep breath, frustration etched across his features. "Only one thing is on my mind: escaping from this goddamn wilderness."

And just like that, the door closed on that conversation. Curiosity nagged at me. I had a good idea of how his father treated him, but I wanted to hear it from his mouth.

Silence swept over us once again. A flicker of movement in the leaves would come and go, the call of a bird whistling through the windless air.

If only I'd chosen differently, I'd be sprawled on my sofa right now, the afternoon sun drifting through my living room windows. Instead, I stood on a dusty trail, my thoughts heavy as storm clouds.

Dark emotions churned in my gut, old memories rising like restless spirits: the pranks that once seemed harmless, the barbed insults, the careless cruelty, and the night Lillian gave up on us all.

My heart thundered, hot rage threatening to boil over.

I clenched my fists until my knuckles ached, forcing the anger back down into its cage.

Then Caiden's voice cut through my turmoil. "We've got a problem." He skidded to a halt so abruptly that pebbles skittered across the path.

My limbs already trembled with exhaustion. "What? Did you have an accident?" I snapped, my tone heavy with fatigue.

"Fuck you," he muttered, dark brows drawing together. "No, there's a ravine. Right in the middle of the path. We'll have to go around it."

A cold dread slid up my spine. I peered over Caiden's broad shoulders. The trail ended in a ragged edge of cracked earth, plunging into a yawning chasm.

Sunlight glinted off jagged stones far below, and the wind whispered up from the depths, carrying dust and distant echoes.

"Looks like there's no hope left," I said, voice flat. "I'm just gonna sit here and wait for something to happen."

Caiden's irritated scowl deepened. "Wait for what?"

"For my knight in shining armor," I shot back. "Or maybe a miracle."

He turned away, scanning the ravine's lip as if it held secret escape routes. Sweat beaded at his hairline, his chest rising and falling beneath his sweat-darkened shirt.

Every muscle in his arms and shoulders stood out, taut like coiled ropes. My gaze flicked over the rigid planes of his back, the sinew of his neck.

My pulse skipped. Heat flushed my cheeks. Why was I even noticing this?

Did I just check out Caiden Baxter? Hell. I needed to snap out of it.

I pushed myself upright. The gravel crunched underfoot. Caiden glanced back. "Princess done marinating?"

I leveled him with a mock-courtly bow. "Madam is refreshed and ready for duty."

He rolled his eyes, impassive. I swept my gaze across the broken trail, peering for any narrow ledge or fallen boulder we could use as a makeshift bridge.

My stomach growled, probably from hunger, or the adrenaline, or both.

"Maybe we can skirt the edge," I suggested, voice steadier than I felt. "Ravines don't go on forever."

He crossed his arms. "I'm not wasting time on some fairy-tale detour."

"Since when did you get to call all the shots?" I shot back, chest tightening.

"I did," he said sharply. "Because I know how to navigate the wilderness better than you."

I feigned an epileptic swoon, clutching my chest. "Oh dear, my intelligence and abilities insulted, what shall I do?"

"Knock it off, Amelia." He threatened.

"Am I annoying you? Did I hit a nerve? So sorry, your highness," I paused and scowled. "Not sorry."

He ignored me, then abruptly barked, "Found something."

My heart lifted. "Really?"

"Yeah," he said, voice wary, "but you might hate it."

We edged a few steps down a narrow berm, the air growing cooler as shadows gathered in the ravine's crevasse. Before us lay a massive fallen fir, its roots ripped up like the skeletal hands of some buried giant. The trunk spanned the abyss, though it stopped short of the far side. Its limbs curled down into the void, gnarled fingers brushing the rocky wall.

"This?" I echoed.

He nodded. "We'll shimmy along the log, then climb the last stretch of the cliff face."

I stared at that moss-speckled wood suspended above a drop that made my knees go weak. My heart hammered. Every instinct screamed no. No heights, no risk, no trial by tree trunk that might snap underfoot.

But there was no other choice. My pulse thudded in my ears as I swallowed hard. The journey wasn't over, not by a long shot.

"You're insane," I said, the words spilling out in disbelief. The thought of navigating that treacherous path exhausted me further.

"Now is not the time to be stubborn," Caiden said, his voice low against the roar of the wind slicing through the ravine.

I pressed my arms across my chest, feeling the coarse weave of my jacket dig into my elbows. "I'm not being stubborn," I shot back, jaw tight. "I'd rather conserve what little energy I have and keep my life than risk it all trying something I'm not capable of."

His brow lifted, a single dark hair arching in silent disbelief. "You really don't have much faith in yourself."

A bitter laugh escaped me as I glared at him. "Yeah. I don't. Sorry to burst your bubble. Must be from all those years of abuse and degradation."

"Don't play the pity card," he snapped, his voice rough with memory. "I've endured plenty of abuse too, from my father. But I'm not going to stand here chatting about it. If you can't believe in yourself, believe in me. We're getting across."

I turned to stare down into the maw of the ravine: sheer rock walls, twisted roots clinging to shale, and a narrow strip of light at the bottom where the forest floor lay bathed in shadow.

I swallowed. "Well, I don't have faith in you, so what's left?"

His answer was soft, but it hit me like a hammer. "Staying alive."

We stood in ragged silence. Our argument had begun to circle like vultures, voices rising and accomplishing nothing. My lungs constricted; I breathed in a shaky, ragged hiss before nodding once.

A silent truce.

Caiden stepped forward first. I watched his boots scrape against the bark, sending a few grains of moss fluttering down like green snow. He leaned back and slid along a thick horizontal branch, body angled, arms tight around the trunk. The branch groaned but held him, its surface dark with damp and lichen.

I held my breath, willing the world to freeze so I could memorize every nuance: how his weight distributed evenly, how his thighs pinched the bark, how his fingertips curled into the wood's deep grooves.

If I failed, it would be on me. No one else.

Halfway down, he paused, looking up with eyes cold and steady. "I suppose you should come on down. I'll stay here in case you slip."

My throat tightened. "You think I can't do it?"

His exhale was a wounded sigh. "If you don't want my help, fine. I'll keep going without you."

A vicious knot of guilt and fear twisted in my gut. I swallowed. "Fine."

I lowered myself onto the branch's edge, calves pressed against its rough surface. The wind whipped past my face, whipping stray hairs into my eyes. My fingers found the bark's ridges, hard and splintered. I pushed off, sliding down inch by inch. My heart hammered as panic curled around my ribs. Every centimeter felt like miles.

"You're doing great," Caiden's voice came from above, flat but piercing through my terror.

I gritted my teeth, teeth chattering against the cold. My last full meal was hours ago, and with every movement, my muscles trembled. The bark ground against my palms, skin tearing, blood warm and sticky on my fingers.

Then, my grip failed. My right hand slipped on a patch of moss. My palm scraped along the trunk, skin shredding against the unforgiving grooves. A gasp tore from my throat.

"Caiden!" I screamed, fingers slipping free, body tilting dangerously toward open air.

"Hold on!" His voice cracked. I heard the scuffle of boots against wood as he began ascending toward me.

I closed my eyes, panic flaring hotter than the midday sun. "Please don't let me die," I sobbed, voice barely above a whisper.

"I'm not going to let you die," he assured me, and there was something raw and honest in his tone.

I felt rough, calloused palms wrap around my waist, gripping me like a vise. His arms were awkward at first, half hugging me, half wrestling to find purchase. Warmth radiated from his body, coursing through my chilled bones.

For a moment, the world stilled. No wind, no roaring abyss, just the beat of his heart and the press of his chest against my back.

The heat faded as his arms slipped, the urgency snapping me awake. I dug my fingers into the bark above my head, muscles screaming in protest, and slowly, painstakingly, hauled myself upright.

Caiden exhaled relief that feathered against my neck.

Was he truly relieved? Happy I was still alive? I shoved the thought aside. There would be time for questions later.

He resumed his descent, and I followed, each movement mirroring his. My breaths came in sharp gasps: inhale, exhale, inhale.

I needed to have faith.

But I lost it long ago. Sometime in my preteen years, when every harsh word from my mother and every cruel taunt from Caiden chipped away at my spirit.

I had become a hollow shell, a cracked house rusting in the rain, haunted by midnight demons.

At last, with trembling relief, I landed on solid ground beside him. He gave me a hand to steady myself; his touch was gentle despite the tremor in his grip.

The tiny alcove at the base of the tree pressed us so close that my back was against his chest, our breaths mingling. My heart thundered with exhaustion.

My legs shook, every fiber of me depleted. All I craved was firm earth beneath my feet. We were two battered souls, forged in darkness and anger, forced together by survival.

"I hope you've got a little energy left," Caiden said, voice low and hoarse, "because you're going to have to climb."

His gaze drifted to the overhanging branches above the ravine wall. I felt guilt prick at my chest for nearly falling, for putting him through those frantic moments.

"We'll see what happens," I said, my voice quiet but determined. My body trembled, but I lifted my chin. I would push forward. I would prove, most of all to myself, that I was stronger than I ever believed.

Caiden's fingers closed around the lowest rung of the twisted vine first.

Above us, the canopy quivered in sunlight, dappling the bark with liquid gold. I measured the climb in heartbeats—thirty seconds, maybe a minute—yet every fiber of me trembled at the thought.

My arms felt as hollow as the trees' knotted hollows, my shoulders screaming after hours on the trail.

Caiden moved as though the rock face were made of silk. His muscles flexed under sweating skin, each vein a pulsing river of effort.

He planted his boots on narrow ledges, then thrust upward, momentum carrying him like a diver launched into open sky. The rock offered him purchase; his body answered without hesitation.

I reached for the same vine and froze. The rough fibers scraped my palm, but my arms refused to bear my weight. I watched Caiden's effortless ascent, disbelief knotting in my chest.

"Grip the branch," he called, voice warm and distant through the leaves. "Push with your feet, then shift your hands, one after the other."

My lungs burned. "I—I'm weaker," I panted, the words scraping against my throat. "You're built for this."

"Don't talk yourself down," he snapped, steady as a cliff face. "Just believe you can do it."

His insistence sliced through my doubt. I couldn't let him win by watching me falter. So, I wedged a foot into a rocky crevice, fingers trembling as I clenched the vine.

My grip felt tenuous, but I hauled upward. Each upward push was agony: muscles ignited, nerves ablaze. My breath came in hollow gasps, each exhale a rattling confession of weakness.

When resignation curled at my mind, a rough hand seized my forearm.

Startled, I looked up into Caiden's face. His jaw was shadowed by the faint stubble of yesterday's shave, his eyes bright with determination. "Pull," he urged, voice low. "I've got you."

With his strength anchoring me, I found one last reserve. I heaved my body above the ledge, shoulders scrabbling for earth, then toppled backward onto mossy ground.

My back hit the loam, and I lay staring at the fractured sky, the blue shards promising something beyond sheer survival.

"We did it," I whispered, heart pounding like a war drum.

Caiden landed beside me with a thud. The forest around us hushed, bearing witness to our small victory. We lay shoulder to shoulder, bodies quaking, breaths mingling in the cool air.

Between our chests, an ember glowed. A fierce, wordless bond ignited by shared peril. It felt less like comfort and more like wildfire, scorching outward from our bones.

But, this was Caiden and me. There was no beauty lingering in the shadows between us, only a scorching inferno that penetrated so deeply into our flesh, leaving a tormented mark on our souls.

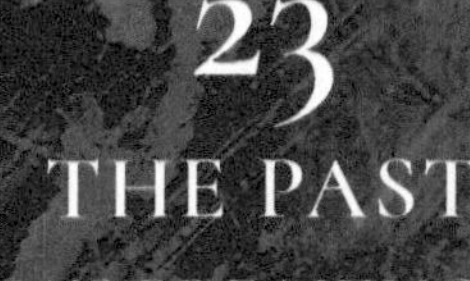

# 23
## THE PAST
### AMELIA'S BREAKING POINT

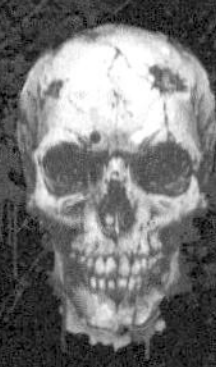

THE KNOWLEDGE OF LILLIAN'S FUNERAL SEVERED MY SOUL into jagged shards, each fragment echoing the emptiness that filled me.

The flowering goodness that once thrived within me evaporated, suffocated by the relentless downpour of grief.

Thank heavens for my grandparents, who stepped in to shoulder the financial burden of the funeral, for my mother was lost in an impenetrable haze, her spirit dulled and distant.

I stood before the mirror, scrutinizing the reflection that stared back at me. My hair fell loosely around my shoulders, framing my face, while the black dress clung tightly to my waist, a bitter reminder of the sorrow that enveloped me.

The girl in the mirror trembled, her mouth quivering as if echoing the turmoil within my heart. I turned away, walking from her gaze and shutting the door behind me, leaving that fragile version of myself in the dark.

The sound of my heels clicked against the wooden floor as I made my way to the living room.

There, I found my mother, slumped in the reclining chair, staring blankly out the window. As if searching for something lost beyond the glass.

I approached her slowly, nudging her shoulder, desperate for a connection. Any sign of the mother I once knew.

For a heartbeat, she remained still. Then she turned to me, her expression a vacant canvas, lips pressed into a thin line. "What is it?" she asked, her voice dragging like molasses in the still air.

"It's time," I replied, my voice barely above a whisper. I hoped she understood. She wore a dress nearly identical to mine, a dark mirror reflecting our shared grief.

She nodded, rising from the chair as if pulled by some invisible string. I wished I could delve into her mind to uncover the depths of her sorrow over the funeral of her daughter. Was the mother I knew, vibrant and full of life, still trapped in there, clawing to the surface beneath the weight of despair?

I suggested driving us to the funeral home, concerned that her focus was elsewhere, and she accepted without protest. In the car, she sat rigid, hands clasped in her lap, her body as still as a statue. A tight silence settled between us, thick and uneasy.

As we arrived at the funeral home, I could see familiar faces among the crowd. Neighbors, acquaintances, and a few distant family members from my mother's side who had come out of obligation, not out of love.

Their eyes averted, guilt settling in their expressions, as they whispered behind hands that once shunned us. My father's family was scattered across states, strangers to me since his departure, a shadowy absence in my life.

I spotted my grandparents seated in the middle pew; their heads bent in muted conversation. I approached, forcing a sad smile, feeling like a ghost haunting my own life. "Hey, long time no see," I murmured.

They looked up, sympathy adorned their expression. "Hey, darling. How are you holding up? I was shocked when I heard of her passing," my grandma said, rising to envelop me in a warm embrace.

I shrugged, masking my pain beneath a veneer of composure. "I'm sad. It was very tragic, but I know Lillian wouldn't want me to dwell." If only they understood the depth of the wound that gaped within me.

"I understand. She was your only sister! It's okay to feel sad, sweetheart," my grandma replied, her voice laced with concern.

"Yeah, I'm still grieving for her." My grandpa joined in, offering a comforting hug and his condolences.

"How's my daughter doing? I've heard about the state she's been in." His eyes shifted toward my mother, who stood beside the coffin, gazing down at Lillian's cold, lifeless body. I couldn't bear to look. The thought of seeing Lillian as a corpse gnawed at me, a visceral reminder that she was gone.

I bit my lip, struggling to articulate my thoughts. "She's grieving too, in her own way. I honestly hope this sparks something in her to try to get better."

My grandma nodded thoughtfully. "Those things take time. I know Judy loves you both, despite how she may be acting. The loss of a daughter is monumental; she must be suffering." The truth weighed upon me like a trench. My mother could only find healing if she chose it, and I had learned there was nothing I could say or do that would change her at this point.

"Yeah, I know she's definitely feeling something," I replied, letting the conversation drift away.

After another embrace with my grandparents, I returned to my mother's side. She remained silent, her face devoid of expression, as she received condolences with mere nods and soft replies consisting of "thank you."

I gently squeezed her hand, hoping to offer some hint of comfort. She glanced at me, her eyes blinking slowly, then withdrew, turning her focus back to the preacher.

In the front row, I found myself unable to tear my gaze from the dark coffin that held Lillian's body.

The more I stared, the more the tears flowed, each sob wracking my shoulders as the pastor's words washed over me like a distant storm, muffled yet powerful enough to ruin me.

A few people stepped up to the microphone to share their memories of her, and I was compelled to do the same.

I wiped my eyes, acutely aware of their puffiness and the devastation etched on my face. As I walked up the steps to the microphone, I scanned the crowd, a lump forming in my throat. I wanted to run, to scream, to escape this unbearable reality.

Taking a shaky breath, I began to speak. "Lillian was my sister. She was funny, smart, and wonderful. Tragically, her life was cut short because she gave up on herself. She had her ups and downs, but she was still my sister, and I love her. It breaks my heart knowing I will never see her again. I will miss her and hope she's looking down on me now, smiling."

My voice cracked, but I steeled myself to continue. "I remember when we were little, she was full of life and light. We would stay up late playing games or spend sun-drenched days in the park. I will cherish those memories forever. She had a kind, genuine soul, and so much potential. May you rest in peace, Lillian."

The sorrowful faces around the room spoke volumes, their downturned eyes and sad sighs spilling over.

They didn't truly know her; they only saw the version Lillian chose to present, the smile that masked her struggles.

I stumbled down the steps, returning to my seat beside my mother, who remained an enigma, her silence both infuriating and heartbreaking.

When it was time to follow the funeral car to the burial site, I gripped the steering wheel, my hands trembling as reality crashed down on me. Lillian was dead. We were about to bury her.

I began to sob quietly, the tears spilling over, though I thought I heard my mother's soft cries beside me.

As we parked and made our way to the grave, tremors shook my body, my vision blurring as I approached the pit.

She's gone.

They were lowering her into the ground forever. A primal urge surged within me, a desperate need to snatch her back from the depths of the earth.

When the coffin was finally lowered, an anguished thought echoed in my mind: *Come back. Don't leave me alone with the monsters.*

I stood frozen at the edge of the grave, terrified to leave her behind. My mother's voice telling me she wanted to leave barely registered in my mind; I was transfixed by the earth that would soon cover my sister.

As the crowd began to disperse, a dark thought coiled within me: *Good riddance.*

I felt a deep loathing for the very people who had turned their backs on Lillian, now feigning sorrow as they paid their respects. They had driven her to this point with their callousness, and now, in the wake of her death, they pretended to care.

But the most unbearable pain came from the absence of Caiden, the boy who had contributed to her downfall, who had not even bothered to show his face.

The wound inside me festered, transforming into a toxic anger, an urge to unleash my pain upon him.

———

"Dante, I need to talk to you." I caught him in the hallway a few days later, his surprise was evident. In that moment, Dante was a pawn, and I intended to use him.

Something inside of me had permanently snapped, and I couldn't care about using the one person who didn't deserve it.

He led me outside to a picnic table; curiosity etched on his face. "What's up?"

"Remember when you asked if there was anything you could do for me?"

"Yeah. The offer still stands." Dante stared at me with open curiosity.

"Well, could I come over to your house tonight? I just... I feel so alone, and I need someone to talk to, especially after the sudden death of my sister." My voice was soft, innocent, though it masked my true intentions.

His brown eyes softened, filled with a pitiful concern. "Of course," he replied, and that was all I needed.

———

Later that night, I crept up the creaking porch stairs, arms wrapped around two dusty bottles of whiskey stolen from my mother's secret stash.

The moonlight pooled through the cracked front door as he swung it open, eyes narrowing at the gleam of glass in my hands.

"What's that for?" His voice was low and curious, a thread of concern twisting around the question.

"Oh, nothing special," I replied, forcing a brittle smile that trembled at the edges. The sweet burn of guilt turned my throat dry. "I just needed a drink, and I thought we could share."

I stepped inside. He shrugged and led me to the sagging couch, where a single lamp cast shadows on the walls. We poured generous glugs of amber liquid into two tumblers, the scent of alcohol stinging my nostrils.

His parents' absence felt like a private stage for whatever I intended.

As I took a slow sip, feeling the warmth spread through my chest like liquid fire, I watched him tilt his head back, draining his glass in a single, greedy gulp.

The streetlight through the blinds painted stripes across his face, coloring his eyes with a drunken glaze. He asked, voice slurring, "So… how're you holding up?"

I let out a ragged sigh, muscles loosening under the haze. "Honestly? Not great. I feel so pathetic and alone. I wish someone would just hold me and tell me it'll okay." I squeezed the empty glass in my hand, vapor of my breath drifting in the cold air.

My confession spilled out like poison: "My sister is dead, all because of Caiden. If he hadn't gotten her pregnant, she might still be alive."

The words cut the silence like a knife. I tasted bitterness on my tongue and let it coat every syllable. "I'm so angry, dammit. I hate him. I want him to pay."

I leaned forward, voice dropping to a whisper that carried a dangerous edge. "You can help me, Dante. Help me get justice."

He blinked, unsteady, caught between loyalty and my desperate plea.

He hesitated. The alcohol had fogged his mind, but I saw the flicker of uncertainty in his eyes. I pressed on, wrapping my fingers around his wrist. "If you really care about me, follow my lead. You know what he did was unforgivable."

He licked his lips, gaze falling to my hand. "But he's my best friend," he murmured, voice cracking.

I echoed Lillian's fierce words as if they were my own: "It doesn't matter. What matters is that he's done horrible things, and he needs to pay." I reminded him of the promise he once made, to do anything for me.

His resolve crumbled. "Okay," he whispered.

Victory bloomed in my chest.

I scooted closer, the coarse fabric of the couch pressing cool against my thighs and captured his lips with mine.

The kiss was a collision, raw desire tangled with the acidic tang of anger.

He responded fiercely, hands gripping my hips as if to anchor himself. His pulse throbbed against my palm, wild and uncertain.

He lifted me easily, the room spinning as he carried me down the dim hallway to his bedroom. The door clicked shut behind us, plunging us into deeper shadow.

Clothes were shed in a frantic dance: a discarded shirt, a stray sock, the rustle of fabric on bare skin. We tumbled onto the bed, sheets twisting around our legs.

His mouth trailed hot, urgent kisses along my collarbone, and every brush of his fingertips sent a jolt through me.

"Touch me," I whispered into the darkness, my voice fierce and trembling. I had never been intimate like this with a person, and it terrified me, but in the haze of my vengeance, I let that terror slip into oblivion.

As Dante explored, pleasure and anger braided together inside me. An intoxicating, poisonous elixir.

My body responded to his touch even as my mind churned with thoughts of revenge. I felt the glowing ember of rage pulse through each vein, delicate yet ruinous.

In that fevered haze, I understood that anger was everything I had left, and I would let it consume every last part of me, whatever the cost.

What happened next was equal parts inevitable and wicked. The alcohol dissolved the last hesitations; the chemical warmth swelled inside me, sparking electricity beneath my skin.

Dante was desperate, a match to my gasoline, hungry for whatever I would give him. And I was all edges and venom, ready to ruin us both if it meant driving a stake through Caiden's heart.

Dante's hands mapped my body with the reverence of a disciple, but my mind hovered above, cold and observing.

His lips bruised my throat, collarbone, the hollow above my heart.

I craved the sting, needed it to prove I was still tangible, that I hadn't drifted into shadow with Lillian.

Each time he groaned, I thought of Caiden, imagined the sear of betrayal that would split his pretty, sneering face when he found out.

I dug my nails into Dante's back, leaving half-moons he'd wear for days, marks I wanted Caiden to see and recognize. The thought alone made me arch harder into every movement, made me whisper Dante's name so loud I hoped the entire block could hear.

I wanted to lose myself in the whiteout, to be remade by sensation, but the venom was always there. Pulsing, multiplying, refusing to let me go.

He cupped my face, breath ragged, whispering my name.

Dante, so careful and sincere, thinking he could rescue me with kindness when I only wanted the world to burn.

He slid inside me, slow at first, but I wouldn't give him the luxury of gentleness. I wrapped my legs around his waist, nails biting into the flesh above his shoulder blades, daring him to go harder, to take what he wanted and leave me raw.

He obliged.

Our bodies collided with an almost holy violence, the headboard rattling, drywall cracking beneath the thunder of our need.

I arched up, teeth grazing the cord of his neck, and he moaned loud enough to shake the windows.

My anger braided with arousal, a double helix of need and hate, and I rode it until my body dissolved, until the past and present and every future pain blurred into a single, shattering scream.

I pressed my thighs tight to his hips, tears mixing into the sweat at our hairline, surrendering to lust because it was the only violence left to me.

I wanted to be filled, bruised, devoured; I wanted to erase everything and start over, to be reborn in the friction and the heat and the noise of it. His hands were everywhere, and so were mine, clawing, pressing, desperate for proof of life.

I rutted into him, not for pleasure to burn away everything that had come before. His breath hitched at my ear. "Amelia, god... you're amazing."

I almost laughed. Amazing.

That was one word for it.

He pinned my wrists to the mattress, but I twisted free, flipping us so I was on top, riding him with wild, reckless urgency. I didn't care about his pleasure, only that I could make him lose himself, make him ache the way I did.

I wanted to split myself open and bleed out all the bad; I wanted him to see what Caiden had broken in me, to see the chaos that I had become.

My body knew what it wanted even if my brain was still somewhere else. Off at the graveside, off in some funhouse mirror where Lillian's dead hands clapped approval at every savage motion.

He watched me with awe and pleasure written on his face. His hands reached up and fondled my breasts, his fingers twisting and squeezing as he allowed me to unravel and take control.

He tried to meet my gaze, brown eyes shining with something too soft, too tentative, and I hated it. I hated him for not hating me, for not seeing the monstrous thing I'd become.

He gripped my waist, steadying me, as if he was the anchor and I was the storm. "You're beautiful," he whispered, and I almost spat in his face.

I pressed my palm to his mouth, fingers digging into the stubble of his jaw, daring him to speak again. He bit the pad of my thumb, just shy of drawing blood, and the pain startled a harsh moan from my lips.

Harder, I thought, I want it to hurt. I wanted the marks, the memories, the proof that I could still be touched, still be moved.

I clawed at his chest, dragging red lines down to his stomach, and he only bucked harder, hands frantic on my ass.

"Fuck, Amelia," he groaned, and I let the word ricochet in my skull like a gunshot.

I rode him until my thighs burned, until my lungs ached with the force of my sobbing breaths, each one more ragged than the last.

I clenched around the throbbing heat inside of me, letting it consume every fiber of my blood.

I let Dante pin me again after a few minutes. He wildly thrusted into me, his chest hammering against mine.

He came with a violence that belonged in war, not love, his muscles spasming under my claws as he jerked himself onto my stomach.

The wave of relief—of obliteration—hit me so hard I blacked out for half a second, the room tilting, his arms the only thing keeping me from falling through the mattress into some abyssal pit where Lillian waited.

After, we lay in the dark, both of us panting.

I stared at the ceiling, counting the cracks, not speaking.

Dante drifted to sleep almost instantly, the way only boys with unbroken hearts could. I listened to his breathing, the steadiness of it, and hated him for it.

I wanted to punch him awake, force him to feel every terrible thing inside of me.

The anger returned, black and bottomless. Overpowering the grief that I should have been feeling. Rage became infused into my bones, as if it was all I would ever be.

*Look away, Lillian. Your sweet sister is too far gone now.*

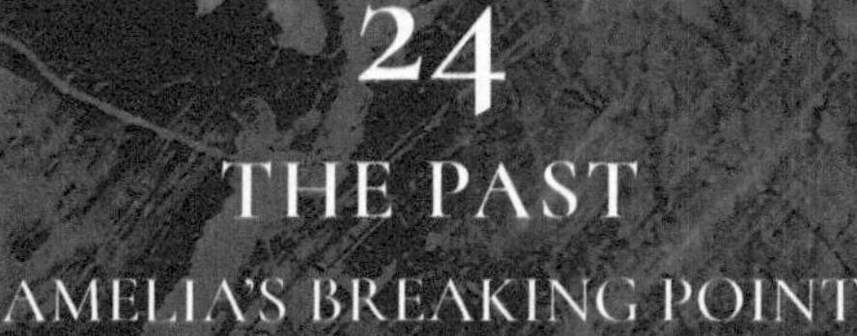

# 24
## THE PAST



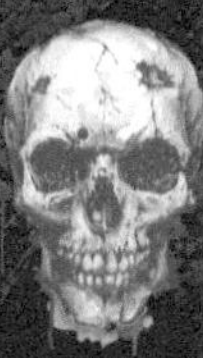

MY SKULL THROBBED LIKE A WAR DRUM, EACH PULSE matching the frantic beat in my chest as consciousness crept back in. Warm weight pressed against me.

Dante, sprawled on his side, his steady snores a low rumble in the hush.

Pale morning light snuck through the gaps in the curtains, painting gold streaks across the rumpled sheets. A twinge of shame flickered in my gut, but I shoved it down.

Caiden needed this lesson in pain. He had to learn, the way I'd learned, how heartbreak carves hollows into your bones. All I craved was for him to taste the emptiness I'd carried since Lillian died.

Her absence loomed behind my eyelids, a velvet shadow that wouldn't lift. Lillian's laughter was buried six feet under, her bright eyes cold in the earth. Revenge was the only fuel left in me.

I wanted Caiden to writhe in hurt. Would she nod, proud of my fury, or turn away in disappointment? I'd never know. The ache in my chest gnawed like a starving beast, hollowing me out from the inside.

A rap at the door shattered the quiet. Footsteps down the hall. A grin slithered over my lips.

Last night, while Dante drifted into dreams, I'd rifled through his phone and sent Caiden a text: *Come by in the morning.*

And he marched right into my trap.

"Dante! Wake up, man!" The voice thundered down the hall. My heart hammered as the footsteps thundered closer, pausing at the door. It swung open on creaking hinges, and there he stood.

Caiden, face pale, eyes blazing.

Dante shifted beside me, hair tousled, cheeks sunken with sleep. He yawned, stretching an arm overhead. "Hey, Caiden... What's up?" His words were soft, drowsy.

Caiden's voice cut the air like shattered glass. "What the fuck, dude?" He strode in, shoulders rigid, nostrils flaring. The room felt smaller all of a sudden, air thickening with his anger.

A sliver of doubt slashed through me. My sister was dead. And I was baiting someone for sport. What would Lillian say if she saw this? A stubborn fly of guilt buzzed at my temples, but I kept it locked down.

Dante rubbed his eyes, sliding off the mattress and tugging on boxers. "It's nothing," he said. "Amelia just needed company. She's been through hell."

His voice was calm, too calm.

Caiden's lips curled with contempt. "I don't give a shit about what Amelia needs. She can rot for all I care. I can't believe you'd sleep with that thing."

The word "thing" landed harshly. Apparently I'm not even a human in his eyes.

Cold rage pooled inside of me.

Dante's jaw clenched. "Chill out, Caiden. That's fucked up. Amelia's not a thing, she's a person. A victim." His tone was sharp, protective.

Caiden turned his glare on me, eyes black as tar. "And you? You've got nothing to say? Poor little Amelia too weak to fight back? You're a coward, just like your whore of a sister." His words slashed into me, each syllable coated in venom.

Lillian lay under the ground—murdered—and here he was, mocking her.

Tears stung my eyes. I couldn't hold his hateful stare.

My throat tightened, every breath tasting like ash. I wanted to scream, to throw myself at him, to make him feel my sorrow.

Then came the crack. Dante's fist snapped forward, meeting Caiden's jaw with a brutal pop. Caiden sagged to the floor, his hand pressed to his cheek, shock flickering across his features. Dante stood over him, knuckles red, chest heaving.

"What the fuck, Dante!" Caiden shrieked, half-crouched, panic in his tone.

"Don't you ever talk to her that way," Dante snarled, spine rigid with fury.

Caiden leapt at him, and they crashed down in a tangle of limbs. Muffled grunts and scuffling sounds filled the room.

I lurched forward, heart hammering. "Stop it! Just stop!" I threw my arms between them, pulling at their torsos, tears blurring the scene.

Dante paused, chest heaving, but Caiden lunged again, forcing me to wedge myself between them, arms trembling.

Dante finally released his grip and rose, bruises blossoming across his skin. He glared down at Caiden. "We're done here."

Breath ragged, Caiden met my eyes one last time—hatred twisted in his gaze—and stumbled from the room, wounded and defeated.

I sank onto the edge of the bed, hands shaking. "I'm sorry, Dante. I... I need to go." In a blur, I yanked on clothes, my voice cracking. He opened his mouth to stop me, but I bolted, racing into the day.

The engine's roar soothed my frayed nerves as I slammed the door shut.

I'd broken Caiden's heart; at least now he knew what loss tasted like.

Days passed in a haunted blur.

Dust motes drifted in sunbeams, and every corner whispered Lillian's name. Her perfume, soft jasmine and vanilla, still clung to the air, a ghost's lingering kiss. I avoided her bedroom; the door stayed shut, dust gathering along the frame like a forgotten tomb.

Silence weighed on me, heavy as lead. Mom moved through the halls like a wraith, lost in her own grief. The image of her in the fog-choked graveyard haunted me. Her head bowed, fingers tracing my sister's name on the stone. I'd watched from a distance, too raw to approach.

Grief burrowed into my marrow, a parasite that hollowed me out, leaving agony in its wake. It was a hurricane, smashing me against memories until I gasped for sanity.

Grief was a ruthless storm. Silent, creeping, capable of shattering the strongest minds. It crashed over you in waves, savage and unrelenting, stripping you bare until only twitching ruins remain. Rising from its wreckage demands a strength I feared I'd never muster.

I've wrestled with this grief my whole life. Loss knocking me flat like a freight train. Even now, I feel it coil around my throat, pressing tight, each heartbeat a pull toward darkness. I'm left a cold vessel, an empty shell shaped by pain. Waiting to see if I can breathe again.

I wandered my house, unanchored, circling from room to room. The kitchen reeked of sour milk and spilled liquor; the living room was a mausoleum of dead plants and dust.

I skirted Lillian's bedroom, the door sealed like a tombstone, its silence denser than lead. I wanted to press my forehead to the wood and beg for a sound—her laughter, her voice, even her anger—but I couldn't.

I drifted instead to my own room, flopping onto the mattress and staring at the ceiling until the lines blurred and strange patterns swam in my vision.

Hours passed, time warping and folding in on itself. I thought about texting Dante. I thought about driving to the cemetery, digging my fingers into the cold dirt above Lillian's coffin just to prove she was real and down there.

Instead, I did nothing. I lay on my back and let the walls close in.

Sometime after dark, a sound split the quiet. Glass shattered. A bottle, maybe two, and then a crash so violent it rattled the pictures in the hallway.

I snapped to, heart thumping, and crept out. The kitchen light flickered, casting a jaundiced pallor on the scene.

Mom was on the floor, half-submerged in a tide of whiskey and orange soda. The bottle was in shards, sticky liquid pooling around her like an ooze.

She wore Lillian's old hoodie, sleeves bunched at her elbows, and her hair was matted to her face as if it had rained indoors. Her feet were bare, toes black with dust.

"Mom." I knelt next to the sticky lake, glass biting into my knees. Her head lolled up, eyes swimming, and for a second, she smiled, wide, grotesque, teeth rimmed in orange.

"I did it, kiddo. I finally out-drank the pain." She made a show of raising a bloody knuckle in victory, then slumped, arm trailing the detritus.

"Let's get you up," I muttered, grabbing her under the armpits. Her body was limp.

She fought me, nails raking my forearm. "Don't touch me," she slurred, then exhaled a sob. "You think you're so much better, judging me from your fucking high horse. But you're just like her, just like Lillian. Think you're special. Think you're too good for this world." She tried to shove me off, but her arms were useless.

I dragged her to the couch. The liquor on her breath was sharp enough to make my eyes water.

She slumped into the cushions, head lolling. "Why'd she do it?" Her voice was small, almost childlike. "Why'd she leave me here with you?"

Before I could respond, she lurched upright, feet skidding through the sticky mess, and pointed at me with a trembling finger. "You!" she hissed, eyes rolling back and then forward again, dilated wide as dimes. "You did this. You killed her. You can't even look at me because you know you're rotten. You're the reason nobody stays. I hate you. I hate you."

My mouth opened, but nothing came out. Not even a squeak. She advanced, half-stumbling, half-floating, like a marionette whose strings had been slashed but not fully severed.

I wanted to back up, but my feet had become part of the floor.

She lunged, caught my wrist in a grip that was all bone and desperation. Her eyes—god, her eyes—were pure blacked out, a bottomless nothing that terrified me.

"You always wanted her gone. Don't lie." Her nails dug into my flesh. "You never loved her like I did. You just want to be the only one left, so you can finally get all the attention you think you deserve."

The words spilled out in a slurry, slaughtering anything in me that still felt like a daughter.

I tried to twist away, to pull free, but she just clamped down harder, breathing through her teeth. "I see you. Don't think I don't see you. You and your fucking secrets."

My vision shimmered; for a second, I thought she might try to bite me. She shook my arm, wild, like she was hoping to rattle Lillian's ghost out of my skin.

"Mom, stop." I meant it to sound forceful, but it came out pathetic. An afterthought. The house echoed the panic in my voice, every surface reflecting back a more frightened version of myself.

She let go suddenly, sending me sprawling. I caught myself on the edge of the coffee table, breath punched out of me, pain jarring up my arm. She stumbled backward, arms flailing, nearly fell into the shards of glass on the kitchen tile.

She collapsed, boneless, at my feet, sobbing into the spilled whiskey. The wetness on her face was equal parts liquor and tears.

I stood over her, body vibrating with the shock of her words, her violence, the living ghost she'd become.

For a long moment, I wanted to leave her there, let her drown in her own mess, let the loneliness finish what Lillian had started.

But the sight of her, crumpled and weeping, twisted something inside me. I crouched, ignoring the sting in my cheek, and stroked her hair.

It was the same color as Lillian's since she dyed it, and for a second, I could almost believe I was comforting my sister instead of the monster who'd made us both this way.

She whimpered, curling in on herself. "Don't leave me. Please, don't leave me." The words were wet and hoarse, her lips grazing my wrist.

I pressed my hand to the back of her head, willing myself to mean it. "I'm not going anywhere," I lied, the words slipping out effortlessly with a sting of bitterness.

She was already snoring, shallow and wet, before I'd finished the sentence. I waited until her breathing settled, then peeled her off the floor and dragged her to her room, half-carrying, half-hauling.

She muttered something about Lillian, about how "She was always the pretty one," and then laughed, a thin and colorless sound that scraped my insides raw.

I stripped the stained hoodie from her shoulders and rolled her into bed, then stood there for a long minute, just watching her sleep.

I wondered when the transformation had happened. When the mother I remembered had been peeled away, and this broken, venomous thing left in her place.

I imagined her body decomposing right there in the sheets, sinking into the mattress one cell at a time until she merged with the house itself. I would find her one morning as a crumpled outline, a greasy silhouette on the sheets.

Maybe then I could finally say goodbye.

I left the room and shut the door quietly, careful not to disturb her. In the hallway, the air was rank with sweat and rotting fruit.

My hands shook as I scrubbed them under hot water at the kitchen sink, trying to scour away the touch of her, the sound of her voice, the words that had fused themselves to my bones.

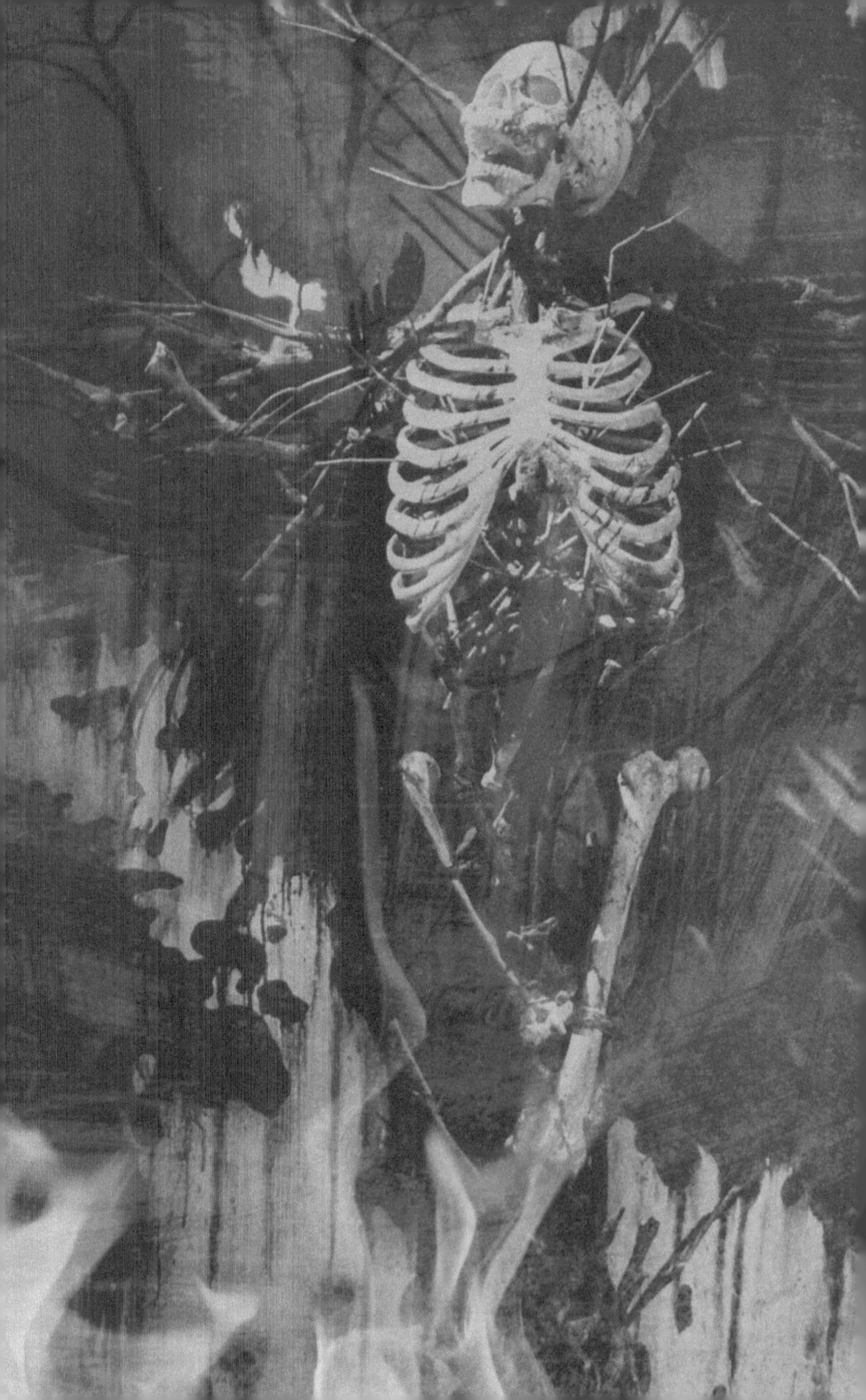

# 25
## THE PRESENT
### AMELIA

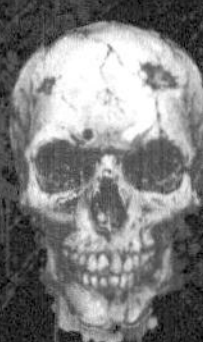

A RAW WIND WHIPPED THROUGH THE TREES, ITS ICY breath raising goosebumps on my arms as I pushed through the dense undergrowth; the mud clung to my shoes, each step a sucking squelch.

Caiden walked a few paces ahead, his jaw set and shoulders tense.

"Can you at least try to not walk so loudly?" I snapped, irritation bubbling beneath the surface as a branch snapped under his foot, sending a shower of leaves cascading to the ground. "We're trying to avoid attracting attention, remember?"

He turned slightly, shooting me a look that was equal parts annoyance and amusement. "What, you think the bears are going to come running just because I stepped on a twig?"

His voice held a hint of sarcasm, softened by an underlying warmth that had developed over the years.

"Maybe not bears, but who knows what else is out there?" I shot back, my own frustration spilling over. "We've been wandering for hours, and you're acting like this is a game."

"Welcome to the wilderness, Amelia," he replied, his tone light but with an edge of seriousness. "You wanted an adventure, remember? This is it."

"Oh, right. Because getting chased by a mountain lion is exactly what I had in mind when I agreed to this retreat." I rolled my eyes, but a small part of me appreciated his attempt at optimism.

"Look, we'll find our way out," he said, his voice steady. "I've been trained for this kind of stuff. Trust me."

I could see the flicker of confidence in his eyes, the same determination that had likely driven him through the challenges of military life. "You've been trained?" I asked, attempting to keep the skepticism out of my voice. "What, did you get a badge for surviving the wilderness?"

"Actually, yes," he shot back, a hint of pride creeping into his tone. "We learned survival tactics during boot camp. I was in some pretty tough environments, and if I can survive those, I can get us out of here."

"Right, because dodging bullets is the same as avoiding getting lost in the woods," I replied dryly, but a part of me acknowledged the strength he had gained from those experiences.

"Hey, it's not just about dodging bullets," he continued, his tone earnest. "It's about staying calm, assessing the situation, and finding a way out. I can do that, Amelia. Just give me a little credit."

I paused, crossing my arms as I considered his words. "I get that you've been through a lot, Caiden. But this isn't boot camp. We don't have a drill sergeant yelling at us to keep moving." My voice softened. "We're alone out here, and it's terrifying."

He turned to me fully, the sunlight filtering through the trees casting a halo around his features. "I know it's scary, but we're stronger than we think. Just remember what I said about staying calm. We'll figure this out."

A silence settled between us. But before I could respond, a sudden rustle in the underbrush caught our attention, making both of us jump.

"What was that?" I whispered, instinctively stepping closer to him.

"Probably just a squirrel or something," he replied, but I could see the tension in his jaw. "Or maybe a bear. You know, since you've been so loud."

"Very funny," I muttered, my heart racing as I scanned the trees, half-expecting something to leap out at us. "This isn't helping."

"Relax. I'm just trying to lighten the mood." He stepped forward, and as he did, he tripped over a hidden root, stumbling and nearly falling into a thicket of brambles. "See? Just nature trying to keep us on our toes."

I couldn't help but laugh, despite the situation. "Well, at least you're good for a laugh. If we make it out of here, I'm going to make sure you sign up for wilderness survival classes."

"And if we don't make it out, at least I'll have a great story about how I was taken down by an angry bush." He grinned, and for a moment, the tension between us felt lighter.

As we continued walking, the terrain began to change. The path narrowed, and the trees closed in around us, creating an almost claustrophobic atmosphere.

Just then, we came upon a section of the forest where the ground was covered in thick, tangled vines and underbrush, the path completely obscured.

"Great," I said, my voice dripping with sarcasm. "Now we have a jungle to contend with. Just what I needed."

Caiden scanned the area, his expression serious. "It looks like this might lead us toward the river if we can get through. But it's going to be messy."

"Messy sounds about right," I replied, eyeing the thicket warily. "Do you really think we can push through this?"

"Sure, why not? It'll be an adventure," he said, his tone teasing but with an undercurrent of determination. "I'll go first. Just follow my lead."

"Of course you will," I muttered, rolling my eyes. "What do I look like, your sidekick?"

"Hey, sidekick or not, I'm still leading the way." He stepped forward and began to push aside the thick vines. They snapped back, slapping against his arms, and he winced, but he pressed on, determination etched across his features.

"Okay, but if you get stuck, I'm not pulling you out," I called after him, a hint of sarcasm masking my concern.

"Only if you promise to take a mental picture of my glorious demise," he replied, his voice muffled by the tangle of foliage.

I followed close behind, trying to navigate the snaking vines that seemed intent on tripping me.

As I moved, I caught my foot in a particularly stubborn root, and before I knew it, I was tumbling forward, crashing into the dense underbrush.

"Fuck," Caiden turned, his expression was a mix of alarm and amusement. "You good?"

"Just peachy!" I shouted back, struggling to untangle myself from the vines that had ensnared my legs like a trap. "You know, this is exactly what I signed up for."

"Need a hand?" he asked, a smirk playing at the corners of his mouth.

"Only if you plan on pulling me out without getting stuck yourself!" I retorted, trying to keep the annoyance out of my voice.

"Alright, alright, let me see what I can do." He stepped forward, crouching down as he reached for me, careful to avoid getting caught in the vines himself.

"Just be careful," I warned, a flash of concern crossing my mind. "These things are like living creatures."

"I'm not afraid of a little greenery," he said, and with a swift tug, he pulled me free.

I stumbled forward, regaining my balance as I turned to face him.

"See? Easy peasy," he said, brushing off his hands as if nothing had happened.

"Yeah, if by 'easy peasy' you mean nearly face-planting into a bush, then sure," I replied, shaking my head. "You're a real pro at this."

"Just wait until we find the river," he said, a glimmer of excitement in his eyes. "That'll really be something to see."

"I'm sure it'll be breathtaking," I said, my voice dripping with sarcasm. "Especially if we end up as bear bait on the way there."

"Optimism isn't your strong suit, is it?" he quipped, nudging me with his elbow as he stepped ahead again.

"Optimism doesn't come naturally when you're navigating through a jungle of doom," I shot back, feeling my irritation simmer beneath the surface. "But I guess I should thank you for the guided tour."

"Anytime, Amelia. Just think of this as character building." I couldn't help but roll my eyes again.

"Character building? More like a crash course in how to get lost and potentially die," I said, glancing around at the impenetrable thicket. "What's next? An obstacle course of angry wildlife?"

"Now that sounds fun," he replied with mock enthusiasm. "Let's add some fire-breathing dragons while we're at it."

"Perfect. I'll bring the marshmallows," I said dryly, pushing through another thick patch of vines that seemed to reach out and grab at my clothes.

Caiden rolled his eyes and shook his head as we continued to push through the tangled underbrush, our banter a temporary reprieve from the reality of our situation.

We pressed on until the underbrush relented and the woods yawned open, exposing a clearing bruised with sunlight and trailing mist.

Here, the wilderness felt less like a deathtrap and more like a sick joke. An endless stage for our misery.

After a while, I spoke again. "You could have just left me back there. Why didn't you?"

"Because I don't want to be like him," he said, barely louder than the wind. "I don't ever want to be like him."

The "him" hung between us, a specter that made me shiver more than the cold.

I opened my mouth to argue, but it was useless. We'd spent so much energy fighting the people who made us that we'd forgotten who we were.

Maybe there was nothing left.

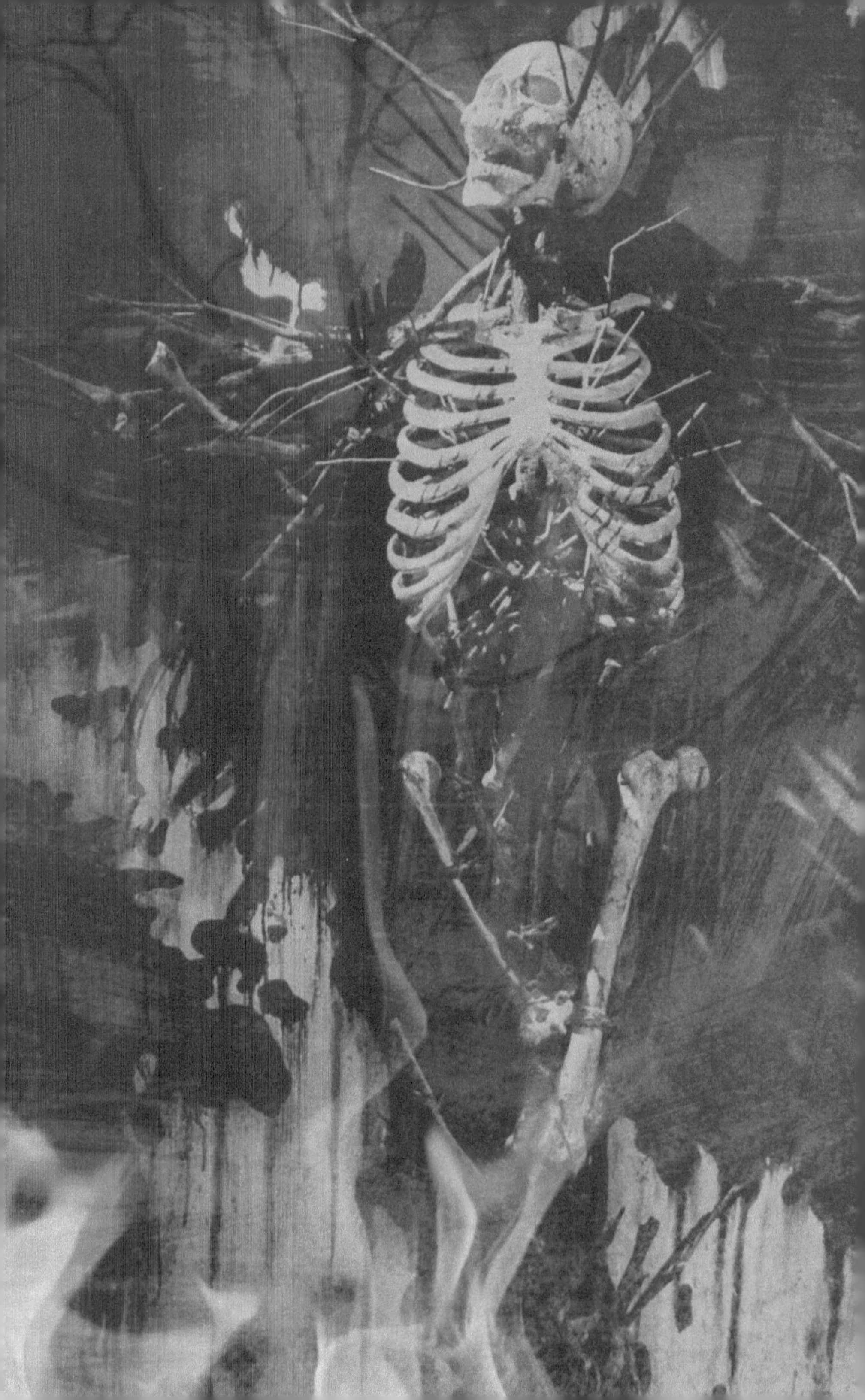

# 26

## THE PRESENT

### CAIDEN

I wish I had never gone on this fucking trip.

The bleeding monster within me fought to escape, to unleash years' worth of rage. Being around Amelia brought that shit out of me.

I forced the beast down, suffocating it. No good came from bleeding out in front of her. She was watching me. Always fucking watching. Probably waiting for me to snap, to give her a reason to bolt and leave me here to rot.

If this had been the Army, I would've left her on the first day. Let the crows pick her bones. But here I was, bushwhacking through brush, and every time I heard her stumble, I had to stop myself from spinning around and screaming. Every single time.

Resentment pulsed under my skin, hot and corrosive. I wanted to fucking disappear. Or push her down a ravine and walk away. Either worked.

She was behind me, breathing too loudly. I could feel her eyes burning into my back, judging me, waiting for me to fail. Typical. Always waiting to see me fuck up so she could crow about it.

"You know you're not a Navy SEAL, right?" she snapped. Even her voice grated. "You can slow down. I'm not dying to impress you."

I clenched my jaw. My fingers curled tight around a low-hanging branch. I nearly tore it off the damn tree. "If you'd keep moving instead of bitching, we'd be halfway out of this forest by now."

"Oh, so we're taking the scenic route so you can show off? Impressive. Really, Caiden."

I gritted my teeth and kept walking, pretending I didn't hear the faint tremor in her voice. Fear? Or just loathing for me? Didn't matter. I'd take either.

"You want a medal?" I threw over my shoulder. "Try keeping up."

"You want to be a martyr, just say so. I'll be right here, collecting your bones after you drop dead."

Red flashed behind my eyes. The pressure built in my skull. But my voice stayed cool. "Don't tempt me. I'd rather lose myself out here than listen to your voice one more second."

She mumbled something, too soft to catch. I didn't care. Wind slapped through the trees. I lost the line of the trail twice, but I never let on. I just doubled down, always forward, even when it ended in a tangle of roots that almost took my fucking ankle off.

Pride wouldn't let me slow down. Not for her. Not for anybody. Even when my legs buckled and the world spun, I kept plowing ahead, just to prove a point. Couldn't be weak. Not in front of her.

But when she tripped, crashed to her knees behind me, I spun so fast my spine cracked. Instinct. Rage.

I caught her wrist before she hit the dirt. Dug my fingers in, hard enough to bruise. "Get up." My voice barely sounded human. More hiss than sound.

She jerked her arm from my grasp, eyes flashing like she'd rather kill me than thank me. "Don't fucking touch me, Caiden." Her lips trembled. Pathetic. I should have let her fall.

But I didn't.

She pushed up onto wobbly knees, hair wild, cheeks flushed, veins standing out in her neck. Every inch of her screamed weakness, and I hated her for it. Hated myself more. Because, for all the venom, I still couldn't just leave her behind. Not after everything. Not now. Not ever.

I turned away, shoulders bunched tight, fists clenched at my sides. I wanted to put my arm through a tree. Instead, I just ground my boots deeper into the muck, shredding the next few yards until the trail dissolved into nothing. "Move," I muttered without turning. "Unless you want to camp here."

She stumbled after me, a curse rattling in her throat. I could feel the heat of her glare knifing holes through my shoulder blades. Still, she followed. Always.

The world shrank to mud, roots, her breath behind me, her boots sucking at every step. Time went feral, lost shape. A delirium of trees, darkness, the ache in my lower back, and a hunger that bit down to the bone and never let go.

She bitched. She always bitched.

"Slow down, monster. Not all of us are built for this." There was blood on her shin, seeping into her sock. She limped, but she wouldn't give it up, not in front of me. That stubbornness almost made me want to grin.

Almost.

"You never quit, do you?" I shot back. "Even when you should."

"I'm not quitting. I just hate you."

"Right back at you."

The brush thickened, lashing her face. I didn't warn her. Let the branches make their marks. At least they were honest about what they were.

Our energy bled out with every step.

I kept checking, every ten steps, to make sure she hadn't vanished. No matter how much I told myself I didn't care, that she could rot for all I gave a shit.

She belonged to me, in this. Suffering, survival, hell, or whatever came next. I couldn't stop protecting her if I tried.

The deeper we went, the darker it got. I felt her getting slower, weaker. I slowed, too, barely. Had to. If she broke down for good, I was fucked. There was nothing else out here. Just us and the endless, suffocating need.

I slowed up at a boulder, pausing, pretending to scan the terrain. Really just waiting for her to catch up without having to admit it. She stumbled into view, raw-boned and pale, arms scratched to shit, hair a wild halo. She could barely look at me without her lips curling.

"Getting tired, princess?" The words slid out. I wanted them to draw blood.

She wiped her mouth with the back of her hand. "Maybe if you stopped acting like a mountain goat on steroids, we wouldn't be lost."

I grinned. "If you'd kept up in the first place, we'd be drinking beer at the resort. Instead, we're watching you break down in real time. It's a show."

She slumped to the ground, back against the cold stone. I didn't know if she was crying or just too empty to care. Her chest shivered with every breath. Watching her fold in on herself did something to me. Not pity, but close, like the ghost of it, sifted through contempt.

I crouched beside her, my shadow blotting out the fading sun. She flinched, lip curling. "Don't touch me."

"Wasn't planning on it." But my hand hovered anyway. Fuck.

She stared up at me, eyes glassy, empty. I nearly spat on the dirt, just to break the spell. "You want to survive or not? 'Cause if you're giving up, let me know."

The corners of her mouth twitched. "You'd want that, wouldn't you?"

"Not really." Each word was a stone in my gut. "If you die, they'll blame me. I'm not going back to that fucking town with your ghost hanging off my neck."

She tried to laugh, but it sounded like choking. "You'd probably just kick my corpse into a ditch."

I imagined it. The weight of her, limp, weightless. The anger that rushed in at the thought. "Don't tempt me."

Our eyes locked for a second. I hated how it made me feel. Like I could break her. Like I could save her.

The thought made my molars grind.

I straightened, looking away. "Get up. We don't have time for your melodrama." I expected her to spit some bullshit, slap back with some sarcastic retort, but for once she just sat there, sucking air, eyes locked on my boots like she wanted to die at my feet. Good. At least then I'd have proof I'd done something right.

She finally got her balance and stood, wobbling, hair falling around her face in a mess of snarls. "You just love bossing people around, don't you?" Not her best, but whatever.

"Better than being a victim." I turned and pushed on, not giving her the satisfaction of looking back.

"Fuck you, Caiden."

"Try it. I dare you." My lips curled. "You're pathetic when you're like this." I kept my voice low, almost gentle. "Was it always an act, or did life just grind you down?"

She stopped, chest heaving. "You don't know anything about me. You think you do, but you never did."

I stepped in, crowding her against a tree, eyes boring into hers. "Bullshit. I know everything about you. You're an open wound, Langston. Always bleeding for someone to notice."

Her jaw clenched. "You're projecting. That's what your dad did, wasn't it? I hear he left bruises where words wouldn't do."

Ice slid through my veins. I slammed my palm against the bark beside her head, the thud snapping through the silence. Her breath caught.

"You want to talk about fathers? I'll bury you under stories that'll make yours look like a fucking episode of Sesame Street," I ground out, leaning in until my shadow swallowed her expression. I watched her throat work, saw the fight spit hot behind her eyes, but she didn't flinch. She never fucking flinched.

"Congratulations on the worst dad trophy," she snapped, too close, breath sour on my cheek. "Still doesn't mean you get to run my life, Caiden." She was trembling, and I felt it all the way down my locked arm. I should have let her go. Should have barked a laugh and shoved off down the trail, left her to gnaw the bark for comfort, but instead I slammed my palm harder against the trunk.

The sound was violence, split and echoing.

I was dizzy with the burn in my jaw, the urge to grab her by the nape and shake her until all the old wounds poured out.

But I didn't.

Instead, I shoved off, shouldering past her so hard I hoped she'd snap a rib just to call my bluff. "You want to keep score, Langston?" I muttered. "You've got your own fucking graveyard, right? Go ahead, drag the corpses out. Let's see who breaks first."

She caught up, boots skidding through the mess of bracken. "You know nothing about my life. Not a goddamn thing," she seethed, eyes digging into my side. "Just cause your daddy was a monster doesn't mean I'm scared of you."

I almost laughed. Almost. "No, you just like playing martyr. Always did."

She hissed. I could hear the exhaustion in it, the weak crackle beneath the rage. "At least I don't shove people until they crumble, asshole."

"Oh, please. You crumbled way before I even touched you." My hands felt electric, restless. It took everything not to punch something. "You think you're the only one who's been chewed up? Look around, princess. Everybody's meat out here."

She tripped beside me, stumbled, and caught herself on a branch. Her knuckles bled fresh red over old scabs. I watched, couldn't stop. The sight of it made my chest hollow out.

I pulled ahead, needing distance, needing air. But she followed, gnawing at my heels. Always.

We kept moving, pushing through a patch of thorns that tore at her shirt. She swore, yanked the sleeve free, and staggered right into my shoulder. I steadied her with a grunt, rough, not gentle, but I was already sick with the stupidity of the reflex.

Her lips twisted. "What, now you're a gentleman?"

I shook her off, barking a dry laugh. "You'd freeze to death if I let you try standing by yourself. You're fucking pathetic, Langston."

"Yeah, well, better pathetic than a sadist." She gripped her arm, cradling it like I'd actually hurt her.

The way she glared told me she hated me for seeing her hurt. I wished I could've told her I didn't give a shit, but that wasn't true. The sight gnawed at me, a dog chewing a bone. I wanted to look away, but couldn't.

Instead, I stood there, jaw clenched, fists jammed into the dirty fabric of my pockets, so tight my fingers tingled. I forced the anger down – always, always forcing it down – and tried to keep my voice calm. Flat.

If I let even a crack show, she'd see what she did to me, that part I could never kill.

"You shouldn't touch anything. You're like glass. Break every time the wind blows."

She shifted on her feet, hair falling in a ragged curtain, arms closing tighter around herself. "Says the guy who can't finish a conversation without throwing something." Her voice rasped, too raw, but she still tried to jab. Always did.

"Yeah, well, I don't see you walking away," I said. I didn't want to see her win. Not even for a second. "You'd wither in five minutes out here without me, and you know it." My words came out rough. The accusation hung like a blade.

"Better that than dying of boredom listening to you jerk yourself off about how tough you are." Her eyes were glassy, desperate, but she still looked straight at me.

I spiked forward, crowding her space. The only way I knew how to get control. "You want tough? Try not to whine every time you get a scratch. Just once."

She shook, the shudder starting in her jaw and rippling down. "You only say that because you're used to pain. You like it, don't you? Makes you feel alive."

I wanted to hit something. I'd spent years making sure I didn't lose it. Letting someone else have that kind of power? No. Never again. I pushed the urge down, but it poured out of my voice anyway: "You have no idea what feeling alive is. You spend your life running from shit. That's your whole personality."

"And you? What are you running from?" Her voice snapped. She didn't care about the answer. I saw it in her eyes, the way she already loaded her next insult behind her teeth.

I leaned in, shadows slicing my face, letting her see how little anything mattered. "Nothing. I take pain. I take whatever I get and keep going. Unlike you."

She flinched, anger or maybe fear. I didn't care. She looked up at me, eyes bright and wet like a wounded animal. "You're just your father's son. That's the only thing real about you."

Something inside me split. I grabbed her chin, not hard, just enough that she had to look up, had to really see me. No ducking. No hiding. Just her and me and the truth between our teeth.

Pretty. Even all scratched up, covered in filth and snot, she was still fucking pretty. Disgusting, how I noticed. More disgusting how it twisted under my ribs, that urge to break her down and keep her standing up. Both.

Her lips parted as if she might spit in my face. "Let go." Fingernails dug into my wrist, not enough to matter. Just enough to show she'd never stop fighting.

"Didn't think you had any fight left." I leaned in, just to crowd her space, let her choke on my shadow. "Feels like you'd rather die out here than admit you can't handle a little pain."

She glared, eyes heated and venomous, but I could see the tremor at the edge of her jaw. "You have no idea what I can handle, Caiden. You never did. You just made sure I was hurting."

I squeezed tighter. "Don't flatter yourself. Hurting you was just for sport."

"Yeah?" She bit the word in half. "You always needed a punching bag, didn't you? Like father, like son. It's the only thing you're good at."

Her words landed hard, but I didn't let her see. I twisted my mouth, bared my teeth in something that wasn't a smile. "Keep talking about my father. See how far that gets you."

I could feel her pulse, wild-insect flutter beneath my thumb. Adrenaline crackled between us. I wanted to shove her. Or pull her close. Maybe both.

Instead, I let go. Turned away. Pretended it didn't matter that for a split second I was tempted to do a hell of a lot more than grab her chin.

She crumpled for half a breath, like she meant to fall. Of course she didn't.

More walking. I slowed, didn't let her see. I was losing strength too. Sun blinding through the canopy, sweat dripping, gnats crawling everywhere. Hell.

"I don't know what's worse," she finally muttered, "the starvation, or your attitude."

It almost made me laugh. Almost. "You love complaining. Secretly, you'd be lost if you couldn't bitch about me."

That got her. She made a sound. A broken laugh, almost a sob. "Classic Caiden. Can't even let me hate you in peace."

"Who said I wanted peace?" My tone rose. I liked the way her jaw clenched, the way her glare boiled.

"Then what do you want?" She stopped in her tracks, goading me with the question. "You want to see me broken? Dead? Or do you just need an audience when you go off the rails?"

Her voice knifed through the trees. I clenched my teeth, tried not to let the venom leak out, but she made it impossible.

Always did.

"I need you to shut up," I bit out. "That's it. That's all I want from you."

"What, reality too much for you? Thought you liked watching me suffer."

"I don't like anything about this," I snarled, voice low. "You think I want to be stuck out here with you? If I could trade you for a rat's corpse, I'd do it in a heartbeat."

She wheeled around on the trail, jaw set. "Yeah, well, you're not exactly top of my list either."

Good. I wanted her angry. I wanted her gnashing her teeth and throwing those looks over her shoulder, the ones that promised she'd eat my heart if she got close enough.

"You want a round of applause for being so fucking stoic?" she spat. "Acting like you're better than suffering. You're not."

"Please." I flashed her a look, all teeth. "I'm built for suffering. It's the only thing that ever made sense."

"If that's the case, shut up and walk." Her tone was flaming, eating through the last of my patience.

But I did. I kept my mouth clamped, nostrils flared, pulse thrashing in my ears. She was behind me, soft panting getting harder, almost frantic. I hated how my body tuned itself to her, every stagger a ripple under my skin.

Log ahead. I stopped dead, let her slam into my back. Felt the shock of it and turned on her before I could stop myself.

"You ever pay attention, or are you just programmed to crash into shit?"

She shoved me, recklessly. Her fingertips dug in, left crescents on my upper arm. "At least I don't storm through life like I'm on a kill mission. You ever try being a human, Caiden?"

Low blow. My chest went tight, a spike of old, familiar rage. I leaned in, crowding her, breath hot against her cheek. "Tried it once. Didn't like it."

Her jaw flexed. "Figures. Humanity's too soft for you. You'd rather stomp around like a pissed-off gorilla."

Cute. She thought she was clever. I braced my wrist against the tree and blocked her in, just to watch her squirm. I wanted to bite back, to snap something that would shut her up for five seconds.

Instead, I leaned in closer, crowding her until I could practically taste her spit and panic.

"You know what else I don't like?" My voice dropped, flat as old blood. "Wasting my time arguing with you. If you'd shut your mouth and use your legs, we'd be out of here already."

She stared at me, lips parted, lashes low. Like she had something to say. I waited for the insult. She swallowed, then shot back, "If I wanted to hear a lecture, I'd call my deadbeat dad."

I clenched my jaw, shoving past her, shoulders colliding on purpose. Let her chew on that. Every step, her muttering dogged my heels. Too close. Always too fucking close.

"You going to pout all day, Baxter?" she goaded, nearly ramming my back. "Or am I supposed to be scared you'll finally snap and toss me off a cliff?"

I kept my eyes on the ground, every muscle screaming at me to stop, but pride wouldn't let me. Not when she was watching, not when quitting meant she won. "Trust me. If I wanted to get rid of you, you'd already be down there." I hooked my chin at the drop-off to our right. She glanced at it, face pale, but she didn't break stride.

Her voice was pure venom. "You're such a coward, Caiden. All threats, no action. Typical."

Heat snapped in my chest. I spun, grabbing her by the upper arm and yanking her flush against me. Her hair whipped my mouth. I bared my teeth in a smile that wasn't a smile.

"You really want to see action, princess?" I shoved her back, just enough to make her stumble over her own feet. She caught herself.

"I forgot. You're only dangerous on paper."

I didn't answer. I couldn't. My head pounded, nerves thrumming like I'd mainlined rage. I wanted to tear into her, rip her down, and see what was underneath. But the other half—the hollow half that knew her too well—just wished she'd stop looking at me like I was something worth hating.

"Your dad really fucked you up, didn't he?"

My hands fisted.

"Fuck off," I spat.

She didn't let it go. Of course not. She never fucking did.

"See," she needled, boots splashing the mud right behind me, "you can't even talk about him. That's what makes you weak, Caiden. You keep pretending it didn't matter."

"I'm not weak," I ground out, nose full of the stink of wet rot and mosquito buzz. "But clearly I'm stuck to dead weight. Maybe your dad should have taught you how to survive, instead of how to cry in people's faces."

She rolled up beside me and had to practically run to close the gap. "He didn't teach me shit," she hissed back, but her breath stuttered. "Guess I learned to cling to life by watching you hate yours."

"You going to whine the whole way, or just until you can't walk?" I shot, eyes never leaving the thin thread of animal trail curling out ahead.

She scowled, hair tangled, jaw set. "I'll walk circles around you, Baxter. Just give me a minute." But her hand shook as she said it. She tried to hide it, tucking close to her side, but I saw.

"What, you want a break? Say the word, and I'll carry you." The disgust flared, but something else twisted with it. A need to see her knocked down, then get back up. To see her crawl. To see her need me.

She flinched at my words, but didn't look away. "You'd love that. Having me helpless. Makes you feel big, right?"

I grinned, teeth bared in the shadows. "Better than watching you dirt-nap in the forest. If you go down, I'm not digging a hole. I'm leaving you for the vultures."

She glared but didn't respond. We walked on.

"Careful," I snapped over my shoulder, right before a low branch caught her across the face. She yelped. Every time she made that noise, my spine twitched. "Eyes forward, princess. Would hate for a stick to do permanent damage."

She scowled, thumb swiping blood off her lip. Her mouth had that wrecked, swollen look. God. "Maybe if you'd warn people, but I guess that's not in your nature, Caiden."

"Warn you, spoon-feed you, carry you, I don't see it on my job description." I grinned at her over my shoulder, all teeth, let her eat that sarcasm. But her glare landed, hot and messy, right in my gut.

The trail twisted, broke. We had to push through ferns, a wall of green shit taller than her. She fumbled one step, and her shoe slid in the muck, ankle rolling. She yelped again.

I caught her. Didn't even think. My grip landed on her hip, hard, and for a split second her body slotted against mine, soft and shaking and filthy. Fuck. My palm was full of her, fingers digging into her bony side. For a beat, we just stood there, clinging through anger, the world narrowing to the mud and my skin pressed to hers.

"You're going to wipe out and take me down with you. At least die with some dignity." I held her one second longer, just to see if she'd fight. She didn't. Her breathing slowed, turned shallow. I watched her tongue dart out, wetting bloody lips. Couldn't look away.

"Shit. Um, thanks for catching me."

If I were smart, I'd shove her off and say something mean to cover my tracks.

Instead, I loosened my grip, but let my hand drag around her hip, thumb tracing just enough to leave a mark. I liked feeling her squirm. She knew it, and I knew it. Her skin, even through fabric, felt hot as a fever.

Her hair was wild, cheeks all burning. My heart hammered. The heat between us flared, suffocating. I didn't back off, not one inch. Just glared down, knowing she'd buckle first. Always did.

I dragged my palm, rough, up the side of her throat. She flinched, breath hissing through her teeth. "What, you scared I'm secretly planning on killing you?" I crooned it low, bending so my face hovered barely an inch from hers.

Her mouth trembled, lips parted. "I'd like to see you try."

Fuck. The way she looked at me. Hell, nobody looked at me that way. Not even my old man, and he was the king of cruel.

She shoved back, but it just pressed us together, root to rib. I felt the outline of her tits through the thin shirt, her chest fluttering like she was on the verge of screaming. Or something else.

She scraped her nails down my forearm. "Get off me, Caiden."

"Nah," I whispered, letting the word land cold on her lips. "You'd miss me."

She rolled her eyes, but the glare was softer, shaky. Her pulse beat against my thumb, crazy-fast. I loosened just enough to let her breathe, but kept her close, locked in my shadow. I didn't trust myself to let go yet. Didn't trust her not to spit in my eye, or worse, beg for more.

She tried to twist, but I pinned her. Just long enough to let her feel what I could do if I wanted.

"You always so mouthy when you're about to eat dirt?" I taunted, letting my grip slide down to the bony point of her hip.

She stilled. I could feel her breathing. Shallow, furious, nothing left to lose. Some part of me wanted to break her completely. The other part? Didn't know what the fuck it wanted.

She smirked. Lips bloody, nose flaring. "I've got more stamina than you, soldier. This what you learned in the Army? Bullying people smaller than you?"

I laughed. Couldn't help it. The sound came out raw. "You think you're small? Princess, you're impossible to miss. Like a siren for suffering. I could spot you in a war zone."

She kicked out, caught my shin, not hard but enough to sting. "Serves you right," she bit out, chin stubborn and high even when she could barely stand. Always more venom than blood in her veins.

She limped past, like she wanted to prove she could outpace me. Nothing but bone and spite, that girl. I watched her hips and the mess of her hair swinging wildly. Too wild. Too pretty, like she could slice me open if I stared too long.

The bush snagged my shoulder as I followed, wet branches lashing my face. I pushed harder, crowding her back.

She noticed. Could see it in the way her shoulders tensed, in how she threw looks at me over her shoulder like daggers. Didn't care. I liked the way she bristled when I was close, like she'd claw my eyes out or kiss me just to shut me up.

She didn't know how close I was to taking her up on both.

I resented every atom of awareness she roused in me.

This wasn't desire. It was a malfunction: hunger, cold, adrenaline, the desperate reality of danger. My instincts betray me because she was the only other living soul within reach. Just that.

I repeated it until the words rang empty.

I hated it. I hated it with a depth that bordered on pain. Hated how effortless it was for her to make my guard slip; how she did it by simply existing, by not even noticing the havoc she was wreaking inside me.

No softness. No longing. No surrender. Wanting her was a disaster. The edge of a cliff, the heart of a wildfire I could never smother if it ever caught hold.

She was everything I'd spent years barricading myself against, the wound at the root, the very reason I had built these walls. And now, she was here, shivering and alive at my side, and I could feel my control eroding, fiber by fiber.

I forced my body to stone; forced my mind blank. Forced myself to resurface every reason why caving to this feeling was a death sentence.

# 27

## THE PAST

### CAIDEN'S CONDITIONING

**16 YEARS OLD**

Half a pack of Camels lay crushed in my jacket pocket, though I had smoked none. I had lifted them from my father's toolbox as an experiment. If I inhaled enough poison, would I become immune to it?

Or would it rearrange the molecules of my rage?

I had learned early, when my father's voice outblared the television and the taste of blood in my mouth became familiar, that the best way to survive was to preempt pain with pain.

Be the hurricane. Get my fist in first, so the next blow, when it came, was only a dull echo. Only a reminder.

I shouldered my backpack and exited the bathroom, moving through the corridor with the slow, deliberate menace of a predator who knew he could not be stopped.

My body, tall and broad and prematurely muscled, parted crowds in a way that was both satisfying and embarrassing. I hated the attention, but I hated being ignored more.

I watched her from the shadowed corner of the hall, arms crossed, my body thrumming with an anticipation that made my teeth ache in my skull.

Amelia.

She stood at her locker, half-turned to shield her notebook from prying eyes, the tawny river of her hair veiling the delicate line of her jaw.

Even from there, I could sense the anxious flutter of her hands as she rifled through the tangle of loose papers and broken pencils.

I wanted to hate her. I told myself to hate her. Day after day, I sharpened that hatred against the strop of my father's misery, whetted it to a blade thin enough to draw blood with a glance.

But the truth was softer, sourer, nothing like what I wished it would be.

Sometimes, when I saw her smile, rare nowadays, more a flicker than an expression, it hollowed something out from my chest, left a cold ache that lingered long after she had gone.

I woke up thinking about that smile, the way she bit her lip when she was nervous, how the tips of her ears went pink when she was caught off-guard.

It was sickening.

I needed to vomit it up, and there was only one way I knew how.

I stalked across the floor, my boots thudding a direct, predatory rhythm.

The other kids in the hallway sensed it and scattered, granting me a berth as though I were a chemical spill.

Only Amelia seemed oblivious, or else so utterly accustomed to danger that she couldn't be bothered to react.

I slammed her locker door shut with a flat palm. The hollow bang echoed off the cinderblock walls.

Amelia jerked back, cradling her hand, eyes sparking with a flash of terror that quickly fell into the bland defeat I had come to expect from her.

"Move," I said, my voice low and even, not a request.

She did, her lips pressed tight, knuckles white where they gripped the strap of her backpack.

I watched her walk away, hunched and guarded, shrinking herself down to nothing, and I felt nothing. Nothing but a cold, crawling disgust.

I rounded on the locker, wrenched it open, and slammed it three more times, each time harder, bracing for the moment when the metal would refuse me and shatter my wrist.

The pain never came. I was too good at this by now.

Later, after school, Dante was waiting by the bike racks, chewing on a strip of beef jerky and watching the sky with the blank patience of someone who expected nothing good to follow the final bell.

I liked that about him. Dante didn't ask questions, didn't pry for explanations. He just existed, a constant presence.

When my shadow stretched across the pavement, Dante spat the jerky stub into the grass and nodded, already knowing we'd be walking to the gas station, then to the quarry, then nowhere at all.

We walked in silence, the sound of our boots crunching gravel louder than any words we might have exchanged.

I felt the old familiar thrum of anxiety in my chest, the anticipation of violence, waiting for my father to materialize from behind a parked car.

But the streets were empty. Even the birds had gone mute, as if the entire town had agreed to vanish for the afternoon and leave me alone with my festering thoughts.

We bought two cans of Monster and a donut at the Kwik Stop, then walked the railroad tracks into the woods, where the town gave up and let nature take over.

Dante peeled the donut in strips and tossed each piece into his mouth, chewing with the languid boredom of a cow.

I sipped my Monster, feeling the fizz burn down my gullet, and imagined it was acid, that it would eat me clean from the inside out.

"You coming to mine, or you gotta check in with the warden first?" Dante said, his voice sludgy with indifference. He didn't look at me, just flicked a lighter over and over, the sparks almost invisible in the broad daylight.

"Not going back there tonight," I muttered, my knuckles white around the handlebars of my bike. I felt the words as a kind of relief, a counting of hours before the next reckoning. "I'll crash at your place if your mom's cool."

"Your dad a dick again?" Dante asked, eyes on the tracks.

I didn't answer. I didn't need to. The bruises on my knuckles spoke louder than words, the way I kept flexing and unflexing my hands as if rehearsing invisible violence. I dragged my boot along the rail and watched the flecks of rust scatter like blood.

"You ever think about doing something else?" Dante continued. "After school, I mean."

I made a noise that was almost a laugh. "Yeah, like what? Move somewhere else? Or maybe just off myself in the gym weight room and save everyone time."

Dante shot me a look, only half joking. "You could join the Army. You'd like that. Free meals. Guns. Nobody gives a shit where you came from."

I considered it, the idea of vanishing into a uniform, letting someone bigger and meaner than my father yell orders at me instead. I pictured my own head shaved, boots shining, a name stitched over my heart like a bandage.

Maybe I'd get so good at killing that the anger would bleed out and leave nothing behind.

I realized, with a kind of sick delight, that maybe I'd even get sent somewhere I could die for real. Make it official. Get a medal for it, if they even bothered to mail one to the ruins of my house.

We cut through the trees, our bodies moving in loose synchrony, the way two stray dogs will walk when neither is quite leader or follower.

If I squinted, I could almost forget who I was, forget the town and its rot, the way everything here seemed pre-digested and shit out before you ever got a taste of real life.

A train screamed by, close enough to vibrate the marrow of my bones, and for a wild second I contemplated stepping in front of it. Just to see if I felt fear, or if the engine would simply flatten me into the perfect shape of my own nothingness.

I didn't, though. I just watched the graffiti flash past, letters warped and melted together, proof that someone else had left their mark on this place before moving the fuck on.

Dante didn't say anything, but I could feel him watching, could sense that my friend was waiting for some sign, some slip of the mask that would reveal what was really going on inside.

He would wait forever, probably. I respected that about him, the willingness to let things rot in silence.

We followed the tracks until the gravel ran out and the woods took over, thick and green and pulsing with the exhale of spring. The runoff from the old quarry had formed a pond, its surface a patchwork of algae scum and bottle-green water.

We sat on the concrete lip of a ruined foundation and watched the wind ripples chase each other across the pond, made bets about which branch would fall next from the rotten birch tree on the far bank.

There was a peace to it, in the way a battlefield goes silent between shots.

Dante rolled a joint with the practiced hands of a priest folding a sacrament. I didn't bother to refuse when it was passed my way. I held the smoke until my lungs spasmed and my vision narrowed to a pinhole.

If I closed my eyes, I could almost pretend it was oxygen. When I exhaled, the world returned, painted in colors I never saw at home.

"You remember five years ago in sixth, when you beat the shit out of Bobby Sandoval?" Dante said, grinding the ash into the concrete. "You knocked a tooth out, man. He still talks about it like it was the best day of his life."

I shrugged, but the memory came back in full.

That was the first time my father had looked at me and grunted something like approval. The only time I'd eaten a real meal that week because of how proud he was of me, instead of standing in the kitchen, staring at the tile while my father sucked down beer and watched baseball.

"He deserved it," I said. "Fucker called me a bastard. Wasn't even original."

"He cried like a bitch, though," Dante said, and laughed.

I found myself grinning, the muscles in my face surprised by the motion. It hurt a little, in a way that felt honest.

We smoked in silence until the joint was spent, then Dante lay back, arms behind his head, eyes half-lidded to the sky.

I felt the darkness at my core, the urge to destroy, but there it ran gently, slowly, like a lazy river instead of a flash flood.

I could almost breathe.

"Wonder what Langston does when she's not drawing?" I mused, stretching my arms, exposing the band of muscle above my hips. "She got friends. Boyfriend."

Dante smirked, but there was a new sharpness to it. "You got some kinda death wish for her, man? You always talk about her."

I almost swung at Dante then and there. The urge came fast and violent, but I channeled it into a sneer. "I don't give a shit about her," I snapped, my voice thick. "Just saying. That's all she is. A sad sack with a pencil."

Dante shrugged, twisted a pebble between his fingers, and flicked it into the pond. "She's not that bad, you know. I had her in class last year. She's nice, not like most of those fake girls. Amelia's..." He trailed off, then shrugged, a small, private smile bunching the corners of his mouth. "Kinda cute, honestly."

The words went off like a car bomb in my head. I sat up straighter, fists clenching, my neck prickling with a cold reptile awareness, like I'd just spotted a knife in a friend's hand. "No, she's fucking not," I shot back, louder than I meant, the words burning on the way out.

Dante looked at me sidelong, testing. "Calm down, man. She's... I dunno. She's nice. Not a drama queen like the rest."

I wanted to grab Dante by the skull and drive his face into the concrete, see if I could knock the softness out of him.

Instead, I balled my hands hard enough to leave bruises on my own thighs.

"You ever talk to her?" Dante pressed, as if he didn't hear the warning in my voice. "Like, really talk?"

"Why the fuck would I?" I snapped. "She's a freak."

Dante shrugged, chewing a hangnail. "Just saying. She's different, is all." He smiled again.

I stood up so fast the world tipped sideways, and for a second I saw it all: the autumn rot along the bank, the scum swirling on the surface, Dante's face split by the line of shadow from the old birch.

"Don't ever say that again," I said, my voice flat. I let the silence stretch, let the threat live in the air, the way my father had taught me.

Dante raised his hands, palms out. "Fine, man. Jesus."

But his eyes never left me, dark and careful. Measuring.

A wind shivered through the trees, and I felt the cold crawl inside my hoodie, settle against my ribs. I wanted to break something, but there was nothing there except Dante, and Dante was the closest thing to family I had left.

It was a sick, twisted dependency.

I jammed my fists in my pockets and stalked away, crunching over dead leaves and brittle sticks, not looking back even when Dante's footsteps followed at a careful distance.

I walked until the trees thinned and the town reasserted itself, until every porch light and warped picket fence reminded me of the world's smallness, the impossibility of escape.

Dante peeled off toward his house without a word, leaving me to pace my own block like a caged animal, circling the perimeter until the streetlights flickered on.

I killed time at the playground, scuffing my boots on the fire-blackened slide, watching as the day's heat bled away into a bruised evening sky.

I didn't want to go home, and I didn't feel like crashing at Dante's house anymore.

I just wanted the ache beneath my skin to stop, for the meat of my body to quiet down and leave me alone with the white noise.

I pictured my father, already half-lobotomized by a bottle, sprawled in his recliner with the TV muttering in the background.

Maybe tonight would be peaceful. Maybe the bastard would just pass out and leave me the hell alone.

I was wrong.

As soon as I slipped through the back door, the stench of vodka and microwave burritos hit me, followed by the pulsing bass of some rock song.

The living room was a disaster of empty cans, ashtrays, and crumpled boxes, and my father lay stretched across the couch in nothing but boxers and a sweat-stained undershirt, eyes half-lidded and mouth hanging slightly open.

The man's chest rose and fell with the slow, heavy rhythm of the nearly dead.

For a minute, I watched him, seeing the future mapped in the bloat of my father's gut and the purple rings beneath his eyes.

I hated the bastard, but more than that, I was afraid of turning into him, of repeating the cycle so many times that the lines between us blurred, and it was impossible to tell where one ended and the other began.

I stepped into the kitchen, the floor sticky underfoot, and opened the fridge. There was nothing but expired milk, a six-pack with one beer left, and a Tupperware container of something that might have once been chili.

I grabbed the beer and popped the top with my teeth, letting the cold foam cut the taste of bile in my throat.

"Boy," the shape on the couch growled, not even opening its eyes. "Bring me a cold one."

I said nothing. I just set the beer down on the coffee table and retreated to the far side of the room, hands tucked into the sleeves of my hoodie.

The old man grunted, took a long swallow, and then finally cracked one eye open.

"You late," he slurred. "Where you been?"

I shrugged. "Out."

"You got a fuckin' attitude on you," my father said, his voice rising. "Come over here."

I didn't want to. I wanted to smash the glass coffee table, hurl the bottle at my father's head and watch it burst, see the old man's skull finally crack and spill out the rot.

But I moved closer, step by step.

"Sit down," my father said, gesturing vaguely at the threadbare armchair across from the couch. I sat, but only at the edge, my body coiled and ready to spring.

My father watched me for a long minute. "You been fighting again?" he finally asked, eyes narrowing. "Heard from the school. You got a problem with authority, boy, and it's gonna get you fucked up real good some day."

My jaw clicked as I clenched it. "Don't see what it matters to you," I said, my voice flat. "You're passed out most days, anyway."

The old man laughed, a dry, wet sound. "You're a smartass. You think I don't see? I see everything."

He levered himself upright, and for a second, I watched the struggle.

He lurched forward, bracing his elbows on his knees so our faces nearly matched, the stench of vodka and rotted teeth an assault all its own. "You wanna be a man, you gotta learn how to take a hit," my father said, slapping a meaty palm against my cheek, "and keep standing. You keep folding up like tissue paper, you'll end up nothing but a stain on the floor."

"I don't fold," I whispered, my voice so thin it almost vanished between us.

"Could've fooled me," he said, wagging his head. "You get that from your bitch of a mother. She ran, and now you run too. You can't even hit back when a man comes at you." He leaned in and spat the words. "If you want to stop being a disappointment, you gotta start hurting people for real. You gotta finish what you start, boy."

I didn't blink. I just stared at his ruined face, every bad decision and old bruise mapped into folds of skin, and saw my own future. Saw that this would be my inheritance, unless I found a way to burn the lineage to ash.

The urge to strike him was tidal, but I kept it coiled inside. Someday, I promised myself. Someday.

"Go to your room," my father finally spat, dismissing me like an animal. "And keep your goddamn mouth shut."

I did, moving through the hall with the stealth of a hunted thing, every sense tuned to the creaks and groans of the house.

I locked myself inside my room and lay on the bed, my hands folded on my chest like a corpse in a casket.

I kept my eyes open, staring up at the sawtooth cracks in the plaster until my neck ached, until the sting of my father's slap simmered down to a numb afterglow.

Sleep was a last resort, a submission I tried to delay as long as possible, because I knew what would wait for me there. The old reruns, the memory loops, my mother's back dissolving into fog as she walked away from the house, the blood-warm taste of my own teeth after a bad night, the way Amelia's eyes looked before she started crying.

Always Amelia, even when I tried to knock her out of my head with fists and venom. It was like a sick addiction.

I pressed the heel of my palm into my eye socket, as if I could mash her image into a pulp and wring it out through my tear ducts. I almost wished she'd fight back, that she'd snap one day and cut me open with a few sharp syllables in front of everyone.

But she always just took it, absorbed the blows like a black sponge, and that made me want to peel her skin off and see what she'd look like underneath.

I hated the need most of all. The sick, pathetic hunger that craved her eyes on me, even if they were full of contempt or terror, because at least then they were real, and pointed at me, and not through me the way the world usually did.

I'd rather be despised than invisible.

I sat up in the darkness, every muscle in my arms and back rigid with a need I could not name. My hands, when I looked at them, were shaking.

Anger mingled with those thoughts, but hatred was easily

blurred. Those feelings were born from something deeper, something pure. I didn't dwell on it, though.

The two emotions blended, anger and Amelia, until they became one.

She made my blood boil. Her existence was a disease to my mind, infecting my bones, devouring me. Amelia was the bane of my heart, leading me into an abyss of agony. She haunted me.

Her innocence, her smile, her pain, her presence. She was a phantom in my shadow, lurking in my dreams.

It swallowed me entirely, until I was a rotting ghost.

# 28

## THE PRESENT

### AMELIA

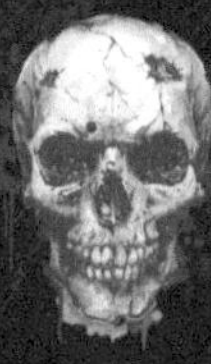

Being stuck out here in the Colorado wilderness was a nightmare. An actual nightmare. It had been a few days since the kayak accident, and I felt as if we were wandering the woodlands in circles, never actually coming any closer to civilization.

The tension was insane. We couldn't go a few minutes without bickering and arguing. There were maybe a few civil moments, but not enough.

The two of us could be bridged by friction alone, by the heat generated from scraping two ruined things together until they caught.

But I knew better: no matter how hard I tried to lose myself to anger, to hatred, to memory, the needle always dropped back in the same groove. His name, my name, our names twinned like wounds.

The fire was dying. The world around us was black and bottomless, the trees a silent jury of skeletons.

I caught myself staring at him, the way his hands hovered over the fire, the raw pink of his knuckles, the scars tracing the backs of his fingers.

He was always marked by violence, even when he wasn't using it.

He noticed me looking, of course. He always noticed. He smirked, lips twisting upward in a way that made me want to claw them off his face.

"You going to keep staring, or are you going to say something?"

he asked, low and almost curious. I could see the spark in his eyes: the challenge, the hunger for a fight.

"I was just wondering if you'd consider throwing yourself into the fire," I said, voice flat. "I hear it's a quick way to get warm."

He scowled. "Ladies first."

A branch snapped somewhere in the woods. I flinched. Caiden didn't, but I could see his muscles tense, every line in his body preparing for disaster.

For a second, I wondered if there was anything he couldn't turn into a contest of endurance, a test to see who would break first.

We sat in silence. The fire gnawed slowly at the wood.

At some point, darkness claimed both of us.

The next morning, I sat up and sucked in the freezing air, my teeth picking up where the night left off, chattering like a machine gun.

I watched Caiden kick dirt over the embers, his hands and forearms streaked with soot.

His back looked bent, tired, as if something had finally managed to gnaw a piece out of him.

I wondered what he saw in the dying glow, what hallucination or memory was haunting him.

Maybe he was reliving some bullet-ridden wasteland, or maybe he was just contemplating the infinite new ways I'd inconvenienced him.

When we started walking again, I could barely keep up.

I let Caiden lead, watched the set of his shoulders, the hard swing of his arms. Sometimes he looked back, just to make sure I hadn't dissolved into the green-black murk.

The path, if you could call it that, was little more than a vein of mud slicing through the trees.

My shoes slipped, my socks congealed with cold water. Every step was a fresh, exquisite misery. I rolled each ache around in my mouth like a stone, savoring it. It was the only taste left to me.

I thought, for the hundredth time, about how easy it would be to just stop. Sit down, lean against a moss-eaten stump, and wait for the earth to reclaim me.

But the memory of Lillian's corpse—rigid, alone, face gone slack and pale—kept me lurching forward. I would not die her death, not if I could help it.

We crested a ridge around midday. My vision wavered at the edges, a feverish haze brightening every leaf, every shadow. I saw the world in halos, like I was already half-ghost.

My knees locked, and I swayed, woozy with hunger and dehydration. I could hear the throb of blood behind my eyes, the world pulsing in and out of focus like a failing satellite feed.

The trees pinwheeled above me, stars blurring into daylight, and for an instant, I was nowhere. Just floating, bodiless, in that gap between misery and oblivion.

Then Caiden's voice cut through, too loud: "Careful, princess. Wouldn't want you passing out and making my life any harder." He was a few steps ahead, standing on a flat outcrop of stone, arms folded, lips pulled into a knife-edged smirk. "Unless you want me to drag your corpse the rest of the way."

I closed my eyes and clenched my fists, nails digging into my palm. "I'm not dead yet," I rasped, the words no more than a strip of sandpaper in my throat.

He didn't move. Just watched, pupil narrowing as if to see how much further I could be pushed before the breaking point. "If you want to die here, just say so. Might save us both some trouble."

I staggered after him, every step an act of violence against my own body. Each muscle screamed rebellion, but I kept moving, unwilling to show him that he was right, that I was weaker than he was, that I was still the victim.

The sun glared down from directly above, a white-hot interrogation lamp. Sweat pooled in the hollows of my neck and spine, but my skin felt cold, as though I was already being digested by the world beneath me, inch by inch.

We kept going. Each hour was a fresh torment. The only food we'd seen was a squirrel, flattened and leaking, in the middle of a game trail. It looked like a prophecy. I watched it for too long, its ruined face, its dark, poppy-seed eyes.

I'd never felt more kinship with a dead thing.

The ground leveled out, and the trees thinned, opening onto what passed for a trail. A weedy tire rut, pocked with puddles, barely navigable.

I followed Caiden in silence, though the throb in my head was a chorus of curses. I wanted to hate him, but my hatred was brittle, all flaking edges and hollow bravado. Mostly, I just wanted to collapse.

He slowed. "Stop dragging your feet," he said, not turning around. "If we lose daylight, we're done."

I couldn't help it. "You're the one who wanted to go north. I told you we should have doubled back to the river."

He wheeled on me. "The river's a trap. It loops back on itself for miles. You want to end up right where we started?"

I laughed, a single note. "Might as well. Maybe we'd find a rescue team. Or a body to eat."

His lip curled. "That's not even funny, Amelia."

"I'm not joking," I said, and I wasn't.

Before he could reply, I slipped on a patch of mud, the world teetering left, and he was there, hand clamped around my elbow to steady me.

The contact was jarring, almost electric, a wild jolt that reminded me I still had a heartbeat. I shook him off so hard my shoulder cracked.

"Don't touch me," I hissed. My voice sounded alien, like a recording of myself played back through a dying tape deck.

"Jesus, I was trying to help. You want to fall and crack your skull open?"

"At least then I wouldn't have to listen to your voice ever again."

He smiled, all teeth. "You'd miss it. Admit it."

I almost laughed. Instead, I pressed two fingers to my temple, willing the headrush away. "The only thing I'd miss is oxygen that isn't contaminated with your narcissism."

We stood there a minute, locked in our old rhythm.

But the old venom had lost some of its bite. We were too tired for real violence, too depleted for anything but the ghost of our old hate.

"Keep moving," he said, turning away. "We'll make camp as soon as we find a dry patch."

I limped after him, pausing to clutch a sapling and breathe through the latest crest of nausea.

We trudged on, the day dissolving into relentless gray. The trail degraded with every mile, until it was just another lie in the landscape, promising escape and delivering only more wilderness.

The only sign of civilization was the occasional beer can rusting in the weeds, or a shattered bottle glinting like a warning.

I thought of all the other lost souls who'd come through here before us. What was left of them, anyway, besides trash?

When we stopped that night, Caiden made camp in silence, his hands moving with rote precision. I watched him, hating his competence, envying it, too.

My own hands shook as I tried to assemble a lean-to from fallen branches. The first one snapped in my grip, the second slipped and landed on my foot. I swore loudly and flung the stick into the trees.

Caiden looked up, eyes hollow. "You want to break your foot? Go ahead. Less work for me in the morning."

"Fuck off," I spat, but there was no heat left in my voice. "Just— fuck off."

He didn't reply, just hunkered down by the fire, stabbing at it with a forked stick. The light flickered off his face, carving out the bones. I sat across from him, knees drawn to my chest, and let the silence fill in the spaces between us.

I slept fitfully, haunted by the howling wind and the hollow ache in my belly.

My dreams were fevered.

Shane and Sabrina, safe and oblivious, laughing in a place made of warmth and food and light. Lillian appeared, her voice muffled and distant, panic in her eyes as she reached for me, but dissolved to river water the moment I touched her.

When dawn bled into the world, gray and cold and merciless, I woke to the sound of Caiden urinating just beyond the fire's ash ring.

That was intimacy, too, I supposed: to know the color and sound of a nemesis's urine before you'd ever seen him truly weep.

We broke camp without words. My body felt less like a vessel and more like a collection of punishments.

My hands shook so badly I couldn't lace my own boots, but I got them on anyway, fingers rigid claws, a parody of willpower.

Around midmorning, we hit the river again.

There was no sign of a bridge. The water was fast and cold, and the noise of it was so loud it seemed to bounce inside my ribcage.

The sight of the water filled me with dread. The memory of the kayak crash whirled throughout my mind.

Caiden planted himself at the bank and stared across, scanning for some trick of geography, some hidden answer in the violence of the current.

The other side was maybe twenty yards, maybe a hundred. It

might as well have been a mile of open sea, for all it mattered to me. I hovered at his shoulder, silent, pulling my arms around myself as if I could wring warmth out of my own bones.

"We're crossing here," he said. No question, no room for negotiation.

"Any particular reason?" My voice was a colorless monotone, scraped raw from cold and sleeplessness.

He spent a long moment chewing the inside of his cheek. "It's the only way forward. If we try to backtrack, we'll lose another day. Maybe more."

I saw the logic, but logic doesn't account for the way the river seemed to pulse, like it was hungry. The rocks that jutted from the water were wet and mossy, spaced just far enough apart to demand a leap of faith with every step.

It was a cartoon-trap: step, slip, crack your skull open, and wash downstream until your bones hooked on a logjam.

He set off, slow and deliberate, weight balanced forward. I watched him, hating the grace of his movement, the way his body seemed to anticipate the rocks' mutiny.

He made it halfway before he turned, beckoned with one flick of the wrist.

My cue. My doom.

I should have told him no. I should have screamed above the river that if he wanted to lead, he could just keep going, vanish into the wild, leave me to rot.

But I was so very tired of arguing, so even my defiance curdled into compliance. The rocks were slicker than glass. I could feel the vibration of the water through the soles of my shoes.

The first two stones were manageable, if insultingly small: just enough space for both feet, but already laced with a skin of ice. The river roared up around me, the sound a low, primal threat.

I had a moment of vertigo, a flash of the kayak—air, water, air, water—then nothing, the cold bloom of losing myself.

My body remembered. My body did not forgive.

"Keep going," Caiden called, his voice clipped, impatient, as if we were late for a train instead of inching across a deathtrap. "Don't overthink it. Just move."

I moved. My legs shook, the fatigue a mutiny of nerves and

sinew. Two more steps and I was within reach; he held his arm out like a lifeline made of thorns.

I reached, but our timing was off, and my shoe caught moss, then lost contact altogether.

For one weightless instant, I hovered, cartoon-like, suspended over nothing, before the world snapped back and I careened into the water.

It was not cold; it was a murder. The river slammed my ribs, knifed the breath out of me, and spun my body under with a violence that was almost personal.

My lungs tried to gasp but filled with wet. I felt my skull strike something hard, and for a second the world went black and red and black again.

My hands clawed upward toward what I thought was light, but my arms felt detached, as if they belonged to something already dead.

I kicked, or tried to. The current only sucked harder, greedy to keep me.

Then hands. A fist in the collar of my shirt, a bruising grip that wrenched me up and sideways, choking me on air and water and shame.

I caught a flash of Caiden's face underwater, warped and monstrous, then we broke the surface together, gasping and clutching at each other, both animals now.

He dragged me onto a rock shelf, half-hauling, half-flinging my body onto the moss. I convulsed, retching river and black spit, my vision flecked with static. His mouth was near my ear, voice a snarl: "What the fuck is wrong with you? I told you not to overthink it!"

He slammed his palm into my back, forcing the water out of me in a series of wet, wracking coughs. Each convulsion sent shards of pain up my throat; I tasted iron and moss and the raw bile of humiliation.

"Jesus, Amelia, you want to die out here? Because you're doing a hell of a job." His face hovered inches from mine, a mask of fury and fear. I could see the pulse hammering in his neck, the quiver in his jaw.

"No! I don't want to die. I'm weak, and it all happened too fast. You could have just let me drown."

For a second, I thought he might hit me, or kiss me, or kill me just to be done with it. Instead, he just stared, eyes so alive with contempt that I flinched away.

"I couldn't do that."

I didn't meet his eyes. "How heroic of you. Well... thank you. For pulling me out."

He huffed in response.

I tried to stand, but my knees buckled, sending me slumping to the wet stone. I tucked my hands under my ribs, hugging the ache, refusing to let him see how close I was to breaking.

He climbed up the bank, mud streaking his calves, and turned to watch my struggle.

I tried to follow, hands clawing at grass, legs trembling, nails splitting, until I finally crested beside him, lungs on fire, river water oozing from my nose and ears and every raw seam in my head.

When I collapsed in the mud, he didn't offer a hand. He just watched, silent, his face a sculpture of judgment and exhaustion.

Above us, the clouds had gone pale, drained of all color, a sky made of dead skin.

I lay there, cheek pressed to the muck, and tried to remember a time before this. Before the hunger, the endless walking, before the river and the pain, and Caiden's voice chiseling at the inside of my skull.

I couldn't. There was only now, only the cold ache in my ribs and the taste of rot in my mouth and the crawling shame of his eyes on me.

"Get up," he said, the words flat and empty.

I didn't move.

He squatted beside me, knees popping in protest, and for a second I thought I saw something like pity in his face. Not true pity, not the soft, saintly stuff for orphans and dogs, but a rougher version, the kind that's just a few molecules away from disgust.

"You break your head?" he asked. "Or are you just going to lie there until you drown in air?"

I rolled onto my back, blinking at the trees that swayed and smeared overhead, and let the silence hang between us. If I answered, I would cry, and I would rather die than let him see that.

I'd rather rot here in the moss and be eaten by foxes, let my bones melt into dust, let the blackness eat me from the inside out.

The only thing keeping me tethered was the hiss of his breath, the dull thump of his heart, or maybe it was just the echo of my own, too stubborn to quit.

He hovered at my shoulder, watching the microquakes in my chest, tracking the tremor in my jaw. I heard his breath, slow and almost thoughtful, as if he were letting the moment settle in before picking at it.

Then, almost gently, he wiped a smear of mud off my temple with his thumb. The motion was so alien it stunned me into stillness.

His touch lingered a fraction of a second too long, as if he didn't trust his own hands to let go.

Then he stood, hauled me roughly by the elbow, and set me upright. I wobbled, but stayed vertical. "Don't die. Not yet," he said, his voice low, almost a growl. "It's too much work to drag a corpse through the woods."

He looked away, jaw tight, and strode off the bank, leaving me alone with the echo of his touch and the cold shudder rippling down my spine.

I hated him for it. More than words, more than silence, I hated him for reminding me I was still alive enough to feel.

That night, the cold chill was still in my bones. The clattering of my teeth and the shivers in my body were enough to keep him awake.

I curled around the last embers of the fire, but nothing in this world could coax the warmth back into my body. Not the feeble flames, not the smothering layers of damp clothing that clung to me like a second, sodden skin.

The cold was an infection, a curse in my marrow, and I hated it as much as I hated who I was sharing it with.

Caiden threw a stick into the blaze, then considered me from across the orange chasm. His face was unreadable, all hard planes in the uncertain light.

I wouldn't meet his gaze, too busy cataloging my own failures: the crawling ache in my ribs, the moss still glued to my thighs, the snot leaking from my nose, which I wiped on the back of my sleeve like a child.

My breathing was off, shallow and fast, as if each inhale cost me something I didn't have to spend.

He leaned back on his elbows, tilting his head to the fractured sky. "You ever stop shaking, or is that a permanent feature now?" he asked, dry as a crypt.

I curled deeper, not dignifying it with an answer. My teeth clicked in reply, the only music the woods cared to provide.

I heard his footsteps crunching across the moss, but I didn't flinch. I let my teeth chatter, let my body shake and rattle itself to pieces. The only sound was the rasp of my own ragged breathing, a death rattle on repeat.

I wished I could quiet myself, dissolve into the mulch and moss, but I was trapped in my own stupid, useless flesh. I wondered if this was what dying was like: a slow, joyless undoing, every cell mutinying against the next.

Then his shadow blotted out the moonlight. He crouched over me, and for a moment I thought he might smother me with his hands, finish what the river had started.

I almost welcomed it. Better to be murdered by a man than by the indifferent cold.

Instead, he reached down and, with a violence that was almost gentle, hooked his arms under my shoulders and dragged me toward the fire. I wanted to snarl, to sink my nails into his face and scream, but I was too tired, too small.

He settled beside me, his back against a boulder, and pulled me up against his chest, locking my arms under his arms, pinning me to him with the patience of a python.

His body was an oven, every inch coiled with heat that radiated straight to my marrow. It was humiliating, the intimacy of it, the way I molded to the shape of him.

I tried to thrash free, but my limbs wouldn't obey. I was shivering so hard the world juddered in and out of focus.

"Stop fighting," he muttered, voice flinty and low. "You'll warm up faster this way." I could hear the effort in his throat, the way he ground the tenderness into something cruel. "Don't flatter yourself, it's like hugging a stiff, rattling corpse."

The heat unraveled me, cell by cell, the knots of cold unspooling into aches, then nothing. My breathing slowed. My teeth stuttered, then fell still. I felt the pulse of his heart in my back, a steady thud, and I tried to hate him for the way it steadied mine.

But I couldn't. All I could do was drift in the space between him and the fire.

# 29

## THE PAST

### AMELIA'S BREAKING POINT

I SPENT THE AFTERNOON CURLED ON THE SAGGING cushions of the old couch, the pages of my novel spread open in my lap.

Outside, the late-afternoon light filtered through dusty curtains, and inside, the hush of the empty house pressed against me.

I clung to each sentence, willing the words to hold off the shadows creeping at the edges of my thoughts. Then a hard, persistent knocking shattered the stillness.

My heart thundered as I shot upright. The couch groaned beneath me, its springs protesting after years of use. Who could possibly be out there?

Everyone who knew this place stayed far away, drawn to gossip about its history of sorrow, afraid of the restless darkness said to swirl behind its cracked wallpaper.

Swallowing hard, I rose and padded toward the front door, every step weighed down by dread and curiosity. The split-second before I opened it stretched into eternity; I felt the air thicken in my lungs.

Then I saw him.

Caiden stumbled into the threshold, the reek of cheap whiskey clinging to him like a second skin. His cheeks were flushed, his eyes wild and bloodshot beneath tangled hair.

The heavy door slammed behind him, and the sound rattled the plaster in the hallway.

He teetered forward, scowling, and I pressed back against the solid oak, my spine finding support in the cool grain.

"You bitch," he growled, voice ragged. "You're the reason I just lost my best friend." Heat radiated from him in pulses. I felt it against my chest, as if I stood too close to a flame.

My legs trembled, and I edged away, my back scraping against the doorframe.

I steadied my chin. "It takes two to end a friendship, Caiden. Blame Dante, not me."

He scowled deeper, brown eyes narrowing to dark slits. "No," he whispered, shocking me with the intensity. "I blame you."

My breath hitched as his fist rose, the knuckles knuckling like polished bone. Every nerve in my body screamed flight, but my feet rooted themselves to the floor.

Then, with a thunderous crack, his fist thudded into the wall beside me. Plaster dust rained down.

I closed my eyes against the impact, my heart lodged in my throat.

When I dared to open them, Caiden clutched his wrist, pale light glinting on fresh blood that dripped between his fingers.

Relief washed through me so hard it left me trembling.

He squeezed his eyelids shut and pressed his forehead into his palms. "Fuck! I can't do it. I'm not a piece of shit like my dad."

I blinked at the vulnerable tilt of his shoulders. He'd been so imposing a moment ago, an angry storm of muscle and menace, and now here he was, shrunken and shaking.

I remembered the rumors, the stories of a boy hardened by cruelty, wielding his rage like a weapon.

Yet in this raw moment, the armor cracked, revealing a frightened child longing for something he couldn't name.

His muttering drifted against my skin. My pulse hammered in my ears. Any word I spoke might ignite him again, but silence felt like an admission of guilt.

Without thinking, I lifted a hand and pressed it against his chest, feeling the rapid thud of his heart beneath my palm.

He jerked back as if I'd struck him. His eyes widened, confusion warring with rage. "What are you doing?" he whispered.

I swallowed around a dry throat. I wished I could explain how the story of his pain mirrored my own, how loneliness had become a shared language between us. "I don't know," I admitted, my voice small.

He ran a hand through his hair, dark brows knitting together. "I don't even know what the fuck I'm doing here."

Silence fell again. I could tell him to leave, that I feared what he might become, but he kept talking. "I told myself I wanted to hurt you, but I fucking can't. I'm an ass with my words, yeah, but I wouldn't ever hit a woman."

I exhaled, the tension in my chest loosening. "Because you're not your father. You're better than him, Caiden."

His jaw clenched. "What do you know about my father? What do you know about me? You don't know a damn thing."

I pressed my lips together, fighting down sudden panic. "I know enough. You're wounded by him. And I... I'm wounded, too. Not in the same way, maybe, but I understand pain."

His face twisted in a hopeless snarl. "I wouldn't even have these issues if it weren't for your druggie mom!" The accusation cut through me like shattered glass.

My pulse jolted. "My mom?"

He spat the words out, venom dripping from each syllable: "Your mom fucked my dad while my mom was still around, after your dad left. My mom found out and left. That's when my dad really let hell rain down on me. He turned into a drunk, abusive asshole. He blamed your mom for the failure of his marriage and burned it into my brain that I need to hate you. So, I learned to fucking hate you."

The air turned electric as the betrayal settled over me.

An affair. My mother's secret, now exposed in bitter confession. The walls of this house felt as if they were closing in, and I struggled to catch my next breath.

He saw the shock in my eyes and lashed out again. "Your mom is a whore, just like you and your sister!"

Pain flared in my chest, hot and stinging. Every part of me trembled with rage. "Fuck you!" I screamed, louder than I'd ever intended. My words reverberated off the hallway walls. "Get the hell out of my house! You're an abusive bastard just like your father, taking your anger out on people who don't deserve it."

He staggered back, shocked, and something like fear flickered across his face.

In that charged moment, I realized how close we'd come to

destruction, how thin the line was between his rage and mine. My own fury surged, a dam finally giving way.

For the first time since I'd known him, he looked small, cornered, vulnerable, empty behind the fury slashing across his face.

I kept coming at him, my voice a blade. "You're right, Caiden. My mom's a mess, and my sister's dead, and you're a wreck because your father broke you. But you don't get to use that as an excuse to make everyone else as miserable as you are. You're not the only one who's lost something."

He trembled, fingers twitching at his sides, blood still trailing down his hand. "No," he said, shaking his head, too forceful, as if he could send the words back inside me with sheer will.

"You want to blame me for everything? Fine. Do it. You want to hit me? Go ahead. But don't pretend you're not just a scared little boy who can't stand feeling powerless." I was screaming, flailing my arms like a woman gone mad.

Suddenly, he lurched forward, chest heaving, limbs rigid with a purpose even he didn't seem to understand. His body crowded mine, but it wasn't violence in his eyes now; it was something raw and pleading. "I *should* hate you," he whispered. "I should want to *kill* you."

But neither of us moved. The moment stretched dark and endless.

I was shaking, every muscle poised for flight, but I didn't move. I wanted him to hit me, to make it real, to give me a wound on the outside that would finally match the ones inside.

"Why don't you?" I challenged.

His face hovered a breath from mine, every line of his jaw clenching with the urge to destroy or collapse or both. I stared into his eyes, searching for the monster I'd always known and seeing only a wild, desperate ache.

For a heartbeat, we were suspended. Two wreckages circling the same fire, waiting for the spark.

He slammed his fist into the wall above my head, hard enough to vibrate the bones of the house, and every nerve in my body fired. "You want me to be like him?" he spat, words trembling. "You want me to prove you right?"

"Go ahead," I snapped back, "Ruin me. Finish me off. I'm a

corpse waiting to be buried at this point, rotten from your fucking torment."

I wanted him to bruise me. Bruise me so badly the ache would finally silence the endless, gnawing clamor in my skull.

He lunged, not with violence, but with hands tangled in my hair, mouth smashing against mine.

Fury sparked between our teeth. I bit down hard enough to taste blood, and he groaned, the sound animal, unguarded.

We tumbled, locked together, toppling to the floor as if gravity was stronger here, as if the house itself demanded our collision.

He pinned my wrists to the floor, face hovering just above mine, blood from his split lip falling hot onto my chin. "You're crazy," he whispered, voice hoarse. "You're fucking insane."

"So are you," I said, and he kissed me again.

I hated myself for letting him in; hated how my mouth met his with equal violence, how my teeth scraped his tongue, drawing out more blood and a guttural sound that was half agony, half pleasure.

We clawed at each other, not with longing but with the blind, animal need to destroy and punish, howling into the kind of kiss that tears at both souls and lips.

His hands pinned and then released, fingers knotting in my hair, jerking my head back so hard I gasped.

I hated him. I hated him so much my whole body vibrated with it, and in that moment, the hate felt electric, almost alive.

This was the only way we could forge our hatred into something physical and punishing.

The more I fought, the deeper he dug in, until my scalp ached from his grip and my jaw threatened to snap under the pressure of his mouth.

My legs thrashed for control, but he was heavier, meaner, and in some sick part of myself, I relished being overpowered, relished feeling something that wasn't numbness or sorrow.

"Is this what you want?" he spat, voice shattering on the question. "You want me to break you?"

He dragged his mouth down my neck, biting hard enough to leave marks, a necklace of bruises, dark as the thoughts that throbbed between us.

We thrashed on the hardwood, knocking into a small table. A lamp fell, glass shattering across the floor.

His hand slid up my shirt, nails raking, and I dug my fingers into the bite wound leaking across his jaw.

We were animals, gnashing at each other, neither willing to yield, neither wanting to win.

It was war, and we needed it.

He ripped my shirt at the collarbone, exposing a patch of skin just to inflict a new wound with his teeth. I wrested my arms free, raked my nails down the side of his neck, satisfied by the blooming red trails.

He pinned my thigh with his knee, ground his hips against me, and my body responded in a way that made me want to rip my own heart out.

I caught him with a knee to the ribs. He grunted, then retaliated by gripping both my wrists above my head, slamming them to the floor so hard I thought my bones would crack.

I writhed, bucked, spat curses, but he only tightened his hold, his face inches above mine, breaths fusing in a hot, angry fog.

"You want to hate me so bad, don't you?" His words were wet and ragged. "You want me to be the monster. Fine."

He bit down on my earlobe, hard enough to draw a shriek, and I twisted my hands until the skin tore at my wrists.

With a growl, he let go, yanking my hips up to meet his. We were pressed together. His sweatpants scrape against my bare skin, every point of contact a new place to fight, a new place to burn.

"Fuck you," I snarled.

He let go with a laugh, but it was the kind of laugh that sounded like a skull cracking. "You'd like that, wouldn't you?" he sneered, grinding his hips into me. His breath was hot and bitter at my ear, teeth sharp on the curve of my jaw. "I bet you're fucking wet for me right now."

The words scraped my skull raw, searing through the last of my resistance.

Hatred pooled between my legs. Of course he could feel it; of course he would use it to humiliate me, to win.

Rage and arousal tangled, a noose tightening at the base of my spine.

"You're disgusting," I gasped, jerking my head away, but his grip held, the pain chaining me to this moment.

He knelt over me, chest heaving, and shoved his hand between my legs, fingers pushing past the waistband of my shorts. He didn't ask, didn't hesitate, just pressed in, fingers grazing my most private area.

My breath snapped into fragments. I gasped, and he laughed, low and guttural.

"You see?" He whispered, nose brushing the curve of my jaw, his breath sour. "You fucking love this. You love when I break you."

The line between hate and want was a razor's edge, and I balanced atop it, desperate not to fall but already slipping.

I wanted obliteration. I wanted to be gutted and left to rot, because maybe then I'd feel something other than the endless, echoing ache.

But I hated him so much that my ribs ached, that my lungs starved for air. And that hate burned almost as bright as this hollowness within.

*I'm doing this for you, Lillian. I want to break him, for you. To hurt him, for you.*

In some parallel universe, this was an erotic movie scene, two beautiful people burning with forbidden passion; in this one, it was two rabid dogs locked together in a death roll, desperate to devour and outlast the other.

Shame spiraled through me, but it only fed the hunger. Hunger to feel something other than this bottomless grief.

I bucked my hips, nearly throwing him off. For a split second, he lost his grip. I seized the chance and brought my knee up, catching him in the thigh.

He swore, tried to pin me again, but I rolled us, straddling his chest, hands braced on his shoulders.

Our faces hovered an inch apart. Neither of us would back down; neither of us wanted to.

My nails dug into his collarbones, and his fingers bruised my waist. His eyes flickered wild, desperate.

I could see myself reflected there. Hair wild, cheeks flushed, lips split. I looked like prey. I looked like a monster.

His hands found my hair, yanked it so hard my scalp burned, and I gasped into his mouth, hating the sound, hating my body for turning against me.

Hate was better than sorrow. Hate was heat and movement.

"Fucking hate you," I spat, shoving my palm against his face, smashing his head back to the floor.

He laughed, a sound unhinged. "Not as much as I hate myself," he said, and bucked again, rolling us so he caged me beneath him, arms braced on either side of my head. He stared down at me, breathing ragged.

My chest heaved, and he just stared, eyes wild and wet and empty.

He just pressed harder, his hips rutting against me, friction building and building until my pulse blurred into a single, vibrating note.

It wasn't arousal; it was annihilation, the need to be ground down to nothing, to finally match the ruin of my insides.

"I could fuck you right here," he said, voice shredded, "and you'd let me. You'd beg for it."

I bucked against his palm, half in protest, half in surrender. "You don't get to have me," I hissed. "Not after what you did."

He began circling my clit in tight, brutal circles, thumb rough against the swollen ache of me, and everything sparkled behind my eyelids, black and glittering.

He hissed, "Filthy little bitch. You don't know what you want."

I tried to arch away, but he crushed my hips to the floor, fingers working at me with a violence that bordered on hatred.

"Fuck you," I gasped, but my own voice came out needy, traitorous.

My cheeks burned with shame, but I rocked against his hand anyway, desperate for the raw sensation, the punishment.

He pressed his palm harder, every nerve sparking white-hot, and I let a whimper slip.

The pressure, the heat, the need. It was all tangled up with grief and anger, a snarl of feelings so dense I couldn't breathe.

I just wanted to feel. In that moment, I forgot about the blame, the anger, the hatred. All I could think about was the sensation of his fingers on me.

My head felt like a crow's wing pinned behind glass, fluttering but hopeless: I was watching myself from very far away. A wet, sickly dream where shame and pleasure were the same color, the same temperature.

I remembered the way my mother used to say, *"A real woman*

*takes what she's given and makes it last."* Maybe that's what I was doing. Making this last, letting every second of it stake a claim inside me.

Caiden made a trail with his mouth towards my ear. "You already gave yourself away to my best friend. Don't pretend you're pure." He ground his hips against my thigh. "You're just a hole. Just like your mom. Just like your sister."

I arched and writhed and then bucked him off, my elbow slamming into his ribs.

He rolled, groaning. His eyes were glassy, unfocused, and wild.

I rolled away, my body burning, skin red and welted where he'd held me.

The whole room spun with anger and disgust, and for a moment, I thought I might throw up. The sight of my own trembling legs, the sticky ache between them, was almost too much to bear.

I thought of Lillian. I wondered if this was how she'd felt, in the final moments before she let go. Split and ruined, wanting to claw herself out of her own skin, the scream of being alive so much sharper than the silence of the grave.

I caught his stare, hateful and wounded. I wondered which one of us had gone further off the edge.

"Don't ever touch me again," I spat, the words raw and blistered from the inside.

This anger within me had bled into destruction.

He sat up, arms braced behind him, a menacing expression on his face. "You're no better than me, Amelia. We're the same fucking animal."

It stung because it was true, or close enough to make me sick. I felt the heat drain from my bones.

"Get out," I said, and the words came out as a frigid whisper. The cold in my voice startled even me. "You're drunk, and you shouldn't even be here."

Caiden's jaw spasmed. For an instant, I thought he might lunge for me again, smash the last of the furniture, put a fist through the television, maybe even put a fist through me.

But instead, he staggered up, legs faltering beneath him, a puppet with its strings sheared.

He didn't look at me as he stumbled his way down the hall, left a smear of blood on the white wall where his hand caught the corner, and slammed his palm twice against the entryway in an animal pulse of violence.

Then he was gone, hurtling through the door, clattering down the porch steps, and into the dying afternoon.

And I was left to deal with the aftermath of my destruction.

The world was a fizzled fuse, a scorched wire, the air still hot and trembling from the current that had passed through it. I lay crumpled on the floor, skin prickling with aftershocks.

My heart fluttered between arrhythmia and inertia, unsure whether to keep beating or surrender.

I traced the crescent cuts his nails left in my flesh, the bruises blooming along my thighs, and felt nothing. Not relief, not satisfaction, not even the expected horror. Just a bottomless emptiness and shock.

My sister's corpse barely cold, my mother evaporated into her bottle, the world already soiled and ruined, and here I was succumbing to my hatred for Caiden in the worst way.

Lillian would never forgive me. If she were watching from whatever secondhand heaven was left for girls like us, she'd spit in my face and call me a traitor. She'd see how easily I let the monster under my bed crawl in and make itself at home.

I wanted to be sick. I wanted to crawl out of my skin, scrape myself raw, leave my own body behind like a snake's old husk, and never look back.

I lay on the ground for a long time, cheek pressed to the splintered wood, waiting for the house to grow cold and for the ache in my limbs to fade.

It didn't. Nothing faded.

The aftermath of what I'd done, what I'd allowed him to do, pressed in harder than the act itself.

I was sick with it, drowning in it, swimming through a soup of regret so thick I feared I'd never claw my way out.

Maybe destruction was the only thing I was ever good at, turning hurt into hunger, swallowing the poison just to see if I could survive it.

My mind replayed the events with sickening clarity. A highlight reel of every gasp, every snarl. The more I tried to blank it out, the louder it became, until I wanted to bash my head against the porcelain just to make it stop.

I dry-heaved over the sink, but nothing came up. There was nothing left in me but acid and ghosts.

I was the architect of my own corruption. I watched the world burn and then poured accelerant on the ashes, desperate for a heat that could cauterize the wound where Lillian had been.

I'd let Caiden touch me. Let him use me, even for a second, and it was a humiliation so vast it eclipsed even the grave.

I wish it were simpler. We give in too easily to the things that are poison, chasing the need to feel better, to forget the pain. Even if that thing we give in to would inevitably destroy us. Even if, on some level of subconsciousness, we hate the thing we are falling into.

When the fire fades, that's all we have left, the darkness and the ache.

I had been gutted and hollowed and left to marinate in my own rot, and in the end, there was nothing but this: The stillness after a disaster, the silence that rings in the skull when the sirens are gone, and all the screaming has burned itself out.

# 30
## THE PAST

### AMELIA'S BREAKING POINT

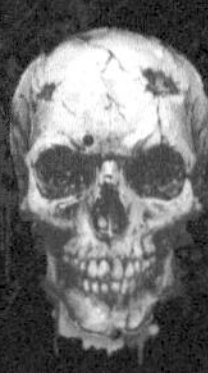

THERE ARE MOMENTS IN LIFE WHEN TIME HALTS, LEAVING one feeling more like a shell than a human being. I reached that point of bottomless emptiness when Lillian died, and now I was plummeting deeper than ever.

Sharing a rage-filled kiss with Caiden, a physical embodiment of our hatred. I remembered what came before it, his confession of a dark secret.

My mother was the reason Caiden's mother had left. A voice in my head whispered insistently that Caiden's mother didn't have to walk away. That was her choice. My mother hadn't forced her to walk through that door and never return.

But if she hadn't slept with Caiden's father, so much pain could have been avoided. I was sure it was my mother who came onto him. After my father left, she had entered a delicate state of mind, spiraling into a version of herself that felt like an utter stranger.

It wouldn't surprise me if she tried to fill the void left by my father with another man.

I tried to confront my mother. Her responses had been nothing but hollow defenses, words that echoed with insincerity.

"Where did you hear that?" she had asked, her voice defensive, as if that was the crux of the issue. Did it really matter where I had found out?

"Does it matter, Mom?" I shot back, my voice trembling with a mix of anger and hurt. "The point is that I know. You slept with someone else's husband! Now his son hates me." My heart pounded in my chest; each beat a reminder of the betrayal that felt like a knife twisting in my gut.

She shrugged, a dismissive gesture that only fueled the fire of my frustration. "That was a long time ago. I was grieving. Brian was there. It just happened. Not my problem that his boy is holding a grudge."

"Are you kidding me?" I exclaimed, disbelief flooding my veins. "Not your problem? This is completely your problem! You started a war between us and the Baxter boys." The words spilled out, a torrent of emotion that I had been holding back for far too long.

"Don't blame me for your battles," she retorted, crossing her arms defensively. "I am dealing with a lot, and I don't need your accusations. Now stop being such a brat!" Her eyes were cold and unwavering; a fortress built against my hurt.

Of course, she wouldn't acknowledge the chaos she had sown. What had I expected? "You're not the only one dealing with grief, Mom," I said, my voice softening, but edged with desperation. "I feel it too, and you are just making it worse by acting this way."

She waved her hand dismissively, a gesture that ignited a fire in my blood. "Leave this alone, Amelia. It is ancient history. I don't need this baggage from you." Her tone was final; a door slamming shut on any hope of reconciliation.

"Fine!" I shouted, my voice breaking with emotion. "But the pain and shame will catch up to you, Mom. When it does, I might not be here to help you through it!"

I turned on my heel, storming out of the room, disgust swirling in my gut for the woman who was supposed to be my mother, yet felt like a stranger instead.

I ached to talk, to pour this poison out of me. Dante had tried to reach me after that night, but I'd vanished.

Now, with desperation tightening my chest, I dialed his number on the faded cream phone in the hall. The ringing shot through the empty rooms like a distress flare.

"Hello?" His voice drifted over the line, distant and warm.

"Dante?" I held my breath.

"Amelia. Are you okay?" His tone was polite, too composed for the chaos I felt roiling inside.

"No." My voice cracked. I traced the chipped porcelain of a nearby vase with trembling fingers. "Can we meet at the park? I need... I need you."

He paused long enough for fear to coil in my gut. "Things got kind of crazy last time."

Tears pricked my eyes. "Please."

His exhale was a soft surrender. "All right. Our usual spot in thirty."

I hung up, heart pounding like a frantic drum.

Thirty minutes later, I sat on the bench beneath the sprawling oak, its ancient limbs creaking overhead. A chill breeze stirred golden leaves across the grass. My leg bounced, and my fingers drummed a restless rhythm on my knee. Each second stretched into an hour.

Then I saw him, striding down the winding path, shoulders squared against the wind. With every step, my pulse slammed harder against my ribs.

"Hey, Amelia."

His soft voice pulled me back from the brink of my spiraling thoughts. The warmth of his presence halted the rising tide of apprehension within me.

I melted when he settled close, his body radiating comfort like a soothing lullaby.

"I'm sorry." The words slipped from my lips, laden with agony.

"Were you just using me to hurt Caiden?" He wasted no time with pleasantries, diving straight into the heart of the matter. I had hoped he wouldn't ask, but Dante was no fool.

"I don't know," I whispered, fear constricting my chest. The truth would send him away, and I desperately wanted him to stay, to wrap me in his arms and be the security blanket that my inner child so craved.

"C'mon, Amelia. Please don't lie to me. I deserve the truth." His voice trembled, revealing the pain behind his words. I realized this was hard for him, too.

"I was upset about Lillian. I don't know. I needed someone to comfort me. To save me from my sadness."

"I can understand that. But I don't remember texting Caiden to come to my house. It makes me think you only wanted to sleep with me to get some sort of revenge on him." He paused, gathering his thoughts, then continued, "I've wanted to be with you for a while now. I like you a lot, Amelia. I wouldn't have texted Caiden, even while drunk, to come over and potentially ruin that night for us."

I felt tears welling up, a wave of sorrow crashing over me. I could feel him drifting away, lost in the fog of all the other people who had left my life.

I was terrible. How could I have done this to him? He had always been sweet. We could have had something extraordinary; he could have been my savior.

Yet, I had ruined it, blinded by my own grief and anger.

I wished I were in the ocean, where the waves could swallow me whole and pull me into the depths of oblivion.

He deserved the truth, even if it meant he would hate me forever.

"I do like you, Dante. I've wanted that too, with you. But my hatred for Caiden runs deeper than my affection for you, and it consumed me." I couldn't bring myself to meet his gaze. I simply couldn't.

"I know. I just wanted to be there for you in any way that I could. I hate what he has done to you, and I don't blame you for what you did."

He wasn't angry?

"You're not mad?" I echoed my surprise aloud.

He shook his head sadly. "I'm disappointed, but not mad. I understand. I just wish you could have talked to me instead of self-destructing and texting Caiden from my phone."

"I know. I'm sorry." The tears continued to flow, a relentless stream. He might not be angry, but the trust between us had shattered, and deep down, I knew we couldn't be friends after this. Perhaps it was for the best.

"I know your sister just died, and you're in a fragile state of mind. I understand, but I need to distance myself for my own happiness. Maybe when things are better, we could try again."

This was it. He was making the speech. I wanted to pull him closer, to beg him to adore me. But another part of me wanted to shove him away, to make it easier for him to leave.

I shut my eyes, battling the conflicting emotions within me.

"Okay. I understand." I struggled to stifle my sobs. Another abandonment. Who did I have left?

My ghosts followed me like sinister shadows; perhaps that was all I had left.

Suddenly, his hand was on my chin, gently pulling my face toward him. I opened my eyes to find his gaze filled with sadness and affection, pain and conflict swirling together.

He leaned in, and I instinctively did the same. When our lips met, it was soft and delicate like feathers brushing against my skin.

The kiss lingered, both of us savoring the moment, the beauty of it flooding through me like a warm embrace. Memories of happiness and safety replayed in my mind like a hazy dream.

I could have experienced that every day. It could have been mine, but I had fallen into the trap of despair. The trap of vengeance and sin. The trap of overwhelming grief.

*But would it really have worked out?* A voice in my head pushed its way in. With the death of my sister, I would not have been able to maintain a stable relationship. A part of me understood that. But it was nice to imagine.

He pulled back, staring deeply into my eyes, searching for something that was no longer there. Then, he looked away.

"I'll see you later, Amelia. Take care of yourself."

He stood and walked away, leaving me on that bench, my lips still tingling from the kiss. My heart ached with an immense weight. I couldn't share the information I had learned about my mother with him; he didn't deserve that burden.

"Bye." My voice barely reached him, lost in the wind, as he faded into the distance.

Goodbye, my almost lover.

# 31
## THE PRESENT
### AMELIA

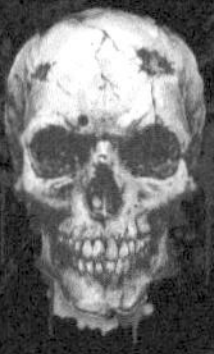

I FELT MYSELF MORPHING INTO A WANDERING GHOST. My limbs moved as if they were no longer my own, each step a laborious effort.

I could feel my weakened heartbeat thumping in my chest, a dull reminder of my existence.

I could see the trees looming around me, yet I did not feel alive. Everything was slow and hazy, the world blurring into a confusing fog of shapes and shadows.

Caiden's pace was weakening bit by bit, his earlier bravado and playfulness dwindling as fatigue set in.

We hadn't spoken about the intimacy of the day I almost drowned in the river, how he saved me, and how he held me to his chest that night to warm me up. He held me all throughout the night, because when I had woken up, his arms were still locked around me.

We were running on adrenaline alone now, our bodies weakened by hunger and strained muscles. The unbearable weight of our situation pressed down on us.

A gnawing pain twisted in my gut, a relentless ache that wouldn't vanish. It felt like something was eating away at my insides. I had never experienced hunger like this, not even on those nights when my mother would forget to make dinner.

Back then, at least I had some choices, even if I still went to bed with my stomach growling.

The hunger I felt now was debilitating, a raw, visceral reminder of my fragility. I now understood the expression of being so hungry you could eat anything.

We had managed to find some fresh water a few times, a small mercy that kept us from completely succumbing to despair. But it wasn't enough.

Almost as if it were a gift from the heavens, Caiden broke the silence, beckoning me over to where he stood a few paces ahead.

Dragging my feet, I stumbled to where he was, my heart momentarily lifting at the prospect of discovery. He pointed to a bush, excitement flickering in his tired eyes.

"Berries," he announced, his voice tinged with a hope I hadn't felt in days.

"Berries?" I echoed, joy bubbling up in me.

Without wasting another second, we both began picking the ripe, round berries, tossing the sweet morsels into our mouths one by one. The taste burst on my tongue, a refreshing jolt that was like a glass of lemonade on a sweltering day.

I could feel life returning, if only for a moment.

But in our elation, we didn't notice the presence that had silently joined us until it was too late.

A deep growl reverberated through the clearing, cutting through the haze of our momentary bliss. We both froze, our instincts kicking in.

Caiden looked first, and then I followed, my mind struggling to process the threat looming before us.

The black bear lifted its massive head, sniffing the air, its beady eyes glinting like the moon on a foggy night. The sight of such a powerful creature sent shockwaves through my body.

I knew black bears were less of a threat than brown bears, but they were still dangerous when cornered. If we stayed still and didn't make any sudden movements, we might be okay.

That's what I hoped. Helplessly.

The creature advanced, inching closer, its musty scent invading my senses. My heart raced, pounding against my chest as it drew nearer.

Just when it seemed the bear would turn away, a small creature scurried beneath us, rustling through the leaves. The bear swiveled its head, catching sight of us, letting out a low, territorial growl.

That's when the panic settled in.

Before I could register what was happening, Caiden pushed me aside, darting into the shadows of the nearby bushes.

The force of his weight sent me sliding toward an opening, leaving me exposed in the bear's line of sight.

I didn't have time to feel hurt by Caiden's actions. The raw fear of staring at the bear, feeling as if my chest were about to explode, was the only thing I could focus on.

I've heard there are two types of people in situations like this: those who take flight and those who fight. Caiden was clearly the type who ran. But me? I was neither.

My legs were numb, my feet glued to the ground, paralyzed by fear.

What would they call that? Freeze mode?

To my relief, a noise came from the opposite direction. The bear turned its head, lowering its snout to the ground as it sniffed, then walked away.

It probably realized I was no threat. Or maybe it sensed how deprived of meat I was; any fat on my body had withered away, leaving only flat skin.

Whatever the reason, it wasn't interested. Not anymore.

In that moment, Caiden crept out from the bushes, and my face fell into an angry scowl as I unleashed the stress I had just endured.

"I can't believe you left me!" I shouted, pushing against his chest in a fit of rage. "You left me to die so you could save yourself! Just when I thought you had a soul, you found a way to disappoint me."

"I know," he replied, the weight of guilt lingering in his tone. "I wasn't thinking. I was desperate not to be mauled to death!"

"So, you decided I should be mauled instead?" My voice dripped with venom, and I could feel the anger coursing through my veins.

This was the Caiden I remembered, the selfish coward, the boy I loathed completely. A tiger can't change its stripes, and neither could he.

"That wouldn't have happened!" he snapped back, frustration evident in his eyes. "Once I got over the panic, I remembered that black bears are the least likely to attack for no reason."

"Well, you realized that a little too late!" I shot back, my voice rising. "You left me exposed in front of a predator that sees human beings as prey. We are in their territory, that's more than enough reason to attack."

I was still shouting, overcome by a whirlwind of emotions. I couldn't stop them; I couldn't control them. They were coming at me full force, feeding off my panic-stricken adrenaline.

"I know. I'm sorry."

Caiden's voice softened, and he didn't meet my eyes. I felt that he was only apologizing to make me shut up.

"Oh, now you want to apologize? Where was your apology when you impregnated my sister and led her to kill herself? Where was your apology after all the cruel things you did and said to me? Huh?" My throat was becoming hoarse from screaming at him.

"I don't need you throwing that in my face right now. Yes, that was all messed up, but don't you toss that at me. You're not all that innocent either."

"I don't know why you can't just take accountability. I wouldn't have had to act out if you didn't bully me into insanity! But of course, you must control the narrative like always," I paused, and he only stared at me, a muted expression on his face. My voice dropped to a whisper. "You might be strong on the outside, but you're weak on the inside. Terrified of allowing yourself to feel or deal with anything. Because if you do, you'll break."

The silence that followed was sharp, biting like ice. We stared at each other, heaving, layered with intense ferocity.

"We should keep moving," Caiden finally said.

Just like that, with one sentence, he shut the door to that conversation, not allowing anything else to slip through into the open, shoving it back into the dusty dark.

We had been getting along a few days ago without any rude remarks or insults, but the days were stretching, and we were withering.

Our malnourished and sleep-deprived state of minds were causing us to turn on each other like feral beasts.

I hoped that we would be rescued before we sank our claws into each other any deeper.

If we wanted to live, we would have to swallow our pride and forget the festering feud that had divided us for so long. But I wondered if it was even possible, given how vulnerable and unwell we were becoming in the unforgiving wilderness, becoming as fragile and cold as the biting wind.

Despair was a slow rot as we continued wandering, and it seeped into everything. The color of the sky, the taste of the air, the way Caiden's voice scraped along my nerves whenever he spoke

We moved on, because that was all we could do.

Forward, forward, until there was no world left to walk through.

I counted steps in my head. One hundred, two hundred. Just to force time to pass.

I thought about all the ways we could die out here: a twisted ankle, a bear's teeth, a slow bleed from the inside out. I wondered which would be quickest, which would leave the fewest regrets.

It should have ended with the bear. It should have ended with the black tongue of the river. It should have ended so many times, but every morning I woke, pressing my face to the filthy sleeve of my jacket, and the forest pressed back, unmoved, undefeated.

Life clung to me like a parasite, and I hated it almost as much as I hated the boy who limped two paces ahead of me, refusing to look back.

I was bone-tired, delirious, running mostly on spite and the scorched memory of every time Caiden had ever wronged me.

Darkness settled in layers. Grief bloomed beneath the cold moonlight. Despite Caiden's presence, I felt undeniably alone. Was it inevitable for us to end up like this? Drenched with remnants of our anger, forced to survive together and not break? Doomed to hate each other and die with each other?

A shadowed presence pressed close to my side. Was it Lillian? Or some other fragment of loss? The black woods shivered around me, and the trees went on and on.

These days, my heart was quiet, like chalk ground down to dust. The shudder of unseen things dragged their hunger through the dark, preying on our exhausted minds.

Time dissolved into fog out here. Bleeding through a haze of our decay. The dark watched us, almost mockingly. I looked closely into the dark, seeking some sort of light. Some sliver of hope. Aching and waiting for a glimpse of something soft.

Nothing moved but the haunt. Nothing answered but the dark. Always. My head pulsed with black static. A scream rose up my throat, but never left the bone.

I was beginning to lose sight of myself, of my hatred, of Caiden, of civilization.

All warmth became memory. Scattered in the ghost-light of the dark. The starless sky was no comfort, cascading like a beastly creature.

The ache of what does not return is spun into the marrow of night. An absence so deep like black water in the bones of winter.

I looked towards the sky.

*Is this how you felt, Lillian? When you slipped away? Empty and alone?*

I thought of my mother. How she might be feeling right now. Would she be cold and lonely too? Would she be wrapped up in her drugs right now? Does she think of me? Or her dead daughter?

*I wish you would come back, mommy. But you won't. And neither will I. Neither will Lillian. Both of your daughters are lost to the darkness, just like you.*

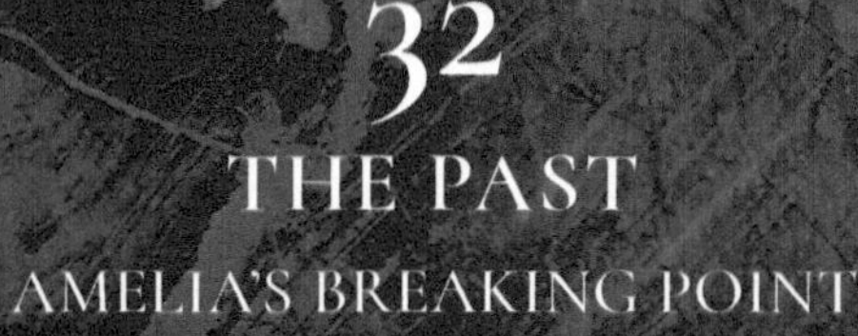

# 32
## THE PAST
### AMELIA'S BREAKING POINT

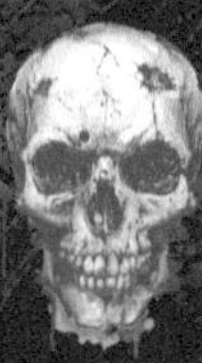

It was graduation day. I stood outside my mother's room, my knuckles poised to knock on the door, but hesitation lingered in the air like a storm cloud.

Tension had thickened between us over the past few days, festering ever since I confronted her about the secret that had come to light.

I approached cautiously, my hand reaching out to touch her shoulder. She flinched at my touch, as if I had startled her from a trance, and the photo slipped from her fingers, clattering against the floor. I caught a glimpse of Lillian's face, frozen in a moment of joy that felt impossibly distant.

"What?" she snapped.

I instinctively recoiled, retracting my sympathy like a wounded animal. For a fleeting moment, I had hoped for a tender word, a flicker of kindness to bridge the chasm that had grown between us. But my hopes sank, drowned in the weight of her indifference.

"Are you coming to my graduation?" I asked, my heart racing with a mix of anticipation and dread.

Her gaze remained fixed on the wall, avoiding mine as if it held some unbearable truth. A sense of dread coiled in my stomach. Was she under the influence of something? Her eyes had a glazed, distant look, as if she were peering into another realm.

She blinked slowly, as if my words took time to reach her. "No, I cannot make it."

A stone dropped within me, sinking deep into the pit of my gut. I had hoped that, despite the grief consuming her, she would want to witness her last daughter's milestone.

I was alive, breathing, yet she seemed utterly indifferent to my existence.

Disappointment crawled into the air between us, erecting walls that felt insurmountable.

"Why do you have to be like this, Mom? I'm graduating; this is huge! You don't even want to support me?" My voice trembled with pent-up frustration.

She clenched her jaw, the muscles taut, before turning away and walking toward the window, a familiar retreat. She had taken to staring out that window more often lately, lost in a world beyond the glass.

"I do not want to go anywhere, Amelia. I lost my daughter; I need time." Her voice was hollow, echoing the void that had replaced her warmth.

Fury ignited within me. Yes, her daughter was dead, my sister was dead. But I was here, alive, and desperate for her acknowledgment.

"Cut the bullshit, Mom. I'm grieving too, but I'm still living my life. I'm alive, and I'm right here, but you don't seem to care!"

My voice, once strong, quivered and cracked, the pain clawing at my heart. It hurt to know that my mother had become a ghost, haunting our home but never truly present. Nothing would ever pull her from the depths of her fragile mind, which seemed to be unraveling.

She turned to face me, her eyes finally meeting mine. "Yes, you are alive. But Lillian was my firstborn."

In that moment, clarity washed over me like a cold wave. I was worth more than the faint echo of my mother's love.

Lillian had always held the favored position in my mother's heart, even as her life spiraled downward into a world of drugs and despair. In the days leading up to Lillian's death, my mother had hardly spoken to her.

I realized that if you truly loved someone, sometimes the best course was to let them be. Just as Dante had left me, though I doubted he had ever really loved me at all.

Someday, she will come back to me. I thought, clinging to a fragile hope that my mother would eventually recognize that her other daughter still existed, still yearned for her affection. I had to believe that; otherwise, despair would swallow me whole.

"Well, Mom, if you have a change of heart, I'll be graduating and stepping into a new chapter of my life. It seems you won't be a part of it." My voice was steady, but the words cut like glass.

Turning away, I walked out of the room, silent tears streaming down my cheeks. Each drop felt like a dagger, piercing the heart of our fractured relationship. The ache of having a mother who couldn't even bear to witness my graduation was a wound that cut deep.

Did she even love me? The question echoed in my mind like a haunting refrain.

I felt like the corpse of a butterfly, my once-vibrant wings now tattered and attached to weary bones. If I floated in an unforgiving sea, it would swallow me whole, dragging me beneath the surface into darkness where no light could penetrate.

As my thoughts drifted back to Lillian and her graduation day, a day filled with laughter, pride, and celebration, an unbearable weight settled within me.

My mother had been there then, smiling, a radiant presence. We had gone out for dinner afterward, a night that felt like a lifetime ago, lost in the shadows of grief.

I collapsed onto my bed, the graduation photo staring back at me. That day felt as distant as a dream long forgotten, a million years adrift in the past.

My mother had failed to keep her promise, and Lillian, sweet Lillian, had chosen to drop out, an act that spiraled into her fateful decision to sleep with Caiden.

The fallout had been catastrophic: a pregnancy that ended in tragedy, leaving her lifeless, a ghost of what could have been.

I gulped hard, choking on the tears that threatened to spill over. I longed for her presence, to hear her voice echoing in my ears, telling me how proud she would have been.

Today, I felt utterly alone. A part of me resisted the idea of attending the ceremony, yet I knew I had to go.

Most of my relatives had turned their backs on us, a direct result of my mother's choices. In that moment, a deep-seated resentment stirred within me. She had not only ruined her life but had also shattered ours.

"Catch a star, Amelia, and make a wish," she used to whisper as she tucked me in at night, her voice a soothing balm to my restless heart. I closed my eyes and finally made that wish.

*Please, get better.*

I ached for the days when she had been a mother, before my father's departure splintered our family.

As I drifted deeper into memory, I found myself lost in an innocent day filled with doves and laughter.

*"Look, Mommy! I am flying!" I shouted, soaring high on the swing, my legs swinging wildly, hair dancing in the warm breeze. She had laughed, her joy lighting up the afternoon, as she snapped a photo with her camera.*

*"You are flying, Amelia! Smile for me, sweetheart," she had encouraged, her voice ringing with pride. I grinned widely at the camera, my happiness radiating like sunlight.*

*I hopped off the swing, my excitement propelling me toward Lillian, who was giggling and playing with another girl on the playground set. "Mommy, can I play with them?" I had asked, my eyes sparkling with anticipation. She nodded, her smile reassuring, but cautioned me to be careful. Lillian showed me the game they were playing.*

*"Okay, Amelia, slide down the slide and then crawl back up," she instructed, her enthusiasm infectious.*

*I stared at the slide, confusion clouding my mind. How could I climb back up? But I wanted to be like Lillian, so I nodded eagerly. "Okay!"*

*With a rush, I slid down the smooth surface, the exhilaration stealing my breath. I stood on my short legs, determined to scramble back up, but gravity had other plans. I tumbled back onto the soft mulch, huffing in frustration. Lillian rushed over, offering her hand. "It's not for everybody," she said gently, her eyes twinkling with empathy.*

*My mother had watched us closely, engaged in conversation with another woman. "Stay close!" she had yelled to her son, who was kicking a ball around with a few other boys. He looked to be my age, his golden hair glimmering in the sunlight. I couldn't help but wonder if I would see him when I started school in a year.*

*"Is Daddy coming to meet us?" I asked, my heart fluttering with excitement. But her response had crushed my hopes. "No, sweetheart. He's busy." The words weighed heavily on me, the realization sinking in that he was not coming. But I brushed it aside, determined to return to the carefree spirit of play with Lillian.*

It was a nice tradition. We would go to the park on Saturdays to play, then go to lunch and have ice cream.

I remember thinking, I never wanted this to end. But it did end, all of it, and soon, it was nothing but a fading memory lost within the changing wind.

All my tears had dried. Lillian should be here, but she was not here. Flipping through memories in my head, I felt as if I were drifting within a cosmic graveyard of sorrow.

It was pointless, hopeless. Reminiscing would not bring her back. I could still imagine her body, lifeless and pale.

I felt shivers run through my spine. Is she here? Could she see me? Was she proud?

Grief was an odd thing; one moment a quiet whisper, the next a deafening roar. A numbness washed over me, my mind a chaotic jumble of everything but my sister's death, the chirping of crickets, the smell of rain, the distant sound of traffic.

The pain was so debilitating on some days that I questioned whether I had the strength to continue. Sometimes, the thought of joining Lillian seemed tempting; we could be angels together, free from the chains of sorrow.

*Would I ever escape these chains?*

I must stay strong. I had to muster courage; Lillian would want me to thrive, not to cry. Yet, when the lights dimmed, all that remained was a desolate bleakness, silence swarming around me like an unwanted shroud.

Her smile haunted my dreams. I sometimes thought I saw her outside my window, a fleeting glimpse of the sister I had lost.

With a sigh, I moved toward my closet, pulling out my graduation attire. I slipped into a simple knee-length white dress and a pair of heels, then draped my robe over my shoulders, hesitating to place the cap atop my head.

It all felt surreal. Despite everything I had endured in the past few years, I had made it. I had done this on my own, without my mother's support. She had chosen her drugs over me, sinking into the depths of a restless loch from which I could not rescue her.

There were moments I wanted to give up. But I didn't. I had survived, and I was damn proud of that.

Yet I still yearned for Lillian. I needed my big sister, but she was long gone.

As I approached her door, I peeked inside once more. She lay on her bed, eyes closed, lost in sleep. I snorted derisively. Typical. She would rather catch up on rest than witness her daughter graduate.

Turning away, the dejection hung heavily in the air. A growing sadness clawed at me. I wanted my mom back, to see her cheer and clap as I received my diploma.

But that moment was lost to me. This only happened once, yet there was no support to be found.

This would likely be one of the last times I would see Caiden, and strangely, that thought brought me a glimmer of happiness.

I was tired of living in fear and grief; it was an exhausting existence. When I finally left, I would leave all my memories behind. A fresh start, devoid of anguish, worries, and visions of death.

I paced back and forth outside my mother's room, glancing inside Lillian's once more. The room, stripped bare and covered in sheets, felt like a ghost town. Dust collected in the corners, and a shiver crawled down my spine.

Home no longer felt like home. It felt like a graveyard, a mausoleum for my lost loved ones.

In the moments leading up to my departure, I wrestled with my emotions, caught between wanting her to be there and knowing I lacked the words to express it.

Eventually, I surrendered to the moment and left.

The school parking lot brimmed with families, laughter, and excited chatter swirling around me. My heart sank a little, a bitter tang of jealousy rising like a dark shadow within me.

I imagined my sister crawling from the grave, running toward me with open arms, or my mother arriving to mend my shattered heart.

But they were mere daydreams, and the reality deepened my pain. I craved belonging, familiarity, and love.

Yet, with every breath I took, that hope withered.

After shoving my way through the crowd, scowling at mothers and daughters who seemed so blissfully unaware, I finally reached the designated area.

As the moment arrived for us to line up toward our seats, cameras flashed, and names were called out. Various speeches filled the air, some inspired me, while others left me bored.

Finally, they began calling names. It felt like an eternity under the sun, its rays beating down on us mercilessly.

When my name finally echoed across the field, a wave of mixed emotions washed over me. Some people cheered, some clapped, but there was no excitement in their actions that resonated with me.

I scanned the crowd, hoping to spot my mother, but there was nobody there who cared about me.

For a fleeting second, though, I thought I saw Lillian's face among the throng, staring blankly at me. The same sensation I had felt outside her room washed over me.

As the principal congratulated me, I thanked him and descended the steps.

My eyes found Caiden's. I held my head high, attempting to project strength, as if to prove I didn't need anyone.

But it was all a façade. My mother's absence mattered. It mattered deeply.

This could be the last time I saw Caiden.

After today, everything would change. But I couldn't settle for peace without confronting him.

I had to say something; I had to see if he felt even a hint of remorse. He was human; he had feelings. He must feel something.

I was a tiger, restless and tense, my breath hot in the confines of the cage, poised to spring.

Eventually, the ceremony concluded. People dispersed, uniting with families and friends, but I remained alone.

I searched frantically for Caiden, pushing my way through the dense throngs of graduates and their jubilant families, each step propelled by a potent mix of grief, pain, and simmering anger.

Memories surged like a relentless tide.

Finding Lillian's lifeless body, witnessing my mother slipping into her own abyss of despair, and enduring years of torment at Caiden's hands.

Finally, I spotted him, isolated from the laughter and chatter of a few friends. An opportunity presented itself; he was alone and unaware, and I felt like a predator zeroing in on my prey.

"Caiden!" I shouted, my voice slicing through the cacophony like a blade.

He turned, his features clouded with confusion as I closed the distance between us, my stride fueled by determination and raw emotion.

"What's wrong with you, huh?" I demanded, shoving his chest with trembling hands, my entire body shaking with a volatile cocktail of rage and despair.

"Fuck off, Amelia," he replied, his tone dark and dismissive, but I refused to back down.

"Are you really going to leave without saying sorry? You killed my sister, and you have nothing to say?" My words were accusing, each one a dagger aimed at his conscience.

"Sorry for what? She did that to herself," he retorted with chilling indifference.

"Oh, really? What about all the times you bullied me?" My voice rose to a scream, oblivious to the stares of those around us, the bystanders who had become an unwitting audience to my unraveling.

He sighed, rubbing his face with an air of exasperation, as if I were nothing more than a bothersome fly.

"I don't know what you're looking for, Amelia," he said, his words void of any trace of remorse.

"God forbid King Caiden looks weak in public. How about you go to my sister's grave and admit you messed up?"

"I'd rather not," he replied, his tone casual and indifferent.

I searched his eyes for any flicker of regret, any sign that he felt something, anything. Surely, he couldn't be that heartless.

"You're an asshole," I spat, my voice raw with emotion.

"Yeah? And you're an annoying bitch," he shot back, his expression remaining as blank and emotionless as a stone.

"If you feel that way, then why did you kiss me and touch me that day when you were drunk? When you showed up at my house."

I was shaking with fury as I stared him down.

Caiden snapped his head towards me. "You want to know why? I wanted to test my hatred for you, and I wanted to see what Dante saw in you. I wanted to see why the fuck he thought you were worth ruining his friendship with me. I wanted to fucking ruin you, to break you."

"Did it work?" I asked.

"Yeah. I do fucking hate you. I don't know why the fuck Dante likes you and why he risked it all to be with you." Caiden stared at me with an expression of pure deadliness and rage.

"I hope you rot," I whispered, my words carried away on the wind like a forlorn wish.

"Real mature, Amelia," he said with a sneer, turning to walk away.

"Don't you walk away from me!" I screeched, my voice cracking with fury.

In a fit of desperation, I tore off one of my heels and hurled it at him, following suit with the other, heedless of the wide-eyed stares from the growing crowd.

I must have looked like a woman unhinged, a spectacle of raw emotion laid bare.

"Piece of shit!" I yelled, watching him disappear into the sea of people, my shoes lying abandoned and dirty on the ground.

In that moment, I blamed him for everything.

I hadn't received my apology, and now I felt like a fool –
Barefoot and humiliated.

My last shred of dignity lay in walking through the crowd without collapsing into a whirlwind of tears.

It hurt to know he didn't care enough to say sorry. It hurt that my mother wasn't here to comfort me, to assure me that everything would be okay.

What was wrong with him? Could he be the devil in disguise?

I left the school, refusing to look back. Instead of driving home, I headed to the park near my neighborhood. Once free from his presence, the weight of my actions settled on me.

"Why do I always do that?" I muttered to myself, feeling pathetic as I sank beneath a tree. I watched the swings sway in the wind, creaking with emptiness, like the void inside me.

I didn't cry. I thought I would, but nothing came.

"I'm sorry, Lillian," I whispered, feeling like I had let her down. I couldn't even manage to extract an apology from Caiden.

Perhaps if my mother had apologized, Lillian would have returned home, and we wouldn't be trapped in this dismal reality.

Her spirit would always haunt me, her voice echoing in my dreams.

Closing my eyes, I let myself drift away like a leaf. In this moment, I longed to run alongside wolves, feeling connected to their souls as they searched for a place to call home. I wished to soar with doves, to flutter my lovely feathers.

I wished to be anywhere but here.

I could leave and forget all of this. Caiden would become a lost memory. Who cared if he didn't care? All that mattered was right here, right now. Everything had happened, and I could not control the stitches of time.

My sister was dead; there was a hole in my heart, and my mother may as well have been dead too. I wondered what she was doing, perhaps sitting by her window, lost in her drugs? I envisioned driving up to my house, seeing her haunted reflection in the glass.

Sitting there, I cleared my head and sank into a warm paradise.

I would survive. I would thrive. I repeated the mantra to myself. Caiden did not matter. Nobody was to blame. I had to keep telling myself that; otherwise, I would be pointing fingers for the rest of my life.

The thought of Caiden made my blood boil, but I had to release that anger if I wanted to live a happy, stable life.

Hatred was like love, yet the opposite. It's an intense, blazing sensation that bubbled within and consumed.

Love illuminated like a star, making you a better, happier person.

Hatred was a swirling, maddening darkness, a never-ending storm. They were opposites, yet they sat side by side, balanced on a thin line, ready to collide.

Hatred is as fragile as crackling fire or thin glass. It burned and built, capable of breaking you.

In the wrong hands, it spiraled out of control, igniting a need for revenge.

It was acceptable to hate those who tormented you, bullied you, and made your life miserable.

One thing I knew was that karma existed.

Someday, Caiden would reap what he had sown. He would feel the same pain and hurt I had endured. And when that day arrived, I would finally find peace, content in the knowledge that he hadn't won. That he had felt the same anguish I carried.

My consuming hatred would never fade, even beyond death, for like love, hatred lasted an eternity.

I stood up, smoothed my dress, and drove back toward home, a shadowy silhouette against the brightness of the day.

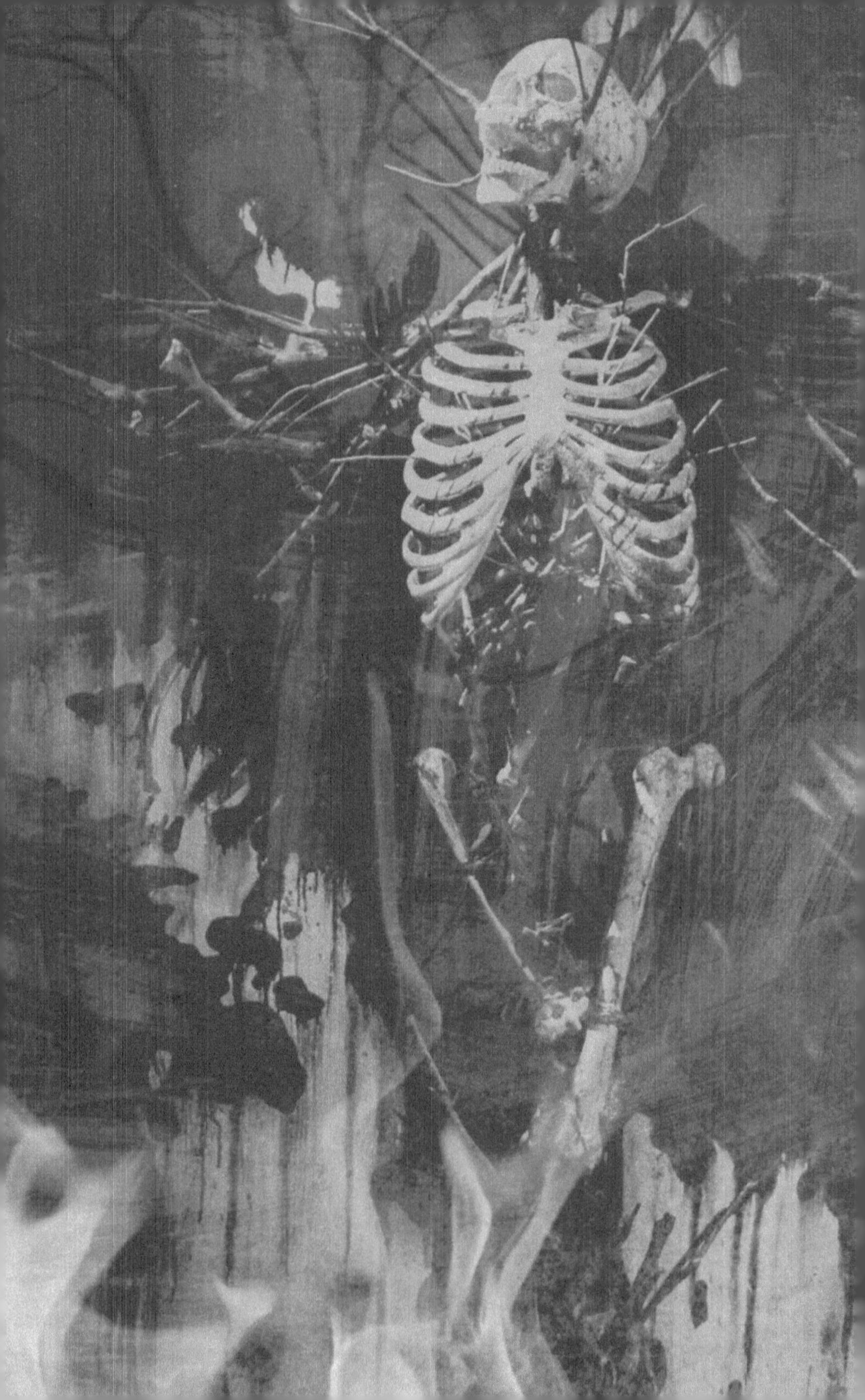

# 33

## THE PRESENT

### AMELIA

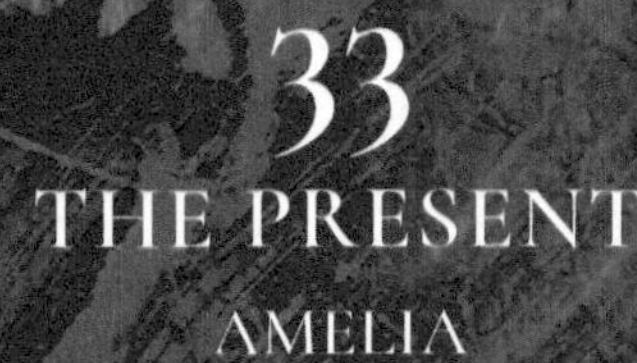

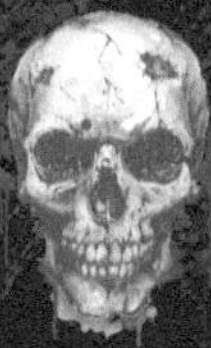

I saw my dead sister today.

We were wandering through the suffocating thickness of the woodland, shadows creeping closer as dusk settled in. A shape flickered at the edge of my vision.

Lillian stood there, hauntingly familiar yet engulfed in an emptiness that sent chills down my spine. I waited for her to speak, but the only sound was the lamentable tone of silence, echoing in the stillness between us.

My insides swarmed, churning with a mix of longing and despair, while the outside of my body remained frozen in place. I couldn't pry my eyes away from her face, so desperately familiar.

When I finally turned to Caiden, my voice trembled with fear. "Do you see her? Lillian? She's right there."

His expression shifted, confusion clouding his features. He looked at me as if I had slipped into madness.

Maybe I had.

That was hours ago, and her face still danced around in my mind, a haunting specter, killing me quietly.

I caught Caiden's eyes darting around, and I wondered if he was hallucinating too.

We hadn't eaten a proper meal in days. A human could only go for so long without food before the body began to shut down, and I felt myself teetering on that precipice.

The trees loomed like ominous shadows, their gnarled branches clawing at the sky. Every rustle sent waves of panic surging through me, as if danger lurked in every corner, waiting to pounce.

I felt the shadows of the past prowling around me, a blend of reality and fractured fragments of my mind, leaving me struggling to discern what was real.

Time stretched into an eternity as we wandered this wilderness. I could feel myself collapsing in on itself, deteriorating slowly. Agony filled my senses; I could hardly focus on putting one foot in front of the other.

*Smack.*

I found myself face down in the damp earth, my limbs sprawled like a weary corpse. It felt as if someone had amputated my legs, and I momentarily wondered if I still possessed them.

Caiden must have realized I was no longer behind him, as two pairs of legs filled my blurred vision.

"What happened?" He knelt beside me, irritation flaring in his eyes as if my falling had inconvenienced him.

"I fell," I managed to croak, a hint of defiance creeping into my voice.

He scoffed, his tone sharp. "I can see that. Did you trip over something? I don't see anything."

Did I trip? The dissociative haze had made a nest within my head, everything swirling into a confusing blur. I knew I had been walking, but my legs felt like lead weights, dragging me down.

"I think I just fell. From exhaustion."

Caiden huffed, and I couldn't help but wonder how he was still standing, still going.

Mentally, I had given up hours ago. There was no light at the end of the tunnel. When I thought about returning to civilization, I envisioned myself in a body bag, buried beneath the ground.

"Yeah, I'm exhausted too. We really need to find food," he said, frustration lacing his words.

I pulled my dirt-covered face up to peer at him, and the sight of his hollow expression sent a shiver down my spine. His brown eyes, usually warm, now appeared deadened.

Golden hues eclipsed by dread.

"Good luck with that," I murmured tiredly, letting my head fall back against the cool earth. A steep heaviness weighed down my eyelids, and I closed my eyes, welcoming the darkness.

"Dammit," he whispered angrily to himself. "You stay here. I'll find something edible."

I didn't bother responding; I wasn't planning to go anywhere. I lay there, completely limp, as time stood still beneath the canopy of trees.

A few times, I thought I heard my name. A distant rumble of footsteps sprinting toward me. When I lifted my head to see if Caiden had returned, I found the surroundings empty, leaving me enveloped in solitude.

The silence was terrifying.

If I listened closely, I could hear the blood rushing through my veins, the air shifting in my lungs with every shaky breath. I could hear the pulsating beat of my heart, echoing like a drum in the stillness.

While lying there, I imagined sinister shadow figures creeping toward me. Their faces twisted and ghastly, long black arms reaching out to pull me into the beyond. Whispers in the wind called to me, coaxing me to follow and wander deeper into the abyss.

I wanted to follow. Almost.

Each hour that passed, the hunger in my stomach dissolved. There was no pang anymore, only a suffocating numbness.

The hope of Caiden's return slowly scattered, and I wondered how many more days it would take until I rotted into the ground.

I turned over onto my back and stared at the dense shade of trees above, a glimpse of sky barely visible through the leaves. Once peaceful, the solitude now felt like a menacing presence, embracing me like a ravenous demon.

"Amelia."

A voice emerged, almost like a devious growl.

My head barely rolled to the side, and I saw Caiden's blurry form approaching. He'd come back?

Before I could speak, he suddenly kneeled next to me. A poisonous look painted over his dark orbs. If he were a creature, it would have appeared he was snarling at me.

"You're so useless. Just lying here while I try to feed us."

"What?" I croaked, taken aback by his sudden fury.

"Poor, sad Amelia. Always so helpless. It should've been you who died. Not your sister."

There weren't any words that left my mouth. All I could do was stare. My heart was pounding as if it were galloping in a race.

"You're not going to say anything, huh? Fine. Maybe I'll finally get some peace without having to hear the sound of your annoying voice. I should just leave you here, let you waste away and be eaten by the wild animals, you never mattered while being alive, so your death won't either."

His words poured out like thunder, surrounding me like a snake curled around prey.

I didn't even realize I was screaming.

"Stop it! Just leave me alone. Please!" My hands were clawing at my skin while tears gushed down my face, mixing with the dirt that coated my face. Screams rushed out, deafening and terrified.

"Amelia! Jesus. Calm down. You're scaring me."

Two hands made their way around my wrist, halting the flesh scratching and hair pulling. I tried to yank away, but the pair of hands were too strong.

My screams eventually stopped. Yet, my body still trembled as if an earthquake was forcing its way through my rattled bones.

I opened my eyes and peered into Caiden's concerned face. His eyes were no longer demonic. He looked normal again.

"Why would you say those things to me?" I whimpered, looking down at the soil upon which I sat.

"What did I say? I came back, and you were screaming." His eyes were wide as he interrogated me.

"You said you wanted me to die. Just now."

Confusion was laced throughout his tone. "I didn't say anything about you dying. Like I said, I came back a second ago, and you were screaming. Telling an imaginary person to leave you alone."

Now I was confused. Did I imagine that? I must have. "I think I need food. And sleep. My mind must be playing tricks on me," I murmured.

"Yeah. You looked like a crazy person. Good thing I brought something back."

If I had energy, I would have recoiled at his comment and bitten back. But there was nothing left, and I probably did just look like someone who had gone insane.

"I thought you weren't going to come back," I whispered defeatedly.

He stood up. "You didn't think I would catch something? I was in the military, I know how to do that."

I shook my head. "No. I thought you weren't coming back at all."

Caiden was quiet for a few moments; I thought he was not going to respond. Until he did. "I'm not going to leave you alone out here. As much as you irritate me, I'm not going to allow another thing to be on my guilty conscience."

A half-smile made its way across my lips. It was faint, but it was there. "That's the nicest thing you've ever said to me."

He chuckled softly.

Once I stood up, he showed me the creature that he had found and cooked. Caiden explained that it took so long because he started his own fire and cooked it before he brought it back.

He wanted me to be able to eat it right away. He also had some for himself before he returned.

The thought that he did something out of pure kindness was enough to warm my heart a little. He was still Caiden, my enemy, but just for today, I wanted to pretend that he wasn't. I wanted to believe that we weren't enemies.

But we were, and we weren't ourselves out here. We were surviving, even if it meant being something other than hateful rivals for a while. Our stomachs were empty; our minds were on the brink of the abyss.

The warmth in my heart scattered, swallowed by frost.

We spent the rest of that day in a cavernous silence, each of us peering into the bruised wilderness as if it might cough up something human.

The faint comfort I'd felt after eating faded fast, replaced by a cold distaste for what I'd swallowed, as if the meat were a violation more than a mercy. Maybe it was. The taste haunted my breath and burrowed in my stomach, refusing to dissolve.

Caiden's mood curdled. He walked ahead, chin tucked, eyes narrow and glassy.

I imagined him replaying my accusations, rehearsing angry retorts, or maybe just counting the hours until we could stop pretending there was any alliance between us.

I wanted to hate him so badly, to let the old, reliable loathing fill me up and crowd out everything else, but it felt dulled, worn out by shock and hunger and the endless horizon of trees.

I just watched his back, the rigid lines of his spine, and wondered what it would feel like to be alone out here with nobody left to despise.

We slept that night in a shallow depression, curled back-to-back like animals, our bodies pressed close against the bitter cold, but each of us holding court with our own nightmares.

I woke to the sound of Caiden breathing hard, as if he was choking on invisible hands. He muttered something, a string of frantic gibberish, and thrashed so violently he nearly rolled into the embers of our dead fire.

I watched him for several minutes, paralyzed by something that wasn't quite fear but wasn't compassion either. It was more like the sick fascination you have watching a wounded thing writhe.

When he woke, he didn't look at me. He just scrubbed his face, refusing to acknowledge the violence that had just poured out of him. I didn't ask. I wasn't sure if I wanted answers or if I just wanted the silence to stretch until it swallowed us both.

We kept on, day after day, following the river until its banks grew marshy and the trees thinned, the sun overhead a white-hot coin that did nothing to warm us.

Sometimes we spoke, but mostly we didn't. It was easier that way. Each hour was another inch the woods tried to claim us, and we were too tired to resist.

My feet were raw, my hands swollen and useless. I stopped feeling the hunger. It was replaced by a buzzing emptiness. A kind of cellular despair that made every sensation float and fade, so that even Caiden's cruelty felt like it was happening to someone else.

I moved through the trees in a trance, numb to everything except the rhythmic crunch of my own battered body.

By now, Caiden and I could barely look at each other.

Sometimes I wondered if our silence made us invisible. If the wild things that prowled these woods caught the scent of our animosity and kept their distance, wary of a darkness that had nothing to do with the forest and everything to do with us.

Our faces had become masks, painted over with mud and old bruises, but the eyes beneath were no longer human.

The further we went, the less I remembered about who I was before. The girl who had fallen through a frozen pond in third grade and never learned to swim, the girl who wore black for weeks after her sister's funeral, the girl who once screamed at Caiden in a school hallway that she hoped he'd die alone, all of them dissolved in the slow wear of frost and filth.

I was just a body, and Caiden was just another body, and we were both being stripped down to the bone.

The next time I saw my sister, she was crouching on a log ahead of me, knees tucked against her chest the way she used to sit on the front porch of our childhood home.

She gave me a look that cut straight through the fog in my brain, a look that asked if I'd finally had enough yet.

I blinked, and she was gone, replaced by Caiden's rigid silhouette. He was waiting, arms crossed, the set of his jaw unforgiving.

———

Caiden's anger and festering resentment turned vicious. He didn't just spit sarcasm or mutter insults like he used to. He stared at me with a calculation that bordered on dangerous, as if he was plotting the best way to excise me from the universe.

When I caught up after falling behind, he'd sneer, "About fucking time," or "Didn't get eaten by your imaginary bears?"

I stopped answering. He could have all the air he wanted; my voice was better spent on the wind.

I could feel the gulf between us growing wider, the weight of history compacted into a single point of mutual revulsion. Our feud was a fire burning hotter the more oxygen we poured into the void.

We found a clearing that night, a patch of moonlit grass ringed by dead trees. The earth was littered with bones. Small ones, scattered by scavengers and gnawed.

Caiden stared at the remains, then at me, and the implication hung between us like a pall: This is how things end out here. You get picked apart, piece by piece.

Our anger boiled over.

We had been sharing a stick of dried meat, something scavenged from the carcass of a forest animal, when Caiden snapped.

He snatched the morsel from my gnarled fingers, his face contorting into something unfamiliar. "You're not even trying," he snarled, spitting flecks of sinew and saliva into the dirt between us. "You want to die, don't you? Well, go ahead. Quit dragging me down with you."

I looked at his cracked lips, the feverish glint in his eye. The thought flickered through me: he could kill me. And I realized that I almost wanted him to. It would end the gnawing ache in my bones, the grinding friction of our mutual loathing, the endless trudge toward nowhere.

But I wasn't going to give him the satisfaction of begging. My hands curled into fists, trembling more from starvation than anger, and I stared him down, letting all the words I'd bottled up ferment into poison.

"Maybe I do want to die," I hissed. "At least I'd be free of you. You think you're some kind of martyr, dragging my useless ass through the woods, but you love this. You love having someone to hate."

He recoiled as if slapped, and for a second, the mask slipped. I saw the raw, naked hurt. Then it was gone, replaced by the familiar sneer.

"You're pathetic," he spat. "Completely fucking pathetic. You always have been."

I laughed. It came out broken, more a bark than a human sound. "Takes one to know one. You're so desperate to prove you're not your father's spawn, you became him twice over. Congratulations. You win."

He lunged. I didn't move.

There was no room for fear, only a thrill of anticipation as his hands closed on my shoulders and shoved me hard into a tree trunk.

The pain stung, and it cut through the gray shroud that had muffled my senses for days. I could feel the ridges of bark bite into my back, feel the warmth of his hands through the threadbare shirt, feel the heat of his hate burning in the scant inches between our faces.

For one unbroken second, we just breathed. His fingers twitched, and for a wild moment I thought he might throttle me, that he might finish what our families and this forest had started.

I wanted him to. I wanted him to do something irreversible, to burn down what was left of us so we could finally be free.

Instead, he let go, shoving me off with a snarl.

I stumbled and caught myself on a rotten log, the sudden gap between us more nauseating than the impact.

We went back to sit on opposite sides of the fire, staring at the same ember and thinking our separate, poisonous thoughts.

# 34

## THE PRESENT

### AMELIA

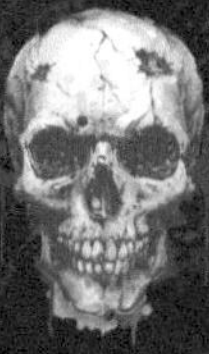

The sky twisted into an ominous beast of inky black, like molten tar churning above us. Heavy clouds writhed with malevolent energy, their undersides illuminated by streaks of pale lightning.

A distant roll of thunder rumbled through the air, vibrating my bones and dredging up the memory of our last kayaking trip. How the wind had snatched at our paddles and sent shivers crawling down my spine.

Now, as I stared up at the furious heavens, cold dread pooled in my gut.

At last, we crested the ridge and dropped into the flatlands, where pines stood as lonely sentinels amid scattered aspens, their pale bark flickering in the dying light.

A narrow stream cut through the meadow.

"Caiden, I think it's going to rain," I murmured, tension tightening my chest.

He didn't pause. His boots crunched against the rocky soil as he kept walking. "No shit, Sherlock," he snapped, sarcasm laced in every syllable.

I wanted to throttle him, but I was too spent for violence. The fatigue in my bones was so deep it felt geological, as if I'd always been made of salt and dust and regret, and every step I took was just the world grinding me down a little more.

We trudged onward, the ache in my calves and soles eclipsed only by the war in my head.

The wind picked up, flinging needles of rain against my face, each drop a cold slap that made my vision blur and double.

My hands were numb. My lips had gone blue. I might have been dying, but it was a slow, boring death.

I thought about Lillian, about how she'd always hated storms. The electric charge in the air would make her hair stand on end, and she'd clap her hands over her ears at the first rumble of thunder.

I wondered if she'd made it to the other side, wherever that was, and if she would be waiting to laugh at me when I finally gave up and crossed over myself. I wondered if she'd forgive me, or if she'd just look at me with that same disappointed silence she'd mastered in life.

We barely made it a quarter mile before the first drops fell, a light drizzle.

I hunched my shoulders and kept walking, every step a sullen admission of defeat, a surrender to the fact that the universe always had one more humiliation up its sleeve.

"Great leadership," I muttered, the words barely audible above the roar of rain. "March us right into a fucking cloudburst. I'm sure that'll get us rescued real quick."

He fired back without turning, his voice slicing through the storm. "Next time, I'll schedule the weather just for you. Maybe get you a golden umbrella to match the attitude."

I wanted to scream, to pick up a rock and split his skull, but the only thing that came out was a bark of laughter.

It surprised us both. The sound was so raw, so unlike me, that I clapped my hand over my mouth and nearly bit through my tongue.

He stopped dead in his tracks. "What," he demanded, "is so goddamn funny right now?"

"I don't know," I said, choking on a fresh wave of giggles. The hysteria came fast, brittle, shattering the numbness that had been calcifying inside me. "It's just you. Me. This. We're in the middle of nowhere. We're going to die out here, and you're still that kid who thinks he's some kind of messiah. It's pathetic. We're pathetic."

He stared at me, rain streaming down the planes of his face, then sloshed through the muck toward the nearest copse of trees.

"We need shelter," he muttered, his hand already peeling wet branches aside. "Unless you want to sleep standing up."

I rolled my eyes and glanced skyward, where the clouds swirled faster now, black veins spreading outward.

A sour gust raced past, wrapping us in its icy grip, and the murmuring breeze sank into a savage howl that echoed between the trunks.

A thunderclap shattered the woods, louder than any beast's roar, and the ground shivered beneath our feet.

My heart lurched. Gooseflesh prickled my arms. "That doesn't sound good," I whispered, wrapping my arms around my ribs.

Caiden's voice was strained. "We might have to wait it out."

"Where?" I protested. "There's nowhere to hide under these trees; the storm's right on top of us." Every instinct screamed that we were trapped, like prey pinned in the jaws of a predator.

He shot me a glance of anger. "I never said we'd find perfect shelter. We just can't stray from our path. We're going to get drenched."

My stomach sank. Back home, I'd curl under my comforter with a mug of tea, let the rain lull me to sleep.

Here, there was no refuge. Just this wild fury waiting to tear through us.

A cold drop struck my cheek. Then another. And another—tiny, stinging beads that blossomed into a full-blown downpour.

Caiden's eyes widened. "Move!" His voice cracked the roar of wind and rain.

He plunged forward between the trunks, and I lunged after him, legs slick with mud. Rain plastered my hair to my face, drumming on my shoulders like a thousand impatient fingers.

The world became a blur of trembling branches and swirling leaves. Each footstep sank into soft earth, and I fought to keep pace.

"Caiden!" I yelled. My voice was swallowed by the storm. "Where—where do we go?"

He pivoted, rain streaking his features, and pointed. "There!" A cluster of thick pines and mature aspens leaned together, their branches interwoven like a cathedral vault. "Under that canopy!"

We scrambled through the storm, branches whipping at our skin, needles and leaves raining down.

Finally, we slammed against the rough bark of the largest pine. I pressed my back to its soaked trunk, the resin's sharp tang cutting through the damp air.

Caiden collapsed beside me, chest heaving, eyes scanning the tempest.

"Why is this happening?" I gasped, voice trembling. "Why won't it stop?"

He drew a shuddering breath, rain streaming off his brow. "I don't know. But panicking won't help."

The storm raged on. I felt the anger bubbling up inside me, a response to the helplessness that threatened to consume us both. "You think I'm not trying? I'm doing my best to keep it together, just like you!"

Caiden scoffed, his hair whipping around his face like a wild animal from the harsh wind. His voice bellowed over the intensity of the downpour. "No. I don't think you are trying. All you've done since we have been out here is complain. I'm sick of it!"

I stood my ground amidst the storm. "Yeah? News flash, buddy, I never wanted to be stuck out here with you. Of course I'm going to complain, I'm trapped in the wilderness with the person I hate the most. I'm probably going to die out here with you. I have every right to be negative!"

The ferocity of my anger whirled as harshly as the storm, engraving a sense of adrenaline within me. It rained furiously, as if a vengeful deity was unleashing its fury upon us.

Darkness fell, a reflection of the turmoil echoing within us, as the sky devoured the last slivers of light.

"I'm so sick of your damn victim mindset." His words were raw with frustration, screaming alongside the howling wind.

"Maybe I wouldn't have a victim mindset if you hadn't made my life miserable. I never deserved that, and you are constantly shutting me down anytime I react to how you treated me."

The sound of my voice rose higher and higher; Caiden and I were clashing into each other amidst the war of the storm. It was poetic in a way.

"You can't blame me for that. I had no choice! You have no idea what I went through with my father. He practically beat it into me that I had to hate you. I was a terrible person, but we can't change the past." His eyes held a darkness that seemed to engulf him, like a poisonous substance.

The darkness drenched me until I was wrapped in his rage.

In the midst of our screaming, the world was collapsing. The trees were bent so low they looked as if they might uproot. Twigs were swirling around us, as though propelled by an unseen power.

The landscape was shrouded in a ruthless, rain-blurred veil, barely recognizable. Cracks of thunder roared above our heads.

"I can blame you," I said, my voice starting low before rising, "You were the one who tormented me. You had a choice, but you chose to be a monster. Just like your father."

He had a sudden, chilling change of expression. His face hardened like stone, as if overtaken by a brutal spirit. "I should have just left you to die by the water after our kayak fell down the waterfall. You have no fucking clue what it was like to be in my shoes. I've tried to be nice, but you are insufferable."

The harsh words he spoke sliced through me. Suddenly, in his presence, I trembled with fear.

Before I could speak, a jab pierced my neck. A numbing sensation crawled over me, my body succumbing to being motionless. Consciousness began to slip in and out.

The rain appeared to melt. The last thing I saw before my eyelids shut was the image of Caiden running towards me. His lips were moving, and I thought I heard my name.

As I fell to the ground, everything went silent and dark, and it felt as if all of my perceptions had ceased.

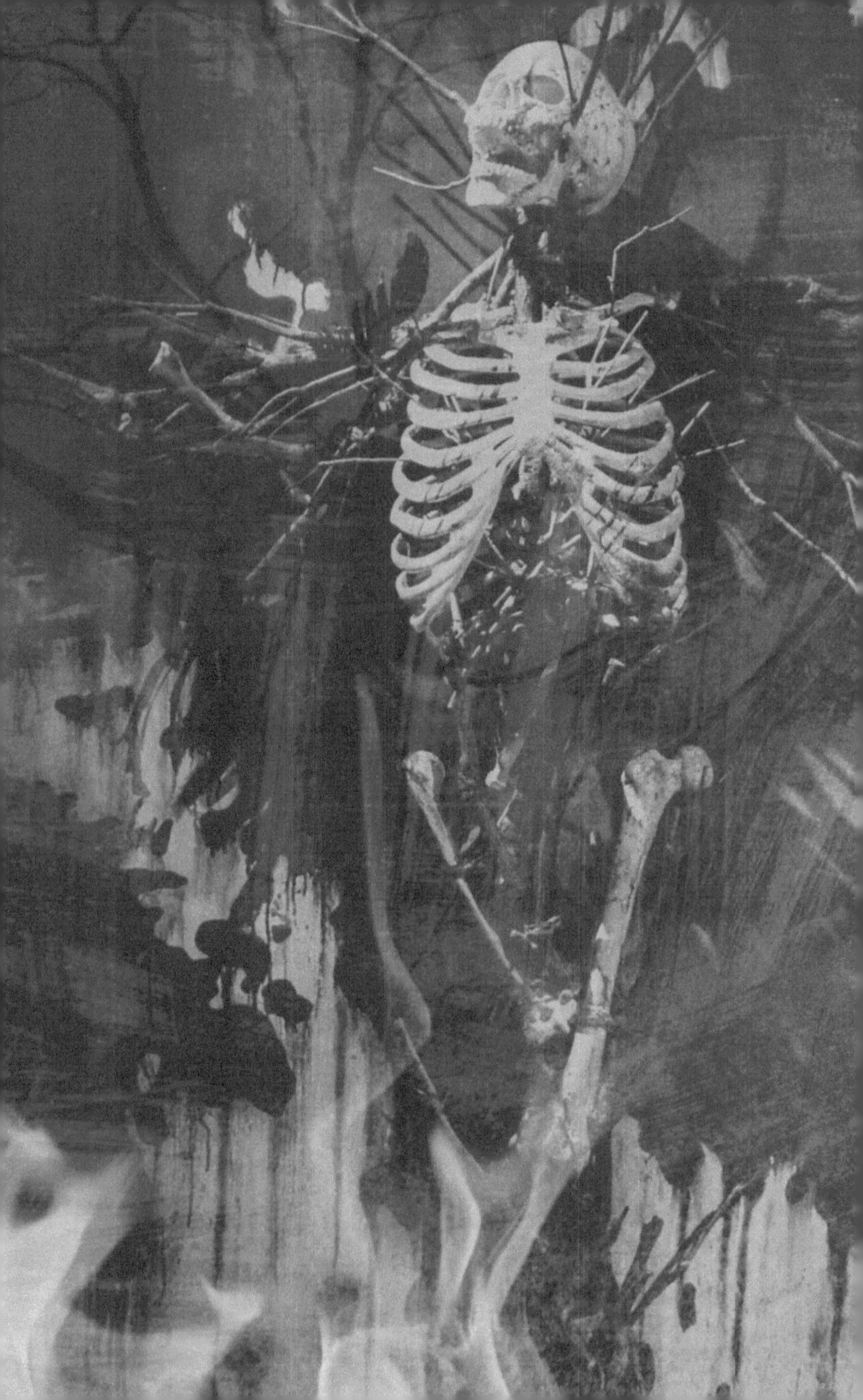

# 35

## THE PRESENT

### AMELIA

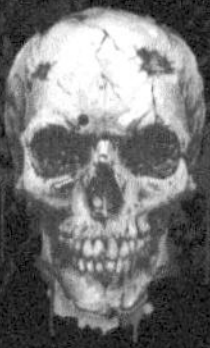

THE BLACKNESS WAS COMFORTING.

When my senses began to come back to me, I wanted to reverse time so I could fall back into sweet oblivion. Silence had fallen, and the sound of rain that I had been hearing was gone. The biting cold wind that had previously enveloped my body was gone. Everything seemed to have evaporated, except me.

*Am I dead?*

The thought hit me like a ton of bricks. Did I want to be dead? I enjoyed the quiet of being unconscious, but when reality settled in, I had a moment of hesitation within my mind.

*I don't want to be dead.*

It was a shocking revelation.

Through the groggy awakening, I could feel my heart beating. I could feel the rising and falling of my chest as I breathed.

The thing that I did not feel was the texture of dirt and rock that I had become accustomed to since Caiden and I became lost in the wilderness. My eyes popped open.

Where the hell was I?

The darkness was thick and suffocating, wrapping around me like a cloak. My head throbbed, and the last memory I had was of Caiden's alarmed face rushing toward me.

I blinked, trying to adjust to the dim moonlight filtering through a small window. How long were we unconscious?

Panic surged through me as I realized I was not outside anymore. "Caiden?" I croaked, my voice hoarse and weak.

I strangely hoped for his presence here with me. If he were here, it meant companionship and a better chance of survival. Although I hate to admit it, his stubborn refusal to give up motivates me to keep going.

"Caiden!" I called out again, a bit louder this time, as I began to find my voice.

After a few moments of deadly silence, I heard a faint groan. I squinted, my eyes straining to see through the surrounding darkness. The small, dusty window let in only a small speck of clarity, and my eyes strained to focus through the dizziness.

Finally, he spoke. "Amelia? Where are we?"

I almost laughed. As if I would know why we were in a dark, cold room. Instead of shooting him a sarcastic comment, I only shrugged. "I don't know. But, I have a bad feeling about this."

"The last thing I remember is you getting hit with some sort of dart, then you collapsed," Caiden spoke groggily, with confusion dancing in his tone.

A dart? The air was cold, and an eerie chill seeped into my bones. My fear was confirmed. We were brought here and trapped. I imagine they would have put us in a clean, comfortable bedroom if they had meant to save us. Not a mysterious dungeon.

"Who the hell could have been out in the middle of nowhere shooting darts in people?" The question hung in the air.

"I don't know. When they show their face, they are going to regret trapping us in here." His tone was cold, and I knew he meant his threat. Something deep in me knew that in the right circumstance, Caiden could seriously hurt somebody.

"I'm scared," I confessed, my essence etched with weary dread.

"I'm not. I'll fucking kill whoever did this. Fuck!" His voice went from conflicted to angry, and I shrank backward from his eruption.

"Maybe this is a misunderstanding." My voice squeaked, and I fell into hopeless delusion.

"A misunderstanding? Are you fucking stupid? Obviously, whoever did this knew what they were doing. Must have been strong as hell to move us into this shitty chamber," Caiden hissed, continuing to explode with fury.

"No need to snap at me. I'm just trying to make sense of this. Or find a little hope in the situation. I need something."

Even in the darkness, I could feel Caiden's intense gaze.

I welcomed the darkness because I don't think I could look him in the eyes. I remember what he had said to me before I got shot with the dart, and his words still stung.

"Sorry. I'm frustrated. I hate feeling helpless."

Surprisingly, he apologized.

"I know the feeling."

Suddenly, a floorboard creaked nearby. We held our breaths, listening. Silence descended again.

Then, a low chuckle echoed through the confined space, sending shivers down my spine. It was a chilling sound, devoid of humor, laced with a predatory satisfaction. "Well, well," a voice, smooth as polished obsidian, slithered into the darkness. "Awake, are we?"

The voice belonged to a man; I was sure of it. Panic surged through me when the realization hit that we weren't alone. How long had the mystery man been there? I wondered.

Caiden shifted near me. I could envision him looking alert, analyzing our surroundings, and trying to spot the man.

The darkness felt less like a refuge now, more like a cage. The chuckle, that chilling echo, was the key turning in the lock.

"Who are you? Come out of the shadows and face us, fucking coward."

Caiden yelled, showing no signs of fear. It was rare for me to witness Caiden being afraid. I wanted him to feel afraid; it would make me feel less like a wimp.

I watched the shadows and waited for an appearance. A pair of eyes, gleaming like embers in the gloom, emerged from the corner.

The man stepped fully into the meager light, his silhouette bleak against the dusty window. There was a barrier between us and the man. It appeared we were confined to a cage-like section of the room.

The man was tall and imposing, his face obscured by a wide-brimmed hat, casting his features into further mystery. He carried himself as a presence of terror. He took a slow, deliberate step towards us, and the air crackled with menace.

"Such a lovely couple," he purred, his voice dangerously low, like a beast's growl. He paused, letting the weight of his words settle before continuing, his tone shifting to a sharper edge. "Let's just say, you two are about to become participants in a very special game."

My blood ran cold.

Caiden, however, remained calm. A sudden change from his explosiveness. "A game, you say?" he challenged, his voice tight with barely contained rage. "I suggest you tell us the rules before this 'game' becomes permanently unwinnable for you."

The man chuckled again, a sound that scraped against my nerves like nails on a chalkboard. He seemed to relish the tension he'd created, his eyes dancing with perverse amusement. "Oh, the rules are simple enough," he drawled, his voice dripping with sinister tones. "Survive."

I swallowed hard, the weight of his words suffocating. "Survive?" I echoed, suspicion creeping into my voice. "What do you mean by that?"

He straightened; I imagined a cruel smile playing on his lips. "You'll see. I have plans for you both. But first, let's make sure you're well-fed and hydrated. You'll need your strength for what's to come."

As he turned to retrieve something from the shadows, I caught a glimpse of the room. A small basement cluttered with forgotten relics of a bygone era. Old furniture stood against the walls, draped in dust, and the air was thick with the smell of decay.

A flickering bulb overhead cast unsettling shadows that danced around us, increasing the sense of entrapment and danger.

"Caiden," I whispered, my voice trembling. "What do we do?"

I could see his shape now, still as a statue. "We wait for an opportunity. We can't let him get the upper hand."

The man returned, holding two cups of murky water and a bowl of what looked like rotten stew. "Eat up," he said cheerfully, the twisted smile never leaving his face. "You'll need your energy. The fun starts soon."

"I'm not eating anything you give us," I shot back, my voice sharper than I intended.

"Ah, feisty, aren't we?" He chuckled, opening the barred door to set the food down. "I admire your spirit. But you'll find that hunger is a powerful motivator."

Caiden's jaw clenched as he stared at the food, then at the man. "What do you want from us?"

The man leaned closer, his expression shifting from amusement to something darker. "I want to see how you both handle a little pressure. You've been through a lot, haven't you? Let's see how much further you can be pushed."

My stomach churned at his words, and I felt a rush of panic. "Are you insane? You can't do this!"

"I can and I will," he replied, his voice low and chilling. "You're in my world now, and I have all the time in the world to play with my little toys."

"Stop this!" Caiden shouted, his anger spilling over. "We're not your playthings! Let us go! I'll rip your throat out."

The man's eyes glinted with sadistic delight. "You're not going anywhere. It's been a while since I've had wanderers in these woods to keep for myself."

He stepped back, allowing us a moment of relief, yet the sense of dread settled heavily in the air. I could feel Caiden's tension beside me, and the reality of our situation clawed at my insides.

"Amelia," he said, urgency creeping into his voice, "we need to find a way out of this."

"I know," I replied, anxiety tightening my chest. "But how? We're trapped down here."

"Not for long," he said. "I'll figure out something."

As the man's laughter echoed in the shadows, I could feel the darkness closing in around us, threatening to engulf us in a nightmare from which there was no escape.

The storm outside was over. We were now trapped in a different kind of storm, where the predator lurked just beyond our reach. Watching, waiting.

# 36

## THE PRESENT

### AMELIA

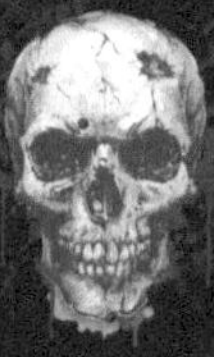

THE DARKNESS SWALLOWED US WHOLE, WRAPPING ITS cold fingers around my throat, suffocating any flicker of hope I clung to.

I pressed my back against the wired wall of the cage, knees pulled to my chest.

The single bulb above cast distorted shadows that danced along the walls, taunting me with the specters of my fears. Every creak, every distant whisper of wind sent jolts of panic coursing through me, tightening the knot of dread in my stomach.

I glanced at Caiden as he paced the confined space, his movements tense, each step echoing like a countdown to some unseen doom. His jaw was set, eyes guarded, but I could sense the storm brewing beneath his stoic facade.

He was a coiled spring, ready to snap at the slightest provocation.

"Would you stop pacing?" I snapped, my voice was sharper than I intended, edged with fear. "It's making my head spin."

He shot me a look, one that could freeze fire. "Better than sitting here like a lamb waiting for slaughter," he replied, irritation lacing his tone. "At least I'm trying to figure a way out of this."

"Right, because we can just wish ourselves out of here," I said, bitterness creeping into my voice. "What do you expect to do? Beat down the door?"

"Maybe if you stopped panicking, we'd have a better chance," he shot back.

I felt the sting of tears prick the corners of my eyes, but I blinked them away. This wasn't the time for weakness. "Do you really think I want to be in this hellhole? You think I'm enjoying this? Your hatred doesn't help."

"Hatred? Maybe I'm just trying to survive here!" he spat, the tension between us thickening like a noose. "You think I'm enjoying being trapped with someone who has lost all hope?"

I recoiled at his words, the truth behind them cutting deeper than any knife. The shadows around me seemed to pulse with life, and I could feel the walls closing in, suffocating me. "You don't know what I'm going through," I whispered, panic clawing at my throat. "I'm scared, and you're not helping."

"Whatever," he spat, his irritation boiling over. "We could actually think of a plan instead of sitting here wallowing in self-pity."

Before I could respond, the door creaked open, and the air shifted.

My heart raced as our captor stepped inside, a looming figure draped in shadow. The dim light flickered over his face, revealing a twisted smile that sent a chill racing through me.

"Well, well, my little pets," he purred, his voice smooth and unsettling. "How delightful it is to see you both still alive. I must admit, I expected to find one of you to be broken by now."

"Get away from us!" I shouted, my voice shaky but defiant.

His laughter echoed in the darkness, a chilling sound that reverberated against the walls. "Oh, my dear, you misunderstand. I'm not here to hurt you... not yet. I'm merely here to observe. To watch as you unravel in the dark."

Caiden stiffened beside me, his eyes narrowing. "What do you want?"

"Want?" He leaned in closer, a predatory glint in his eye. "I want to see the fear in your eyes. The way it twists your mind and turns you against each other. The way it makes you beg for mercy."

I felt a wave of nausea wash over me as his words sank in. "You're sick," I whispered, my voice trembling.

"Sick?" he echoed, feigning offense. "Oh, no, my dear. I'm simply a connoisseur of human suffering. I find it fascinating. The way people react when they realize their lives are slipping through their fingers. You're both so entertaining to watch."

His gaze shifted between Caiden and me, and I could feel the weight of his scrutiny, as if he were peeling back our layers, exposing our fears for his amusement. "You're both so young, so full of potential. And yet, here you are, trapped in a filthy basement, reduced to mere playthings. Doesn't it make you question everything you thought you knew about yourselves?"

"Shut up!" Caiden snapped, fists clenched at his sides. "You're nothing. Just a coward hiding in the dark."

The captor's smile widened, a glimmer of madness dancing in his eyes. "Ah, but I'm the one with all the power, aren't I? I control the narrative here. You're just pawns in my game." He took a step closer, leaning in as if sharing a secret. "And there's nothing more delicious than watching someone's hope crumble, piece by piece."

I felt the walls closing in, the shadows creeping closer, whispering doubts in my ears. Panic surged within me, threatening to consume me whole. "What do you want from us?" I managed to choke out, my breath hitching in my throat.

"I want to see how far you'll go to survive," he said, his voice dripping with malice. "How much pain you can endure before you turn on each other. It's a beautiful dance, really, a waltz of desperation and despair. And I have a front-row seat."

"Stop!" I shouted, my voice breaking. "You can't keep doing this to us!"

He chuckled softly, a sound devoid of warmth. "Oh, but I can. And I will. The longer you remain here, the more you'll unravel. You'll see your true selves, the monsters lurking beneath the surface. I'm merely the catalyst."

I could feel Caiden's anger simmering beside me. "You're just a motherfucker hiding behind your games," he said, his voice low and steady. "You think you can break us? You're wrong."

"Am I?" the captor retorted, amusement dancing in his eyes. "Or are you simply too afraid to face the truth? Fear is a powerful motivator, my dear boy. And I intend to use it to its fullest potential."

As he stepped back, the shadows seemed to close in, the darkness wrapping around us like a vice. I felt the weight of despair pressing down on me, the panic threatening to spill over.

As the door creaked shut behind our captor, the sudden silence in the basement felt deafening. I drew in a shaky breath, trying to calm my racing heart, but the darkness throbbed with the echoes of his taunts.

The shadows felt more alive now, crawling along the walls, whispering my deepest fears.

"Did you hear him?" I said, my voice was trembling. "He wants us to break. He thinks it's some sort of game."

Caiden turned sharply, his eyes blazing in the dim light. "And you think cowering in the corner is going to help? He's right about one thing: you're giving up way too easily."

"Giving up?" I screamed, the words bursting from me like a dam breaking. "You think I'm giving up? Look at us! We're trapped in this nightmare because of him. I'm scared, Caiden. I can't take much more of this."

"Exactly! And that's the problem. You're too busy panicking to think," Caiden snapped, his voice rising. "We need a plan, and right now, you're just dragging us down."

I felt the sting of tears in my eyes, the weight of his words crashing over me. "What do you want from me? I'm terrified. Every moment we spend here, I feel myself slipping away. I'm losing it, Caiden. I don't know how to keep fighting when it feels like I'm drowning."

"Drowning?" He laughed again, a cold, humorless sound. "You're drowning in your own self-pity! We're in hell, Amelia. And you're just sitting there waiting for someone to save you! I don't want to be here either. But I'm not going to let fear cripple me. That's not who I am."

"Then why are you taking it out on me?" I shouted, the words escaping before I could hold them back. "Why do you think I'm the problem? I'm not the one who brought us here."

His eyes narrowed, and for a fleeting moment, I glimpsed the vulnerability behind his anger before it vanished, replaced by a hard mask. "You're right. You didn't bring us here. But you need to wake up. We can't afford to lose focus or hope. If we do, we're finished."

"I'm trying," I cried, my voice breaking. "I'm trying to hold it together, but he's in our heads. He's playing with us like we're toys, and I don't know how much longer I can stand it."

"Then you need to stop wallowing in your fear!" Caiden's voice dropped to a low growl, his temper boiling just beneath the surface. "You think I want to sit here and listen to you spiral? I'm trying to survive. Like I've always done."

"I admire that, but you're in denial about how screwed we are," I shouted, stepping forward, anger flaring in my chest. "You think you're the only one who wants to survive? Every moment we spend here, I'm fighting the urge to lose my mind. I'm terrified. And you know what? Maybe that's okay."

His eyes flashed with anger, and I saw the struggle within him, fear mixed with a desperate need to stay strong. "You think being scared is okay? You think that's going to help us?"

"I'm scared because I don't want to die here! I don't want to be another victim." Tears spilled over, hot against my cheeks. "But I also don't want to be yelled at by the one person who's supposed to be on my side."

"On your side?" Caiden's incredulity painted his features with disdain. "I'm just trying to keep myself alive. If you can't handle that, then maybe you're not cut out for this."

The words hit me like a slap, and I recoiled, his dismissal was painful. "You think I wanted to be here, trapped with you and that monster? I'm trying my best."

"Your best isn't good enough!" he barked, his frustration boiling over, sending a wave of heat through me.

The finality of his words bit into me, and I felt the last remnants of my hope slipping away.

We were both spiraling, caught in a whirlwind of fear and anger, and I wondered how much longer we could endure before we broke completely.

As the shadows closed in around us, I realized that in our desperate fight for survival, we were becoming each other's worst enemies. And in the darkness of that basement, I feared we might not only lose ourselves but also each other.

# 37
## THE PRESENT
### AMELIA

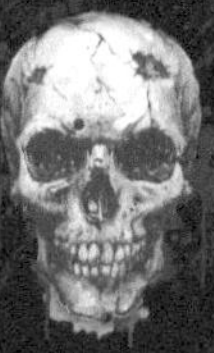

Sunlight, fractured and weak, filtered through a grimy window high in the wall, yet the basement remained stubbornly dim. This half-light illuminated our surroundings with chilling clarity: we were ensnared in a wire cage, its tall, barred metal door firmly shut.

The cage sat in a damp, unfinished basement; I could just make out the worn concrete steps of a staircase leading upwards toward a shadowy abyss at the far end of the room.

Since our encounter with the kidnapper, a dreadful silence had settled over us.

Caiden, slumped against the opposite wall, sat rigid with silent fury, his face a mask of shock and barely contained rage.

We were both too stunned to speak.

I thought I heard the skittering of a rat's claws across the concrete floor. It was a tiny, unsettling sound in the stillness.

In the half-darkness, my mind wandered into the darkest depths. Everything had led me to this desolate place, to this cage, and to this hopeless situation.

Trapped here with Caiden, I replayed a vision of the man slaughtering us. We would bleed out in the darkness, our slow, agonizing deaths mirroring our bleeding souls.

Shadows danced in the periphery of my vision, twisting into monstrous shapes.

Paranoia, icy and insidious, coiled through my veins like a venomous snake. My head throbbed with immense pressure, as if it might explode.

I squeezed my eyes shut, trying to count my breaths, to regain some sense of control.

We were alone. We were going to die. The crushing weight of that reality settled upon me.

My stomach growled in protest. A small plate of food sat untouched on the floor near the cage.

But even the possibility of food was tainted by fear. Could it be poisoned? Was it safe to eat?

The gnawing hunger in my stomach was a constant, painful reminder of our last meal, hours ago. Far too long. A desperate urge overcame me.

Maybe it would not be so bad to eat this mysterious food.

I pulled the plate closer, picking up a piece of bread. The meat beside it remained unidentified, its origin a disturbing unknown.

"What are you doing?" Caiden's voice cut through the tense silence, startling me.

"I'm hungry," I mumbled, the pathetic weakness of my confession echoing in the quiet room. I knew that consuming this food was playing into his hands, feeding his perverse game of control.

"Eating that food is doing what he wants," Caiden pressed. "We need to show him that he cannot control us."

His logic was undeniably rational, but the overwhelming feeling of hunger eclipsed any reasoned argument.

I bit into the stale bread, relishing the taste of real food despite its bitter flavor.

"Dammit, Amelia. You never listen to me."

"I don't care what you think, Caiden. I'm starving."

"You're so weak. Did you ever stop to think that maybe that food is drugged?" Caiden insisted, voicing what I had already anxiously considered.

"I thought about it. But at this point, we're going to die, so I can't care about that."

My words emerged as a melancholic song, filling the air and wrapping around me with its tune.

"We are not going to die. If the military and living with my father taught me one thing, it's that I survive," he paused, eyeing me carefully. "It's kill or be killed."

"You keep bringing up your father, but how am I supposed to understand if you never explain it further?"

He sat there, defenses built around him, but I pushed to break through them, to unravel his heart and dissect it.

Caiden fell quiet for a few minutes. I didn't think he would respond. The sound of breathing filled the chilled air.

A 'drip' echoed every few seconds from somewhere in the deepened shadows. I had to remind myself that I was still here. I was alive.

"My father was a cruel man, Amelia. If it wasn't for him, I would've never learned to loathe you." His voice emerged slowly, tinged with sadness.

Through the darkness, I could see his pain. His head hung low, his eyes searching the floor as if rummaging through memories. His broad appearance seemed sunken and small.

Like me, he had lost an unfortunate amount of weight.

In the dim light, I saw him exposed, and it hurt.

"What do you mean by that? When you say, 'learned to loathe me'?" He had given me snippets of his father's cruelty but never the whole story. I wanted to understand. If I did, perhaps I could set aside my anger, and we could work together. We could survive.

Caiden heaved a sigh, deep from his soul. "Fuck. I really don't want to go into his torture. But I probably should." His voice drifted off, and I waited. I wouldn't push him, not now. He was battling with his demons, torn between two sides of a bitter conflict.

"My father had controlled me since my mother left. He would beat me, degrade me, and isolate me. If I didn't obey, he would become furious. He told me that if I wanted to live in his home, I had to make you my enemy, since you're Judy's daughter, and in his drunk and deluded mind it seemed to matter to him," he paused, the tension in his shoulders tightening as he squeezed his eyes shut.

He was tormented.

"At first, I only complied to make him happy. So, I could go for a day or two without being bruised. But then, I learned to hate you, and it became a sick part of me."

"I'm sorry, Caiden. That's awful."

In that moment, I knew I meant it. No matter what Caiden had done to me, he was just a child, bearing the weight of his father's rage. He had done what he thought was best at the time. How could I blame him?

I should have. I wanted to. But still, even after all the trauma, my heart held softness.

He didn't say anything, so I kept talking.

"You did what you had to do to survive. Though knowing that doesn't take away my anger from your torment," I paused, contemplating my next question. "Do you still hate me? Your father isn't here, so could it be something that's undoable without his presence?"

His reply was instant. A harsh, anguished tone cutting through the silence, his demeanor stormy as the chaotic sea. "My father haunts me, Amelia. He's in my blood. His ghost follows me every fucking day. Even now, I'm fighting the urge to torture you. It's all I know."

"Well, I hope a day comes when he no longer haunts you. I say that because I am still haunted by my sister and my mother. For different reasons, but they follow me like a shadow."

"I hope so too."

We were plunged back into a bleak silence.

That silence endured until the creak of a door opened, and footsteps began thumping down the stairs. The beat of my heart immediately quickened, and panic barged its way into the small area once more.

"I see my pets are bonding." His voice, like a creeping beast in the night, wove through the atmosphere and struck me like lightning.

I glanced at Caiden; he glared at the mystery man.

"Whatever you're planning on doing to us, you'd better do it now. Otherwise, you're a dead man," Caiden warned, his tone gravelly and dark.

A shiver spiked throughout my spine. The vision of Caiden murdering the mystery man was a terrifying thought. I had witnessed my father hit my mother, and that was scary enough.

I couldn't imagine witnessing a murder.

"Watch your mouth, young man. I'm the boss around here. Don't worry; you have some time before your time is up. I like to play with my pets before I slaughter them. It's more fun."

He chuckled, a low, rough sound. The glint in his eye, however, held no amusement; it was the cold gleam of a predator sizing up its prey.

I was struck with dread. I couldn't scream. I couldn't cry. All I could do was sit and contemplate his words.

My insides swarmed.

Each second stretched into an eternity. His words echoed in the hollow chambers of my mind, a chilling symphony of impending doom.

I tried to swallow, but my throat felt constricted. Escape seemed impossible, a cruel joke in this macabre game of cat and mouse.

"Now, where were we? Ah yes, your contribution to the fun."

"Fuck you, you sick fucker," Caiden shouted, jumping up from where he stood.

Before he could storm over to my side of the cage, right next to where the mystery man stood outside, a glass barrier descended from above.

Caiden was trapped on the other side; we were now divided.

A cruel, demonic laugh tore from the man's throat. "Did you think I would let my pets roam freely without a plan? No. I built this cage with the intention of dividing it. To fill my subjects with fear."

I looked up to where his eyes went. The barrier had come from above. It had been built into the ceiling, a clever mechanical device that could be lowered and lifted. But how?

I glanced back at the man. He stood close to the cage from the outside, and I could see a device in his hands, a button.

Of course.

My stomach sank a little more. He had thought of everything.

The cage felt smaller. Claustrophobic. The walls closed in, and each breath became a struggle.

"Dammit!" Caiden bellowed with furious intensity. His foot ascended and kicked the barrier, but it was pointless. It may have been transparent, but it was thick.

He kicked it again. And again, screaming a string of curses at the man.

A pleasurable tint filled the man's eyes as he watched, a slow smile playing on his lips. The realization hit me like a physical blow, a sickening feeling that twisted my stomach and clouded my mind.

He enjoyed this. He found a perverse pleasure in our agony; the sounds of our choked breaths and desperate cries were a symphony to his ears.

"Caiden, stop! You're giving him what he wants. Look at him! He's enjoying this." The thoughts reeling through my head tumbled out in a torrent of words. Watching Caiden tear himself apart, the raw agony in his eyes was unbearable.

Caiden heard my desperation. Thankfully, the barrier wasn't soundproof. He halted his destruction but stood defiantly, a murderous expression filling his dark eyes.

"Now, sit and be a good pet. I want to be able to play with my female pet, but I can't have you rushing at me like a bull."

Oh god.

A sickening feeling washed over me. He wanted to play with me. I wanted to pretend I didn't know what he meant, but the horrors of my experiences knew exactly what he intended. I slid to the edge of the cage, pressing against the barrier.

The door opened, but I was frozen in place. Caiden's voice rang out, urging me to run. But I couldn't. My eyesight clouded, and I felt heavily sedated.

Then, the answer struck me: the food. Caiden's accusation of it being drugged. His plan was to drug me so I couldn't resist him when he came to assault me.

His shadowy figure towered over me, a coldness sweeping through the air. He was smiling deviously, and I felt as if I were in a nightmare.

I cowered on the ground, my hands curled around my knees, helpless to fight.

Caiden was banging his hands against the glass, screaming words, but I couldn't focus on what they were.

With a slow, deliberate movement, the mystery man bent down, his eyes intense. I felt his hands on me, a physical and unsettling sensation. The texture was rough, the temperature cold, much like a glacier's icy surface.

A blurred dream was all that came after. A chaotic jumble of half-remembered sensations, like a fading echo.

A blackness, thick and suffocating, descended, pressing down on me as my mind drifted to a distant, unknown place. My muscles coiled tight, each fiber screaming in protest, on the verge of shattering.

I longed to escape into the boundless cerulean sky, its azure expanse a tempting invitation, so I closed my eyes and imagined soaring among the clouds.

I grasped at anything to shift my focus away from the distressing violation taking place.

# 38

## THE PRESENT

### AMELIA

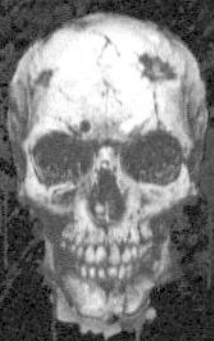

The man's departure unleashed a monstrous darkness; it swelled, grew, and filled the space with a chilling, deep dread and suffocating silence.

The light had disappeared, and obsidian hues fluttered through the singular window. There weren't any stars glimmering, that I knew.

It was as if the darkness had swallowed the outside, and we were falling into a black hole.

Not even the moonlight was noticeable; its presence was now a forgotten ghost.

Silence dripped sorrowfully. The barrier hadn't moved, and I was thrown into an isolated terror.

I knew Caiden was on the other side, but I couldn't see him. I couldn't hear him. He was so far wedged into the shadows that he blended with them perfectly.

I opened my mouth to speak, but nothing slipped out. My senses were frozen in time, coated with a seemingly permanent shock. Time moved slowly, and I wondered if time was passing at all.

At this point, it was unknown how long we had been gone for. I wondered if Shane and Sabrina were looking for us. If they were, they had given up by now.

We were far gone, and rescue was becoming a lost hope.

I tried to imagine my home. My home that I was never going to see again. The image was faint, like a blurry picture taken from a distance.

Once that image fled my mind, it wandered to further memories. Childhood. Lillian's face fell in and out of my head. My mother's scrutinizing and haunted face went round and round, like screams of terror in my mind.

Nights and days filled with isolation and panic. Walking alone with my sorrows, feeling like a phantom in my own home.

The thoughts landed on Caiden. The contempt in his eyes burned with each abusive word, like a hateful fire. The sting of his actions coursed through me like a hurricane.

Each small thing felt like a crushing weight, and the turmoil in my body manifested as dreadful flames. I was corruption incarnate, a two-legged monster sinking deeper into the viscous, crimson pools of blood, the coppery tang infecting me.

He sat there, unmoving, uncaring, and my soul fell deeper into dusk.

Hours passed by in this dark stillness. I was too weak to do anything other than collapse further into myself like a dying star. Seeking comfort from Caiden was not an option; he was in his own hell in the dark on the other side.

A darkened inferno was raining down onto me, and I no longer fought it but welcomed it, succumbing to its fatal grip.

I was startled awake by a sudden, animal scream.

My own, I realized, when my throat burned a moment later. I'd slept, or perhaps just slipped into some state of suspended terror, and now my body had remembered how to react.

I watched the sun's rays bleach the world gray and then disappear altogether.

Light and dark, light and dark, until I was sure my mind was splitting on the axis of it.

Hunger gnawed, then retreated, and returned sharper, always sharper, until I could hear my own bones chewing on my flesh.

I hallucinated, I think.

Sometimes the glass sweated blood; sometimes the cinderblock walls leered with faces I'd seen in my worst memories.

Sometimes the rats came out and spoke with my father's voice, or my mother's, or Lillian's, and I did not bother to answer because I could not tell if I still possessed a mouth.

I watched Caiden the whole time.

Even in the haze of waking nightmares and real nightmares, I counted every time his ribs moved up and down, the way he pressed his forehead to the glass as if wishing to bash straight through it by willpower alone.

He scared me less now than before.

Maybe that was the point of our captor's design: whittle us down to the gristle, burn away the old rot, so that all that remained was the most basic and desperate urge to survive.

When the food came, I ate. He did too.

Some of it made me sick, and some of it made me sleep for so long that waking up felt like being born again in a world where I had never known sunlight.

Sometimes, when I woke, the tray was gone, and I could not recall eating at all.

Maybe I had eaten my own tongue out of madness. Maybe I had willed myself hollow.

The barrier was warm now, smeared with our sweat and the condensation of desperate breath. Caiden had started pressing his lips to it, as if breathing the ghost of me would keep him alive.

When I touched my face to the glass, I could almost hear his pulse, slow and thick as oil.

Once, in the hours before dawn, I heard him sob. He tried to hide it, but the sound traveled through the barrier anyway, warped into a sick, animal whimper.

I lay on my side and watched the ceiling rotate slowly overhead.

If I closed my eyes, the world swung like a pendulum, and I could almost believe, for a split second, that I'd wake up outside, with the wind in my hair and a forest to run through.

———

The walls were closing in, day by day.

Each moment I spent in this cage, I felt haunted by the mysterious man who trapped us in here. Tormenting us, taunting us, breaking me apart.

I could still feel the phantom touch of his cold and sickening hands on me.

The darkness didn't help. It intensified the suffocation and helplessness.

I slept in bursts, each waking worse than the last. My body ached. My fingers tingled with an electric panic that crawled up my arms.

I didn't want to move, didn't want to even open my eyes and look at Caiden through the milky glass, but the claustrophobia was a weight on my chest, a parasite feeding off every shaky breath.

Sometimes I sat up, curled so tight I was almost fetal, and pressed my forehead to the cage wall until my skin went numb. Sometimes I paced my half of the cell, circling like a caged rat, the rhythm of my bare feet on concrete the only sound I could control.

But mostly, I just lay there, feeling my heart pound out a warning.

Not safe, not safe, not safe.

The man hadn't come back in a while. Maybe hours. Maybe days. I'd lost all sense of time, and the thought clawed at me, a raw animal terror that I was already dead, that I'd never left the forest, that this was hell, and my punishment was to keep reliving the same panic over and over without end.

I jammed my hands between my knees and squeezed, trying to slow the tremor, but it only made the rest of me shake harder.

My mouth was dry. My tongue felt like a clump of dirty cotton.

I tried to count my breaths—four in, six out, like Mom taught me years ago— but they kept getting stuck on the inhale, a catch in my throat that made me want to scream.

My ribs stuttered; the world tilted.

The panic attack came on so fast that I didn't recognize it as panic. Only the roaring certainty that I was dying, for real this time, my heart exploding in my chest, my breath dissolving into nothing.

The world blanched into a white, howling noise.

I clawed at the wire, blinding myself with tears I didn't even feel, and all I could do was choke on half-formed syllables that never made it past my lips.

On the other side of the glass, Caiden's shadow jerked upright, a rapid, almost predatory lunge, as if he'd been hoping for the chance to witness my final collapse.

"You're breathing too fast," Caiden said, voice muffled but clear enough to cut through. "You're going to black out."

His face was a blur behind the glass, a shape that resolved slowly into a real boy, a boy I hated, a boy I needed.

He pressed his palm to the divider. "You're fine. It's just air. You're panicking yourself into it."

I tried to tell him to go fuck himself, but all that came out was a wet, animal sob.

My chest caved in, then ballooned out.

I was a malfunctioning machine, spiraling into brokenness.

"I can't," I gasped. "I can't—I can't—"

The words broke up in my throat, stuttered into shreds by the convulsions of my lungs. My whole body felt like a chewed wire, twitching and sparking and not quite dead.

He dragged his fingers down the surface, smearing a streak between us. "You're not dying, Amelia. You're just losing your shit."

He sounded so calm, it made me want to rip my own face off.

But then his voice cracked, a hairline fracture running through the practiced apathy. "Look at me. Not the walls. Me."

I tried, but the world was blurry, tunneling in and out, edges sharpening then softening like a bad dream.

He kept talking, voice low and regular, counting for me. "In on two, out for four. Listen to me. I'm counting. That's all."

And I did. I followed the rhythm: in on his command, out when he let me. I focused on the fog his mouth made against the glass.

I watched it appear and vanish.

I could have killed him for the way his voice slid between my ears, bypassing the rest of me. I could have killed myself for how badly I wanted to obey.

But I did as he said, because the alternative was obliteration.

Slowly, my lungs stopped convulsing, the tremor stilled to a shiver. Bile pooled at the back of my throat, but at least I was breathing.

My body remembered the bruises, the bruises remembered my body. I was here, and I was alive, and that was the worst part.

He watched me with a predator's patience. "Better," he said, and his hand lingered on the glass, fingers splayed as if he might break through.

"Don't tell me what to do," I said, voice a ruin, all gravel and salt. "You're not my keeper."

His mouth twitched, a ghost of a smile. "You sure about that?"

I pressed my palms together until my knuckles turned white.

He was still there, staring at me. "Try to sleep," he finally said, soft now, almost defeated. "You'll need it for whatever comes next."

I curled up, knees to chest, and let the sweat dry to a tacky film.

I listened to the silence, to the far-off, dripping tap of a world that had gone on without us, to the rhythmic pulse of my own blood, always, always reminding me that I remained.

Each time I blinked, the cage returned: the concrete, the rust, the stink of old metal and urine, the ghostly afterimage of Caiden's face when I had nearly drowned in the river.

How many times could a person die and wake up in the same body?

The ache in my skull had matured to a steady, buzzing halo; when I pressed my fingers to my temples, I half-expected them to sink through scalp and bone, burrowing in to scoop out the rot inside.

It was late.

I could tell by the way the yellow bulb overhead seemed to ooze rather than shine, casting everything in a sickly, buttery pallor.

There was no sound from above, not even the footsteps of our captor.

That should have been comforting, but instead the quiet only sharpened the edges of my thoughts, made the dread more acute.

I could not stop reliving what had happened, the heavy, blunt fact of it, the way I'd dissociated just enough to survive, only to have the memory flood back in with a vengeance as soon as my guard was down.

I craved oblivion. I wanted it more than I would ever admit to anyone, even myself.

Oblivion: the erasure of what had happened in this room, the reset of all my inner clocks, the mercy of waking up somewhere else —anywhere else, even if it meant being back in that surging, freezing river, gasping Caiden's name as the undertow peeled the skin off my bones.

Instead, I was left with the gnawing knowledge that nothing would ever really end, not for me.

I would keep cycling through these deaths and rebirths, each time a little less myself, until they finally carted out what was left and the world could get on with forgetting me.

# 39

## THE PRESENT

### CAIDEN

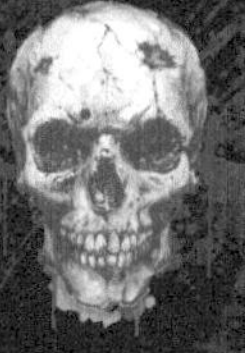

I paced the cage, round and round like a starving animal, boots carving out the same useless path in the concrete. There were scuff marks now, black tattoos from soles that couldn't stop moving. I couldn't make myself sit. Not for long.

Amelia sat in the opposite cage.

I tried to ignore her, but she was always there. A reflection, a wound, a problem I couldn't solve.

"You're making me dizzy," she snapped. Her voice cracked, raspy and thin, but she forced it out anyway. "Just stop. Please. I can't watch you anymore."

"You're dizzy because we're malnourished. Not because my boots are touching the floor." My voice was rougher than I meant. I didn't care.

She scowled, fingers digging into her arms. "You think you're so smart."

Another lap. My body ached, knees and ankles, and every place I'd been bruised in the past week reminded me they existed. "Smarter than you."

"If you were so smart, we wouldn't be here."

The words hit harder than they should. My jaw locked. "You want to blame me? Go ahead. It's not going to change anything."

She closed her eyes, head thumping back against the wall. "Just fucking stand still for once."

"I don't remember promoting you to warden," I muttered.

"Better than pacing like a caged wolf. You're not going to find a way out by wearing a hole in the floor."

I stopped. Only for a second. Then my muscles twitched, and I found myself moving again, slower this time, eyes fixed on the ground. I hated the cage. Hated the glass. Hated that every time I saw her, I remembered things I'd buried alive.

"You done?" Her words were a challenge. She wanted me to come over there, wanted me to fight her, maybe even hit the glass and see if it would bleed.

"I'll be done when he lets us out."

She stared at me, face unreadable. I didn't know what she was thinking. Didn't care, I told myself.

I kept moving. The sound of each step bounced off the concrete, making the space feel smaller.

She sighed. She sounded so damn tired. "Why do you do this?"

My laugh was empty. "Why do you care?"

"Because I have to look at you all day."

"Well, lucky you."

The fight drained out of her face. "Go to hell."

I almost smiled. "Already here."

That was when the light cut out.

Not a flicker. Not a warning. Just instant, predatory dark.

A fist closed around my throat. My skin prickled. The world collapsed. Cage, concrete, the thin barrier of glass between us. It was erased in a matter of seconds. My body forgot how to breathe. The darkness pressed against my eyes like I'd never see again.

Somewhere on the other side of the glass, I heard her gasp. Her breath stuttered, high and shaky. "Caiden?"

I didn't answer right away. I was too busy counting my heartbeats. They pounded so loud I was sure she could hear them.

The dark started to invent things. My brain tried to make sense of the nothing, tried to conjure shapes out of the thick black.

Corners became movement. Shadows became bodies. I could have sworn I felt someone in the cage with me, moving just out of arm's reach.

I tasted old panic.

My father's voice surfaced out of nowhere, low and amused, like smoke curling under a door. *Look at you now.*

I hated that. Hated how much of him was still under my skin, years after they put him in the ground. I hated that even trapped, even as a grown man, I couldn't shake the memory of being small, of listening for footsteps, knowing they'd get closer, knowing there was nowhere to hide.

I tried to remember what the basement at home had smelled like. Booze. Sweat. Decay. This place was colder, cleaner, and more precise. But the principle was the same: nowhere to run, nowhere to fight. Just endure.

Another voice cut through the black. "Are you there?"

I recognized the fear in her words. I'd heard it before, under bridges, in motel rooms, in places kids weren't supposed to hide. The ache almost made me laugh.

"I'm here," I said. My voice sounded too loud. Too human.

Something about her silence made my gut twist.

The darkness pulsed. My brain kept generating monsters, eyes, and teeth in every angle. I braced against the wall, fingers digging into the cold concrete, willing myself not to lose it.

I wondered if she could hear my breathing. If she could sense, somehow, that I was just as scared as she was.

She whispered, "Don't leave me."

"I'm not going anywhere." The words came out before I could stop them. I hated the softness in my voice. Hated that even after everything, my first instinct was to keep her from falling apart.

"I can't see anything," she said, voice barely a thread.

"I know." My hands flexed uselessly. "It's just dark. That's all."

I'd been in worse. That's what I told myself.

The dark pressed closer, cold hands around my neck.

I remember closets. I remember blankets wrapped over my head, trying to stifle every sound so nobody would find me. I remember the way his shadow fell through the crack under the door, stretching, growing, swallowing everything.

The urge to scream rattled in my chest like a trapped fly. Instead, I pressed my forehead against the bars, breathing slow and steady, counting off numbers in my head. Anything to keep the emptiness from overflowing.

Was Amelia crying? I couldn't tell. Maybe it was just the sound of her breath snagging on her ribs.

"You still breathing?" I growled.

"Not sure," she whispered.

I let my head hang. "Start counting. It helps."

"What?"

"Just do it. Count to five. Then start over."

She didn't answer, but I could almost feel her concentrating. The quiet between us buzzed.

I pictured her on the other side of the glass, hugging her knees, eyes wide and white in the dark. I wanted to punch something. I wanted to break through, just to touch her shoulder, just to prove she was still real.

The air felt like glass shards cutting my throat.

Why was he doing this? The psychopath upstairs. I imagined him sitting in the light, watching us on some hidden camera, grinning at the panic. Flicking the switch on and off, just to remind himself he owned us.

What was it about people like him, always needing to own something helpless?

The seconds dragged. I felt each one crawl under my skin and make a home there.

I pictured my father's laugh. I wanted to be better than him. But sometimes, in the dark, I wondered if the rot had gotten into my bones too.

Would I survive this? Would she?

I started talking, just to fill the space. "He's probably just fucking with us. He wants us scared."

"He's succeeding," she said.

"What else is new?"

I heard her shift, heard her knuckles crack. "Is he going to kill us?"

I didn't want to answer. "Not if I can help it."

A beat. Then: "You really think you can stop him?"

"I'll try."

"You always say that," she snapped.

"What do you want from me, a guarantee? Nothing in life is guaranteed."

The words echoed, bitter as bile. My father had taught me that.

The dark thickened, pressed against my skull.

I wanted to blame her for something. Anything. Maybe if I could hate her enough, I wouldn't care what happened in the end. But hate and fear started to feel the same, down in the marrow.

My hands wouldn't stop shaking.

"Are you scared?" she asked suddenly.

I waited. "Yeah," I said. "I am."

The silence between us was grave.

Then, without warning, the light snapped back on.

Pain hit my eyes. Everything was flooded with white. I blinked, trying to adjust, trying not to look as relieved as I was.

She hunched away from the glare, like she'd been shot.

We stared at each other through the smeared glass. I saw her, all of her: the trembling lips, the haunted eyes, the bruises on her wrists. Barely hanging on.

She saw me too. And I didn't like what was staring back.

The world was smaller now. The cage, the memory, her presence. All of it heavier.

Above us, something creaked. Footsteps on the stairs. I knew what came next.

But in that moment, it was just us. Naked and shaking.

Maybe that was the worst part.

———

The footsteps grew louder. Wood groaning under boots, relentless and heavy. Each step pulled the world tighter around my throat. I watched the door, watched the tiny rectangle of light at the top of the basement stairs grow and then shrink as he blocked it out.

The kidnapper came down slow, savoring the moment like he was walking into a surprise party. Everything about him reeked of patience, like a wolf that knew the sheep could never escape.

He stood on the lowest step, his hands loose at his sides. His eyes flickered over both cages, then fixed on me. He smiled. No warmth in it.

His voice was soft, almost kind. "Isn't it peaceful? How quiet it gets down here at night?"

I didn't answer. Neither did Amelia.

He smiled wider, showing molars. He rested his hand on the mesh of the cage, close enough that I could see the veins crawling up his wrist. He held the silence as if it was a living thing.

The knife appeared from his belt. Smooth, practiced, the movement so casual it made my skin crawl. I couldn't stop staring at the blade. The edge gleamed, a thin thread of light in the basement gloom.

"I was thinking," he said. "If I opened the cage right now, which one of you would try for the knife first?"

Neither of us breathed.

He looked at me. Then at her. "Or maybe you'd both just freeze. Bunnies in a snare." He tapped the point of the blade against the steel. "You ever see what happens when two animals are cornered? Sometimes they rip each other apart for the hell of it."

I gritted my teeth. "Why don't you open it and find out?"

His head tilted, like I was something in a petri dish. "Bravery. I like that. You talk big. But what do you do when the door actually opens?"

I stepped up to the bars, as close as I could get, hands wrapping around cold metal. "I'd kill you."

"No," he said, voice gentle, as if he was explaining math to a child. "You'd try. You'd fail." His gaze slid to Amelia. "But I wonder, which of you has more to lose?"

The room throbbed with silence. I could hear her breathing, thin and sick, like a dying animal.

He crouched, coming level with my eyes. "You think you're a hero. She thinks you'll save her."

I wanted to leap at him, wrap my hands around his throat. But all I could do was stand there, the rage boiling in my head, heart pounding out of rhythm.

He watched me simmer, let the moment drag. "You want to know what I think?" The knife drifted towards the lock, slow and deliberate. He ran the tip around the edge, tapping metal against metal.

"I think you both make a lot of noise, but at the end of the day, you're just scared kids. That's what you'll always be. Scared and weak and waiting for someone to save you."

He stood up, brushing dust from his knees. "I could let you out right now. Set the two of you loose. But then the fun would be over. Where's the art in that?"

He paced in front of the cages, slicing the air with the knife, watching our eyes follow every movement. The bastard was getting off on it.

Amelia whimpered, soft, barely a sound at all.

He grinned. "She's the one who would run," he said to me. "Not you. You're the one who stays and takes the punishment."

"Try me," I spat.

He pressed his face close to the bars, shadows eating the lines of his jaw. "You think pain scares me? I was born in it." He tapped the knife against his temple. "Up here, you either learn to love the dark or the dark eats you alive."

He stepped back, studied us with that blank, cold stare. "Sleep tight, pets."

He left as silently as he'd come, footsteps fading into the ceiling, leaving a bruise of dread behind.

For a minute, the only sound was the hum of the basement light and our twin heartbeats battering the air.

Then, from the other side of the glass: "Caiden."

I swallowed. "Yeah?"

Her voice trembled. "I don't want to die here."

I closed my eyes. A thousand memories crashed together. Every bruise, every scream, every time I'd failed to protect anything. But something was different now. The violence in my blood had a name and a purpose.

"You won't." My voice sounded alien. "I'll get you out. I promise."

Afraid to say the rest out loud: I would do anything. Anything. Break every bone in my body. Rip out his heart. Sell my own soul. I would burn the world to keep her breathing.

But that thought scared me almost as much as the knife.

I pressed my palm to the glass, watching her mirror me. We sat in our boxes, caged and broken, but not dead yet.

I wouldn't let it end that way. Let him play his games. Let him turn the dark on and off. We'd find a way out.

Even if it killed me.

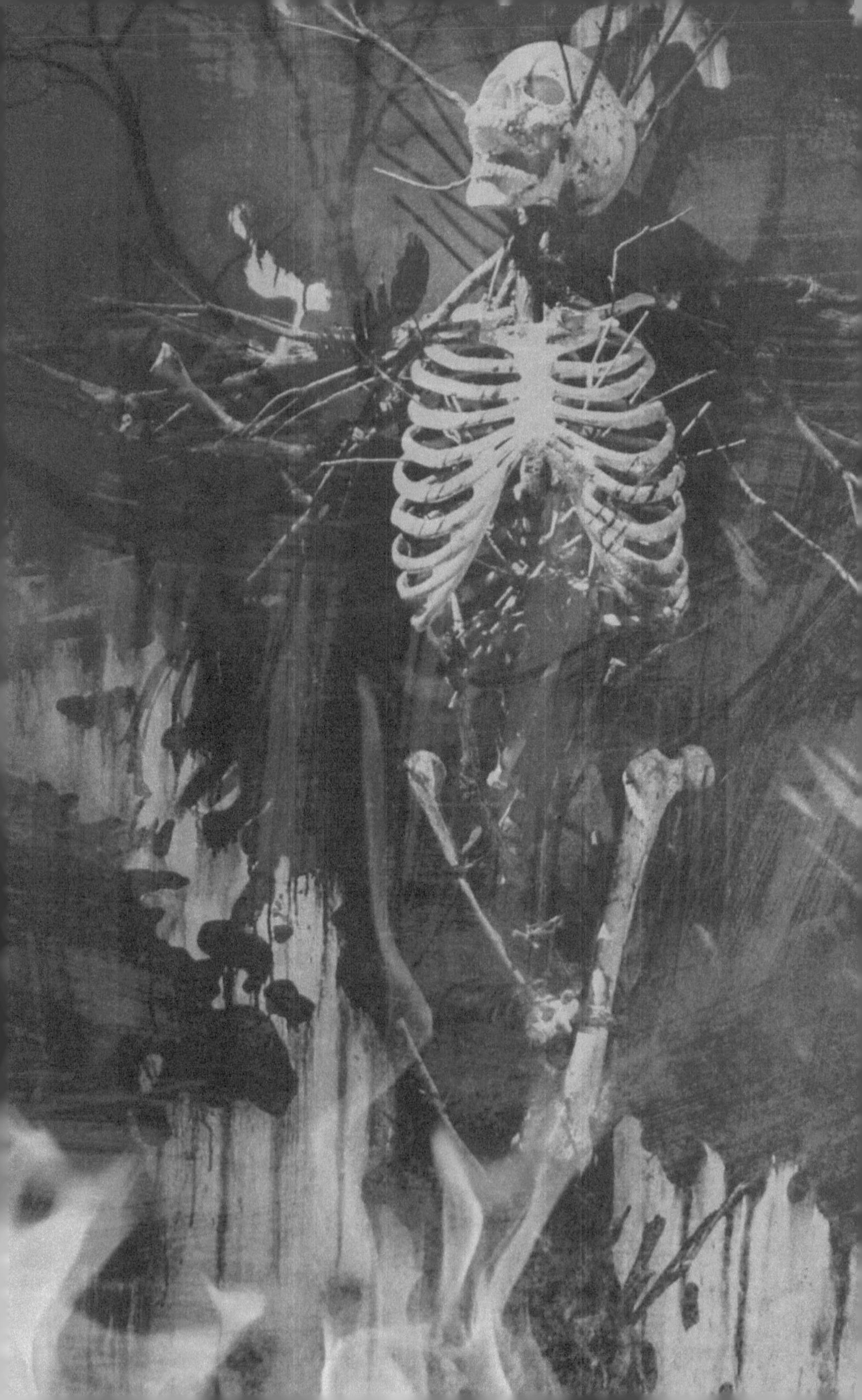

# 40

## THE PAST

### CAIDEN'S CONDITIONING

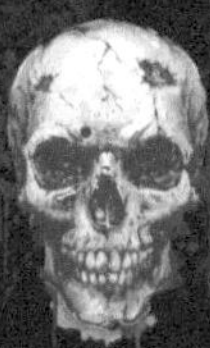

**18 YEARS OLD**

I was halfway through senior year, counting the days until graduation.

The day when I could maybe escape, the day when I could maybe be free. But freedom was an empty dream, and I knew the inevitable was suffering in the claws of my father.

Today, something was bubbling inside me. I could feel it the second I woke up. The heat in my blood, the sorrow in my heart, the loudness of my father.

My hatred for Amelia was blooming into something dark, possessing me like a fucking hungry beast.

But last night, I had a dream. No, a memory.

I dreamt of Amelia. Her innocence, her hair, her scent, how fucking adorable she was when we were kids.

I woke sweating. The dream was simple. We were back in the park when my voice had a higher tone, and my knuckles were still pink and unscarred.

Amelia was perched on a swing, chattering about birdsong and the shape of clouds, her hands waving with frantic, childish energy.

In the dream, her teeth were blindingly white, and her laugh made the leaves vibrate. I'd wanted to reach over and touch her, just to see if she was real, if her skin was as soft as I remembered, but even in the dream I lurched to violence instead, snatching a caterpillar out of her hand and crushing it in my fist. She cried.

I woke up furious at myself for even in fantasy being so pathetically transparent.

I sat up and rubbed my face hard, trying to shake the sleep off, but the rage didn't go with it. It never did.

I got dressed fast. Jeans. Hoodie. Boots.

When I walked out, the living room was a mess. Empty cans. Ash. A half-crushed chip bag under the coffee table. My father sat in his chair like a king on a throne made of rot, one hand resting on a bottle.

He didn't look at me at first.

He never did, not in a normal way. He only looked at me when he wanted to prove something. When he needed a target. When he wanted to remind himself, he still owned something in this miserable house.

I tried to move past like I didn't exist. Like I wasn't a pulse he could crush with one sentence.

He spoke anyway. "You going to school today, or you planning to be a worthless piece of shit your whole life?"

I stopped with my hand on the doorframe. My stomach twisted, but my face stayed blank.

"Going," I muttered.

He snorted. "Sure. Good. Maybe you'll learn something. Like how to stop embarrassing me."

Embarrassing him. How fucking ironic.

I didn't respond. If I responded, it would turn into a fight. If it turned into a fight, something would break. If something broke, it would be me.

So I swallowed my words like broken glass and walked out the door.

At school, her presence haunted me with the persistence of a toothache. I saw her everywhere: at her locker, bent over an overdue library book; in chem lab, mouth set in a thin, haunted line; at the edge of the quad, squinting into the wind, hair a living flame.

I wanted her wrecked. I wanted her to fall apart the way I did every time I caught my father's shadow on the wall.

Yet I also felt a weird, painful burn in my chest every time I caught sight of her, a tangle of panicked want and loathing, a chemical spiral that left me dizzy and raw.

I hadn't thought about these feelings in years. But now, they were in my vision, pulsing and burning.

Friday lunch, the cafeteria was a madhouse, and I took my usual place at the end of the table, a kingdom of empty milk cartons and poverty-tier pizza.

Dante sat across from me.

The air felt electric. Like something was about to happen, something stupid and irreversible.

I spotted her, as I always did. Amelia, hunched over her lunch tray, poking at the limp green beans like maybe they'd bite back.

She looked more hollow than usual. A little less color in her cheeks, her eyes rimmed dark like she hadn't slept in a week. I hated myself for noticing.

Dante nudged me, noticing who I was staring at. "You see Amelia's hair? Looks like she's not doing so well."

His face held concern, and I scowled.

"She looks like a corpse," I replied, but the words tasted sour. "Maybe she finally realized nobody cares if she breathes."

Dante raised an eyebrow, and I could tell my friend was reading me, weighing the danger of pushing further. "Shit, man, you're obsessed. Just admit you want to rail her."

My jaw flexed.

I wanted to punch Dante in the mouth for saying that. But it was true, a sick, festering truth, and the urge coiled hotter than ever.

I hated her, I did. But sometimes, the pull of hatred and the lust of desire became a confusing haze in my head.

"Fuck off," I muttered, stabbing my fork into a clotted wad of mashed potato.

Images conjured in my mind that made my pulse throb: Amelia's mouth, parted with surprise, the soft arch of her throat when she laughed.

I forced the thoughts down, hid them beneath the layered misery that shielded me from myself.

"She's nothing," I spat, louder than intended. Other heads turned. I felt the heat rise in my neck.

I stood abruptly, chair scraping across the floor, and stalked out of the cafeteria, leaving the tray and my friend behind.

I didn't stop moving till I reached the gym, its echoing darkness a sterile and familiar comfort.

I ducked into the empty weight room, let the clang and grind of metal be the only sound. I loaded the bar with more than I could handle, let it pin me to the bench until my arms shook and my vision blurred at the edges.

Every rep was a red purge, a wrenching away of the weakness. I thought of Amelia. Her delicate neck, the light in her eyes when she stood up for herself.

I pictured her hands, how they'd shake when I got too close, how she would go pale and shiver even when it wasn't cold.

I kept pushing, letting the weight crash down, black stars swimming at the edges of my vision, until I lost count of the sets and couldn't feel my arms anymore.

After, I sat on the rubber matting, sweat soaking through my cutoffs, and let my head fall back against the wall. The world pulsed with each beat of my heart.

I didn't want to move, ever again. But even there, in my exhaustion, the images of Amelia wouldn't leave me. They layered over the ceiling tiles, invaded the bloodshot dark when I closed my eyes.

I was fucked, and I knew it.

After the workout, I showered in the empty locker room, letting the hot water scald me until my skin was streaked red. I scrubbed harder than I needed, trying to sand away the feeling that I was unclean, that something formless and shameful was crawling just under my skin.

I caught my face in the mirror. There was no softness left in my features, only harsh lines and angry shadows. I looked older than I should, like my father in a certain light, and that terrified me more than anything.

I ditched the rest of afternoon classes, prowling the length of the football field until my legs ached and my thoughts spun out into static.

The sun was pale and useless this late in the year, but I craved its warmth like a junkie. I lay on my back beneath the home bleachers, squinting through the bars at the empty sky, and let the chill leech through my clothes.

For the first time in years, I let myself feel the thing I'd spent a lifetime beating to death. The want. It was a pure, destructive force, the untamable animal inside me, and it hurt in a way that almost felt good.

I thought of the dream again. Amelia, the swing, her hair catching gold in the sun, and the ache in my chest flared so bright it made me want to scream or laugh or both.

There was something in her that called to all the ruined pieces of myself, some echo of softness I'd never been allowed to keep.

When the last bell of the school day rang, I lingered in the empty quad, watching the slow migration of students leaving the school.

I flexed my bruised knuckles, rolling my thumb over the scabbed skin, and searched for her. Amelia.

She always cut through the courtyard at this time of day, her gait quick and stilted, her eyes locked on a point somewhere beyond the horizon. I could almost time her presence to the minute; there was a discipline to her misery, a schedule for her pain.

And there she was. A distant shape, arms cradling textbooks across her chest, dark hair streaming behind her like a flag of surrender.

I pressed my tongue to the cut inside my cheek, tasted salt and metal, and for an instant the world tunneled to just the two of us, all noise and color collapsing into a single point of gravity.

I hated how my body reacted, how the sight of her sent a current through my nerves, how my heart stuttered and then snapped into double-time.

It felt like weakness. Worse, it felt like hunger.

I stayed hidden, just watching.

She didn't notice me at first; her eyes flicked left and right, scanning for threats but never seeing the ones that mattered. When she finally sensed me there, her pace faltered. She tightened her grip on her books, as if the extra pressure would keep her from shattering on the spot.

She was close enough now that I could hear the faint rattle of her breath, the uneven steps she took to keep her distance. I could have reached out and grabbed the strap of her backpack, reeled her in like a fish on a trembling line. The urge was there, as always, to close the gap. To see if she'd fight back or just crumple and cry.

But I didn't.

I took the long way home, a route through side streets and half-abandoned lots, letting the chill of late spring scrape the heat from my skin.

The memory of the dream clung to me, damp and persistent, the way cigarette smoke clings to a thrift store jacket. I flexed my hands until my knuckles cracked, as if I could squeeze the image of her out through my palms, but it only grew sharper, more insistent.

By the time I reached my house, the sky had gone the color of old bruises, and the porch light buzzed with a swarm of moths.

I stood at the edge of the driveway for a full minute, staring at the warped siding and the sagging gutters, wondering if tonight was one of the good ones. If my father were so far gone, he wouldn't notice me at all.

I pushed through the front door, letting it slam behind me, and the smell hit me like a punch: piss, sweat, the metallic sweetness of spilled beer gone sour.

The TV blared a sports recap show, the volume cranked to a level that made every word sound like a threat. My father was in the battered armchair, a plastic liter bottle of cheap vodka balanced precariously on his thigh.

"Look who it is," my father said, not turning. "The prodigal shithead. Home before midnight for once."

I didn't bother with a response. I moved to the kitchen, the soles of my boots sticking to the floor, and opened the fridge for something to eat.

I grabbed a slice of bologna and folded it into my mouth in one bite, chewing without tasting, then washed it down with water straight from the faucet.

I'd almost made it to my room when my father called out again, his voice slurred. "Hey! Get your ass in here."

I paused, every muscle in my body hardening with dread. I considered ignoring the summons, but that always made it worse in the long run.

I walked into the living room, arms crossed over my chest. The bastard didn't even look up.

"You skipping school again?" he asked, eyes glued to the TV. "Got a message from the office. Said you're about to flunk out if you don't get your shit together."

"Don't care," I muttered.

My father made a show of sighing, as if the weight of

disappointment was crushing his ribcage. "You're a fuck-up, you know that? You're gonna end up like your mother, running away from everything." He raised the vodka bottle in a silent toast, eyes bloodshot and yellow at the edges. "At least she had the sense to leave."

The old rage surged up, raw and electric, but I ground my teeth and looked at the floor. If I didn't respond, I could sometimes ride out the abuse until it burned itself down to cinders.

But tonight, my father was in a mood. "Look at me when I talk to you," he shouted, and when I didn't, the bottle flew across the room, smashing on the wall above me, liquor fanning out in a sticky comet as the bottle wrecked itself against the drywall.

I didn't flinch, but the sound did something to me. Snapped the last filament of self-control inside my chest.

"Clean that up, you little shit," my father spat, not even watching for a reaction.

I went to the kitchen, dug out the crusted mop, and blotted the puddle of vodka from the carpet, the stench burning my nostrils. The urge to burn the house to its bones, to torch everything and walk into the ash, pulsed white-hot under my skin.

I almost did it. Almost set the rag on fire and chucked it onto the couch, to see if my father would even notice before he was part of the smoke.

But the memory from that morning cut through, stopped me cold: Amelia's voice as a kid, the way she'd said my name like it was something precious, not something broken and thrown away.

I'd killed that feeling a thousand times, buried it deep, and yet there it was, alive and kicking at the inside of my skull. It made me want to scream, or punch the emptiness into submission, or just find a way to shut it up for good.

I finished the cleaning, tucked the mop away, and stared at the red-hot line of my knuckles where I'd clenched the handle too tightly.

I wiped the spill, rinsed my hands, and headed for the door.

"Where do you think you're going?" my father barked, now fully upright.

"Out," I replied, my voice flat as a gravestone.

"Don't come back here unless you plan to act like a man," he said, then dropped back into the chair.

That's when I snapped. "I'm more of a fucking man than you. Your own wife couldn't stand you and left. She left me here with a goddamn monster."

My father lurched out of the chair, the remote thumping to the floor and batteries rolling under the couch.

His face was angry, veins throbbing in his temple, mouth wet and trembling with words that wanted to be fists. "You little fuck. I should have left you at the hospital. I should have drowned you in the goddamn bathtub the minute I found out you were mine."

I almost laughed. It was the same threats, the same spit-streaked litany of disappointment and hate. What was new was the way a part of me, a very small and haunting part, felt nothing at all.

"I gave you everything. I put a roof over your head. I showed you how to be strong. And all you do is whine and mouth off, just like her. Useless."

He continued to advance. A slow, rolling threat.

"You're drunk," I spat. "You're always drunk. Your threats don't mean shit to me anymore. You don't even know why you're angry anymore."

My father sneered, as if reading my mind. He knuckled his bloodshot eyes and jabbed a finger in my direction. "You think you're better than this? Than me? You want to know what a real man does? He takes what he wants. He gets even, and he doesn't whine about his fucking feelings."

My jaw tightened, feeling the muscles jump in my cheek. "You ever think maybe that's why everyone leaves you?" I asked, the words landing with less force than I meant.

My father just laughed. A dry, rattling sound.

"Yeah? Well, at least when I fucked up, I got something out of it." He wiped his mouth with the back of his hand and leaned in, voice dropping to a hiss. "You know what your problem is, Caiden? You got your mother's softness in you. All that hope, all that wishing. That's why she ran."

The room spun a little, his voice, the TV, the tang of blood and rot all swirling together in a way that was almost psychedelic. I could see the rage in his eyes, but underneath it, there was something else. Fear. Or maybe regret, but more likely just terror that I would become something he couldn't control.

"You wanna act like a man?" he sneered. "Then you gotta kill what's soft in you. You gotta break it before it breaks you. That's all women are good for, son, breaking men. They'll smile at you while they stick a knife in your gut, and they'll walk away laughing. You need to be meaner. Maybe you might actually be loved if you're meaner."

My face went cold, skin stretched over bone, my mouth opening and closing but only spit and air emerging.

There was no winning. Not with my father, not with myself, not with Amelia, not even with the world. It was all just a sick, looping game, and every night I told myself I didn't care, I didn't want her, I didn't feel, but then I dreamed of her and woke up wanting to set something on fire.

Maybe my father was right. Maybe I needed to be crueler. Perhaps I was only good at crippling hearts with my words and bleeding them out.

I had to get out. I was a human fire alarm, nerves screaming, every fiber in my body ready to start a riot.

I scraped together my wallet and a pack of crumpled Camels and walked out, not sure where I was going, only that it had to be away.

The cold hit me in the face, wind biting through my hoodie, but I liked the pain. It was real, uncomplicated, nothing to decode.

The streets were empty except for the blinking neon above Duffy's, the only bar in a ten-mile radius that would serve a kid who could barely grow a beard.

My fake ID was a joke, Dante had made it on a laminator in the school library, but the bartenders at Duffy's didn't give a shit.

All they cared about was that you didn't puke on the pool table or start a fight you couldn't finish.

I pushed through the door. The regulars were hunched like gargoyles around the bar, eyes glassy and indifferent.

I liked that about this place. Nobody cared who you were or what you were running from. You slid money across the counter, and the bartender slid oblivion right back at you.

I took a seat at the end, near the jukebox, and nursed a whiskey Coke with both hands, staring at the TV above the bar. Some sitcom played to a captive audience of zero. I drank until my jaw unclenched, until the edges of my anger went fuzzy and loose.

After maybe forty minutes, I noticed her.

Lillian Langston, Amelia's older sister.

She had already graduated from high school, but I remembered seeing her when she still went to our school. She was three years older, so I never interacted with her much.

But something pulled me to her. She did look similar to Amelia in the face. Maybe that's why I went over to her. Or maybe I was just sad and needed comfort.

She was a little drunk, but managed to keep her eyeliner from smudging, which was more than could be said for the state of her hands, ringed with purple marker, some old cigarette burn on the web between thumb and finger.

Lillian was slouched against the bar, two empty shot glasses already lined up and a third sweating beneath her palm. Her hair, darker than Amelia's and long enough to tangle in the little bowl of peanuts, fell in ropes around her face.

She looked like she'd given up on pretending to care.

I ordered another drink, then sidled up beside her, not even sure what words would come out.

In the muted light, her resemblance to Amelia was uncanny, but the effect was like seeing a photo after too many generations of photocopying. The lines blurred, a little more haunted around the eyes.

She didn't look at me when she spoke, just stared into the bar mirror, lips tight around the rim of her glass. "I know you," she said, voice flat and steady. "You're that Baxter kid. The one makes my little sister cry."

I almost retorted with something mean, but it didn't land right. Instead, I took a long drink of whiskey, letting the burn recalibrate my insides. "She used to cry a lot. Now she just looks empty," I said finally, twisting a cocktail napkin until it tore.

Lillian just shrugged. "We all lost our will to cry. Life is all about emptiness now." She tapped the rim of her glass, empty except for a curl of melting ice. "What are you doing here?"

I shrugged and scanned the room as if the answer might be on a TV screen. "Avoiding home. You?"

She grinned, though it was a sad twist of the lips. "Me too. My mom is being a drugged-up bitch. Needed to escape for a little bit."

She looked at me finally, and there was nothing in her eyes but the weary, feral light of someone who had run out of things to lose.

"I get that," I said. "My dad's an alcoholic. He's in one of his asshole moods tonight." I didn't really mean to say it out loud, but the whiskey was working fast and loose.

Lillian nodded in a way that told me she understood. She sighed and changed the subject before it got too dark. "You're not even old enough to be in here, are you?"

I shook my head. "Not by a long shot. I'm eighteen."

She seemed to like that answer and slid her empty glass next to mine. "You want to get out of here? I got some weed and more alcohol at my place. Mom's on a bender, so she won't be home. Or conscious. Pretty sure Amelia left for the night to escape my mom, so we'll be alone."

I'd never been to the Langston house, but I could draw the blueprint from memory. The ghost of Amelia in every doorway, the quiet rooms.

I wasn't sure what came over me, but I agreed. I needed a distraction, even if it was with the sister of my enemy.

Or maybe, just for a night, I wanted to be with somebody who reminded me of Amelia, just so I could have that sick taste of being near her, just to see what it might feel like.

I followed her out, side by side, into the night. I hopped into her car since I had walked to the bar, and she drove in silence toward her house.

The driveway was edged with garden gnomes, their faces bleached and split by the cold. The house itself sagged at the porch, a rash of moss crawling up the shingles, the porch light dangling from a cord like a hanged man's tooth.

Lillian waited at the door, keys in hand, her hair wild and unbrushed. She didn't say anything until the door shut behind us.

She padded ahead on bare feet, stepping over it with practiced indifference. I caught the glint of her eyes in a hallway mirror and saw how little she cared about the mess, how little she cared about anything at all.

She led me to her room, all the way through a living room where the TV was tuned to static and a framed photo of the Langston girls glared at me from above the mantel. I didn't look too closely at it. I didn't want to see Amelia's face or feel the old guilt gnawing from the inside out.

Lillian flopped down on her bed and patted beside her.

"Sit, man. You look like you're about to bolt through the window."

She fished a joint from her nightstand and flicked a battered Zippo to life, the flame licking up with a sweet, chemical snap.

I sat, more than a foot of space between us, and stared at the posters on the wall. Elliott Smith, some poet I didn't know, a glossy cutout of a wolf's head with the tongue scribbled in blue Sharpie.

She lit the joint, inhaled, and watched me through a half-lidded gaze as she exhaled. "You can relax. I'm not gonna bite. Unless you want." She grinned, showing teeth. "So. Baxter boy. What do you want to talk about?"

I took the joint when she offered. I was no stranger to weed, but this was strong, chemical and bright, and it crackled down my throat in a rush.

I coughed, wiped my mouth, and handed it back. "Wasn't planning to talk," I said, my voice rougher than intended.

"Not planning to hook up either?" she teased, but there was no real threat behind it. She was just watching me, seeing what made me squirm.

I shrugged. "I just didn't want to be at home."

She stared into the dark corner above her desk, where a string of fairy lights had half-burned out. "You want a drink?"

"Sure."

She got up, winding her way through piles of laundry and books, and came back with bottles. She handed me one and watched me drink, then poured herself the same in a cup. "To bad decisions," she toasted.

The burn was glorious. Sweet, just enough to drown out the static. I felt my whole body loosen, my limbs buzzing, and my mind going white at the edges.

Everything in the room softened, lost its angles.

Except for Lillian, who somehow, through the haze, became clearer.

She perched on the bed across from me with her legs curled underneath her, swigging vodka like it was nothing more than water. "You're a quiet one, aren't you?" she said.

I shrugged, not trusting myself to speak. I was tight-wired, jittery; the inside of my head buzzed with the beginnings of a migraine and the clamor of everything I'd tried not to feel.

The joint spun between us, a slow spiral from her lips to mine, and I took it each time with fake nonchalance, holding the smoke until my lungs crackled.

The room was hot, but the booze and weed made my skin tingle, brought every nerve to the surface.

Lillian watched me with a smirk, like she was waiting for me to break and didn't even care if I did. "You're not very fun, you know," she said. "I thought you'd be all brooding and rage. You're famous for it."

I ignored the bait and knocked back more vodka. "I'm just tired tonight," I said. "Tired of being angry."

She shrugged, and for a moment she looked almost childlike, hunched there, drinking with a stranger and pretending it didn't matter.

"So what's your deal?" she said. "You always look like you want to punch the world. Or maybe just yourself. Which is it?"

I didn't answer. I just drank and let the warmth spread from my chest to my fingertips.

"It's complicated," I mumbled.

Lillian laughed. "It's always complicated. That's what everyone says before they do something stupid." She leaned in, close enough that I could see the tremble in the hand that held her glass. "You ever try just letting it out? Not the hitting. The talking."

I rolled the bottle between my palms, thinking how stupid it would sound to spill my guts to the sister of the girl I'd spent years tormenting.

I was supposed to hate her, and everything about this house, but instead it felt weirdly safe, almost comfortable. Like I'd stumbled into a parallel reality where nobody expected shit from me.

"What about talking it out with my sister?" Lillian cocked her head and studied me. "Resolving whatever anger you have toward her."

A bitter laugh pushed out of me. There was no way I could explain the origin of my hatred, how it all came back to my father, and the abandonment of my mother. "I don't know," I said. "Amelia gets under my skin. Always has. She's weak, but she's not. Makes me feel like shit just by existing. There's no fixing it."

Lillian's smile faded. She took another hit. "She's not as delicate as you think," she said. "You think you're the only one walking around with splinters inside?"

She let the bitterness hang there, then shrugged it off. "You two are more alike than you know."

That scraped something raw inside me. I didn't respond. I drank instead.

"It's easier," I muttered. "To numb it."

I drank until the room began to spin.

"Maybe I just need to get her out of my head. Beat it out, fuck it out, whatever works."

"If you want to fuck her out, you'll have to get in line," Lillian shot back. She uncapped the vodka and poured them both another, the overflow beading on her knuckles. "I'm only half kidding. Guys have been sniffing around her since middle school and she barely looks at them. You think you're the first one to want a piece?"

I grimaced, the burn in my stomach suddenly colder. I didn't want a piece, I wanted the whole fucked-up animal thing, wanted to turn her inside out and see what was left, if there was anything beneath the rot and brokenness.

I drained my glass, waited for the world to come back into focus. "I was never in line," I said, voice thick. "I'm not even in the running."

Lillian watched me like she was measuring how close I was to the edge. "If not with Amelia," she said, voice low, "I can help with being a distraction. Only if you want."

I heard the dare in her voice, the recklessness. I should have left, should have put my head through the window and walked back into the sleepy churn of my father's disappointment.

Instead, I reached for the joint, took another hit, and let the smoke spool tight in my chest. "You saying you want to help?" I asked, my words thick with the warp of vodka and weed.

Lillian tilted her chin, her hair swinging forward to curtain her face. "I'm saying you don't have to be alone with your poison."

I didn't answer. I just watched the way she moved on the bed, the way she rolled the joint between her thumb and forefinger, the way her mouth curled around the filter. If I squinted, I could almost see Amelia's shape in her. The same set of brow, the same dark drift in her eyes.

Something in me twisted nasty. I wanted to insult her, to cut the moment open with cruelty, but nothing worth saying came to mind. My tongue felt huge and useless in my mouth.

Lillian slid to the edge of the bed, her thigh pressing against mine. "You ever just let go, Caiden?" she said, her voice low. "Or do you always have to be holding the knife?"

I flinched at the sound of my name. It was too intimate, too real. For a second, it was Amelia's voice saying it, not this older echo, but the girl I'd spent years trying to erase from my own bones.

I put the joint to my lips and inhaled until my vision swam. When the smoke left my lungs, I felt a little lighter, a little more suspended. As if, if I cut every anchor, I might just float through the ceiling and dissolve with the heat.

I didn't look at her for a long time. I just let the burn trickle through the veins in my hands, let the numbness work its way up my arms. I closed my eyes and waited for the feeling to crest, but Lillian's thigh was an insistent heat next to mine. It was a reminder: I'm here. I'm not allowed to drift. Not when the world is made of corners and people who never fucking leave you alone.

"Why are you doing this?" I asked, hating myself for how pathetic it sounded.

She shrugged then took the Camels from my jacket and sparked one up as easy and thoughtless as breathing. "Why does anyone do anything?" she said. "We're all just flailing around, trying not to choke, giving in to whatever will distract us from the dark."

I watched the cigarette smolder between her lips, the orange pulse bright each time she sucked in, and for a moment I thought about how easy it would be to just reach over and touch her. Her mouth was the same shape as Amelia's when she frowned, and the idea made my skin crawl. But it also made my heart ratchet up a notch.

Lillian exhaled, blowing a stream of smoke at the ceiling, and time seemed to dilate. Everything slowed to the birth of a single thought—

I didn't want to leave. I wanted to feed the animal. To see how far I could press her, or myself, before something broke for good. It was selfish, it was trash, but the hunger inside me didn't give a shit about dignity.

She tipped the last of the vodka into her mouth, wiped her lips with the back of her hand, then did something I didn't expect.

She stood up abruptly, teetered for a moment, and peeled her dress up and over her head in one practiced move, letting it drop to the carpet as she stepped out of it. She stood there in a black bra and lace panties, and for a second I couldn't breathe.

Her skin was as pale as a crescent moon. She shivered, and for a minute neither of us spoke.

My tongue felt replaced with glass, and the sight made me dizzy with a new kind of tension. There was a sick irony to it: sitting in the Langston house, in the room where all the ghosts of my childhood enemies and obsessions were crammed into the carpet and the walls, being seduced into something ugly and reckless by the sister of the girl who had ruined me.

The bile of the day was still hot in my throat, my father's words and the memory of that dream clinging to my skin. I wanted to smash a window, punch a crater in the drywall, run until my legs snapped.

Instead, I just watched Lillian: the sway of her hips as she knelt back onto the bed, the way she didn't bother to cover herself, the way she met my gaze head-on, unapologetic.

"Don't overthink it, Baxter," she said, her voice thick and slurred but laced with a strange clarity. "You look like you're about to run, or puke."

I should have been numb to everything by now, too empty to even register the churn. But my skin prickled with every movement she made, and the animal inside me.

Not the one that fought, not the one that grew strong on hate, but the other one, the one that hungered and starved and pawed at the insides of my ribcage.

I hated this, hated her, hated myself. Mostly myself, for being so weak, for wanting anything at all. I wanted to scream at her to put her dress back on, to roll back the last ten minutes, to erase the sight of her body and the raw need crawling up my limbs. But I did nothing.

She climbed across the bed, movements smooth and deliberate, the practiced confidence of a girl who'd learned exactly how to weaponize her own body.

She stopped a foot from me, kneeling, bare thighs folded under her, arms loose and patient. "It's not complicated," she said, voice softer now, almost slurred, like she was talking to herself more than to me. "It's just chemicals and meat. The body wants what it wants, so you give it something. Then it's quiet for a while."

I sat there, hands limp, and watched her as she climbed onto my lap.

It was Lillian's weight, the warmth of her bare skin pressing through my jeans, that snapped the last thread of resistance.

She straddled me, thighs bracketing my hips, the trembling in her hands at odds with the tilt of her chin. I didn't know if it was the vodka or the weed or just the loneliness, but I let her settle there, let her nudge my hands to her waist, let her pull my mouth to hers.

Her lips were soft, parted, and insistent, tasting of cinnamon and smoke.

I kissed her back only because it was easier than refusing, because I knew how to be wanted only in the context of being used, and Lillian, god, she was using me, using me to patch some hole in her own chest.

Her hands slipped under my shirt, fingers cold and restless against my belly, then up to my chest, tracing lines over my ribs as if she could feel the ugly things I kept caged inside.

She broke the kiss, forehead pressed tight to mine, hair curtaining our faces. In the dim, I saw her swallow.

"You okay?" she whispered, voice rough with need or sadness or both.

I almost said no. But I didn't. Just gripped her hips harder, dragging her against me in a rhythm that was half plea, half punishment. I wanted to hate her for how easily she'd found the switches to flip, for how she'd peeled away my armor with so little effort.

But mostly I hated myself for letting it happen, for wanting it to happen, because being with Lillian was the closest thing to Amelia Langston, to feeding my hunger.

I was inside the warmth of Lillian, but what I wanted was to be outside myself. That was the whole point, wasn't it? To push my own body out to the perimeter, let it become a set piece while the rest of me—the hungry core—hid somewhere unreachable and watched the show.

The vodka burned, the weed made everything feel underwater, my fingers tingling like they were waking from a decade's sleep.

Lillian's mouth was open against my neck, her voice a ragged, fading echo, but I paid no attention to the words.

I watched the ceiling, counted the chips in the paint, and the constellations of black mold creeping along the plaster. I did not want to see her face. I did not want to see my own expression reflected in her wide eyes.

I pressed my palm over her breastbone as she rocked above me, feeling the frantic triphammer of her heart, and for a second I thought of crushing down, hard, seeing what noise she'd make if I really tried.

That was the echo of my father, the violence curled in the roots of my DNA, the urge to take and hollow and leave the rest for crows. But I didn't. I just held her steady, a hand to anchor her as she bit her own lip and let her body work out whatever it needed to.

She was nothing like Amelia. Not in the way that mattered. Her hair was black, not gold; her laughter, even when it bubbled up, was never light, never easy. She was brittle, all edges and scabs and nerves.

I kissed her back with a violence just shy of cruelty, let her grind against me in stuttering desperation, let her teeth scrape over my jaw and ear and neck.

When she pushed my jeans down, I felt exposed, not in the way of being naked, but in the way of being peeled, each layer coming off with a raw, wet sound.

She ground her hips down, and I felt myself harden with a speed I'd never known, like my body was only waiting for the right ache to betray me. I was glass, hollowed and fragile, every cell strung tight.

My hands flexed on her thighs, not guiding so much as holding on; I needed the pressure, the proof of her, the heat beneath her skin.

The room was roaring with our breath, her hair falling in a tangle that lashed my face, the vodka searing my throat, the world reduced to the wet friction and the slip of skin against skin.

She shimmied her hips and arched, a gasp whispering out of her mouth, and then she reached between us, pulled my hard-on free, and held it, just for a moment.

She fitted me to the seam of black lace, shoved the panties aside, and rubbed herself against me, wet and shuddering. She was hot, fevered, a tremor in her thighs as she rocked forward, taking me in.

As she slid down onto me, I saw a flash of her face, a wetness in her eyes that looked nothing like pleasure. I knew that look. I wore it every day. The look of someone clawing for meaning inside a burning house.

Her head tipped back, jaw slack, and for a moment I let myself believe I was somewhere else, someone else, not a Baxter or a monster or a freak, just a piece of meat in the dark, being used for its only available purpose.

I let her, let the animal take over, let the rhythm of want and forgetting erase every other thought. I gripped her hips with such force that my thumbs left white ovals in her skin, watched her move above me, watched the muscles in her neck tense and relax and tense again.

I didn't close my eyes, not once. I stared past her, at the wall, at the photo of her and Amelia taped up by the dresser. The younger one, bright-haired and oblivious; the older one, dark and already stained with the knowledge of how things went wrong. They looked like sisters in the way that violence and tenderness can be sisters, sharing the same bone structure but none of the gentleness.

She rode me, rough and fast, a parody of pleasure. I wondered if she was pretending or desperate enough to need it real. Her hands clutched at my shoulders, nails biting through the thin cotton of my shirt, and I let the small pain anchor me to the moment.

I wasn't gentle either as we fucked each other. Why would I be? I was never shown gentleness; the closest I'd ever come was the echo of a soft voice before the door slammed or the memory of hands that only touched to hurt.

She didn't look at me, but I felt her face at my neck, her breath hot and erratic. I sensed the trembling in her arms, the ghost of a sob in the way her mouth pressed hard against my skin.

She was grinding down on me now, her thighs locked around my hips, her hands braced on my shoulders as if she needed to hold me underwater.

I wrapped my arms around her, squeezing until she squeaked, until the air in her lungs hissed past my ear. It was a mockery of comfort, but she didn't ask for less. She clawed at my hair, dragging my head back to expose the pale line of my throat, and bit at the skin there.

This frenzy was born of needing not to feel, not to think, not to be alone with the sick twins of loneliness and longing. She ground out a rhythm, faster and faster until the headboard hammered the wall.

I let myself thrust up into her, hard enough to bruise, hard enough to make her grunt and dig her fingers deeper into my back.

Her round breasts bounced in my face. I caught her nipple in my mouth, bit down almost too hard, used my free hand to fondle the other, and heard her gasp. A wordless whine that might have been a plea for more or less. Didn't matter.

I was not there, not really. Not with her. I was a thousand miles back in time, a thousand miles forward, orbiting the same doomed sun. Lillian's hands on me, Lillian's heat, Lillian's hair stuck to my cheek, none of it was her, not really. I was fucking the vacancy she left behind.

I almost wanted to call her by the wrong name, wanted to spit out *"Amelia"* just to see what it would do to the animal clinging to the inside of my ribs. But I kept it inside, let the syllables dissolve on my tongue, because even at my worst, I wasn't sure I could stand the honesty of it.

I drove myself up into Lillian, hard and jerking, needing to fill the hollow she'd found in me. The one I spent every day trying to shore up with hate and violence.

My hands found her ass, rough and possessive, pulling her down, guiding her angles with a control that was more plea than dominance.

She hissed when I pinched, then twisted her hips so I was forced deep inside, nerves sparking in her belly and mine. The pressure built, white-hot, a spiral of want and misery and the need to be needed.

She pressed her palm to my chest, bracing herself, and sweat ran in cold lines from her hair to my bare skin. I watched her fingers creep down, sliding over her ribs to the soaked triangle between her legs. She rubbed herself in little circles, her breath coming fast and higher with each round.

I was hypnotized: by the sight of her, by the furious concentration on her face, by the shattered little moans. I didn't stop. I couldn't. I was inside her, every thrust was an electric storm up my spine, every spasm a riot of hate and longing and the sick, raw need to leave a mark that would never, ever fade.

I heard myself groan, and for a second, I felt the split–felt myself fracture along fault lines, one side watching from the ceiling while the other bucked and clawed and burned with the need to belong, even if only as a wound.

I held her steady and let her ride me, her face gone slack with concentration, the wet slap of flesh on flesh loud in the shivery air of the room. She pressed her forehead to mine.

When she came, her thighs clamped around me, and she ground her hips in a tight spiral, little tremors juddering through the bones of her pelvis. She made a low, keening sound and let the shudder work through her until her nails went slack on my skin.

I could have lasted longer, but I didn't want to. I'd spent a lifetime holding back, choking out everything that made me weak.

For once, I let the animal win. I bit down on the curve of her shoulder, hard enough to leave a mark, and came inside her with a violence that left me lightheaded, nails digging rivers into the small of her back.

The sound that broke from my chest wasn't pleasure, not even close. It was release. The pure and perfect silence that follows an explosion.

When I was done, I collapsed back, dizzy, the world gone white and then pitch black, my heart rabbiting out of control as if it wanted to leap right out of my chest and leave my body behind for good.

Lillian rolled off me, panting, her hair stuck damp to her cheeks. She laughed once, then pulled the rumpled comforter over her chest like a shield.

We lay there side by side, eyes fixed to the ceiling, breathing in sync and out of time. I didn't say anything. There was nothing to say.

I closed my eyes. I wanted to pretend it was Amelia I'd just fucked, wanted to believe that somewhere, in some possible world, the gap between her and me wasn't just a nightmare.

I chased that thought beyond the edges of consciousness, inside the hot bell of Lillian's room, in the aftershocks of sweat and raw skin. I felt nothing as my body collapsed into the mattress.

I felt everything, and that was worse.

Just for one night, I gave in and allowed myself to hate her a little less, knowing that tomorrow the monster would return, and I would fall right back into the grip of darkness and rage.

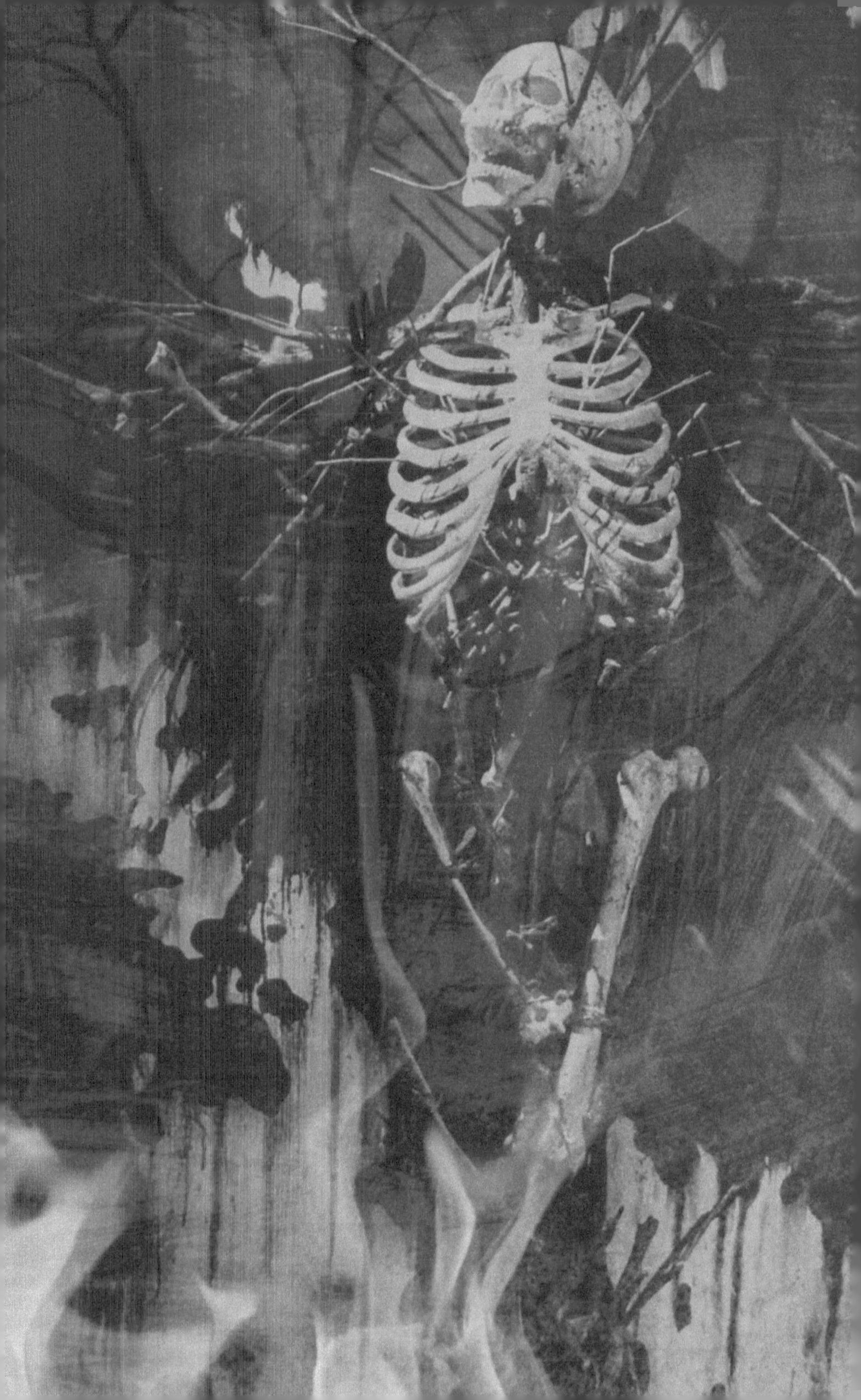

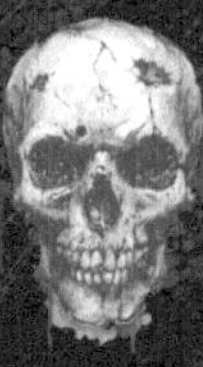

# 41

# THE PRESENT

## AMELIA

The stench of urine invaded my senses, further corroding my already fragile sanity. The man who demanded we call him "master" had provided each of us a bucket to relieve ourselves in.

At first, I had refused. It felt inhumane, a blatant effort to degrade us. But the pressing need to empty my bladder became overwhelmingly consuming, and I reluctantly accepted my fate.

Whenever one of us needed to go, we exchanged a silent understanding and told the other to close their eyes.

Caiden had already witnessed my assault, yet I had been too drugged to fully grasp the humiliation of it.

The thought of him seeing me exposed, urinating in a bucket, was unbearable. I couldn't bear to witness him in such a vulnerable state either.

We agreed to preserve whatever shreds of dignity we had left.

The man came and went, sauntering down into our makeshift prison to toy with our minds, or with me alone. He provided one meager meal each day, a small plate of stale and unsavory scraps, barely enough to sustain us.

My body felt drained, and I could see Caiden's energy waning with each passing hour. I suspected he was drugging Caiden too.

We didn't utter any words for a while, until the door creaked open slowly, the rusty sound echoing in the stillness. The man flung the cage door wide, the hollow sound reverberating in the dim room as he tossed the plate of food inside, scattering scraps across the filthy floor.

He was humming a tune I almost recognized. A children's lullaby, grotesquely out of place.

"Slop is here for my pets," he sneered, his voice dripping with mockery.

He turned his attention to Caiden, who was normally hunched in the corner but now stood defiantly, silently challenging the man with his brooding demeanor.

"Get back to the wall," the man commanded, his gravelly voice vibrating with menace.

"No. How about you lift that wall and face me like a man? Coward," Caiden snapped, a sudden strength overtaking his previous hollowed and grim demeanor. His eyes locked onto the man, a vein pulsing in his clenched fists.

"Get back! Don't make me say it again." The man's voice darkened, a threatening growl that filled the room.

"No." Caiden's voice was firm, possessing an unwavering stubbornness.

What happened next was entirely unexpected. A fiery intensity ignited in the man's eyes as he turned, his hand a blur as it lashed out, connecting painfully with my face.

A scream, high-pitched and filled with terror, erupted from my lips.

"Every moment that you defy me, she gets hurt."

His voice was cold, devoid of emotion, a chilling instrument that betrayed no remorse.

Caiden stared at me, helpless and broken on the ground. His gaze swept over me, his chest heaving, anguish etched across his features.

"This isn't over," he muttered as he retreated, his shoulders loosening under the weight of forced obedience.

The man remained still, a predator savoring his control.

"Because of that little act of disobedience, I realize I've been too generous. Each day, you both will decide who gets food and who starves. Today, the girl gets food. Tomorrow, you decide."

With that, he slammed the door shut, leaving us in a suffocating silence, dread creeping into our hearts once more.

The pain in my face intensified, becoming a throbbing, unbearable pressure. I winced at the sensation.

"I wish he would just kill us already," I whispered into the dark, not expecting an answer.

Caiden groaned in response, a sound of irritation. He remained silent for a moment before what he said shocked me.

"You know, this feels like my own personal hell. I keep thinking that maybe I am in hell, and this is my punishment for my actions. Maybe I deserve to rot in here."

Each syllable was a lament, and it tore at my heart.

"Why do you say that?" My question hung in the air, filled with uncertainty.

"Watching you get hurt and humiliated, unable to do anything to help, it's fucking with my mind. I know you think I'm heartless, but I'm not. I can't stand witnessing that."

He took a deep breath, his gaze distant yet piercing. "I've carried resentment like a burden for so long, letting it shape my perception of you. But watching you suffer like this, it's shattering me, and my hatred is losing power over me." A raw honesty colored his voice, revealing a vulnerability he had long hidden. "I'm grappling with fucked up things, trying to untangle this mess in my mind. Everything is so fucking blurred."

"Thank you for telling me that."

A whisper, faint and trembling, was all I could manage. His confession, soft and gentle like a lullaby, calmed the turbulent storm raging in my heart.

"It was pretty fucking hard. But I'm not exactly thinking clearly in here, being sleep-deprived and malnourished."

I blinked, processing his words. "So, did you mean what you just said?"

A beat of silence lingered between us.

"Yeah, I did. I know that."

That was all I needed, and it made me want to cry.

Tears welled up, one by one, then streamed down my face. They poured forth, burning like acid against my skin. Everything that had been building inside of me flooded over.

The pain, the misery, the exhaustion burst forth, uncontrolled, a raw and visceral cry.

Every sob was humiliating. I tried to swallow them, to let the tears trickle back down my throat and drown the thing inside me that still cared, but I couldn't.

I pressed my forehead to the cold glass, feeling my teeth chatter as the violence of my crying shook me. It was a child's cry, animal and shuddering, the kind you hope will never be heard by another living soul.

I hated myself for it, and I hated Caiden for being there to witness it. I hated the world for making us its playthings.

I pressed my fists to my eyes, hard enough to color the world with starbursts, and tried to carve out a space in my head where I could be numb again.

But the numbness was gone; it had been replaced by this raw, weeping nerve that stretched from skin to bone.

I cried until my lungs ached, until the noise of it drowned out the low, grating hum of the man's generator somewhere overhead.

Until nothing existed but the sound of my own undoing.

It left me emptied, wrung out like a sponge, and when I finally looked up, Caiden was staring at me through the glass, his face slack with defeat.

For the longest time, we just watched each other. There weren't any words left, nothing to say that hadn't already been scraped out of us.

We were past blame, past apology, past anger.

All that remained was the shared humiliation of being turned into shivering, broken things, and the knowledge that it had taken this much suffering to finally strip us down to that.

It made it worse, somehow, to have no enemy to punch, only the echo of your own hate.

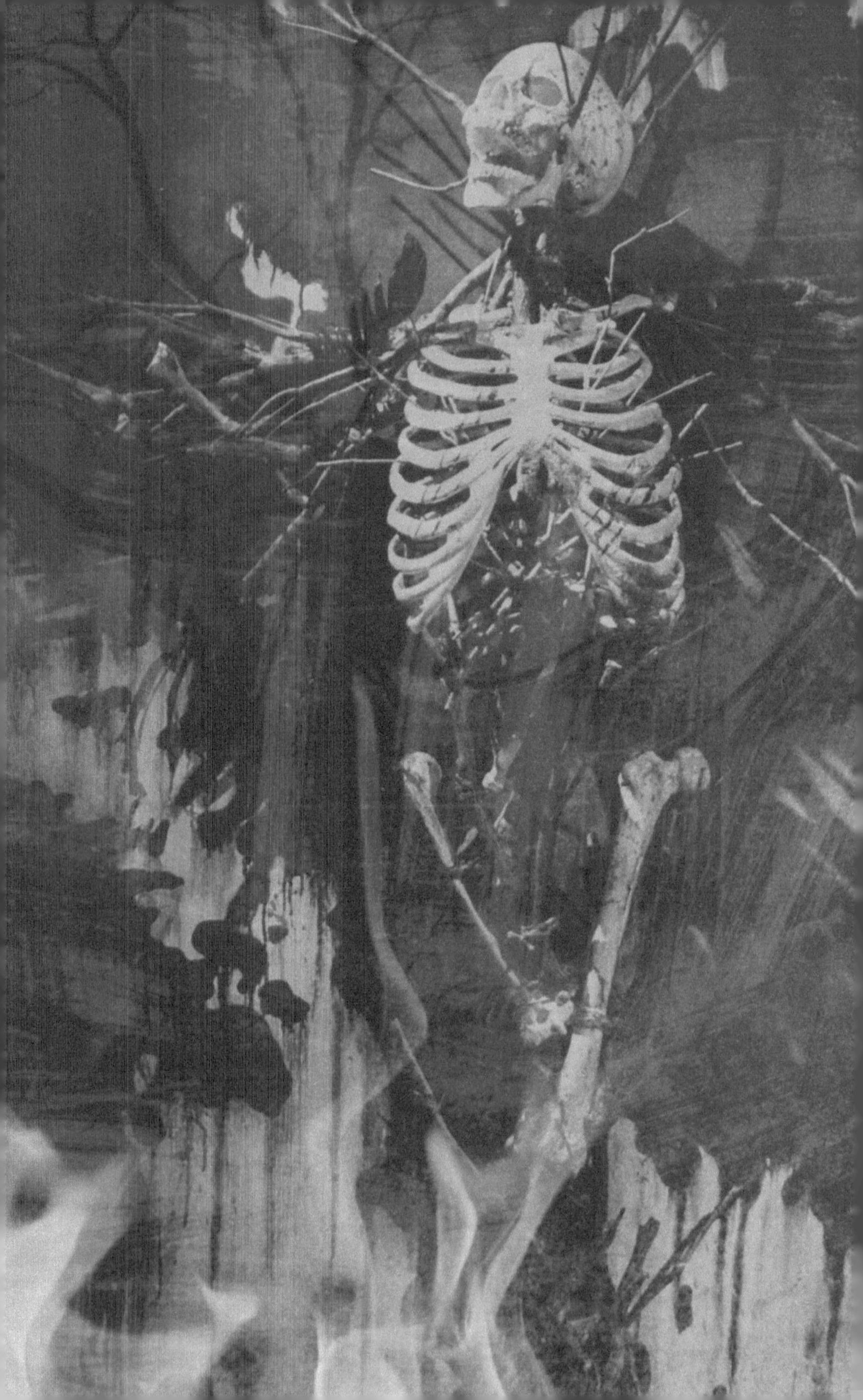

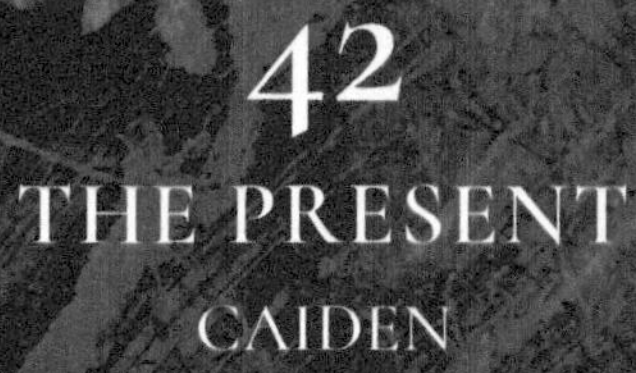

# 42

## THE PRESENT

### CAIDEN

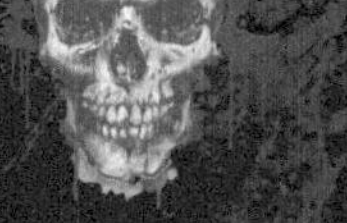

There was nothing left except the dark.

It pressed up against my skin, breathing with me, getting in the cracks between my ribs and winding tighter with every exhale.

Maybe it had always been there, even before this place. Before Colorado, before the glass, before the bastard who called himself our keeper. Maybe the darkness was waiting for someone like me. Someone who deserved a cage.

But there were worse things than dark. Like the way the cold worked into your bones so deep you forgot what it meant to be warm. Or the way the glass between me and Amelia caught the light, turned her face into a ghost in the reflection if you looked at it just so. Or the way the bastard upstairs could come down at any moment, split the silence wide open with his voice, his boots, whatever sick game he had that day.

Tonight, even the shadows felt brittle. Like they'd break if you moved too fast.

My hands wouldn't stop shaking. The urge was always the same. Put my fist through the glass, bleeding out if I had to, just as long as I could reach her. But the cage was smarter than I was. The cage always won.

*Stomp. Stomp. Stomp.*

His boots on the stairs. He wanted us to hear. Wanted the panic to settle in before he even hit the basement floor. I pressed my spine into the concrete behind me, fists curled in my lap, watching the door at the top of the stairs.

I counted the seconds. Sometimes it was five. Sometimes ten. Tonight, it took longer. Maybe he wanted to make sure we knew who owned the time down here.

The door burst open, light spilling down the steps and cutting stripes into the dark. He filled the doorway. A bear of a man, face cold and blank, mouth twisted into something that might've been a smile if you squinted.

He took his time coming down the stairs. I thought about what I'd do if he opened my cage first. Break his knees, bite his throat out if I had to. But he never did. He always saved me for last.

He carried something in his hand. Metal, glinting. Knife? Crowbar? I didn't care. I wanted him to try it.

He stopped at the glass, looking from me to her, back to me again. Slowly, he set the tool down on top of the metal feeding slot in the glass. Then he crouched, peering through at me like a scientist with a rat.

"My favorite time of day," he said. "Playtime for the pets. Have you two learned anything since our last conversation?" He rapped his knuckles on the divider, ignoring the way I bared my teeth.

I spat at the glass. "Come closer. Let's see who eats whom."

He laughed; it echoed off the walls. "Still so much fight." He glanced at Amelia, eyes raking over her tiny frame. "This one's more interesting. You're so quiet, dear. You don't even whimper." He faked a pout, eyes dead as stone. "We might have to fix that tonight."

Amelia shrank further against the wall. I wanted to rip the glass out of its fucking tracks. My pulse thundered in my head, louder than his footsteps, louder than anything. I slammed my fist into the barrier, hard enough to jar my shoulder. "Touch her and I'll—"

He rose, slow and deliberate, like a curtain coming up on an act he's played a hundred times.

"You'll what?" He cocked his head, pitying. "You're behind glass. You're less than a pet. You're a curiosity. You exist because I allow it, boy."

He turned his back on me. Dismissed me, like I was nothing. Then he stalked to the door of Amelia's cage, unlocking it with a casual twist of his wrist, the heavy iron swinging open with a groan so loud it hurt.

Amelia didn't scream. Not even when he grabbed her by the shoulder and hauled her up. She fought him—shoulder twisting, feet kicking—but it was useless. He was built to break things, and she felt so small. I thought he might snap her bones just for the thrill.

I shoved both fists against the glass, yelling her name, my voice breaking raw. It didn't matter. The sound died in the blackness between us.

He shoved her to her knees in the middle of the cage, yanking her head up by her hair until her throat was exposed. I could see the fine tremor running through her. Fear, maybe, or something worse. But her eyes stayed on mine. Locked in, like a lifeline.

He crouched beside her, face inches away, hand curling around the back of her neck. The show was for me, I understood that now. Everything was for an audience.

"See, this one's perfect. Submissive, but stubborn. She's not like you; she knows her place." He pressed a gloved hand to the side of her face, thumb stroking her cheek. "Still pretty. Even after all this." He pinched her chin, turning her face toward the glass, letting me see the way her lips trembled.

I wanted to break every tooth in his head.

"I could make her scream. Would you like that?" he asked, not looking at me. "Would it make you feel alive, to see her cry?"

"Go to hell," I whispered, voice shaking. "You sick freak."

He smiled, all teeth and emptiness. "Already there, pet. And you brought her with you."

His hand fisted in her hair, yanking it back until she gasped, a sound so small it barely made it through the glass. He brought the knife to her throat, letting the edge skate up over her skin. Not cutting, just reminding her (and me) how easy it would be.

I slammed my fists into the barrier again, throat raw. "Let her go! You want pain? Come here. Don't hide behind her."

He ignored me. He always did.

He leaned in, mouth beside her ear, whispering things I couldn't hear. Whatever he said, it made her flinch. Then he let her go, shoving her to the ground.

She didn't make a sound. Not once. Not even when she hit the floor.

"You see?" He turned to me, triumphant. "You could learn from her. You scream, you threaten, you rattle your cage. It's pathetic."

I panted, hands aching. I wanted to tear his spine out.

"What do you want from us?" I spat. "We're not fucking pets!"

He laughed again, a low, wet sound. "You're whatever I need you to be. Creatures in a box. Born to be watched. Born to suffer."

He lingered in the doorway, backlit by the sick yellow light from the stairs. Then, the door slammed shut. His boots retreated, up and up and up until even the sound died. The bulb overhead buzzed, throwing weird shadows on the walls.

She lay where he'd left her, hair spilled over her face like blood. I pressed my forehead to the glass, hating myself for not being enough. Hating him more.

Sometimes I wished I'd never come out of the cage my father made for me. Sometimes I wished I'd stayed an animal.

But I couldn't stop watching her. Couldn't stop wanting to pull her onto my side of the world, where no one could touch her. Couldn't stop wanting to hurt him in ways that would make even hell look like a holiday.

I slid down the glass until I was sitting, breathing in the dark. My hands shook. My knees ached. Every inch of me wanted violence.

We were pets. We were prey. And until I broke this cage, I was nothing.

I watched her for a long time, cataloging every inch, every tremor. Waiting for her to move, waiting for the next storm.

———

When the echoes finally died, all that was left was the scrape of my own breathing and the faint, humiliating buzz of the basement bulb. I could smell metal. Blood, maybe, or maybe just the memory of it.

She didn't move. Not at first.

I pressed two fingers to my temple, grinding them into the bone, like I could push out the headache that had been burning there for hours. It never worked. I looked at her through the glass, watched the way her shoulders shook, just once, before she forced them still again.

The urge to smash the barrier ripped through me. A violence I didn't recognize, bigger than anything my old man had ever managed to make me feel. I wanted to kill. Wanted to gut him, paint the walls with his insides. Not just for me. Not this time.

For her.

Which was fucked up. Because I didn't care. Not about her, not really. She was baggage, leftover from a life that didn't want either of us. I told myself that every hour. But right then, I wanted him dead so hard my teeth ached.

I couldn't say any of that. Couldn't say anything, not at first.

"Amelia." The word almost caught in my throat, like a bone. I coughed it up, bitter. "He didn't cut you badly, did he?"

A long pause. Her head still stayed down, hair hiding everything.

"Hey." I tried again, rougher. "You alive over there, or do I gotta start talking to myself?"

Nothing. Not even a twitch.

I glared at the ceiling. Typical. She'd rather freeze herself solid than let anyone see her bleed.

The darkness crawled closer, licking at the edges of my vision. My pulse was sick and slow.

I leaned my head back against the concrete and let the words fall out before I could stop myself.

"Remember that winter around second grade?" My voice sounded all wrong. Too soft, like I'd borrowed it from someone weaker. "The one where your mom left you in the freezing rain? I guess she was too fucked up on drugs to pick you up."

I could feel the ghost of a laugh, somewhere in the back of my chest. It hurt.

"I saw you. I did. I'm the one who left the jacket by the school doors so you would see it when you went to sit on the steps like a sad little puppy."

A faint sound. Could've been a laugh, could've been a sob. I didn't dare look too close.

I kept going, needing the noise.

"I even followed you home. Just to make sure you made it there. You never knew that the jacket belonged to me, so I didn't ask for it back."

Silence again.

I wanted to bite the words out of my mouth. Why the fuck was I talking about this? The past was a wound. The past didn't heal.

I slammed the brakes on that train of thought, voice sharpening.

"Anyway. Don't get any ideas. Just bored as hell and needed to kill the silence."

I risked a glance at her. She'd lifted her face just enough that I could see the shine on her cheek, maybe a tear, maybe just sweat. She wiped it away with the back of her hand. Her wrist was shaking.

"You don't have to..." she started, voice ragged. She cleared her throat, tried again. "You don't have to pretend."

That stung. Deep.

"Pretend what?" My words snapped like bone. "That there's any point to this? That we're getting out?"

Her jaw tightened. I recognized that set to her mouth.

"You...you didn't have to say that stuff," she mumbled at last.

I grinned, humorless. "Why not? You said it yourself once. We're both just bad memories in the making. No point fighting it."

She huffed out an unsteady breath. I could see goosebumps on her arms, even from this distance. The cold sank in, deep as marrow.

I pressed my palm to the glass, the way you might press a hand to a grave.

"You ever wonder if people like us are just born wrong?" The words came out bleak, a flat fact. "Like, maybe there's a glitch in the code. Some people get love and safety. Some get cages. Some get glass walls and freaks with knives."

She didn't answer. But I knew she was listening.

The quiet swelled. Thickened. It was almost comforting, in a sick way.

"I don't know," she said at last. "Maybe it's just...bad luck. Maybe we both just got unlucky."

For some reason, I wanted to laugh. I wanted to break something. Instead, I slumped against the far wall, exhaustion stretching me thin.

I said: "When we get out of here, we should wreck his goddamn house."

She startled, a reluctant smile tugging at the edge of her mouth. "You think we're getting out?"

I bared my teeth, all challenge. "We're not dying down here. Not without turning the tables first."

That felt like a promise. I hated the hope in it.

I forced myself to look at her, even with all the bruises, she was still here. Still fighting. Not dead yet.

"We'll make it hurt," I murmured. "For everything he did to us."

For what he did to you, I almost added. But that would have been too much. Too fucking sentimental.

I let the silence fill back in.

Eventually, she whispered, "You think we'll remember all this? After?"

I considered that. Rolled it around in my head.

"The bad shit, yeah," I said. "Never goes away. But maybe the rest, too." My voice got softer, more dangerous: "The parts where we kept each other sane, even for a second."

I regretted it as soon as it left my mouth.

I threw a punch at the air, tried to kill the softness before it grew mold.

"Don't read into it," I warned. "You know me."

She nodded, hair hiding her again.

But I could see her hands. Splayed out on the floor, reaching for the warmth that wasn't coming.

Goosebumps danced up my own arms.

The silence turned unbearable. Coiled like an animal in the dark.

I wanted to protect her. I wanted to destroy the world. I wanted to shatter the glass and crawl through, just to feel something that wasn't helplessness. Just to fucking mean something.

But I sat in my cage, counting the seconds, talking to a girl I once hated, a girl I still hated, a girl I would kill for if someone gave me the chance.

That was the truth. The only one that mattered now.

In the end, we curled into the silence. Two ghosts in a basement, alive because neither of us knew how to die.

I closed my eyes and let the dark settle in.

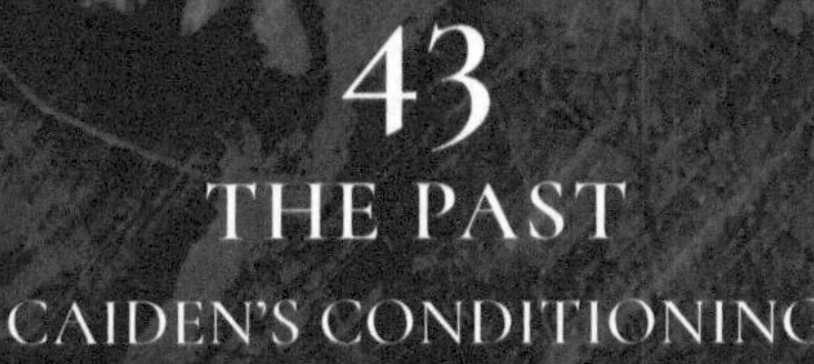

# 43

## THE PAST

### CAIDEN'S CONDITIONING

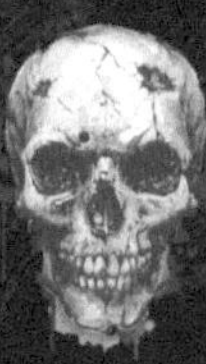

Lillian was dead. Her name still echoed through the town, whispered behind hands, scribbled on bathroom stalls. She's now just another ghost everyone pretended to mourn while they waited for the next distraction.

Even in death, she found a way to haunt me. Not that I deserved to think about her. I'd torn her apart just as much as anyone. Maybe more.

And then there was Amelia.

She moved through the crowd like she didn't belong to anybody, but the truth was, she belonged to every cruel joke, every rumor, every filthy stare. My stares most of all. I couldn't look away. Couldn't stop tracking her, like some broken compass that always spun toward disaster.

Then that day, when I found myself at her house.

I wanted to wreck her. I needed to. But I'd left her shaking in the hallway, her eyes full of something I couldn't name. Fear, maybe. Disgust. Or the same sick want curdling my veins.

She's been avoiding me since. Not that I blamed her. Every time I saw the curve of her jaw as she stared through me in the halls, I remembered the taste of her.

Dante had his hands on her. That part throbbed like an infected wound. I could still see his fucking face, the way he looked at her like she was something precious, something to protect.

He didn't know shit about her. He wouldn't know what to do with a girl built from trauma and barbed wire.

Amelia was mine. Mine to torment. Mine to control. Mine to break. Mine to ruin.

The next day, I caught her after last period. She was alone by the bike racks, shoving her books into her bag with more force than necessary. I saw the tremor in her fingers, the way she tried to pretend she wasn't looking for an escape route.

I grinned slowly. "Slumming it today, Langston? Where's your bodyguard?"

She rolled her eyes, but her spine went rigid. "Go away."

I stepped closer. She didn't back down, just glared, daring me. "You look like shit."

She should've run. But she just squared her shoulders and glared harder, lip trembling like she was biting down on her own words. Sometimes I wondered what it would take to really break her. Sometimes I wondered if I even could.

Her jaw clenched. "Go to hell."

"Already live there."

For a second, we stood there, locked in some silent war, not breathing. I couldn't look away from the way her breaths went shallow, the little pulse at her throat jumping beneath her skin.

The whole world spun around us. I waited for her to blink, to fall apart, to run. She just stared, eyes burning.

I left her there, watching me walk away.

I kept moving, ghost-shadows trailing behind. My head is full of her, always. I didn't know how to stop.

———

The bag swung back, heavy, stupid. I hit it again, harder. Fist—thud—recoil—thud. My body stung with sweat and old bruises. My skin reeked of rage.

This was the only place that made sense.

The gym at dawn, nobody around except some retired lifter in the corner, watching cable news with the sound off. I didn't care. Every time my knuckles slammed into the bag, it was like the world shrank. Like all the shit inside me could explode outward, leave nothing but emptiness behind.

Didn't work. Never did. But I kept trying. Maybe if I hit hard enough, the ghosts would finally scatter.

Amelia.

Always fucking Amelia.

I told myself I hated her. I did. But the memory of her stuck inside me like a fishhook. Then, I'd think about how she and Dante were intimate together, and my anger would augment.

Fist. Bag. Fist. Bag.

My father always said nothing soft survives. He drilled it into me the same way he drilled his fists into my ribs: Hate is strength. Love is weakness. If you have to pick, pick anger. Don't let them see you hurt.

Funny. If he could see me now, he'd probably laugh. He'd spit in my face. Tell me I was a fucking embarrassment, letting some pathetic girl bend me out of shape. Letting her crawl under my skin, fuck with my head, ruin my appetite for destruction.

But maybe he'd be proud, too. Proud of how I made her look at me with terror and hate all mixed up. Proud that I learned how to break her, even if I never meant to.

Maybe that was the whole point.

I hit the bag again. Hard enough that my knuckles split. Blood smeared across the leather. I liked the sting. I focused on it and let it drown out the rest.

Why her? Why did it have to be her?

She was nothing. Just another soft, trembling kid, all shadows and panic attacks, barely holding herself together. I should've forgotten her years ago. But now every time I closed my eyes, I saw her.

Sometimes wanting me, just as wrecked.

It made me sick. It made me hard.

I ground my teeth. Slammed my fist until sensation blurred into numbness.

I told myself I was just wired wrong. That it was biology. My father's voice in my skull: *They're all snakes, every last one. They'll sink their teeth into you if you let them.*

But that wasn't it. I knew it wasn't.

I needed her to hate me. More than I needed air. Needed her to look at me and see a monster. Needed her to understand that I'd never let her win.

But I wanted her, too. Wanted her like a sickness.

I looked down at my hands. Blood, sweat, raw skin. Nothing pretty about it. I hit the bag again.

I was a walking cliché. Abused kid, brainwashed to hate, can't stop wrecking everything good. Maybe the only thing real about me was violence. Maybe that was all I'd ever be.

Amelia was a symptom. Not a cause. If she wasn't around, I'd have found someone else to fuck up. Ruin. Destroy.

I wondered if she knew that.

I wondered if Dante did.

Thinking about his hands on her made me want to put my fist through his teeth.

He'd never get it. He'd never understand what it was like to be raised on violence and told it was love. He saw her as something fragile to cherish. I saw her as an addiction to kill or be killed by.

I kept pounding the bag. My arms burned. My breath came rough. Sweat ran down my spine, pooling at the waistband of my shorts. I wanted to puke, scream, or laugh.

She was everywhere. No matter what I did, I couldn't scrape her out.

I threw one last punch, hardest yet.

I leaned my forehead against the bag, heart rattling in my chest. Nothing left but the ache.

Maybe if I kept going, eventually I'd shatter. Maybe then I'd finally get some peace.

Or maybe not. Maybe this was forever.

Goddamn it.

I wiped blood on my shorts, flexed my fingers. Stepped back and glared at the bag, as if it could glare back.

I thought about that day again. I remembered what it felt like to own her, even for a second. It was the only time I'd felt whole in months.

I'd never stop wanting to ruin her.

I wrapped my hands tighter, took a breath that tasted like blood and old sweat, and started hitting again.

Harder this time.

———

I tracked Dante down by the benches behind McLean's Pharmacy. He sat there, hunched, knuckles white on his phone. He looked up the moment I got close.

Didn't jump. Didn't run.

Of course he didn't. He was always too steady, too fucking solid. The opposite of me in every way.

I didn't bother slowing down. Just stopped right in front of him, let the anger splatter everywhere.

"Got a minute?" My voice cracked.

He sighed. Shoved his phone in his pocket. "Not really. But you're gonna talk anyway."

"Don't get smart."

He shrugged, jaw tight. "What do you want, Caiden?"

I could've said anything. Should've said nothing. Instead, I went straight for the only thing that mattered.

"You fucked her." Didn't bother making it sound nice. "You fucked Amelia."

His brows flicked up, just for a second. "That's what you're here for?"

"You gonna deny it?"

He shook his head slowly. "No. I'm not denying it. You walked in and saw the aftermath for yourself."

My fists clenched.

"You think you're better than me?" I spat.

He looked away, out at the cars passing on Main. "I think—" He hesitated, tongue wetting his lower lip. "I think I'm done with you, man. For real."

That stung. More than it should've.

"Bullshit."

He grimaced. "You just can't stop, can you? Wrecking her. Wrecking everyone. It was never a game for her, Caiden. You just don't get it."

"Oh, and you do? What, you're her white knight now?"

He stood up, fast enough that the bench groaned. But I didn't back down.

"I'm not trying to be anything. I just care about her." His voice was quiet but made of stone. "I care. That's more than you ever did."

I laughed. "You don't know what the fuck you're talking about."

"Don't I?" He glared. "I saw how you looked at her. Like you wanted to break her. Maybe you succeeded. But I'm done being part of it."

I took a step closer, shoulders bunching. "You're gonna ditch me for her?"

He didn't move. "Yeah. I am."

"You're pathetic."

"Maybe." He shook his head, lips pressed thin. "But not as pathetic as you."

Everything inside me curled tight, ready to blow.

"I should put you through the wall," I growled.

He just looked at me, tired. "Yeah. Maybe you should."

But I couldn't do it. Not really. Not after he said it like that.

He shook his head, shoulders slumping. "We're not friends anymore, Caiden. Can't do it. Not after what you did. Not after how you treat her."

He turned to leave. No hesitation.

I shouted after him. "She's poison! You're too fucking blind to see it."

Dante paused, just for a second, long enough to twist the knife.

"Maybe I'd rather be poisoned than end up like you."

And then he was gone, footsteps echoing down the cracked sidewalk.

I wanted to scream. Wanted to punch something, anything.

I was alone. Again.

The taste of bitter burned my tongue. Dante, gone. Amelia, everywhere.

I shoved my hands in my pockets, fists tight around my own brokenness.

Fuck them. Fuck everyone.

All I had left was anger.

And it wasn't nearly enough.

———

I found her behind the school, where the dumpsters reeked of rot and bleach. Perfect. No one would hear us. No one would care.

She caught sight of me, and everything in her tensed like a deer seeing the flash of a rifle. But she didn't run.

Brave. Or stupid. Didn't matter.

I cut off every escape route, my shadow swallowing hers.

"You think you're something special?" I sneered, voice already shaking with the need to hurt. "Running around fucking every guy in town?"

She flinched, but her eyes went cold as glass. "Fuck you."

I laughed. "Bet you already tried."

Her body shook, hands clamped white on her books. "You're obsessed. Why don't you just leave me alone?"

"Because you don't deserve peace," I said, stepping closer. "After what you did to Lillian by fucking Dante the night of her funeral—after what you did to me? You're just a cheap replacement. Think Dante gives a shit about you? He's using you. Everyone is."

She opened her mouth, maybe to scream, maybe to spit. "Don't talk about her. You don't get to talk about my sister."

"Oh, but you can go around acting just like her? Screwing anything with a pulse, hoping someone finally notices you exist?"

She went grey, but she didn't back down. "You're the one who started it. You ruined everything, you ruined—" Her voice hitched. "You ruined Lillian. You ruin everything you touch."

Something in my chest cracked. But I pushed harder.

"At least I'm not so desperate I'll spread my legs for anyone who asks."

She slapped me. Hard. Palm stinging, skin on fire.

I barely felt it. Not compared to what came next.

"You know what?" I hissed, nose to nose now. "You're gonna end up just like your dead fucking sister. Maybe sooner, if you keep acting like this."

She recoiled, but the rage in her eyes could've burned me alive. "You're evil. You fucking monster. I wish you had never touched me. I wish I had never fucking met you."

For a second, I almost said I was sorry. Almost.

Instead—"I feel the same. Only thing I regret is not walking away the second I laid eyes on you."

She glared, tears streaking her face, but her hands were steady. "You're sick. You're empty. That's why no one can stand you. Not Dante. Not anyone."

I smiled, all teeth, too bright. "Guess it takes one to know one."

She turned and ran, books forgotten, footsteps echoing down the alley.

I watched her go, every part of me screaming to chase after, to pull her back, and make her fight more.

Instead, I stayed. Let the silence crawl back in.

For a long time, all I could taste was the guilt, bitter and rotten. What I'd said about Lillian. What I kept saying, every time, like I wanted to break her for good.

But then Dad's voice, greasy and thick, oozed through my skull. *Don't feel bad, boy. Don't you dare.*

If you let up, even for a second, they'll bury you. Violence is the only thing anyone respects.

I dug my nails into my palms until pain flickered white.

Anger, shame, self-loathing. There wasn't a name for the color it made when it mixed. The only thing I knew was I had to stay hard, had to stay mean. Anything else was death.

So I stood there, breathing in the stink of the dumpsters, until the urge to chase her faded.

And when I finally moved, it was like stepping through molasses, everything slow and heavy.

I almost hoped I'd never see her again.

But I already knew that was a lie.

I walked.

Didn't know where I was going, just that I couldn't stay. The sky behind me bled out orange, then faded to bruised purple, then grey. Dusk crept in, slow and final.

Every step echoed. Every shadow got longer.

Crows screamed overhead, black shapes flapping from one dead tree to another. They landed on the power lines, eyeing me like they knew exactly what kind of monster shuffled past their kingdom.

The streets emptied. Doors slammed. Lights blinked out, one by one, as if the world wanted to forget it ever held me.

Didn't blame it. I'd want to forget me, too.

I kept walking, out past the school, past the football field stripped bare by winter. The chain-link fence rattled in the wind, rattled like bones. The parking lot was empty except for trash bags blown up against the wheels of a rusted-out car.

Everything was silent. The only sound was the echo of my own footsteps and the crows, cawing like they were calling me home.

Hadn't realized how dark it was getting. How cold, too. I dug my hands in my pockets, hunched my shoulders, tried to shrink down so the shadows wouldn't rip me apart.

Didn't work.

I saw Amelia everywhere. I saw Lillian, too, eyes glazed with disappointment.

They were all ghosts now, haunting my every step.

I wanted to blame them. Wanted to scream that none of this was my fault.

But I knew better. It's always the monster's fault for being born.

Dad would've laughed to see me like this. Face raw, knuckles split, a trail of pain behind me. He'd be proud I wrecked Amelia so good. He'd be proud I chased away my only friend. Proud that I learned the only lesson he ever bothered to teach:

Keep hurting them until they can't hurt you.

Even if it means destroying yourself in the process.

I stopped by the playground at the edge of town, the one nobody used anymore. Swings creaked back and forth in the wind. The sand beneath them was scattered with broken glass.

I watched the sun wink out behind the treeline. Just black and blue and nothing.

Didn't feel relief. Didn't feel anything but the hollow, only the edge of emptiness where a heart should be.

Maybe I could stay here forever. Maybe the dark would finish what I couldn't.

Crows circled overhead, cawing louder.

I threw my head back, screamed at them until my voice cracked.

They screamed back. Their answer was the only thing that made sense.

I walked some more, loops and circles, until I didn't know where I was or what time it was. Only that the world was empty, and I was the only thing left crawling through the wreckage.

No hope. No redemption. Just the shadows, and me, and the way anger kept the emptiness from swallowing me whole.

Maybe that was enough. Maybe that was all there ever was.

*Am I a man or a monster? I know now, Dad. I'm a monster. Just like you.*

I could never return to that sweet, innocent boy who dreamed of a mother's warmth and the companionship of Amelia. The girl who

I once craved, but now she's the girl who I feel a consuming hatred for.

A battle, forever, of hunger and hate. But hate would always win because that's who I was. A boy filled with rage, emptiness, and violence.

I could never be saved.

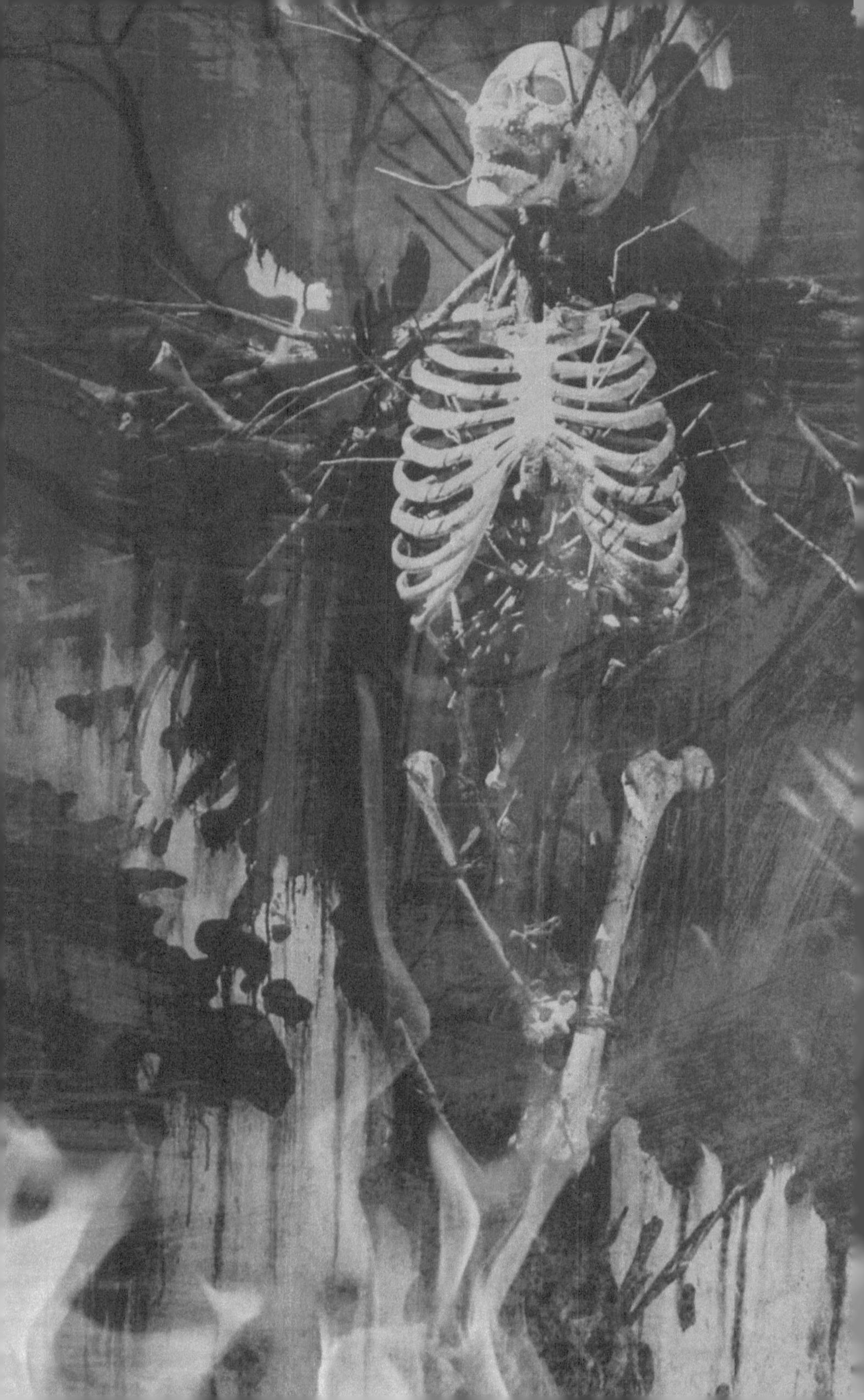

# 44

## THE PRESENT

### CAIDEN

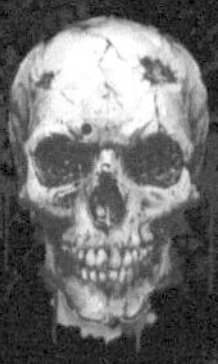

The basement made me raw. As if it were splitting me open and dissecting my deepest, darkest depths.

A few days in, and I started understanding the rules without him having to say them out loud. The light stayed on because darkness made people too honest. The food came when he felt like it because hunger made people obedient. The glass stayed between Amelia and me because distance made us resent each other in new ways.

He was building us into exactly what he wanted.

I hated him for it. I hated myself for falling into the pattern anyway.

Amelia sat on her side of the barrier, legs pulled in, arms wrapped around her knees.

Watching her do that made something in my chest go hot. Protective wasn't a word I wanted. It sounded too noble. Too soft. What I felt was possessive, almost.

As if the thought of anyone touching her wrong made my hands itch.

I sat with my back against the wire, head tipped forward, staring at the concrete. I tried not to watch her.

Tried.

The basement was silent except for the bulb buzzing overhead and the slow drip of water somewhere behind the wall. Each drop landed with a soft, wet click. It sounded like time leaking away.

Amelia shifted, and the scrape of her shirt against the concrete made my jaw tighten. She sucked in a breath, then another, like her lungs were forgetting their job.

Panic.

I could see it on her skin. In the way her shoulders climbed toward her ears. In the way her gaze darted to the stairs, even though nothing had moved.

I hated panic. I hated it because it was loud and contagious, and it made people do stupid things.

I hated it because it reminded me of myself.

"Breathe," I said, low.

She didn't look at me. "Don't tell me what to do."

I clenched my jaw. "Fine. Don't breathe."

Her head snapped up, eyes flashing. "You're such an asshole."

"Yeah," I muttered. "And you're still alive. Keep it that way."

She stared at me through the glass like she wanted to throw herself at it just to prove she could. Like she wanted to hit me because she couldn't hit him.

Then her gaze dropped. The light in her eyes dimmed again.

The old hate wanted to rise. It wanted to take control because hate was easy. Hate had a script. Hate didn't ask me to be careful with my words.

But something else kept pushing through the cracks. Something that made me notice her shaking, that made me hate the way the bruises looked on her skin. Something that made me want to climb through the glass like an animal and rip his throat out with my teeth if he came near her again.

It pissed me off because none of it made sense. She was Amelia. The girl I'd sworn I hated. The girl I'd spent years turning into the villain because my father needed one. Now my body kept betraying me, leaning toward her like she was warmth in a cold world.

I rubbed my palms together, trying to ground myself. My hands were rough, scabbed, and dirty. I looked like a man who belonged in cages.

Her voice came out small, hoarse. "How long do you think it's been?"

Since what? Since sunlight? Since the last time we heard a step on the stairs? Or since anyone gave a fuck that we were alive?

I flexed my fingers, feeling pins and needles up my arm. "I stopped counting."

Lie. I always counted.

She picked at a splinter in the wood, eyes jumping to the far wall, anywhere but me. "You think he's coming back?"

I snorted. "Bet on it."

She made a sound, almost a laugh, but not really. It was too watery, too thin. "You're optimistic."

"Just realistic. Guys like him don't leave things unfinished." I let my head knock back against the wall, the jolt echoing in my jaw. "He likes the game too much."

Her jaw tightened.

I could see her throat working, the way she swallowed hard, like maybe the words hurt. She wrapped her arms tighter. Shaking.

I watched. Couldn't look away. Even when I wanted to. It was like a sickness.

The awful part? I wanted to cross to her, pull her over to my side of the glass, tell her it wouldn't happen again. That was the lie I'd want to tell. But if I was over there, I might hurt her. I was always better at hurting. My father made sure I was good at it.

So I leaned back and let the meanness run the show.

"Figured you'd be used to this kind of thing by now," I said. "You were always good at being pathetic."

Her head snapped up. For a second, the fear was gone, replaced by that old fire. The hate she had for me was the one thing that tied us together.

She bared her teeth like a cornered animal. "If I'm so pathetic, why are you stuck here too?" Her voice wavered, but she went on. "Not so tough now, are you?"

I grinned, all teeth. "Tough enough not to cry about it."

Her lips pressed together. I'd hit a nerve.

Good.

She looked away, shoulders curled forward, breathing slow and deliberate. Counting, maybe. Trying to regain control.

I stretched my legs again, this time pressing the heel of my boot into the edge of the glass barrier between us. It thudded, cold and hollow. I liked the sound. I liked the way it made her flinch.

"Do you ever..." She hesitated. "Never mind."

I cocked my head. "Say it."

She glared, but it was weak. "Do you ever think about... what happens next?"

I shrugged, lazy. "Doesn't matter. We get out, or we don't."

She was quiet for a long time. The kind of quiet that might've meant something if we weren't half-dead in a basement.

Finally, she muttered, "You really don't care, do you?"

I wanted to laugh. Or scream. I wanted to bash my head against the wall until the feeling went away.

Instead, I said, "I care enough to keep talking to you."

It was almost true.

She didn't reply. Her feet shifted again.

I grinned, splitting the silence. "You cold?"

She gritted her teeth, a slow nod. "What's it to you?"

"Nothing." I rolled my neck. "Just curious how long you'll last."

This time, there was no comeback. Just a deep breath, air shivering in and out through her cracked lips.

But she didn't give in. She never did. Not even when it would have been easier.

The hopeless part? I respected her for it.

And if I respected her—if I cared, at all—it would kill us both. Or maybe just me.

I heard a creak above, floorboards settling. My pulse kicked up. A jolt, then nothing. The darkness pressed closer, the glass a slippery, funhouse reflection of my own face, bloodshot eyes, and a smear of stubble. Just a fucked-up animal in a box.

So I talked, just to keep my teeth from chattering. "You ever think about high school?"

She blinked. Stunned. Didn't expect that.

"No," she whispered. "Why would I?"

I shrugged. "Easy to forget when things were simple."

Her face twisted. Bitter. "Simple? We hated each other."

I almost said, did we? I didn't. I caught the instinct, crushed it.

"Some things never change," I said.

And for a moment, that was it. The world shrunk down to the drip of water, the ache in my temple, and her breathing, ragged and stubborn, across the glass.

I closed my eyes, counting the seconds between each sound. Easier than watching her come apart in slow motion.

Easier than watching myself do the same.

I stayed awake, teeth clenched, and let the hunger eat me alive.

———

The dark was a beast with a hundred teeth.

Sometimes it bit you slowly. Sometimes it clamped down hard, straight through flesh and bone. That's what it felt like as the minutes crawled by.

We stilled in our corners, caught in the glue of exhaustion. I thought maybe she'd finally drifted off, but then—

A sound.

I jerked upright, all nerves. At first, I thought it was her. A breath snagged, a throat catching, something weak and breakable in the dark. I almost called her name, but then the sound grew, and my blood iced over.

Crying. Sobbing. Deep, stuttering, horrible. The kind that made your skin crawl. It was a woman's voice, warping in the echo of the basement, all the syllables slurred and overlapping.

Amelia snapped to, eyes wide. She glanced at me, panic splayed raw over her face.

"Do you hear that?" she whispered, barely moving her lips.

No way she didn't hear it. The crying saturated the space, filled up every crack, and made the glass between us vibrate. It was everywhere at once. Like the sound was trapped under our skin.

I went still, ears straining. It got louder, a fever pitch, then dipped again, breathless, desperate. My hands curled. Instinct. I wanted a weapon. I wanted a reason to kill something.

Her voice trembled. "Is there someone else down here?"

I shook my head slowly. "Doesn't sound... right."

Because it didn't. The sound didn't change when we talked. Didn't change with the room. It looped. Broken, mechanical, just a second off.

She cringed, clutching her knees. "Make it stop, make it stop..."

I almost snapped at her, just to drown it out. But I was too locked in, pulse slamming, every muscle tensed. I scanned the blackness, body humming, but there was nothing. No footsteps. No doors. Just that endless, pitiful sobbing.

Then I got it. The bile crawled up my throat.

He was fucking with us. The psycho. He'd run wiring through

the guts of this place, let the ghosts haunt us when he didn't want to come down himself.

A recording. A trick.

Rage firebombed through me. I slammed my palm into the barrier. The echo thundered back, but the crying kept going.

"Fuck you!" I roared at the walls, voice shredded. "You think this is going to break us?"

Nothing. Just the noise, skipping, on and on.

Amelia flinched with every outburst, her nails digging into her elbows so deeply I thought she'd draw blood.

"He wants us to lose it," I growled, but my voice sounded thin, even to me. "It's all a goddamn show."

Her head jerked. "Why?"

I snorted. "Because he can. Because he likes it."

Her breathing came shallow, dizzying, and fast. I could see her shaking.

And I wanted to punch the wall until my fists caved in.

But I didn't. I just watched the way the sound hollowed out her eyes and turned her into something brittle, the kind of break that never heals right.

The sobbing trailed off, slow at first, then cut. The silence after was sharp enough to bleed.

We sat in it. Hours, maybe. Or just a handful of minutes stretched into torture.

It got worse after the crying stopped.

Not the echo, no, the echo lingered, haunted every scrap of silence, but the real horror was the way time folded in on itself. An hour could've been a day, or a minute. The dark didn't care. All it wanted was for us to forget what shape we were supposed to be.

I tried to nurse my anger, wrap it up like a shield, but the truth was transparent: every time she looked small, I felt like a piece of shit.

Reminded me of those days after school, when my father would dish out his lessons, and I'd run to the creek and punch rocks until my knuckles bled. Reminded me of the last time I saw her cry and how much easier it had been to hurt her than admit what it did to me.

She startled me, voice a soft, bruised thing. "Why do you do that?"

I blinked, picking up a splinter from the floor. "Do what?"

She rolled her eyes, but it was weak. "Act like you hate me every time you do something... nice."

"Nothing about this is nice," I said, voice flat.

She set her jaw. "You know what I mean."

I did. Fuck, I did.

But I couldn't tell her the truth. I couldn't tell her hate was the only rope I had, and if I let go, I'd drown. So I spit it out.

"It's easier than listening to you talk."

She flinched, just a flicker. But she didn't look away.

I kept going, because I didn't know how to stop.

The silence that followed was suffocating. The only sound was the drip—drip—drip—and her breathing, fast and tight.

But in my head, everything screamed.

Easier than wanting you and remembering I used to want you before my father made me believe wanting was weakness. Easier than admitting I'm protective of you and I don't know why. Easier than looking at you now and seeing what I did to you. What I could do if I let myself care.

The dark got thicker. Amelia pulled her knees up, chin locked between them, and I watched her, couldn't not watch. Every time her breath skipped, my heart went with it. Every time she shut her eyes, I wanted to make sure she opened them again.

The world was a tunnel, narrowing down to us, the glass, and the sound of water seeping from a pipe or the ceiling. For a while, nothing moved.

I stayed awake.

Sleep was an ambush, sleep was death. I needed to be ready, in case psycho decided to come back. I needed to be awake for her.

If she slept, she didn't have to see me. If she slept, she was safer.

I let my own eyes close, but only for a second at a time. When I opened them, I scanned for her, making sure she was where I left her, making sure she was breathing still.

I didn't need to like her. Didn't need her to forgive me. All I needed was to know she'd wake up in the morning, shake out her hair, glare at me, and keep fighting.

Maybe that was the sickness. Maybe that was my cage.

She slipped under, at last, sleep dragging her down. She looked breakable, like a glass doll on the other side of the wall.

I wanted to reach through. I wanted to smash my fist through the barrier and pull her in.

But all I did was sit. And watch. And promise myself: no matter what, she'd see daylight again. The water dripped. The dark pressed in. And I stayed awake. Just to keep her safe.

Hating her had always been easy. This was the hard part.

# 45

## THE PRESENT

### AMELIA

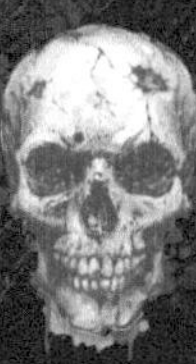

Caiden was supposed to be my enemy, but in here, he felt like my lifeline.

I was sure we would both die, but at least we'd do it as one creature, not two halves left to rot. Instead, I pressed my palm to the glass and mouthed his name.

His eyes flickered, followed my hand, the motion slow and underwater. He didn't speak. I could tell his mouth was too dry.

We spent hours like that. Our bodies on either side of the sweating sheet, tracing each other's outlines, inventing a language of gestures and sighs.

It was the closest I'd ever been to him, and the farthest.

I thought about other times we were close. Not like this, but back in school days. Times when he would shove me in the hallway, or watch me from a distance, a violent hunger whirling in his eyes.

One time, he'd grabbed me by the wrist and yanked me into the locker room, slammed me against the cold blue metal, and hissed in my ear that I was "already a ghost, just didn't know it yet."

At the time, I'd thought he meant to kill me.

Now I wondered if he'd only meant to claim some piece of me, to see if he could draw blood with words alone.

There was nothing left to bleed now, but I felt myself craving any closeness, any friction.

He was the only heat in this world.

I watched as he slumped, legs sprawled. His face was ruinous, but I still recognized the old glint beneath the scum of exhaustion.

He caught me staring.

"What? You want something?" His voice was barely a whisper, husked and raw, but it curled around me like a ribbon, tight and mean.

I pressed my hand harder to the sheet of glass between us, willing it to shatter, or soften, or dissolve. "I never thought anything could be worse than you tormenting me," I said, the words forming in my mouth before I could stop them. "Shows how stupid I was."

He didn't answer. Instead, he looked away, rolling his head into the crook of his arm as if he could hide inside himself and never come out. "What's worse," he said, finally, "me tormenting you, or me being the only thing left?"

His tone was colder than the glass between us. I had no answer.

He closed his eyes, lashes clumped and caked with sweat. "You're the only one who doesn't let me forget who I am," he muttered. "It's fucked up, but it helps."

A long pause, punctuated by the rasp of his breath. "That's all I've got."

"We should have let the river take us," I said, and meant it, but my hand stayed pressed to the glass, unwilling to let go, to float away.

He opened one eye, bloodshot and yellow around the edges. "You were always the quitter," he said. "I just finish things."

I watched the ripple of his chest, the way his shoulders trembled under the thin skin. I tried to hate him for being right, for being the one who could hold on until the very end, but the feeling wouldn't come.

It was burned out by fatigue, or maybe I'd just lost my taste for it. He was all I had, and in that deprivation, every cell in me bent toward his gravity, the way a plant will always strain toward the only source of light.

We didn't touch, couldn't, but the hunger for connection swelled with each hour alone together.

I whispered, "I used to wish you'd die. Really die, like in the woods, or a car crash, or some jail cell. Now I wish you'd just keep talking so I could remember what a voice sounded like."

He didn't open his eyes, just smiled, slack and mean. "You get sentimental in captivity, Langston?"

"Fuck you," I said.

"You wish."

That sparked something inside of me. I thought about the times he drunkenly kissed me. One time, I kissed back, and other times I froze. Paralyzed by fear.

"Why did you kiss me those years ago? When you'd be drunk and angry. Why did you do it?"

His mouth curled, more snarl than smile. "I don't remember half that shit."

"I hated you for it."

My voice cracked, but I steadied it on the next breath. "I hated you for making me want something I couldn't even name yet."

He pressed his forehead to the glass, and for a moment, I imagined the skin melting away, the bone beneath. "You think I wanted to want you?" he rasped. "You think that's what I fucking wanted?"

The ache in my chest doubled. "Then why did you keep doing it?"

"Because," he bit out, "it was the only thing that made me feel less than dead. That's what you were. A reminder that I might still have a pulse. Even if I had to make you bleed to prove it. And maybe I liked how it affected you. Made me feel powerful. I don't fucking know. I don't think when I drink, I just act."

He closed his eyes then, maybe ashamed, maybe just past caring.

I pressed my fingers to the barrier, tracing the outline of his skull. "You always were such a goddamn coward," I said. "Couldn't let yourself be human, not even for one second."

He nodded. "It's easier that way. Being a heartless monster. Once you start caring, you start dying. That's the law. You know it as well as I do."

I watched his face, the way the cheekbones jutted out now, every edge sharpened by hunger and sleeplessness. He looked like a photograph left in bleach.

All the color leached out. Only the shadow remained.

I said, "You could have at least pretended not to hate me. It would have made this a little easier."

He shrugged. "Didn't want to make it easier."

I let my head fall against the divider. The glass was humid.

I wanted to punch through, but I wanted to curl up in the

farthest corner and never hear his voice again. I hated how I needed him now, how I felt every flicker of his attention as if it were electricity through my bones.

I could hear his breath, faint on the other side. His lips parted like he might say something, but the words clotted behind his teeth. "Do you even know what I am?" I said, voice raw, straining to be heard through the glass. "I'm not what you think, not some fragile, broken—" The words jammed in my throat, and I didn't finish.

Didn't need to. He already knew. He'd always known.

He scraped a finger down the divider, a tiny shriek of plastic, then let his hand drop. "I know what you are, Amelia. You're the only thing that's ever made me want to be something different."

I was boiling with the wish to reach him, to wring his neck or drag him close or just touch his skin. The urge was so wild it made me dizzy, nauseous. I thought about what the man upstairs wanted. That we break, that we give up.

But I didn't want to give up. Not quite. Not if he was still breathing.

I curled up on my side, spine to the divider, and tried to think about anywhere but here: Lillian's laugh, the way the tile in our kitchen always stayed cold even in summer, the ache of being fourteen and wanting to crawl out of my own skin.

Every memory was haunted by Caiden, a flicker at the edges, a shadow in the picture.

It was always him, even when I wanted it to be anyone else.

Caiden was picking at a scab on his elbow, eyes glassy, mouth half open like he'd been caught mid-curse and never got to finish.

He looked up, and I caught the flash of anger there, the old reflex, but then it dimmed to something worse. Pity.

I wanted to bite him for it.

"You keep staring," he said. "Didn't know you were so into horror shows."

"I'm just waiting for you to finally decay into slime," I said, not even looking away. "You'd be more pleasant company that way. Maybe I could use your corpse as a pillow."

He shrugged, picking at a strip of peeling skin. "Go for it. Not like you ever wanted anything else from me."

I rolled to my back. There were old water stains that looked like the silhouettes of bodies, or countries, or maybe just the last places people had been alive in this house.

"You think he's coming back?" I asked, voice flat.

"He's upstairs. I can hear him sometimes. Pacing. Or crying, maybe. He's got problems."

"Takes a psycho to know a psycho," I said.

He rolled his eyes, but the lines in his face thawed a little. "You want to hear a joke?"

"No."

He told it anyway: "What's the difference between a basement and a coffin?"

I sighed. "Surprise me."

"In a coffin, at least somebody gives you flowers when you finally shut up."

I barked a laugh. "I could almost smother you if I could reach through the divider. You're not funny, you know that, right?"

He grinned, or at least showed his teeth. "You keep saying that, but you keep listening."

He was always better at making you want to die than at making you feel alive, but here, at the bottom of the food chain, maybe that was a kindness.

Maybe he was the closest thing to comfort I'd ever get.

I felt the panic rising, the urge to claw out of my skin.

I pressed my face to the divider, exhaling until the sweat on my upper lip fogged the spot, and watched him, blurry and distorted, on the other side.

He mimicked me, his breath the same, and for a moment our fog blots kissed, merged, evaporated.

I didn't want to let go, but I wanted to run, to bash my head against the wall until there was nothing left to think or feel.

I wanted both. I wanted Caiden to crawl through the glass and smother me, to eat me alive if it meant I wouldn't die alone.

Instead, he said, voice lower than before, "If you had to choose, would you rather starve to death or be shredded by that bastard upstairs?"

I thought about it. "Starvation is easier. You get to hallucinate a little before the end. Plus, your body eats itself. It's poetic, in a way. The only time you're truly self-sufficient."

He snorted. "That's the most you answer I ever heard."

"And you?" I said, curious in spite of myself.

"I'd rather be eaten. At least there's a fight. At least you don't die for nothing." His throat flexed. "My dad would respect that."

I made a disgusted noise, deep in my chest, the way you do when you smell something rotten but are too tired to move away. "Don't start talking about your dad like he's a role model."

He shrugged, dragging the edge of his heel along the concrete. "We're all monsters in here. Some of us just get caught."

He didn't look at me when he said it, which made it worse.

The words burrowed into my skin, into the scar tissue I'd so carefully formed over the last decade.

I wanted to refute it, to claw the accusation out of the air and shove it down his throat, but I knew he wasn't wrong. Not really. I'd learned early how to bite, how to make the bad thing happen first, so at least you could say you saw it coming.

I pressed my knees to my chest, bony under the thin fabric. "I never wanted to hurt anyone," I said, voice low. "I just didn't want to be the one getting slaughtered." My tongue was thick, words sticky as glue. "You made it so easy to hate you, Caiden. Maybe that was your plan all along."

"Doesn't matter now," he said. "We're just ghosts. Ghosts don't get to pick their enemies."

A wind rattled the basement window, cold coming in through the cracks. I shivered.

Caiden raked his nails down the divider, making a sound like a dying animal. "You cold?"

"Freezing." I wrapped my arms around myself, but it was useless; I was too thin for insulation, just a rack of bones and spite wrapped in a soiled T-shirt.

He looked me over. "You look like you're already decomposing." The way he said it, I almost smiled.

"Good," I said. "I hope it speeds things up."

He pressed his cheek to the glass. "You'd haunt this place just to piss me off, wouldn't you?"

"If it's the last thing I do."

I tried to keep my voice steady, but there was a tremor in it that matched the one in my hands. I could feel the panic, deep and poisonous, worming its way through my marrow.

I didn't want to die. I just didn't want to live like this.

"Bet you'd make a hot ghost," he said, deadpan. "That's your whole thing, right? Haunting people."

"My whole thing is surviving you," I snapped, and for a moment we just stared at each other, neither of us willing to blink first.

"You think he'll make us eat each other?" I asked, the words coming out slurred and dreamy.

Caiden's head jerked up. He glared at me through the film of condensation and grease. "You wish," he said, but there was no bite left in it.

"You'd taste like shit," I said, just to keep the silence from congealing around us. "Too bitter."

He rolled his eyes. "You're the one who'd taste bad. Like old chicken, left in the sun too long. All string and gristle."

I laughed, or tried to, but it came out as a cough, the sound echoing off the damp stone. "That would be an ironic way to go. Eaten and digested by my childhood enemy."

He ignored that, retreating into himself again, shoulders hunched and face turned away.

The glass was smeared with our fingerprints, with the oil and sweat of two bodies refusing oblivion.

We didn't talk much after that. The room crept into the night, the only light coming from the jaundiced bulb in the stairwell, barely enough to silhouette the glass divider.

Hours passed.

The quiet was almost absolute, except for the occasional rattle of pipes or the distant, arrhythmic footsteps of the man upstairs.

I wondered what he was doing. Sleeping, maybe. Or sitting at his table, staring into the black, listening to the silence to see if we'd begun to turn on each other yet.

I pressed my ear to the divider. I could hear Caiden's breath, slow and ragged, and the soft thud of his head as he knocked it against the glass in slow, measured intervals.

Maybe he was counting time, maybe just keeping himself awake. I wondered if he was still awake at all.

I was about to say something—anything, just to break the tension—when the door at the top of the stairs shrieked open.

The sound rumbled through the basement, dragging me up from whatever half-sleep I'd managed to claw out for myself.

Caiden jerked upright, too, eyes snapping to the stairwell. For a second, neither of us moved. The steps came slow and deliberate, as though the man wanted to savor the moment, to make the horror last as long as possible.

The metal stairs groaned under his weight. I felt my pulse spike and my throat close up. In that instant, I wanted to disappear into the concrete, become nothing but bone and dust, something the man wouldn't bother with.

He stepped into the pool of yellow light, smirking. His teeth were too white, his smile too wide, and he looked at us like a farmer checking his livestock before a slaughter. "Awake?" he called, voice syrupy and false. "Or did my little pets finally wear each other out?"

I said nothing. I watched the way his hands hovered by the buttons on his remote, the way he eyed the divider, calculating, always calculating.

Caiden spat at the floor, baring his teeth. "Come in here and say that, you coward."

The man's eyes flashed with something feral. "I said you'd break first, and guess what? You did."

He stepped forward, knelt so his face was level with mine through the divider.

I wanted to back away, but I couldn't. My body was a dead weight, fused to the dirty concrete. "You look paler than usual, darling," he whispered, lowering his voice. "Maybe you need a little special attention."

His gaze slithered over my face, then dropped lower, cataloging every tremor, every bruise.

I heard Caiden's fists battering the glass, a primal bellow ripped from his throat. The man didn't even flinch. His tongue curled over his teeth, wetting his lips like he could taste my fear through the glass.

In the sick fluorescence of the basement, his face was a mask. Something below animal.

"Don't you fucking touch her!" Caiden's voice was brutal, thunderous, but the divider turned it soft and distant, like a memory of violence instead of the real thing.

"You remind me of a dog I once had as a child," he said, voice drifting, as he stared at Caiden. "It bit and bit, until one day my father broke its jaw with a brick. Still tried to bite with its mouth hanging open. That's what you are. That's what you'll always be. An animal with nothing but its bite left."

"Fuck you," Caiden snapped.

The man ignored him.

"You know, at first I wasn't sure which of you would make the better subject. But in the end, it's always the girl." He said this like it was a law of science, a principle etched into the marrow of the universe.

He unlocked the cage on my side with a flourish, the click echoing through the basement like a gunshot. I tried to scramble away, but my body was spent; I managed only a pathetic crab-walk to the far corner, clutching my knees to my chest.

Caiden's shout vibrated the glass, a wordless, animal sound, but there was nothing he could do.

The man stood over me, silhouette tall and precise, his expression one of infinite patience, as if he could wait forever for me to exhaust myself.

"Don't make this harder than it has to be," he said, and he grabbed my shoulder, anchoring me to the filthy slab of concrete.

I thought I'd panic, or scream, but there wasn't enough air left in my body.

I just watched him, eyes wide, time stretching into a dream.

I could see each pore on his face, the sick shine of saliva webbing his lips, the slow dilation of his pupils as his hand closed around my throat. Not tight enough to kill, just enough to make me want the next breath more than anything.

His fingers dug into the bruises already mapped across my skin. It was almost an act of cartography: charting pain, tracing the fault lines of every old wound, every remembered violation.

I heard Caiden's body strike the glass again, a dull, meaty thud, and the man's smile crept wider, savoring the sound.

On some level, I knew he was doing it for Caiden, for the way it made him howl, the way his rage fogged the divider and left it streaked with spit and blood.

We were the show, the dark mirror, and every twitch of agony was a gift to the audience.

He pressed his mouth to my ear, the breath hot and reeking of old cigarettes. "You're going to thank me for this," he whispered. "You're going to remember me for the rest of your short, beautiful life."

I heard Caiden's fists, the scrape of his body against the divider, the animal grunt in his throat.

The man seemed to savor it; he tilted his head, listening to our misery as if it were a composition he'd written himself.

He turned me to face the glass, so I could see Caiden, so Caiden could see me.

I tried to avert my eyes, but the man's fist closed in the nest of my hair and jerked my chin up until my gaze met Caiden's through the greasy, smudged partition.

There was a helplessness in Caiden's face I'd never seen before, and it felt like a new kind of death.

The next part was fast, and slow, and endless.

I was loopy from the drugged food, but still there.

Everything after that was a stuttering reel, the world breaking into single frames: his hand clamped at the base of my skull; my body going numb except for a thick, burning ache everywhere he touched; the wet click of his tongue; the animal, senseless noises from the other side of the glass.

My face was mashed flat against the divider, Caiden's eyes just inches away, wide and crazed and wet.

I didn't cry or scream or beg. There wasn't any point. I'd been emptied, scraped out by days of fear and hunger and previous iterations of this exact trauma.

I watched myself from outside my body, a ghost watching a meat puppet, and I realized this was probably the only way to survive it.

It was a performance, a ritual, I realized. The man had done this before. I could tell by the way he spaced his words, the way he forced me to watch the reflection of myself as he pulled my hair, the way he adjusted my hips for the best view, the best angle of despair.

It was calculated. He liked to see the ruin he made.

In the sick darkness, I had a moment of clarity.

The times Caiden had come onto me when we were teenagers, there was some part of me that wanted it. Always. A demented, deprived part of me that yearned to be filled with something other than hollowness.

Despite the anger, despite the hatred.

This was nothing like how it was with Caiden.

Being wanted and being consumed were two different things. I'd always known that, even when I pretended not to, even when I let myself believe that there was something sickly romantic about our mutual destruction.

Caiden was hunger and violence and hate, but he was always human. He was always, at the root, my equal. We could hurt each other, but never erase.

The man was nothing but devouring. He was the black hole at the center of the world, and we were the scraps flung into his event horizon.

It was not an act of wanting, not a collapse of mutual fury or the old, sick ache for absolution through pain.

It was nothing, and that was the point. It was obliteration made flesh. A destruction so complete it left no space for memory or hunger or even hate.

I was only a body here, a sack of needs, a thing to puncture and drain.

I'd spent my whole life fighting not to be an object, and now, at the bottom of it all, that was all I was. A shape for his pleasure, a reflection of my own agony, a thing to shred.

There was no power, no transaction, not even the pretense of hunger. Only the fulfillment of some ritual humiliation, the satisfaction of seeing the animal break.

And I knew he would never stop until he had spooned the last remnants of warmth off my bones.

Afterward, the man zipped his pants. "You see, son?" he said, not even looking at Caiden. "Nothing in the world can keep a woman from being just what she is. No matter how you cage 'em, they'll always show you their true nature."

Caiden made a sound that was half growl, half sob.

My face was a mask of nothing, but inside, my brain curled in on itself, a snail recoiling from the knife.

I saw the man retreat, his footsteps a slow waltz, the door closing behind him with a wet, metallic sigh.

I collapsed, ragged and boneless, onto the filthy cement.

Not even the rats dared approach. I was a beacon of rot, a blend of old agony and fresh shame.

I think I slept, or maybe I just blacked out and woke with a migraine that made my teeth ache.

A warmth pressed to the glass: Caiden's hand. He was still there, still a living, breathing animal.

He hadn't looked away. He hadn't left. I wanted to hate him for it, but for once I couldn't tell if I was more afraid of being seen or of being left alone in the dark.

At the end of the day, I was grateful for Caiden's presence, and I realized that we could never go back to how it was when we were kids.

The darkness between us had been eclipsed by some sort of strange new light, a bond forged in pain.

# 46

## THE PRESENT

### AMELIA

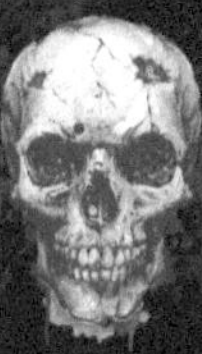

I LOST COUNT OF THE DAYS DOWN HERE. SOME DAYS, WE were left in the darkness. Going hours without anything to remind us that we were alive.

Shadows screamed and slithered around me. Sleep never came easily. When I did fall into an exhausted slumber, my dreams were filled with nightmares of blood and terror.

I would wake soon after, not being able to fall back into blissful unconsciousness.

For so long, I found comfort in the quiet embrace of the darkness, a solace found in the stillness of night. But now, it was a daunting terror, lathered with haunting shapes and sounds.

The hunger in my body was pushing me over the edge.

If we were taking too long to choose who gets to eat, he wouldn't feed us at all. Testing our limits on how long we could go without food, as if we were his personal experiments.

The next time he came down, I was ready. It was as if I were a hungry lion trapped in tiny confinement, needing to run free.

His malicious presence filled the basement as he entered, his feet making almost no sound on the old floorboards; it felt like a predator stalking its prey.

"How are my precious pets today?" His question hung in the air, a harsh sound; there was no kindness in his voice.

Caiden spoke up. "How do you think? Why the fuck am I still

alive? I've been thinking about it. All you've done is mess with Amelia, not me. So, what the fuck is my use? Why not get it over with and kill me?" His words spilled out in a wild rage.

"I must admit, my pet, it does fill me with splendid delight to know you are witnessing her torture, helpless to step in. That is your use: to play the bystander role in my games. It fills me with a deep pleasure."

A cruel laugh escaped the man's lips, echoing in the confined space. He took a slow step closer, his eyes glinting with a wicked satisfaction.

Caiden flinched, but his defiance remained. "You're a coward," he spat, the word a tiny spark against the overwhelming darkness. "Too afraid to just end it. Just kill us both and get it over with." The air stung with the weight of terror and simmering rage, the distant drip, drip, drip of water somewhere in the dampness of the basement echoed the 'tick tick' of time slipping away.

"In time, I will. That's a promise." His voice darkened, and his cruel smile faltered. He stepped closer, opening the door to the cage.

"But for now," he whispered, his voice a venomous caress, "the game continues." The drip, drip, drip of water seemed to mock their desperate stillness, a relentless counterpoint to the mounting tension.

A small whimper escaped my mouth and pierced the silence, a chilling soundtrack to our impending doom.

He stepped backward; the cage door was still open. My legs itched to run.

"You have one minute to try and escape." his words seemed too good to be true, and I stayed where I was in the cage. He noticed my hesitation.

"You hear me? I said run," his voice was commanding as he barked his order, and my body instantly uncoiled in response.

I ran, my heart pounding like a drum, as if the room had burst into flames.

The sound of Caiden's voice, strained and far off, barely reached me, yet I continued onward. Panic tightened its grip, and my thoughts scattered like leaves in the wind, leaving me incapable of rational thought.

The dark pressed in while my feet moved without direction across the rough, cold floorboards.

I ran up the creaking, old wooden stairs, my feet slipping on the worn steps. Time was almost up. I burst through the door, a wave of bright light momentarily blinding me, and I stumbled, my hands flailing as I fell onto the hard floor.

Once my eyesight refocused, I glanced around, taking in the blurry shapes slowly sharpening into focus. I was in a cabin. The air had an unpleasant, musty fragrance. Decay filtered through the senses, as if something dead were rotting.

I didn't take any time to observe the surroundings or think of a rational plan. I kept running. The front door was right there. I reached for the doorknob, but it was too late.

Time was up.

The man's grip on my waist was like iron, pulling me roughly backwards Terror choked my scream as my arms thrashed, his grip like a vise around my body. He dragged me back down the stairs, across the floor, back into the cage. He tossed me onto the floor.

"Bastard!" I screamed out, tears dripping from my eyes. Freedom was so close. It was right there in my grip, but it slipped away like a hopeless dream. I felt the familiar sting of failure, a hollow ache in my chest.

His harsh, mocking laughter echoed in my ears, a cruel sound that grated on my nerves. "You almost had it, but you must be silly to think I would actually let you go."

"What?" I choked out.

"It was part of the game, my little mouse. As I said, I thoroughly enjoy pushing my pets to their limits. Giving you breadcrumbs of hope, only to yank them away. It was something I got used to growing up, and now I thrive off of doing it to others."

He leaned closer, his eyes glinting with a sick amusement. "Tell me," he whispered, his breath cascading into me, "did you enjoy the taste of freedom? The fleeting glimpse of escape?" The cage door clanged shut, the metallic sound a final, brutal sting to my failed attempt.

The drip, drip, drip continued, a maddening metronome counting down to an uncertain future. A future where the game, it seemed, would never truly end.

As he left the basement, the sound of his laughter faded, replaced by a pouring silence, as the horror of what we'd witnessed settled in.

# 47
## THE PRESENT

### AMELIA

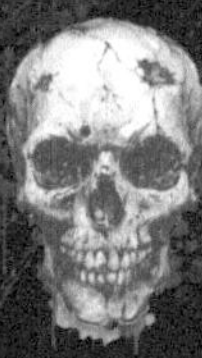

THE CAGE BECAME A UNIVERSE OF ROT. I WATCHED MY own hands shake, wondering at what point they'd stopped being mine.

Hunger wrung me out and left me feverish; my skin crawled, and every now and then I'd scratch until I bled, just to feel something.

I tried to remember the feeling of sunlight on my shoulders, or the way it felt to run, or to laugh. These memories came in fits, then sputtered out.

Mostly, I existed only to count the seconds between my own shuddering breaths.

Sometimes my body ached for touch so much that I pressed myself to the glass, desperate for the simple pressure of another human. Sometimes I shivered away, curled up so tightly I could not tell where my own limbs began or ended.

I whispered to the darkness because silence terrified me more than the idea of being heard.

I started talking to him. Not always so, he would answer; not even because I expected him to listen, but because every word I spoke aloud was like scraping my nails against the inside of my skull, and the pain meant I still existed.

Sometimes I told him about the dreams, or the shapes I saw in the corner, or the memory of a bird I watched once as a child, its wings snapping against a windowpane over and over until it broke its neck.

He didn't respond.

I wasn't sure he heard me at all. Some nights, he went so still I wondered if he had willed himself out of existence, and a not-small part of me envied him for it.

Once, I pressed my face to the warm glass and said, "Do you remember that time you threw a snowball at my eye?"

He didn't flinch. Maybe he was asleep, or maybe the memory hurt too much. I closed my eyes and let the silence pool around me.

It was a stupid memory. I tried again. "You used to sit behind me in algebra, and you'd flick the back of my neck with your eraser. I hated it. I still hate it."

The condensation on the glass trembled, collecting into rivulets that cut lines through our fingerprints. The silence pressed back, thicker than ever.

I started telling Caiden the stories I had kept to myself, revealing secrets I'd never shared with anyone, not even with my own thoughts, not even when I feared death.

"I always knew Lillian was going to kill herself," I confessed, "and I hated her for making it so obvious." I looked at him, admitting, "There were times I wished you'd get expelled, locked up, anything that would make you disappear.

I paused and added, "Mom was already rotting from the inside long before she stopped breathing. The last thing she ever said that made sense was, 'You're the only one left. Don't be like me, Melly.' I've already failed her, Caiden."

I told him how I used to draw versions of myself that weren't so small, brittle, and breakable. "Every time I did, I swear I could feel something warm under my hands, like I was holding on to the ghost of a future," I said, hoping he understood the depth of my longing.

Maybe I hoped Caiden would snap, or scream, or at least acknowledge that I was still here, that I wasn't just a reflection against the glass.

He never did. Not even when I told the stories that involved him

I told him how, sometimes, when I was a child, I would hide beneath my bed and pretend the dust and old socks were stalactites in a cave, and if I made myself very quiet, the monsters would walk right past.

How even now, when I inhaled the bitter tang of mold and rust, I could imagine I was somewhere else, expelled from time, floating between worlds.

I told him about the first time I saw a dead thing, a rabbit my mother's car had clipped on the way to the pharmacy. The way its body twitched after the impact, the way I thought it would get up and run, but it didn't.

I told him how she scraped it from the tire with a stick, face blank and efficient, and how she said, "Life is harder than death, Melly. Remember that."

I had never known whether she was warning me or herself.

I told Caiden how much I hated the sound of my own name in his mouth, how I'd rehearsed every possible comeback to his taunts but always said nothing, because I was more afraid of his father than I was of him.

I told him how sometimes I pictured the two of us growing up somewhere else, somewhere without chain-link fences or screaming mothers or the taste of metal in every bite of food.

I told him how I walked until I could not feel my legs one day, and ended up sitting on the Baxter front steps, staring at the black hole that was their living room window.

I said that I wanted to throw a rock through it, but couldn't.

Eventually, even my confessions ran out. I'd scraped through every memory until the marrow was visible, until shame and exhaustion coiled together and left me numb. I'd told him that I hated him those years ago, and that I hated myself more for letting it matter.

I began to lose grip on the boundary between memory and hallucination. The past swelled, sticky and insistent, until it eclipsed the present entirely.

In the dark and in the day, my nervous system revolted.

The cold glass propping up my cheek became a portal, and I fell through it, cascading backward through the years so fast I felt my stomach twist. Some were hallucinations, others were warped memories.

I was standing in the hallway of our Violet Road house, fourteen feet bare and icy against the floor. Lillian was at the kitchen table, bent over a notebook, her hair a fog of static. Mom was slumped in the recliner, one eye open, a cigarette trembling in her fingers.

A poltergeist memory: A shadowed voice, echoing through the drywall, "You're a fucking disease, Judy." The sound reverberated.

Lillian looked up at me and smiled, but her teeth were the jagged shards of a broken glass. "You're next, Amelia."

I blinked, and I was in the school gym again, thighs chafing against cheap polyester shorts, sweat-slicked hair sticking to my neck.

Caiden's voice rang out from the bleachers, pitched high and cruel, "Hey, Langston! Is your mom still a sex worker, or is she, like, retired?"

Laughter, shrill and rising. I could smell the raw gym floor, the mildewed towels, the desperate sweat of girls who wanted to be anywhere else.

I remembered the red bloom of humiliation spreading from my collar to my scalp. I remembered the way my fists clenched, the urge to jump the bleachers and tear his voice out at the roots.

Instead, I did what I'd always done. I shut my mouth and endured.

Even when I knew I should have screamed, or fought, or run, I stayed still and silent.

Back in the dark, I counted the ribs exposed at his neck, the way his Adam's apple bobbed when he swallowed.

I wondered if he also replayed every miserable second of our youth, or if the poison in his father's house had burned those memories out of him.

The memories grew darker, more insistent.

The sound of crashing glass and shrill arguments, the clang of my mother's voice, the way she'd drag me and Lillian down the hallway by our wrists, nails sharp as sewing needles, when her moods turned. The salty bite of tears I could never let loose in front of her.

The way, when she'd finally crashed out on the couch, her breath thick and rattling, Lillian and I would creep barefoot to the laundry closet and curl up inside, knees under our chins, hands laced together, like that would keep us safe from whatever skeletons thrashed their way through the drywall.

Sometimes, I'd wake up shaking in the dark, clutching my knees so hard I'd leave bruises.

The scratch of my mother's laugh would fill the silence, echoing down the stairwell and through the vents, spiderwebbing every surface in the house. *You're not special, Melly. You're just like me. Just like your sister. Just like every woman who ever clawed her way through this world and still ended up nowhere.*

I remembered the night she OD'd in the tub, the way the water was streaked with her hair dye and rusty with blood from her knees, the way the paramedics spoke in low, bored voices, as if this was a routine plumbing problem and not the slow erasure of a person.

I remembered the way they looked at me, the girl with the tangled hair, and how I had wanted nothing more than for one of them to reach out and touch me, just once, to prove I was real.

But they didn't. Nobody did, until the next day, when Lillian and I returned home and found Mom on the couch, an ice pack taped to her temple, already lighting up again. *Don't ever call the ambulance unless I stop breathing for real. You hear me, Amelia? Don't play the victim. I'm fine.*

Sometime's, I saw Lillian in the dark basement. Her voice was the same as it had always been: soft and mocking, just short of kind. *You're really doing it, are you? Rotting away with the boy who ruined you. That's so you, Amelia. You never could let go.*

Sometimes she'd bring souvenirs from the past. A sliver of bloody glass, a cigarette stub, a yellowed library card with my name misspelled in loopy fourth-grade cursive. She'd hold them up and shake her head, a private joke at my expense.

*You always wanted to be seen. Well, you got your wish.* She'd vanish then, leaving me with the echo of her laughter and a film of shame that clung to my skin. I wanted to ask her if it hurt, dying alone, choking on your own breath.

When I saw Caiden through the glass, I sometimes saw him as the boy with the dirt-crusted knees and wild, furious eyes, the boy who'd chased me down the railroad tracks and dared me to jump the creek, who'd smiled like hell itself couldn't touch him.

Sometimes he was just a hollow echo of that boy, all tendon and hunger, bruised in places the light never reached. Sometimes, under the sick-yellow bulb, he was hardly even human, slumped against the wall like a heap of forgotten laundry.

I remembered the first time he hurt me on purpose. Not with words, but with his hands. A shove in the hallway, a twist of my wrist during gym class, marking me purple where nobody could see.

He'd sneered something about not being weak, about how nobody in Pathosbury cared if you cried. I'd wanted to punch him so hard his nose collapsed, but I couldn't. I was too scared of him, of myself, of becoming what everyone seemed to expect me to become.

I remembered the night he'd followed me down to the river, the last day of junior year. I'd gone to smoke, to scream at the wind and kick rocks into the muddy water, to burn off the nerve endings he'd spent years fraying.

He'd appeared behind me, as silent as a stray dog, eyes glittering in the dusk. "You don't have to be here," he'd said, as if he was granting me permission. "You can just leave. Nobody would give a shit."

I laughed, and the sound had come out like a cough. "Fuck off, Caiden," I had told him, but he hadn't moved.

When I tried to step past, he grabbed my arm, hard, so hard I tasted iron, and spun me into him.

I felt his breath on my neck, the tremble in his hands, and the way he wanted to say something real but didn't know how, so instead he squeezed tighter, fingers digging into the meat of my shoulder until I yelped.

"You're not better than the rest of us," he whispered, then shoved me again, not quite letting go.

I'd hit him that time, hard enough to split the skin over his cheekbone, hard enough to satisfy us both.

He'd laughed then, a ragged, wild sound, and I remembered that laugh more clearly than any of my mother's lullabies.

Afterward, I'd stumbled home, fist throbbing, heart raw, and stared at my bruised knuckle for hours, not sure if I was proud or ashamed.

Now, watching him through the glass, I wondered if he remembered that night. Or if all the memories had blurred together into one long series of hurts and retaliations, a relay of damage passed down until we lost track of who'd started it.

Sometimes I'd let myself believe we were just animals in a cage, stripped of our histories and motives, surviving by base instinct. Sometimes I wanted to believe there was meaning in the pain, that it made us special, or holy, or at least not completely empty.

But then the man would come, and the world would shrink to the size of a fist again.

The next time I slept, the dreams came in a flood.

I was running down the railroad tracks, legs made of concrete, every step heavier than the last. I could hear Lillian's voice behind me, chanting in time with the slam of my feet. "Run, Melly, run, or you'll end up like me."

Only it wasn't Lillian's voice at all, it was his, the man upstairs.

The sky sagged overhead like a dead lung, and every step took me closer to the end of everything.

I woke gasping, cheek pressed to the glass, and found Caiden staring straight at me.

He looked different: the haunted, wary edge was gone, replaced with something scraped raw and almost childlike.

I realized I'd been speaking in my sleep, mouthing the words "don't leave," over and over. I hated him for hearing that, for knowing that even now I needed him here.

He moved his hand, slowly, so I could see he meant no threat, and pressed his palm to the spot opposite mine. My fingers hovered, then settled onto the glass, separated by a millimeter of plastic and vacuum.

His hand was bigger, bones stark under the skin, but the lines of our hands fit together like two halves of an old wound.

We stayed like that for a long time, not speaking, just breathing in sync. The world beyond the glass was a smear of shadow and sickly light, but in here, for a moment, I could almost imagine we'd made a place of our own.

Not safe, not sane, but ours.

The man interrupted us with the thunder of boots. He stormed in, kicking at the tray with enough force to send the food skittering across the concrete and shattering the silence.

His voice was a drill through my skull: "Hands off the glass, lovebirds. Unless you want a reason to need stitches."

Caiden's hand snapped away. Mine did not. I pressed harder, glaring back with the only currency I had left: spite.

The man grinned at me. Today he wore a different coat, something bristly and red that looked like it had been skinned from a living thing.

He paced, eyes flicking from me to Caiden, back again. His shadow bent around him, a greedy black tongue licking at the wire.

He stopped directly in front of me, crouching low so that our faces were almost level. His eyes were jaundiced, ringed with cracked red like old paint.

"Do you know how many days it's been?" he whispered, as if we were co-conspirators. "I do. I always do. That's the fun of it."

I didn't answer. I wouldn't give him the pleasure.

He leaned closer, his lips brushing the mesh. "I like the way you look at him. Even after all this. Still think he'll save you, do you?"

I looked past him to Caiden's face. Not for comfort, but for proof that I wasn't just a figment in the man's fever dream.

Caiden stared straight through us both, jaw clenched so tight a vein pulsed at his neck.

He circled the cage, slow at first, then faster. Like a coyote testing the perimeter of a campfire. He bared his teeth in a parody of a grin. "You're just animals," he spat, "and animals can be trained to do anything. Even love each other."

He let the words hang. He wanted to see if they would ruin us.

The man left us with only our hunger and the memory of his words.

I hated that a part of me was still counting on Caiden. I hated more that the part was growing.

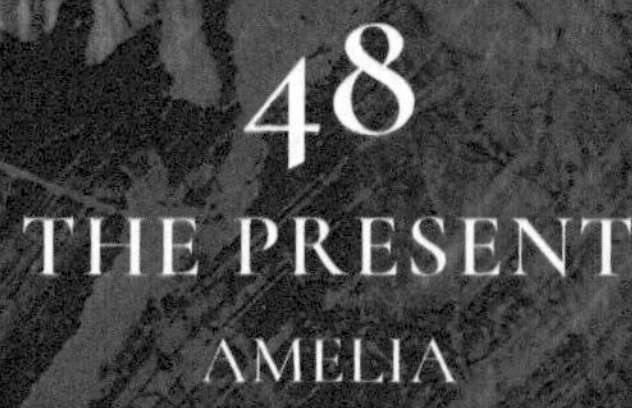

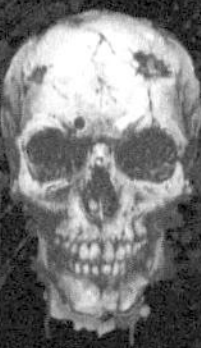

# 48

## THE PRESENT

### AMELIA

A TUMULTUOUS STORM BREWED INSIDE OF ME, COLORS crashing and merging into a frenzied maelstrom.

My adolescent instinct screamed for flight, to break free from this raw moment of his unexpected vulnerability.

This was Caiden, tangled in the web of my longstanding resentments, struggling under the unanticipated weight of his candor.

Yet, beneath the layers of past grievances, a warmth simmered from his revelation, a shared darkness binding us. We were reflections of each other, shadows cloaked in trauma, anger, and guilt.

Our parents, lost to the relentless grip of addiction, had carved out destructive paths we seemed doomed to tread.

We faced each other stripped of defenses, laid bare in this icy prison of despair. Confronting our inner demons, we grappled with the cruel fate that had ensnared us.

But as the morbid darkness pressed in, my mind teetered on the brink of collapse. I clung desperately to a fragile glimmer of hope, flickering like a candle on the verge of extinction.

My thoughts ricocheted wildly around Caiden.

He's deceiving me. He's toying with my sanity. He's vile. He's my adversary. Don't trust him.

The cacophony of frantic whispers assailed me, each one a merciless echo driving me ever closer to the precipice of madness.

"Caiden?" My voice trembled, a desperate plea for clarity amidst the chaos. I needed something to halt this insanity, to ground me back in reality.

"What?" His response fell flat, different from the raw openness that had engulfed him just moments before.

"Um, I was wondering about something you said before we were captured. Did you mean what you said about wishing you had left me for dead?" I held my breath as I waited.

The silence stretched before his response, an agonizing wait that felt like stepping onto flaming coals. My heart pounded with each second that passed.

"No, I didn't mean it. I was mad." He confessed.

"Okay. That's good," I uttered pathetically, a fragile relief tinged with regret.

Here I was, longing for him to open his heart again, to wrap me in feathers of solace.

This weakened state had shifted my perception of Caiden, igniting a craving for his compassion and companionship.

Yet his demeanor had hardened once more, the subtle shift in his posture and the tightening of his jaw betraying the internal struggle he was battling.

It felt as though he read my mind with what he said next.

"Doesn't mean anything. I can't allow myself to give in to this fucking yearning that I've carried beneath all the anger and hatred."

Caiden sat in the shadows of the cage as he snapped at me, a sudden anger tearing through his voice.

"Yearning?" I whispered, fear coiling tightly in my chest as I awaited his answer.

"Yes. Yearning for you. My father made me hate you. But before that, I craved you." Shock coursed through me as his words tumbled out, lathered with anger.

"Fuck!" Caiden snarled, smacking the barrier with his hand.

My body shrank back from the force of his blow against the glass. He held his head in his hands, squeezing his eyes shut, the muscles in his arms flexing and tensing.

He was a broken shell of a man, grappling with demons that clawed at him like a ravenous beast.

"I'm sorry." I wasn't sure what else to say. What could one say to that? Caiden, who had tormented me for years, had just confessed to an intimidating and forbidden truth.

"What the fuck are you sorry for? I'm the piece of shit here. I fucking hate myself, and I always will. All I wanted for all those years was for you to hate me too, so I could feel less guilty about my behavior."

Caiden snarled, and he smacked the barrier again; the violent force sent a fearful tremor through my body

"You felt guilty?" I had always viewed Caiden as a cruel monster, devoid of remorse, much like our kidnapper. Along the way, I had forgotten that he was human too, battling his own hell.

"I did at first. But over the years, bullying you became too easy, and I started to enjoy it. I buried that guilt and pity so deep that it evaporated." He turned away, staring into the darkness, avoiding my gaze.

A spark of anger ignited within me, hot and sudden, as I recalled who I was speaking with. I couldn't let his muddled words cloud my thoughts.

He was Caiden.

I hated him. He hated me.

The chilling confession that he had enjoyed making my life miserable snaked around me, its icy grip constricting my breath as my heart pounded in my ears.

It made me forget the softened feelings I had been having for him in this cage, and suddenly, he was the boy who bullied me again.

"Who the fuck do you think you are? You think you can bully me to the point of crushing my soul and make it up with some goddamn confessions that probably aren't even true? How fucking pathetic." The words surged out of me, and I reveled in the rush of adrenaline.

I needed that release.

"No, I know I can't make it up. I just thought I'd be honest before we die." Caiden spoke in such a hopeless way, and it terrified me.

"I thought you said we would make it out of here?"

He shook his head, anger radiating off his body like heat from a flame. "You were right about me. I'm a fucking coward. I'm tough and confident on the outside, but I'm no use to you. You need to save yourself, Amelia."

"Fuck you, Caiden. Fuck you for making me feel small and weak, for giving me hope only to yank it away and abandon me completely. If you're going to give up, then that's reason enough for me to fight because we can't both sit here and wither until that sadistic fucker kills us. This is not how I want to die."

"Whatever," Caiden murmured, refusing to meet my gaze. He had retreated further away, isolating himself until I was left alone with the darkness once again.

He was lost in his own madness, and I was close behind.

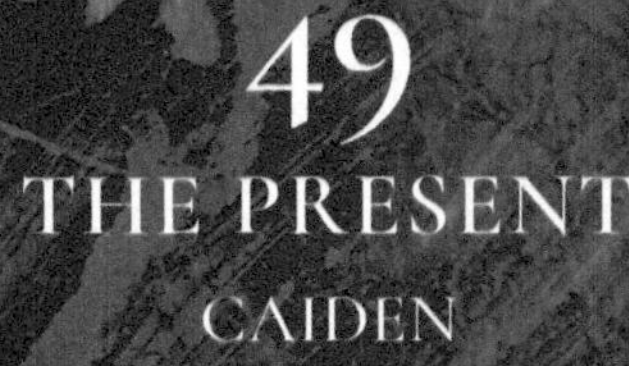

# 49

## THE PRESENT

### CAIDEN

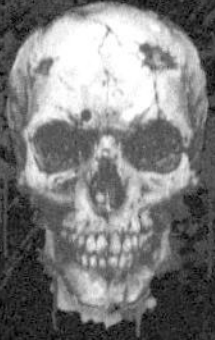

THE DRIP OF WATER SOMEWHERE IN THE BASEMENT sounded like a countdown. The buzz of the bulb overhead sounded like a nerve being rubbed raw. Even my own breathing felt loud, like the walls were listening for it.

I hated that the wire let me see everything while trapping me anyway. See the concrete. See the stairs. See the dark mouth of the doorway above. See the stains I kept refusing to stare at long enough to understand.

The visibility was its own cruelty. A reminder that freedom was right there, just out of reach, like a fucking taunt.

Time slipped sideways down here. It wasn't measured in sunsets or meals. It was measured in how often he came down the stairs. In the times that the light flickered. In the way that my body started to feel like it belonged to the basement. Like the damp had crawled into my bones and planted roots.

I sat with my back against the wire, knees bent, forearms resting on them, head tipped forward like I was trying to keep my thoughts from spilling out. The shirt on my skin was stiff with sweat and grime. My knuckles were split again. I kept reopening the cuts without meaning to, picking at the scabs when the anger got too loud. It was something to control. Something to ruin that wasn't her.

Amelia sat across the cage. She'd been quieter since I opened my mouth. Since I said the thing I shouldn't have said. The thing that made my skin crawl with regret every time I replayed it.

Craving.

I wanted the old distance. The old hatred. The simplicity of it. Hate was easy. Hate was a script my father wrote and made me memorize. Hate gave me somewhere to put the chaos.

This was messy and vulnerable. This was me handing her a weapon and pretending it wouldn't hurt when she used it.

I stared at the glass until my eyes burned. It had smudges from our palms. Old prints layered over new ones. Evidence of proximity without touch.

Close enough to see the exhaustion in her face. The crack in her lower lip. The bruise blooming along her jawline from where he'd grabbed her too hard. Close enough to watch her breathe, to count each rise and fall like it mattered, like her lungs were the only thing keeping mine working.

Not close enough to fix a damn thing.

The bulb flickered. Buzzed. Steadied.

My jaw clenched.

I'd started hating the light almost as much as the dark. The light meant visibility. Surveillance. Being watched. It meant he could come down at any second and see us exactly like this.

The dark was worse, though.

The dark made my mind loud.

In the dark, the basement didn't just feel like a cage. It felt like my childhood house. The hallway. The heaviness in the walls. The certainty that footsteps meant impact.

I could handle a lot of things. Cold. Hunger. Pain.

But the sound of a man moving above me made something primal wake up under my ribs.

A part of me that wanted to become the weapon my father always said I was.

I pressed the heel of my hand to my forehead, hard enough to see sparks.

Amelia shifted on the other side of the glass. A small movement, careful, like even changing position, cost her something. Her shoulder slid higher against the wall. She dragged a hand over her face, palm trembling.

She was slipping. Not physically. Not yet.

But I could see it in her eyes, in the way she stared through the floor like she was already gone somewhere else. Helplessness wasn't loud with her. It was quiet. It was a slow surrender. It was her trying to shrink so the pain couldn't find her.

I hated it. I hated watching it. I hated that I couldn't reach across the glass and grab her shoulders and shake her back to life. I hated that the thought of touching her made my throat go dry.

Because that's what craving was, wasn't it? A need so immense it buried you.

I stared at her hair, at the curve of her neck, and I remembered being fourteen and seeing that same curve when she bent over her locker. I remembered the sudden punch in my gut, the heat, the confusion. I remembered how I'd turned that confusion into cruelty because my father's voice lived in my skull like a parasite.

Hate her. Hurt her. Make her pay. For your mother leaving. For Judy. For everything.

My father had died a few months after graduation. Alcohol poisoning. Like the bottle finally got tired of pretending it wasn't killing him and just did it outright.

I'd thought I'd feel relief. I'd expected freedom. What I got was a ghost. What I got was his voice still running my life, still deciding what I was allowed to feel. What I was allowed to want.

Even dead, he'd owned me.

I dug my fingernails into my palm until pain flared and grounded me.

My muscles tightened on instinct. I sat up straighter, shoulders rolling back, face smoothing into the dead calm I wore like armor. If he wanted fear, he wasn't getting it from my expression. He could earn it the hard way.

Amelia's voice came muffled through the glass. I couldn't make out the words, but the tone was thin with exhaustion. She was trying to speak like she didn't care.

Like she hadn't been reduced to a shaking animal in a cage.

I leaned closer to the glass, not because I wanted conversation, but because ignoring her felt dangerous. Not for her. For me. For whatever was building inside my chest.

"What?" I said flatly.

Her eyes flicked up, annoyed that I'd responded at all. She said something again, clearer this time, still muffled but readable.

"Do you think he's coming back?"

She was trying to plan. Trying to anchor herself to something predictable. She needed an answer to cling to.

I didn't have one.

"I don't know," I said.

Her jaw clenched. She snapped back, words blurred by the barrier but obvious in shape.

"You never know anything."

I leaned in closer, my breath fogging the glass. "None of us know anything," I said, harsher than necessary. "That's the point."

I shifted away from the glass, needing space that didn't exist. "Don't fucking look at me like that," I muttered.

Her mouth parted. She looked like she wanted to argue, then thought better of it. She sank back against the wall, eyes dropping again.

Silence returned, heavy as wet cloth.

I stared at the concrete floor and let the darkness in my head creep forward anyway. It came whether I wanted it or not.

Images.

Pathosbury. The hallways. Her locker. Her face when I shoved her too hard and pretended it was an accident. The way her eyes would flare, defiant, even when she was scared.

Lillian.

Her laugh. Her hands on my shirt. The way she'd looked at me like I was something worth knowing, and I'd taken it because I was selfish and angry and starving for affection I didn't know how to ask for.

Then the consequences. The spiral. The pregnancy. The way everything turned black and final.

The word suicide still didn't feel real in my mouth. It felt like a story that belonged to someone else, something tragic you read about and put down.

Except it was welded into us.

Into Amelia. Into me.

I clenched my jaw until it ached, trying to grind down the guilt like it was bone. It didn't go away. It never went away. It just waited.

My father's voice crawled up from the pit of memory, thick with whiskey and contempt.

*You ruin everything you touch.*

I swallowed hard. I wanted to punch something. The wire. The wall. My own face. Instead, I sat still and let the rage boil, contained, because I'd learned early what happened when rage escaped.

People got hurt. Mostly the wrong people.

Amelia made a soft sound across the glass. Not a sob. Not a word. A sound like her breath caught on something sharp.

I looked up fast.

She was staring at the corner of the room, eyes wide and glassy, shoulders drawn tight.

Hallucinations. Again.

The basement loved those. It fed them. It cultivated them like mold.

I watched her for a long second, my chest tight, and told myself not to move. Not to react. If I reacted, it became real. If I reacted, he won.

Amelia whispered something to the corner, barely moving her lips.

My stomach turned.

I stood up, slow and controlled, because if I moved too quickly, my body would show how scared I was that she was slipping. I stepped closer to the glass, staring hard at her until her eyes flicked to mine.

"Stop," I said.

Her brows knitted together.

"Stop talking to whatever the fuck that is," I said, voice low. "It isn't real."

Her eyes flashed with anger, immediate and defensive. "I know."

"You don't," I snapped.

She sat up straighter, fury giving her a brief spine. "Don't tell me what I know."

I leaned forward until my forehead nearly touched the glass. "Then act like it," I said.

Her lips pressed tight. Her eyes were wet with rage, not tears. "You don't get to act like you care," she said, slow and deliberate, like she wanted each word to land.

My stomach clenched.

There it was. The truth she kept throwing at me like a rock. I deserved it. I also hated it.

Because caring was not some noble thing I was choosing. It was a weakness that had crawled under my skin and made itself at home. It was a craving I hadn't asked for, a hunger that made the rest of my hungers feel simple.

I forced my face colder. "I don't care," I lied.

Amelia stared at me like she wanted to believe it because believing it would hurt less. Then she looked away, shoulders slumping again.

The lie tasted like ash.

I backed away from the glass and sat down hard against the wire, letting my head hit it once. The impact sent a dull pain through my skull. It felt deserved. It felt like punishment.

A few days in this cage and I was unraveling. Not with tears. Not with dramatic speeches. With this quiet rot inside me, this slow realization that hatred had been my shield, and without it, I didn't know what the hell to do with what I felt.

What I'd always felt, buried under my father's orders.

I remembered a night in high school, after practice, walking home alone.

I'd seen Amelia down the street under a streetlight, hair catching the glow, face tilted up like she was thinking about something far away. I'd stopped behind a tree like a creep and watched her for a long minute.

Not because I wanted to hurt her.

Because I wanted to walk up and say her name like it meant something.

Then I'd heard my father's truck on the road, and the spell broke, and I'd gone home and swallowed the longing like it was poison.

Craving. I'd always had it. I'd just been trained to translate it into cruelty.

Now the translation was failing. Now I was stuck in a cage with her, and the old hate didn't fit anymore, and the guilt was too big to hold, and the fear was so constant it made my teeth ache.

I stared at my hands.

These hands had shoved her. Grabbed her. Hurt her. These hands had touched her sister. These hands wanted to touch Amelia now, not even in some pretty fantasy, but in that raw, desperate way that meant I needed proof she was still alive.

I hated myself for it. I hated myself for everything.

Amelia was turned away now, back to the corner, back to staring at nothing.

And I hated myself again.

I sat back down against the wire, head tipped forward, and let the darkness in my head roll closer. Let it remind me of everything I'd done. Everything I'd ruined. Let it whisper that this cage was my punishment.

The worst part was that a piece of me agreed.

If there was any justice in the world, Amelia would not be trapped in here with me. And if there was any justice in the world, the craving I admitted would die in my throat before it ever got the chance to become something real.

Justice was a fairytale.

This was just a basement. A cage. A glass wall. Two people slowly being stripped down to whatever they really were beneath hate, beneath guilt, beneath fear.

I stared at the barrier until my eyes blurred.

Then I closed them, not to sleep, but to hold myself still.

If I let the storm out, I would become my father. If I became my father, Amelia would not survive me, even if she survived this.

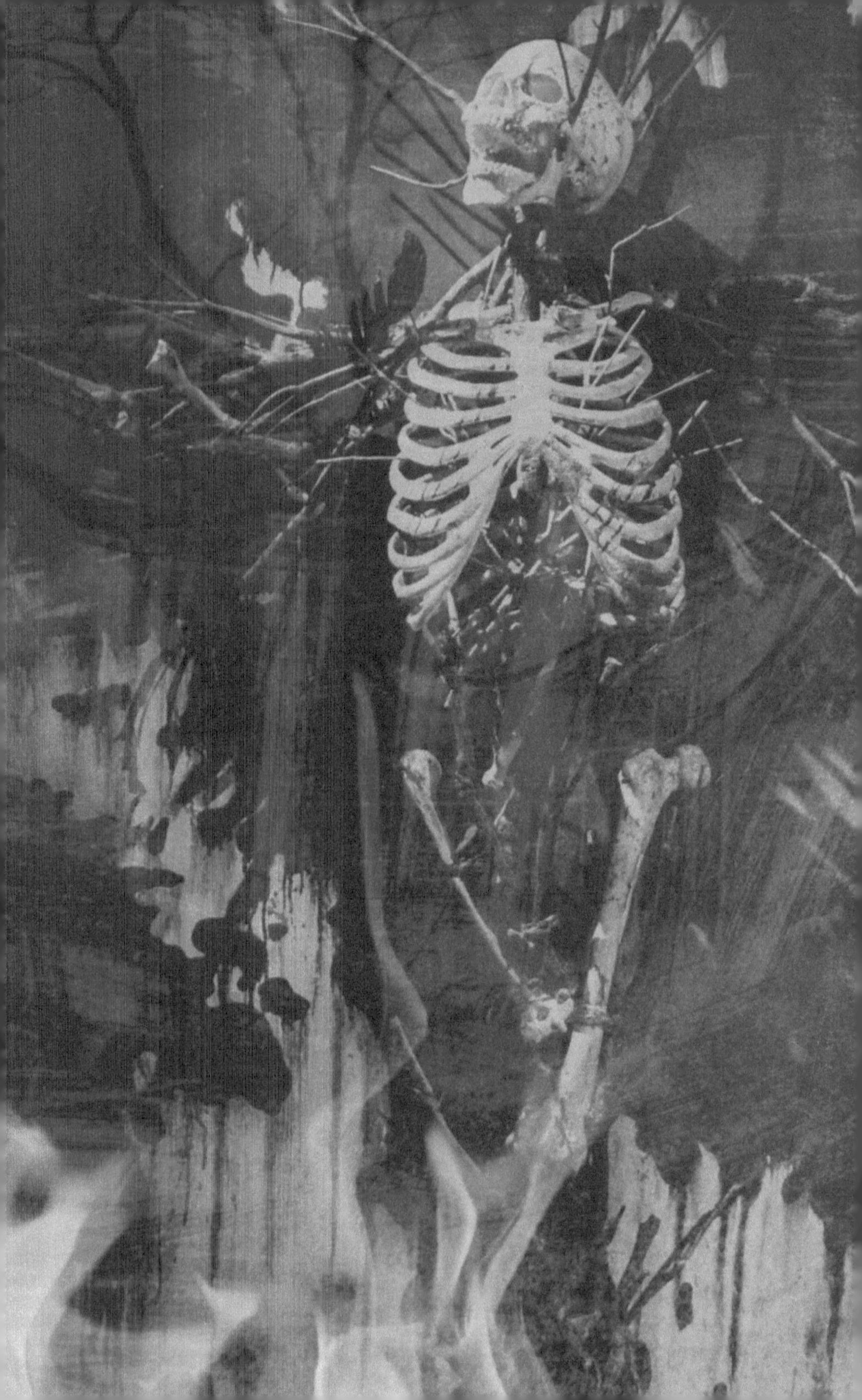

# 50

## THE PRESENT

### AMELIA

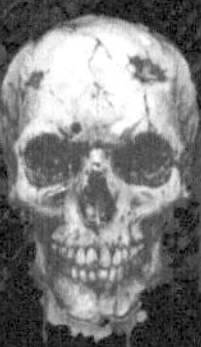

As the empty hours dragged on, I replayed every possible scenario in my head, contemplating all that could go wrong. Anything could happen, but I had to try.

Something deep in my gut told me we were running out of time. His demeanor had shifted lately, as if he anticipated something exciting on the horizon.

When it came time to decide who would receive food, he began giving us larger portions, as if fattening us up for slaughter.

A terrifying thought crept into my mind: he intended to cut us up and eat us. It made a twisted kind of sense.

Out here, in the middle of nowhere, he must have seized any opportunity for sustenance.

I peered at Caiden, the daylight streaming through the small window, illuminating his hunched figure in the corner. I inched closer to the barrier, placing my hand against the glass.

"Caiden." I needed to ignite his adrenaline. He was lost in the dark lately, more so than I. We were both breaking, but he wrestled with something dark and disturbed within his mind.

No answer.

"Caiden," I yelled louder, tapping on the glass.

He turned his head slightly. "What?" His voice was dull, devoid of vitality.

"I was just checking to see if you were still conscious. You haven't said much." Though my voice was weak, a tremor coursed through it as I fought to keep my tone steady.

"I've just been contemplating. Keeping to myself."

"I can see that," I breathed out, wondering how to break through him.

Silence enveloped us again. A sigh escaped my lips. He could scarcely look at me. I wasn't surprised; I knew he felt a kind of second-hand shame every time the man came down to "play with me," as he put it.

I was grateful for the drugged food, numbing my senses as he intruded upon my body.

"Please say something," I pleaded, desperate to see that fire in his eyes again. The brokenness that cloaked him was disheartening. All my life, he had been strong and tough, never backing down.

But now, he was a shell of who he used to be.

Now, more than ever, I needed that fierce and angry Caiden.

"What do you want me to say? There's nothing left. I'm done," he spoke dully, a monotone rasp barely audible.

"Come on, Caiden. I need you to wake the hell up," I snapped at him fiercely. "You kept telling me that I shouldn't give up, so I'm doing the same for you. We have to cling to whatever tiny bit of sanity and clarity we have left, for our own sakes. I have a bad feeling that our time is running out."

"You're probably right."

I waited, but he didn't say anything more.

"And? What will you do about it? If there's any tiny bit of humanity left in you, then be a man for once in your life and work with me here."

My words aimed to push him, and they did.

"I am a fucking man. I've survived a lot of tough shit. My father, the military, being kicked out of my home because my girlfriend didn't want anything to do with my drunk ass anymore," he yelled, angry, though I could see that he was angrier with himself.

Surprise washed over me. He had a girlfriend? That must have been what he and Shane talked about when Shane asked if he needed a place to stay.

The thought of Caiden being loving and affectionate was disturbing, almost surreal, a complete contradiction to his usual demeanor.

A sliver of doubt remained; I couldn't fully grasp that he was capable of such a thing. But my mind didn't linger on that topic for long.

"Exactly. You're stronger than you know. So, get angry. Get energized. Take all that frustration about how hard life has been and let it fuel you. That's what I'm trying to do. But I can't do it by myself." I took a breath and poured out my next sentence. "You *owe* me this. After everything you've put me through. After impregnating my sister, leading to her suicide, you owe me."

His head snapped upwards, nostrils flaring, eyes burning.

That was the Caiden I remembered.

"That was not my fault. Yeah, I had sex with her, but I was fucking depressed that night and needed somebody. I didn't push her to kill herself. But you know what the sickest thing about that was?"

His voice was stone and flames.

I remained silent.

He continued.

"I wanted it to be you. I had a passing thought while I was with her. She looked so much like you in the face, and that tiny part of me that craved you? I wished it had been you instead," he screamed, his eyes wide and bloodshot, a snarl twisting his lips.

"Don't say such things."

His words crashed down on me, and I could only whisper back, feeling utterly helpless and small.

I should have felt flattered by the praise, but instead, a hollow feeling resided deep within. The ache in my heart intensified, a dull throb mirroring the emptiness I felt.

"I can't keep holding all this in, dammit. It's eating me from the inside out. I never meant to impregnate her. When you told me about it, I wanted to push it aside and pretend it didn't happen. I'm a fucking coward, Amelia. It's all I will be because of my alcoholic father. He molded me into who I am, and I wish I could strangle him for it." His words tumbled out in a torrent, cascading over me like a waterfall. He paced within his small cage, fists clenched, his shouts echoing off the cold walls. He was a furious madman coming undone.

Perhaps I had pushed him too far.

His confession of "craving me" hung in the air still, threaded with lament and shock.

I was overwhelmed by a rush of memories, each encounter replaying in my mind like a movie. His hatred was a venomous snake, his words poisoned arrows, his anger a roaring inferno. I knew he had told me he loathed me completely. He even reveled in being cruel.

But the awareness of a hidden, deep part of him that yearned for me sent shivers down my spine, pulling me into a dizzying spiral of emotions.

I could only sit and watch as he unraveled. It was as if he were a volcano erupting, years of suppressed feelings exploding outward.

"Fuck! I fucking hate myself." He slammed his palm against the glass, acting like an enraged beast.

The sound reverberated through the space, deafening in contrast to the sudden silence that followed.

He slumped against the wall, the fury draining from him, leaving behind a hollow shell. Tears welled in his eyes, tracing silent paths down his cheeks, mirroring the rivers of regret carving their way through his soul.

The rage had spent itself, leaving only the raw, exposed wound of his self-loathing. For a long moment, ragged breaths filled the space, an aftermath to the emotional cyclone that had just passed.

Then, a choked sob escaped his lips, followed by another, and another, until the sound became a relentless, heart-wrenching wail.

In that moment, the man I had known, the monster he had become, seemed to vanish, leaving only a broken, vulnerable boy clinging to the shattered remnants of his past.

Seeing him so broken, a cold dread washed over me, shattering my composure.

This was Caiden, but he was no longer my enemy; he was my parallel. Something deep within shifted, and I leaned against the glass, pressing my palm against the barrier.

"Caiden. It's okay."

My voice, soft as a gentle blanket, aimed to wrap around him and soothe his pain.

"No. It's not. I've done horrible things, Amelia. This is my punishment." As he spoke, his voice came out as a trembling choke.

I shook my head. "This is not your punishment. This is your redemption. Prove to me that you can do the right thing."

His eyes burned into mine, a silent scream in their depths as his rage subsided, leaving only a simmering ember of fury. "Fine. I still don't know how I should feel. I'm being torn in both directions, and I don't fucking know what the right or wrong thing is. But I want to survive. I know that. It's all I know how to do, survive." His gaze softened for only a second. "Thank you for reminding me of that."

A wave of complex emotions washed over me as I nodded, my heart pounding a rhythm of anticipation and anxiety.

His words struck a chord; the sensation of being pulled between two opposing forces mirrored my own inner turmoil, a painful tug-of-war within my soul.

Caiden, the architect of my suffering and Lillian's demise.

But I also saw a broken, damaged man, his eyes haunted, his shoulders slumped from a life of being brainwashed and abused.

The silent battle between anger and pity was a tempest of conflicting emotions, a furious storm versus a gentle rain. The question of our future after the escape hung heavily. Would we return to the old ways, or would this adventure forge a new era for us? The taste of uncertainty filled the air.

We would either be pulled apart or pulled together, and I wasn't sure which outcome I wanted.

# 51

# THE PRESENT (WITH FLASHBACK)

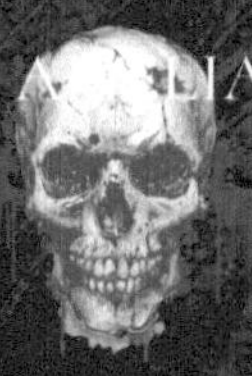

AMELIA

*My mother lay passed out on the lawn.*

*Lillian and I had awakened, ready for school, but the house was silent, and our mother's bedroom stood empty.*

*After wandering through the quiet halls, we spotted her shape outside, curled up on the grass. The rising sun cast long shadows across her sleeping form, transforming our home into an ominous scene.*

*"Is Momma okay?" Lillian had frowned as I turned to her, seeking answers about our mother's behavior.*

*Lillian shook her head. "No, I don't think so." She grabbed a blanket from the closet and stepped outside, draping it over our mother.*

*"Are we going to wake her up? We're going to be late for school."*

*Lillian sighed and walked back inside to finish getting ready. "Mom is going through a lot, Amelia. She won't appreciate being nagged about that. I doubt she'll be well enough to drive anyway."*

*"If Dad were here, he could take us." My tone emerged bitter, memories of our father's recent abandonment sinking their teeth into me. Our mother hadn't provided many details; she had only said that he was dangerous and that he didn't love us.*

*That sentence had carved a deep gash in my soul. A raw, bleeding wound that pulsed with agonizing pain, one that would have a long-standing effect.*

*Lillian remained silent; the grief between us was a blanket woven from shared loss and unvoiced fears.*

*The silence stretched, interrupted only by the chirping of birds, an eerily cheerful contrast to the anxiety knotting in my stomach.*

*School suddenly felt insignificant. The problem of our mother pressed down upon me, her figure sprawled on the lawn like a discarded doll, a sorrowful symbol of a family fractured beyond repair.*

*But Lillian moved on more quickly than I did. She yanked me inside and ordered me to finish getting ready. Eventually, we made our way, walking down the road together.*

*It took longer to reach the elementary school since we were on foot, and we barely made it on time. Lillian dropped me off at my classroom and then went her separate way to her designated class.*

*The day dragged slowly, the events surrounding my mother replaying in my mind. Seeing her like that left a hollow sadness within me, one that branded me unlovable, invisible.*

*At recess, I sat alone on the grass. A cacophony of joyous shouts and squeals filled the air as children tumbled and played, their energy radiating around me. The sounds taunted my internal turmoil, as if to say, 'This will never be you.'*

*The world faded away for a short time; I felt unseen, unheard, a silent observer in my own life. I could have melted into the shadows like a ghost, and nobody would have noticed.*

*That thought, a faint whisper in the back of my mind, lingered until a body settled beside me. I nearly jumped away, surprise etched on my features.*

*"Hello," the boy said, gazing at me with wide, curious eyes.*

*"Hi," came my quiet, shy response. I had seen him before at school, but his name escaped me like a fleeting shadow.*

*"What are you doing over here by yourself?"*

*My hands fiddled nervously with the grass. "I just don't feel like pretending to be happy."*

*"Why aren't you happy?" He continued to ask questions, his eyes warm and inviting. I leaned into that warmth, relishing the fact that someone was noticing me.*

*"I don't think my momma loves me. I keep thinking she's going to leave like my dad did." The words spilled from my mouth before I could stop them, and I immediately shrank back in shame for oversharing with this boy.*

*But instead of laughing at me, he sat there with an expression of kindness.*

*"I'm sorry. I can understand feeling forgotten. My mom left too."*

*His smile was soft and delicate, barely a twitch of his lips, yet somehow meaningful. His sorrow hung heavily in the air, and I felt seen, the weight of his pain connecting us.*

*"Yeah, it's not a fun feeling." The boy didn't push any further after my response but sat with me in the grass. His presence offered an odd comfort.*

*"I'm Caiden, by the way. You're Amelia, right?"*

*Caiden. It was a nice name. Unique.*

*I imagined our friendship, Caiden and Amelia, two inseparable kids formed by a shared sadness. There was a magnetic pull toward him.*

*He was cute with his boyish features. The way his hair danced in the breeze, how his eyes shimmered like the hues of moonlight and sunlight.*

*I had never had such thoughts about a boy before, but I embraced them in that moment.*

*His face seemed familiar, too, as though we had shared a moment like this before.*

*"Caiden," the name rolled off my tongue. "Nice to meet you. But how did you know my name?"*

*He shrugged, as if it didn't mean much, but his expression said otherwise. "I've seen you around, and I pay attention sometimes. You seem like a nice girl."*

*The softness within me intensified, and I smiled back at him, hoping this connection would last. Perhaps I wouldn't feel so empty and alone, and I could sink into him as if he were a blanket.*

The memory struck me like a physical blow, leaving me breathless and weeping silently in the shadowed corners of the cage, each tear a hot drop against my skin.

A bitter taste filled my mouth as I mourned the loss of our innocence, the missed chances echoing in my memories.

His gentle nature, like a soft, delicate flower, infused me with a comforting warmth, akin to sunshine breaking through clouds.

But the petals decayed, their tender texture turning brittle and crumbling, and the sunshine was swallowed by a barren, starless blackness, silent and opaque.

We can never go back. Our innocence was slaughtered too soon.

Time just keeps spinning. A maddening blur. We just keep circling this carousel of hateful rage and tragedy. Always finding the dark, never reaching the light.

I cried in the dark. I wept for our lost innocence, for something that we could never go back to.

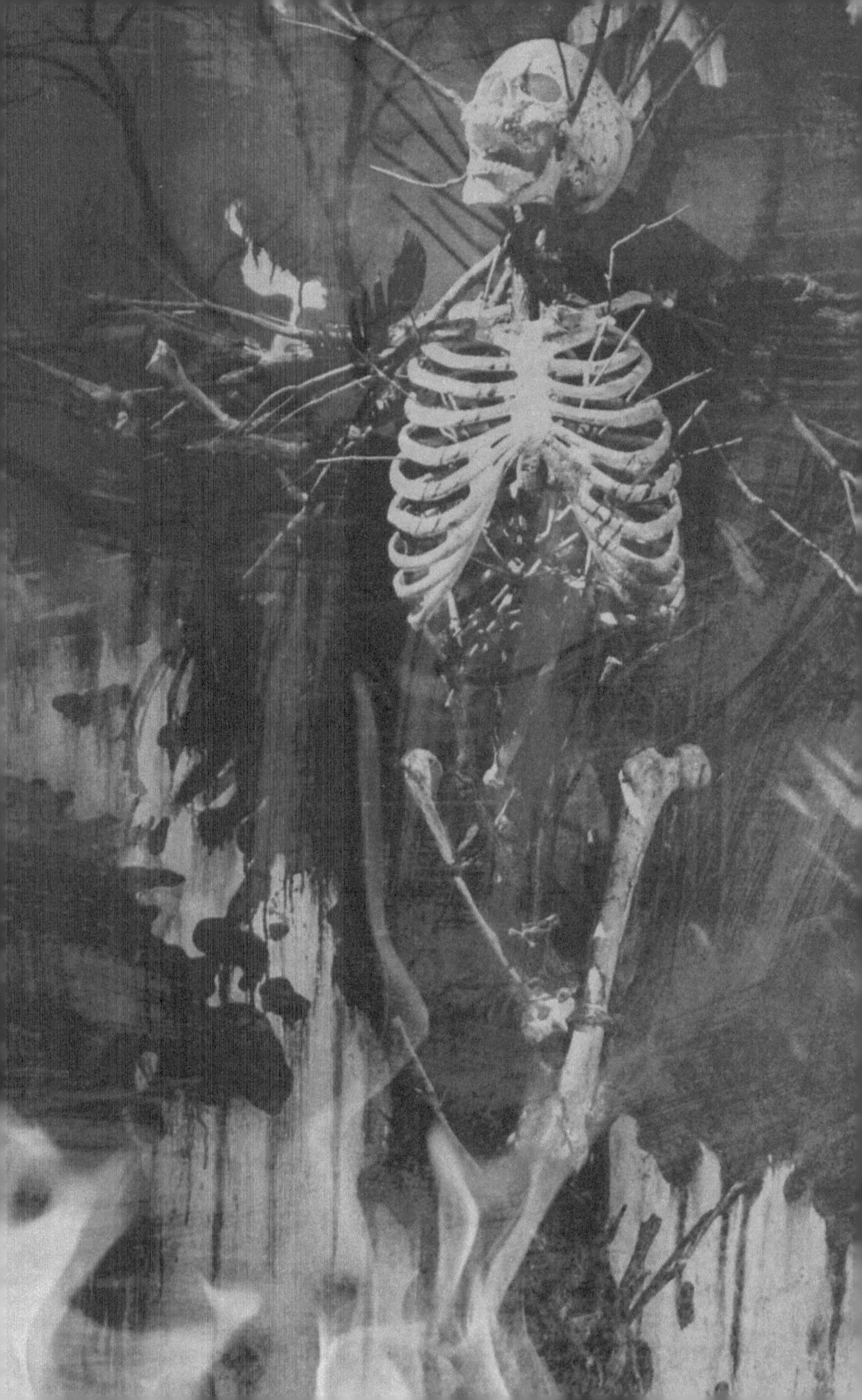

# 5²

# THE PRESENT

## AMELIA

I ALWAYS DREADED THE MOMENTS WHEN THE BASEMENT door would open with a heavy and slow creak.

It meant the arrival of our tormentor.

When the bolt scraped back, it sounded like a guillotine being readied. I pressed my hands to the glass, not for comfort or hope, but just to anchor myself to something that proved I was still here. Still real.

He trailed a smell of wilted lilies and machine oil, a bouquet of death and industry.

I saw his mouth before I saw his eyes. A crescent, wide and white. He smiled as if we were old friends meeting for cocktails. "My pets," he crooned, and the word was a caress and a threat in equal measure, "I do hope the accommodations are to your liking."

He circled, as always, making a show of ignoring us for as long as he pleased.

He always stopped and stared at Caiden first, as if the very sight of him was a slow-motion car wreck he could not get enough of. "You look different today," he observed, cocking his head. "Did you two have a lover's quarrel, or are the rats finally winning?" He grinned, showing teeth that did not look real, as though he'd filed them to points for aesthetic effect. "You should know that hunger is not fatal, but apathy is. Most of my prior tenants have succumbed to the latter long before the former."

He drifted closer, and I felt his eyes crawling over my skin; I have never in my life felt so truly naked. "Do you dream about me?" he asked, as though inquiring after a pet's digestion. "Do you see me in the static of your nightmares?"

I spat at the floor, but my mouth was so parched it only sent a fleck of grayish foam to my lap.

He studied me with the patience of a botanist watching a mold bloom. "I want you to know," he said, voice soft, "that I find your progress exhilarating. You are transforming marvelously. Not just physically, though I see the desperation in your eyes, the hunger that has nothing to do with food. No, my dear, the real change is happening in your soul."

I didn't look at him.

I looked at Caiden, who was coiled against the opposite wall, a statue of scorched earth.

Caiden's eyes, which had once been so alive with hate, now looked fossilized. Like something that had already died, been excavated, and was now on display for a sadist's amusement.

The man leaned closer. "Tell me, have you reached any epiphanies in the dark? Found god? Or perhaps, found each other?" He grinned, a wet slit in the mask of his face. "I wonder what it's like to love someone you also wish would die. Isn't that a peculiar kind of hunger?"

I thought I would be sick. He put his palm to the cage right where my forehead had just been. I flinched without meaning to.

"Fuck you," Caiden said, his voice so hoarse it sounded like sandpaper on bone.

The man did not acknowledge him. "You want to know the secret of the universe, my dear?" he asked me directly. "It's entropy. Everything falls apart, and the only thing that matters is how beautiful the ruins can be."

He let that echo. His hand slipped from the glass.

He turned away and circled Caiden's side of the cage on the outside. "You want to kill me," the man murmured. "I can see it. You would rip the skin from my face with your teeth if you could, if I let you." He cocked his head, as if listening to some secret music. "That's good," he said. "Very good. I prefer my subjects with bite." A pause. "But you'll never touch me, son. Not really. You'll only dream of it until the hunger is all you are."

Then, pivoting with a showman's flourish, he spun back toward me. "As for you, you're different. You think your anger makes you special, but it's your capacity for shame that truly sets you apart." He leaned in, his face so close I could see the pattern of stubble on his jaw, the way his smile never touched his eyes. "You hate yourself for how much you want to live," he said. "You'd eat the flesh off his bones if I asked, and then you'd pray for forgiveness. You'd still beg for seconds."

I tried to punch him through the cage, but my knuckles thudded dully, the divide as thick and final as a tombstone. The man laughed. "You see? The animal is always closer to the surface than you'd like to believe."

He straightened, smoothing the lapels of his suit as if about to deliver a eulogy. "You know, I used to believe that the greatest tragedy was how fragile the human body is. But I was wrong."

He knelt. "It's the mind. The mind is so much easier to break apart than any bone."

He started to rap his knuckles along the wire, a slow and arrhythmic percussion that set my nerves to jangling. "You ever wonder," he said, "why some animals eat their young? Or why, in a famine, mothers will take the food from their children's mouths, even if it means the children wither and die?" He drew a finger down the mesh, eyes locked to mine. "Because when the world ends, every bond is a noose."

He rose to full height, looming over the cage as he surveyed us. "This is not about you," he said, almost gentle. "It never was. It's about the moment you realize you're replaceable, and how quickly you'll trade dignity for a few more minutes of breath."

He turned to Caiden and smiled. "Our strong boy is starting to believe this. See how he sits now, how the violence is still there but it's gone all quiet? That's the real mutation, the final adaptation." He flicked his eyes to me. "And you. You keep hoping someone will come. That's your mistake. Hope is a trick of the brain, a parasite that keeps you running in place. I wonder how long it will last."

He reached into his pocket and pulled out a small, battered notebook, the kind my mother used to make grocery lists in when there was still a point to pretending we would have food.

He flipped it open and read a line aloud, as if we were schoolchildren: "In the end, all things turn to hunger. Not anger, not even fear. Hunger. It's the only honest thing left after you've burned everything else to the ground. Then, there's just decay."

The man snapped the notebook shut and looked at me with something almost like affection. "I think you'll find that's true, soon enough."

He lingered, then suddenly reached through the mesh, fast as a striking snake, and grabbed a handful of my hair.

I gasped as he yanked my head forward, cheek bone pressed hard against the wire.

For a split second I was certain he would break my skull open just to hear the sound it made. He inhaled deeply, like he was savoring perfume. "You smell like an animal, too. All fear and wasted hope."

He released me with a shove that rattled the cage and left my scalp burning.

Caiden leapt to his feet, fists balled, ready to charge the glass, but the man only turned to him with a smile of bare, predatory joy. "Does it hurt, watching me touch her?" he said, voice syrupy and slow. "Do you wish it was you?"

Caiden spat, a red thread trailing from his split lip. "I wish I could kill you."

The man's laugh was genuine and sick, the kind of laugh you hear in an empty slaughterhouse after midnight.

"The animal in you will lose its fight, in time." He turned to me, fingers twitching on the bars, as if itching to stroke my cheek but knowing restraint was more exquisite than contact. "Would you like to see what the face of mercy looks like?" he asked, and before I could answer—before my mind could even assemble the shape of the word "no"—he reached into the cage and slapped my face, hard.

I remember the sound before the pain, a hollow pop like a glass bulb imploding. My head snapped to the side and the world fractured into a kaleidoscope of black and red.

I reeled, collapsed against the back wall, vision swimming with spots. I wanted to scream, but the shock was so complete it left me mute, gaping at the man whose face had contorted into delight.

He didn't break anything with the slap, but I felt broken.

"Stop!" Caiden thundered, and the man only smiled, shaking out his hand, flexing the fingers as if enjoying the ache. "You want pain? Next time, direct it where it's deserved," Caiden hissed, a low sound. "You come in here and do it to me. You leave her the fuck alone."

His fists hammered the glass with a force I thought might finally, miraculously, break it. It only gave a little, vibrating like a tuning fork.

The man made a show of considering, one eyebrow raised. "Noble, in a lost-dog sort of way," he said, "but you misunderstand the nature of my experiment. She's not a control variable; she's the crucible." He lifted one finger, waggling it as if scolding a stubborn child. "If I broke you, what fun would that be for her? I want her to witness how even the most promising specimens can be reduced to pulp by their own appetites."

He turned on his heel, surveying us with the practiced detachment of a surgeon mapping out his next incision. "I'll be back to check the results of my hypothesis," he said, voice gone brisk and businesslike. "Try not to disappoint me."

With that, he swept up the stairs, each footfall receding with the finality of a judge's gavel.

The door banged shut, leaving only the trembling air and the taste of blood on my tongue.

I rolled onto my side and spat the coppery mix onto my sleeve, eyes watering.

The pain radiated, but I was used to pain. I understood it, could metabolize it into something that almost felt like clarity.

But what I could not metabolize was the knowledge that I wanted to kill him, to feel my hands around his throat, to watch his smile collapse beneath my fingers.

Across the glass, Caiden's face was pressed to the glass, his mouth twisted in a rictus of rage that was so naked I could almost taste the acid of it.

For a second I thought he might smash his way through by force of will alone; he slammed his hand against the divider, again, and again, and again.

He stared at me, his eyes wild, as if silently begging me to survive this. To outlast it, outlast even him.

I crawled to the glass, cheek hot and throbbing, and pressed my palm to where his face hovered.

He mirrored me, and we stayed like that, breathing the air between us.

I couldn't tell if I was comforting him, or the other way around.

The violence receded, but it left an afterburn in the air: the man's words, the way he'd described me, the black hunger that seemed to be the only real thing left inside me.

I hated that he was right.

What terrified me was not the pain, but the clarity, the sense that I could become whatever monster he wanted, given enough time and pressure. I could taste the animal in my spit, the way it curdled around my tongue.

Eventually, the pain faded. Replaced by an emptiness so vast I thought it might swallow me whole.

I tried to feel anger at Caiden for his uselessness, his inability to save either of us, but it was like poking a corpse with a stick.

I didn't feel hatred. I didn't feel anything.

The silence blossomed. The darkness pressed in around us, but I was grateful for it.

Darkness hid the worst of our wounds, made us secret again, unobservable, unspectacular.

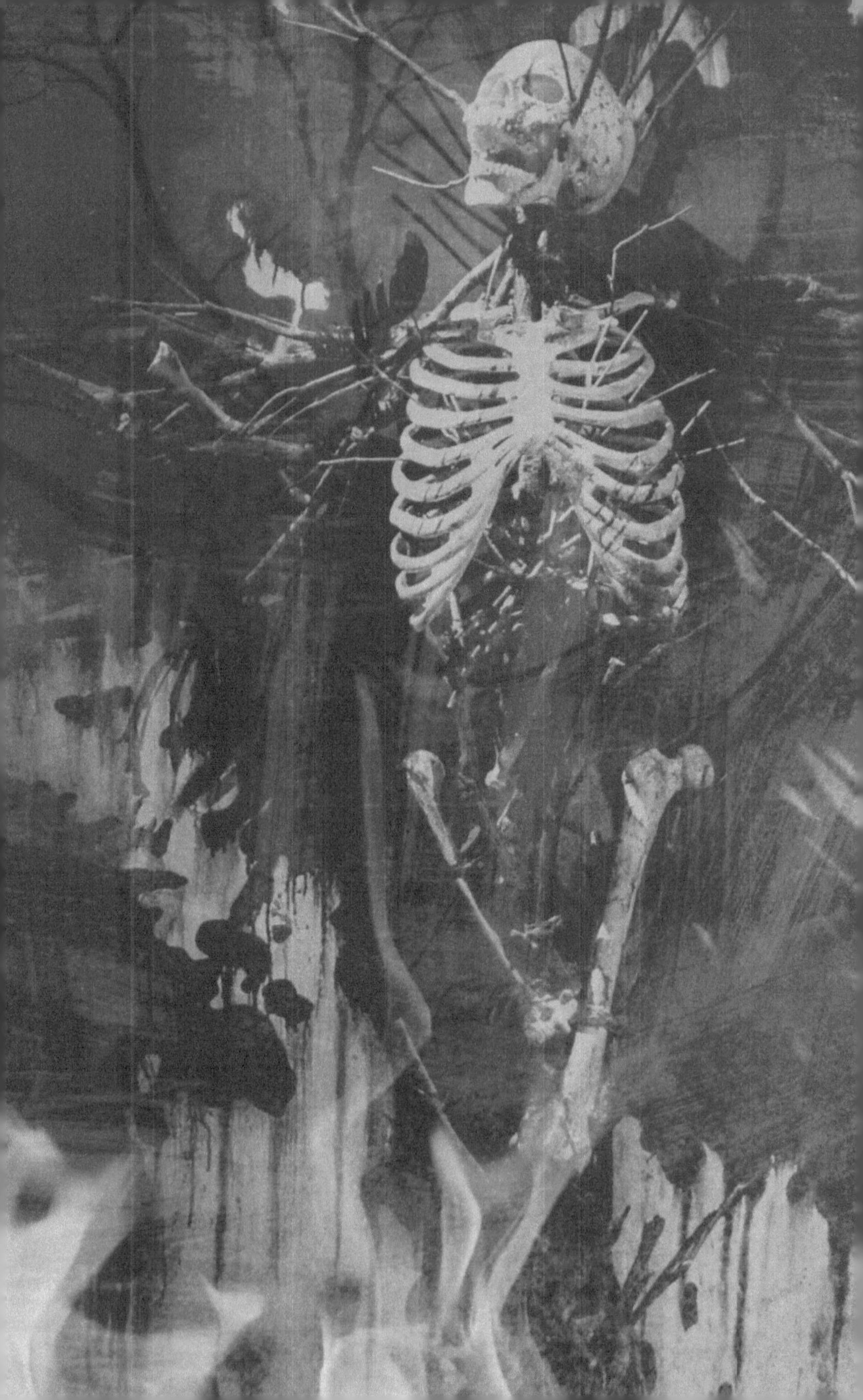

# 53

## THE PRESENT

### AMELIA

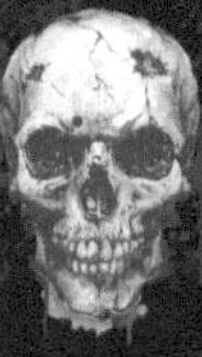

The isolation slowly eroded my sanity.

Caiden stood just beyond the barrier of the cage, yet he felt impossibly far away, and I stumbled deeper into the shadows. My flesh had grown cold from the absence of warmth; I longed to be held.

In this warped atmosphere, I yearned for that person to be Caiden, for he was all I had in this desolate room. We were two ghosts adrift in decay, bound by our desperate need to reclaim the light.

Civilization felt like a distant memory, a dreamlike dystopia where safety and security had become forgotten luxuries. The thought echoed in my mind: we cannot die down here.

That was my driving force. I refused to succumb to another corrupt experience; I would survive.

Yet, I often wondered what my mental state would be once we escaped. Would I still be the same person I was before this wilderness retreat?

Silence enveloped us, stretching time into an unbearable eternity. Each moment forced me to question my senses. Was I truly here? Was Caiden really there? The scents of decay drifted in and out, and strange sounds erupted from the depths of the basement.

It was crippling.

My breath hitched in a ragged gasp, caught in the suffocating stillness. Was this madness, or merely the result of prolonged deprivation?

The line between reality and insanity blurred, the very fabric of my existence fraying at the edges.

I pressed my forehead to the wire mesh, letting the cold pattern imprint itself on my skin. The ache in my jaw had faded to a dull pulse, but the memory lingered, a sourness behind my eyes that refused to drain away.

I could not stop thinking about the precision of his violence, the way he'd calibrated the force of his hand to stun but not shatter, to mark me without marring.

He wanted us intact, or at least recognizable—to ourselves, to each other, to whatever god might be watching.

I thought about what he'd said, about mothers eating their young. I imagined mine, gaunt and trembling, dragging me to the mouth of some deep, wet cave and gnawing my limbs until I was nothing but a shorn, voiceless stump.

I imagined myself doing the same to Caiden, if pressed hard enough. I didn't want to, but the urge curled in my belly like a parasite, whispering that one day I would be grateful to have someone softer than bone to bite down on.

I wondered if he thought about eating me, too. If he would, if the man came down here and put a raw knife to the floor between us and said, "One survives."

I didn't know if I would win, but I wasn't sure I would mind losing. Maybe it would feel better to finally be consumed, to be useful.

The drip, drip, drip from somewhere overhead kept time. I let the sound fill my skull, a metronome counting out the cycles of my own decay.

We were less than animals now. We were carrion, waiting for the flies.

A memory rose, unbidden, of the science textbook from eighth grade. There was a diagram of decomposition, a time lapse of a mouse rotting in a glass box.

First the skin sloughs, then the eyes burst, then the organs blacken and collapse like wet tissue. At the end, there's only a yellow-brown skeleton and a puddle of everything that used to matter.

I remembered thinking, even then, that the mouse looked peaceful at the end.

Then, the creaking of a door shattered my tormented thoughts. My stomach dropped; I recognized that sound.

It meant he was here, our sadistic kidnapper.

"Good afternoon, my pets," he drawled, his chilling voice slithering like a serpent, crawling over us.

Neither Caiden nor I responded, we knew there was no point in doing so, and it only seemed to infuriate him.

"I do not appreciate being ignored. Bad pets will get hurt."

His voice, a chilling rasp, faded into the empty room, revealing the sinister nature of his soul. I opened my mouth to speak, but Caiden shook his head, a silent act of rebellion.

A low chuckle rumbled from the darkness, a prelude to inevitable cruelty. Dread clung to the shadows.

He knew we were defying him. The game had begun, and we were mere pawns in his twisted, macabre entertainment.

"Feeling adventurous today, are we? I can be adventurous too." A darkness threaded through his tone as he stalked closer, his face pressing against the wires of the cage.

His eyes, two chips of obsidian, gleamed in the dim light, and a cruel smile twisted his lips, a grotesque parody of amusement. He reached out, a long, pale finger tracing the bars, sending an icy shiver down my spine that had nothing to do with the cold.

This was more than a game; it was a meticulous dissection of our will, a slow, agonizing dance with fear. As the metallic clang of a nearby instrument echoed through the chamber, a fresh wave of nausea washed over me.

"Maybe my friend here can talk some sense into you foolish subjects. I've been itching to play with my favorite tool for a while." He lifted his hand to reveal the silver gleam of a knife. The sight of that blade sent a jolt of panic through me.

Caiden's eyes widened, mirroring my own terror as they locked with mine. A silent plea passed between us, a desperate pact forged in the crucible of fear.

The game, it seemed, had just begun its most brutal act. His cruelty loomed like a dark cloud, a chilling foreshadowing of our impending demise.

We had to escape today.

The knife glinted ominously as he traced it menacingly along the wires. "I truly love this part of the game."

The door to the cage opened, and he slid inside like a deadly creature of the night. His low chuckle vibrated through the air, reminiscent of a rattlesnake's warning.

"Don't do this," I whispered, succumbing to pitiful and desperate pleas.

"You wanted some adventure, right? You got it."

He crouched, his face a canvas of chilling detail, so close I could smell his breath, feel the weight of his harsh gaze. He hadn't fed us yet; my energy was nearing its end.

All I could do was lie there as he roughly pushed me onto my back, proceeding to straddle me.

His weight pressed down, a suffocating burden mirroring the crushing weight of despair. The cold steel of the knife felt impossibly close, a promise whispered on the edge of a blade.

Then came a sudden pain in my stomach, a searing white-hot sensation that ripped through the numbness.

A scream tore from my throat, swallowed by the echoing chamber, lost in the symphony of his cruel amusement.

Caiden's loud plea morphed into a strangled gasp, his eyes wide pools of terror reflecting the flickering light pooling through the window.

We were in the finale of his game.

A stream of blood began to trickle from the small cut on my flesh, dripping onto the cold floor. It was a minuscule wound, but enough to bleed.

"Fuck! Leave her alone. Hurt me instead, you sadistic bastard." Caiden's voice, high-pitched and ragged with pure terror, sliced through the stillness, leaving a chilling trail of fear in its wake.

"You will get your turn, in time. It's been a while since I had two pets to cut up and eat. I'll be set with a meal for weeks. I've been short on portions having to feed my last subject to you both."

He was feeding us human meat.

Nausea churned within me, and a coldness, deep as the sea, ran through my veins.

Panic seized me, and I fell into fight mode.

We were going to die and become the food that he consumed. That thought alone reignited my will to live.

My vision blurred, the metallic tang of blood filling my senses. Adrenaline surged through my veins, a fierce and desperate ally.

I kicked, a wild and desperate lashing out against his weight, aiming for anything that could disrupt his sadistic ritual.

He grunted, momentarily surprised by my unexpected resistance. That split second was all I needed.

With a surge of strength born of pure terror, I hurled my body into his, long enough to grasp the object he held in his pocket. I had seen him slip it in there, and I blindly hoped it was still with him.

If not, I was definitely going to die today.

Joy surged through me as my fingers brushed the hard metal. Frantically, I slid my fingers over it and felt the button.

Without hesitation, I pressed it. It took only a few seconds, but those moments allowed me to release the barrier.

The glass began to slide upwards, and Caiden was ready.

The instant he had enough room, he dove beneath and charged towards the man like a bull intent on inflicting damage.

But the man was quicker.

He smacked me in the face, the sting of the blow igniting the bruise that had already marinated on my skin.

I fell backward, and he seized my hair, yanking me upward.

"Fucking bitch," the man spat, dark rage distorting his features.

The monster within him erupted, and I trembled in its wake.

Caiden halted in his tracks, his eyes wide with realization; the man had the knife pressed against my neck.

"Go back to your side of the cage, or I'll cut her throat like the pig that she is." Caiden and I both knew he meant every word.

I silently pleaded with Caiden to stand down, mouthing silent words of surrender.

Escape felt like a fleeting dream. It was all we had, but in my frenzy of panic, it appeared that he had regained the upper hand, and we had lost.

The overpowering pressure of his grip conjured visions of death in my mind. My fate narrowed down to the glint of steel against my flesh and the choice Caiden had to make.

"Fuck you."

That was all Caiden managed before he charged towards the man.

In the critical seconds before he reached, the man had enough time to begin sliding the edge against my skin.

The blade missed my neck but drew a cut between my neck and shoulder blade.

My bloodcurdling scream sliced through the darkness.

The pressure subsided as the man was knocked to the ground. A high-pitched clang echoed across the floor as the knife fell.

Blood, warm and wet, seeped down my chest, as my body slumped to the ground, the liquid coating my limbs.

I watched in horror as Caiden and the man tumbled together in the half-dark, thrashing and clawing at each other like wild animals.

"I told you not to fucking touch her!" Veins bulging in his neck, Caiden screamed, his fists pounding against the man in a murderous rage, a primal roar escaping his lips.

I could faintly make out his expression; a deadly glint entered his eyes, his face a mask of furious rage, his jaw clenched tight.

The man shoved him away for a moment, tackling him with brutal force.

"Caiden! Watch out!" I screamed as I saw the man grab the knife, aiming for Caiden's chest.

To my relief, Caiden had quick reflexes. He swiveled his body at the last second, kicking the man off him.

It all happened so quickly, a blur of motion and sound. The man grunted, pain and frustration mingling in the sound. He shouted obscenities, spitting with rage, his threats laced with venom.

In a swift movement, Caiden sprang toward him, catching him off guard. The blade flashed in Caiden's hand, a silver streak of hope.

Sounds of flesh tearing, wet and sickening, filled the air, blending with Caiden's furious shouts.

Then, all fell silent, leaving only our ragged breaths.

Caiden collapsed to the ground beside the motionless, bleeding body. I sat there, transfixed, the echo of the event resonating in my ears, a silent hum in the sudden stillness.

"I told that motherfucker I'd kill him," Caiden finally murmured, breaking the deathly quiet.

"We're free," my whispered voice echoed, a bell of hope ringing loud in the aftermath.

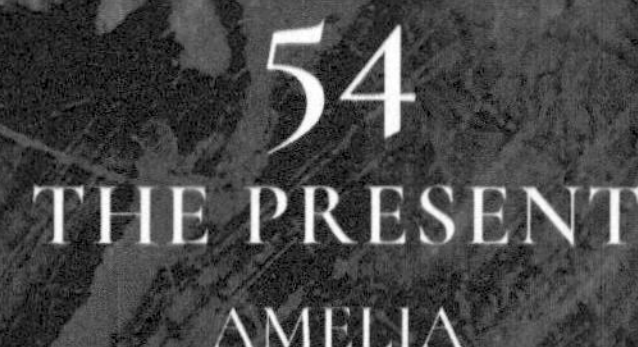

# 54
## THE PRESENT
### AMELIA

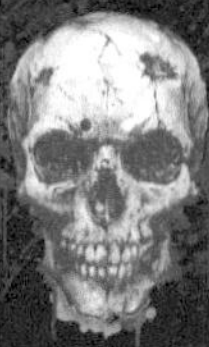

The blood, still warm upon my skin, pulsed with a sickening rhythm. My vision swam, veiling the scene in a blur of red and shadow.

Silence stretched around us, broken only by the incessant drip, drip, drip of blood onto the grimy floor. The stench of violence and fear clung to the air, a grim testament to what we had just endured.

We had survived, yet the victory felt hollow, stained crimson with the price we had paid.

Minutes crawled by as we sat there, drenched in shock and weighed down by fatigue.

Finally, we sprang to our feet, the freedom we craved manifesting as a chaotic scramble of stumbling feet and pounding hearts, a desperate flight into the echoing darkness of the chamber, towards the ascending stairs.

We hurried through the basement door and emerged into the dim light of the cabin.

Before I could make it to the front door, Caiden halted me. "You need to get your wound cleaned up before we go back out into the wilderness."

I glanced down at the blood trickling down my body and realized he was right. I couldn't risk an infection.

In haste, we scurried through the cabin, searching for anything that could help us.

A battered first-aid kit, long forgotten in a dusty corner, yielded antiseptic wipes and a roll of ragged bandage.

Caiden, his own wounds ignored for the moment, worked quickly and efficiently, his hands surprisingly gentle as he cleaned and dressed my gashes.

Warmth seeped through me, and I embraced his touch. After being isolated in the shadows, my only experiences with touch had been harsh and cruel, inflicted by the hands of a sadist.

Caiden's touch was a savior.

The cabin, a refuge from the horrors we had escaped, felt strangely small. The scent of antiseptic fought a losing battle against the lingering metallic tang of blood.

When he finished, he looked at me, his gaze was weary yet resolute. "Let's get out of here," he said, his voice rough but firm. The weight of what he had done hung between us, an understanding etched into the lines of our faces.

Freedom, it seemed, had a bitter aftertaste.

"Should we gather more supplies?" I inquired, wanting to be prepared this time if we were to return to the wild.

"Right. Good idea."

Caiden turned away, and I sensed a sudden distance forming between us. The cage had held more than just demons; it had held our inner turmoil, a maelstrom of memories, bitter resentments, and childhood wounds.

A haunted chill lingered in the air after those confessions, each word a ghost whispering in the silence.

Neither of us dared to bring up what had been spoken in that cage. I wondered if we would ever speak of it.

We moved with quiet purpose, discovering a large backpack and stuffing it with anything useful we could find. Rope, knives, tape, cloth, bottles of water from the fridge, and canned food.

Then we came across a freezer. Caiden and I opened it, and inside lay a human body, the scent of decay strong and overwhelming. I screamed and fell backward.

"Shit." Caiden shut the freezer, a terror settling between us. A sickening realization slithered through my mind: we could have been the dead body rotting inside if things had played out differently.

Once back in the main area, I paused to observe the surroundings of the sadist who now bled out in his own dark and deadly chamber below us, succumbing to the fate of the victims he had slaughtered.

The interior was dimly lit, the only illumination coming from flickering candles haphazardly placed around the room, their wax drippings pooling on the timeworn wooden table.

The walls were lined with rough-hewn logs, darkened by age and something more sinister. Stains that may have been blood caked and dried, providing a grim testament to the cabin's dark history.

The furnishings were sparse and utilitarian. A battered old armchair sat in one corner, threadbare and stained, while a wooden table dominated the center of the room, littered with various tools, some for mundane tasks, but many that hinted at more deadly uses.

Among them lay a child's toy: a faded, cracked action figure, its paint chipped and eyes missing. The juxtaposition of innocence and horror sent a chill down my spine.

The walls were adorned with strange carvings, crude etchings that depicted scenes of violence and despair, a haunting diary of the killer's mind.

A rusty meat cleaver, a set of knives glinting menacingly in the candlelight, and an array of hooks hung from a nearby wall, each one seemingly waiting for an unfortunate soul.

The floorboards creaked beneath my feet, the sound echoing in the silence as if the cabin itself were alive, trapping secrets within its walls.

The air was thick with a nauseating combination of smells: the acrid scent of decay mingled with the earthy musk of damp wood and the faint, metallic tang of blood.

There lingered a hint of something sweet, perhaps the remains of a long-forgotten meal or herbs used to mask other odors.

A small, grimy window looked out upon the dense wilderness, its panes cracked and smeared, allowing only slivers of moonlight to filter through.

Outside, the wind rustled the leaves, but inside, the quiet was suffocating. A small fireplace, cold and empty, was surrounded by a pile of logs, with ash and soot caked in the corners.

The cabin reflected its owner, a place where humanity had been stripped away, leaving only the raw instincts of survival and a twisted aura.

I found myself wondering who this man had been before he became a sadistic killer.

Or perhaps he had always been like this?

I recalled something he mentioned, how his behavior towards us had been something he endured while growing up. The thought made me imagine how horrific his childhood must have been.

A diary sat on the edge of the table, and without thinking, I grabbed the journal and stuffed it into the backpack.

"If you're ready, I'm ready," Caiden said, standing by the front door, his face worn with exhaustion. His shirt hung loosely on his body, covered with a mixture of blood, dirt, and other stains.

We were filthy, tired, and blood-stained. Yet, neither of us dared to suggest washing ourselves or sleeping in his bed.

He pushed the door open, revealing the bruised twilight sky and the battered landscape beyond. The stars twinkled like a million tiny diamonds scattered across the inky canvas of night.

A symbol of hope, in my eyes.

Yet, the wilderness took on a more haunting tone. The wind howled softly through the trees, creating an eerie symphony that echoed through the valleys, and the temperature began to drop, a chilling reminder of their precarious situation.

Our mission was far from over, but we had survived this traumatic and horrific experience. If we could get through that, we could get through anything.

As we left the cabin behind, a dark thought struck me. I envisioned all the tormented souls trapped in that dark space, the ones who hadn't been as lucky, the ones who had succumbed to the edge of the knife.

Those souls would haunt me until the day I died, especially our captor, who would rot into the sinister floorboards.

# 55

## THE PRESENT

### AMELIA

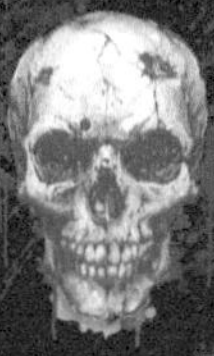

After we left the cabin, we gobbled up some of the canned food before collapsing by a cluster of trees. Drained of spirit.

As daylight broke, we found ourselves on the move again, not knowing where we were headed but determined to go as far away from the cabin as possible.

Silence enveloped us, broken only by the rustle of unseen creatures and the crunch of twigs underfoot, becoming our constant companion. A gnawing hunger crept back, but fear, a more potent appetite, drove us deeper into the emerald shadows of the forest.

Neither of us knew what to say. The tension hung stiffly, a presence that loomed over us like a dark shadow.

As we walked, I became acutely aware of the pain shooting through my feet. Our shoes, torn and weathered, turned each step into a painful ache. The stench that emanated from our bodies was nearly unbearable, but we had no choice; we had to endure it.

After what felt like hours of trudging through the woods, the trees began to thin and shrink until they finally disappeared. I glanced around, a surge of glee filling my body.

We had returned to the rocky flatland. Water flowed around us as we stumbled upon a large opening, the woodland retreating behind us.

"Fuck it," I whispered, shedding my shoes and sprinting towards

483

the water. I dove in, the cool liquid enveloping me as a smile broke across my face for the first time in days, cleansing my body and spirit.

"What do you think you're doing?" Caiden exclaimed, approaching the spot where I floated in the water.

"I'm soaking in the freedom," I murmured, closing my eyes and letting my heartbeat slow to a calming rhythm.

"Well, hurry up. I want to cover as much ground as possible."

I rolled my eyes and looked at him. He stood in the sunlight, a frown etched onto his face.

"Loosen up, Caiden. Why don't you come into the water with me and clean yourself? You stink."

I splashed some water towards him.

He hesitated, his brow furrowing as if he might argue, but then a small smile played at the corners of his lips. For the first time since the cabin, the tension seemed to crack.

He kicked off his own battered shoes, the sound oddly loud in the sudden quiet, and cautiously waded into the cool water.

The sun warmed our skin, and for a few precious moments, the fear and exhaustion washed away, replaced by the simple relief of fresh water and shared silence.

"This is pretty nice," Caiden confessed, allowing the water to cleanse us of stress and filth.

"I told you so. Maybe you should listen to me more often," I said tiredly, savoring the calm waves between us that momentarily overshadowed our usual bickering and resentment.

"If I did that, we probably wouldn't have made it through some situations," he retorted, but there was no bitterness in his voice; it sounded light and feathery.

I realized he was right. He had guided us through many harrowing situations, keeping me going when I felt like giving up.

"Yeah, good point."

But as soon as I spoke, my mind spiraled back to the cage, the image of that sadist with a knife to my neck, demanding Caiden to back down.

Yet, Caiden had charged at him instead.

"Why did you attack that psycho when he had the knife to my neck? You knew he could have killed me." Instead of letting the thought fade, I allowed it to engulf me, a fire igniting within.

He glanced at me, a dark expression overtaking his features. "It was the only chance we had."

"But I could have died! He could have sliced my neck in an instant."

I remembered how close the knife was to the skin, how easy it would have been for it to slice into my flesh fatally.

Caiden looked away, shrugging. "It was a chance I had to take. I had a feeling you'd be alright. It was kill or be killed."

A sudden storm of anger erupted within me, and I quickly waded out of the water, yanking a piece of cloth from the pack to dry myself.

Sensing my fury, Caiden followed me out of the water, his tall figure looming over me.

"You're mad. Why? Why do you have to ruin any good moment we have?"

With an exasperated grunt, I threw my hands in the air, glaring at him. "Why am I mad? Maybe because you risked my life all to save yourself!"

Caiden's nostrils flared as he moved closer, his feet pounding against the terrain. "Are you fucking kidding me? I wasn't saving myself! I was saving you. Saving us! He was going to kill us if I didn't do something. You could at least be grateful that I saved your life, again."

The tension returned, crackling in the air like a fire on the verge of igniting, making the hairs on my arms stand on end. It wrapped around us with ferocity, a chilling blast that cut through my skin and made my teeth chatter.

"No, you risked my life! You could have waited until he didn't have a knife against me!"

"You are so goddamn impossible." Caiden shook his head, staring me down with equal anger.

He was so close now that our breaths collided, and I felt myself falling into the swirling depths of his brown eyes.

But what left me breathless was watching his gaze flick down to my lips, then lower to my chest, where my damp t-shirt clung to my body, outlining the shape of my breasts, my nipples poking through the fabric.

My cheeks flushed crimson as an intense heat surged through me, a wave of fire that sent shivers through my blood and tingles down to my thighs.

His gaze lingered there, a trace of something unreadable flashing in his eyes before he abruptly looked away, his Adam's apple bobbing.

The anger seemed to dissipate, replaced by a strange, almost awkward silence.

He ran a hand through his wet hair, the gesture revealing the strain beneath his controlled exterior. The tension remained, but it had shifted, morphing into something heavier, more intimate.

He cleared his throat, the sound low and rough. "Look," he began, his voice softer now, "I... I didn't mean to scare you. I wouldn't have let you die. That's a promise."

His jaw set tight as he peered at me, analyzing my every movement. I nodded, the rise of anger ebbing as I dissolved into his softness.

"I know. I shouldn't have blown up like that. I don't know what came over me. Too much has happened in the past few days."

"Yeah. It's fine. I get it." He looked away, his eyes tracing the rippling waves.

We put our shoes back on and drank some of the water, stumbling through fragments of tension intermingled with something intimate and profound.

My heart pounded; the thought of opening the door to something forbidden and unknown terrified me, and I sensed a similar unease in him.

Yet, a rush of thrilling curiosity surged within me.

I spent that whole day and much of that night gnawing on the memory of his gaze. How it had lit on my body, lingered, then retreated as if burned.

I told myself it disgusted me. I told myself it was proof that he was every inch his father's spawn, that even now, even after all we'd survived, I was just a thing to be consumed.

But it was a lie, and the lie soured in my mouth, rancid and persistent.

This old anger was transforming into something that tasted like longing and disaster. That terrified me.

I couldn't sleep that night. I told Caiden I was going to keep watch, though both of us knew I was too exhausted to last more than a few hours.

I perched on a boulder by the water, knees hugged to my chest, and watched the moon's reflection shiver on the surface.

I tried to meditate on the beauty of the world, to remind myself that it still existed, that it hadn't all been eaten away by cruelty and hunger.

But every time I closed my eyes, I saw the blood pooling under that man's face, saw the edge of the knife flashing in two directions at once. I saw the glimmer in Caiden's eyes when he'd finally killed for me.

I was so tired of being a victim that I barely noticed the moment I started to become the monster.

When the sky tilted from blue to pale yellow, I crept back to where Caiden slept. He was curled on his side like a kicked dog, his face stripped of anger, just soft with exhaustion and a thin film of sweat.

I knelt beside him and watched the way his eyelids twitched, the muscle beneath jerking at some remembered pain. I wondered if he was dreaming of his father, or the cage, or of me. Possibly all three.

I reached out and brushed a stray hair from his forehead.

The contact startled him awake, and for a moment, he looked at me like he didn't recognize my face in the morning light.

Maybe he didn't. Maybe we were both strangers now, two new creatures with nothing left but hunger and the memory of what we used to be.

"What?" was all he said, but the word came out on a breath that was ragged, almost pleading.

"It's daytime."

We stared at each other, and then he nodded.

We shouldered the pack, picked a direction, and started walking.

It wasn't until the afternoon that we ran into the first sign of other human life: a dead hiker, collapsed in a tangle of sage and rock. He'd been there a year maybe, or longer. What was left of him was all bone and mummified sinew, the rags of his clothes fluttering around the frame. His ribcage gaped, a hollow birdcage, and the sockets where his eyes had been stared straight up at the cloudless sky.

I stood over him, hypnotized, unable to look away.

Caiden knelt, his face unreadable, and searched the dead hiker's pockets with a gentleness that nearly broke me. He found a battered lighter, a half-empty bottle of iodine, and a wallet with a faded photo stuffed behind a driver's license.

The man's name was Steven. His picture showed him with a woman and a boy, arms around each other at a backyard barbecue. Smiles too big for the camera, faces alight with a hunger for something.

I took the photo from Caiden, numb, and turned it over in my hands. Some animal in my chest wanted to scream, to warn the woman and child that this was what would become of Steven, all meat peeled away by time and loneliness.

I slipped the photo back into the wallet, hands suddenly shaking.

I wondered if that's what I would become. A leftover, a corpse for the next lost animal to discover.

I thought: this could have been us. This almost was us.

I thought of the man in the cabin, how easily he could have made us this, and how easy it would be for the world to forget what we looked like before we were reduced to bone and dirt.

We left the corpse behind, but parts of it clung to us. The empty sockets, the decay, the glint of hope made monstrous by abandonment.

I watched Caiden from behind as we trudged on. His spine was a straight, stubborn line; his shoulders hunched with the effort of dragging himself into each new step.

In the daylight, with no fences or monsters or wire to separate us, he was both less and more than I remembered. Less menace, more ruin. I could see the seams where he'd split open.

I wondered if he knew how visible it was.

By sundown, we'd walked out of the dead man's shadow but not his orbit.

We ate cold beans with our fingers and drank river water, then huddled together in a hollow beneath a fallen tree for warmth.

I kept my face angled away from him, safe in the shadow of a root, but I could feel his eyes on me.

I wanted to ask him what he saw, but I was afraid of the answer. Instead, I asked, "Do you think he was running away, or running toward something?" meaning Steven, or maybe myself, or maybe all of us.

Caiden's voice was a rasp. "Does it matter?"

I thought about it. "Maybe not. Maybe, if you're lost, one direction is as good as another."

We lay there, silent, the only sound the wind sighing through the needles overhead.

I thought I would not sleep, but I did, and my dreams crawled with the faces of the dead: Steven, the man in the cabin, my mother, Lillian—each one blinking in and out like dying stars, their eyes wide and flat.

———

I woke to the touch of Caiden's hand on my shoulder, gentle as a whisper. He didn't draw back when I startled, just let his palm rest there, warm and solid. His fingers weren't the claws I remembered from our youth, the bludgeons of violence; they were simply fingers, roughened by the world but not by malice.

I shivered and let myself lean into him, just a little.

"When we get out of here," he said, low enough that I had to tilt my head to hear, "I want you to forget all of this."

"That's not how memory works," I said, sharper than I meant. I didn't want him to stop. The warmth pulsing from his hand was the only thing keeping me from shattering.

He shook his head, lips twisted in a smile. "It is if you try hard enough. I did it for years. You just fake it until the memories get tired and quit."

"Is that what you did with me?" I asked, and there was a challenge in it. I wanted him to lie, and I wanted him to confess, both at once.

He didn't answer right away, but when he finally did, he kept his voice so low it was almost a rumor, "I tried. I never could."

He withdrew his hand and wrapped his arms around his knees, chin on wrist, and stared into the dark as if it would yield an answer if only he watched long enough.

A hollow ache shivered deep in my bones, some longing that had no shape and no voice, something so old and so unfinished it could only express itself as want.

The silence expanded and held, made sacred by fatigue and animal warmth.

I could sense the hunger in him too. Not the simple need for food, but the deeper, blacker hunger that had gnawed at us both since childhood.

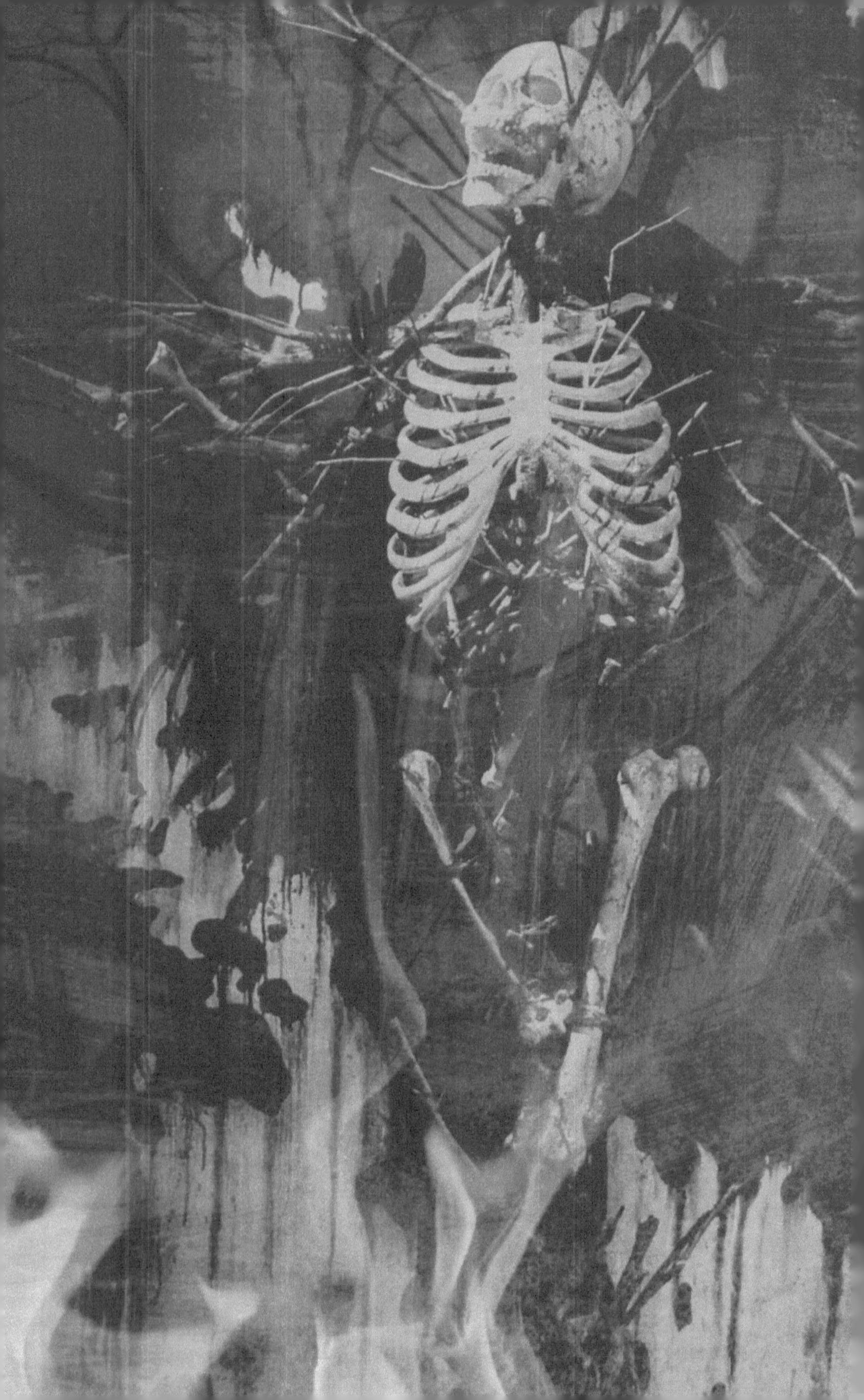

# 56

## THE PRESENT

### CAIDEN

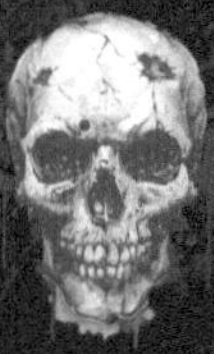

The woods felt different after a cage.

We stumbled through undergrowth with the kind of urgency that wasn't hope. It was flight. My nerves were still convinced the cabin had hands reaching after us.

Amelia walked a few steps ahead, arms wrapped tight around herself. Her gait was uneven, stiff. Like her joints had forgotten how to exist without concrete under them.

I kept my face calm. I kept my shoulders loose, my pace steady, like I wasn't shaking on the inside. Like my hands weren't still remembering the feel of a handle in my grip. Like I hadn't taken a life and felt it end.

Every time I blinked, I saw it.

Not the gore. Not the mess. The *moment*.

The split second where I crossed a line I couldn't uncross and realized I didn't feel regret first.

I felt relief. That was the part that made me sick.

I didn't kill him because I'm a hero. I killed him because my storm finally found a target it could justify. He'd put his hands on her, and he'd made her eyes go hollow; he'd turned us into entertainment. Something in me snapped and said enough.

The wilderness swallowed sound the way water swallowed bodies. It made our footsteps softer, our breathing louder.

We crested a ridge and the trees thinned for a bit, a ripple of sun turning her hair almost blue-black.

She hesitated, one hand wrapped around her skinny wrist like it was the only thing keeping her anchored. We hadn't talked about what happened. Not really. I think both of us knew it would break us open if we did.

"Think we're getting closer to the river?" She cleared her throat, eyes darting to my hands before she looked away.

"Looks like it," I said. It was all I could manage. There are only so many words after you kill a man.

She nodded, picking at the blood under her nails. Wasn't even her blood, mostly. I caught the tremor in her shoulders; she shoved it down like she always did.

We kept walking.

The undergrowth was thick, grabbing at our legs. Branches cracked under my boots, and every so often, a crow called, like it couldn't wait to pick apart what was left of us.

"Do you think..." She trailed off, hesitated, like maybe it was better to say nothing. Then: "Do you think it's colder now, or is that just me?"

I almost laughed. Of course she was cold. She'd lost weight since we first got locked in. Cheekbones cutting sharp, wrists all bone, skin nearly translucent with shock and starvation. The sun did nothing out here. It was always cold, always damp. But more than that, I knew the kind of cold she was talking about.

I grunted. "Probably both."

She looked at me sidelong. I could feel her staring at the blood on my hands, the way it had dried in the cracks. She shivered. "My fingers are freezing."

It just happened.

I reached out and took her hand. Her fingers were icy, trembling. I pressed them between mine, trying to rub some heat back in. For a second, neither of us breathed.

I could feel her pulse in her knuckles, the faint twitch of her heartbeat. She blinked at me, eyes huge and wild, and I thought about kissing her just to see what would happen.

Instead, I let go like I'd been burned.

She jerked her hand back, hiding it in her sleeve.

We stood there in the silence, surrounded by the hush of the woods, and I could feel the tension spiking between us.

"Sorry," I muttered, though I wasn't sure what for. Touching her, or stopping. Or wanting to do it again.

She exhaled, a faint, shaky laugh. "No, it's... Thank you."

We didn't move for a long second. I studied the ground. My hands twitched, remembering the knife, remembering skin parting and bone giving way and the weird relief of being able to do something—anything—to fight back.

"I keep thinking it's over," she said softly. "But it doesn't feel over."

"Yeah." My voice was rough. "I know what you mean."

We started walking again. Every time her shoulder brushed mine, a jolt went down my spine, as if the violence of the escape had rewired me and now even something gentle, something as simple as warming her hand, hurt more than the wounds I carried.

Time spun out, unspooling between us. The trees got denser, the ground dipped and rose. Once, when I lost my balance, she caught my arm without thinking, steadying me. Her hand was so small I almost laughed. She let go quickly, like she'd remembered herself too late.

The ghosts followed us. Him, the bastard I killed, the basement, the bulb, the smile. My father, watching from somewhere in the rot beneath the earth, probably laughing that his son turned out just like him.

But she was here, alive, and so was I. Maybe that was the only reason I could stand the blood, the ache, the memory.

Amelia broke the silence again. "Do you think anyone's looking for us yet?" Her voice was too loud in the hush, but it was better than the quiet.

"They'll come," I said, whether I believed it or not. "They have to."

She nodded, but didn't look convinced.

For a while, the only sound was our breathing and the squelch of mud under our shoes. She started humming to herself, a weird, twitchy melody, probably just to prove she was still alive. I tried not to look at her lips.

She stumbled on a root and almost went down. I caught her

elbow, steadied her. Held on a beat too long, then forced myself to let go.

The light faded, and the cold came up out of the ground, gnawing at the edges of us. Her lips turned pale. She wrapped her arms around herself, trying to steal warmth from her ribs.

"Langston," I said.

She looked up. "Yeah?"

"If you're cold, say something."

She gave me a look. Half challenge, half something I couldn't name. "You'll just let me freeze?"

I wanted to say, I'd murder a thousand men to keep you warm. Instead, I swallowed and shrugged.

Her mouth twitched like she could hear the words I didn't say.

For a while longer, we were silent. I kept my hands jammed in my pockets, afraid of what I'd do if I let them out again.

When the woods finally opened into a low dip that smelled faintly of water, I let out a slow breath. We were still lost. Still haunted by what we'd done. But the space between us was crackling, tense, alive.

I could still feel her pulse in my hands.

I wanted to scratch.

———

The river was less a destination and more a line we crossed, like some mythic boundary between then and now.

We stumbled through the brush until it opened up, and there it was: not wide, but fast, the current chewing up pebbles and broken twigs, spitting them out downstream. I crouched at the bank, the mud cold under my knees.

Amelia dropped beside me, her hair in her face, her breathing shallow. We didn't say anything for a while. Just sat there, both pretending the river mattered more than the silence chewing at our guts.

I watched my hands as I cupped river water and drank. The motion was automatic. Blood had gotten under my nails, dark and stubborn, and it wouldn't scrub out, not even in this icy current. I stared down at my own reflection, and for a second, I saw him. The kidnapper, or maybe my father, or maybe just the version of myself I killed back in that cabin. Haunted, hollowed, still hungry for something I couldn't name.

The water shivered with every movement, distorting my face. I didn't look away.

Amelia broke the silence. "You ever wonder if you're a good person?"

I snorted into my hand, water dripping down my wrist. "No point. Never have been."

She didn't laugh. She was watching me, the way you look at a wild animal. "I mean. After... everything. Does it ever get to you? Do you feel—"

She couldn't say it.

So I said it for her. "Guilty?"

She nodded, lips pressed thin, eyes fixed right on me.

I shrugged, kept watching my reflection ripple and come apart. "No."

She waited. Let it hang. Wouldn't let me have the lie.

Finally, I broke first. "That's bullshit. Of course I do. I feel—" Words caught. I wanted to punch something, or maybe just dig my hands raw in the gravel until I bled out all over again. "I feel fucking sick. Not 'cause I did it, but 'cause I had to. Or maybe 'cause I'd do it again. Hell, maybe it's 'cause I don't regret any of it. I'm guilty for not being guilty enough. Does that even make sense?"

She blinked, slowly, like she had to process it.

"It makes sense," she said, quiet. "I think. You're angry."

"Yeah. I am." My voice scraped against my teeth. "He touched you. He hurt you. I wanted him dead. I wanted to be the one who did it." The confession was raw. My own words almost made me flinch.

Amelia didn't flinch. She just pulled her knees to her chest and stared at the river, its relentless motion chewing at the edges of the bank.

"It doesn't go away," she said after a while. "The sick feeling. I thought if I ever got free, it would stop. But it's still there. Like the air's thinner now."

I nodded. Couldn't stand the idea of touching her, not right now, not with these hands.

"Do you think we'll forget?" she asked.

"No." I let the syllable drop into the water, let it get carried away. "We don't get to forget."

She shivered. The wind cut sideways, yanking at her hair. The urge to reach out again, to warm her up, hit so hard I had to clench my fists just to keep from moving.

I dunked my hands in the river, let the cold bite into my bones. Rubbed at my skin until it stung. It didn't take the blood away, didn't clean me up. Just made me remember. This was who I was, now. The cage, the kill, the girl beside me looking for a reason not to be afraid.

She drifted closer, almost leaning into my side, but not quite. The tension between us is as sharp as that knife in the dark.

"If you could go back," she asked, "would you do it differently?"

I thought about it. About letting him live, about walking away, about the look on Amelia's face every time he touched her. Maybe there was a better version of me somewhere, but I'd never met him.

"No," I said, meaning it. "I'd just do it faster."

She let out a breath, shaky but edged with relief, and her hand brushed my arm. Light, careful, as if she needed to make sure I was real.

For a moment, all the violence and horror and guilt dissolved into something else. Something raw, dazzling, a cracked mercy.

I looked down at my hands again, the blood trapped under the nails, and wondered if it would ever come out.

"I don't know what I feel," she said, voice shaky. "I don't know how I'm supposed to feel. I hate you. I hated you. Then you saved me. Then you..." Her throat worked. "Then you killed him."

I swallowed hard.

Saved her.

Like I'd earned that word.

The truth was uglier. I hadn't saved her because I'm good. I'd saved her because I couldn't stand the idea of her breaking under someone else's hands. Because something protective had snapped awake in me like a guard dog unchained.

Because craving wasn't just lust. It was need. It was possession. It was fear.

Amelia stood too, wobbling slightly. She steadied herself on a rock, jaw clenched.

"We need to keep moving," I said, afraid of what might come out if I said anything else.

She nodded. "Yeah."

We moved deeper into the wilderness, away from the cabin, away from the road we still hadn't found, away from everything that felt like safety. The forest was damp and shadowed.

As we walked, Amelia slowed more than once. She stumbled on a root, caught herself, then kept going like nothing had happened.

I noticed. Of course I noticed.

I stayed close enough to catch her if she went down. I told myself it was practical. She was smaller. Weaker right now. Dehydrated. Running on fumes. I told myself it wasn't because the thought of her falling made my chest constrict.

The wind shifted. Leaves rattled. Somewhere in the distance, a bird called. The forest didn't care what we'd survived. It only cared about what we could survive next.

My fear wasn't the wilderness anymore.

It was the way my feelings for Amelia were rising like something undead. The way the protective instinct didn't feel like a choice. The way guilt and shame sat heavy in my chest, mixing with something that looked too much like wanting.

I stared at her profile, the line of her cheek, the way she hugged herself like she was trying to keep the pieces in.

I hated that I wanted to be the one holding her instead.

I kept my eyes on the trees, on the darkening path ahead, on anything that wasn't her face.

But my mind kept circling back to the cabin, the moment my hands moved. To the fact that I'd crossed a line for her.

A line I used to pretend I'd never cross for anyone. And now that I had, the terror wasn't the killing.

It was what it revealed.

That the boy who hated her had been built out of someone else's poison. And the man who protected her might be real. That possibility sat in my chest.

I stood there in the fading light, jaw clenched, hands still dirty with a past I couldn't scrub off.

And when Amelia finally stood and started walking again, I fell into step behind her without a word.

Close enough to catch her if she fell. Far enough to pretend it meant nothing because pretending was the only thing keeping me from admitting the truth.

That I was afraid of the woods. And I was more afraid of her.

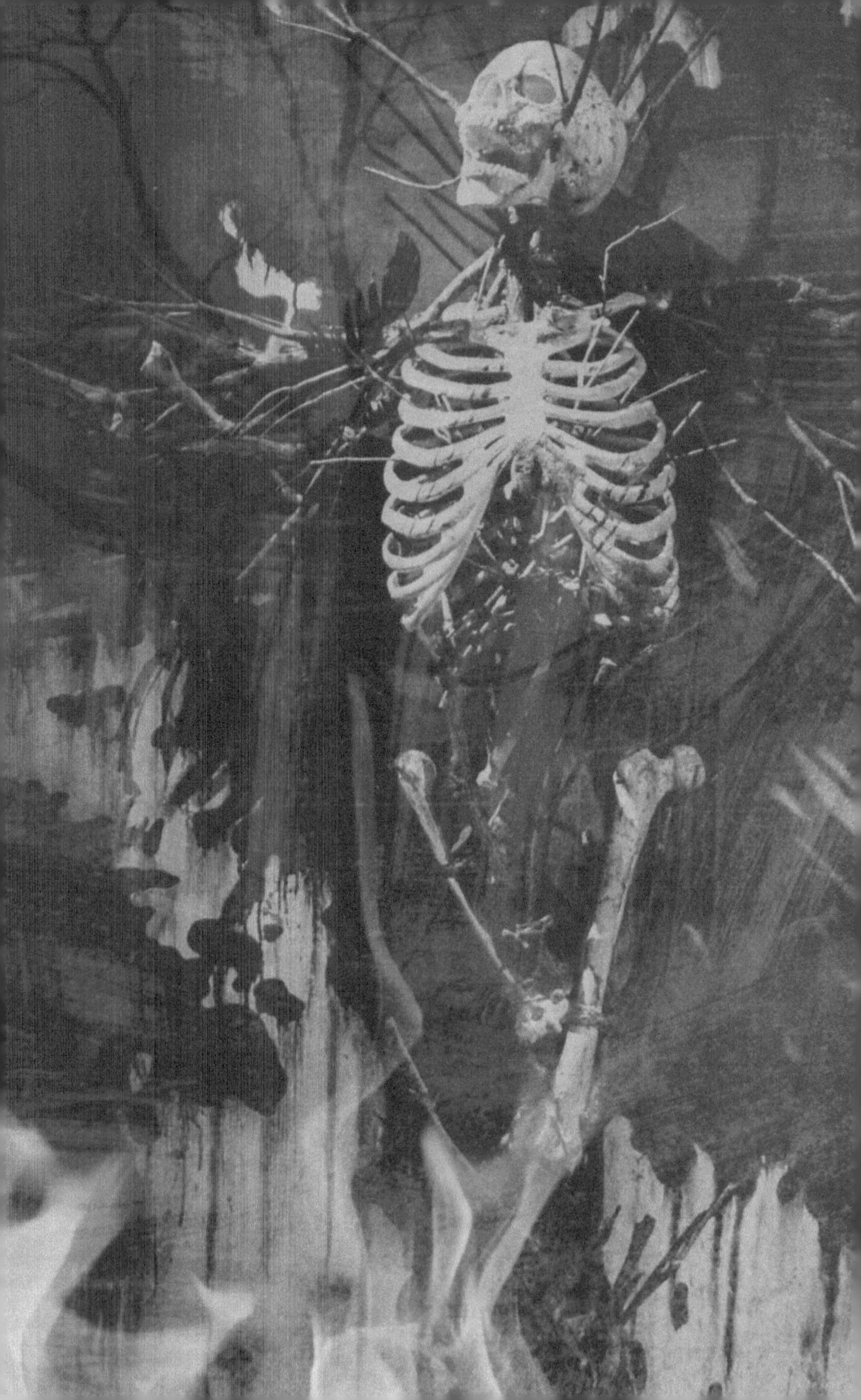

# 57

## THE PRESENT

### AMELIA

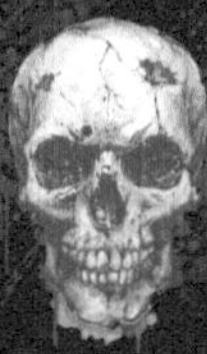

The wilderness cascaded endlessly before us, a vast expanse of rocky mountains and flatlands both majestic and utterly desolate.

A cold, biting wind constantly reminded us of the approaching night, which draped the world in a fog of eerie silence.

Each gust whispered through the tall grass and jagged stones, carrying echoes of our shared terror, haunting memories clinging to us like shadows.

The man's voice still rang in my ears, a hawk's screech.

The forest felt alive, watching, waiting. Every twig snap echoed, a reminder that we were not alone, igniting a primal fear within me.

I glanced at Caiden; his face was a mask of concentration, but the tension coiling in his shoulders betrayed his calm.

We were both on edge, our bodies weary from our escape, our minds too frazzled for rest. Exhaustion weighed down my limbs, each step a struggle against the fatigue threatening to overwhelm me.

My body ached from my ordeal in the cage, the knife wound still stinging, a worry that it might become infected despite Caiden's bandages.

A feverish sweat prickled the back of my neck, and the bloody bandage clung to me, hot and sticky.

Every time I lifted my arm, a pain flared where the knife had bitten, a sick reminder of how close I'd come to being meat for the next freezer batch.

The thought alone made me shudder. I could almost imagine the man's awful hands tearing into me, could smell the rot wafting up from that chest in the cabin, taste the coppery tang of his meal.

I wanted to scream, to spit out the taste of terror, but the woods seemed to swallow all noise, trapping us in a suffocating hush.

The sky above us hung low and bruised, clouds trailing scraps of moonlight that painted the world in sickly blue.

After hours, my legs were numb, my feet laced with blisters, but I pressed on, driven by nothing but the animal urge to stay alive.

Caiden stumbled beside me, his shirt stiff with dried gore, despite our brief swim to cleanse ourselves. A wild look haunted his face. He caught me glancing and turned away, jaw set in a hard line.

We walked until our shadows vanished, until the fire on the horizon traded places with a creeping pallor that threatened to swallow us whole.

The mountains were not the adventure I'd fantasized about as a child, nor the pretty tragedy I'd painted in my sketchbooks after Lillian's death.

The land here was a bruised and battered canvas, scrubbed raw and left for dead.

We stumbled into a gully, the rocks slick with patches of lichen, the descent unforgiving. My ankle twisted and I tasted gravel, the pain a blinding white that made me gasp. The hum of panic rose again, a tide that refused to recede.

Caiden hobbled down after me, flinching as he landed, barely suppressing a hiss.

"You good?" His voice was shredded, every syllable sandpaper.

"Yeah." My lips barely moved around the lie. I pawed at the ground, hauling myself upright. The wound in my shoulder burned, blood blooming anew through the ragged bandage, but I forced myself up.

We followed the gully, the world reduced to a corridor of stone and shadow. Somewhere overhead, the moon played peekaboo with the clouds, throwing the rocks into a nightmare chiaroscuro.

We were prey, scurrying through a landscape carved by predators, every shadow a snare.

My mind circled sickly, returning to the freezer's eyeless stare, the way my captor's blood had painted everything in sticky finality. I tasted metal in my mouth.

I thought about how, after all this, we'd still be nobody's priority. The world would keep grinding, the search parties half-assed and useless, the people who loved us already mourning or forgetting.

I pictured my mother numbed out in a stained bathrobe, fumbling for her cigarette as the sheriff's car rolled up, the headline already printed in her eyes.

Lillian's ghost flickered at the edge of my thoughts, a warning or a curse.

The gully ended in a wide, stony fan, a graveyard of shattered boulders sloping down to a moonlit creek.

I stumbled again, my balance wrecked, and sat hard on a rock, breath rasping in the cold air.

Caiden dropped beside me. He pressed his palms to his knees, head bowed, sweat streaking the dirt on his face.

Neither of us spoke for a long time.

Somewhere upstream, something splashed. The notion of being hunted, even by a dumb animal, made me laugh, a dry sound that clawed up my throat and died.

Caiden turned, the whites of his eyes stark in the gloom.

"I keep thinking he's still out there," I said.

He nodded, silent.

"Like, if I look away from you for one second, he's going to be there. With the knife. Or a gun. Or just his hands."

"Yeah," Caiden muttered. "It's fucked. But I killed him, I know I did."

He worked his jaw, then reached into the backpack for the last bottle of water. He held it out to me, not meeting my eyes.

I took it, screwed the cap off, and drank. The water burned down my throat.

Eventually, we came to an open plain, grass and sagebrush bowing in the wind, the slopes on either side hunched like the backs of starving dogs.

We walked in a line. Two pathetic figures bruised and bandaged, each footfall sinking us deeper into the wasteland. The wind tried to push us back, its teeth gnawing at our skin until we huddled closer, sharing what little body heat we could.

The moon, swollen and predatory, hovered just above the horizon, watching us with a pale, unsleeping eye.

The ground here was flat, but the stones conspired against us.

Every few steps my sneaker would catch on a rock, pitching me forward; every time, Caiden grabbed my arm, steadying me, but his hand lingered as if to memorize the shape of me.

I could feel his own tremor, the shared current of fear and adrenaline.

Neither of us mentioned it. Neither of us dared.

We circled a patch of burnt grass, blackened and brittle as bone, and ducked behind a boulder to escape the wind. I collapsed, my legs trembling.

In the darkness, Caiden's eyes seemed to glow. Like a wolf's gaze, wild and haunted.

My own mind was a tangle: the freezer, the knife, Lillian's laughter in the distance, the possibility that this whole thing was a fevered nightmare and I'd wake up alone in a white room.

The wind howled, a high keening that reminded me of the way the man's voice had twisted the air in the basement, whistling through the cracks and into the soft tissue of my skull.

I found myself straining to hear it now, half-certain that any moment he'd step from behind a tree, dragging a snare wire and wearing that polite, hollow smile.

I shivered, not from cold but from the sick certainty that trauma isn't something you outrun; it's a parasite, it curls up under your skin and waits for night.

Our kidnapper was dead, yet I felt as if he would jump out and attack us.

It was a dread that was engraved deep into my bones. I wondered if I would ever feel safe again.

A raven landed on a rock, its obsidian eyes seeming to pierce my growing darkness, mirroring the unease that coiled in my gut.

Caiden glanced at me, as if sensing my unease, but did not speak. I embraced the security of his presence, grateful that I had somebody else to endure this with, being lost out here in the Colorado wilderness.

Suddenly, a low howl ripped through the stillness.

Caiden's hand instinctively reached for mine, his knuckles white against my skin, pulling me towards him.

My body stiffened at the contact, and a shiver enveloped me.

The raven took flight, its shadow a fleeting omen against the rapidly darkening sky.

Panic, raw and visceral, threatened to overwhelm me, but I clung to Caiden's hand, the shared tension a fragile lifeline in the invading dusk.

Each step was a battle against the crescendo of fear, the wilderness itself seeming to conspire against our escape.

My head drooped. My eyelids fluttered. Caiden's shoulder pressed against mine, anchoring me to the stone, to his warmth, to the reality that we were not alone and not safe and, maybe worst of all, not dead.

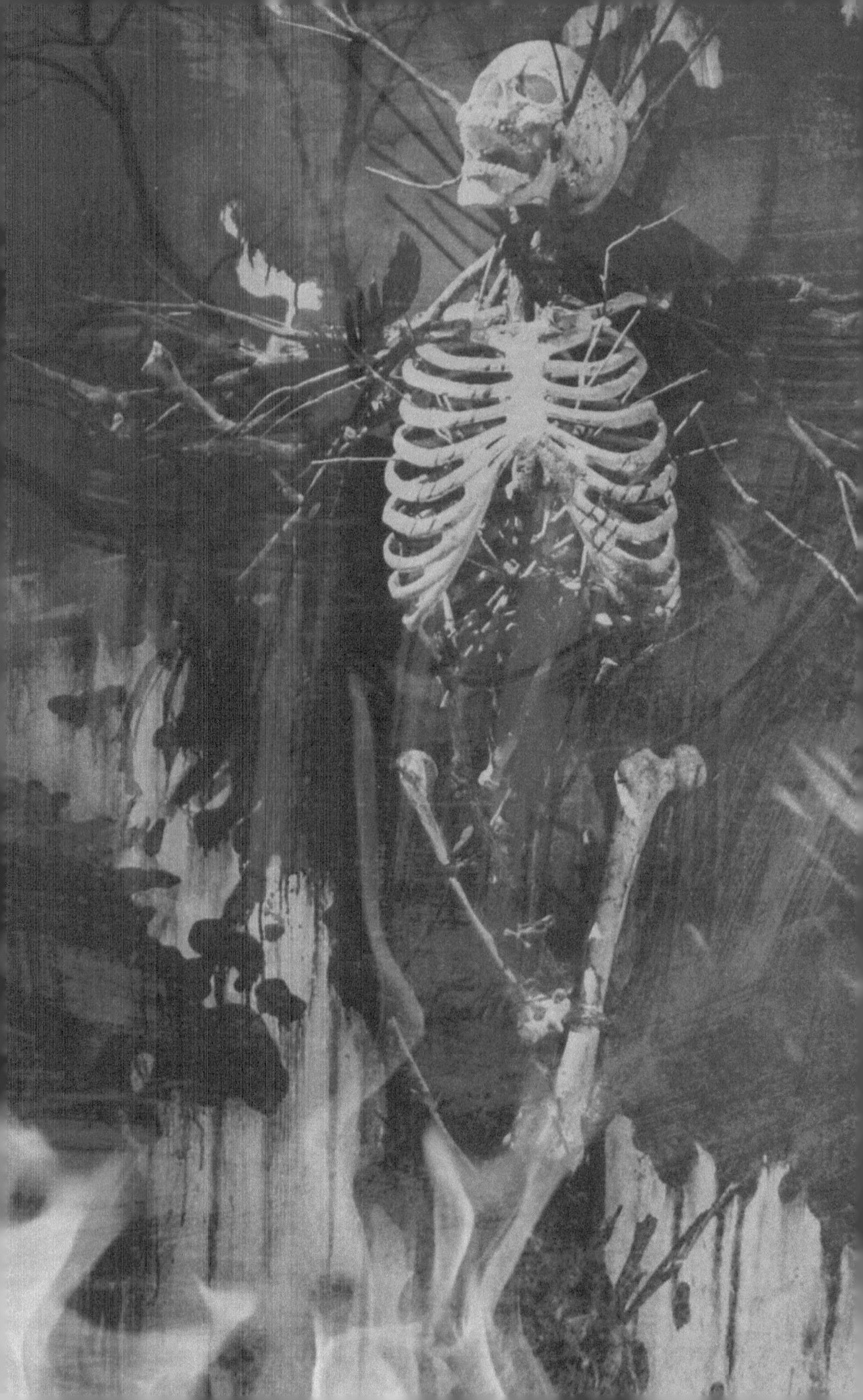

# 58

## THE PRESENT

### AMELIA

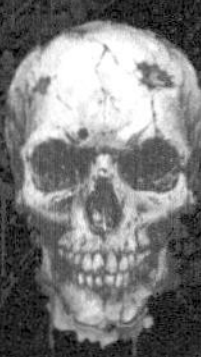

Caiden and I had fallen asleep next to each other in the wilderness, and I awoke with him pressed up against me from behind.

I woke just after sunrise. The cold bit deep, and my shoulder throbbed like a hymn for everything ugly that had happened.

I could see my own breath, each exhale a ghost. I shifted, and something heavy tightened around my middle.

His arm. Caiden's arm, banded across me, hand buried under the hem of my shirt as if he'd tried to climb inside me for warmth while we slept.

My body went rigid.

At first, I could not move. My brain spat static and white-noise instructions—run, bite, scream—but none of it made it past the locked gates of my jaw.

I could not even muster a sound. His chest pressed against my back, radiating heat, anchoring me to the cold earth beneath.

The thing that frightened me most was not the weight of him, but how I wanted, for a moment, not to move. How my skin prickled at every point of contact, how the salt of his palm on my stomach felt more real than any touch I'd ever known.

If I shifted, if I so much as blinked, he would know I was awake. I didn't want him to know. I didn't want to explain why I hadn't shoved him off, or why the idea of being alone in the cold was suddenly worse than being trapped in this tangle of bruised limbs and borrowed heat.

The animal in me stirred. I hated it, but also wanted it. To be held, to be wanted, to let the ache inside me find its answer in the press of his body. I wanted him to suffocate the memory of our kidnapper and the wire and the cage, to kill it with the violence of his presence.

I did not want him to wake up and see me like this: exposed, caught in the act of needing.

I jerked forward, dislodging his arm, and rolled a few feet away so violently I almost retched.

The movement startled him awake. He sat up, instantly alert, his face wrenched into an animal grimace.

He looked at me, hair wild, eyes black with hunger or fear, and for a long moment we just stared at each other.

Neither of us said a word, but the silence was louder than a gunshot.

His stare, wild and bare, made my skin crawl with something that wasn't disgust. Not quite. I wanted to spit, to scream invective at him, but my jaw wouldn't unhinge.

In the freeze-frame of dawn, I couldn't tell if I was more afraid of being touched or of never being held again.

Caiden broke the trance first. He scrabbled to his feet, brushing the dirt off with quick, savage motions, refusing to look at me.

I crossed my arms over my stomach, feeling the imprint of his palm like a brand. My body was a contradiction of needs.

Bone-deep shame, vibrating want.

"We have to move," he said.

He turned away, hauling the pack over one shoulder. I trailed after, slow at first, anger and embarrassment sticking to me, and made every step echo with the memory of his hand pressed flat to my skin.

I wanted to scrape him off, to pretend it had never happened. I wanted to scream at him for being what he was. But I also wanted to grab his hand and put it back.

The sun was already high, burning the dew from the grass, and my wound had crusted into an ache. We followed a dirt ridge, picking our way through scrub and shale, the world already shimmering with heat.

My lips were cracked. I licked them, tasting salt and iron, the aftershock of fear like a fever under my sweat.

I refused to look at Caiden, but I kept close enough to hear his footsteps, to note the way his breathing shifted when the path narrowed, and our arms brushed.

We stopped at a trickle of water, the stream barely wider than a piss trail.

I knelt and drank, then splashed the freezing water onto my face. It shocked me clear for a moment, blurring the edges of the memory.

I watched Caiden lean over the bank, cupping his hands. His arms were strong and bruised and beautiful in a way I hated myself for noticing. There was a rawness to him now, as if the wild had stripped away the shell of menace and left only the animal, hungry and hounded.

He caught me watching. For a second, he simply blinked, and for a moment, there was nothing in his face but pure, blank need.

My chest clenched.

I let the water chill my wrists, my temples, the wound on my shoulder. The cold seeped in and numbed the world for a minute, and I let myself believe that the fever had broken, that I could walk on without memory.

But then I stood, and he was waiting for me, gaze pinned to my face as if he'd never seen me before.

"Does it still hurt?" he asked, and for a second I thought he meant the shoulder, but his eyes darted to my stomach, then away.

"Not really," I lied. My voice was steadier than I expected.

He nodded, like he knew it was a lie and didn't blame me for it. We followed the creek until the banks widened into a low, stony basin.

There was a scattering of driftwood, bleached and splintered, and I settled onto one of the logs while Caiden picked his way along the waterline. He crouched, poking at the mud, then stood and stretched, the movement pulling his shirt taut over the ladder of his ribs.

I watched him, not bothering to hide it.

I was starving. Not just for food, though the ache in my belly was a black hole, gnawing at the integrity of my skin from the inside out. It was everything. The need to be seen, to be wanted, to be more than a discarded scab on the edge of the world.

And when I looked at Caiden, I recognized the same hunger, a shadow-self that stalked the edges of his body.

He was the only person alive who knew what the inside of that cage had done to me, who had seen the animal curled up in my spine and didn't try to kill it.

Maybe because he'd had his own animal, and maybe because he wanted to see how long we'd last.

Caiden drifted back to where I sat, and the air between us was as dense as the day after a funeral. He dropped onto the log beside me, letting our knees touch, not by accident.

His thigh was warm through the shredded fabric, and the proximity made my skin prickle. He looked out over the basin, his hands twisting in his lap.

"We should figure out where to go next," he said, but his voice was softer than I remembered, all the edges worn away. "We're running out of food. And the bandage—" He made a vague gesture at my shoulder, the gesture useless and almost apologetic. "You'll need antibiotics. Soon."

I watched the ants migrate up the driftwood, all order and hunger and single-minded survival. "You think there's anyone out here looking for us?"

His face went still. "No." He shook his head. "There's nobody. Not for a while, at least."

He didn't say what we both understood, that we weren't the kind of kids anyone came looking for. Not quickly. Maybe not at all.

I picked at a splinter, tried to pluck a word or two from the mist in my head. "The freezer," I said, and my voice came out thin, crimped. "Do you think he ate all of them?"

He stared at his hands, flexing the fingers. "He definitely ate some." He didn't elaborate. The silence made my teeth ache.

"Would you eat me?" I asked it like a joke, but my mouth was too dry, my tongue heavy as a stone.

"I'd eat the fuck out of you."

The words hung in the air. My brain flared, then shorted out, unable to decide if I wanted to laugh or run or just lie down in the mud and let the ants do their work.

The way he said it, deadpan, but with a twist of heat behind it, forced my skin to erupt in goosebumps.

He met my eyes and didn't look away.

"Was that a joke?" I managed, voice so dry it cracked.

He shrugged. "Depends if you want me to be serious."

The way the wind sculpted his face, the wolfish cut of his jaw, made me want to bite something myself.

"You're disgusting," I said, but my voice was trembling, the words failing to land between us as anything but a dare.

He leaned closer, enough that I could smell the sweat and riverwater on his neck. "You're the one who asked."

For a beat, we sat there, knees pressed together, the rest of the world narrowing to two sets of teeth and a single thumping pulse.

"You wouldn't like it. I'm all gristle and spite."

"I like gristle," Caiden said, and his mouth tugged at one corner, almost a grin. "Spite's the best flavor."

His thigh pressed harder against mine, deliberate now. I didn't flinch. I let the heat seep through, let my own hunger bloom behind the wall of my chest.

There was a gravity to the moment, a slow drift.

He looked at my mouth, then back to my eyes, and for the first time since childhood, I understood what it meant to want something so badly you could almost feel the shape of it in your bones.

I should have been repulsed by him, but I wasn't. The horror had torn everything else out of me, and in the riptide, it left only want. Raw and simple.

I felt the want in my jaw, in the way my tongue pressed against my teeth, in the hard ache at the base of my skull.

I wanted, and I hated that I wanted, but I was starving for it, for the violence and the tenderness collapsed together until I couldn't tell which was which.

But this was Caiden, I shouldn't have this hunger inside of me towards him, but it's there, and I'm terrified it won't ever go away.

It was wrong, so wrong.

I watched the shadow of a hawk spiral over the dry creek bed, and I thought, not long now.

Whatever Caiden and I had become—whatever wolves or scavengers we'd turned into—there wasn't much left in us but the will to be the last one gnawing on the bone.

The thing was, I didn't want to be the last. I wanted him to stay, despite our past, even if it meant I kept eating until there was nothing left but the two of us, empty and toothy and sated on each other's ruin.

I wanted to ask him if he blamed me for any of it, if he would have left me in the freezer if the choice was there, but I could not make my tongue move.

So I just sat, letting the sweat bake over me, feeling the wound throb and the riot of wants settle into a hard, black seed.

We did not move for the better part of an hour. There was nothing to wait for, but neither of us wanted to move. The exhaustion was not just in muscle, but in nerve: a weariness of having survived, of having to keep surviving, day after day.

Eventually, I fished a can of beans from the pack, wedged it between my thighs, and cracked it with the knife.

I took a spoonful, then another, but the food made no impression on my hunger. I passed the can to Caiden, who scooped up a mouthful and swallowed without comment.

The intimacy of the moment was so raw I wanted to laugh. We had shared a cage, a wound, a killer; now we shared a spoon, the backwash of our spit swirling together with the chemical tang of the beans.

I remembered a time, not so long ago, when the idea of touching anything that had passed Caiden's mouth would have made me gag.

Now, the idea of not sharing it was what made me sick.

When he handed it back, his hand lingered, thumb grazing the inside of my wrist.

It was not an accident.

I stared at the point of contact, feeling the pulse there.

I wanted to say something, but the words jammed in my throat. He watched me, all focus, all waiting, as if to see what I would do next.

"We're not gonna die out here," he said finally. "I refuse."

I made a noise that might have been a laugh, a cough, or a sob. I wasn't sure. I was too tired to check.

"Good," I said. "Because I'm not done hating you yet."

The words had no teeth, no venom, but he seemed to understand the new gravity of them. The way "hate" was a lifeline now, a chain that held us together when everything else was wind and bone.

He grunted, and the silence held for a few more cycles before he stood. His fingers hooked through the can's rim, and he lobbed it into the creek where it spun in an eddy, gleaming silver under the sky. "Let's go then," he said, voice gruff with something like hope.

We walked. The sun climbed and baked the earth around us, the heat a relentless press that made the sweat roll down our necks and soak the bandages.

My shoulder throbbed in time with my heartbeat, each step sending a new jolt of fire into my arm. I said nothing about it. He didn't ask.

The terrain was monotonous and hostile, every rise and dip echoing the ache inside my limbs. We tracked the creek for a mile, maybe two, until the water vanished into a dry gravel bed.

I wanted to stop, to curl up in the little hollow and sleep until the next century, but Caiden just kept moving, head down, eyes glued to the horizon.

When I lagged, he waited. When I stumbled, he caught me. No words passed between us, but his hand on my elbow or the small of my back kept me upright and moving, putting himself in front of the worst of the wind.

When I looked at him, I saw the old Caiden—the bastard, the bully, the monster—but I also saw the shadow of the boy from the playground, the one who'd sat quietly beside me and watched the sky.

I hated how much I needed both of those versions of him. I hated how my body responded to the closeness, the heat, the memory of his hand on my stomach. I hated that the hate was now a thin film over muscle and bone, a web that bound us together even as it threatened to rot us from the inside out.

When the sun began to slant, orange and mad, we crested the first rise of the day and saw nothing but a new, wider valley, another stretch of rock and rippling heat.

Caiden stopped, sweat streaking his face, and let out a low, guttural "Fuck."

He tilted his head back and closed his eyes, and for a second, I thought he might cry. I almost wanted him to. It would make it easier, maybe, to forgive him for all the ways he'd failed to be a monster.

Instead, he turned to me and said, "If we don't see water soon, we're going to have to slow down. You're bleeding again."

I looked at my arm. The bandage had become useless, blood seeping up and blooming through the gauze. It didn't hurt as much as it should have.

"I can keep going," I said. My voice felt like it belonged to someone else, some tougher animal that didn't know how to shut up.

He gave me a look and shrugged. "Fine. But if you fall over, I'm not carrying you."

A sick thrill ran through me at the thought of him carrying me. I imagined it: his arms under my knees and back, his jaw clenched against the effort, his breath damp on my face.

I wanted to snap at him, to say he'd never have the strength, but the words dried up in my mouth. The idea of being weightless in his arms made my body hum with a longing that had nothing to do with safety, or maybe everything to do with it.

He started down the other side of the ridge, boots crunching the crust of earth. I followed, letting my weight carry me forward, letting gravity do the work.

At the bottom, a wash of stone and eroded sand gave way to a patch of green. Grass, stunted and burnt, but it meant water. Somewhere underground, some trickle feeds the fragile roots.

My mouth flooded with anticipation. I could have devoured the landscape.

We searched for the source, kicking at rocks and poking at the dirt. When I found the seep, I almost cried.

We knelt, scooping at the liquid with our hands, sucking it from the ground like desperate animals. In the moment, I was nothing but thirst and want, lapping up the taste of life like it was the last drug on earth.

He watched me drink, and in his eyes I saw an echo of the fever that burned in my own. The way his lips parted, the way his gaze traveled my jaw, my throat, the curve of my shoulder, made the skin go hot under the bandages.

I wiped my mouth with the back of my hand, daring him to look away.

He didn't. His voice was soft, almost tender. "You have dirt on your face."

"Yeah? So do you."

He reached out, thumb brushing the smudge from my cheek. The touch was electric, a jolt straight to the base of my spine.

I flinched, but didn't pull away. His hand lingered.

We crouched there, side by side, the silence between us suddenly taut and humming. I wanted to say something stupid, to break the tension, but all I managed was, "What?"

It came out defensive, as if I needed to remind him that I wasn't prey.

He didn't answer. His thumb moved, slow, deliberate, tracing the edge of my jaw.

For a second, I thought he would kiss me, and I wanted it too much to find words for the wanting. The ache moved through me, a pulse that rewrote every old hurt into something raw and new.

Instead, he just said, "You should rest," and stood, his hand falling away.

I watched the muscles in his back flex under the thin shirt as he walked back toward the patch of shade. I hated him for stopping. I hated myself for wanting him not to. I hated that we had nothing else in the world, no other horizon but our own ruin.

But I followed, because I didn't want to be alone with the old ghosts.

We huddled under the shelter of a boulder, knees drawn up, the heat radiating off the rock like a fever. I peeled the sodden bandage from my shoulder and wiped at the blood.

Caiden watched, face gone shuttered and blank, but his hands twitched in his lap, restless.

"How bad is it?" he asked.

I flexed my arm, wincing. "Not bad enough to die from."

He grunted, the sound a soft rumble. "You're such a liar."

"Yeah," I said. "I know." My voice was too thin to sound like anything but defeat.

He dragged a hand over his face, and I watched the lines it left in the grime, the way the muscles bunched in his jaw.

He looked up, finally, eyes catching on mine with a ferocity that made me want to crawl out of my own skin. "You always were," he said, something almost gentle in the words. "You lied to everyone. But you never lied to me. Maybe you tried, but I could always see through it."

I almost laughed. "That's because you never believed anything I said. Or even cared. I didn't feel the need to try to put on a mask."

He leaned forward, elbows on knees, eyes fixed on me. "I believed you," he said. "You just never knew what you wanted."

The words sliced. I thought of all the things I'd ever wanted. My sister alive, my mother sober, my own skin to fit better, the violence to stop.

Now, all I wanted was a can of beans, a handful of water, and this moment to last longer than the next disaster.

"We should keep moving," he said, already up. "If we stay in one place too long, predators will start circling."

I stood, the ache in my shoulder now a dull, needy throb, and followed. The sun was sinking, the sky bruised purple.

We walked in silence, the rhythm of our steps a counterpoint to the howl of the wind. Each mile hollowed out something deeper in me, and the hunger for Caiden—for the gravity of him—grew as relentless as thirst.

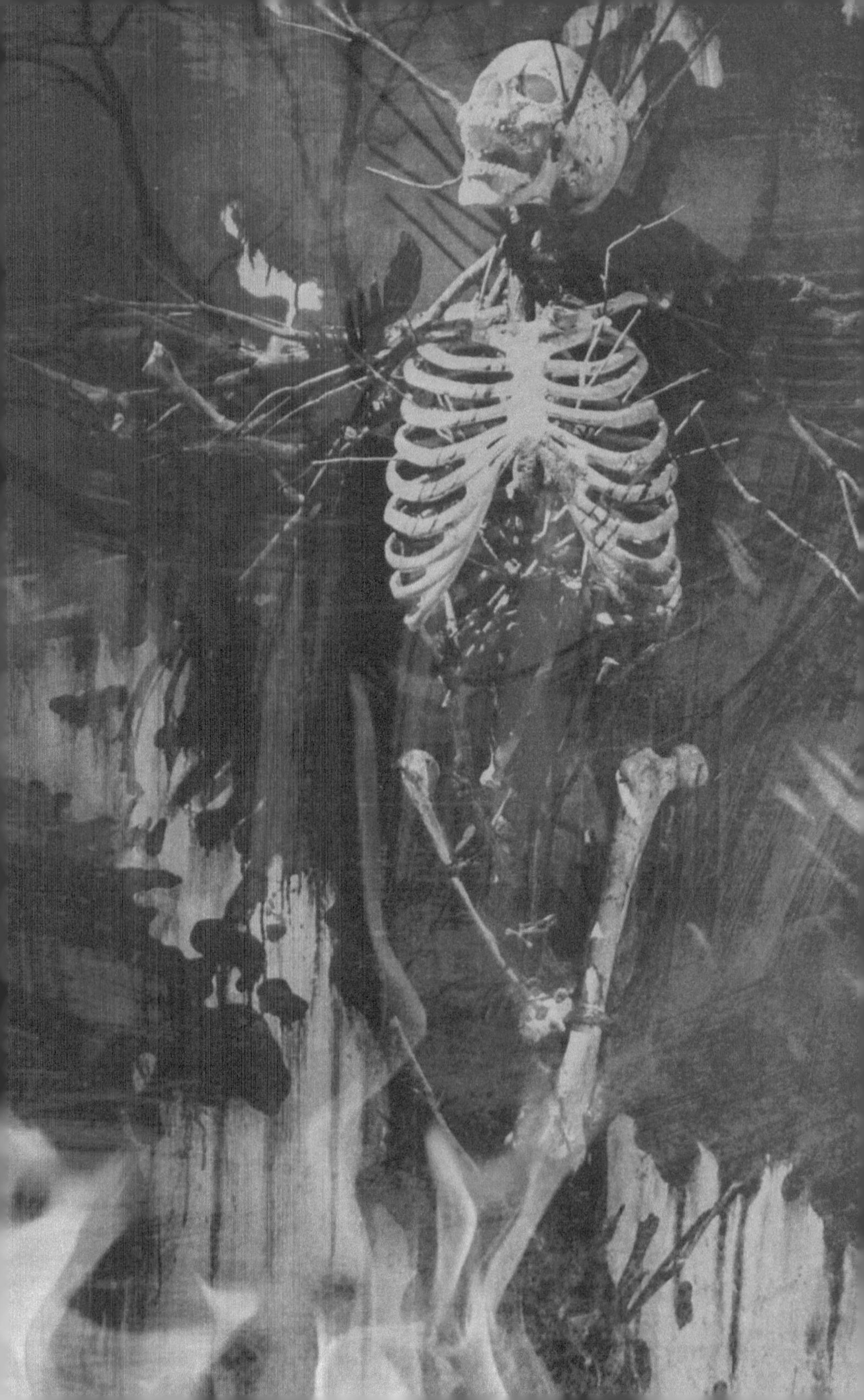

# 59

## THE PRESENT

### AMELIA

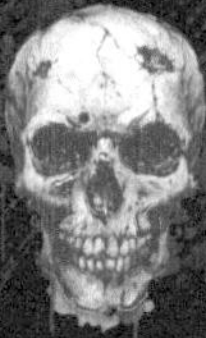

Caiden and I found ourselves ensnared in a game of silent glances and fragile tensions, wandering through the rugged terrain of the Colorado wilderness, where something wild and dangerous fluttered between us.

Initially, we had been enemies; the tension between us was thick enough to cleave with a knife.

Yet, as we navigated the unforgiving landscape together, side by side through countless hardships, our mutual distrust began to erode unexpectedly, blurring the lines that separated foe from friend.

I wasn't sure what we were.

He wasn't either. The silent question etched into the beautiful landscape that mirrored the uncertainty within our hearts. Each shared sunrise and every perilous mountain pass we conquered together chipped away at the hatred that had once defined us, leaving behind something fragile yet undeniably powerful.

It wasn't friendship, not exactly.

But I couldn't deny the unsettling paradox; our connection felt both wrong and right, simultaneously thrilling and terrifying.

We were two opposing forces, a lamentable storm and a raging fire, destined to collide in a cataclysmic clash, yet drawn together like magnets.

I had once thought that our story would end in a deadly explosion, but everything had changed, and we were slowly becoming the essence of starlight, something delicate and soft born from a cosmic collision.

We walked a tightrope, both terrified of falling, yet a part of me longed to surrender to something that felt inevitable.

The later hours found us hiking a ridge in the thinning sun, the world around us a shimmering haze of heat and dry light that had stripped away all illusions of safety.

The rocks were slippery underfoot, and the wind had a serrated edge, slashing at our exposed skin. We walked without speaking, our shadows long and distorted, twin stains on the landscape.

A red-tailed hawk traced circles overhead, casting its flickering shadow back and forth as we wound through the mini-valleys of the flatland.

I thought of my own shadow, the way it stuck to my heels no matter how I turned, a darkness that refused to burn away even at the world's brightest noon.

Caiden kept pace a yard ahead of me, hands shoved deep in his pockets, shoulders hunched against the world. The trailing light made his hair look almost golden, a boy from some other universe who had not learned that everything he touched would rot.

It was absurd, this aura of innocence, when I remembered the way his hands had closed around another man's throat; how he'd watched the last gurgled breath without looking away.

But even that memory had softened in retrospect, blurred by the way he'd bandaged my shoulder and forced water on me, how he'd slept beside me without once making a move, except for that one accidental hand under my shirt, which I'd not been able to stop thinking about since.

I wanted to blame him for everything. The hunger, the pain, the way my body now ached not just from injury but from proximity. The way I'd caught myself wanting the pressure of his palm, the roughness of his fingers, wanting his mouth.

Not just to touch but to be devoured, as if something in me could only be made real by being consumed by him. It was monstrous, but I didn't care.

He was a beautiful disaster, broken in the same ways I was. Maybe that was why I couldn't hate him, even when I needed to.

I stumbled, numb-footed, and he caught my elbow, holding me

upright longer than necessary. His hands were large and calloused and trembling just a little.

I pulled free, but only because I feared I might never let go.

We rested for a moment on a slanted rock. Caiden huddled close, our knees touching. I let myself lean into him, surrendering to the body heat and the unspoken truce.

For a moment, we were something other than victims, other than enemies.

Eventually, the bandages on my shoulder bloomed red again.

Caiden noticed, his gaze lingering on the stain. He said nothing, just pressed his hand over it, stemmed the bleeding with a fierce, silent pressure.

I remembered the way he'd screamed my name in the darkness of that hell-cabin, the way his fists had splintered the closet door. The way he'd killed a man, for me. How could I ever explain how those memories felt, sacred and obscene, a communion of violence?

I shivered, and his arm slipped around my shoulders.

I let it happen because resisting was pointless.

When I glanced at him, I found his gaze already fixed on me.

I swallowed hard, my heartbeat quickening, my cheeks flushing a vivid shade of scarlet.

"Caiden?" I whispered, my breath catching in my throat.

"Yeah?" His voice came out low and husky, a gentle murmur, like the wind whispering through the trees.

I felt an intense yearning to have him whisper to me in the dark, surrounded by flickering candlelight, while I lay beneath him. The image ignited my mind, and despite my efforts to shake it away, it persisted, urging me to give in.

"I don't want to be enemies anymore," I confessed, my voice a fragile whisper that barely reached him.

His intense gaze narrowed as he scrutinized me, as if trying to decipher the truth hidden in my words. "Really?" he asked, skepticism laced with a hint of intrigue.

My eyes fell to the ground, a surge of vulnerability enveloping me. I bit my lip, feeling the heat rise in my cheeks, and with a surge of courage, I dared to meet his eyes.

They burned into mine, a primal heat simmering just beneath the surface, threatening to consume us both.

"Yeah," I murmured, my voice trembling. "I've been thinking

about what's happened between us, and it's changed my perspective."

He shifted closer, the space between us shrinking, the air thickening with an undeniable tension that pulsed like a living thing. The heat wrapped around us, binding us in its fervent embrace.

"What perspective do you have now?" His voice was a low, confident rumble, as if he already knew the answer but hungered to hear it from my lips.

"Don't make me say it," I pleaded softly, my heart pounding in my chest, a wild rhythm that matched the intensity of the moment.

But shifted again, closing the remaining distance, his presence overwhelming, intoxicating. "Say it," he demanded, his voice a caress that sent shivers racing down my spine.

"I think I crave you too," I breathed, the admission hanging between us, a confession that ignited the spark of desire into a blazing inferno.

His breath hitched, mirroring mine. The tension, once a battlefield, now crackled with a different kind of energy, raw and intimate.

He reached out with his other hand, his fingers brushing against mine, sending a jolt coursing through my entire being. The touch was tentative, hesitant, yet charged with a power that defied words.

For a long moment, we sat suspended between the past and the future, the Colorado wilderness a silent witness to the growing flame between us.

Then, he leaned in, his lips a whisper away from mine, and the world around us dissolved into the intoxicating promise of something new, something dangerous, something breathtakingly beautiful.

This was Caiden, once my nightmarish tormentor, but now, he was my Caiden. The one who saved me, the one who survived with me, the one who revealed that beauty could exist even in the dark.

Our faces drew closer, his eyes, once a storm of darkness, now clouded with golden flames, burning bright with passion in my vision.

In a hypnotic state, I allowed myself to move closer, inhaling the essence of him, any thought of the past fading from my mind.

In this moment, he was a beautiful man woven from broken, fragmented threads.

I wanted this feeling to consume me, to dig deeper into his heart and nestle within it.

Just as our lips were about to touch, a whirring sound sliced through the air above us. Our heads snapped upward, startled by the sudden loudness that interrupted our quiet intimacy.

We jumped back from each other, realizing what had invaded our moment.

A helicopter.

"We're here! Oh my God!" Our screams echoed through the vast expanse, raw and ragged, as we waved our arms and jumped, our throats burning from the exertion.

The helicopter descended, a beacon of hope against the sprawling landscape, bringing the reality of rescue closer with every passing second.

Finally, after days of believing we would perish out there together, we were saved.

As the helicopter landed and the pilot stepped out, Caiden and I exchanged knowing, nervous glances.

Out there, we had been Caiden and Amelia, two souls bound by survival, connection, and trauma. But none of us knew what awaited us once we returned to reality.

I only hoped we wouldn't revert to being eternal enemies now that we were on the brink of moving past it.

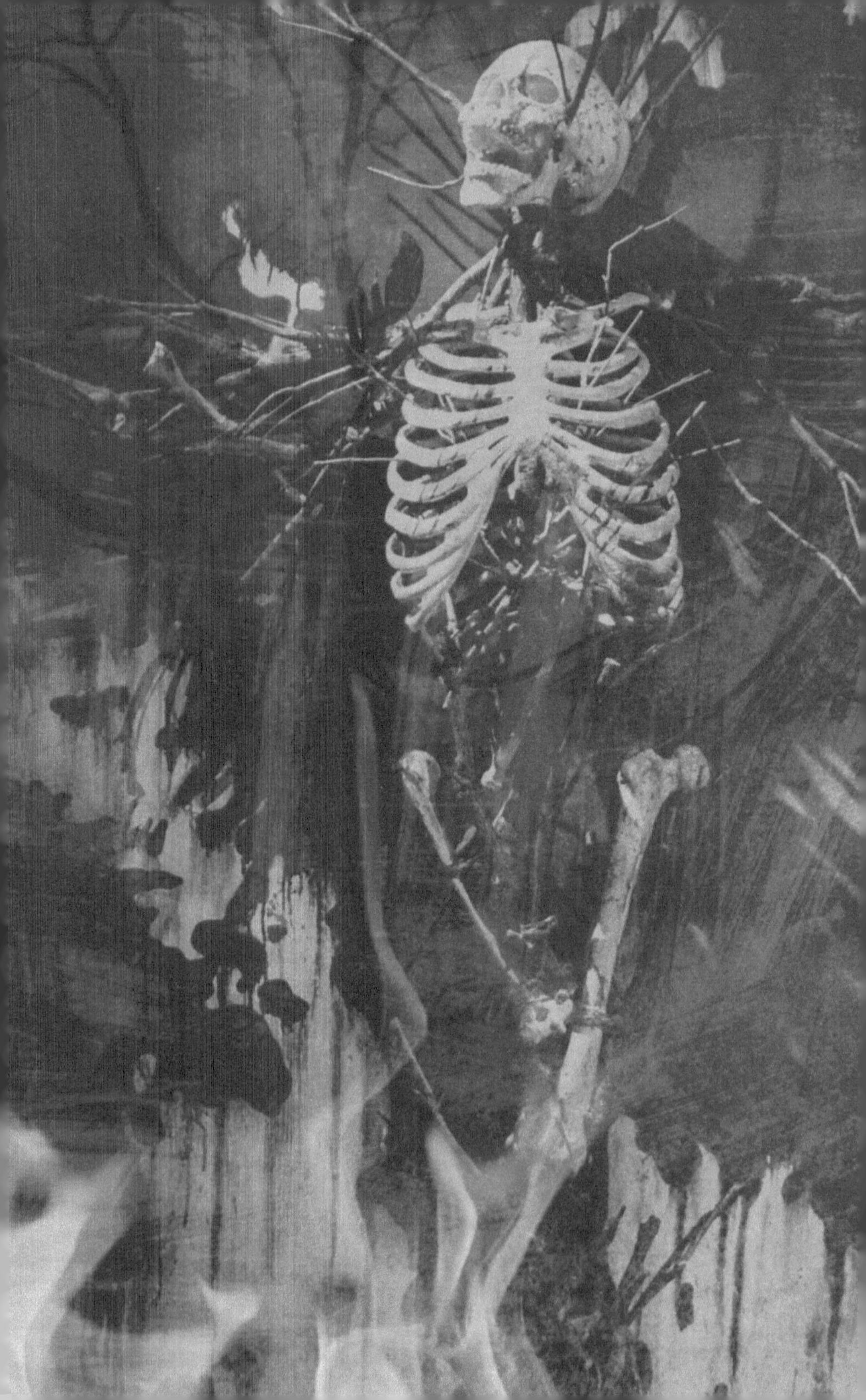

# 60

## THE PRESENT

### AMELIA

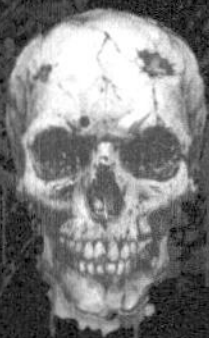

THE SIGHT OF CIVILIZATION WAS A SWEET RELIEF, A BALM for the raw wounds we carried. The first few days had blurred into a whirlwind of confusion and disbelief. In a last-ditch effort to find us, they had sent out a helicopter, and it was successful.

Once we landed, Sabrina and Shane rushed to greet us, their arms enveloping us in tight embraces, their voices bursting with relief and joy that we were alive.

Caiden and I stood off to the side, our clothes filthy and wrinkled, our expressions hollowed by exhaustion and the haunting memories of what we had endured.

I glanced at him, and he met my gaze; we both felt the weight of our trauma. It was too much to process, too surreal to comprehend. Not long ago, we had faced death, and now we stood in fresh clothes, surrounded by warmth and light.

As we recounted the horrors of the cabin and the monster who had lurked within, the police revealed that many had gone missing in the wilderness over the years, with most never to be found again. Somehow, they had discovered the cabin.

Later, we saw on the news that a gruesome collection of bones had been unearthed from beneath the floorboards. The body found in the freezer was identified as a hiker who had disappeared months before.

They also discovered the lifeless body of the killer, his remains grotesquely marred with bloodied gashes.

A DNA test confirmed his identity: Blake Hill. The police files told a chilling story of a boy turned monster. Blake had murdered his father in cold blood after enduring years of torment and abuse.

His father, plagued by psychotic tendencies, had imprisoned Blake in their basement, subjecting him to horrific games. He even kidnapped other children, forcing Blake to witness their torture and eventual demise. The mother, complicit in the madness, was just as deranged as her husband.

Though she killed herself long before Blake escaped.

Eventually, Blake vanished from society, his sanity eroded by trauma. He retreated to the very cabin that had once belonged to his family, allowing his torment to fester in isolation, transforming him into the emotionless killer he had become.

He was doomed to replay the horrors of his past, desperately seeking validation in the twisted echoes of his memories.

It was a tragic tale, and I almost felt pity for him.

I still possessed the diary I had stolen from the table, though I had yet to open it. Now, it lay in the drawer of my nightstand, a ghost haunting my thoughts. I couldn't bring myself to throw it away.

Most nights, I sought solace with Shane and Sabrina. I couldn't bear the thought of sleeping alone; the nightmares threatened to consume me.

Some nights, I envisioned Blake hovering over me, that sinister smile freezing my bones, his predatory gaze penetrating my very soul. His cold hands would close around my throat, and I would wake, breathless and terrified.

Haunted by Blake Hill.

Tonight was no different from most nights since our rescue two weeks earlier. I lay in their guest bedroom, tossing and turning as sweat poured across my skin, fevered tremors shaking my body.

I awoke with a scream, panting, my eyes darting around the room, expecting Blake to leap from the shadows with his knife.

The door creaked open, and I shrank lower in bed, paralyzed by fear. He's here.

A tall figure stepped inside, and I whimpered helplessly.

To my surprise, the figure settled onto the edge of the bed and flicked on the lamp.

It was Caiden.

"I thought you were Blake Hill," I murmured, my voice shaky.

A flash of concern crossed his face, but it disappeared as quickly as it had come. Since our rescue, we had barely spoken.

The harrowing moments we shared on that mountain felt like a distant memory, overshadowed by the realities of civilization. Even sharing the same house wasn't enough to bridge the chasm between us. We only saw each other at night, when I sought refuge from my nightmares.

Since our return, we had both avoided one another, terrified of the emotions lurking beneath the surface. If I let myself get too close to him, I risked being hurt again. There was too much baggage, too many dark feelings that refused to fade.

That wouldn't disappear just because we had shared some intimate moments while fighting for our lives.

We were malnourished, exhausted, and traumatized. We needed to cling to one another; we needed that closeness. At least, that's what I told myself to alleviate the sudden distance I felt.

Everything was different now. We were ourselves again, and there was no reason to hold onto a distorted bond forged in struggle.

We had faced death together; it was what anyone would do in such circumstances.

"Nope. It's just me. Blake is dead, Amelia. He can't hurt you."

I scowled, hating the way he stared at me, as if I were insane.

"I know that," I snapped, frustration bubbling to the surface. "But he's still haunting my nightmares. I wake up feeling like he's going to jump out and attack me."

"I heard you scream and thought you were hurt. Good to know it was just a nightmare." He turned to leave.

"Really, Caiden? Can't you show at least a little empathy? How come you heard me and not Shane or Sabrina?" I interrogated, feeling a familiar flash of anger.

"A nightmare can't hurt you, Amelia. I'd rather you have a nightmare than relive that situation with him. I'm hurting too, from what we went through, but we're safe now." His demeanor shifted, his voice rising with anger. "I was already awake. I couldn't sleep. So, I figured I'd check on you after your scream."

"Why can't you sleep?"

He sighed, exasperation etched on his face. "Like I said, I'm hurting too, from our experience and other things. But knowing you're physically okay, I'll let you get back to sleep."

He turned to leave, but a wave of cold dread washed over me at the thought of being left alone.

"Wait." My voice trembled, a small cry filled with desperation. He paused, his hand hovering over the doorknob but not turning back.

"Can you stay? Just until I fall asleep? Once I wake up, it's hard to drift off again. I just need to feel safe." Each syllable was a quiet plea, layered with irony; I was begging Caiden for safety and comfort, even though his presence had kept me alive in that cage.

A part of me clung to that connection.

I expected him to walk out, but instead, he shut the door and turned to face me. He looked at me, and I could see the tension unraveling in him as I lay there with messy hair, my chest peeking out from the covers, wearing a loose shirt and flushed cheeks.

The desperation on my face must have been enough to convey the urgency of my need for safety and comfort.

"Yeah. Okay. I'll stay." He tentatively walked toward the bed, sitting slowly, as if he expected me to lash out at him.

He laid down on the other side, maintaining a careful distance.

"Thank you," I whispered into the darkness. He didn't respond, so I continued, my voice barely a breath above the silence.

"This reminds me of the time we shared a bed at the motel. I remember waking up in a panic, realizing I had crawled into bed with you."

He scoffed softly, a hint of disbelief threading through his tone. "Why is that such a bad thing? I'm not diseased."

"I know… but at the time, I harbored so many terrible thoughts about you. Being that close felt like torture. It filled me with anger and helplessness." I laid there staring at the ceiling.

I felt the bed shift, and I could sense him turning to look at me. It was dark, but I could always feel his heated gaze, a warmth that wrapped around me like a blanket.

"Can I confess something?" he murmured, his voice low and laced with vulnerability.

He felt too close, yet not close enough.

"What?" My voice came out raspy, barely a whisper.

"That night in the motel, I thought you looked damn sexy in what you were wearing to bed. That thin shirt, those shorts that rode up your thighs... Goddamn."

His words enveloped me, stirring something deep within. In an instant, our lips met, the taste of him unexpectedly sweet against my tongue.

The kiss was rapid and heated, not slow or romantic. Hatred and passion fused in an embrace, blending into one, twisting into a complex thread of clashing lips and entangled hearts.

He groaned, flipping me onto my back, his hands roaming freely, pushing his body into mine. I wove my fingers through his thick, chocolate-hued hair, pulling him closer, our lips dancing together in a rhythm all their own.

My thighs tingled again, a red-hot sensation surging through my body, causing my legs to wrap around his waist, yanking him closer. I yearned to immerse myself in his essence entirely, to savor this moment before it slipped away.

"Caiden," I breathed, my voice a breathless moan as his lips trailed from mine to my cheek, then down my neck, his kisses igniting goosebumps on my skin.

Caiden let out another groan, devouring me with an intensity that left me breathless.

But then he stopped, his dark eyes blazing with barely contained heat, a wild, beastly passion consuming him.

"Shit," he muttered softly, as if the word itself was a confession of weakness.

His hand hovered over my stomach, fingers flexing in the air. For a moment, I thought he would slam his fist down on me, on the bed, on his own chest.

I reached up, unsure, every cell in my body screaming for his touch, but the chasm between us had grown wider in an instant.

His hunger was rabid and dangerous, and I wanted it to devour me, even as another part of me shrank from its heat. I wanted him to break me open and pour himself inside, to fill the empty, haunted places that nothing else could reach.

His eyes flicked to mine, dark as obsidian, and for a moment I saw the violence there, barely leashed beneath the surface.

He kissed me again. My body arched beneath his, electricity

crackling down my spine, my pulse leapt in every inch of skin he touched. The taste of him filled my mouth and drowned the lingering terror.

His hands found my waist, then slid up, one palm braced against the angle of my ribs, the other digging into my hair.

In the half-light, his silhouette loomed above me, all hard lines and rough edges, shadow and heat. I should have recoiled. I should have clawed at his shoulders, spat in his face, told him I hated him.

Instead, I let him in.

His tongue parted my lips, slow and cautious, waiting for me to bite. I didn't, not this time. I chased him back, lips bruising, teeth scraping, matching his ferocity.

His hand snaked under my shirt, palm sliding over bare skin, and it was like being branded. Too hot, too sudden.

He cupped my breast, thumb rough against the nipple, and the sensation was so jarringly intimate that it yanked me out of the frenzy.

My mind splintered; I was raw and trembling, but not in the way I had wanted.

The room blurred. The pressure on my chest was suddenly suffocating, every touch reminding me of the hands that had pinned me, the ones that had left bruises on my skin and poison in my lungs.

I gasped, a thin whine catching in my throat, and pushed him off me with both hands.

He fell back, stunned, as if I'd struck him.

For a second, we stared at each other, both panting, his pupils dilated so wide his eyes looked black and hollow.

"What the fuck was that for?" he demanded, rolling over to the other side of the bed, the sheets rustling in frustration.

"We can't do this. I'm sorry. I shouldn't have let it go that far. You're Caiden. I'm Amelia. It's not right," I stammered, my heart pounding like a drum in the silence of the room.

Caiden had made my young life a whirlwind of misery, but now, everything felt different. A small, persistent voice in my mind nudged at me, trying to make sense of the chaos.

I shook it away forcefully. This was wrong.

"Seriously? You're using that excuse? Stop being so damn dramatic," he shot back, his voice tinged with disbelief. "I thought we were past that. I can't fucking control this craving anymore now that I've had a taste of it. All the reasons I convinced myself to hate you have flown out the window. All that's left is this overwhelming desire to have you."

I glared at him through the shadows, my heart caught between anger and longing. Despite his tough exterior, I could see the hurt in his eyes, a crack in the facade he fought so hard to maintain.

"Maybe you should stop thinking of yourself. I was molested by Blake, remember? That's a big part of this too. In the heat of the moment, it didn't matter, but reality caught up with me, and now I just can't do it."

I hoped he would understand, but this was Caiden. His emotions were a labyrinth I struggled to navigate.

"Fine. I see how it is. I remind you of Blake," he said, bitterness creeping into his voice.

"No. Well, yes. Sort of. Touching me reminds me of his torment. You're nowhere near who he was as a person, but I just need space. Okay? I need to breathe and figure out what this means."

Caiden shifted off the bed, the distance between us growing unbearably vast, each inch amplifying the tension in the air.

"Sure. This is why I was holding myself back. I was afraid it wouldn't be right or that I would hurt you," he replied, anger seeping into his words.

"You didn't hurt me, at least not right now. I just need space to think. This is all too much, too soon," I whispered, my heart aching with the weight of my words.

"Yeah. Don't worry about explaining yourself. I get it. Sleep well, Amelia," he said, his tone resigned.

He dove out the door, shutting it behind him with a finality that echoed in the silence, leaving me alone in the dark, tears slipping soundlessly down my cheeks, each drop a testament to my turmoil.

I wanted him to come back, to fill the emptiness that had suddenly engulfed me.

Yet, paradoxically, I also wanted him to stay gone, to give me the space I desperately craved.

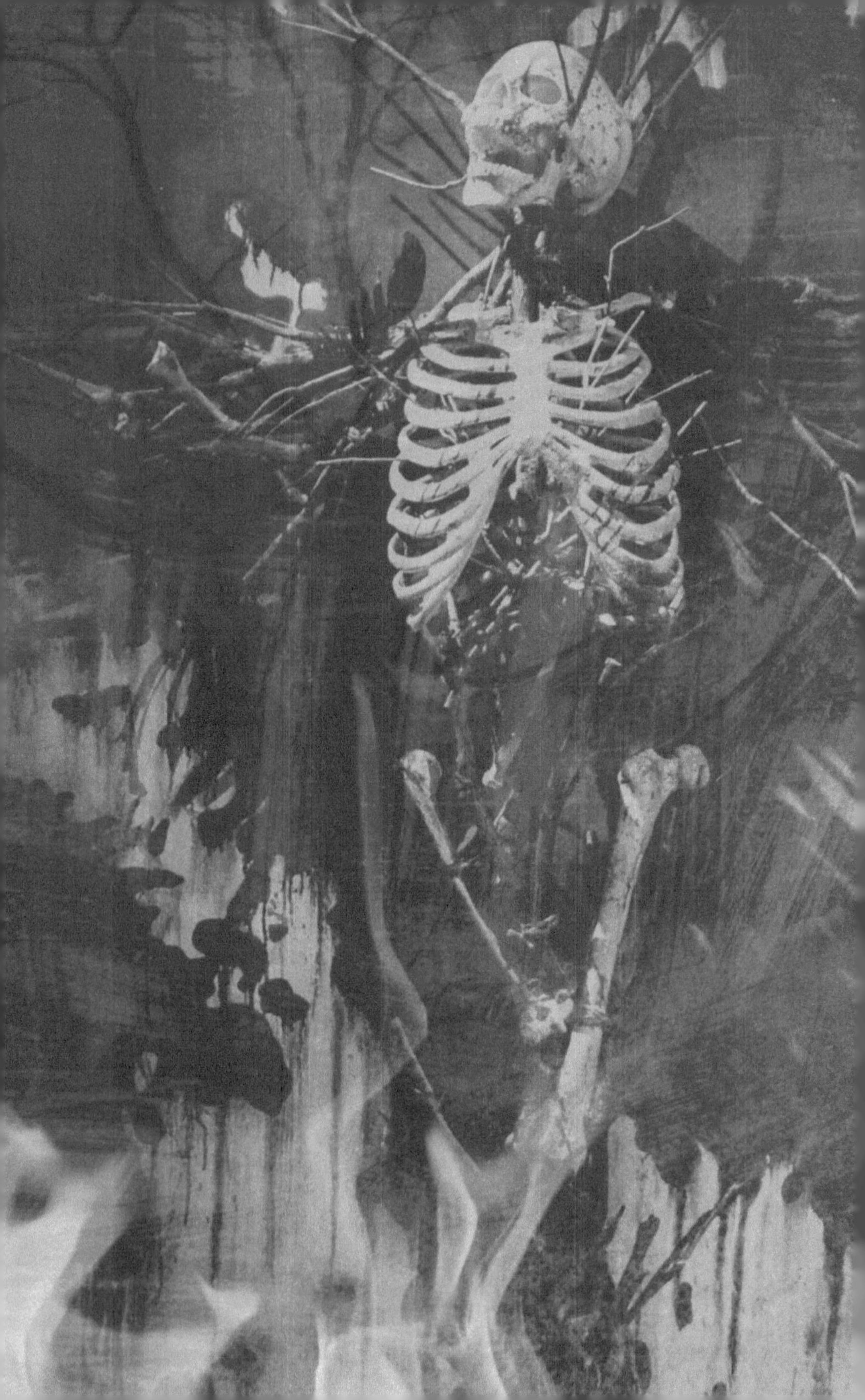

# 61

## THE PRESENT

### AMELIA

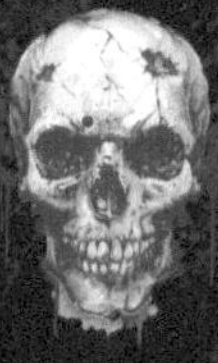

I began passing the time by reading Blake's journal. I knew I shouldn't, but with the increased hours spent at home, the temptation was too great to resist. I rarely stayed at Sabrina's house anymore, not with Caiden living there.

Blake's writings unfolded in detailed paragraphs, chronicling his days with an unsettling clarity. He delved into themes of shadows, isolation, and visions of death, painting vivid pictures of the taste of flesh on his tongue and the thrill he derived from slicing his knife through skin.

One entry struck particularly deep; it revealed how he had come to understand his father's twisted desires.

He expressed, in a sickening way, that he felt he had inherited his father's spirit after killing him, viewing that act as his eternal punishment for the slaughter of his parents.

He detailed the torment of his victims. Playing mind games, indulging in knife play, depriving them of sleep and food, pushing them to their breaking points.

He would grant them a fleeting glimmer of hope, only to extinguish it with their final moments, relishing the panic in their eyes as they faded into lifelessness.

I should stop reading, but I couldn't.

Sleep continued to elude me. I had writing deadlines to meet for the company I worked for, yet my work was slipping into disarray. Some days, I sat in the dark, my gaze tracing the shadows, fearing they would consume me. I felt myself sinking deeper into the abyss, helpless to pull back as memories of the cage engulfed me.

On those nights, I yearned for Caiden. I needed him to save me, to hold me, to protect me. But then, the memory of cradling my dead sister would crash over me, dragging the weight of rage back into my chest.

A deep shame washed over me as I recalled my kiss with Caiden, the very act that felt like a betrayal of Lillian's memory.

I was terrible. He was terrible. We were both terrible.

A battlefield raged within my mind, and I felt utterly powerless against its fury.

Amidst my secluded turmoil, a knock reverberated through the air. My body tensed, realization dawning that someone was at the door.

Cautiously, I stood and made my way to the entrance. Peeking through the peephole, relief flooded me when I saw Sabrina's familiar face.

I opened the door, welcoming her inside.

"Amelia! Hey, how are you? I haven't seen you in a few days," she said, stepping through the threshold and enveloping me in a quick hug. I shrugged and sank onto the black couch.

"Not doing well." I didn't bother lying.

She settled beside me, her wide, sad gaze fixed on my face. I despised that expression, the one brimming with pity.

"I got worried when you said you weren't coming by at night. Did something happen?"

"I just don't want to be a burden, that's all." How could I explain that my reluctance stemmed from Caiden? He was Shane's stepbrother; he deserved to occupy that space more than I did.

"Honey, you are not a burden. We enjoy having you around and knowing that you are safe." Her voice was warm and genuine.

"Am I safe, though? I don't feel safe. Not when I sleep, not when I'm awake. I still feel the terror that haunted me in the wilderness."

"I'm sorry. I know healing will be a long process. Why don't you share your feelings with Caiden? He went through it too; it could be beneficial for both of you to bond over it and find solace together."

Her suggestions were logical, and it would work if we had a normal relationship.

"No. There's too much history with Caiden." My voice dripped with bitterness.

She furrowed her brows, confusion clouding her features. "History? What do you mean? Being lost together? I know he's been concerned about you. He asked about you the other day and wanted to know if you were okay."

That revelation ignited my temper. "No! I'm not okay. He and I kissed. I kissed my childhood enemy. At this point, I'm not even sure what we are. We endured so much together out there, and it changed how we felt. But now that we're back, it feels like we've reverted to where we began."

Sabrina's hand flew to her mouth in surprise. "You and Caiden knew each other? From years ago? Why didn't you say anything? And when did you kiss?" Her shocked tone shifted to excitement as she asked her last question.

I let out a strangled groan, burying my face in my hands. "Yes. We practically hated each other. He bullied me, and I loathed him for it. All because my drug-addicted mother had an affair with his dad, which led to his mom abandoning them and leaving Caiden with his abusive, alcoholic father. Both our lives spiraled downward after that."

I glanced up at her silent expression. "I didn't mention it because I didn't want to ruin the trip."

"And the kiss?" She inquired.

"It happened in the guest bedroom after I had a nightmare. I flipped out and told him to leave."

"Oh, sweetie... I don't claim to know every twisted knot of your past, and honestly, it doesn't change how I feel about you. But I do know Caiden cares; he's practically unraveling over something, and I have a hunch it ties back to that kiss you two shared. You owe it to both of you to talk it out."

I felt the familiar flutter of panic in my chest, my inner child screaming to run, to hide.

But my grown-up self—the one who'd learned that pain doesn't heal itself—nudged me forward. I couldn't outrun this forever.

A cold shiver raced down my spine as I eased open the mental door I'd bolted shut for so long. Light spilled through the crack, warm and golden, illuminating a future where laughter echoed in sunlit rooms, where Caiden's hand fit perfectly in mine.

My chest tightened at the sight of it, how soft the promise looked. Did I deserve a future so gentle? Did I dare risk another heartbreak?

Every instinct warned me: Caiden Baxter was forbidden territory. And yet, there were nights when I closed my eyes and pictured his arms around me, safe and steady.

I remembered him once—before anger and revenge warped our paths—innocent, kind. What might have grown between us had we never become enemies? Childhood allies who blossomed into something more?

A tender, aching thought whispered that maybe, in another life, we were already blissfully in love.

"I'll talk to him," I finally whispered, my voice trembling like a candle in the breeze. "But not yet. Every time I see him, I'm dragged back to that cage, to the pain."

Sabrina reached across the couch and brushed a hand over my shoulder. "Avoiding it won't make it hurt any less. Sometimes you have to stare pain in the face to break its power."

I rolled my eyes, though her words stung with truth. "Ugh. Must you always be so wise?"

She laughed softly, a warm bell in the dim living room. "That's what best friends do. I can't let you bury yourself in misery."

I hated that she was right.

"Is that all you came here for?" I asked, trying to shift the mood.

Her eyes danced with excitement. "Actually... Shane and I decided to move the wedding up. With everything going on, we all need a little sparkle in our lives. We're tying the knot in two weeks. I'm hoping, you'll still be my maid of honor?"

A genuine smile blossomed across my face, lighting me from the inside out. She deserved every ounce of happiness her heart could hold—and more.

"That's wonderful, Sabrina. I wouldn't miss it for the world."

She squealed, hugging me so fiercely my ribs ached. "Yay! It's going to be magical, I promise."

"I'll hold you to that," I teased, nestling into her embrace.

We lingered a while longer, sipping tea and laughing softly as the evening shadows stretched.

She reminded me—again—to call Caiden, and I gave her my solemn vow.

Yet the instant her front door clicked shut behind her, doubt crept in like a chill through the cracks. I curled up beneath the blankets, the ghost of uncertainty whispering over my skin as I stared at the ceiling, lost in the cold hush of my own doubts.

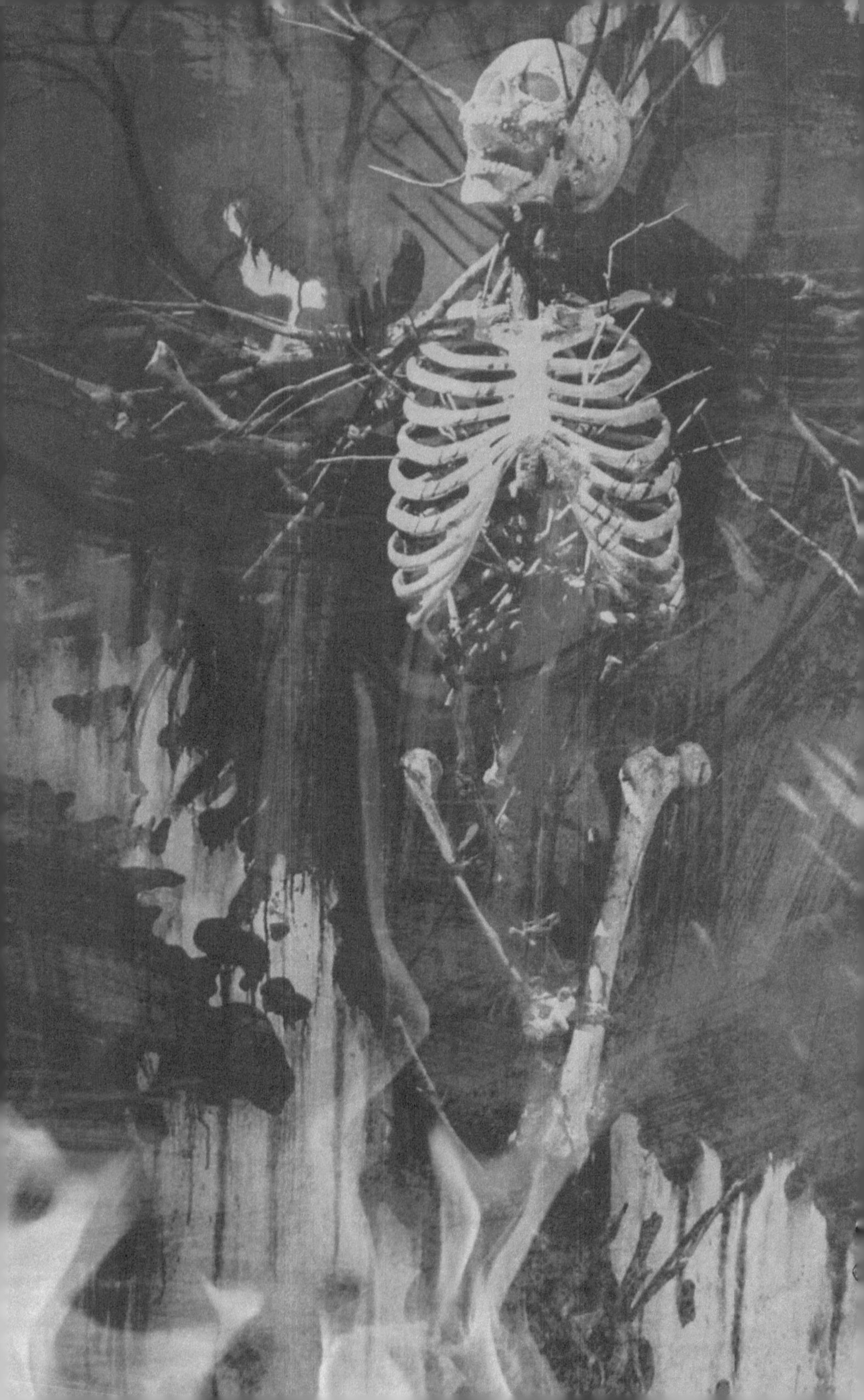

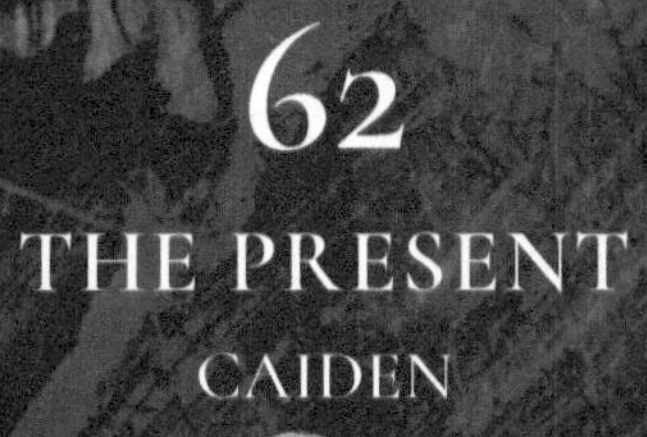

# 62

## THE PRESENT

### CAIDEN

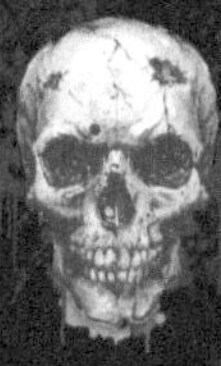


belong to me.

Shane called it "making space." A home. A fresh start. He said it like the words weren't knives.

I lay on the pullout couch and stared at the underside of the stairs. The wood slats looked like ribs. Like a cage. Like the cabin, if you stripped the horror down to its bones and painted it suburban beige.

I kept hearing the knife.

Not the real one. The one I used that went in and didn't come out clean. The one that changed the weight of my hands forever.

I thought I would feel more human once we got out. Instead, all I felt was more.

Emptier, sure. But the emptiness just made room for the hunger. It was a different kind of craving now. Raw and clawing. It made my hands shake, made my chest ache. Made everything about her a goddamn trigger.

Her shadow through frosted glass, the tiny indents her shoes left by the entryway, the shampoo she used, still clinging to the guest towels.

If I concentrated, I could hear her up there right now. I could always pick out her voice. Even if she only whispered, I would hear it. I was wired that way. Ruined that way.

Sabrina was working her usual campaign. "Please, Amelia, just stay for dinner. I already made too much—"

A soft reply, almost impossible to catch. But I caught it: "I don't want to be a bother. I really should—"

"Come on. Shane will be so disappointed if you bail. He said he's making his specialty."

A pause. The silence means she's thinking about it. Means she'll stay.

My jaw locked so tight it hurt.

I didn't want to go up there. Not really. Not when I'd barely figured out how to be human around her again. Not after everything she saw. The way I broke in Colorado, the way I lost control. Not after what I did to her the night we got back. The hunger I let loose, the way I tore at her in Shane and Sabrina's guest bedroom, like if I devoured her mouth, maybe I could erase the hell from both our bones.

She let me in. Gave herself up for a second, wild and desperate. I was drunk on her then. But when it was over, when she looked at me with those too-wide eyes, she seemed so fragile. So terrified of what I'd done to her, or maybe terrified of herself for wanting it.

I hadn't touched her since. Because I didn't want to break her again. Because I was afraid of myself, of what I'd do if I let myself have her.

Except I wanted to. Every fucked up, mangled bit of me wanted to. I fantasized about it. About putting my hands around her throat and kissing her until she couldn't breathe, about pinning her to the wall and swallowing her cries. About what it would be like if she didn't push me away.

I could have stayed down here, I told myself. I could have stayed safe, in the dark, unmoving. I didn't need the heat of her, the way her voice stung every nerve. But that was a fucking lie. I was weak. I was an addict, and she was the poison.

The stairs creaked under my feet. My hands shook as I opened the basement door.

Light burned my eyes, too sudden, too bright. I blinked, caught the blurred shapes.

Shane at the stove, Sabrina plating something up, and Amelia standing there, twisting her hands. Her hair was down. She looked like she was ready to bolt, her body turned toward the exit even as she nodded along with Sabrina's chatter.

I hovered at the edge of the kitchen like a ghost. She didn't see me at first.

"You made it," Shane said, a forced brightness in his voice.

I grunted. My eyes caught on Amelia. I didn't want to look at her, but I couldn't stop.

She didn't look at me at all.

I wondered if she was replaying that night, the same as I did.

Maybe I was wrong. Maybe she didn't even think about it. Maybe I was the only one haunted.

But the ache in my chest said she did. Said she burned for it just as much as I did, and hated herself for it.

I stood at the edge of the room, not moving, not breathing, waiting to see if she'd meet my eye. She didn't.

She always did that when she felt exposed.

God, I craved her. Even when I hated her, I wanted her. Especially then. That was the curse. Hatred and desire, always tangled together, always pulling me back to her.

My hands curled into fists. I forced my voice steady. "What's for dinner?"

Sabrina looked over, startled to see me out of my hole. "Oh! Pasta. Shane's recipe."

Amelia gave a small shudder, so slight I almost missed it.

She hadn't expected to see me. That was good. It would keep her on edge. Maybe if she were on edge, she'd stop haunting me.

But even now, with the whole room between us, she took up too much space. I could feel her. Smell her. Want her.

I would keep my distance, I promised myself. Act like I didn't care. Like I hadn't memorized every inch of her skin, every sound she made when she broke.

But I was a liar. I'd always been a liar.

I followed the others into the dining room, every muscle tense, feeling like a wolf among sheep. If I so much as touched her, I knew I'd never stop.

So I wouldn't.

I would sit there, and I would pretend.

But if she met my eye, if she reached for me, if she so much as whispered my name—

God help us both.

Dinner was nothing. Just an act. Four strangers playing house, pretending there's no history bleeding through the cracks in the drywall.

Shane set down plates with that practiced ease, eyes bright with some breed of optimism I'd never understand. Sabrina hovered behind him, a nervous hurricane of words and movement. You could hear her energy in the way she set the forks.

Amelia sat across from me.

Not beside me. Across. As far away as the table would allow, tucked small between her hair and the shadows, like she could disappear if she tried hard enough.

But she couldn't. Not from me.

Shane poured the wine. "Look, I know it's not five-star, but I think you'll be impressed. Maybe even convert you, Sabrina."

She grinned. "Anything's better than my cooking." A pointed look at Amelia. "Except for your lasagna. Still dreaming about it."

A nothing laugh from Amelia. Fragile, like glass about to crack. "Not a high bar. I lived mostly on cereal and instant ramen for years."

My jaw flexed. My eyes flicked to her hands, small and quick, twirling pasta in practiced motions. I remembered those hands. Fisted in my shirt, clawing at my neck, trembling when I kissed her. She was doing it again. Hiding the tremor. She always tried so fucking hard not to be seen.

I wanted to see her. I wanted to see every raw nerve.

Sabrina beamed. "You should cook for us next time, then."

Her head snapped up too fast, startled. "Maybe," she mumbled. "If you're brave."

Shane shot me a knowing look. "You could use some tips from Amelia, right, Caiden?"

Every word hit like gravel in my throat. I shrugged. "Doubt she wants my help."

A twitch in her lips. Not quite a smile, not quite a snarl.

Sabrina was relentless. "You're practically family now. It'd be nice. Healing, you know?"

I wanted to laugh. I wanted to scream. Nothing about this was healing.

I shoved food into my mouth, chewing hard enough to feel my teeth grind.

Sometimes I caught her looking at me. Just a flick. Just the smallest glance, like she couldn't help herself. Like she remembered how I kissed her in that room, dragging her down with me, drowning her in the heat and the hunger. I could feel it in the way she held every muscle tight, waiting for me to snap.

She was scared. Of me, or of herself, or both.

I could have told her I was scared, too. But I'd never say that out loud.

Shane and Sabrina kept up the chatter, trading war stories about open houses and work and shit that didn't matter. Sabrina's voice got sharp whenever she asked Amelia about her writing. Like she wanted to pull her closer, make her feel welcome. Amelia answered with half-sentences. Never offering more than she had to.

I envied that. The ability to be quiet, to hide. I'd spent my whole life being too fucking loud.

I pushed away from the table when I was done. Couldn't take another second.

The others followed, drifting toward the living room. Some movie was queued up already, light from the TV flickering across the couch.

Amelia hesitated in the doorway, one hand braced against the frame. She looked up, caught me staring. For a second, the whole fucking world froze.

Then she looked away.

I took my place on the couch, putting just enough distance between us so it wouldn't look obvious. But I could feel her. Feel the gravity of her, the ache in my bones.

Shane gave a whistle. "Movie time. Everyone ready?"

Sabrina snuggled in beside him, her laughter too bright. "Don't fall asleep, boys."

I could have laughed at that. But all my humor was gone.

Amelia sat next to me, her whole body tense. She wouldn't let herself relax. Wouldn't dare touch me.

I wanted her to.

But I didn't move.

I just let the ache build, let it rip me open from the inside. I deserved it.

The credits started rolling. The lights went low.

I wondered if she would ever forgive me.

But more than that, I wondered what it would take for me to forgive myself.

The movie was boring. I couldn't even tell you the plot, the names of the actors. Every cell in my body was tuned to how close she sat, the heat radiating off her legs, the slow, inevitable way her thigh drifted until it was pressed flush against mine. I pretended not to notice, but I noticed everything.

She didn't move away. She never did, not when it mattered.

At first, I kept a safe inch between us. As the movie sagged on, she leaned in, maybe by accident, maybe on purpose. I tracked the hitch in her breath when our knees brushed. I tested it, subtle, shifting just enough that her weight shifted too. Electric. I was starving.

Her hair smelled like wind and water.

I wanted to drag her onto my lap and devour her. I wanted to pin her wrists and ask her if she hated me or if she just needed a reason to give in. But I sat stone-still, jaw grinding, fists jammed between my thighs so I didn't reach for her.

On TV, a couple kissed in the rain. Laughter, wet faces, and desperate hands. I barely saw them.

Shane started nodding off, slumped at the end of the couch, and Sabrina yawned theatrically. "We're grabbing ice cream. You two want any?"

I shook my head. Amelia didn't answer.

They were gone. Just like that. We were alone. The silence was total. My blood roared in my ears.

She spoke without looking at me. "Why do you do that?"

I blinked. "Do what?"

She laughed, but it wasn't funny. "One second you act like I'm not here, the next—"

A flash in her eyes. "The next you're...right here. Like you'd kill anyone who even looked at me wrong. Then you pull away. Like you want to punish me for something. Why?"

I breathed through my teeth, scared my hands would shake. "You're imagining things."

She turned, biting hard on her bottom lip, searching my face. "You kissed me. That night. Then you disappeared."

I closed my eyes. "You shoved me off."

"I—" She caught herself, a tremor in her voice. "I didn't want to. I was scared."

I was quiet for a long time. Then: "Scared of me?"

"No." A rush of air, like she couldn't believe I'd even ask. "Not of you. Of what I wanted. Of how it felt."

I shifted, fingers digging into my thighs. "Sure didn't seem like you liked it."

She laughed, a broken sound. "I liked it. That's the problem. I didn't want it to stop."

I couldn't take it. I turned toward her, so close now I could taste the heat coming off her skin. I reached up, thumb grazing her jaw, just to see if she'd flinch.

She didn't.

She tilted her face up, eyes on my mouth. "Why are you like this?" she whispered.

"I don't know." My voice was shredded. "You fuck me up."

Her hand found my wrist, squeezing just enough to ground me. "I hate it."

"I do too."

She licked her lips. "So...what, then? Just keep pretending?"

"If we didn't pretend, I'd probably ruin you."

Her laugh was like breaking glass. "Too late."

I leaned in, helpless, aiming for her mouth. But footsteps pounded down the hall and I jerked back, pulse wild, hands falling to my lap like I'd been caught stealing.

She scooted away. Gone.

Sabrina bustled in with bowls, giving us a look. "Everything okay?"

"Yeah," Amelia said, voice paper-thin.

She stood, stiff and deliberate, and thanked them for dinner. At the door, she didn't look back.

I sat on the couch, insides scraping raw, watching her silhouette vanish in the porch light. I let the fire in my chest burn, contained, furious, starving.

I didn't follow. But I wanted to.

Fuck, I wanted to.

It wasn't normal anymore, not for me. All I could think was how close I'd been to losing control, not in violence, but in wanting.

That was the most dangerous kind of losing control.

Possessive thoughts kept licking up inside my skull like fire.

*If anyone else touched her like I did, I'd break something.*

I hated myself for it.

I hated my father for building this in me. Rage as love. Control as safety. Possession as proof. I hated Amelia for making me want what I didn't deserve. And I hated myself most of all because the hate didn't erase the truth.

It only fed it.

Wanting her wasn't a sweet feeling. It was a slow, consuming violence, and I was losing the fight to keep it caged.

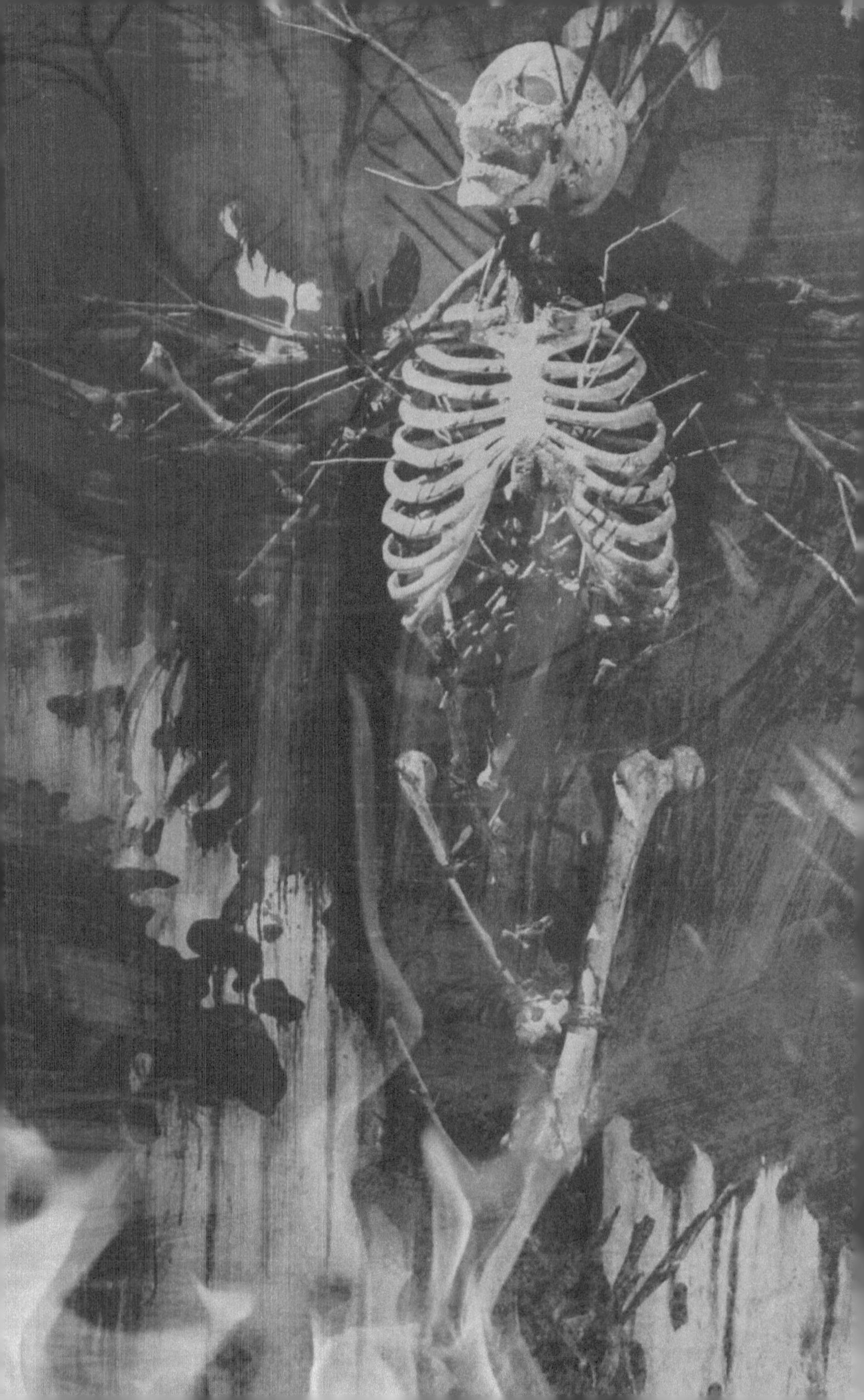

# 63

## THE PRESENT

### AMELIA

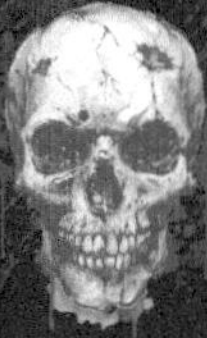

TODAY WAS THE DAY OF THE WEDDING, AND INSTEAD OF joy, my heart ached.

I stared at myself in the full-length mirror. The blue dress hugged my curves, ending at the knees and revealing smooth, tanned skin.

My dark brown hair was curled and neatly arranged around my head, framing my face perfectly. The scar on my flesh, a reminder of past struggles, was now concealed under layers of makeup.

With my porcelain skin and bright eyes, I appeared like a delicate, flawless doll.

But if anyone could glimpse the turmoil within, the deafening roar of my inner struggles and the bitter sting of unshed tears, they would see my carefully constructed composure begin to crumble, revealing my true, vulnerable self.

I refused to wallow any longer. With a practiced smile, I walked out the front door, steeling myself for the day ahead.

The drive to the estate lasted around an hour and a half. I arrived early to help prepare Sabrina and found her in the wedding suite, radiant and glowing with excitement.

"Amelia! You made it!" she exclaimed, her voice a melody of happiness.

I settled down next to her, smoothing the fabric of my dress. "Of course! I wouldn't miss your wedding. This place is beautiful, by the way."

Sabrina beamed, her enthusiasm infectious. "Right? We're getting married in the gardens, and then we'll have the reception by the lake."

"How many people will be here?" I asked, my curiosity piqued.

She waved her hand dismissively, as if my anxiety were trivial. "Oh, don't worry. Not many. Just a few friends, my parents, Shane's parents, and some other family members."

I nodded along, but my eyes widened when realization hit me. "Wait. Shane's mom will be here? She's Caiden's mom too. Has he even seen her since she left?"

Sabrina shrugged, her expression thoughtful. "Shane hasn't told me much about that. But I assume he hasn't seen her since he was a kid. It's got to be a bit weird for him."

"Weird? Caiden's going to freak out. Her abandonment left a huge scar on him and his dad. It set off a chain reaction of events." My words tumbled out, fueled by the anxiety building within me.

The thought of Caiden confronting his mother sent shivers down my spine.

Sabrina placed a calming hand on my arm. "Amelia, it'll be okay. Caiden knows she's coming. He said he's ready to face her."

Caiden actually willing to confront something? That notion seemed bizarre to me. Perhaps he had changed.

"Okay, if you say so."

A part of me remained unconvinced, unsettled by the uncertainty that loomed ahead. But perhaps this was needed. Caiden needed to face his past to move forward.

Time passed swiftly, and before long, it was time for the wedding.

"Good luck," I told Sabrina, stepping away to find my place at the altar.

"Luck is on my side today," she replied, her smile endearing.

I walked through the winding hall, the old wood creaking beneath my feet, and stepped outside into a picturesque scene bathed in the golden light of the setting sun. The warmth of the sun kissed my skin, while the melodic symphony of birds filled the air, a joyful chorus that contrasted sharply with my inner turmoil.

The stunning gardens showcased vibrant rows of flowers, their perfume fluttered in the air, interspersed with enchanting statues. Everyone was seated, and the ceremony was beginning.

I waited patiently for my turn to walk down the pathway to the altar, where I would stand next to Sabrina.

As I stood there, I felt a pair of eyes on me. I turned to see Caiden. His gaze was intense, a mixture of apprehension and something else. Hope?

A hesitant smile graced his lips, a departure from the guarded demeanor I knew so well. The years melted away, leaving only the boy I had once known, vulnerable and searching.

My carefully constructed composure threatened to shatter.

The music swelled, signaling my cue. Taking a deep breath, I walked towards him, towards the altar, and towards the unknown.

As we walked side by side, his hand brushed against mine, sending a shiver down my spine from the unexpected contact.

Butterflies stirred in my stomach, their wings beating a frantic rhythm against my ribs. Was I scared, excited, or simply nervous?

The memory of our heated kiss pressed against me, yet I focused hard on placing one foot in front of the other.

Once at the altar, we took our designated sides, awaiting the bride and groom. Their parents sat in the front row, and I followed Caiden's gaze to where he was looking.

His mother.

I carefully observed his expression, which was a canvas of shifting emotions.

She caught his eye, and familiarity flickered across her face. A mother would always recognize her son.

I held my breath, praying Caiden wouldn't break.

As the music shifted, a sweet violin began its melody, the notes like honey in the air.

Shane stood at the front, near Caiden, who patted his back in a gesture of camaraderie.

Now it was Sabrina's turn. Sunlight glinted off the silver threads in her dress as she glided down the soft grass, her expression serene and almost ethereal.

"She looks like an angel," I heard Shane mutter, his gaze filled with awe.

My heart leapt as I stole a glance at Caiden; his gaze held an intensity that consumed my being.

Time seemed to stop as Sabrina reached the altar, her eyes

locking with her groom's. The scene unfolding was a silent testament to the bond about to be solidified.

Then the ceremony began, a blur of vows and promises, tears and laughter, a love story unfolding before us.

My own anxieties melted away, replaced by a quiet joy as I witnessed their happiness. The lingering scent of lilies and the warmth of the sun created an atmosphere of peace, a fitting backdrop for their love.

But it ended all too soon.

The wedding reception was a haze of speeches, each one filled with laughter and the clinking of glasses.

Caiden and I were coincidentally sat next to each other.

I stole a glance at him. His dark hair was tousled, and his brown eyes were sharper than I remembered, reflecting the flickering light of the chandeliers above. He seemed more at ease, yet a storm brewed beneath his calm facade.

"Enjoying the festivities?" he asked, his voice low and intimate, just for me.

I nodded, though my heartbeat betrayed me. "Yeah, it's beautiful. Everything is perfect." I cleared my throat, trying to mask the emotions swirling within. "You look nice and cleaned up."

His lips curved into a smirk, but the intensity in his gaze lingered. "You know, I never thought I'd see you in a dress like that," he chuckled softly, his tone playful yet edged with something deeper.

I felt the heat creep up my neck. "Well, I didn't think I'd be standing next to you at this wedding," I shot back, the words slipping out before I could stop them.

His laughter was genuine, a warm sound that spread through me. "Yeah, you would have thought we'd never get along after everything."

There was a flicker of something in his eyes, a shared memory of our shared struggles, and suddenly, the distance between us felt both electrifying and suffocating.

As the night wore on, the music shifted to something more upbeat, drawing couples to the dance floor.

I watched as Sabrina and Shane twirled, lost in their world. The joy radiating from them was infectious, and I couldn't help but smile.

But as I turned back to Caiden, my heart sank a little.

"Do you think they'll be happy?" I asked, the question escaping my lips before I could think it through.

"Who knows?" he replied, his voice somber. "It's hard to tell these days. Happiness is fleeting."

His words carried a weight, a reflection of his own scars, those from his mother's abandonment and the years of resentment that had shaped him.

I wanted to reach out to bridge the gap I felt between us, but the memories of our childhood hostility loomed large.

"Caiden," I began, hesitating. The truth was, I wanted to understand him, to strip back the layers that had been built over years of bitterness and hurt. "What will you do when you interact with her? Your mother?"

He stiffened slightly at the mention of her, his jaw tightening. "I don't know," he admitted, his voice low. "Maybe I'll just walk away. I've spent so many years trying to forget that she existed."

"You deserve to confront her," I said softly, my heart racing. "You deserve to have your say."

He turned to me, his eyes searching mine, and for a fleeting moment, I saw the boy who had once been my fiercest opponent. "And what if I don't want to?" he challenged, but there was no malice in his tone, only a vulnerability that made my breath hitch.

"Then don't," I whispered, a strange mix of fear and desire coursing through me. "But you can't keep running from it. Not forever."

Just then, the music changed to a slow ballad, and couples began to sway together. My heart thudded in my chest as Caiden looked at me.

"Dance with me," he said suddenly, the command more of a plea wrapped in bravado.

I hesitated, the past swirling around us like a storm, but something deep inside me yearned to break free.

I nodded, and he stood, extending his hand toward me. With a mixture of trepidation and exhilaration, I placed my palm in his.

As we stepped onto the dance floor, I felt the world fade away; the lights dimmed, and the crowd melted into a blur.

It was just us, standing on the cliff of something unknown.

His hand wrapped around my waist, pulling me closer, and I

could feel the warmth radiating from his body, igniting every nerve ending.

"You're nervous," he murmured, his breath hot against my ear, sending shivers down my spine.

"Maybe a little," I admitted, my voice barely above a whisper.

"Don't be," he replied, his tone softening as he pulled me tighter. "We're not enemies anymore, Amelia. Not after what we've been through."

I looked up into his eyes, searching for the truth in his words. The vulnerability reflected at me was intoxicating. "But what if—"

He cut me off, leaning closer, his lips barely brushing against my ear. "What if we just let go?"

And at that moment, I knew. I knew that this slow burn was about to ignite into something neither of us could control. The lingering kiss we had shared weeks ago had only been a taste of what was beneath the surface.

Then, he pulled back slightly, enough to search my eyes again, his expression a mixture of hope and fear, as if he were waiting for me to give him permission.

His dark hair framed his face, and those deep brown eyes, swirling with emotions, held me captive.

Just then, I felt a flutter of movement beside us.

A tall figure with tousled light brown hair and bright blue eyes approached, flashing a charming smile.

It was Alex, one of Shane's friends, and from the way he looked at me, I could tell he was intrigued.

"Hey, Amelia!" he called out, his voice warm and inviting. "You look stunning tonight."

"Thanks, Alex," I replied, trying to ignore the way Caiden's posture stiffened beside me. "You look good too."

"Care for a dance?" he asked, extending a hand toward me.

I hesitated, glancing at Caiden, who was suddenly very tense, his jaw clenched as he watched Alex like a hawk.

"Uh, I—"

But before I could finish my thought, Caiden stepped forward, a low, protective growl in his voice. "Sorry, but I think she's busy."

Alex raised an eyebrow, surprised by the sudden possessiveness oozing from Caiden. "Just one dance, man. It's just a friendly offer."

"Yeah, well, she's not interested," Caiden shot back, his eyes narrowing, and the tension in the air shifted, thickening like fog.

"Actually...," I started, feeling caught in the middle. The intensity between me and Caiden was so thick that I could barely breathe.

I needed to escape.

"I'll dance with you."

Leaving a bristling Caiden, I stepped away towards Alex, who continued to grin, shooting Caiden one last glance as if to gloat.

He took my hand and led me to the dance floor, spinning me into a carefree twirl that made me laugh. For a moment, I lost myself in the rhythm, the vibrant energy of the celebration washing over me.

But even as I danced, I could feel Caiden's eyes boring into my back. A glance over my shoulder confirmed it: he was watching us, his expression darkening with every passing second.

My heart raced.

"Is everything okay?" Alex asked, pulling me closer as we swayed to the beat.

"Yeah, of course," I replied, forcing a smile. But my thoughts were elsewhere.

I watched as Caiden shifted uncomfortably on the sidelines, his hands clenched into fists at his sides, his jaw set tight.

It was clear he didn't like the sight of me dancing with Alex.

"Come on, let loose a little!" Alex encouraged, his laughter bright and carefree.

I tried to enjoy the moment, but the tension wrapped around me like a cloak.

I glanced back at Caiden, and my heart sank. He had turned away, storming off in the opposite direction.

"Where's he going?" Alex asked, following my gaze.

"I don't know," I admitted, unease settling in my stomach.

And then I saw it. Caiden, approaching his mother, who stood awkwardly at the edge of the reception, her face a blend of apprehension and longing.

"Caiden, no," I whispered under my breath, but it was too late.

He stormed up to her, his voice rising above the crowd. "What the hell are you doing here?" he shouted, the raw fury spilling out, a dam breaking under the pressure of years of pent-up resentment.

Her eyes widened in shock, and I felt a pang of sympathy for her. "Caiden, please, I—"

"Don't 'please' me!" he exploded. "You think you can just show up after all this time? You left us! You left me!"

The guests around us began to turn their heads, whispers rippling through the crowd like a wave. I could see Shane's face twist in concern, knowing all too well the weight of Caiden's history with his mom.

"Caiden, I'm sorry," his mother pleaded, her voice trembling. "I wanted to explain—"

"Explain what? That you abandoned me for another family? That you didn't even care enough to check on me?" He stepped closer, his voice menacing. "Do you have any idea what that did to me? To my father? Do you know how much torture I endured? I was a fucking kid! I was a kid who needed his mom, but I was left alone with a monster."

I felt my heart race, torn between intervening and letting him unleash this storm.

"Caiden, please," she said, her voice breaking as tears welled up in her eyes.

He shook his head, his face a mask of rage and hurt. "You don't get to apologize now. You lost the right to that a long time ago."

The crowd shifted uneasily, whispers growing louder, but Caiden didn't seem to care. He was in a world of his own, consumed by the confrontation.

"I've spent my whole life wondering why I wasn't good enough for you," he continued, his voice rising. "Wondering what was wrong with me. You think showing up here changes anything? You think I want to hear your excuses?"

"Caiden!" I called out, unable to stay silent any longer. I stepped away from Alex, my instincts pulling me toward him, but he didn't look back.

"Just stay out of this, Amelia!" he snapped, his eyes blazing with fury.

"Caiden, please! Just come walk with me," I pleaded, but my voice was drowned out by the murmurs of the crowd.

"Do you have any idea what it's like to feel abandoned?" he continued, his gaze fixed on his mother. "You think you can waltz back into my life like nothing happened?"

His mother's face fell; anguish etched across her features. "I didn't mean to hurt you. I was young and scared. I thought I was doing what was best."

"Best for whom?" he shot back, his voice like ice. "Best for you? Because it sure as hell wasn't for me or my dad."

I stepped closer, wanting to reach out, to pull him back from the edge. "Caiden, come on. Let's just talk—"

But he cut me off again, his anger spilling over. "I don't want to talk, Amelia! Not now! Fuck off."

My heart sank, the distance between us growing impossibly wide. I wanted to help him, to ease his pain, but I felt powerless as I watched him confront his mother.

"Caiden, please," she pleaded one last time, her voice breaking as tears streamed down her cheeks.

"I'm done," he declared, his voice shaking with emotion. "I'm done with you, with this. You made your choice a long time ago."

And with that, he turned on his heel, storming away from her, his fists clenched at his sides.

It broke my heart to watch him unravel like this.

"Caiden!" I called again, desperation clawing at my throat. But he didn't stop. He walked away from it all, from his mother, from the reception, from me.

"Amelia, you okay?" Alex asked, concern evident in his voice as he stepped closer to me.

I shook my head, my heart aching. "No, I'm not okay."

"Maybe I should go after him," I said, taking a step forward, but Alex gently caught my arm.

"Let him cool off. He needs to process this."

But I could feel the tug of my heart, the urge to reach out to him, to remind him that he wasn't alone. "I can't just leave him like this," I insisted, my voice trembling.

"Amelia," Alex said softly, "you can't fix everything. Sometimes, you need to let people handle their pain in their own way."

I nodded, but the worry in my chest wouldn't dissipate.

As the music played on and the guests resumed their conversations, I felt the heaviness of what had just transpired settle around me.

And as I stood there, surrounded by laughter and celebration, a single tear escaped, tracing a path down my cheek, mirroring the silent storm raging within me.

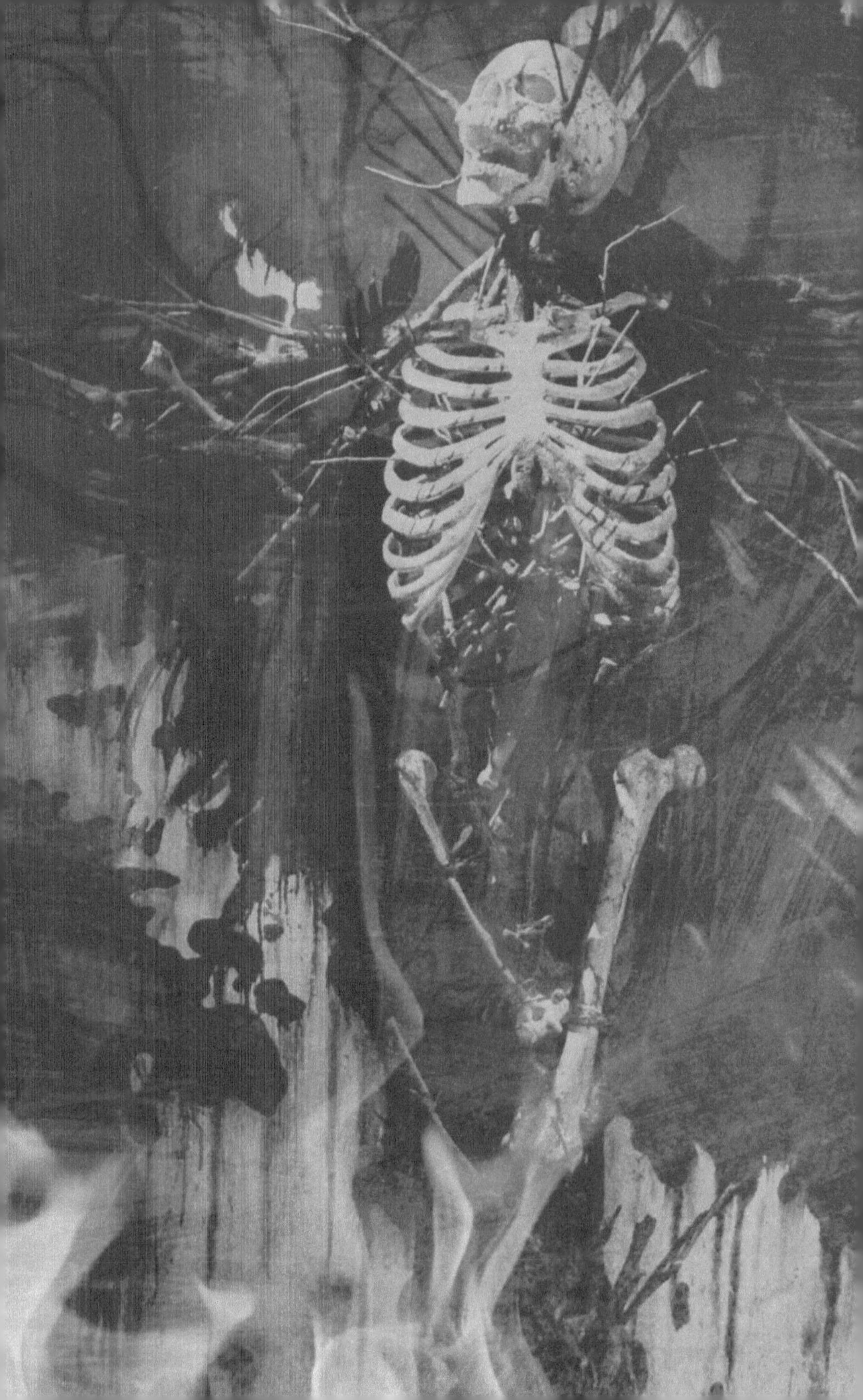

# 64

## THE PRESENT

### AMELIA

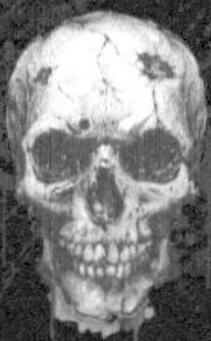

A week had passed since Shane and Sabrina's wedding, and the chaos of that day still echoed in my mind like a distant storm rumbling on the horizon.

Even in this new place, I couldn't escape the turmoil that lingered between me and Caiden. It caught up to me ever since I discovered that Caiden is Shane's half-brother, and I felt as if I were a teenager again.

After the wedding, Caiden had shut himself off from me, retreating into the temporary home he shared with Shane and Sabrina.

I had tried reaching out, but my texts and calls had gone unanswered, leaving me feeling more helpless than I ever had before.

The silence was a dreadful thing, a suffocating blanket woven from festering resentment. Each day felt heavier than the last, the vibrant joy of the wedding now a faded photograph, its colors bleached by the encroaching grey of our unresolved conflict.

I found myself drawn to the old pier, its weathered wood a comforting contrast to the turmoil within me.

The rhythmic crash of waves against the pilings was a hypnotic counterpoint to the beat of my heart, a constant reminder that even amidst the storm, the lake continued its relentless rhythm.

Perhaps, I thought while watching the gulls wheel overhead, it was time to let go of the rope, to allow the tide to carry away the debris of the past, even if it meant facing the tempest alone.

The wind whipped through my hair, mirroring the chaotic thoughts swirling within.

Letting go wouldn't be easy; the connection to Caiden, despite its tumultuous nature, was a lifeline, however frayed. But clinging to it, to the hope of reconciliation, felt like clinging to a sinking ship.

The pier, stretching out into the grey expanse, seemed to offer a path, a solitary journey towards calmer waters.

Tonight, I would write him a letter. Not an apology, not a plea, but a simple explanation, an acknowledgment of the storm we were both weathering.

Perhaps, just perhaps, in the quiet space between the words, a fragile bridge could begin to form.

As the sun dipped lower, casting an orange glow across the water, I pulled my notebook and a pen out of my satchel.

The faint sound of laughter drifted from the distance, reminding me of the warmth of community I had found here, yet it felt distant and unreachable.

Words poured out of me as I wrote, filling the page with my thoughts. The scratching of my pen was the only sound.

I was finishing the last paragraph when my phone buzzed against the slats of the bench.

Sabrina's name lit up the screen, the display a sudden flare in the evening dusk. I almost didn't answer. I didn't trust my voice not to crack, didn't trust my composure not to unravel with a single, well-meaning question.

But I thumbed the green circle anyway, bracing for the inevitable concern.

"Hey," I said, aiming for breezy but landing closer to bitter.

"Amelia! I'm so glad you picked up. I was about to call in a search party," Sabrina chirped.

In the background, I could hear Shane's muffled voice and the clatter of kitchenware, the auditory fingerprints of domestic bliss.

"Are you free tonight?"

"I wasn't planning on doing anything," I said, which was true as far as it went. "Why?"

"Dinner at ours. It's nothing fancy, but I don't want to be the only girl there. Please? I'll die of boredom if I have to listen to them talk football and lawn fertilizer all night."

A spasm of panic gripped my chest.

"I don't think I'd be much fun tonight," I said.

"Which is exactly why you should come," Sabrina said lightly. "Don't make me drag you here myself."

"I'll think about it," I said, and to my own surprise, I meant it. "Who's coming, exactly?"

Sabrina hesitated just half a beat, but I caught it anyway. "Shane's friends. And, uh, Caiden will be here. But don't worry, I already warned him to behave."

My throat closed in reflex. I waited for the familiar ache to break me open, but instead, I felt a kind of numb clarity.

The idea of seeing him made my skin itch and my pulse stutter, but there was no part of my heart left that wasn't already bruised.

"Alright. I'll come. But I'm warning you, if anyone brings up fantasy football, I'm leaving."

"You're an angel! See you at seven," Sabrina said, already moving on, her voice curling with warmth. She hung up before I could change my mind.

I let the phone drop into my lap and watched the gulls spiral over the water, arabesques of hunger and perseverance.

I told myself I was stronger than this, that if I could survive the cage and the wilderness and the endless return to daylight, I could survive one meal with Caiden.

I drove back to my small home and changed into something nice but casual. A violet-hued cotton blouse and jeans.

Tonight would be the first time I'd see Caiden since the wedding, and I wasn't sure what to expect. Would he be angry? Would he still be closed off?

The uncertainty gnawed at me, but I forced myself to remember that this was an opportunity to bridge the distance that had grown between us.

When I arrived at Shane and Sabrina's house, the familiar scent of grilled chicken and roasted vegetables wafted through the air, mingling with the sound of laughter that spilled from the open patio doors.

My heart raced as I stepped inside, the warmth of the home enveloping me like a comforting blanket.

"Amelia!" Sabrina called, her face lighting up as she spotted me. "You made it!"

"Wouldn't miss it," I replied, trying to sound upbeat despite the butterflies in my stomach.

"Dinner's almost ready. Caiden is in the backyard, helping with the grill," she added, her eyes sparkling with excitement.

I nodded, my heart pounding as I made my way to the back patio.

As I stepped outside, I spotted Caiden standing near the grill, his back toward me. He looked different. More rugged, perhaps, with a tension in his posture that had me worried.

"Hey, Caiden," I said, my voice tentative as I approached.

He turned, and the moment our eyes met, I felt a jolt of electricity. There was an intensity in his gaze that sent my heart racing, but it was clouded by something darker. Anger, frustration, and unresolved pain.

"Hey," he replied, his tone curt, as if he were bracing himself for a confrontation.

"Dinner smells great," I said, trying to keep the mood light.

"Yeah, well, Shane's the one who's cooking," he said, returning his focus to the grill.

I felt a twinge of disappointment at his dismissal, but I pressed on. "I'm glad to see you. I've been worried about you."

He stiffened, turning slightly away from me. "You shouldn't be. I'm fine."

"Caiden—" I started, but he cut me off, a flash of anger igniting in his eyes.

"Why do you keep trying to save me? I don't need saving," he snapped, his voice rising slightly.

The bite in his words stung, and I took a step back, my stomach churning. "I'm not trying to save you. I just want to be here for you, to help you."

"Help me?" he echoed, disbelief etched across his features. "You don't even know what you're getting into."

"Then let me in," I pleaded, my heart racing. "I can't just stand back and watch you push everyone away, not after what we went through."

"Maybe it's better this way," he said, his voice dropping to a near whisper, but the hurt in his eyes betrayed the bravado.

I sighed, then pulled the letter out of my pocket. "I want you to read this."

He hesitated, his eyes flickering from the letter to my face. "What is it?"

"Just read it. Please. It's just some things I needed to be honest with you about. So much has changed since Colorado."

I kept the letter in my hand, extended towards Caiden.

With a resigned sigh, he took the letter, his fingers brushing against mine.

The contact sent a jolt through me, a reminder of the connection we shared. But just as quickly, he pulled back, his expression guarded.

Just then, Shane and Sabrina stepped outside, breaking the tension. "Dinner's ready!" Shane called with a bright smile on his face.

As we gathered around the table, I could feel Caiden's anger simmering beneath the surface. He sat across from me, his brow furrowed.

As we ate, the conversation flowed around us, but I found it difficult to focus.

My gaze kept drifting to Caiden, who seemed lost in his thoughts, a storm brewing behind his dark eyes.

I was desperate to reach him, to break through the walls he had built, but each time I opened my mouth, the words felt stuck in my throat.

It wasn't until Alex arrived that the tension shifted. He came bounding in with his usual charm, his smile brightening the room. "Hey, everyone!" he exclaimed, his gaze landing on me. "Amelia! You look fantastic!"

"Thanks, Alex," I said, trying to keep my tone light, but I could feel Caiden tense at the compliment.

"Are you ready for some fun?" Alex asked, clearly in high spirits. "I brought a game for us to play after dinner. It's going to be epic."

"Sounds great!" Sabrina replied, her enthusiasm infectious.

As the evening wore on, I couldn't help but notice Caiden's eyes narrowing each time Alex flirted with me.

It was a subtle thing. Just a glance, a slight tightening of his jaw. But it spoke volumes, igniting a possessiveness.

At one point, Alex leaned in closer to me, his voice lowered as he joked about something that happened at work. A bright, carefree laugh escaped my lips, yet Caiden's burning stare pierced me.

"Amelia, you should definitely join us for a hike this weekend," Alex suggested, his eyes sparkling with excitement. "It'll be a blast!"

"Yeah, maybe," I replied, stealing a glance at Caiden, who was now visibly irritated.

"Right, because that's exactly what she needs, more outdoor adventures," Caiden said, his tone dripping with sarcasm.

I felt the shift in the air, and the laughter around the table faded, replaced by an awkward silence. "What's that supposed to mean?" I asked, my voice was steady, though my heart raced.

"Nothing," he replied, his jaw clenched. "Just that some people aren't cut out for—"

"Cut out for what?" I shot back, my frustration bubbling over. "For living life? For having fun?"

"Amelia," Sabrina interjected, sensing the tension rising. "Why don't we all just enjoy dinner?"

After dinner, as we moved to the living room for games, I took a deep breath, my heart pounding.

I couldn't bear the tension another second. I feigned interest in the game that Alex had brought. A sickly-sweet party charade that required far more social lubrication than any of us possessed. While my eyes kept drifting to Caiden, who brooded in the corner, jaw ticking, eyes flat and dangerous.

A knife in a drawer, waiting for a hand to draw it.

The game itself was a fever dream of laughter and humiliation; I watched Shane perform a ludicrous pantomime of "pterodactyl mating season, and Sabrina dissolved into gleeful peals at his dinosaur squawks.

I laughed too, but it was a mechanical sound, the kind my mother used to make in the good years, before her pills stripped the brightness from her throat.

Alex dominated the room, his energy relentless, his confidence engineered to absorb every photon of attention.

His hands were always in motion, like he was conjuring the air, and he kept finding excuses to brush them against my arm, the small of my back, the inside of my wrist.

"Amelia, you are absolutely brilliant at these clues," Alex

enthused, locking his gaze onto me, blue eyes alight. "I'd want you on my team for any game night, hands down."

The compliment was harmless, but it sent a jagged ripple through the air. Caiden's gaze flicked up. He looked at Alex, then at me, then back down at his cards.

His knuckles whitened, gripping the plastic so hard it warped.

Shane, predictably, made a joke to cut the tension: "Let's not all fight over Amelia's superior intellect, gentlemen; she's got enough brilliance for the whole table."

The room laughed, but the sound felt hollow; a bell rang in a crypt. I smiled, but my mouth was dry, the inside of my cheeks bitten raw.

I wondered if they could see it, that every jibe and touch from Alex was another bone in the graveyard Caiden and I haunted.

As the night wore on, laughter and games filled the room, but I felt like an outsider, trapped in my head. My gaze kept drifting to Caiden, who was now sitting across the room, his expression hard to read.

And then I noticed Alex watching me, a hint of something more in his eyes. It sent a shiver down my spine, reminding me of the growing connection between us.

As I glanced over at Caiden, I saw the pain etched on his face, the internal struggle that mirrored my own. And in that moment, I knew this was far from over.

The scent of Alex's cologne hung in the air as I sat beside him, his arm casually draped across the couch, grazing my neck, while I locked eyes with Caiden, his face a mask of seething anger.

*Two can play at this game, Caiden.*

I sent a silent challenge to him with my gaze. He shifted in his seat. The brown specks of his eyes were adorned with an inner heat that caused my stomach to flip and twist.

Caiden watched as I leaned into Alex, giggling like a giddy schoolgirl at something he said.

The game ended, but Alex's arm remained where it was, a comforting weight against my side, it was a nice change from the iciness radiating from Caiden across the room.

He didn't speak, didn't touch, but the intensity in his eyes promised a continuation, a battle waged not with words, but with actions.

With the silent language of hearts entangled and torn, battling within the fury of winter and the delicacy of starlight.

The storm within us raged on, a prelude to a confrontation that felt both inevitable and terrifying. This tension is unresolved and electric.

Alex stood and stretched, his shirt riding up to reveal a stripe of tanned skin. He caught me looking and winked, so deftly I wondered if he'd been practicing in the mirror.

"You want to try that new gelato place around the corner?" he asked, pitching his voice low, just for me. "I hear they have blood orange. Your favorite, right?"

I managed a nod, because what else was I supposed to do? Say that every flavor tasted like teeth and regret now?

Alex offered his arm, and I took it. The others watched with varying degrees of amusement, but when I glanced back at Caiden, I saw the vein in his temple pulsing, his jaw set like concrete.

He didn't say a word, only stared at the wall, as if he could bore a hole through it and escape into the blackness beyond.

I let myself get to the bottom of the porch steps before the chill of the night air bit into my arms, and I remembered too late that I'd forgotten my bag.

"I'll grab it," Alex offered, but I shook my head, already halfway back up the walk.

Inside, the house was quieter; the laughter had faded, and the lights were low, everyone else gone off to their own corners. I grabbed my purse from the counter.

As I turned, I nearly smashed straight into Caiden: six feet of silent fury, standing in the half-lit hallway like a warning.

He didn't move.

I tried to brush past him, but his hand shot out, catching my wrist. The grip was tight, but not cruel; his thumb pressed right over the flutter of my pulse.

"Are you seriously going to fuck him?" he whispered, not even looking at me. "Is this just for show, or are you actually that desperate?"

I tried to yank my arm free, but I was held captive by the force of his strength. "You don't get to police what I do."

He laughed. "No, I guess I don't. You're a free woman."

He stared at me, his face a study in rage and hunger.

The silence between us was like the vacuum after an explosion, where the only thing left is the ringing in your ears and the pressure in your chest.

"You want to pretend?" he said, voice low and lethal, each word weighed out in ounces of venom. "Go ahead. Play house with him. See if it fixes anything."

I tried to wrench my hand away again, but he held me, thumb tracing the line of my pulse as if he could erase it, as if he could pull the blood right out of me. "Let go," I said, but my voice was thin and unconvincing, a child's voice, a ghost's.

He made a sound. Half laugh, half snarl. "You don't actually want me to let go."

I hated that he was right.

Even as shame flushed through me, even as I imagined Alex waiting outside with his easy smile and his clean hands, I didn't want to be free of Caiden's grip.

I wanted him to pin me here, to force me to admit that nothing about me had changed except the cut of my scars. On some level, I wanted to be ruined all over again, but this time with intention, with a witness.

"Why are you doing this?" I whispered.

His breath was hot against my face, something dark and chemical, like gasoline on a summer sidewalk. "You know what I want. I want you to admit that nothing, nothing, will ever satisfy you except this."

His hand on my wrist tightened, and I felt the bones in my arm grind together, but I didn't make a sound.

The pain was a relief from the ache that gnawed at my insides every waking hour.

I had no answer.

All the words I'd ever stockpiled bled out of me at once, leaving only the hush of my own shallow breathing.

The truth was, even in my best moments, I was half-invisible, a shadow stitched together from scraps of other people's longing.

If Alex wanted to fuck a ghost, who was I to stop him?

If Caiden wanted to break me open just to see if anything was left inside, maybe that was the only thing I deserved.

He pressed me against the hallway wall, the drywall cool through my shirt, his hand still locked around my wrist.

His thighs caged mine, and I knew if I tried to run, he'd let me, but he'd follow, and I'd let him catch me.

My pulse stuttered. From fear or want, I couldn't tell. Maybe they were the same thing, in the end.

He brought my hand to his chest, where the beat of his heart was frantic as a sparrow's wings. "You think Alex knows what you look like when you're scared? When you're starving? You could be anyone for him."

His words thrummed through my bones; the truth in them hurt more than the grip that left bruises on my skin.

I finally wrenched myself free, but even then, the heat of his touch lingered like a chemical burn. "And for you?" I spat, my voice shaking. "What am I for you, Caiden? Just another thing to break?"

He shook his head, almost violently. "No. Never that."

He reached out, and this time I let him, too numb or too desperate to resist. His hands settled on my hips, fingers biting through denim to the flesh beneath, anchoring me where I stood.

"I can't stop thinking about you." He said it like an accusation, as if I'd infected him somehow. "I hate you for it."

I wanted to laugh, but my throat had closed around the sound. "So what now, Caiden?" I asked, voice cracked open. "You want to drag me into a room and prove you're the only one who matters?"

He looked startled, then something like hunger flashed across his face. "I want you to stop lying to yourself, you're not fooling me," he said, and with no warning at all, he bent and kissed me.

It was greedy, filthy, ruthless. A claim staked with teeth. I could feel the anger in it, the months of wanting and not having, the years of training himself to hate what he could not have.

My hands clutched his shirt, either to push him off or pull him closer, but I didn't know which, and when his tongue forced my mouth open, something inside me uncoiled in response.

There was nothing careful about it; this was not a kiss meant for healing. It was a cage, its door thrown open just so I could see what it meant to be trapped.

He lifted me easily, pushing me up against the wall so my feet left the floor. My back collided with the plaster, and the sound must have been loud, but I only heard his breath in my ear, ragged and near feral.

He held me there as if I weighed nothing, as if letting go was not an option, and I realized in that moment how much I wanted this, how much I needed someone to eclipse my own will.

His teeth dragged down my throat, scraping past the collarbone to the hollow at its base, and I heard myself gasp, the sound animal and unhinged.

His hands roamed—back, ribs, ass—nothing tentative, nothing gentle. He gripped the meat of my thigh and hiked it up around his waist, pressing himself so close I could feel the bulge in his jeans, hot and urgent against me.

There was no air left between us.

"You want to go, go to him," he hissed against my ear, but his hand squeezed tighter. "See if you can be touched by him without thinking about this fucking hunger."

He let go, sudden and sharp, like a dog unclenching its jaw.

My arm hung at my side, numb and tingling.

He stepped back.

For a split second, I caught the look in his eyes, how starved he was, how deeply, perfectly broken.

Then he slammed the door and was gone.

I watched the shadow of him all the way to the end, confused and hot all over. One minute, he was distant and cold. Then, suddenly, he was possessive and all hunger.

I sighed and let myself out into the night, into Alex's waiting arms.

We went to the gelato place, and I smiled and laughed and tried to be normal, to be someone who could enjoy the clean, citrus tang of blood orange on the tongue.

But it all tasted like memory, like the sweetness you only recognize after it's gone. Alex touched my hand and told stories, and I nodded along, but the heat of Caiden's mouth lingered, a ghost on my lips.

And as I lay in bed that night, I felt uncertainty press down on me, knowing that whatever came next would shape the course of our lives.

# AUTHORS NOTE

Thank you to anybody who made it to the end of Hearts Entangled In Winter's Fury!

Do not worry, book two is on its way which will continue the tension and relationship between Caiden and Amelia, as well as introducing a love triangle conflict with Alex, Amelia and Caiden, and going deeper into facing their past and ghosts when they have to return to their hometown. While also exploring themes of yearning, desire, obsession, possession, inner conflict, grief, trauma consequences, redemption, angst, etc. You will also get more insight into their own inner healing when it comes to the abuse and trauma from their parents. Let's just say, they have to revisit old wounds.

Book 1 is a story that I was inspired to write based on a one-word prompt: hate. I can still remember sitting down to type it out. It was originally a short thing, maybe 3-4 pages. There was no happy ending. Just raw, consuming hatred and pain.

The more I experimented with this story, the more I realized that the best way to end it was to make them fall in love. (So, of course, I had to tone down the abuse and cruelty between the two of them)

But, with all their slow-burning angst and wounds, it'll take more than one book for them to come together and fully resolve their issues! So, stay tuned for more. Book two will contain both Amelia's and Caiden's POV.

I am so thrilled with the outcome of this book. It is a precious project that I hold dear to my heart, exploring so many themes that may resonate with others as well as myself.

I tried to make their pain and trauma as authentic as possible. I myself dealt with a drug addict parent, parental emotional/verbal abuse and abandonment, anger, grief, loss of a family member to suicide (my father), betrayal, emptiness, loneliness, identity crisis, minor sexual abuse and addiction issues myself. I poured a lot of myself into this book, especially into Amelia.

I started this book's journey when I was 14 years old. I was an edgy, depressed, angry, and anxious teen pouring my inner conflict and emotions into things I wrote. Dealing with a lot of family issues and unresolved trauma/grief/personal issues.

I would write it, delete, rewrite, delete, rewrite, and so on. For a long time, I could not commit to it. I took multiple-year breaks from this novel. But I just kept coming back to Amelia and Caiden. I wanted, *needed*, to finish their story.

Now, at 25, I finally put it to rest. And decided to continue their story in two more books!

Please be sure to leave a review on Amazon/Goodreads and let me know your thoughts! And feel free to share with other book lovers!

# ABOUT THE AUTHOR AND SOCIAL LINKS

Donna Kessler is a self-taught writer residing in North Carolina. She has been a lifelong lover of reading, writing and poetry, even publishing a poetry book called Swirling Emotions in 2020! She began reading when she was a toddler, and began writing at the age of 9. She enjoys writing about dark, traumatic and tragic themes with emotional depth. Her favorite genres to read and write are dark romance (or general romance), horror/mystery, poetry and anything psychological. She has one dog and also enjoys painting, psychology, spirituality, cleaning, collecting and caring for animals! Her main motivation to write is to express her own struggles/emotions, and to bring comfort/consolation to other readers. Her main hope is that readers will find her books and truly connect with the emotional depth and the characters or the relationships.

Instagram: @donnakesslerauthor
TikTok: @authordonnajill
POETRY IG: @donnapoetess
Substack: @donnapoetess
Wesbite: donnakesslerauthor.com
FACEBOOK GROUP NAME FOR THIS BOOK SERIES CONTAINING UPDATES, INFO, DETAIL, DISCUSSION AND MORE: <u>Haunted Darkness Of Our Ruin dark romance series</u>